"Do I have t

Gillander chuckle⸺ rein and sit with me, my⸺

Blade felt as thou⸺ his spine. The invitation⸺mon sense he had. With a⸺tting himself loose, he swung his leg over and dismounted. Cincy put her muzzle up and rolled her eyes, the whites showing, but stayed put in a ground-tie, as promised.

Thomas sat also. He reached out and his hand passed through the frayed cuffs and spindly forearms. He had expected it, but he had not expected the icy chill that accompanied the action.

Gillander put his hands out, palms facing. Thomas mimicked the action, his hands moving until almost, but not quite touching. As the warmth of his body touched the icy barrier of death, his aura flared out, and a corona of blue fire ringed the four hands.

"I have to move and move fast. The night Denethan attacked and you saved the perimeter—you moved time. I want to know how. Now tell me," Blade said, "and tell me true, or I'll find a way to rip the guts out of you as surely as I would Denethan's."

The ghost grinned.

Books by Charles Ingrid
in DAW Omnibus Editions

THE
MARKED MAN
OMNIBUS

THE MARKED MAN
THE LAST RECALL

CHARLES INGRID

DAW BOOKS, INC.
DONALD A. WOLLHEIM, FOUNDER
375 Hudson Street, New York, NY 10014
ELIZABETH R. WOLLHEIM
SHEILA E. GILBERT
PUBLISHERS
www.dawbooks.com

Dedicated to Paula, unsung heroine.
Thanks for polishing the words.

THE
MARKED MAN

Chapter 1

He spotted the body half-hidden under the rotting hulk of an '02 hovercar. Mesquite and oleander had crowded the car until the corpse was only one of the dark and twisted shadows in the dirt. The dead man wore patrolman's clothing.

Thomas Blade reined in. He sat still for a moment, and watched the ears of his gelding flick back and forth. A raucously chattering crow circled low and flew in to shred at the victim's sprawling arm. The horse's ears pricked, then relaxed. Satisfied that they were alone, Blade swung a leg over and dismounted. He dropped the reins. The crow protested his approach and left with a flap of tattered black wings.

The body had been dead a while. Two days, probably, from the smell and lividity. The throat had been worried at by crows and ants and sowbugs, but it looked to be the death wound. The ragged edges had not been slit cleanly—something had torn it open.

Blade wiped his hands on his knees, then absently touched the chevron scar marking his brow. There were a lot of things out here which could have killed the man, but he didn't like speculating.

He straightened up. A wind smelling of sea and salt tugged at the long white scarf about his neck. On a clear day like today, from where he stood on the ravaged coast of the Los Angeles basin, Catalina could still be seen. Blade toed the body. "You're a suspicious son of a bitch," he said to himself. But patrolmen didn't stop to check the view, and, from the grooves in the dirt, the body had been dragged in and hidden. Predators behaved differently than murderers. Blade got the groundsheet out of his bedroll. The gelding rolled a white eye at him, reacting to the stench of death amid the already pungent odor of the disintegrating car. He sidestepped when Blade attempted to mount up, malodorous bundle under his arm. Thomas cursed the horse and pulled himself up anyway. The groundsheet would absorb most of the smell for the time being. He'd be down at the big house soon where Charles would not be pleased to know that someone or something had taken out one of his patrolmen.

He took the horse around in a cautious circle, examining the ground and brush for more information, then reined about toward his original destination. He almost overlooked the snare lines set in the heavy brush above what was obviously a jackrabbit run.

Blade did not get down to look at the snare. He knew nester work when he saw it, but he wondered whether discovering the snare was coincidental or important. Charlie didn't like nesters and neither did Blade, and it would be convenient if the blame for the patrolman's death fell that way. Thomas distrusted convenience.

The canvas-shrouded body stuck out awkwardly across the gelding's withers. Its shadow crossed the snare as the horse shifted uneasily. Blade made up his mind, clucked the horse into a trot, and headed for the big house.

The big house was a magnificent, if timeworn, manor house of stone and flagstone and red-tiled roofing where sparrows and pigeons quarreled among the eaves. The crescent drive was hand-cut across the grounds and the sun glittered off the '96 Cadillac coach sitting in the driveway, its antique carcass waxed to within an inch of its metallic life. Thomas thought briefly of its biodegradable counterpart that he'd left moldering in the foothills. He squeezed the gelding into a lope.

A man broke into a greeting run from the driveway's far end. "Thomas! They've been asking for you!"

The crescent drive and the stables just downhill bustled with life. There were small carriages and carts and horses picketed all over the grounds. Blade smiled wryly. All the secretive plans of the past years were now up in smoke. The head groom reached for his gelding's headstall. "Looks like you've brought an uninvited guest."

Thomas dismounted, took his hat off, and settled it on the saddle horn. The sea wind dried his fine blond hair quickly.

"From what I've seen, there's no such thing as an uninvited guest. Who's here?"

"Every governor and mayor Charlie could call in. They've been sitting in the big house arguing for the last day or two."

"Where's Charles now?"

"In the schoolhouse. He told me to tell you, no trouble." But the servant did not look very menacing as he delivered his warning.

"You're a little late on that one, Weber. Take that bundle down to the cold house and see if you can make it a touch more palatable. And don't let Veronica see it."

The groom nodded. He stroked the gelding gently with his third hand. "Who was it?"

"One of the sentries. Now I can't tell you any more, so don't ask."

"All right, then. What did you bring for a wedding present?"

Blade patted Weber's shoulder. "Now that would be telling." He pivoted on a boot heel, then pulled on his yellow-gold mustache. "Not a word until the kids open it . . . I've got three more laser disks. The machine still working?"

"Impeccably. About the only thing around here, besides me, that does." Weber watched as Blade took off his saddle pack. Hoisting it over his shoulder, he made his way to the group of outbuildings used for schoolrooms.

The doors and windows had been left open to catch the breeze off the ocean cliffs. He took a moment to collect his wits. He could hear the drone of young voices in response to the lecturer. It took him back a few years as he moved quietly within the shadows to stand where Charles Warden could not see him. The teacher of the class, an elderly man, sat tucked up in his corner as though trying to avoid notice altogether while the Director of Water and Power was speaking to his students.

The DWP had begun to run a little to fat, Blade noticed, but was still an imposing man. The children seated at small desks and on the floor ranged in ages, sexes, and races, and with few exceptions, had their attention fixed on him. At his back was a multicolored plastimap of the old United States.

Blade smiled in spite of himself. So this wedding was to be the launch of a number of pet projects. Charlie was inside the schoolroom now, hoping to whip up the imagination of future cartographers.

"What good does it do, sir," a reedy voice piped up, "to know their names if the states aren't there anymore?"

"Ah, but that's the point," Charlie said. He paced back and forth in front of the children. His neck was florid above his collar, a sure sign of excitement. "We know that much of the country was devastated, both by the 'Star Wars' reprisal and by the plagues that followed—but we don't know who's there and who isn't. There are bound to be pockets of people who still exist."

"What happened?"

Charles paused a moment, looking into the face of the solemn girlchild who asked him. She knew the catechism, of course, they all did, but large-eyed Alma seemed in quest of an ultimate truth. The DWP cleared his throat. "We don't really know. We can guess. Two incoming asteroids of tremendous size struck North America. Attempts to deflect or destroy them evidently set off the 'Star Wars' defense network accidentally. That, in turn, set off limited nuclear war. And, that in turn, set off nuclear havoc in third-world countries such as India and South Africa, which had unregulated and unauthorized nuclear weaponry. After the destruction and what we called nuclear winter, we know that parts of China and Russia managed to survive—parts of Europe are rumored to have made it, too. And South America. We lost the African continent, of course, but we still get radio signals we cannot quite decipher or locate. So you must know your countries, states, and counties as they were, until we can get the mappers out and back again to tell us how our world is *now*. For the first time, we have a stable enough population here to let you go, if you want to."

"Anywhere?" A small dark boy, legs folded gracefully under him, spoke up.

"Wellll." Charlie turned around and looked at the map. He pulled at the slateboard and brought down a map of California. His back to the children, he began to delineate areas with a blunt finger. "We know, of course, what the asteroid strikes here and here left—"

"Us!" the children shouted out.

"Well, it left this massive fjord over what used to be Santa Barbara, and this crater here in the greater L.A. basin was made on the bounce—Nevada took the heaviest brunt—and the nuclear strike wiped out most of the Bay Area here and the upper part of the state and the far east coast here. Chinese Vancouver took over the greater Seattle area, but we have a massive break from upper Washington all the way down to San Francisco. This area was never densely populated and we don't know what happened after the radiation and plagues." Without skipping a beat or turning around, he said, "What do you think, Thomas?"

The children let out squeals of surprise and delight as he stepped out of the shadows, dust motes swirling about him to diffuse sunlight. "I think," he said quietly, "that anyone who goes out to map the world will be a great adventurer."

Charlie smiled broadly. He added, "I'll turn this class back to Protector Wyethe."

As the spindly, white-haired man stood up from his stool in the corner, the DWP caught Blade's attention and guided him back outside.

"What do you think?" Charles Warden asked him as they stepped away from earshot of the classrooms.

"I think you ought to be ashamed of yourself," Blade answered. "Sending lambs out into the wilderness with the wolfrats."

Charlie gave him a resentful look and a sigh. "Has to happen sometime. You know it and I know it. What we don't know can kill us."

"What we do know can kill us. I brought in one of your outermost sentries with me."

"Who?"

"No one I trained. Weber took him to the cold house. He's not in good shape, even for a corpse, but his throat had been ripped out."

Charlie's eyelids flickered. "Predators?"

Blade shook his head. "I don't think so. I think a lizard got him."

"*Shit.* Don't say anything to Ronnie or anyone else in the house, will you?"

Blade quirked his brow. He felt that oddly shaped scar pucker as he did so. "That depends on who you've got in the house."

"I've got everybody in the house, dammit, and you know it."

"I know it now, but this isn't what we discussed months ago. We discussed discretion—we discussed out-and-out secrecy. You're going to have unwanted visitors, if you don't already."

Charles stopped in his tracks. His bulky shoulders tensed and shifted under his shirt. "I have my reasons, Thomas."

"Of course," he said smoothly and proceeded to the elegantly carved oaken doors of the big house. Beyond, the sounds of laughter and muffled talk, even the clink of fine crystal pre-Disaster glasses could be heard. "Coming in with me?"

"No. I need some time with the body. Keep Ronnie busy and stay civilized."

Thomas watched him walk around the far end of the house. There had been mullioned windows here, in the front, but for defense they'd been boarded up long ago. No one could watch him as he stood there until he could shake off his vulnerability, don bravado like a fine cloak, then kick the door in.

Someone screamed. The sound climbed, then truncated. The crowd in the foyer turned, drinks in hand, saw him, and faces brightened. Thomas recognized what Charles would call "his political crowd." He threaded his way through. A male voice followed after. "Veronica! Hide the virgins."

Laughter shrieked and blushing faces turned away from him. But they shrank away from him rather than brush shoulders, this crowd. And why not? They were more than a little afraid of him. He was, after all, the executioner.

He passed a tray of lemon drops. He was uncommonly fond of lemon drops. He dipped a hand in and filled a pocket. He caught a fleeting glimpse of himself in a gold-veined mirror. The tail of his white scarf floated behind him, caught in the draft created by his swaggering gait. His fine gold hair was cut a little too long over the ears and brushed the collar of his battered brown leather jacket. The hairline was too far back, revealing too much of a lean face. *Twenty years from now,* he thought, *I'll be bald as an egg.* The notion made him frown as an elegant woman in a dress of Alice blue emerged from an alcove at the foyer's end.

Henna accented her long brown hair. One slender hand curved about a champagne glass, as she hooked the other along his outstretched arm and brought it down gracefully to her level. "Thomas! Behave yourself. Charles is worried enough about things without you."

He kissed her temple. "But, Auntie, isn't that why I was invited?"

"Lord Protector," she said smoothly, the tone of her voice reminding him of both his office and his duty, "you were invited because we love you. Now come with me and let me present you." Her nose wrinkled slightly. "Really, Thomas, couldn't you have stopped at the bathhouses on the way in?"

"Water and time are money."

"Ummm." She didn't sound convinced.

"I'll get there as soon as I can," he reassured her, as they walked into the great room of the house.

The wedding of Charles' and Veronica's daughter had brought out the big cannons, Blade could see. The mayors he knew because of his circuit riding as judge and executioner, but the others he knew only by reputation. As his gaze swept across the room, he saw no fewer than five Protectors. Those, plus himself and Wyethe in the classroom, meant Charles had called in the entire group. The county barriers and the people living behind them were vulnerable to any attack, physical or psychic, that might be launched on them. Blade felt his jaws clench in anger.

The cattle baron from Santa Barbara gave him an acknowledging nod. Thomas noted that his new jacket had been smartly cut to both accommodate and hide his tail as neatly as possible. His perpetually bald wife had a new wig as well. They were lean and tanned from hard work, but their clothes spoke of prosperity.

Veronica did not miss the look nor did she miss Charles' entrance from the rear of the manor house, his face pale. "Boyd, I can see you and Delia know Thomas. Take him under your wing, will you? I have some other things to do and he's not a social animal."

"Just an animal." Thomas smiled engagingly, but it did little to change the pallor of Delia's own expression. He could not blame her, really. The last time they'd met, he'd been there to put her eldest son to death. He looked past Delia to watch Veronica corner her husband. The DWP looked unhappy for a fleeting second.

Before Boyd could react to his newest duties, Delia's lip curled and she began to speak. Or tried to. Her voice was drowned out by the squeals of the children as they caught sight of him, a pack of them emerging from the kitchen and racing across the massive room heedless of the crowd they scattered. Wyethe must have let them out for good behavior.

"Thomas! Thomas! Thomas!"

The corner of his mouth quirked. He was always undone by the children. They knew him for what he was. It was fortunate the adults didn't—they attributed Thomas' popularity to the toys and odd things he was always bringing up from the ruins. It was the children who knew how to spot a free soul and unfettered heart when they saw one.

He flipped the ends of his scarf back over his dark brown leather jacket as he got to his knees in order to talk to the clamoring children. Quiet Alma, as soulful as her name, smiled up at him and touched the patched knee of his riding and tracking trousers. He patted her hand back. Behind her, Stefan watched solemnly, his hair white-blond, courtesy of his Russian blood. His mother had come over on a boat fifteen years ago, most of her fellow voyagers dead from the journey, too frail to last the arduous trip from their snow-blasted lands. She'd worked in Blade's county for many years and he'd taught Stefan to shoot. But when he'd lost his mother, he'd come here. The DWP took in all orphans. He gave Thomas a quiet nod. But the others were anything but quiet, bouncing and cheering his presence.

They drew Veronica's attention away from Charles and she said, "Honestly, Thomas. When you're ready, I'll have you announced."

He looked up, irony mirrored in his brown eyes. "I think everyone here knows my name already."

She made a noise of disapproval and stalked off, her heels making a staccato noise on the flooring. He watched her go, knowing that her agitation was not caused by him but by what she'd just learned from the DWP. Amid soft laughter, Thomas shrugged and turned back to the children who were tugging on the strings of his saddle pack. Even the bride and groom were on their knees like everyone else, her swirled party dress crumpled under her. He reached out and touched the girl on her shoulder where the gown exposed soft skin. "Jennifer . . . you'd better get up before I get in trouble. That's no way to treat such a pretty dress."

Blondely beautiful, the twelve-year-old wrinkled her nose a second, then nodded and got to her feet. The groom, thirteen-year-old Ramos, darkly handsome even though his features had not quite delineated themselves, stood up bearing Thomas' pack. It was his right to ask, and so he did.

"What did you bring?"

Thomas shook his head. "A wedding present, but you won't know what it is until you open it. Bad luck, you know." He fought the impulse to reach out and brush Ramos' straying black hair from his forehead. Young, both of them. He sighed. The world around him seemed to go in pairs, and now it was pairing off younger and younger—although these two were special indeed.

"Thomas!"

He craned his neck and saw Charles bearing down on them through the crowd. He grinned at the children. "I think I'm being called."

Ramos bore the pack off to the ballroom, where long tables held packages of glittering splendor and threw the canvas pack to the head of the table, where it reigned by virtue of its own difference. The boy stroked the pack before bolting off to join the herd of children as they clattered past him, headed toward the kitchen. Alma lagged behind for a moment. He threw her a kiss.

"Go on, big eyes. I'll be here for the party."

The child nodded, then turned and raced after her friends.

Thomas watched wistfully before turning back to Charles who said, "Was it necessary to kick in the door?"

Blade reflected for a moment and decided that it probably hadn't been, but it had seemed appropriate at the time. "It wasn't latched."

"No, but your boot left a notch in it. Antique, Thomas, a genuine oak antique, and you left a mark in it that—"

"Will always remind you of Jennifer's wedding day," Thomas interrupted smoothly. "Congratulations, Charlie." He played out the lie that they had not met outside the classrooms, though few seemed interested in their conversation.

"Thank you." The big man paused. "Come in the study with me."

The way he said it, Thomas knew he didn't have a choice, and he followed in his friend's wake, trying not to walk on his heels. Macaulay's *The Way Things Work* was open on the massive desktop. Thomas knew Charlie had been attacking another knotty problem.

Charles gave him a glass and tapped an aromatic, amber liquor into it.

"Must be serious," Thomas said as he took the glass and sat down. The sweet smell of herbed stuffing issued from the couch. "You've given me the serious stuff to drink."

"You're right . . . one of Denethan's raiders tore his throat out. That was Franco, one of my best."

"I didn't train him." Charlie's glance flickered over Thomas as he answered that, and he knew the DWP had identified the arrogance in his tone. How could Franco have been one of the DWP's best sentries if Thomas had not trained him?

Charlie drained his shot glass. "Have you heard anything?"

"Heard anything about what?"

"Thomas! About the wedding, on the streets or anywhere else."

"No, but then, I already knew. What's this all about? You've got a block full of carriages and now you're worried about discretion? Who in the hell gave you permission to call in the Protectors? Worried about the Lizard of Oz?"

"Water rights give me the permission. As for the Lizard—is nothing sacred?"

"Lighten up, man. *The Wizard of Oz* is a brilliant political satire. And if I hadn't found the disk for it, none of you would even be dissecting it for dinner conversation today." Blade grinned humorlessly. "And if it applies to our nemesis from the Mojave, so much the better."

Thomas eyed Charlie as the burly man sat down in a leather chair. Air wheezed out of the chair discreetly as the DWP squeezed in. Blade sipped the whiskey and waited for the mellow sting to leave his tongue before adding, "Isn't that why I'm here? Isn't that why all seven of us are here, at one time, in one place, as seven Protectors haven't been since the early days? Because you're afraid—no, petrified—that Denethan will somehow find a way to come at you and your little Adam and Eve."

"It's no joke, Thomas."

"I wasn't making a joke. We all know that Denethan would love to take out our two genetically pure beauties before they have a chance to bear children who might—just might—bring back a pure human race. I saw the guards up on the hills. I rode right through them and I'm here to tell you that if Denethan uses his wind raiders, we're dead meat, just like the sentry I brought in. All seven Protectors, the children, and every one of your hypocritical wedding guests."

Charlie took out a handkerchief and mopped his sweating brow. His thick salt-and-pepper hair was plastered to his skull with perspiration. His full neck bulged outside the confines of the tight neckline, adding purple to the scarring on the side of his neck. Blade, finding himself staring, looked away, out the window, to the windmills busily churning in the sea breeze off the cliffs. He was aware of the increase in tension that followed his words.

Charles said softly, "I know you're angry because I didn't follow your advice."

"That wasn't advice I gave you. I thought we were taking security precautions and making plans for their future."

"I had to do it differently, and I won't have you calling my guests names."

Thomas took another draft. "The fact is, we're all here to celebrate the mating of two pure specimens—when it's our own mutations that have kept us alive this long. Genetic splicing came along just in time to keep the disaster from annihilating us. And now you and the others are busily trying to undo what made us survivors."

Charlie looked at him bleakly. "I suppose you side with Denethan."

Thomas glared back. Then he tossed off the last of his drink. "I'll pretend I didn't hear that. I'll pretend it's because you're under a lot of stress that you suggested I have anything to do with that reptilian monstrosity in the Mojave. Because if I didn't have a good imagination, Charlie, I'd have to take you outside and carve you up, just out of principle."

Charlie let out a gusty sigh. "You know I didn't mean it. But you're right about one thing—I'm scared. I wouldn't have all the Protectors here at one time if I wasn't—and if it wasn't for the future of the human race, you guys wouldn't have agreed to come. Jesus." And the aging man buried his face in his hands.

Thomas relented. "He's heard, Charlie. Denethan's tentacles stretch all over L.A. The only question is: did he hear in time to do something about it? We don't know, and we won't until something happens." Thomas stood up abruptly and poured himself a refill. "Where's the ceremony? I saw the Caddy out front."

"At the sea bowl." Charles raised his face. He mopped it quickly, but his eyes had reddened.

"Good choice. Lots of nature. I like it there," Thomas said thoughtfully, as he moved past his old friend to the picture window. "We might have a chance yet."

"Do you think so?"

Thomas' answer was interrupted by Veronica, as she opened the door and stuck her head in. "Art Bartholomew is whipping everybody up over the water share allotments again." Veronica's icy blue stare pinioned Thomas for a minute, then she smiled. "Being a good boy?"

Thomas shrugged. "Give me a break, Ronnie."

She flushed at her nickname and left them alone in the study. In the sudden silence, he could hear the scold and song of the birds outside. He turned back to the DWP.

"What's this about Bartholomew?"

"Politics. You wouldn't be interested."

"Why don't you just cut off his water altogether? He's got a well, he'll get along for a while. Give him an appreciation for the system."

"I've never used water to make anyone toe the line and it won't be done in the counties as long as I'm DWP. And Art has a fine appreciation for the system. He wants to be Director of Water and Power when I pack it in. That's why he's here, drinking my booze and celebrating my daughter's wedding."

"Just as long as you duck when he decides to bury the hatchet." Thomas finished off his drink.

"Tell me I'm doing the right thing," Charles said heavily as he got to his feet.

"You're doing the right thing," Thomas answered automatically. He paused. "Politically. The people out there have a right to be polarized into this. But as for the kids—I think I'd just take the two of them and tell them to make love and babies for the rest of their lives. No muss, no fuss. This," and Thomas, indicated the celebration with a wave of his hands, "this is going to pull Denethan's attention to us."

"I can't do that. They have to be gotten out, and gotten out now. Ten years have passed, and the plague is showing up again. Nesters, mostly, but I can't afford to lose anybody."

Thomas grew silent. The eleven-year plague was a mutating virus that attached itself to the DNA—inflicting even worse abominations on them than genetic engineering had—and it was uncontrollable. Luckily, short-lived, but women and men once infected had to be sterilized or pass on genetic changes too monstrous to face. Nesters lived outside the system, by choice. "Then send them away quietly. Why wine and dine all your friends and enemies?"

"I don't have much of a choice." Charlie's neck, where he had his immature gills cut out, pulsed. "Politically." He opened the study door. "Shall we go?"

Chapter 2

"What is an Art Bartholomew?" Thomas asked, easing his way from the muffled quiet of the study back into the cheerful din of the outer rooms.

Veronica pointed her chin at a warty little man on the far side of the room, talking enthusiastically and waving his hands. He had attracted a crowd of his own, much like dung attracts flies. Thomas pulled at a corner of his mustache as Veronica said, "I told you not to invite him, Charles."

"I couldn't very well leave him out. Besides, this is an opportunity to get some things settled without having to put them to a vote. You might as well come, too." He looked at Blade. The scars above his collar line pulsed slightly.

"Right."

Bartholomew's voice seemed to rise with every step closer they took, as though their approach enflamed him. Charles was at the edge of the crowd when Gray Walton took him by the elbow.

"A word, Director, if you please."

Gray Walton was black, and his brown eyes shone with a keen earnestness from his burled skin. Charles stepped back, away from Bartholomew's audience. "What is it, Gray?"

"My daughter gave birth yesterday."

"She did? Congratulations, man. . . ." Charles paused, seeing the too bright gaze in Gray's eyes. The two turned away to exchange quiet words Thomas was not privy to. He edged past them to listen to Bartholomew.

"Water isn't politics, he says. Bullshit. If it wasn't, he wouldn't be Director of Water and Power. The problem is to use it politically. Take water rights away from the nesters and let them dry up and blow away in the wind."

"You know that's not policy." Thomas raised his voice as the man paused in his tirade.

"Policy? The policy is nothing more than situational ethics, anyway."

"Nothing is ever black and white."

Bartholomew fixed an intent gaze on him. Then the warty man smiled. "You, of all people, should be first to judge."

The crowd parted a little at seeing Thomas in their midst. He felt himself smiling. "On the contrary, Bartholomew. As executioner and Protector, I'm the last one to judge a situation. I only come in when the accusation has been proved or disproved, a neutral party. I truth-read and I carry out the sentence, but I make no moral decisions."

"And that leaves you innocent?"

"No, it leaves me disinterested. Which leads me to ask: what do you hope to gain from additional damming in your county? As I recall, you have fairly heavy rains, but with a lot of runoff. In order to deny water rights to the nesters, we'd have to build an earthen dam . . . then you'd have quite a little reservoir of your own. No way to test the water or filter the contaminants out of it—but you wouldn't have to come to the DWP then, would you? Unless, of course, your people want clean water."

Bartholomew closed his mouth tightly for a moment, then said, "I won't countenance such accusations by responding to them."

"I bet you won't." Thomas turned away. He bumped into Charlie's bulk.

"Defusing the situation?"

"Trying to."

His friend made a funny sound at the back of his throat, a half-growl. "No duels this time."

"Who, me?" Thomas spotted a clear area by the patio doors, which were open to gather in the late afternoon breeze. He headed for them. In his wake, he heard a strong female voice saying, "Soap's your best insecticide. Nothing dangerous and it kills the infestation all the same."

"Not these bugs it doesn't. I picked one off my bushes the size of my thumb . . ."

*   *   *

Charlie followed him out to the patio. They stood, facing into the wind. Blade watched the windmills generating energy for this tiny square of civilization. After a long moment, he said, "As long as the wind blows inshore, Denethan can't launch his wind raiders. The minute it changes . . ." and he let his voice trail off.

"Have you felt anything yet?"

Blade looked at him. "Why me? You've got six other Protectors here to ask."

"Because you're more sensitive."

Thomas thought of a scornful reply, then discarded it. Instead, he took a mediative breath. He had not felt the black wave of despair and fear that Denethan usually launched along with a physical assault for years. He did not feel it now. He shook his head. "Nothing. But that doesn't mean our lizard man isn't out there waiting and watching."

The patio doors reopened with a squeak, bringing both men around. This time they faced three governors, one of whom, from Thomas' own county, was on his tiptoes from drink.

"Valdees."

"Blade. So he roped you in here, too?" The chunky, graying man with skin like burnished leather lifted his glass.

"I sense a request," Charles said. He eyed the other two governors, the woman tall and lanky like her counterpart.

"We want the nesters cleaned out." Her voice was clipped, emotionless.

Charles answered, "You're talking murder."

"No. We're talking war. I don't advocate Bartholomew's method of taking away their water. That's cruel."

"And it takes too long," Thigpen added. He had not spoken yet, but stood back as if weighing the speech of his peers.

Charles shook his head. "I'm the Director of Water and Power. Water's life, and I'll give that to you. If you want death, you're going to have to find yourself a general."

"There's that," Valdees said. "You're quick enough to fight if the filtration station is threatened."

"But I don't want to do it as a full-time job. Governors, I invited you all here for this occasion to air some of these grievances. But I can't give you a snap answer for them, and I don't think you really want that from me, do you?"

Governor Irlene shook her head, her dark hair threatening to break free from its glittering net. "No. What we do want is a guarantee that you'll sit down and talk with us."

"All seven mayors and governors? Or just you three?"

"The three of us, first." Thigpen took a step forward. "The nesters are vermin. Something has to be done."

Charles nodded gravely. "Then we'll talk," he said.

The trio left as quietly as they had come. Thomas took a deep breath and could smell himself. "That reminds me," he said. "Veronica recommended a visit to the bathhouse. Any hot water left?"

Something in his question struck Charles as funny and the man put his head back and bellowed with laughter. Blade could still hear him faintly as he walked across the lawn toward the bathhouses in the deepening afternoon shadows.

Charles joined him in the immense wooden tub, awakening him from a half-drowsed dream. His mood had become much more somber. He washed first on the deck, rinsed, and in a wreath of foam, sat down next to Blade. The water level immediately surged up, covering Thomas' reach for the dagger he'd brought in with him. Charlie said, "At ease," as if knowing he'd be armed.

Blade gave him a baleful glance. Then, after a moment, he said, "How come, if I'm a good fifteen years younger than you, you've got twice the hair I have?"

Charles grinned wickedly. "Ronnie and good genes," he answered.

They laughed together, then sighed.

Finally, the DWP said, "We're going to have to do something about the nesters. They're using up valuable grazing land and runoff water."

"And?"

"And they're unclean. And they've chosen to stay that way, and outside our laws. We're walking a fine line here, just to stay alive, and they've chosen not to be a part of that commitment."

"Show me a death warrant for each one and I'll take them one at a time. But I won't stand by if you declare war on them. What about the ones who are born on the other side? They didn't choose that life."

"Then bring them back."

"Maybe I will." Thomas stroked his scarred brow. "One of

them, or a creature of one of them, gave this to me. A token. Could have taken my head off, but didn't."

"I know."

"But do you know what it means?"

Charlie shook his head, spraying water like a wet dog. Thomas paused, watching him, then said, "I don't know what it means either. But I do know they could have killed me and didn't."

The DWP answered only, "If the plague starts in, we may not have any choice."

Thomas decided not to answer him. They sat in the immense wooden vat until the water chilled.

The wedding day dawned fiercely clear and clean. Thomas left his hat with Weber to be brushed and blocked, took his gelding, and went up into the scrub hills surrounding the settlement.

He spotted the sentries long before they gave any indication of sensing him. One got to his feet, grunted his intentions to the second and moved out of sight behind a stand of blooming red and white oleander. He ground-tied the horse and made his way around behind their position. A swift movement and the garrote was around the neck of the chunky woman nearest him. Her hands went up and he twisted the loop a touch.

"Down there," and he nodded to the manor house, "down there, they're having a party. Up here, you're working. You're supposed to make sure the people down there are safe while they're having a good time."

A necklace of tiny crimson beads welled up from the garrote. The woman husked, "Who?"

"Blade," he said. "And be glad it's me." He brought the guard to her knees with a bit more pressure. "Next time, neither of us could be so lucky."

Her hands had stayed at her neck, fingers rigid and coiled, not to free the loop but to jab at his eyes. It was the only correct thing she'd tried to do. With a grim smile, Blade twisted the loop a fraction more and left her kneeling, dazed and clawing at the garrote that was biting into her fleshy neck. It was a spare.

*   *   *

Veronica was livid when he returned. "Where have you been?" The air was filled with the whickering of horses and the creak of harness as carriages pulled into the procession.

"Checking on the security. The wind's about to change, Ronnie, and when it does, we all need to be ready." His gelding skittered sideways under him. "Where's Charlie? We're riding shotgun."

"Oh, no," she said firmly. "You're driving one of the guests." She watched him dismount, took him by the arm, and led him to a small VW cart.

The woman inside, young and blonde, full-cheeked and with a thickened waistline, smiled prettily at him. Her rouged cheeks pinked genuinely as he seated himself next to her and took up the reins. His muscular thigh brushed her fleshy one.

"Sir Thomas Blade," Veronica said formally, the hem of her dress of antiqued ivory lace in danger of being stepped on by his gelding. She reined him back. "This is Shellyann. I told her you'd escort her today." She gave the gelding a no-nonsense slap across the nose as he clicked his teeth at her sleeve and left them to their own devices.

The line of coaches pulled away and he turned his attention gratefully to the trail ahead, as he clucked to the mule team pulling them.

"Lord Protector," the woman repeated softly. "I'm Shellyann. Is it true what they say?"

There were two kinds of women, thought Thomas. Those who were repelled and a little frightened by what he did, and those who were excited.

The last thing he felt like was flirtatious conversation. He allowed a glance at his carriage mate. More of Veronica's matchmaking, no doubt. "That depends on what they say."

"Are you in the ruins often?"

That surprised him, a little. Most of them wanted to know if he was really an assassin and executioner. "Sometimes, on the fringes. No one goes In-City. Rest assured, madame, I do not glow in the dark."

Shellyann blushed again. The heat of the sun overhead and the weight of her party dress made her face dewy with perspiration. She looked away, saying, "I hope to test that statement myself . . . later."

Thomas clucked to the mules. One of the children's carriages, a van made convertible, was directly in front of them. The children hung over its sides, scolding and crying out to him, individual words melding in a din of enthusiasm. He thought he spotted a sturdy blond toddler who waved with more vigor than the others. "Is he yours?"

"Why, yes, I—how did you know?"

"Your waistline, Veronica's intentions, and his obvious love for you. Where's his father?"

"Dead." Shellyann looked at him. "But I am proven a fertile woman."

"Indeed." Blade sank into his own thoughts then, and the woman, with an expression that said she'd been insulted, lapsed into silence as well.

The road wound like a serpent across the peninsula. Eucalyptus limbs waved beside the path's edges and shed their scented bark, gray-green leaves fluttering in the wind. The grass was golden, dry, awaiting the beginning of what passed for a rainy season. Soon they would be brown, brittle, and dangerous. Blade had often warned Charlie about living in the foothills because of brush fires, but it did no good. Just as Charlie's warnings to him to stay out of the borders were ignored by Blade.

A cry to the fore of the caravan rang back, and Blade pulled his team to a halt, right against the bumper of the chop-topped van holding the children. The blond leaned over and cried, "I love you, Mummy."

"I love you too, dear," she called back. To Blade, she said anxiously, "What's the matter?"

He stood in the VW. Ahead, he could see the point riders pulling their rifles as their horses milled about restlessly. The road hairpinned down and around. Soon, they would be making the immense horseshoe turn that led past an enormous, ancient campus, and on to the sea bowls. He didn't like what he saw. The riders were too nervous. The scarf pulled at his throat. "I can't tell," he said, finally. "It could be javelinas or maybe coyotes."

"Or nothing."

Blade doubted that. Although his mule team was calm, the horses ahead were too nervous, their nostrils cupped wine-red against the wind. He looked down at Shellyann. "Can you drive?"

"Of course. If I have to."

"Good. You know who I am. You know what I may have to do."

She lowered her eyes. "Yes, Lord Protector."

Charlie came loping down the road on his half-Clydesdale gelding, the reins of a riderless horse in his hand. He stopped alongside the carriage. "Care to mount up, Thomas?"

Thomas stepped off the door frame and swung effortlessly aboard the black mare. He nodded to Shellyann. "May we meet again," he said.

The woman's bow-shaped mouth tightened as they rode off. Overhead, thin wisps of clouds moved across the sky in a high wind. But Blade sensed a change in the air. As he drew to the fore of the line with Charlie, he saw one of the point riders tap a vial into the hollow barrel of his rifle. He recognized the chemical.

His head snapped back toward Charlie. "No defoliants."

"Why not?"

"For god's sake, man, the peninsula is just getting back to normal. Would you contaminate what you've worked for all these years?"

Charlie sat his horse heavily, his jowls working. Then he turned to the guard and said, "Put it away, Castro."

"Something's in the tall grass, sir."

"Then we'll flush it out."

"The chemical's quicker." Castro sat, stiff-necked.

"And more harmful. Do as I say."

Sardonically, the guard said, "Yes, sir," and unloaded the vial carefully. His flat brown-eyed gaze swept across Blade in amusement. For a fleeting moment, Blade wished this man had been guarding up on the ridge instead of the woman. This one, Blade would have killed cheerfully without a second thought.

Wyethe rode up in his Protector's robes, his elbows flapping and the high, thin strands of his white hair blowing in the wind. The sun had reddened his pale face. He squinted nervously behind his glasses.

"What's happening?"

"You tell me," Blade said as he stretched in his stirrups, trying to gain a better view across the tall grass.

Wyethe said, "I d-d-don't like it."

Charles made a strangled noise at the back of his throat. He settled for waving his point riders into the grass. The arrogant sentry rode in first, his back straight as a ramrod.

A silence fell over the caravan, and over the broken road, and across the grassy field.

It was broken by a high-pitched squeal of anger and Castro pitched headfirst over his horse as the beast bolted in panic. A pack of wild pigs burst out of the undergrowth, ill-tempered and in a hurry.

The javelinas swept over him, squealing and grunting, their slotted feet and tusks tearing him to ribbons. He screamed once, tossed out of the grassy cover like a rag doll, but he was done for before Blade could reach him. In a wave of bristles and tusks, the beasts snorted and broke over the road, scattering riders on unnerved horses while the mule teams lifted their heads wisely and watched the javelinas disappear downhill into a gully.

Blade ground his palm onto the saddle horn. The rider, whoever he'd been, had been a lean and dangerous man. The javelinas had saved Thomas the trouble of doing something about him later. He watched the beasts grunting and disappearing into a gully.

Charlie steadied his pistol on his left wrist and fired, bringing down the boar at the rear. He signaled his guard. "Go get him, Stein. The wedding table can use some fresh meat."

His man nodded.

Wyethe shivered. "Lady" Nolan rode up then, on a mincing, cream-colored mule with one brown eye and one blue one, uncannily like those of his rider. She tilted her straw hat back. Wisps of light brown hair escaped as she did so. "What is it?" she asked.

"Javelinas. Gone now."

She wrinkled her nose slightly and looked at Blade with the blue eye. He had the eerie feeling she equally thoroughly examined Wyethe with the brown one. "We'd better get this procession underway. I don't like the barometric pressure."

"It's dropping?"

She nodded. "Rapidly."

Charles overheard and understood immediately. He waved the procession on. To Blade, he said, "What about Stein?"

"He can catch up with us. The carriages are slow enough."

The seven Protectors eventually grouped at the head of the

caravan, each drawn by his or her Intuition. If they had lacked such Intuition, they would not be Protectors. Four were women. Three men, and two of them older, white-haired, or bald. Of the men, only Blade was virile and vigorous. Three of the women were young enough . . . but none of them really caught his eye.

And yet Blade understood more than most that it would be disastrous if he did not marry and procreate soon. And if it were with another Protector, so that their talents might be passed on, so much the better. Thomas flexed his neck and looked up at the blue sky. It was not that he had not had his dalliances. It was only that his heart had never seemed too interested in what the rest of his body was doing. He found it highly ironic now that he was leading a marriage procession.

In two hours, they had reached the crest and were heading down its winding road to the immense leveled-off field before the sea bowls. Blade reined back. Blue sky had fled, pursued by gray. His ears registered the dropping pressure and he swallowed carefully to ease it. His scarf lay limply about his neck. The sky rumbled.

Lady Nolan let out a high cry, punctuated by, "Here it comes."

Charlie wheeled his horse. He gave a piercing whistle. "Head 'em in and get set up in the buildings! Hurry!"

Whips cracked. The mules broke into a run, their sleek pelts glistening with sweat and a patina of fine dirt. The carriages rocked unsteadily behind them. The children hung over the sides of their vans, whooping with excitement. The train of the bride's white lace dress streamed out a window. Blade watched Veronica gallop past, keeping pace, her face pale, for she knew the danger.

Wyethe muttered, "D-D-Denethan."

Lady Nolan fought her mule to a standstill as his stablemates went hurtling past. "Mindstorm," she said. It meant a storm of black panic and fear, driving strong men to irrational acts. For some paranormal reason, it would also create a turbulent weather front. Blade had seen strong winds and even rain accompany a sending from Denethan.

No one of them was strong enough to block Denethan. It would take all seven.

"Not here," Blade called. He spurred his black mare at the

heel of the caravan, and followed it to the outbuildings of the sea bowl.

It had been built before. None of them were exactly sure if it had been for religious ceremonies or entertainment, but the massive park and aquarium structures had stood the test of time well. Inside, one of the restaurant's kitchens had already been cleaned and stocked for the wedding banquet.

As for the bowls themselves, the locks and equipment and pumps were complicated enough that they were no longer maintained, except for the very outermost pool, at the edge of the docks. Blade hadn't been there in almost a year. He liked to think the sea bowls had been constructed for religious purposes.

He reined the mare to a halt and touched her lathered neck. The beast minced a sidestep or two, as the other six joined him.

Charlie waited, on foot, poised as though he was seriously considering running away and joining his guests in the temporary safety of the building.

Lady Nolan looked at him. "Go inside, Charlie," she said softly. "We'll hold it off here as best we can. Get the wedding done." The rising wind tore her hat from her head, and only its ribbons tied about her throat held it.

"But I need at least one of you inside as a bodyguard."

"Charlie, if you can't trust your own guests, then we can't help you. We need all seven to stand against the storm . . . and even then, we might not be enough. You know that. Marry the children and send them off while we have a chance."

· He couldn't meet her eyes—either of them—and turned away abruptly.

Blade dismounted and held Wyethe's mousy brown stallion as the Protector got down. The older man clamped his jaw tight against his fearful stuttering.

The sky blackened. Phosphorescent bolts stalked overhead, sizzling and striking at one another.

"Jesus," said Alderman. "When did he learn to do that?"

The plump, brown-skinned woman named Oletha muttered grimly. "He'll have our range soon."

"Clasp hands."

Blade's hand was squeezed tightly by Wyethe on one side and reassuringly by Lady Nolan on the other. He planted his booted feet firmly on the asphalt. His intuition sent his thoughts questing deep into the earth. Man sculpted creations of natural elements . . . he could feel the power and memory rooted in them. Blade felt the tiny bridges and interferences of synthetics. He had no power over or from synthetics. That was Denethan's strength, he'd been told. Blade gritted his teeth. His heart began to pound in involuntary reaction to the despair aimed at them.

The mindstorm broke. It lashed and battered at their minds, frizzling the synapses of their brains, short-circuiting their rationalities, searing their dreams. He felt Wyethe's palm go sweaty.

The air crackled. He smelled ozone. He shut his eyes against the intensity, but the blues and greens of the lightning burned through his lids.

Lady Nolan said tightly, "Let it go no farther than us." Each slow word was paced by a hard-fought determination to speak.

They made a shield against the sea bowls. The storm whirled and funneled down at them, at their very toes, lashing across the broken parking field. Chunks of asphalt exploded and flew off into nothingness. Stalking men, stick figures of lightning, ranged about them.

Blade realized that Denethan would kill them all to get to the children. Sweat dripped down his forehead and cut a path over his taut face.

Alderman went to his knees, slack in the lineup of Protectors, his bald pate crimson with the sudden pounding of his blood pressure.

Power speared Blade. From the blackened sky, a funnel dropped and began to twirl its deadly way toward them, the field and lot churning at its base. On its heels came the roar of a power mightier than anything he'd ever felt before. He dropped hands instinctively and stepped forward.

Lady Nolan let out a tiny cry of fear.

Blade looked into the storm. He unwound it in his mind, feeling the fury of it and trying to send it streaming away from them. He held up his left hand, and then, in defiance that smacked across the field, slammed his right fist into his palm. "Storm break!"

He had broken the line. The Protectors at his back might not stand without him. He most certainly couldn't stand alone against Denethan. But he threw his chin up. Overhead, the clouds boiled. Patches of blue broke through, and his scarf bannered from his neck.

"Thomas! Come back! He's too strong!"

Thomas grinned. He stood rooted in his elements. The enemy had parapsychology and he did, too, and more, he had the witchery of his elements, his time, behind him. He felt the storm give and then the fear drain as though he stood alone, a lightning rod that grounded Denethan's hatred. He stretched his hands up and felt the last vestige of his Intuition crackle outward, smashing the black funnel whirling toward him.

Oletha gave a cry and fainted dead away.

Charlie held up a punch glass. "To the Protectors!"

The hall rang with the toast. Blade felt himself blush beneath his weathered tan and was glad that few would be able to discern it. Lady Nolan, recovered from the outlay of psychic energy, arched the eyebrow over her brown eye.

"Modesty, Thomas?"

"I know, it ill becomes me." Thomas stood uncomfortably in the banquet hall. Veronica had taken his hat and he felt overexposed. He nodded toward the children, who stood shyly, their hands clasped, surrounded by adults and watched at a distance by their friends, separated for all time by a ritual they scarcely understood. "I think I'll wander around for a while. I'm not needed here anymore."

Nolan placed a hand on his arm. "Be careful," she said. "You have no reserves left."

The corner of his mouth quirked. "Neither does Denethan at the moment, if we're lucky."

"An assassin doesn't rely on Intuition," she said. She sniffed. "Now I've mothered you enough. Go on."

It was late afternoon when Blade stepped out into the sunlight. A cold wind smelling of sea and fog blew up the hill. It was the scent of the sea that drew him.

One of the secondary sea bowls had been filled. Thomas approached it cautiously, by way of the tunnel of the amphitheater. He ran a hand through its salted water.

The water was bitter and acidic. It stung his hand and he drew it out quickly. Nothing of the Pacific could live long in this water. One of the pumps, perhaps, was fouling the chemical mix. He passed that bowl by and went down to the grand one, the one that opened onto the Pacific itself. He stepped back and sat on a concrete and aluminum step. The aluminum was corroded and pitted. It dug at the smooth denim of his jeans.

He watched the sea bowl. It had a movement and life all its own. He'd spent one summer exploring the area and knew that down below was a huge window through which the secrets of the sea pool could be seen. But if he went down below, then he couldn't watch the surface up here.

And, he told himself, *nothing swam there anyhow.* He knew. He reached up and gently unwound the long white scarf from about his neck.

His gills sprang pulsing to attention.

He was tired. His Intuition had been drained away to return when it would, a fickle thing, like that of most Protectors, but better than having nothing. He sat, his hands loosely resting on his knees, staring into the hypnotic flow of the water.

Like a bright lance, the last glow of the sun off the water blinded him. Thomas sat up straight. He wondered how long he'd been sitting in the stands. *Long enough,* he thought, and stood.

A star danced on the brow of the water. It drew him. Blade wandered down the asphalt pathway to the water's edge where the water gate was open. Whatever creatures of the sea were once penned here had long ago been freed. Three summers ago he'd stood here and had been privileged to see a wild porpoise swim in, circle, and then swim out.

He anchored himself at the sea bowl's edge, scarf fluttering forgotten from his left hand. The star was the sun's reflection in the mirror of the water, the water that called to him now. His gills feathered in the salty wind. He breathed deeply, using them as they had been intended.

Blade shivered. *Why not?* he thought. He shed his jacket, kicked his boots off and dove in.

As he came up, the setting sun lit the water with fire, its rays shattered into a million hard diamonds bobbing on the surface. He sputtered—the Pacific was cold this time of year. He treaded water for a moment, his eyes dazzled.

And then he saw what had broken water in front of him, had come swimming through the sea gate and into the bowl, and was now watching him.

She was three times his size, nearly twice that of any dolphin or porpoise he'd ever seen. Her skin was azure blue and turquoise. The water sheeted off her like a gossamer veil as she tail-walked toward him. Blade had no doubt he was viewing a goddess. He held a hand up and she dove, spraying him with foam, and then arced up from below him, her hide grazing his hand as she surfaced.

They swam in tandem, dancing, he and the dolphin goddess. When she dove below, taking him with her, the salt water tanged through his gills and he wondered if he would live long enough to swim with her, embraced in her fins. But, unafraid, he sank in the dark sparkling water, whirling and twirling to the rhythm of her desires. When at last they gained the surface again, Blade broke into the air, gasping and gulping with exhilaration.

The dolphin smiled at him. She opened her jaw and took his hand in it gently, and bit down, her sharp teeth making a pattern of crimson diamonds down the back of his skin. The salt water stung in it. Blade shuddered as she let him go, knowing he'd been marked for the dolphin's own as surely as if he had been tattooed or banded.

A last whirl in the iridescent water, then she looked at him with an ancient wisdom, leaped the sea gate, and was gone.

Blade floated weakly in the water. He touched the chevron mark over his brow with a limp hand. He'd been marked for the second time. It was a mysticism, a spirituality he had not yet reached.

He swam to the concrete lip of the pool and pulled himself out.

Chapter 3

"To the newlyweds!" Charles said. His voice rang out gruffly over the muffled noise of merrymakers, but enough of them heard him that they echoed the toast.

Blade stood inside the restaurant archway, a blanket that smelled faintly of dog and mule thrown over his shoulders to dry him. He shrugged into it. Shock and giggles had greeted his wet condition.

From a shadowy corner to his right, he heard a whisper. "A jealous husband threw him in. Can you imagine? He just got here yesterday."

He turned an inquiring face toward the corner and the whispering stopped. "And so legends beget legends," he said wryly and strode into the main hall, ignoring the silence that followed him.

Charles captured him with a beefy arm. "Thank you, Thomas. That was nice."

"What was?"

" 'And so legends beget legends,' " Charles quoted. "An apt followup to my toast. I won't tell you what I heard about you falling in. Still wet?"

"Not quite. And I won't tell you what I saw when I jumped in." Irritated, Blade looked around for more interesting and infinitely more sober company.

But something in Blade's manner pierced Charles. He straightened up and set his champagne glass down. "The kids won't leave for a few minutes. I've got time. Come with me, and tell me what you saw."

In a quiet corner booth of the restaurant, Charles snagged Blade a cognac snifter off a passing tray and forced it into his hands. "I'm not as drunk as I appear," he said. "Nor you as fool-ish. I can't believe you decided to take a dive. What happened? Rumor has it you lost a fight with a jealous husband."

Thomas had replaced his white scarf. It rubbed over the del-icate, sensitive edges of his gills as he turned his head and looked harshly at Charles. "I was alone, and I jumped. Maybe you've forgotten why we went back to the sea and what we owe it."

Charles sat back. His fleshy neck overflowed the neckline of the tuxedo and his scars flushed purple. "I haven't forgotten," he said haltingly. He rubbed his neck. "What did you see?"

"A dolphin as big as an orca. Incredible. She came in from the open sea, over the sea gate . . . she danced for me. Then she marked me." Almost shyly, Thomas laid his hand and wrist down on the tabletop for Charles to see. The toothmarks had dried, crusted blood on them, but the pattern to come could be seen. "Have you ever heard of anything like that?"

Charles sucked in his breath and shook his head. "Never." He commandeered the untouched cognac snifter. "Maybe it's better not to ask questions."

He quaffed the cognac and jumped slightly as a young voice interrupted, "Daddy . . . it's time."

Jennifer withdrew her hand from her father's shoulder. She looked a little flushed, and the hem of her wedding dress had been grayed by dragging it on the floor while she danced. She stared at Thomas with wide gray-blue eyes, and blushed.

"Jenny! Yes, of course." Charles got to his feet much quicker than his bulk and inebriation should have allowed. "Come on, Thomas."

The restaurant crowd pushed outside. Charles went to a canvas-draped shape on the parking lot and, with a snap of his wrist, uncovered the paralight sitting on the asphalt. It was a gleaming antique relic from days of old and looked hardly big enough to hold two teenagers.

Thomas sucked in his breath. "Charlie, the wind raiders—"

"Come on. Denethan's already had his try at us. You broke the mindstorm. He won't be able to muster up anything else for days."

Blade looked at his old friend. "You knew that. You counted on that, didn't you? Even if you had to sacrifice the seven of us." At Charles' back, Lady Nolan swayed, and she looked at Thomas with outrage.

"Grow up. We do what we have to. Anyway, the sun's going down. Ramos has been piloting for several years. Even I won't know where he's taking her."

Veronica had steered Jennifer out into the evening, and she stood, her hands showing elegant knuckles as she gripped her daughter's shoulders tightly. She kissed Jennifer. "You remember what I told you."

"I will, Momma. Don't worry." Jenny hugged her mother vigorously. "We'll be back soon."

He felt a little out of balance as the rush of Intuition flooding him made his ears pound.

"With children," dark Ramos said. He grinned suddenly. "Like puppies!"

"God, let's hope not," Wyethe muttered. He stood on his toes. "Let's get this thing in the air." His fine white hair fluttered about his ears.

The wedding guests stood on the edge of the broken field as the paralight buzzed into motion and sped down the lot. It lifted easily, wafting into the sunset. Thomas blinked as the frail aircraft banked and headed north, up the coast. He knew the boy wouldn't fly much farther at night and that the fuel wouldn't let him get more than three or four days by horseback anyway. From there, they'd travel on foot to whatever sanctuary Charlie had found for them. He'd seen the packs on the floor of the aircraft.

Charles stood, his head craned back, as he watched the circling paralight. Jennifer's white wedding dress came floating out of the sky like a cloud and settled among them, to shocked gasps and a few titters. He smiled grimly as Veronica gathered up the dress and crushed it to her bosom. "Let's hope Ramos can steer by the stars like we taught him," he said to nobody in particular. "Come on, everybody! We've food and drink to finish off!"

At the door, Blade caught Charles by the elbow. "I'm leaving."

"So soon?"

He nodded. "You don't need me anymore. I'll take the black mare—she's fresher. You keep my gelding till I come by again."

"All right." Charles hesitated, then reached out and grabbed Thomas in an immense bear hug. "They'll be all right, won't they?"

"I'm sure they will," Blade answered. He knew then that Charles knew he was going to follow them, as far as he could, to ensure their safety. This was what his old friend had really wanted of him, and known he could not ask. For a Lord Protector to leave his county for the needs of a few, weighed against the needs of many, could not be asked. But it could be volunteered. Still, Thomas said nothing. It was better Charles not have his guesses confirmed if Denethan came hunting answers.

Chapter 4

From the look of it, the wedding reception was doomed to hang on all night and into the wee hours of the morning. That would make it more difficult for Thomas to evade the lovely thighs of Shellyann and leave the party unnoticed unless he left right now. Which was fine with Blade, for he wanted to stay as close on the trail of the paralight as possible. Charles followed him to the outbuilding being used for stabling where Blade ran his hand over his packs and discovered Charlie had brought along everything he might need to follow Jennifer and Ramos. There was even a crinkly bag of lemon drops. He said nothing about having been shamefully manipulated as he took the black mare's reins and led her outside, his friend at his heels.

They faced each other awkwardly in the twilight, the warmth of Charles' bear hug already stolen away by the wind off the ocean.

Blade wrapped his white scarf closer about his neck and ran his fingers about the collar of his jacket. The movement reassured him that he still had his three garrotes and two shuriken in place. Then he said, "I don't want to be seen following after. Pull your sentries in or make sure they're looking in the other direction." He would leave no witnesses to testify that he, the Lord Protector, had abandoned his post.

Charlie, however, took things in hand by summoning Wyethe and Alderman. When the two Protectors stumbled out of the building holding each other up and congratulating Charles on a splendid party, he interrupted brusquely, "Veronica says she's worried. I want to be sure Denethan can't bring his wind raiders."

Alderman's shining head glowed with an alcoholic flush.

His job presumably finished for the day, he hadn't stinted in partaking of the celebration. He stammered, "Projection. You want a Projection . . . Wyethe, I can't think!" The two men leaned against each other in confusion.

Thomas dug down in his pocket. His hand emerged wrapped about a smooth gray stone, a beach pebble ground down by sand and tide. He dropped the object into Alderman's palm. A spark arced between his hand and the other Protector's. "Here," Thomas said. "Use my pebble. Cast up a fog."

"Thank you, Blade," the old man got out. He made a fist about the pebble as though to keep its potency from leaking out. He and Wyethe strode shoulder to shoulder down the slope of landscaping toward the sea bowls, where it would be easiest to Project a low coastal fog. Blade watched them go, knowing theirs would have been illusion but now, based on his pebble and power, it would be real.

Veronica had been on edge all afternoon and he wondered fleetingly if it was due to more than hosting the wedding and giving her only daughter in marriage at such a young age. Ronnie's sharp blue eyes occasionally saw more than was visible to others. He caught Charlie's elbow as the DWP took a lumbering step after his weathermen.

"Where's Ronnie?"

"Inside, with the others. Leave her alone, Thomas, please. She won't tell you anything. This is just . . . a precaution. And it will give you better cover to leave." Charles put out his great, callused hand. "We'll be sitting down to council tomorrow. We'll come up with a workable plan for the nesters, but I won't do anything until you get back."

They locked grips. "I can't thank you enough—" the burly man began, and his voice choked to a halt.

"Then don't. I'll take extra water shares." Thomas loosened his friend's hand, took the mare's reins and swung up as the first wisps of fog began to creep up the slope. He shrugged into the collar of his leather jacket, felt the silken wrap of his scarf bunch up comfortably, and did not look back even as Charles yelled, "Good luck, Thomas. The mare's called Cindy."

The mist shrouded the peninsula completely by the time he reined the mare to a stop on the low crest overlooking the massive trail which led north up the coast and bordered the disaster-pocked basin. It hid fields he had not seen in a decade, and he didn't know if he could bear to look upon them now, assuming fog did not hug them in its obscuring embrace.

No more defoliant, he'd said. *The land was just recovering,* and Charles had ordered the vials put away. Unconsciously, Blade patted his jacket, feeling the inside pockets lined with similar vials.

But Thomas felt no guilt as he looked the area over now. *A single man was not a bad trade,* he thought. He'd seen these fields burning, plowed with the bone shards of the dead, ten years ago, in the last great battle against Denethan, before both sides had downscaled to hit and run raids, the cost of out-and-out war being too great.

His fingers twitched about the reins. He could ride around, far around, out of his way, but the night would have brought the paralight down, somewhere close to Zuma Beach, he guessed, and the fog would both hide the children and keep them there for the several days it would take him to catch up. There were ruins beckoning to him from the other side of the highway. He eyed them warily. Without his gauges they could be death traps for him as as they'd been for those who had died within the area during the Disasters.

The mare stomped uneasily, as if reading his own edginess, then stepped out across the field, her legs pushing the mist into swirls of gray as she took the short way across in answer to Blade's desire. He gave her her head, even as the mists coalesced around them and his curse came to life.

There was a borderline between parapsychology and witchery, a border which no man he had ever known could cross, save himself. He knew of no one else who could cast a fog with a painstakingly charmed pebble or who could see what haunted him now.

Never look at a ghost directly, his old mentor had told him. Gillander had trained him well to follow in his footsteps as a Lord Protector. Neither of them had figured the teacher would not be around to see his pupil succeed him. Perhaps Cindy saw the ghost as Blade did, for her ears pricked, then flattened, but the squeeze of Blade's legs about her barrel kept her to an easy trot, as he did not look at the apparition, but to the left of it, so that it could approach his right brain sensitivity as he'd been taught.

But he'd also learned never to meet a ghost on its own ground if he could help it, and drew the phantasm with them to where the fields leveled off and the broken edge of asphalt bordered them. He fought the mare to a stop and kept her curbed against shying as the manifestation caught up with him, its image in his peripheral vision.

The corner of his vision shimmered as if caught in a teardrop. Through it, he saw the mists gather and solidify until a rawboned man stood there, one shoulder hunched against a wind that did not blow in Thomas' twilight. He had no colors but white and gray and darkness and was difficult to see against the road. But he was there. No doubt of it.

His trousers bagged at the knees, and the frayed cuffs of the jacket were rolled back, and Blade could even see the stretched-out elastic suspenders underneath the jacket. Gillander, he recalled suddenly, had been a ruin crawler, too, and the elastic suspenders were a proud relic of a hazardous trip. They could no longer make elastic. Gillander was not bald, but his hairline had receded perilously far, and his colorless hair stood in a thatch as though he'd just run his fingers through it.

The ghost pointed a finger at him. Almost simultaneously, Thomas' skin prickled. The black mare shivered under him.

"Made me run hard enough to keep up with you."

"You could have stayed resting," Blade answered mildly.

"With you about, treading on my bones? Hardly. I've waited a long time to catch you riding by. How long has it been?"

"Ten years, give or take a few weeks."

The ghost mumbled a bit. Its image wavered, then flared into substance and color. "Look at me," it ordered.

"And be caught by you? Gill, you taught me better."

"I hadn't time to teach you everything. Who's Lord Protector in my place? You?"

Blade didn't answer. His mare pivoted suddenly, bringing his line of sight straight into those intense gray-green eyes of the ghost. Having met the calamity, he would not flinch from it. He stared until the phantasm gave, blinked, looked away. Not until then would Thomas acknowledge the patch of skin on the back of his neck that had gone ice cold, and the beads of sweat under the band of his hat.

"You are strong," Gillander said, and it was his voice that remained insubstantial. "You'll have to be."

"I know."

"What's it been like?"

"Since you've gone?" Thomas considered the ghost's question. He answered slowly, "Heaven and hell. We prosper, we dwindle. And the mutant keeps his distance, but harries at us."

"Do they know what to do with you?"

"I guess," Thomas answered flatly. "They made me executioner."

"Hah! Figures. They could never see beyond. Projections, Truth-reading, Thought-influence or Blocking, a little Precognition. What you can do, my boy, goes beyond that."

"Sometimes."

Gillander shrugged. "That's as may be. The sixth sense is a tricky one, and magic even shyer. How about water?"

"Some. Charles is working on an answer to that."

The ghost rubbed its forearms as though cold. "The ground is dry," it said. "My bones are brittle. This is a poor place you left me."

The tone of the apparition's voice bored through Thomas. He had not left Gill to die, he'd been driven off. But it was futile to argue with the dead. Thomas had much that Gillander's phantasm coveted.

The ghost sensed a lack of sympathy. It shrugged, pointing out a track across the ruins. "Are you going In-City tonight?"

"Perhaps. I haven't been here in a long time."

Gillander's thrice-broken nose twitched. "No wolfrats out yet. You might have some luck, Thomas. Be careful you don't catch more than you bargained for. You're being followed."

"I know," Thomas said levelly to the first and then reacted speechlessly to the last, touching his heels to Cindy's flanks, whirling her, but seeing nothing in the night.

The after-essence of his aged mentor was smiling when Thomas turned back, the black mare quivering between his suddenly tense calves. "You," Blade said harshly, "are only a retention of my memories. Wishful thinking. I'm tired of you."

Gillander shook his head. "Sorry, boy. I'm more than that. A manifestation of your curse, if you will. I no more wanted to be drawn up than you wished to be haunted. But here it is. Work with it or not, as you will." The ghost sat, Indian-style, upon the ground, Fog hissed and disappeared as though boiled out of existence.

"Who's following me?"

Patchy eyebrows raised. "Now you confuse me with Omnipotence. That I don't know, and you have a bit of time left. Spend it with me?"

"Do I have to cross your palms with silver?"

Gillander chuckled. "It would be difficult to try. Drop rein and sit with me, my boy."

Blade felt as though he had an iron bar frozen against his spine. The invitation went counter to every ounce of common sense he had. With a swiftness of movement as though cutting himself loose, he swung his leg over and dismounted. Cindy put her muzzle up and rolled her eyes, the whites showing, but stayed put in a ground-tie, as promised.

Thomas sat also. He reached out and his hand passed through the frayed cuffs and spindly forearms. He had expected it, but he had not expected the icy chill that accompanied the action.

Gillander put his hands out, palms facing. Thomas mimicked the action, his hands moving until almost, but not quite touching. As the warmth of his body touched the icy barrier of death, his aura flared out, and a corona of blue fire ringed the four hands.

"I have to move and move fast. The night Denethan attacked and you saved the perimeter—you moved time. I want to know how. Now tell me," Blade said, "and tell me true, or I'll find a way to rip the guts out of you as surely as I would Denethan's."

The ghost grinned.

Chapter 5

The sight of Gillander's bared teeth almost changed Thomas' mind. He shrugged mentally, and let his breathing even out and his thoughts shift into a more receptive mode. He felt his gills flare, prickling against the scarf. The auras of their nearly touching palms became clearer, more sharply defined.

"What do you wish me to tell you first?" the ghost asked mildly.

"Whatever you would have me know, Gill." Thomas bit back his sharper, more urgent needs.

"Then I would tell you that a Protector never, ever, leaves his territory. You are tied to it. Your energies are rooted there."

A sharp pebble under one lean hip ground at Blade. He nodded in answer to the ghost. "I know."

"Then you may not realize this. You're a naturalist, my boy. Your energies are grounded, bled out by artificial things. You feel it without realizing it—that's why the ruins excite you. There you're as blind as any man, walking the edge, and your blood runs hotter, knowing the danger."

His head shook in denial, an independent movement that Thomas had not ordered.

A whuff of disapproval as the other's aura flared, orange-red, against his hands. "The more fool you."

Blade felt his gaze narrow despite his attempt to stay aloof yet receptive. "I'm an enforcerer as well as a Protector," he said sharply. "My skills in that domain move with me."

"A murderer." The ghost sighed. The scent of his breath, faintly foul, drifted past Thomas' face. "Not what I would have taught you if I had had the time."

"Then teach me now."

"Impossible!" Gillander clucked his tongue over his teeth, making a sound as physical as if he still existed in flesh and blood, bone and ivory. "Still . . . what are you doing tromping on my deathbed?"

"Trailing."

"Someone important, I gather. Most important if you want to know how I moved time itself."

Blade said nothing. The ghost reared up high, elongating itself in the torso until it towered above his body. He did not even look up, forcing Gillander to shrink back in order to meet his eyes.

"For god's sake," his old mentor sputtered. "Do you think I would tell your secrets even now? To whom? I hate Denethan more than ever. Out there, on that hillside, my bones rub cartilage of his folk . . . my flesh decayed next to their scales. I smell the stink of their wrongness. They are not even human!"

Thomas relented. He said only, "I'm following hope."

The night grew very chill about them, though the fog from the coast gave them a wide berth and hesitated even to cross the broken road track Blade could see clearly through Gillander's opaque form.

"Saaa," murmured the old man. "Babes. Charles found his genetic pair. I knew we were close . . . and he's sent them away to hide them. How are they traveling, Thomas? Did you brew up this mist? It stinks of the sea."

"No." He felt his face twist in a smile. "Wyethe and Alderman."

"Ha! I'd like to give those two old farts an ache in their joints for that." Gillander wavered a little. Red flames came to life in his eyes, then died out. "But I interrupted you, boy."

"I'm trailing a paralight."

"It'll be beached, then. Just enough range to get them away from Denethan's gliders, probably." Gillander sucked hollow teeth in thought.

"Yes."

"How many riders?"

"Just two."

The flame points winked up again. "You'll never keep up by horseback. That contraption travels as far in an hour as you can in a day."

"There's a lot of fog this time of year," Thomas answered noncommittally.

"You'll need more than fog to keep out of Denethan's way. Ah. Now I know why you palaver with ghosts. Do I hear Denethan following? No. But I have no ears for wind raiders . . . I can only hear what strikes the ground. Hoofbeats. Yours and those of that other who follows you. Perhaps I'm wrong. Perhaps fog will stand you better than I thought. Although . . ." and Gillander's reedy voice hung on the word.

Blade's attention wandered. The ghost seemed mainly lonely despite Thomas' original hopes for real information. The broken cityscape beckoned. Under slabs of concrete and rusted wire forms stabbing the night like lethal spears lay the secrets of a dead city. And despite what Gillander had offered earlier, wolfrats were running across the horizon. He saw the flashes of their red eyes, tiny pinpricks of rodent hunger, as they loped across concrete canyons. A coyote yipped once sharply, as if in defiance, but even a coyote did not dare the ruins alone when the wolfrats were out.

The ghost noticed what drew his gaze. "The ruins make you itch, don't they? You were always as curious as a catling, Thomas." At the sound of his name, Blade looked back, caught by the power of the ghost's voice. "Want me to keep on teaching you? Then I offer you the thing you want. That's right, my boy. Listen to me well."

Sparks rippled about the corona of their upheld hands. They broke off and drifted away, fireflylike, until they hissed out as they reached the curling edges of the mist.

"You want to trail without being seen, keep up with the wind, and learn the secrets of the land. I can give you the ghost road, boy. My gift to you—an' my curse, too. But when you take the ghost road, power changes. You don't need to worry or wonder about paralights or wind raiders."

Blade's legs had gone numb. "Ghost road?" he repeated.

"That's right. You want it, don't you? I can tell."

He wanted nothing like it, knew nothing of it to know if he needed it or not, but he'd given Gillander too much of his trust and now the phantasm had him, gripped his being tightly between psychic teeth.

"It'll take you where you want to go, and when, and even a few places you don't! You've got to be careful. The resonances will be able to find you there—you'll be open to 'em, Thomas. I can't protect you from that—I'm a resonance myself. You'll be walking the bones of the dead, boy, drawing up their hatred and their joy and their fear to fuel you. It's a tough road to walk. You lose yourself, bit by bit. And there are things, Thomas, which transcend our normal dimensions and can find you on the ghost road. Pure evil, most like, though a good un gets through now and then. It'll kill you if you walk it too long, and twist and turn you long before that. Walk it too long, and you'll be one of the primeval ones, and the only fuel you can draw on is the hate and fear."

Thomas started thinking about the shuriken in his left cuff, the special one, made of cast iron, guaranteed to ground any vibration. Warrantied to drain away ghosts, a lightning rod for the supernatural. The blue-orange corona of their hands trembled as his fingers twitched. Gillander clucked again as if he read Blade's thoughts.

"Not nice. But you need a trial, I know. A lesson. Walk tonight, Thomas, on the ghost road. The wolfrats won't even scent you. But watch your back, because the ghosts will."

The corona flared suddenly, arcing out until his eyes watered from the glare and he shut them tight, tears leaking under his lids, the flare blasting through his eyelids which bled red from the inside. Then it got dark and very quiet.

Thomas woke still and cold, legs aching from being folded under him. His eyes were crusty and he rubbed them gently, feeling the grit stinging as he buffed it away with cautious fingertips. The ground was dank. The fog had gone, and the black mare grazed on scattered tufts of grass. Moonlight swayed overhead as he got to his feet, staggering like an arthritic old man. Lady Nolan had warned him about psychic backlash, and he'd just had a doozy of one, glad that it had been confined to hallucination. One booted foot was still numb and he stamped, trying to wake it into pins and needles. He tramped on something, caught it in the air as it flew toward his face, and opened his hand to look at it.

Your key, Thomas, to the ghost road.

A bleached-out skeletal finger rested in the palm of his hand. The bones of the little finger, misshapen through natural propensity—a crooked finger. A memory flashed through Thomas of Gillander matching hands with him, and the mentor's crooked small finger.

"For shrewdness, my boy," the spindly teacher had told him when they'd both been younger and Gill still alive. He had visions of Gillander clutching the dowsing rods, crooked little finger stuck out stubbornly from his right hand and framed by his worn sleeve cuff.

Of all the finger bones buried on this war field, how many would be crooked? He did not feel like calculating the odds. It did not matter. He knew whose bones he had. He could feel them radiating the hate and despair of matter bereft of soul and consigned to decay in the earth.

Thomas clenched his hand about the gift. He slipped the finger bones inside his jacket where they rattled next to a vial of poison. With a slap to the grazing mare's neck, he warded her quickly with a few mesquite twigs and left her there within a triangle of protection. His numbed foot quickly came to life as he jumped to the broken track and made his way down into the fringe of wreckage, willing to sacrifice some time exploring the ghost road in the hope of finding something to use against Denethan and his minions.

Light was always the problem in the ruins and being on the ghost road didn't change that. The best finds were underneath, below concrete slabs that might shift weight even as he sidled below into caverns of darkness that held stillness and death. Thomas disliked the inconvenience of carrying a lantern or torch, but he had little choice if he wanted to see what he might unearth. He swung underneath a jaw of concrete and dropped into the darkness, scattering a wolfrat's nest as he hit. It was empty and its stench burst cloudlike about him. He choked as he kicked free.

A tangled square of metal tried to bite into his ankle. He picked it up. The makeshift torch illuminated painted letters: E R NCH ARMS. Time and erosion had made the rest illegible. This building was likely to have been a dwelling, then, rather than a place of business. Thomas liked dwellings though he found most of their contents incomprehensible, ground to dust, and what had survived that, undecipherable. He dropped the crumpled sign and moved farther into the ruin.

The building had been thoroughly looted already. The stalls held little but rusty scraps of the cars stripped apart here, though the concrete still retained oil and grease spots, soaked into the cement. Signs of ransacking were everywhere amid the spoor of wolfrats that littered the garage flooring. He had a little time if he was cautious—the giant rodents would not be hunting here in their own warren. They would be coursing above—but would soon return, and if they came back hungry, his future held dire portents. Thomas raised his torch a little higher. The pillars bore the signatures of the gangs who had reigned here. Thomas scratched his chin. Before or after the demise of the building?

He fingered one of the markings as he passed it. The paint was still slick, viable, the signature meant to last the test of time. Charlie had an archivist who could probably read it, but the paint had long outlasted the regime of the signer.

Even here, in the bottom of the building, Thomas could see layers of life. What had happened here, just to this one building? Had it been in decline or had it been brought down by one of the Disasters?

Before Thomas could search further, he heard the click-clack of nails trotting along the concrete. Torchlight reflected in beady slants of crimson as the wolfrats returned to their tunnels.

As big or bigger than a coyote, the rodents trotted along their hunting grounds, scaled tails sliding behind them. Thomas froze, then reached for his shuriken and tossed it, hoping to bring down at least one of the rodents before they charged him.

With a whisper like the wind, the shuriken sank deep into the rodent's body. It keeled over with a shriek. Thomas sucked his breath in. How could he affect them from another dimension— and how vulnerable was he to the hunters? The pack halted uneasily and cast about, their rodent teeth showing like sabers as their lips curled back. They milled about yet could not see him though he stood less than ten feet away and their stink nearly choked him. Crimson beams flickered toward him. They sensed him, he knew they did, and he knew Gillander had lied to him about this. Part of the trial, he supposed. He put his hand inside his vest and cupped the bone. He sifted through its anger and dismay until he found a flicker of hope and drew on that.

The hair rose on the back of Thomas' neck. He dropped his torch and stamped it out, as the flame seemed to draw the rats' attention, and the glowing eyes blinked, shuttering him away from their sight. Then the death squeals of their wounded companion grew louder as a packmate decided to feed. In a frenzy, the pack turned on its own and tore it limb from limb.

He did not know if he was grateful or had merely lost his mind. And he did not know if he had the strength to walk on the bones of the dead.

Denethan awoke from his nap as the moon rose and saw his men seated around the fires, drinking beer and fermented asses' milk. They looked as one to him when the firelight illuminated his profile. He could see that they had worked diligently even during his rest . . . catapult towers lay ready to be installed, to launch wind raiders soaring off the cliffs.

Their whispers hushed, so that they could hear him speak.

"I have failed," he said. "But my powers have shown that this war will be won by warriors, and we are all warriors here!"

They shouted in agreement.

Their noise pleased him.

"We are not less than the wind in the desert."

"No!" they answered him.

"We are not less than the sand on the beaches."

"No!"

"And we are not less than men!"

"No! No! No!"

Denethan raised his palms. They quieted. "You've sworn blood oath to this raid. We all know that many of us here will not return. Take care, even so. My powers tell me that the plague is about. Take no prisoners except the children. And take pride in what we are about to accomplish!"

They jumped to their feet and their cries echoed. Denethan bowed his head and returned to his tent. The night air chilled him, and he was weary. The Protectors had grown much stronger than he'd expected. They had turned aside his Projection and one . . . yes, one had even been mighty enough to take up his thought and create new strength. He vowed they would not prove strong enough to stop him.

The black mare sensed Thomas as he crossed the broken track, and she put her head up with an inquiring whicker. The moon appeared to be no lower in the sky as he kicked apart the mesquite twigs forming a ward on the horse, and picked them up to return to his pack to be used again. As he slipped the twigs in and fastened the flap down, he paused in thought. Had time actually stopped while he was on the ghost road?

"How did you like the ghost road, my boy?" a reedy voice inquired at his back.

"You're not there," Thomas said without turning. "You're the product of psychic burnout."

"You're angry with me."

"You lied to me! I brought down a wolfrat."

"Just a tiny one. So I misled you. I'm a ghost, after all, and jealous of the life and spirit which animates you, no matter how much I loved you in life. Remember your lessons. Use the bones I left you. When and if you wish to travel the ghost road, meditate on them. Do what I showed you. Just remember—the ghosts can reach you. They'll leech the life out of you, if they can. But you're a smart boy, and quick, too. Oh, and remember that time is like the snake swallowing itself. There is no time for you on the ghost road, but you are dying with every step you take."

Thomas turned then, and saw the wispy, amorphous form of Gillander drifting next to him. "Nice," he said. "How long do I get?"

"I don't know. I've never had to worry about it before." His mentor smiled. "So don't push it, Thomas."

"Right." Thomas turned back to the mare and swung up.

The ghost trotted to keep up. "Leaving so soon?"

"Thought I might," the executioner said. "We both agree I'm being followed." He paused, then added, "Thanks, Gill. And rest in peace."

"I'll try," the ghost shouted after him.

Brush along the ridge crackled as Thomas crept along it and then lowered himself into position. He could hear the sound of hoofbeats drawing near. Only a fool rode in the dark—or someone desperate to catch up with him.

He fingered his throwing star. The night flared with the heat of the trailing horse. He could hear its lusty breath and the creak of leather. When it got close enough to smell, it would be within striking distance. Thomas tensed.

His nostrils filled with the stink of horse and lather and he rose from the brush, his arm going back in a smooth motion.

The wall-eyed mule half-reared in startlement, and the woman on its back pitched head over heels to the ground.

Chapter 6

She was too busy falling to kill him and for that Thomas was grateful. Unable to stop the release of the throwing star, he gave an extra twist with his wrist, sending the shuriken off its target by mere inches. As it soared into the night, the mule came to ground and stood protectively over its mistress.

Lady Nolan rolled to her side, gasping for air. In a moment, her face reddened and she got out, "Shit. And I was worried about you."

Thomas moved then, knowing she'd identified him and he was no longer a target for retaliation. He lifted her to her feet. "Are you all right?"

"No thanks to you." She rubbed one buttock.

"What are you doing out here?"

She looked at him in the dusky moonlight, her blue eye paled to silver. "Nice reception."

"I lost my best shuriken because of you," he pointed out. "And you wouldn't have been too hospitable to me if you hadn't been in midair."

"Perhaps." Her slender hands went back and she retied the traveling scarf that held back her hair. "However, I was following you. Therefore, I wouldn't have been too surprised if I had caught up." Her brown eye glinted at him.

Thomas caught her mule's reins and the cream-colored beast put up its head, giving him the same blue-eyed, brown-eyed stare.

"Thank you," he said tersely.

"You're welcome. I figured you wouldn't even be able to put wards up. Fog or no fog, Denethan's crew is bound to be out here, somewhere." Lady took her mount's reins from him. "I suggest we move off the bones of the dead."

Thomas backtracked, hoping for a gleam of metal in the moonlight. The Protector watched him a moment, then sighed.

"Your favorite?"

"My most accurate."

"Heaven forfend." She held out her right hand, fingers twitched, closed her brown eye, and the shuriken came gliding slowly out of the night. She caught it and tossed it deftly to him. Her face paled with this telekinetic effort.

Thomas replaced it in the collar of his jacket.

"No thanks necessary," the woman said, as she put boot in stirrup and mounted up.

Blade grinned. "And none given. But you keep showing off and neither of us will be in any shape to set wards."

Over a low-banked fire that held off the chill of the fog, Thomas said quietly, "Now tell me the real reason you were following me."

She looked up from the battered tin mug she cradled in her creased palms.

"And tell me the truth," he added, not saying what he meant, but her eyes widened slightly.

"Because you'd hate to have to kill me? Blade, you have depths I never imagined." She sighed, pushing her booted feet forward and crossing them at the ankles. "There are now five Protectors."

He straightened. "What happened? Who did we lose?"

"Nobody, you nit. But you abandoned your post—and so did I. For the same reason, I imagine . . . following the children."

An intense heat boiled up inside Thomas. "Damn Charlie—"

"No." She held up her right hand. "I had no idea he'd spent the day manipulating you. I had decided on my own. Jennifer is too young to send off that way and Charlie wouldn't tell me where he'd sent them. Quaker County is small enough that Oletha can cover them as well. I had—" She gave a low laugh. "I had an unquenchable desire to be a midwife."

Thomas shifted uneasily.

"I know," she said gently. "You travel alone. But when I found that sentry bound and gagged . . . I knew when I touched him you'd done it. So I sat there on Murphy—" At its name, the mule's long ears flicked, then it went back to grazing. "I sat there and tried to figure out what the hell you were doing. Then it came to me that you were doing what I was doing. Only you're more ruthless about not wanting any witnesses."

"Oh?"

Lady smiled. "I was just going to sit and have a mug of tea with the sentry—and drug his cup."

"Poison beats a chop to the neck for subtlety any day."

She looked away. The firelight made the round planes of her face even softer, almost cherubic, but Thomas realized that when he'd lifted her off the ground earlier, she'd been much lighter than he expected, and well-muscled. Her beauty was in curves rather than well-defined bone structure.

"I'm sorry."

"Oh, you don't have to be. We're in a dirty business, Thomas. I know that. Although I don't think the DWP has ever had quite as efficient an assassin as you are."

"Thank you."

She looked back quickly, muttered, "Good god, you think I'm complimenting you," and emptied her teacup out. "I'm going to take advantage of what's left of the night."

Thomas watched her settle back onto her saddle and blanket. He kicked apart the coals to settle the fire down even more, and lay back himself. Perhaps in the morning he'd think of a solution to his problem.

He shrugged into his worn leather jacket. Vials clinked together in the inner pockets as he did so, and among them clicked the finger bones of a dead man. When he slept, he dreamed of nothing, not even ghosts.

He awoke to the mule's bray. It sounded akin to the wail of a dying cat and hung on the fog-damp air of the morning. The beast had put its all into the gut-wrenching noise and stood exhausted, sucking air back into its lungs. Lady Nolan bounded to her feet, kicking aside a tangle of saddle blanket. She went quickly to her mount, slipping one arm about its neck and pinching its nostrils shut with her free hand as she brought its head to her chest and cradled it there as if in apology for gagging it.

Blade felt the tingle of power down his spine, that black unreasoning fear which gave Denethan's attacking raiders the edge in any fight. He rolled to his knees and cast about.

Lady felt it, too. She looked at Thomas, as wild-eyed as the beast she tried to calm. "Denethan."

"Has to be. On the wind." He made a lunge for the black mare as she began to lift her head for a whicker.

"How do you know?"

The mare shivered under his touch and stamped in the dust. He didn't know how he knew, he did just did, and he bit off, "That's his fastest way in."

Lady took her hand off the mule's muzzle, shaded her eyes and then pointed. "Catapults off those peaks, riding the thermals in—"

Thomas looked in the direction she indicated and felt his blood chill. To have launched so close to Charlie's—Denethan must have built catapults at the base of the peninsula. How could he have gotten in so close without being challenged?

He uncoiled. He was wasting time wondering about the mechanics of the invasion. The giant batwings sculling closer to them would have them spotted soon, if they didn't already.

"Across the track," he hissed to Lady. "Under the concrete."

"Rats—" she began in protest and then broke off. She kicked her dun-colored saddle under the furze bushes lining the campsite. Blade followed suit. He'd taken the nosepiece off Cindy, letting the headstall hang about her throat as if it were a catch instead of a bridle, Lady had done the same, so now they gathered up the loose reins and hustled the mounts across the broken roadtrack and into the shadow of the ruins. Cindy did as bade, but the mule planted front hooves stubbornly and refused to duck in under the overhang until Lady stepped back and planted a swift kick against its lean haunch. With a half-bleat of protest, the mule joined the black mare. Lady crowded in next and stood shoulder to shoulder with Thomas.

"You can't blame him," she muttered. "Mules have more sense than horses. None of us should be in here."

Thomas was unslinging his pack from his shoulder. He plucked out a vial and opened his rifle.

He ignored Lady's wide-eyed stare.

"You can't do that—it'll do no good without a direct hit and even then—if you hit a wing instead of the fuselage—the vial will simply bounce off."

Thomas did not look up as he dropped the vial into the firing chamber. Then, carefully, he searched a vest pocket until he came up with the ring he was looking for.

Even in the shadow, the exquisitely cut marquis diamond flashed.

"My god. That thing's worth a fortune."

"It will be if it saves our hides." Thomas raked the diamond edge across the handblown glass vial. It rasped as it etched a V-cut into the glass. he went back over the etching several times before he was satisfied. "Now," he murmured. "If it survives the firing, it should be weak enough to shatter on impact—any impact."

Lady Nolan had a hand up to her mouth and was backed up against her mule's flanks. The two chemicals inside the vial boiled about each other in a lethal dance. With a grunt of satisfaction for the mayhem he was about to cause, Thomas lifted the rifle.

The wind raiders drifting across the morning swirled and eddied, cankers on the face of the sky, great blots of corruption, meeting wing tip to wing tip as if conferring, then looping about. They flew unerringly toward the ruins, but in spiral search patterns. He calculated their most likely path.

Pleased, Thomas said, "They're just reconnoitering. They didn't spot us."

"Then let them go."

"No. They're between us and Zuma Beach."

"Zuma . . . the children? You know where they are?"

"I can guess where they are . . . or were, until the fog lifted." Thomas watched the raiders swoop about again. He began to squeeze the trigger.

"You can't possibly get them both."

"I don't have to," Thomas answered absently, his concentration on his target. "Bring one down, the second will come to us—or head back to report. Either way, the odds are more to my liking." He heard her begin to pace, then blocked her out. There was nothing in his sight or mind but the corridor his missile would travel and its intended destination.

The two wind raiders began to pull together as if magnetized. He squeezed the trigger back and felt the rifle jump in his cradled hold as it fired. Without looking, he wound back into position and tapped the firing chamber open for another vial.

"Jesus, you're a bloody bastard," Nolan was in the midst of saying, "no wonder you keep the glass smiths busy—" when the bullet struck and shattered and both wind raiders were engulfed in a cloud of noxious smoke. They tumbled to the earth like singed butterflies.

"Both of them," Lady breathed in astonishment as the raiders hit the ground, and Blade saw a dark figure tumble out, get to its feet, and run.

He dropped his rifle and sprinted after it.

"Thomas, no!" she cried, and the enemy stopped, turned, and angled toward the sound of her voice.

A sane man, or a sane *human,* would have kept running for freedom. *But not one of Denethan's ilk,* Blade told himself as he circled. *Stay clear of its teeth and claws.* He sped across the open ground, closing on his target. He pulled the throwing star from his collar as he jumped a wicked-looking chunk of asphalt. Quarry in his sights, something from below hit him in midair, shoulder into his torso, driving the wind out of him as he hit and rolled.

Two! Thomas cursed himself for not having seen the second one escape the noxious cloud of the wreckage. He had no time to worry about Lady Nolan as the being clutched him tightly and brought up its feet to begin clawing at his stomach. Blade kneed him in a region generally vulnerable and the lizard man recoiled with a hiss of pain. Thomas shuddered in revulsion and fought against the band of muscle holding his arms down, shuriken still gripped uselessly in his hand. They tumbled about on the earth—the field of bones—and Thomas saw a broken end spearing upward, out of the dry ground as if blossoming from there.

He wrestled his own lean bulk against that of the other, even as the lizard man snapped in Thomas' face, carrion-smelling fangs missing his cheek by a fraction of an inch. As he bucked backward, he ground his heels in and propelled himself upward. His attacker lost his grip, falling back, and Thomas lunged forward.

The being fell onto the bone with a scream and a bubbling hiss. The lizard man convulsed, his clawed feet drumming in pain.

Then the being looked at Thomas, and he saw the poison sacs behind the ears begin to bulge, and the lipless mouth pucker. "Mercy," the begin croaked, even as Thomas brought his hand up and slashed the throwing star across the exposed throat. Unspat poison drooled from the enemy's lips as the being's head lolled to one side and his thin, oddly formed chest sucked in for one last breath.

Thomas got shakily to his feet. He looked at his shuriken, where a nasty green film stained the metal. He started to wipe it off, then changed his mind. A poisoned edge might come in handy.

A high shriek tore the air behind him. Thomas whirled, Lady Nolan brought to mind again, and made for the concrete cave. A second shriek tore out of the darkness and a figure came stumbling out, sank to its knees, then toppled over. Thomas slowed to a deliberate walk. The creature struggled to pull a charm from around his neck and just as stubbornly, the charm twisted to garrote him. Thomas caught up with him where he lay, spent, lips gone ashen. He kicked the creature once, in the ribs. The vicious blow spent what little breath the being had and he expired with a rattling gasp.

Thomas looked down. This beast was even more vile than the other . . . the visible skin was patterned in beige and gray scales. He could see little human remaining in the being except for the wide open blue eyes, now glazing over in death. The creature wore a leather overvest and thin cotton pants, ballooning about its travesty of legs. Around its neck, the thongs of a medallion it wore had constricted until they cut into the wattle of reptilian skin. Lady Nolan had strangled it with its own amulet.

Thomas reached down. He snapped the amulet off and then ground it into dust beneath his boot heel. A sooty, oily smoke puffed out and dissipated. He spat. It was just as well Lady had killed him—Denethan's man would never have suffered interrogation.

The Protector stumbled out of the cave a second later, her face gray from her psychic endeavor, her hands shaking. Thomas went to her and took her elbow quickly, steadying her.

"Is he?"

"Yes. Both of them." He helped her to sit down in the sunshine and fresh air. The black mare whickered after him inquiringly, and he led both mounts out. There had been quite a struggle inside, from the torn and bruised grass and the dirt kicked up. The mule had a welt down its right foreleg. Thomas examined the cut. His forte was not Healing and he could not ask Lady to expend any more energy. He would have to keep it clean and hope the wound did not fester, but Denethan's carrion-eating troopers carried a poison of their own in their claws.

Lady Nolan looked up as he reemerged. The color had returned to her cheeks, but she sat hunched up, her arms about her knees. Her blouse had been torn and she'd knotted it together, but sat hiding the tear like a mortal wound, hugging it from sight.

Thomas decided to examine the body instead. Revulsion soured the taste in his mouth.

He toed the body over so as not to see its face any more, its saurian travesty of a human expression, with eyes as startlingly blue as those of the child bride he was trailing.

"It's not worth it," he said.

Lady Nolan cleared her throat. "What?"

He had been thinking aloud, but turned toward her. "I said it wasn't worth it. Better to die out as the human race than become *that*."

She got to her feet and stood unsteadily as if facing a high wind. "Then," she said with determination and drew herself up. "We'd better find the children before they do."

Chapter 7

Thomas looked over the bodies. He'd retrieved his rifle and the tack. Beyond, the two wind raiders burned, the smoke rising from them foul and rank smelling. He breathed deeply and felt his gills stir beneath the scarf as if to cleanse the odorous air. "We'll leave the bodies where they fell." The palms of his hands itched in agreement. He had no desire to touch the lizard folk again.

"The blood scent will draw the wolfrats."

"Exactly. They won't leave a trace. As for the raiders . . ."

Lady uncoiled and stood up. "They'll be in ashes soon."

The feather-light touch of power, however unwanted, scaled his spine. He cast about, looking over the hillocks, greenery starting to wilt in the sun's warmth. Far away, corrupted shadows drifted over the hills. "Damn." He grabbed for Cindy's reins.

"What is it?"

"More raiders. Come on." He headed back toward the cityscape.

She set her heels. "I won't go back in there."

"What choice do you have?"

The cream mule stamped a hoof and one ear flicked forward and then back. For a second, Thomas had the weird sensation that the beast was part and parcel of her ability, like an antenna probing the world. She was still pale. Her fingers plucked unconsciously at her knotted blouse. Then she reached out and took her mount in hand. "If you don't feel it, I can't tell you what it's like—but I can almost hear them, Thomas. Like an echo from yesterday."

He fell in step with her, saying, "Sticks and stones can break my bones, but words can never hurt me."

She flashed a look at him. "Any child can tell you words form the major part of his arsenal. But you know that."

They reached the edge of the overhang. Thomas looked over his shoulder. He could just barely see the batwings now. He slapped a hand to the mule's haunch as the animal slowed to his mistress' reluctant pace. "I hear them, too," he said softly. "But they can't touch us."

Or they would not be able to until he took the ghost road, and if Denethan's pursuers were hot on their heels, it was a course he might be forced into. Yet he would be exposing himself to mysteries he had not explored and did not know the rules to, except that his own life fueled every step. But he clamped his jaws shut as Lady Nolan led her mule into the shadows. Time enough for her to know later.

He angled their flight north and west, determined not to let Denethan's men drive them out of their way. As the sun climbed, and the blue sky filled with its brownish haze, Lady became more and more taciturn. They wound their way through leaning walls of concrete and wood, wood so frail with dry rot that when the mule brushed one beam, it disintegrated into powder and splinters. Lady froze as the debris showered her, nostrils pinched as she held back a cough.

Thomas looked up as a batwing shadowed them, then sailed onward.

She cleared her throat. "Did he see us?"

"I don't think so. We'll be underground again in a minute." He nodded ahead to a yawning gap in the ruins.

She shuddered. "The wolfrats will be out soon."

He thought. *Sooner than that—it's always night down below*—but said nothing to her. His leather jacket creaked as he reached up to pat the black mare's shoulder.

On the heels of his silence, she added defiantly, "You don't care, do you? You've a reputation for exploring the cities."

"I've a reputation for a lot of things," he answered. "Less than half of which is true. But I do explore when I can, under the right circumstances."

Darkness swallowed them, but it was fleeting. She blinked rapidly to adjust to the dappled lighting. The tunnel was open-roofed in spots, so he did not bother with a torch. He would have put a hand out to steady her, but she put her hand through her stirrup and leaned on the mule instead. She stumbled anyway and as he threw a hand out to help, she peered at him through the murky visibility.

She laughed. "At least I can testify that you don't glow in the dark."

He flushed, knowing that Shellyann had been discussing her hopeful prospects. "Not yet. But I suggest we wait until we're done here. I don't have my gauges with me . . . this area could be quite hazardous."

"Life is hazardous. This is damned dangerous."

He had no defense there. A sound echoed behind them and both mule and horse pricked their ears alertly.

"Coyote," Lady identified.

"This time of day?" Thomas turned and sighted back the way they had walked. Memory of the coyote he'd heard at night stirred inside him. He reached out, shoving at Lady's elbow. "Run for it. Go as fast as you can."

Still she hesitated. "Why?"

"Coyotes stay out of the ruins—that's the territory of the wolfrats. Unless that coyote is being driven to trail a prey. That's one of Denethan's tricks."

She began to stumble forward into the patchy dark of the tunnel. She spat out a pungent curse and added, "They were right about you. You're trouble."

"But worth it." Thomas grinned fiercely and broke into a jog to keep up with her. The tunnels were mostly laid with ties and rails, but a few spurs were bare, always leading back to the main corridor. The yip-yip-yaroo at their heels grew fainter. He began to think they had outrun the trackers when Lady threw up her hand and came to an abrupt halt.

Fresh air dried the sweat on his face. He took the time to run an inquiring hand down the black mare's left foreleg. She'd tripped up badly in the murk, but he felt no heat in the leg nor did she wince as he probed it deftly. The mule licked at his scratch, but the edges of the wound looked clean, despite the reputation of lizard scratches. Without looking up, he said, "Okay. Whenever you've caught your breath."

"I'm not leaving without *her*," Lady answered.

Thomas looked up sharply and shouldered her aside. Hud-

dled in a beam of light that broke through from a fiberglass cor-
rugated roof, was a dirty-faced girl. He hadn't heard her snivel-
ing over the animals' and his own panting, but now that his
senses were alerted to her presence, her sounds of misery were
deafening.

"Sweet heaven," he muttered. "She's a nester, a squatter.
Leave her be, we've got enough on our hands as it is."

"She's in trouble."

"She's an outcast and she wouldn't be here if she hadn't
chosen to be."

"She or her family couldn't pay Charlie's water tax, that's
what you mean."

He was shoulder to shoulder with Lady Nolan and now
leaned on her ever so gently. "She chose to be here. We haven't
the time to argue the justice of it now. The rest of her tribe will
slaughter us and suck the marrow out of our bones after they've
roasted us. Come on."

Lady looked at him in the thinning darkness. He kept his
face still, but the gaze of her eyes pierced him. "You'll kill her,"
the Protector said, "after we pass through, to keep her from
talking."

He shifted weight. "That's the law for nesters." Then, softly,
"At least it'll be quick."

"She's a human being."

"So are the kids we're trying to catch up with."

"And," Lady said, her voice lowering in emphasis, "she's in
labor."

He saw the awkward thrust of the girl's body, her knees
spread as she squatted in the shaft of light, chewing on her
knuckles and staring fearfully toward them.

He looked away. The girl let out another muffled groan and
began panting rapidly.

He couldn't close her out of his senses. "Oh, shit," he said,
and dropped the mare's reins. Almost as one, he and Lady
moved forward to her aid, Lady talking rapidly.

"We can't leave her here to the rats or Denethan's coyotes."

"We're not taking her with us."

Lady said nothing, but her mouth set firmly as she reached
the girl's side and smoothed back a mane of tangled hair to reveal the teen's haggard face.

Thomas stood over them. If the girl's family had fled their

holding, unable to pay for even enough water shares for their
own gardens, then where were the rest of her kin? As he
watched the swollen belly ripple under the rags of her gar-
ments, he thought it more likely she'd fled on her own—unable
to prove who the father of her baby was. Unlike Shellyann, who
could take pride in her maternity as a proven woman, this runaway likely had been soiled with nester seed.

An even worse sin in Charlie's quest for genetic purity.

The girl stopped panting, her temporary paralysis fled, and
like a snake, she lunged toward the pointed stick that stood
leaning in the corner.

Lady drew back, startled. The tapered end jabbed the air
where her blue eye had just been.

"Git away from me!"

"We want to help."

Even illuminated by the rays of light filtering down, the
girl's face was so filthy he could not tell the color of her skin.
She gave him a feral, sideways glance, even as she jabbed her
crude weapon at Lady's face a second time. Then a paroxysm
of labor struck and she doubled over, unable to hold the stick
steady. It clattered to the ground at her feet. She began to pant
and Lady reached out to hold her shoulders steady. Thomas
could sense the warmth and calmness she sent out for the
other's comfort. The girl would have none of it. She struck out
with a strength born of desperation and Lady Nolan went
rolling.

Thomas charged at her and half-picked her up, pinning her
arms against her sides. She rolled wild eyes at him, then
dropped her chin and began to sob. He loosened his grip and
she withdrew an arm cautiously as Lady got to her feet.

The girl traced the chevron scar on his left brow. "You've
been marked by *them*," she said so quiet he didn't think Lady
could catch her words.

"What? What do you mean?"

She looked at him shrewdly. "If you don't know, you'll
know when *they* want you to." She licked dry lips. "Help me.
Please." Another pain shuddered through her and he lowered
her into the cradle of Lady's arms."

"How long have you been out here alone?"

"Four, five months. I ca—can't remember." The girl bit
her lip.

"Couldn't prove the sire?"

She looked up from between strands of matted hair and tossed her head contemptuously. "Oh, I know who's the father all right. But when I told, they didn't believe me. Made it harder for all of us, so I ran off."

Lady had a smudge on her cheekbone where the girl had hit her. Her lips thinned slightly as she looked up. "Tell me," she said. "I'm a Protector. You're doing well, but if—"

"I'm not for dying, not this time." The girl's eyelids flickered. "But it's my own dad that got me pregnant."

Lady sucked in her breath sharply, but there was a wet mushing sound, and the ground beneath the squatting girl's feet grew damp and glistening.

The girl let out a startled chirp. Lady smoothed her brow and said, "That's the waters. It won't be long now."

Thomas stepped back to give the two room. He drew his knife from his wrist sheath. Lady's glance frowned briefly at him. "To cut the cord," he said defensively.

The runaway put her hand upon Lady's wrist. "I trust him," she said softly. "He's been marked."

Thomas moved away to pace uneasily.

He did not know if either Lady or the girl could hear it over the groans and pants of labor, but the muffled yowls of the coyotes drifted through the tunnels toward them. Whatever ground they'd gained was rapidly being eaten away. The miracle of birth was going to be the death of them all.

Chapter 8

A Protector of a county is just that, a protector. Sometimes an enforcer, particularly for the politics of water, but most times a judge, an arbitrator, and a shield. A Protector came to his duty with no name but the one he or she'd been born with, forsaking his own family, for the greater one of the community. Thomas had chosen his last name for his avocation and been awarded his knighthood for performance above the beyond the call of duty—but Lady had been so named at birth, and her surname of Nolan had been taken from that of her mentor.

Thomas stood now, at sentry, listening to the rhythmic panting of the girl behind him. He'd stood through enough births to know this might not be an easy one—that women sometimes broke their waters, then suffered through another day of labor, but he also knew he could not wait. The moment he heard the howls grow closer, when and if the howls grew closer, he would end the young mother's agony, his difficult choice already having been made for the good of the majority.

And he knew that Lady Nolan knew his decision as well. She coached the girl now, he could hear her calming voice though his own senses were pitched toward the outer world and the enemy trailing them. The hypnotic lull of her voice occasionally broke through his concentration and he found himself breathing in time with her. He pivoted toward them in irritation just as the girl let out a low wail and Lady gasped, "Thomas, help me! I'm exhausted."

He lowered himself at Lady's side. He could see a thatch of hair crowning, and knew the girl wailed because the birthing was stretching tender skin. He entwined his arms about Lady's, reached out with knife point and gingerly nicked the membrane, knowing that a clean cut would be better than a tear.

Lady cried out in triumph, "Now, push!"

The girl did so, and the baby's head came free. Thomas jerked his hands back as Lady reached for the infant. The Protector leaned on him or he would have thrust himself away, as a cold chill swept over him. He swallowed hard though his mouth had gone dry.

"Lady—"

"Not now, Thomas." She gave the young mother a too bright smile, her voice frayed. She was more spent than the mother. "The worst is over. One more push and I've got him."

"It . . . feels good to push."

"I know. Just go with it—now."

The baby slipped out, covered with the waxy coating some babies have, tiny thatch of hair sticking up on end, private parts red and swollen with the indignity of birth—all that Thomas had seen before. What he had not seen before was a babe with three legs . . . or perhaps that grotesquerie was a tail . . . and the wail that burbled out of its frog face was scarcely recognizable as a human sound. Unconsciously, he held the knife ready.

Lady Nolan took it from his numb fingers and deftly cut the cord. "Lean back, and take a breath. Then we've got a few more pushes."

"The baby?"

The woman was still. She'd taken off her traveling scarf and now wrapped the child in it for warmth. The girl leaned back against the tunnel wall. She turned her pale face toward Thomas as Lady swaddled the newborn from view. "What is it?" she asked, her voice edged in panic at what she'd read from Thomas' expression. "What's wrong with my baby?"

"Nothing, little one." Lady attuned her voice to its most soothing modulation, the strain showing in her face.

"It's the eleven year plague. Nothing else explains the monstrosity," said Thomas.

"No!"

"It has to be," Thomas protested.

"Father mated daughter . . . that's reason enough." Lady lost control of her voice. She looked to the girl, "But he's alive and that's all that matters. *Life.*"

Cat-quick, the disheveled girl snatched the child from

Nolan, child and knife, and unrolled the bundle which began to cry in distress. Her voice joined her son's in fear and horror. Too swiftly for either of them to prevent it, she struck with the knife and the child's cry stopped abruptly. She ripped the bloodstained scarf from the body and let it fall to ground. Her own body shuddered and expelled the afterbirth, one bloody monstrosity deposited on the cavern floor next to another. She bound herself as Lady Nolan let out a soft moan and toppled to the dirt, spent beyond her psychic reserves, all so that this mother and child could live. He swept Lady's hair from her face and checked her neck pulse. She'd be all right. He looked up to find the girl with the knife at the ready.

Thomas stood, keeping himself loose and prepared for action. Light angling in, illuminated her gamine face. She put her chin up. "Don't be following me."

"You can't go far. At least stay with us long enough to get out of the ruins."

Her lip lifted in an animal sneer. "I don't want to leave. This here's my home. I'm clean now, right? No more birthing monsters?"

"Maybe." His tongue felt like cotton. "The plague strikes differently. It could be you and your baby, or just the baby."

"I never heard of any plague."

He lifted his right hand. "They don't talk about it much. It comes in cycles. You're too young to remember. . . ."

"Don't come any closer. My lover will be coming for me."

"Your lover?"

She smiled then, and the smile transformed her into a sepia-hued madonna. The transformation confused Thomas long enough for her to reach out and touch his brow softly, murmuring a word as her fingers caressed his scar.

He heard her add, "You don't want to meet him just yet." The sound cut through the cord of his consciousness like a knife and he fell as though she'd stoned him.

He awoke to dusk, the yip-yaroo of the hunters ringing in his ears. He got to his knees and shook his head, groping for alertness. He heard Lady stir.

"Thomas?"

"I'm here. Are you all right?"

"Spent, that's all. What happened to you?"

"She nailed me," Blade lied. He had no more idea of what she'd done to him than why she put such store by his marking. He saw the knife lying on the ground in front of him and picked it up as he stood.

The babe and its afterbirth were gone, dirt scraped into a mound at the tunnel's side, a mound marked with stones and a pointed stick made into a crude wooden cross.

Lady, braced against the tunnel walls, put her hand to her mouth. "Oh, Thomas—she buried him."

The mound would not last when the coyotes came through. With a muffled curse, Thomas, his legs still weak at the knees, wove his way to the black mare. What in hell had that little bitch done to him? He pulled out his canteen, and the mesquite twigs that could carry the psychometric echoes of a telepathic warn-off. He returned, wiping his mouth from a long pull of the warmish water, and handed the canteen to Lady. As she took a similar drink, he squatted over the mound and set up the wards to protect it. When he finished, he ran his hand over the cross and pulled away a tuft of thick, brown hair . . . coarse and musky smelling between his fingers . . . and distinctly not human. Something else had been down there with them and the girl. He tucked it out of sight in his jacket pocket.

When Lady handed the canteen back, her eyes glinted moistly as she said, "Thank you."

He did not ask her for what she thanked him. A second howl pierced the silence. Lady scrubbed her eyes and said, "We've got to get out of here."

He shook his head. "Too close. We're done already."

"You can't be serious about making a stand here!"

"No." He reached inside his jacket again, and this time removed a dead man's finger bones. "But you may not like this idea any better."

The mule proved more stubborn. It stood with hooves planted firmly, long ears twitching forward and back, back and forward, as Lady pulled on its bridle. "Come on, Murphy. What's done is done!"

Thomas bypassed them, leading the black mare. A fine sweat dappled his brow. The road he'd opened before them crossed over the hatred and misery of a thousand million souls. The feeling of walking on it clawed at his guts. He didn't know what he felt, but he knew every step on the ghost road would weaken him. "You can't blame him, Lady."

"Don't want to blame him. I just want to *move* him." Lady backed up and Murphy, sensing the windup to a powerful kick in the haunches, hastily broke into a trot.

Thomas scratched his nose to muffle his response as Lady cursed and ran to catch up.

They strode in silence for a time. Lady's hair, without a scarf to hold it back, fluffed about her face, softening the lines of her chin and jaw even more. There was a thread or two of gray in her hair, but Thomas had seen the young go gray before and now he thought absently that she probably wasn't much, if any, older than he was. It was her talent for mothering that aged her. He thought about the flower-bedecked straw hat she'd worn for the wedding. She'd probably woven it herself with strong, capable hands.

She looked toward him as if netted by his thoughts. "Would you have killed it if she hadn't?"

His mouth pulled. "You always ask the hard questions, don't you?"

"Someone has to." The set of her face etched about her eyes, the beginning of wrinkles.

"Probably. It was plague-born."

"You don't know for sure!"

He put a comforting hand on the black mare's shoulder as the tension in their voices alarmed the animal. "The girl seemed unmarked enough. There was no reason for the baby to have been so deformed. All I know about the plague is what we all know—it's a constantly mutating virus that attaches itself to our DNA and changes it. It causes abominations far worse than the adaptive ones given us years ago. If it goes on unchecked, there'll be nothing human left of us. We might as well never have crawled out of the sea!" Unconsciously, he took his hand from Cindy and fingered the scarf about his neck.

Lady's mouth half-opened, but then she shut it firmly on whatever it was she had been about to say. Instead she said, "The only chance we have seems to be that it's a very short-lived virus. It attacks a few and then becomes dormant for another decade."

"It only needs to attack a few," Thomas said bitterly. "There're so few of us left."

"Life is still life," she argued.

He flicked a glance at her as she walked along, the peculiar dusk of the ghost road paling her face. "I refuse," he answered, "to argue the quality of life."

"But you can't! You don't know what their potentials are, or what they think and feel."

"I know what I think. I know what I feel. That's enough for me."

"You really hate those gills, don't you?"

Her voice did not invite his answer, so he didn't, but he could feel his face turn hot. He tugged savagely on Cindy's headstall, pulling the black mare into the lead as the tunnel narrowed down and he had an excuse for walking alone. The aforementioned gills stirred, prickled into erection, and he ignored their throbbing in his neck.

Without those gills, he could never dance with dolphins. Nor could his ancestors have lived in the ocean environment until the earth had stopped revolting. But they were not what he would have chosen when the genes were being spliced. He might have chosen wings instead, to have flown above all this—

Lady stumbled at his heels. "Rats!" she said hoarsely, her throat gone tight with fear.

Thomas swung about. The mule threw its head up, shying away and bolting past him, its passage pinning the smaller black mare up against the wall. The mule stopped where the tunnel widened and came about, teeth bared, ready for a stand.

Blade slapped a hand up against his saddlebags, found the rifle sheath, and pulled it free. He pushed Lady behind him and could feel her trembling. He heard the rush of their clawed feet upon the packed dirt and rail way now, and the slither of their scaled tails behind them. As the pack rounded the bend, the dusk caught the glow of their slanted, crimson eyes.

He put a free hand back to pat Lady Nolan comfortingly. "Remember, we're on the ghost road. They shouldn't be any menace to us."

Her whisper back was tense. "Pat me there again and you'll have more than wolfrats to worry about."

Thomas chuckled as he opened the rifle's firing chamber, just in case, and tapped a vial into it.

The pack stopped just into their neck of the tunnel and

milled about. They were a lean and mangy bunch, coyote-high at the shoulders, their tails dragging behind, scaled and scarred. They pulled back lips into rodent snarls, whiskers quivering as they sniffed the air. Predator primeval and it appeared they could hunt the ghost road as well as any other.

"They don't look unaware of us," whispered Lady.

"My thoughts," muttered Thomas. He locked the rifle into position and lifted it.

The lead rat, a beast of mingled gray and brown, with a white patch on his forehead that bled away into a transparent ear, put his muzzle up, winding the air enthusiastically. At his haunch, a brown and white spotted rat lifted its leg and peed upon the track, filling the tunnel with its pungent odor. The rats milled about their leader then, unsure about going either forward or backward. They mumbled jaws at each other, rodent tusks clashing.

The lead rat lowered his muzzle a tad and looked dead on at Blade. He could feel the heat of the beast's hunger. He knew the beast had to sense him. Perhaps Gillander's bones could shade the four of them only so well. Perhaps his blood still ran hot.

With a sudden squeal, the wolfrat launched himself at them, his packmates shrilling and charging behind him.

Chapter 9

"Damn you, Gill," Thomas said as he pulled the trigger and whirled to hotfoot it out of there. From behind his left ear, a wheezy whisper answered, "So I was wrong about the wolfrats. Sorry, m'boy."

Lady had already taken to her heels, beating on the haunches of the black mare and screaming harshly at the mule which retreated with a defiant bray. Thomas pointed to a broken bank, leading above despite its treacherous footing. "Up there!"

"Above?"

"You got a better idea?"

She didn't. She threw herself on the embankment to claw her way up. Behind them, the rats emitted bloodthirsty squeals even as the magnesium/water vial shattered in the tunnel and burst into a flare as the two mixed. White fire stabbed at Thomas as he whipped both the mare and mule out of the tunnel, their reins flapping as they bucked and crow-hopped over Lady and onto the lip of the embankment.

He took a running leap. His fingers found a purchase, and he kicked his boots up as the bank crumbled under his soles. Something caught at him and he looked back to see a rat fall back, teeth clashing, his boot heel scarred from one saber-toothed fang.

"Thomas!" Lady swung at him, caught his forearm and pulled with all her strength, both colored eyes blazing in determination.

He scrambled up beside her. The rats milled about below, working themselves into a frenzy to follow. The leader leaped futilely, his face blistered and bloody from the magnesium flare. Blade didn't have enough throwing stars to handle the pack. Close range combat looked more favorable, particularly if he could take them on as they came up the bank. He pulled his knife.

"I'll take 'em one at a time. You kick back the others, if you can."

Lady pulled on his arm. "Thomas, listen!"

Over the high-pitched rage of the wolfrats, he heard the suddenly crystal clear yip-yaroo of the coyotes.

"Jesus! Doesn't anything work on this ghost road?"

Gillander sounded peeved. "There's a knack to it you haven't quite got yet—"

"Shit!" he answered the ghost. "I haven't got the time to learn!" He took a swipe at the first rat clambering out of the tunnel after them.

It made a high-pitched chirp and lunged at his thighs, whiskers peeled back against snarling, pointed jaws. Its left eye was clouded and its gray pelt blistered. And it was hungry. Drool rolled off its saber teeth as it snapped at him. Thomas kicked it under its head and as it reared back in pain, he slashed across the exposed throat. With a peculiar sound, Lady kicked it off the rim and it fell, squealing and bleeding, among its packmates.

The wolfrats immediately attacked it themselves. Lady's face was greenish as she staggered back to him as they forgot their original prey.

"Let's get out of here," she begged.

Thomas threw a quick look over the edge to see how busy they'd be. The leader lifted his wedge-shaped head to return the look, then went back to tearing and crunching the carcass still quivering in its death throes.

"Looks good to me," he said, and followed Lady Nolan who'd already made a decision and was throwing a leg over the mule's saddle.

The black mare was not so accommodating. Thomas made a grab for her headstall, but the sound of the feeding frenzy down in the tunnel had made her wild-eyed and she shied away from his touch. Lady leaned in her stirrups to make a grab at the reins; she missed and nearly lost her seat. Thomas spread his hands and coaxed the mare nearer.

"Thomas!"

Lady's warning paired with the howl of coyotes. Thomas

whirled. He could not see through the cityscape, but the beasts were close on their heels, they had to be!

He turned back around and lunged at the mare, grabbing the stirrup as she bunched up, ready to bolt, the whites of her eyes showing in maddened panic. He snubbed her with her own reins and mounted, loosening the reins as soon as he had both feet firmly in the stirrups. She gave a little hop, ramming the shoulder of Lady's mule.

The coyotes broke the shadows of the corner, dun forms fleeting across the eerie dusk of the ghost road. Their eyes gleamed yellow and green. They were silent predators leaping broken canyons. Their tongues lolled pinkly out of their grinning mouths. It was no longer necessary to howl to give away their prey—they were found!

"Get out of here!"

Lady looked at him, her face sheet-white. "Not without you!"

"You've got no choice. I'm in between and here's where I'm going to stay! Now, get! I'll catch up."

"No. Not without you!"

Thomas gripped the mare as hard as he could. He looked over his shoulder. The coyotes seemed almost to be in slow motion, bounding across the asphalt chunks of what had been a six lane road.

"Don't argue with me!"

"I won't go without you."

He slapped the ends of the reins against the mule's cream-colored butt. "Get out of here!"

The mule had more sense than its rider and charged into movement even as Lady Nolan shouted defiance and hauled back on its reins. Pink foam sprayed from its open mouth as the bit cut in.

Thomas slewed the mare around to face the coyote pack just in time to see them launch themselves at him. He reached deeper into the despair and hatred that was the foundation of the road, felt his chest grow chill, and his mind darken. But he had it—he had the fabric of the ghost road and wrapped it tightly about him like a shroud.

The leader came at him and a second leaped at the black mare's heels, wolflike, to hamstring her. He caught a glimpse of flashing eyes and ivory jaws. He threw his right arm up as he tossed the knife into his left hand and the mare let out a pealing whinny of fear.

Hotter than fire, the coyote passed through his form as though he wasn't even there. The predator tumbled to the lip of the ditch and bounded to his feet, head low and growling.

The entire pack ran through him, each beast a brand—and not one of them able to touch his flesh. Thomas kneed the mare after the mule and she plunged forward, her neck lathered gray and her hide shivering. The mule showed its heels to her and the mare plowed along in its wake.

"There," said Gill behind his left ear. "Satisfied?"

Behind came the sounds of coyote pack meeting wolfrat pack. Thomas shrugged deeper into his leather jacket. He did not understand what was physical and what was not on this ghost road—only that he could not trust his senses, any of them. And if he stayed in this dimension of cold unlife, he would need a death shroud indeed.

He rode hard after Lady Nolan and watched her brown hair streaming loose on the wind.

He examined the coyote dung on the patchy road and then stood up, eying the sun and clouds overhead. He said to Lady's blue eye, "Three days old, I'd say." He'd thought he'd never get warm again, but real time beat down on him and he'd not go back to the ghost road unless it were a matter of life and death. His heart beat sluggishly and his legs were still ice-cold numb from the knees down.

"So you were nearly savaged by a pack of animals three days gone?"

"Looks like it." It was warm inside his leather jacket. He thought of taking it off and lashing it behind the saddle, but things were too tense to risk losing it if he were unseated or lost the mare. He mounted up and scanned the curving foothills. "Zuma Beach is on the other side of that."

"Good. I'm for riding a little farther."

"Hungry?"

"God, yes." She swept her hair back from her forehead. "And I can hear Murphy's stomach cranking from here."

"The ghost road. It bends time somehow, I think."

"So this morning is actually two or three days from when we thought it was."

He shrugged.

"I thought you were supposed to save time."

"We made great time once we left the tunnel," he pointed out. It was her turn to shrug.

"Where are the children?"

"Who knows? From the dew on the ground, I'd say there's been quite a bit of fog through here. Maybe they're still grounded most of the day."

"And they're low on fuel." The two of them had discussed the backpacks Thomas had seen. Soon their quarry would be on foot and much easier to follow.

He nodded. Cindy fell into step with the mule. Lady rode silently for a handspan of yards, then said, "Would you have killed that girl?"

"Don't think so."

"But you said the baby was plagued."

"I'm no doctor. I don't know what went on inside her body. The baby was obvious."

She fell silent again for a while. Then, "I could be contaminated. Or you."

"Doubtful. The contagion takes more exposure than that."

"But the virus is airborne."

He looked over at her. "Are you afraid?"

"Shit, yes. And you are, too."

He felt the morning breeze through his thinning hairline. His wrist itched where the dolphin's teeth had scarred him. He rubbed it absently. "Not for myself," he said, reluctantly.

"Like Denethan?"

"Like me." He heeled the mare ahead of the mule, and left Lady behind as he followed the broken road toward the coastal foothills and the wide beaches he knew lay beyond.

When the mental whiplash flicked him, he thought perhaps it was her, lashing out in anger.

Then he realized that her Talent lay in Telekinesis and Healing. Not this attack that fried around the edges of his thoughts. He reeled in the saddle. Instinctively, he flung up an arm to protect his skull. He couldn't get a shield up; the ghost road had drained him dry.

"Thomas! What is it?"

The air crackled. He could barely hear Lady's alarmed

words through the static. He opened his mouth to speak. His words sounded with the blue flash of lightning and ozone stink.

"Mindstorm. . . ."

Lady grabbed up the reins from him. He doubled over, the saddle horn gouging his rib cage.

Denethan was reaching for him. He could see it if he closed his eyes!

Blade shuddered. He knew he could break Denethan. He'd done it before. There had to be reserves inside him that he could tap. Desperately he reached deep into his determination. He half-formed a shield and hunched under it.

The two mounts stood in the road, the mare dancing nervously under her burden. Blade rolled an eye at Lady.

"The beach! Ride for it. Lead me."

Lady nodded. He lolled back in the saddle and let himself go to war.

Denethan straightened. His smile thinned. *He had him.* His coyote trackers had found something warm and vital— something so hot and pure that it was like molten rock. It had cooled, but now as he searched northward, he had felt it again—and it was his quarry!

He recognized the shield that had broken his sending before. Powerful, this one . . . the light to his dark, two sides of the same coin. He recognized the kinship immediately. The rock throne cradled his form, brought the sun's warmth to him, as the lethargy of nighttime crept away. His concentration waned slightly as his adjunct stole up to him and said, "The catapults are ready."

"Not now! I have him! Get away from me. Post a watch. Send me the scribe." All this through gritted teeth. Denethan dare not lose the contact, not when he had spent the better part of two days searching for it. Who was this unknown wrestling with him? He had Talent, no doubt of that—Denethan could not reach anyone without it—was he one of the fabled Protectors? If so. . . .

Denethan drummed his nails upon the rock. He could not have contact without Talent—and yet the better the contact, the better the ability of the other to defeat him. It was like a handshake . . . the more openhanded, the more sincere the gesture, unless the other got a grip on him that could bring him to his knees.

"I am here, Denethan," the scribe said mildly and curled up on a rock near Denethan's feet.

The man opened his eyes a slit and saw the scribe. The scribe was aged, had worked for Denethan's father. His thin hair was blue-white, his eyelids sagged over weary eyes, but the hand that held the pen was steady. Denethan closed his eyes again as soon as he ascertained that the other hand and two supple, bared feet were empty of weapons.

Although, as Denethan well knew, even a pen could be a weapon. His father's life had ended with one buried in his jugular.

He spared enough energy to signal the other to wait silently and record what Denethan said.

Chapter 10

Lady Nolan rode slowly. She let her mule pick out its own road in its wisdom and watched Thomas instead. His weather-beaten face paled as the trance dragged him under like a drowning man, and she wondered if he would awaken again. There were lines carved like deep crevices in his face and his eyes looked sunken. The ghost road had taken a terrible toll and left him almost defenseless against Denethan's psychic attack.

Never in all the learned history of Protectors had they dueled with an enemy such as this. She had felt it when Thomas broke Denethan's storm before and she could feel the incandescent energies now . . . she was like a moth twirling in the light motes before a lantern, drawn to it and knowing that for the sake of her life she must not enter.

She reached over and gently disentangled Thomas' now limp white scarf from around his neck. His gills were flared, rose-pink with exertion. She dampened the scarf with the meager supply left in her canteen and replaced it hopefully. Thomas' head bobbled about on his neck.

She watched anxiously for burnout, the sudden nova of power that could leave him a mere shell of a being. Her mentor Nolan had been destroyed doing mental exercises he was no longer empowered to do. Burnout was like the brilliant guttering of a candle just before it drowned in its own melted wax.

The sky darkened. Her ears popped as the air pressure dropped suddenly, and thunder rumbled. Lady looked about. Clouds of slate and ebony arced over the browning foothills. She smelled rain as well as salt air. But the swirl of activity covered a small area and she and Blade were its epicenter.

Lightning struck behind them on the road. The air filled with the smell of burning pitch. The ground thrilled as the shock wave rolled under them, and both mounts danced nervously. The display was not as dark and dangerous as that which had threatened them on the peninsula. Both Denethan and Thomas had to be nearing the bottom of their stamina.

Cindy stumbled, nearly pitching Thomas over her neck. He did not react to save himself—Lady caught him and almost lost her own seat. She looked about her in irritation, wondering if she should lash him to the saddle, and not finding a spare strap to do it with. She reined up Murphy, dropping back to the black mare's flanks to search Thomas' saddlebags.

She found the rope almost immediately. She pulled out the coil, relieved she would not have to paw through his personal effects further. He mumbled as she tied his wrists together and loosely tethered him to the saddle horn. She kept the end of the rope wrapped about her own saddle horn to jerk him free if she needed to. Better he should fall than be dragged by the mare if she bolted.

Irritation crawled up her spine. Sweat dripped down the back of her neck, under the mane of her hair. She blew, angling her breath toward her forehead, cooling her face briefly, wishing for her straw hat. If only rain would fall. A wind current tore through, expiring as quickly as it came up. She thought of the paralight on a storm-ridden thermal and fretted over Jennifer and Ramos. Several fat drops of water beat down and stopped.

The clouds swirled away, boiled off by a relentless sun. Did that mean Thomas held, or even was winning? She dared not guess, but kept the mule and the mare pointed relentlessly toward Zuma Beach. Her hair crackled in the residual static electricity that hovered about Thomas like an aura.

She was not used to extended riding, and her thighs chafed horribly as the high noon sun beat down on her head and they rode through the foothills, and down to the beach side. The ocean's sparkle hit her sight with a blinding flash of gray-blue, but its breeze brought a welcoming coolness to her flushed cheeks.

She pulled both animals to a halt. Thomas stirred for the first time in the last several hours. His lips were cracked. They were glued together and flakes sloughed apart reluctantly as he mumbled something.

Lady leaned close. "What is it, Thomas?"

"Ground. Ground me."

Puzzled, she straightened. Was that what he had said, or was he groaning? Why not, "Let me down?"

He convulsed. His feet came free of the stirrups. Uncertainly, Lady pulled the rope free, reached over and pushed.

He fell like a wet bag of grain. Sand clouds puffed up about his body. She watched a moment, then dismounted herself, her knees locking up for a moment. She staggered over and knelt beside Thomas' motionless form.

He didn't look as though he were still breathing.

"Shit." She tore at the neck of his shirt, laying it open so she could feel for a pulse in his neck. Beneath the white silk scarf, the gills fluttered madly, gasping for air. The rest of his body seemed not to be functioning. Did he dream he was swimming? If so, the dream would be fatal. She pounded the heel of her hand on his sternum. "Breathe, Thomas, dammit, breathe!"

Denethan had him. Thomas worried at the mindstorm that engulfed him, a maelstrom in his ocean of thought that threatened to suck him down and bury him forever, so far below the surface of consciousness that he could never return. He had to breathe and could not, to think and speak, and could not. He could not form a cogent thought . . . but he had to, it was the lifeline he needed to cling to.

He thought of the enemy. Denethan could not deny him that thought or he would deny himself—possibly even destroy himself. Thomas clung to it, a buoy in the miasma pulling him down. He fought the fear and panic that the other fed him—told his heart that it was strong enough to keep beating. He fought back to the surface, a long, slow fight that ached in his very bones. Gillander spoke behind his left ear . . . a niche reserved for haunts, Thomas supposed. "Remember your grounding, boy. You pull your strength from the earth. Denethan's a mademan. He pulls his from artifices. Get yourself to ground!"

The Lizard of Oz did not want to let him go, not yet, but Thomas had one last strike left in him. He lashed out, and as suddenly found himself washed ashore, in the midst of grit and sand. He could feel its burning warmth beneath him and reached out to anchor himself with Lady's strength, if she was still with him.

* * *

Denethan reeled back. The scribe motioned to a nearby servant and took up a bucket of water and a sponge and laved his face, the inside of his wrists, the nape of his neck.

"He was strong," the old scribe said.

"Yes." Denethan leaned back and half-closed his eyes. "Strong and hateful. Before I find the children, before I deal with any of the others—him, I will have to kill." He coiled in the sunlight, drawing in energy for a new strike.

He lunged upward into her face so suddenly she screamed. His eyes opened, pupils rolled back in their sockets. In reflex, she slapped him across the face and fell back in the sand.

He sat straight up, threw his head back and collapsed. This time, he breathed. Noisily, gustily, like a spent runner. The mark of her hand was the only spot of color on his face.

He opened his eyes as she knelt forward. His parched lips struggled to form words. She leaned close to catch them. His life, their lives, might depend upon it.

His lips worked to shape words, "Lemon drop?"

Lady slapped him again, this time with pleasure.

Thomas chewed gingerly. The bread had gone stale after three days in the pack, but the smoked fish was none the worse and the cheese perhaps aged even smoother. He looked pensively across the beach to the markings of high tide. The paralight had been here. Been here, camped for two days by the looks of it, and flown on. Lady sat across the fire, her arms hugging her legs, rounded chin resting on her knees. The ocean appeared to fascinate her.

He cleared his throat. "I didn't know you cared—"

"Knock it off, Thomas." She nailed him with that two-color stare.

He shrugged, unable to meet either eye.

"You did a stupid thing, engaging him instead of just shielding. I thought I was going to be packing around a goddamn potato for the rest of the trip." She pointed a finger at him. "And we've lost Jennifer. So I don't want to hear it."

"Right. I apologize."

Her gaze softened slightly as he made an effort to chew the last crust of his sandwich. He washed it down with a swig of water and held his cup out for more.

"Just remind me to let you do some swinging next time we get cornered."

"Thomas!"

She threw the whole damn canteen at him with some most unladylike words.

He awoke on the beach, the night fog creeping in across the phosphorescent waves, cold seeping into his bones. He felt hot and his chest was tight, and as he looked across the water, he thought he saw a dolphin, tail-walking the foam. He wiped a trembling hand across his forehead. He brought it down covered in briny sweat. Lady's stubborn back faced him across the campfire's embers. She lay curled under a spare saddle blanket. The ghost road had played havoc with his senses. He wondered what effect it had had on hers.

He pitched his voice to reach her, but what came out was a dry croak that died in the heavy sea air.

He tried to roll out from under his jacket. His joints had gone to mush. All he could do was lie on the damp sand like a broken doll. He was in trouble, and he knew it. They called it breakout fever . . . usually adolescents got it when they were developing their psychic powers as they crossed into puberty. The worse cases either had the power burned out of them . . . or died. This was the psychic backlash Lady had feared.

A shiver convulsed him. He bore it silently, sweating and shaking. When it was done, he made one last effort to contact Lady before he passed out.

"Lady!"

His plea was nothing but a feather gliding on the wind.

Born to be a Healer, she heard it even in her dreams. "Thomas?"

She was making her way to his side when he slid under.

Chapter 11

Fever dreams.

No, not dreams. Memories.

Thomas had never seen a block prepare for war before. Men crawled like giant ants over the foundations and up and down the streets. He stood at the window, watching the supplies for fortifications being hauled away. Rusting car bodies, salvaged to use for carriages, were filled with sacks of sand to be dumped as barriers. He saw the frames roll by, thinking of all the pride of fallen men resting in those cars. The DWP liked to restore them and use them for dress carriages. Not now. Those frames awaiting restoration had other, less esoteric uses in store.

"Been thinking of a name, boy?" Gillander spoke from the corner where he sat, legs crossed Indian-style, a lap writing desk balanced on his bony kneecaps.

Thomas let a smile through as he looked back over his shoulder. "Not yet. Besides, it's a little early, isn't it?"

"Not necessarily. Last name for a Protector's like ordering a pair of boots while your voice is still changin'. Takes time to find the right fit and settle into it."

The tall boy returned from the window to sit at his teacher's side. "Maybe," he said, "but I won't need a surname if you retire and you've already told me I've still got a lot to learn."

"Now there's truth in that," Gillander agreed. "What's going on out there?"

"Preparations. Lots of them. I don't understand most of it. Sure hate to see those cars going for barriers. Wish they could use the melty ones."

Gillander wrinkled his face, long skinny nose moving with

the grimace. "We've been smelting those things down for decades. It's vanity keepin' 'em round. More putty than metal in most of them bodies now, anyways."

"Charlie likes them."

"Charles would. They go with his high falutin' job."

Thomas lapsed into silence. "But water's important," he said, finally, mildly.

"Course it is. It's life! And keepin' it pumpin' through and clean and rationing it, that's the most important job around here. Allotting the shares and enforcing the law. But you see," and Gillander tapped a lean finger on the writing desk, "Charlie inherited that job. There's a few around here waiting to see if he's bit off more than he can chew. He's got to do more than parade around in his fancy carriages to convince people."

"You talk like Charlie has to fight people around here, too."

"Maybe yes, maybe no." Gillander looked at him shrewdly. "He's going to need a lean, mean bodyguard."

Thomas felt his cheeks heat up and he turned around, unable to continue meeting his teacher's stare. Had Gill seen him working out? It wasn't like he'd ducked out on his mental exercises or anything. Uncomfortable on the floor, Thomas surged to his feet and returned to the window.

"War is a fascinatin' thing," Gill commented.

A shiver like cold goose feet walking down his spine shook Thomas. He said, "And it's horrible, too." He looked at his teacher from the safety of the window. He felt the change sweep over him, the change that came when he realized he was remembering, or dreaming, instead of living this experience. His voice dropped suddenly, hitting an adult register. He groped for what it was he wanted to say. "What's it like being dead?"

Gillander grinned. The late afternoon light slanting from behind Thomas struck his eyes, making them reflect like cats' eyes, red pinpoints of flame. "It's having time to do things over, like havin' this conversation now instead of the one we had fightin' over your training for Charlie."

Thomas shook uncontrollably. "What's happening now? Am I dreaming? I don't understand!"

"No," his teacher answered sadly. "Not yet."

"You can't tell me—" his voice went up again, cracking. "You can't tell me what to do! I want to know how to shoot a rifle. I want—I want to know those moves with your hands and feet. I want—"

"You want to know how to kill," Gill interrupted.

"I don't want to sit around cobbling people's old shoes when I'm not being a Protector!"

"There's nothing wrong with being a cobbler. People need souls, too."

"Soles," Thomas shouted. "You mean soles!"

"Do I?" Gillander's form began to grow misty-opaque and disappear as though the angled sunlight ate it away. "Do I?"

Confused, Thomas threw himself at the door and tore it open. He bolted outside, gasping for air.

Outside the small building, it was night. He saw Charlie walking by with one of his overseers, saying, "They won't attack at night. They're sluggish at night. . . ."

Blinking at the sudden loss of the sun, Thomas turned around. He'd been fighting with Gillander over his training. Nervously, he wiped the back of his hand across his mouth. He had lost time somewhere—an hour or two of sunset and dusk— and perhaps he'd lost more than just time.

He cast about. Fires glowed on the hills. Fires for bivouacking troops, and for signals. Embers banked in the event of the conflagration of war.

Seeing him hesitating in the shadows, Charles turned and pointed at him. "Who are you?"

The DWP was a big-shouldered man, in his prime. His gills flared in challenge. Thomas straightened. He hid his gills under a muffler his mother had knitted. It was clumsy, hot, and chafing. This man wore his gills like epaulets, badges of honor and rank.

That was in the days before Charlie had his cut out . . . I kept mine because I liked swimming with the dolphins too much. . . .

"I'm Thomas, sir. Apprenticed to Gillander."

"Oh." The massive man looked him over briefly, then said mildly, "Shouldn't you stay close to your mentor, son? there's likely to be quite a power drain when Denethan hits."

Guiltily, stammering, "Y-yes, sir," and knowing there was no going back to Gillander. Not just yet.

The DWP swung around, rejoined his aide, and strode off to the big house chosen as headquarters for the line. Shortly, halfway up the lane, a slender woman joined him. She carried a fair-haired toddler. He put an arm around them both. Thomas heard, "Veronica . . ." drifting back on the evening wind, then nothing.

With a feeling that he only had his skin halfway on, Thomas made his way to a ridge and stood on it, looking at the approaches to the peninsula. Absentmindedly, he patted down his blue-tick shirt. He usually carried a spare garrote or two. He was empty-handed this night.

But he wasn't himself. He knew it and could do nothing about it. As he overlooked the pockmarked basin, he heard it now as he'd heard it then . . . a wind raider skulking on the night breeze from off the peninsula, downwind, so as not to alert anyone. So as not to make the signal fires gutter low and then flare up with the message of its passing.

He had no time to scramble down off the ridge. Now, as then, he threw his head back and yelled with both voices, exterior and interior, so that everyone could hear. "Enemy, coming in, south downwind!"

And now, as then, the hills erupted in fire as the troops of the desert mutant known as Denethan made their own sunlight.

He himself, killed one of the Protectors with that scream of warning. No one blamed him for it. She was an old woman with fuzzy iron-colored hair and a knack for finding lost things. She'd been the one who'd taught him to dowse water, a Talent that Charles did not encourage because all water needed to be cleansed and metered. In later years, Thomas would find dowsing invaluable as he also found Charlie did not control the wilderness. He was not the one who discovered her body—he could no longer remember who did—sitting in her rocking chair, next to one of the armory sheds, her tatting in her lap. Her head was nodding upon her chest, and crimson leaked from both her ears.

The Protectors were not allowed at the front. Thomas remembered thinking that sometime around dawn, after the moon had smoldered and gone dark with the battle, and lizard backs rippled around the tiny knoll where he and his Protector had taken a stand. Gillander grabbed up his sweating hand.

"Run for it, m'boy."

Panic-stricken, Thomas gazed across the enemy ranks. He

could, perhaps, make it back up the long sloping field. But Gill was too spent, and Thomas was not strong enough to carry him. "We'll hold them here," he said, and his words came out far braver and stronger than he felt.

"No." Gillander shook his head. He tapped his temple. "Charlie's bringing out the missile guns. They're going to use the defoliants. Get out. Get out now, and I'll do the holding."

This land would be ablaze—ablaze and toxic. The small fires Denethan's men had set during the night to keep their blood warm would be as nothing to what Charles had planned. Even young Thomas could comprehend the horror about to erupt.

He turned and ran, without a good-bye. He ran as he'd never run before, once or twice skittering past a mutant soldier like a flushed rabbit, too quick to be sighted or caught. He ran for Nolan and the other Protectors, but mainly Nolan because he was good with TK and if anyone could pluck Gillander out of thin air, whisk him out from under the enemy's nose, Nolan could.

But Nolan had not survived the night's war either. Lady wept over him . . . funny, Thomas had not remembered her that well before . . . her eighteen lush years to his fourteen a threshold he could not cross then . . . and his only hope then had been to go to Charles.

Out of breath and with a stitch in his side that threatened to double him over, he found the ridge where the missile guns squatted and a handful of men paced at their bases.

Charles did not remember who he was. He looked at him evenly. Thomas had somehow grown in inch or two since their meeting last night. The big man's pepper-colored hair looked as if he'd just run a hand through it, and his eyes, once the color of freshly dried tobacco, now looked murky and tired. "What do you want?"

"I'm here to—to guide your placements."

"A little young for gun fire control, aren't you?"

Thomas gulped down the "yes, sir, no, sir" that became garbled somewhere in his throat where his gills intersected his windpipe and answered, "I just came in over the fields where the line broke late last night. *Do you want to know where they are or don't you?*"

Charles reached out with a massive hand and gripped his

collarbone so tightly he could hear the bones move and he would carry the bruise for a month. "Tell me the truth" was all that the DWP said to his impertinence.

A soft cloth salved his wound now and he heard a gentle voice murmur, "You're just dreaming, Thomas. Come back to me."

He stirred in his wandering. He did not want to remember the morning Charles stalked the battlefield, unconquerable, beating back the lines of desert mutants, roaring his defiance at Denethan, repairing breaches, and Thomas strode shadowlike in his wake, searching the fields for Gillander.

The battle was over when Thomas found him. He sank to his knees beside the sere carcass that bore little resemblance to his teacher and cried. He beat his fist into the gory soil.

"You *moved,* damn you. You *moved.* I saved the knoll for you, but you *moved.*"

The dead could not answer him back. And worse, the dead could not hear him explain why he had run without saying good-bye. He had never intended that to be the last time he ever spoke to Gillander.

A month later, his bruises faded to a sickish yellow, he packed up his kit and left for the ruins, in search of a murdering squatter who, it was said, knew a hundred different ways to kill a man. Only Veronica and Charlie knew that his prodigious TK powers had been dampened, lost, leaving him almost deaf and mute. He could Truth-read and Project, but the other Talents had been striped from him. That was okay. He still had his hands.

He found the squatter and brought him in for bounty, dead, but not until after a year and a half of scholarship from him. Then Thomas went back to the ruins, combing them, for the murdering squatter who had known a hundred different ways to kill a man had had a gentle, inquiring side to him, like Gillander, and had been searching for civilization in those times when his sanity came upon him.

When Thomas came back, it was to take up his role as Protector, having chosen the surname Blade for the weapon he most liked to use, and a chevron scar quirked his left brow sardonically.

He had not found any answers in the ruins. Or rather, he'd found too many: fire, quake, decay. And he had been found by something intelligent living on the north edge of the L.A. basin, where the Cleveland National Forest edged down to the foothills. Something that had reared at him out of the night, with a hoarse cry, and marked him as its meat.

Or disciple.

Thomas mumbled in his delusion and cried for the lack of knowledge. Lady Nolan reached across the sand and took his calloused hand in hers, and murmured soft words he could not quite hear.

Chapter 12

"You're deluded if you think Denethan is holed up somewhere in the foothills, sweating through breakout fever."

"I didn't say that," Thomas answered evenly, if weakly. "I said, he's as spent as I am. So the night and day we lost isn't. Hopefully."

His retort didn't mollify Lady. She viciously stabbed a stick into the campfire, stirring up ashes and embers. "Who told you to go on the offensive anyway? Did you think you could stick one of your knives into him?"

Thomas felt his lips curl. "I wouldn't waste one of my knives on him," he muttered.

"No? Then you had no business taking the offensive! If you can't handle it, don't do it! I can't—we—can't afford to lose you."

"I almost had him." Thomas, not listening, stared at the fire dancing on the sands. "I almost had him at the wedding."

"That was then! We were all linked. Yesterday he almost had you."

Thomas looked at her fiercely. "You don't think I can do it. But I can. We're bound now. He's like a shadow to my every thought and all I have to do is look for him."

Lady sat back and tucked her knees up. She was far enough back from the fire so her eyes were shadowed as she answered somberly, "You probably can. But we can't afford to find out. Your symptoms were those of breakout fever, but I've never seen that in an already realized Talent. Twins are thought-tied, sometimes. Why not mortal foes? So what are we going to do now?"

"We catch up with the paralight. The tide's wiped out most

of the sign, so there's nothing to lead Denethan on if we're careful in the morning. We ride hard and hope our luck holds."

Lady mumbled, "If it weren't for bad luck, we'd have no luck at all."

Thomas grinned at her. "Toss you for the blanket? Or we could share it?"

She rose up. "It's my mule and my blanket. You got it last night because you were ill. Tonight you can molder on the sand for all I care." She stalked off, rounding the boulders that tumbled onto the sand where the mountain met the shore, to make her evening ablutions. Thomas watched her go, thinking that she probably had been lying to him when she'd said she preferred to sleep with her mule.

Probably.

The noon sun was hidden under a bank of clouds, the kind of clouds that leaned on Southern California oppressively until the sun burned them away into a kind of haze. There was no rain in them . . . they were dove gray against a nondescript sky. Thomas reined in the black mare and stretched in his saddle, eyeing the horizon from under the protective shade of his wrist. The clear, crisp days of February were nearly gone.

The mule rattled to a stop at the mare's heels. Lady's face, pink with sunburn, was framed by damp tendrils of hair.

"He has more sense than any of us," she remarked, also stretching in the saddle. "Another mile and he won't go for me at all."

Blade cast a glance at the cream mount that seemed to know it was under consideration and looked up, eyes rolling. Its hide shone with lather.

"We'll break for half an hour. No longer." He swung down and Cindy quivered in relief. She lipped at her bit, foam dripping He dampened a rag and wiped her mouth down, then cupped a hand and let her suck up a bit of water.

Lady said mournfully, "We're low on water, too."

"Not likely to find any around here. The ground's too thirsty."

The Protector looked to her left at the ocean, where water rolled gently with the tide, gray-blue under the overcast sky. "There's no drinking that."

"Not yet, anyway." He looped Cindy's reins over the saddle

horn so she could wander and crop whatever shoots of grass she found in the wash cutting across their trail. The mule followed after, with a flip of its tufted tail.

Lady sat down abruptly, after first examining the dun-colored dirt for ants or other biting disasters. She settled her canteen in her lap and lifted her hair off her neck. "Thinking of Charlie's dream?"

"It's more than a dream—it used to be a reality, once."

"Once," she echoed. Her left eye, the blue one, seemed to catch a touch of the ocean's reflection. "You and he seemed obsessed with the past."

"If he gets the aqueduct repaired, he can bring runoff from as far away as Santa Barbara. . . ." Thomas twirled a pair of rods in his hand, preoccupied.

She fanned herself. "I refuse to argue politics with you."

"Politics?"

"Water is politics, Thomas, you know that. At least in our society. Charles may be DWP, but he's not above criticism. The aqueduct is a serious liability for him, particularly if he can't get it operating. He's had to delegate a lot of authority on other projects."

"And the more diffuse his power gets—"

She nodded, "The less power he has. I don't have as much faith in democracy as he does."

"Now who's arguing politics?"

"Not arguing, just commenting." Lady gazed serenely at the grazing mare and mule. She wet her lips from the canteen and gave a wistful sigh.

Thomas checked out the wash as well, noting the streak of green brush that ran down its eroded side. "Well," he said, "I wouldn't want you to be offended by my political opinions, so why don't you sit back while I do a little dowsing."

"Dowsing? Really?" She sat up straight and looked at him with a delighted expression. "I've never seen it done. Does it work?"

He shrugged. "No time like the present to see." He gave her a hand up. "Just don't jiggle my elbows."

Her eyebrow quirked. "Pardon me. I didn't intend to touch anything that was off limits."

Thomas felt heat washing his face as he approached the cut. He showed her one of the metal rods. It was two hands long, with a three-finger length at the end bent at right angles for a handle. He held the rods loosely in his fists, pointing ahead, parallel but separated. He began to walk slowly but deliberately across the ground.

As he approached the line of greenery, the rods began to slowly drift apart. He made no attempt to tighten his grip and did not stop walking until the swing was abrupt and complete.

Lady caught up with him. She looked down at the rods and the green path beneath them. She looked up at him. "It doesn't take an idiot to know there's been water through here," she said, "or there wouldn't be any vegetation."

"And it doesn't take a pair of dowsing rods either," he answered her. "But this is a wash—the rainwater came flooding through here and left. Or did it? If there's a decent water table level, we might hit some by digging."

She waved her hand down the length of the erosion. "Where might you suggest? Or are you the one going to be doing the digging?"

"I'll dig. But not here." He paced to the start of the greenery, settled his rods loosely in his fists again and began to pace the length of the wash. The rods would not stay parallel in his hold—they wavered back and forth—as Lady trotted next to him, saying, "It's psychosomatic."

Suddenly the rods swung violently outward, the one on his right bringing her to a quick halt. She looked downward at dirt as fine as ash, drifting over the toes of her boots. "Dig here?"

"Don't move." He shoved the drowsing rods into her hands and caught up with his black mare. His breakdown shovel was in the far pack. He returned, snapping it into place. Lady, somewhat apprehensive, had not so much as twitched.

Grinning, he shouldered her off the area. "You can breathe now."

She gave him an evil look as she moved out of his way. He began to dig.

By the end of their half-hour break, the mule had come back out of curiosity. Its nostrils were flared as it nodded, and Lady pushed it out of the way for the billionth time. She eyed Thomas in his hole.

"I'm not impressed."

"Oh?" Thomas paused, and wiped the sweat off his upper lip

as it seeped into his fine mustache. The ends hung sullenly. He pointed at Murphy. "Tell him that."

She looked at the mule. "Him?"

"Him. Why do you think he's crowding you? He can smell it." Thomas dove the spade a little deeper, then lifted the shovel close to Lady's face. "Run your fingers through that and tell me it's not damp."

But she could see the difference in the texture. See and smell it. As she watched, Blade drove the shovel down three more times, and suddenly his boot leather began to turn dark as water trickled into the bottom of the hole. He quickly shoveled out the mud a few more times, then held his hand out and Lady helped him out of the hole. He grabbed hold of the mule's headstall. "Let it seep in and fill a little before you water him."

"Is it clean?"

"It's not toxic, if that's what you mean. Not out here. We'll fill our canteens after the animals have drunk and the silt settles down a little."

She looked after him. "You could put Charles Warden out of business."

Thomas stopped in his tracks, the shovel between his hands, as he began breaking it down. He met her gaze. "If I wanted to," he said. "But I'd have to dig a hell of a lot of holes to water Southern California."

The tension lines fled from her face with her sudden gasp of laughter. The mule nudged her aside and she turned her attention to wrestling with it until the water level came up enough to water the two beasts.

Lady packed the last of the filled canteens. As she fastened down the flaps on her pack, she said, "I thought dowsing was a folk art."

"It is. But the DWP has discouraged it." Thomas didn't look up as he shifted the contents of his pack about a bit, getting ready to put the dowsing rods away.

"I thought anyone could do it, if they wanted to."

His chin came up. He smiled slowly. "Like to have a go at it?"

"Daring me?"

"Why not?"

"All right." She took the rods from his grip. "What do I do?"

He led her into the wash. "Let's do an easy one first. The water hole's over there, ten paces. Let's see if you can locate it."

Lady rolled her eyes skeptically. He shrugged. "Hold the rods like this. Think: *water.* Then blank your mind. And don't try to move the rods. Keep your fists level and flexible. If the rods swing out, they swing out. If they don't, they don't."

"But I know the water's there."

He nodded.

The woman looked at him, started to say something, then firmly closed her lips. He noticed that they settled automatically into a half-smile, without conscious effort. Abruptly, he took his hands away from her fists. "Go to it."

She hesitated briefly, then strode out confidently. He watched her walking past, her tan blouse open at the neck, revealing fair skin that freckled faintly rather than tanned, her long, denim riding skirt down to her ankled boots, the color pattern of brown and blue repeating itself. An intentioned echo of her eyes? The rods wobbled a bit and he yelled out, "Hold them a little firmer." Then he watched her stride closer and closer to the hole, her strides becoming shorter and more hesitant. The rods stayed parallel in her hold.

At the pit's edge, she stopped and threw him a baleful glance over her shoulder. "Nothing happened."

He joined her. "Then I guess you're not a dowser." He reached for the rods, she held them out of his grasp.

"One more time."

"All right."

"Blindfold me this time."

"And have you fall into the hole?"

Her jawline tensed. "I've been wet before."

Wet, but not defeated. He fought the grin teasing the corners of his mouth. "All right, then." He reached for the white scarf about his throat. It was not there. Thomas looked down and saw his reflection in the still, murky surface of the watering hole. His grin fled.

"Where's my scarf?"

Lady gave him a puzzled look, small lines forming in the center of her brow. "In my pack, I suppose. I took it off when you were sick."

"Why?"

"You breathed easier. And I needed something to wipe your

face down." She called after him as he headed for the mule and
began rummaging through Lady's saddlebags, looking for the
silken fabric. "What's wrong?"

"Nothing." His fingers snagged up the scarf and he drew it
out of the pack, heedless of the disarray he left behind. He
wound it around his neck, protecting and hiding his gills, and
thus changing his reflection to mask what he saw as the inhu-
manity of his own image. He took the rods from her. "We've
lost time."

"All right." She trailed him back to their mounts. "I say you
cheated."

"And I say you can't dowse." He mounted up and kicked
Cindy into a swinging trot, not caring whether Lady Nolan
stayed with him.

He slowed down when the mare's neck became white with
foam, and she put her head down, blowing in exhaustion. Lady
Nolan reined in.

"We can't keep this pace up."

He looked out over an ocean turned sullen and gray, the sand
rippling in glistening patterns as the tide shifted. "I told you it
would be a hard trail."

"It's not the trail I'm worried about." She wrapped a leg
about the saddle horn, her long skirt pulling back, showing a
shapely, if pale, calf. Most of the women from his Protectorate
had taken to wearing slacks for riding, or shorter skirts. She
drew her hair back with her hands and twisted it quickly into a
knot, tucking it into place at the nape of her neck. It wouldn't
stay there, of course, three or four loping strides of the mule and
it would come down.

Thomas reached into his inside jacket pockets. Vials tinkled
and his hand brushed the ivoried finger bones several times—
damn things appeared to change pockets at will—and he finally
found what he needed. He stretched out his palm to Lady. Two
long hairpins lay across it.

She snatched them up. "Wherever did you get them—" the
rest of her words cut off as she pinned her hair back.

"I use 'em for lock picks. Take care of those two. I can't
spare any more."

She dropped her hands back to her reins. With a slight shake
of her hand, she put her heel to the mule's flank, pressing him

back to the trail. By leading them out, she moderated the pace. Thomas watched her back—ramrod straight in the saddle, yet at ease, at one with the mule's rhythmic walk.

He put his hand inside his jacket again, checking the remaining hairpins. For some reason, the finger bones now resided in that slit.

The ghost road would save him—them—the hard trail days ahead. But he was feeling the toll of his fight with Denethan as much as his pressing need to find Charlie's children. He didn't think he could afford to travel the ghost road now. He remembered the deathlike chill and despair too well. Was that where Denethan drew his attacking Projection from? From the hopelessness of a thousand million dead? Perhaps.

He remembered the flickering reflection of himself in the water, gills exposed. Denethan was hunting, and the eleven year plague had begun its cycle. And Thomas knew he couldn't afford not to follow the ghost road. He had to catch up with Jennifer and Ramos before Denethan did.

The bones were in his hand almost before he slipped his fingers inside his jacket.

Chapter 13

He didn't tell her until late afternoon what he had decided. A red-tailed hawk, too young to have the russet tail feathers accenting his speckled body, sailed the cooling thermals of the ocean. For a fleeting moment, his outspread wings spanned behind Lady's face, giving her an ethereal appearance. She had pulled the mule to a halt on the bluffs, and they were silhouetted against the lowering sun as though they rode the sky. Their trail had intersected the old Coast Highway and they now rode alongside its wasted track.

"No," was all she said. The denial was written in the sudden pallor beneath her sunburn.

"You're here at my sufferance," Thomas answered. He flicked Cindy's reins, and the black mare shifted uneasily.

"You can't leave me behind."

He did not answer. If he took the ghost road alone, they both knew that he could and would.

The hawk circled and disappeared, skimming the bluffs behind Thomas.

He waited for the tears and disappointment, but they didn't come. Lady lifted her head and pulled her shoulders back.

"You couldn't have come this far without me," she said.

"I'll be the first to admit it."

She eyed him closely, tiny lines furrowing between her off-color eyes. The hairpins still held her hair back, except for tiny wisps along her forehead that twisted in the breeze now, catching the last glinting gold of sunlight. "Damn it, Thomas. You've just been through breakout fever. Not too many grown men can boast that."

"I weathered it with your help. I'm not ungrateful."

"I don't want grateful! I want you alive." She slumped then and turned her face away, veiling her expression from him. "You're draining yourself. Psychic reserves are precarious, you and I both know that. You can't go on forever."

Thomas felt a stab of guilt for treating her coldly. She'd been an able partner thus far. If anyone was responsible for slowing them down, it was himself—yet he was punishing her for it. He kneed the mare alongside the mule.

"Then come with me."

She shook her head. "I don't think you can maintain the road for both of us. You think you're well, but we won't know until you're rested, and then it could be too late. Thomas, breakout fever could well have burned you dry." She dared to look back at him then.

Her words jolted him. He had never suffered breakout when young . . . he'd been apprenticed to Gillander when he was ten. He'd seen other boys come and go . . . he'd never wondered why. Breakout could kill, yes, he knew that, but he'd never come to the realization that it could also sear the power out of him, leaving him just another mutated husk of a human.

"I dowsed the water—"

"I was measuring you. No Talent used there, and I'll be damned if I know *how* you did it."

"I'd feel it if it was gone."

"Like Nolan? He never knew he was finished until he tried the impossible and it killed him. I can't let that happen to you!"

For a moment, the fever memory of a younger and weeping Lady interfaced over that of the one pleading with him now. He shook free of the memory and the feelings it evoked. "I'd feel it," he repeated.

The mule stamped. Its movement brought them closer together, knees touching. He grew aware of her scent—orange blossoms and hot sun as well as mule—as he leaned nearer.

The corner of her mouth quirked, as if she could read his sudden thought. Lady said softly, "I've never known a burned-out psychic who wasn't impotent as well."

He reached out and pulled her from the mule into his arms, saying, "I think we can settle that issue here and now."

No fog came in from the ocean that night. Firelight glowed off the banked embers, illuminating the black mare as she slept,

head down, and the mule as it determinedly chewed a few this-
tles. Lady rested her head on his bare shoulder, murmuring,
"Now we're even farther behind."

"And this time it is most definitely your fault." He tucked a
strand of her hair behind her ear so that it could no longer tickle
his neck.

"My fault! You grabbed me."

"Yes, but you just sat there waiting to be grabbed."

She put a knuckle into his ribs. "I was arguing. You were the
one who got—"

He put his hand over her mouth. She subsided. He said
softly, "We're not going to make very good time joined at the
pelvis."

"I know that," she muttered through his hand, her breath
coming in warm, moist bursts.

"Then we'll sleep a while, and take the ghost road."

That truly silenced her. He added, in his most gentle voice,
"We've no choice."

She nodded, and threw her arm over his stomach, her touch
light and comforting. He lay still, waiting for her to say something, then realized he was listening to her low and rhythmic
breathing. There was a dampness on his shoulder where she
leaned her head, but he could not tell if she had kissed him—or
if she had cried a bit before she fell asleep. Thomas clamped his
jaws shut tightly and tried to find sleep himself.

The ghost road was darker than he remembered, colored
pale ash and charcoal rather than sepia. A spear of ice pierced
him from his bowels to his throat, but he said nothing. Lady
looked at him curiously as they crossed into the shadow rim of
the other world, her hands in the air fussing with her hair. She
finished pinning the loose strands back and remarked, "It must
make a difference what hour you summon it at. We were nearly
in daylight last time."

"It's time displacement. Anyway you look at it, it shouldn't
make a difference." Thomas looked about. He would have, and
did, trust the live Gillander with his life. The dead one, he had
doubts about. He didn't like the twilight effect casting too many
shadows to hide too many possible enemies. He tucked the ends
of his scarf into his collar, felt the comforting coils of his gar-

rotes and dropped his hands back to the reins. He wondered how long he could stand the cold. "The choice has been made."

Lady clucked to the mule and Murphy stepped out smartly along the broken highway that hugged the rugged coastline. The black mare fell in behind. Thomas took advantage of riding at Lady's rear to loosen his rifle in its sheath. He tapped the firing chamber open and dropped a small but potent vial inside. He closed the chamber slowly and hoped his companion did not hear the distinctive click it made when it shut. If she did, Lady said nothing. She put the mule at point and held it there.

They rounded the bend. Thomas kept his hearing focused, listening for coyotes in the foothills behind them, or the low whoosh a wind raider coming in overhead might make. He heard nothing but the click of their mounts' hooves on the rock and sand track or the occasional retort as one kicked aside a chunk of asphalt. Lady twisted around.

"Why isn't this whole? Shouldn't we be riding in a time period when all this flourished?"

He shrugged. "I don't know. Isn't one of your Talents a sense of time? The bones didn't come with a set of instructions."

Not true, Gill said snippily at his left shoulder.

Overriding his voice, Lady said, "That's true." She paused, a small frown line appearing across her eyebrows. "Nothing. It's as though the thought itself repels."

Thomas pondered the dubious rules he knew of the road. That the coyotes could sense them but be physically unable to touch them while the wolfrats could both sense and reach them had no logical basis. Unless, of course, the wolfrats had their own psychic abilities, on some instinctive level. He knew that some animals possessed a keen sense of direction and had been known to travel hundreds of miles through unknown territory to return to their home ground. Could wolfrats sense prey even through layers of time? Why, then, would they ever hunger? The thought of being ravaged by beasts unrestricted by time and place chilled him.

But, as a hunter himself, he knew that not all hunts were successful.

The wolfrat filled an ecological niche as a very successful scavenger/predator of the city ruins. And although he had not heard of packs reported in the foothills, he knew he could not discount them as a hazard along the ghost road along with whatever troops of Denethan searched the coasts.

For now the road was quiet. For now they were safe.

Lady put her hand up and wheeled the mule around. "Off the road!" she cried out, and kneed the panicked mule past Thomas.

Thomas had been dozing in the saddle. He shook himself awake with a curse. The black mare, bit clenched in her teeth, danced a savage dance by the roadside. Then he saw what it was Lady had seen.

Fireballs, low and level, curving across the terrain at them. They sped down at an incredible rate, the wind roaring in their passage. Cindy reared as he kicked her after the mule. He fought her heaving panic to bring her back to all fours and get her out of the fireballs' pathway. The mare squealed. He threw himself forward as he felt her start to lose her balance—and the last thing he wanted to do was have her go over backward and fall on him, him with a vestful of poisons, explosives, and other chemicals. He kicked his feet free to bail out if his weight did not right her.

There was a moment of soundless agony. He could feel her trembling as she balanced on her hindquarters. Could see the fireballs coming in at them like comets. Could feel his hands frozen in an attempt to bring Cindy down, unable to pull his rifle. Could see Lady, riding in under their chins, throwing herself at the headstall to pull the mare down.

They all came together at once as time resumed. Cindy came to earth, tearing her headstall out of Lady's hand.

The Protector looked up, her jaw dropping open in astonishment. "What is that?"

He shoved his boots deep in his stirrups as the clinking vials stilled. His heart rattled against his rib cage once or twice before settling. He looked up, and saw it also—so massive that the fireballs it had thrown seemed mere specks. It was dark with an orange corona, and it was curving along the horizon toward them. The wind sucked in, hot and dry. His ears popped. He stared at the apocalypse descending.

"Light . . . light, sound, and fury." Lady turned her mule and sat, considering the ghost road. The unknown mass grew larger and larger until it threatened to flame up and blot out the eastern sky. This part of the ghost road had been a highway. He could feel it now, a lane of despair, people piled upon it, rushing to get out, to leave, unable to go anywhere. Beneath their feet was a common grave site the depth of which frightened him.

Lady said softly, "What night is this?"

He wondered if it could touch them on the ghost road. He faced the asteroid. "I think this is the night the world died."

"No!"

"They tried to flee the city. This is one of the roads they took. Too many, trying to leave all at once." He loved her, and he stared at her soft profile delineated by the orange-black mass hurtling toward them.

He twitched the mare's reins. "We can run for it."

Lady brought her mule around to pace him. "I wonder if we'll be able to see them."

The spear that felt like it was piercing him turned in its wound. He stifled a gasp. "Why would you want to see them?"

"I'd give my soul if I could find out what they thought. Do you think they knew anything of what happened to the roads or the cities? Were they fleeing from disaster or driving straight into it?" Lady looked at him pensively. "That's why you like the ruins. I used to think it was because the gadgets fascinated you. How they worked and why and if they still could. You were always bringing back laser disks and the like. But that wasn't it at all, was it?"

"No. I guess we share a morbid fascination. I can't figure them out. Did they know when they spliced such and such a gene what they would create? How could they ignore the damage they were inflicting?" His left hand rose to his scared neck. "Or were they just playing at life?"

"You know the gills were intentional. We all had them a hundred, a hundred and twenty years ago. The ocean was the only safe environment we had left." Lady stroked her mule soothingly.

"Except for the desert mutations," Thomas argued. "And what we don't know about genetic splicing could fill books. The eleven year plague looks like an intentionally adaptive, evolving virus that attaches to the DNA chain. What genius let that loose? If they meant us to survive, they did it back asswards."

She put her hand out and placed it on his thigh. His muscles tensed under her touch. "I don't think they had much chance to plan."

"And I don't think they gave a damn one way or the other. But I'd like to *know*. I'd like to know just what they had in mind when they created things like me and Denethan." He reined away from her, kicking the mare viciously in the flank, as he shouted, "That thing is going to hit in minutes. I don't know what it'll do to us or the ghost road."

Thomas rode vigorously into the twilight, jaw set, his ears ringing with the roar of his own thoughts. He worked alone, he was used to it, and, dammit, he was not used to having his mind laid open like a raw wound for Lady Nolan to probe whenever she felt like it just to see if he was hurting. He couldn't protect her here. Hell, he couldn't even protect himself. He was unsure what they were about to witness and whether they would survive it.

The mare, still unnerved, responded when he touched heel to her, and began to canter over the foothill. It curved and broke away, downhill, back toward the ocean. He heard the mule braying faintly behind him, then nothing, and knew he was alone until they caught up, which was fine with him. Cindy's ears flicked forward and back, trying to sense if he wished more speed or not.

Both mare and mule came to a skidding halt as thunder boomed. The Protectors turned in their saddles. Beyond them was a vast expanse of light . . . thousands and thousands of small lights . . . shining in the night, white light being colored a garish orange as the burning asteroid swept close and filled the sky. Then it impacted. Blade shrank back and threw his arm up to shade his eyes. Then he heard it, a wail that grew as other voices fed it until he knew he must be hearing the cry of a million throats. The ground shuddered, throwing his mare to her knees and staggering the mule about. Then, silence. The night went dark as if nothing had ever happened.

Cindy heaved back up. Blade grabbed for the saddle horn to steady himself.

"Are you all right?" he asked Lady.

"Yes. Did you . . . did you hear that?"

He had thought perhaps the wail had been meant for his ears alone. But even in the dim light of the half-moon, he could see her ashen face. "Yes," he said briefly. "I heard it." He turned the mare on the road. "I don't want to be around to see the rest of it." He kicked his horse into a trot.

The broken track of the Coast Highway intersected with another, a faint, shattered line out of the east, off the sere dark foothills of the interior. Cindy put her ears back and charged ahead, gaining speed as she flung herself down the curving slope. Thomas rocked back in the saddle slightly to balance the mare, but he let her keep the bit. At the bottom, he reined her in, knowing he must wait for Lady to catch up. The sound of the mule's hooves drumming upon the ground drowned out his faint call. Murphy came downhill in a high-stepping trot. Lady's face was flushed when she pulled in beside Thomas. "That's quite a road!"

"Yes," he said. "I believe they called it Deadman's Curve."

Chapter 14

He said nothing to her of his ghosts, wanting to, but hesitating until the time had long since passed when he could have mentioned it without her wondering why he had waited so long. They seemed to hang on him, a clammy fog of misery. If she saw ghosts of her own, she never mentioned them to him either.

They stopped for a break. He got out of his saddle stiffly, feeling like an old man. He chafed his hands for warmth and stomped his feet, icy numb. Lady put hobbles on the mare and mule while he found a freshet of water and filled the canteens. They squatted in a gully eroded by the ocean and the broken road. Lady offered a thistle flower to the mule who gave her a disdainful look.

"They won't eat," she said, "but they're going to have to be grazed or we'll lose them. They're losing flesh. Haven't we been on this road of death long enough?"

"Almost," he said. A cornmeal cake crumbled in his mouth, as lifeless as the scene around them. "I'd like to cover another landing site. We've probably missed one."

"And if you can't find it?"

"Then we've lost the trail. I've no Talent for Seeking. You?"

Surprise rippled over her expression. "No Talent for Seeking? Thomas, you've more talents than most people have fingers."

He shook his head. "Not me."

She closed her mouth firmly instead of arguing. He broke off another piece of cornbread and passed it to her, along with a jar of honeycomb Veronica had packed for him. She took the jar and put a sticky finger to her mouth wryly.

"It's lost its flavor, too."

"Use it anyway. There might be some value to it." He watched her eat, with dainty yet matter-of-fact movements. She seemed to be unaware of his stare.

Not everything had lost its appeal. Uncomfortably, he got up and walked out of sight.

The urine he released was a pallid stream against the twilight background. As it pooled into the ashy ground, he found himself wondering if it were night or day outside the ghost road. He refastened his fly, thinking about making love to Lady Nolan once more, but not here. Not where he could not smell the salt breeze and flowers in her hair, or taste the mild flavor of her soft skin. Not where nothing cared for the living. Not where his flesh felt like the icy skin of death.

A branch cracked. Its pop shattered the unnatural silence of the landscape. Thomas froze. Then he located the sound's direction and followed it.

He climbed uphill to skirt the draw, and lay on his stomach to look down at it. Below, three figures squatted around a flat rock, drawing and quartering a wild cat. Sprawled beyond them was the wind raider the three had flown to get this far. He stared for a moment, then a pins and needles tingling began in his boots and hands. Blade lifted a hand and spread it before his face. He'd lost the ghost road. Without conscious thought, he'd lost it and now they were vulnerable to the predators below.

Grounded, the wind raider looked like a large, ungainly blot. Without a catapult or jumping off a sea cliff, it would not be possible to get it back into the air. The raiders seemed unconcerned. It had served its purpose by bringing them this far. They passed each other the bloody bits of their kill, unworried about the black rivulets falling between their fingers or the lack of a fire to cook their meal.

He held his breath. As feeling crept back into his body, he tried to focus for a projection. His thoughts whirled unsteadily. He had no strength for an attack, the ghost road had sapped him. It would have to be the hard way. He drew out a blade and a garrote and gathered himself for a leap.

He took out one by landing on it. Its neck went with a pop as the other two were knocked on their rumps, raw meat flying out of their hands. Thomas sprang, burying his knife hilt-deep in the second who had recovered well enough to charge him. As the third jumped on his back, he flung the garrote over his head, found a neck and brought his hands together, tightening the loop as the men atop him and below him began to die.

He shrugged off the dead weight as the thrashing stopped. He skinned back the grimacing lips to find ordinary, if somewhat decayed, teeth. He kicked the ashen dirt in their faces, thinking that this trio was more manlike than he'd grown to expect from Denethan. He cleaned his loop on the dead man's breeches and replaced it in his collar.

The knife was a little messier to retrieve, but he had no intention of leaving it behind. He cleansed it as well as he was able to before slipping it into his boot.

He took one last look at the three dead men before turning to Lady. He put his hand inside his vest where the finger bones seemed to leap into his grip, and his blood went chill.

She was repacking his saddlebags when he came back. She did not seem to have noticed that they had lost the road and gained it again though she looked troubled beneath the sheen of her sunburn. "Trouble?"

"Nothing to speak of," he answered. "We need to hurry. We're running out of time on the ghost road."

She turned a disturbed gaze toward him but asked no questions.

They found one of the landing sites. It was in a lee, on the bluffs overlooking the ocean, its grass yellowing already in a spring that had begun dry and would likely get drier. Poppies had been broken and snapped off by the weight of the paralight. Lady dismounted, picked up a broken stem and twirled it in her fingers. It spun in her fingers, gray petals and blackened stem. He watched her toss it to the ground and look up at him, one eye darker than the other, both somehow colorless. He had a sudden desire to see color in her gaze.

"How long ago?"

He frowned. As he looked out over the meadow, he could see the present or near present images superimposed on those of the past. He could see Ramos chasing Jennifer across the grass, her white buttocks still slender as a child's, flashing like a rabbit's flagging tail as she raced away from him. He wrenched his sight away from the two naked children and back to Lady.

"Yesterday. Perhaps even this morning. What do you think?"

"This morning. The sap still runs in the flower. I couldn't see it, but I could feel it."

He nodded and held the mule steady while she remounted. They rode hard until they crested the bluffs above Carpin, and he put his hand out to halt her. The twilight revealed his worse nightmare. He took the finger bones out of his pocket to break the ghost road. His hands were like ice and the thought struck him for a moment that, if not frostbite, he had chilblains.

With a roar, sound and scent and color returned to the world. It brought the reek of fire.

Lady's lips pressed together thinly as she looked down on the plains, and ocean, and ruins in front of them. Thin columns of dark smoke rose into the air from twisted shadows at the base of the ruins.

"God," she said. "We're too late."

Chapter 15

"No sunrise this morning," Charlie said, as he reached out and pulled Veronica to his side. The low hanging clouds showed pink briefly, hiding the errant sun. She had not been sleeping well for the last few weeks, and he'd gotten out of bed early to trail her outdoors this morning. She stood on the sweeping expanse of land behind their house, land that had once been groomed as part of the estate. She shifted uneasily in his arms.

"Missing Jennifer?"

His wife did not look at him, her stance and attention aimed northward. But she answered, "Need you ask?"

"No. I guess not. I heard last night that Lady Nolan's gone, as well as Sir Thomas." He loosened his embrace. "The children'll be as safe with them as anyone."

Veronica looked at him. She had aged somewhat but admirably since his first infatuation with her. Gray brushed her chestnut hair at the temples, but her skin stayed clear and firm. There were fine wrinkles about her eyes whether she frowned or smiled, though. Her brow arched. "It would have been safest not to send them at all."

He looked over the expanse, thinking that he disliked the overcast mornings that burned away to too bright afternoons. He liked the days that started out crisp and clear and stayed that way, even though the ocean breeze could have a bite to it.

Veronica stirred within the shelter of his arms. "I didn't come out to look for them," she said softly. "Enjoy the view, Charles. It's likely to be the last sunrise we'll ever see."

He spun her about roughly. "What the hell are you talking about?"

"I'm talking about the attack." She smiled gently. "I love

you, Charlie. I loved you when I first met you, and I loved you when you sent Jennifer away, and I love you now. I want you to know that."

Charles staggered back a step. "Who's attacking? When?" He cursed himself for not recognizing the half-trance of a Seeing.

"They're coming, love, and this time, you can't stop them." His wife's eyes rolled back in her head and she collapsed with a weary sigh. He caught her up. "Ronnie! Wake up! Are they coming at us here or at the plant?" But she was gone, passed beyond his awakening.

He lifted his head and bellowed for help.

They left their mounts tethered above, but even that far removed, Cindy spread her nostrils at the scent and rolled her eyes. Lady took her skinning knife from her belt sheath and cut as much sweet grass as she could reach hastily and threw it in front of the animals before scrambling down the slope after Blade.

After the sterility of the ghost road, the stench of the carnage hit them like a fist. The air swarmed with the buzz of flies, and stank with fire and earth. Lady Nolan staggered to a halt, and put her fist to her mouth.

"God," she said, and gagged.

He pushed her away, so that she couldn't see the bodies, and so that he could not hear her heaving too clearly. His own stomach knotted up against his spine. He staggered, unable to control limbs so cold they might as well be stone. Finally and ironically, thanks to the glittering fire, he warmed enough to approach the bodies.

As near as he could tell, at least they've been burned in one piece, thrown clear of the paralight wreckage. Denethan's men had not torn them limb from limb. It was one of the few mercies he could grant their dying. They had not been immolated. They had died first, and the raiders had burned them afterward. Strands of Jennifer's light blonde hair lay streamered over the charred ground, incongruous against her blackened skull. Bones of her hand were entwined with those of the boy's.

Thomas wrenched his gaze away to the paralight. He could see the flashburn along the fuselage. A vial bullet, then, such as the one he'd fired at the wind raiders days ago, had caught them. They'd gone down burning, helpless, wedged inside the paralight's body, seeing their death surge up before them even as they flamed. He hoped they'd hit the ground before the burning had gotten too bad.

With a sigh, he turned back and caught Lady by her shoulders and steadied her trembling form. "They didn't suffer."

His words caught her mid-gulp. "Wha-what?"

He reflected that she wasn't a woman who looked beautiful crying. Her face had gone blotchy and swollen. "They died on impact. Denethan's men brought them down, but never got to them after that."

"T-thank God for small favors." She hiccoughed roughly. "Oh, Thomas." She twisted abruptly in his hands and barreled into him, catching him up in a desperate embrace and where his jacket fell open, his shirt became wet as she began to cry in sobs whose ache he could feel echoing in his own sorrow. But he could not cry as she did, so he stood there and held her. He envied her her emotions.

He could not tag his own so easily. Did he sorrow because he'd failed in his mission? Or because they were children, too young to die any kind of death—or did he mourn the loss of tomorrow's children, to be born without gills or third arms and other mutations. The gills could be bred out, of course. He knew families with several generations gillfree, but it was a very strong recessive trait and one that could return at any time. He himself was such a throwback. And Charles—

He let go of Lady so abruptly that she rocked back on her heels. A shock thrilled through him.

"Charlie's in trouble," he said. "Come on—we've got to hurry!"

She dried her face on her sleeve and scurried after him as he took the slope in leaping strides. "Thomas! What is it?"

"We've got to get back and get back *now.*"

She panted to a stop behind him as he gathered up the black mare's reins. He pulled his scarf off his neck.

"I'm not going anywhere else until you explain."

"I haven't time. Will your mule lead blindfolded?"

"I don't know. He's always been sensible—*Thomas, will you tell me what's happening?*"

"We've got to get back. I'm no going to be late this time if I have to walk on water." He pulled the finger bones out of his vest and looked over the span at the Pacific Ocean. The coast-line sparkled back at him.

"What—oh, no. You can't be serious. You look half-dead now. And your hands—it's as if you've been frozen!"

"Listen. The ghost road isn't real—it's time displacement. But even by land, we can't get back in time, and I can guarantee you, Denethan's men are still out there between us and the peninsula. We can't take days going home."

"You might as well suggest flying."

He looked over the edge of the bluff as if considering, then shook his head. "No, the paralight's in no condition."

She planted her feet stubbornly. "Do you expect to walk over water?"

His brows went up. "You've lost your senses. I know the area. There's a man-made marine not too far from here. I recognize the shape of the bay and breakwater. It's not been salvaged too badly. With any luck, we'll find a fiberglass boat shell in good enough shape to hold us. I can rig a sail—if you can convince the mule and horse to stay quiet once we load them—can you?"

"Boat back?"

"It's the best way. And if we can do it in ghost time, we might only lose a day or two."

She threw her arms about him and let out a shaky laugh. "It's not the days I'm worried about losing. What about Charlie? I feel nothing."

Thomas shrugged. "Who's got the worst reputation as Protector?"

"Why, you, I suppose. You're the executioner."

"And if you were going to Protect something very valuable, wouldn't you send your most fearsome Protector to do it?"

"Yes, but—I don't understand."

"You will," Thomas said bitterly. "If we're too late."

Alderman collapsed, his thin chest wheezing. One of the boys darted out and dragged his body back. Charlie saw the movement from the corner of his eye. With the loss of another Protector, he was as good as whipped and he knew it.

Veronica handed him a loaded rifle. "At least they haven't gotten into the plant," she whispered, her gentle voice gone hoarse with the day's fighting.

"No."

They both knew the enemy would use it to bring him down—that Charlie would surrender if they broke through the water station's defenses and threatened to destroy it. The DWP would never let the plant be sacrificed in his place. He had been betrayed and now he was being destroyed.

Veronica rubbed one eye. She let out a tiny sob. "Oh, Charlie! I can see Jennifer—she's waiting for us."

He turned a deaf ear toward his wife, cradled the rifle into position and sighted on a target. It would be dark soon. As he fired and watched the hillside explode, he wondered if the warfare would get better or worse when night fell. His wife sobbed brokenly at his shoulder. Even if he survived this day, even if he could somehow gather his ragged troops together and win, he'd lost his wife. Her mind was as broken as the sounds of her grief. He pulled the trigger, releasing the second chamber. He handed the rifle to her. "Damn it, Ronnie. Keep loading!"

She stared blankly at him for a moment, then nodded and took the weapon. Her trembling fingers brushed his gently. She whispered, "I love you," then she bent quickly to the open case of vials and began to load the rifle.

The sea on the ghost road was as black as obsidian. Their wake cut white foam into streams behind them. The peaks and valleys of the waves seemed not to move, as though they rode a crystal sculpture of an ocean.

Lady sat hunched between the two mounts, each hand an anchor to their bridles. Her face was pale, her eyes closed, as she concentrated the Talent she had for animals to keep them calm.

Thomas had all he could do to keep the wind from blowing the sail out. He could not ask for better direction. The coastline skimmed behind them and he hung on the boom to keep it from swinging around and clipping the animals. A line to the rudder was wrapped about his wrist as the sailboat plowed across the currents.

A massive gray shape slid close under the dark waves. He looked across the starboard bow, and his jaw clenched. The presence was as long as the twenty-four-foot long boat he sailed. It circled, then came closer, pacing them. It rolled, breaking surface, and he looked at dorsal fins and a flat, dead eye.

The shark grinned. Then it dove, disappearing rapidly. Thomas leaned far out, trying to keep it in view, but his rigging reins drew him back. Primeval forces, he thought. If it could get to him—

There was a hard bump below his feet as though something had hit the bottom of the boat.

"Thomas! What is it?"

"Nothing," he said quickly. He ducked under the boom and went to the port side, at the bow.

Foam churned. But nothing appeared.

He spun on his heels and, straining his eyes, tried to see in the murk behind the boat, but all he saw was the dazzling comet tail of their wake crossing that murky curtain, and it blinded him momentarily. The mark on his wrist itched and he rubbed it absently, thinking of the dolphin goddess. The sea roared at him, covering him with foam.

He turned and faced a bottomless pit of teeth. The shark came at him, biting the air before his face. A scream tore from his throat and he felt the abrupt shift of the boat as the mare reacted, throwing herself back wildly. The boom swung, dragging him half behind it before he caught himself and collapsed the sail—the rigging pulling him literally out of the shark's jaws.

"Keep her down!" he shouted at Lady as the woman cried, "What is it?" Her eyes were opened wide, but she stayed down and brought the mare to her knees behind her.

Spray drenched him as something scraped up alongside the boat. "Just think of it as another big wolfrat!" He pulled his knife and cut himself free from the tangled line. "Watch the boom!"

It swung back, but not too close to them, and danced with the erratic movement of the boat.

The sailboat drummed with another blow from down below.

Thomas fished inside his vest. He grabbed two or three vials without looking and scrambled back to the bow. He nicked his wrist and hung over the side, watching the darkness of his blood disappear into the midnight water.

His hand throbbed. The fingers clutching the vials grew numb. The boat skewed sideways against the waves and he knew they were taking on water. Not much, but enough.

Lady saw it rise. She screamed as his vision filled with a gray wall and white teeth, slashing savagely at his hand.

Thomas dropped the vials even as he threw himself back in reflex. The shark reared up against the boat, forcing its body out of the ghost water, thrashing against the bow. He could smell it and knew that it crossed the ghost road, that it was not held to mortal boundaries. Then it fell back, unable to throw itself into the boat after him. Blade crawled back to where Lady sat, one arm wrapped about the mule's neck, her skinning knife to its throat, her face streaked with tears.

He took the knife from her as she said, "I was going to throw him over. To save you. To make it let you go."

He grinned weakly. "If it had gotten me, there wouldn't have been enough to let go."

There was a flash and a deafening explosion behind the boat. He shaded his eyes and she tightened her grip on the animals.

"I think I managed to give it indigestion anyway," he said.

"How could it—how could it touch us?"

"I don't know. Gillander warned me . . . there are some things the road cannot contain. Basic forces. Pure evil, he said." He stroked her flank, where she could not feel his cold touch upon bare skin.

She made a funny noise, then said, "I think you'd better stop fooling round and start bailing."

"Right," he said.

Even on the ghost sea, Thomas recognized the point where the sea bowls cupped out from the shoreline. They were nearly home. There was a strand of beach not far from the bluffs where Charlie's house reigned, and as he pulled out the finger bones to bring them off the ghost sea, he felt a moment of misgiving.

"Shouldn't we bring the boat in first?"

He nodded. "I think so. Bring 'em to their knees. I don't want the boom to hit them. I've got to tack us in."

Lady clucked sweetly to the mule to bring it down. The mare was difficult—her black knees already scabbed from rough treatment earlier. Reluctantly, she went, with Lady making soothing noises and stroking her muzzle.

Tired in every fiber of his body, he began to fight the sailboat to make it do what he wanted it to.

* * *

Denethan scanned the scorched grass, and the massive house, and the bodies lying everywhere. His men ranged through, trotting like hounds across the grounds.

"Take no prisoners," he said flatly. The carnage was not of his making, but an enemy was an enemy.

"No, sir," his fighters called in response. He looked around again, senses probing briefly, without waste. His eyes could tell him about the slaughter here as easily as his Talents.

On the outskirts, where the last charge had finally broken, he found the body of a large, burly man, curled protectively over what had once been a beautiful woman. It appeared that he had broken her neck himself with one swift twist before being overrun.

Denethan ran a nail tip across the insignia sewn over his breast pocket. The DWP. He eyed the corpse. There was no flavor here of the man who'd faced him down earlier, but he had no doubt that this was the body of one of his most formidable enemies.

He touched a boot toe to the carcass gently.

"We'll leave them," he announced loudly. "If there're any survivors in the hills, they can creep out after we're gone and do whatever they want to with the bodies."

He signaled to his troops and they left with him. What he searched for was elsewhere.

Charlie held his breath another few minutes, then let it out raggedly, and opened his eyes. His vision stayed blurred. He was still alive, but would not be for long.

Ronnie had been wrong about him, though. He *had* seen another sunset. Now he lay waiting for . . . what, he was no longer sure. He moved his hand searchingly and found her chill one, and cradled it, rubbing his thumb back and forth across the circlet of gold which had once bound them together. Strange. There had been no looting.

The black mare let out a strangled whinny as Thomas cut her with the reins, whipping her up the curving roadway. The signs of warfare stained his vision everywhere he looked. For a moment he wondered if the ghost road had brought them to another time, but he knew better.

Lady let out a tiny cry as they drew close to the manor

house. Carrion crows took flight at their approach. She pulled the mule to a stumbling halt and half-dismounted, half-fell out of the saddle.

"Everyone," she whispered hoarsely. "Did you See it, Thomas? Why didn't you tell me?"

Numbly, he shook his head. Following the signs, he went around to the back of the house and saw where the final breach had been made. Charles' body curved about Veronica's frail one, her blue dress crimson-splattered with his blood. He dropped from the saddle.

The mare shied away from the sandbag barrier and the wooden crates still with vials of ammo cradled within. He stepped over broken bodies to reach Charlie. He dropped a hand on his old friend's shoulder.

The carcass was still warm. He felt a quivering breath go through it beneath his hand.

He jerked the body over, and, as Charlie's eyes came open, he leaned down savagely and cried, "Where're the children, you bastard! Where did you send our real hope?"

Chapter 16

Lady caught up with them. She hammered at Thomas' back, crying, "For god's sake, leave him alone! Can't you see he's dying! Thomas, let go of him!"

But a thin smile, coated with pale blood, etched Charlie's face. "If . . . I wasn't a dead man, I would be. Right, Thomas? And I don't blame you." He coughed weakly and Blade let go of his shirt. His head dropped back to pillow on Lady Nolan as the Protector took his head and shoulders into her lap.

With an expertise born of practice and Talent, she ran her fingers lightly over his face and chest. Then she looked up at Thomas and shook her head. Blade stepped back and squatted down, trail soreness in his legs, his shoulders aching as if yoked to the world. His Intuition had fled him, bled dry by the ghost road, but he didn't have to Truth-read Charlie to get truth. "Tell me something I don't know," he said bitterly to the woman. "Tell me why this man sent his only daughter and another man's son off to be *butchered*. Tell me why he made sure Denethan would follow his decoys by making sure I would draw the lizard's attention."

Charles' lip worked soundlessly. The shiny scars at the sides of his neck where gills had been cut out bulged purple and the dying man gasped for breath. Lady's brow furrowed in empathy. She gazed at Blade with pain in her eyes, silently pleading for his good behavior.

But Charles reached for and grabbed up Thomas' hand. "Be still," he got out laboriously. His forehead shone with sweat. "You know what I did. I . . . only wonder how."

Thomas grasped his friend's neck in a rough caress. "Your gills, damn it all. Your gills! How could Jennifer be genetically pure just one generation removed when we both know of families two, even three generations removed carrying that recessive mutation!"

Nolan sucked in her breath. "They died for nothing? You sent them out to draw Denethan's attention?" The horror of what she'd seen on the outskirts of Carpin flooded her eyes. The blue turned icy, but the brown brimmed with an unshed tear.

"Ramos . . . maybe. But we had our pair . . . didn't want . . . anyone to know . . . needed a decoy. Denethan had been sniffing around lately. Knew he wasn't bottled up in the Mojave anymore. Who but Thomas would find out . . . sent my own daughter out as decoy . . . hoped he could keep her safe anyway. . . ." The dying man's eyes flickered to his friend's face.

"You knew Denethan would follow them if I went after."

"Your . . . reputation. Ronnie's idea . . . internal spies . . . had to throw them off. We thought you were good enough anyway. . . ." His eyes clouded. "Jennifer?"

Thomas shook his head briefly. He said only, "They didn't suffer."

"Veronica knew . . . two days ago. I didn't believe her." Charlie still held the stiff hand of his dead wife. He squeezed it tighter.

Lady said to Blade, "And you knew about this. That's why you drove us to get home!"

Thomas shook his head. "Not about this. Only that the children weren't what we were told. I had no idea about the attack. I did not think Denethan would be ahead of us." He turned away from the astonishment on her face.

His friend's eyes had closed. Thomas raised his free hand to Lady's and gripped it so tightly she could hear bones move. She bit her lip to keep from crying out.

"Keep him here. Just another moment or two—"

Instead of protesting, she nodded sharply. "I—I'll try."

Charlie opened his eyes and squinted, tears running from the corners of them. "It's dark, Thomas. Is it still sunrise?"

"No. Mid-morning, a little later."

"She said . . . we wouldn't see another sunrise. She was wrong . . . everyone dead but me. Denethan kicked me . . ." He moved his hand feebly, rubbing his rib cage.

Lady pressed her right hand to his forehead and bowed her

head in concentration. The strain began to show on her already tired face.

"Charlie," Thomas leaned close and whispered urgently. "Did the children get away? Who were they?"

"Alma and . . . Stefan. But I told you . . . already, didn't I? I was . . . waiting for you . . ."

Lady whispered, "I'm losing him."

Sweet-eyed Alma and blond Stefan, whose genes had sailed all the way from the other side of the world. Thomas rocked back. "Where?"

"To the College Vaults." Too spent for words, his old friend closed his eyes tightly. After a shuddering breath, he added "We didn't plan to send out Alma and Stefan . . . until after searches had stopped. The way would have been clear then. . . ."

Blade nodded and then added, because Charles could no longer see him, "Yes, except that it led back to you again. You old fool."

"Yes." To Lady Nolan. "I'm cold. Can't you keep me warm?"

"No," she whispered. "Not now."

The frame of what had once been a massive, vital man seemed to shrink as he trembled from the cold. Then he coughed again, and drew a long, painstaking breath. "We were betrayed." Then, "Ronnie?" He put a hand up, brushing Thomas' face without knowing it. "Thomas, I've . . . got to go. Ronnie's waiting . . . and there . . . Jenny. . . ."

The Protector lifted Lady's hand from the man's forehead saying only, "Let him go." He pressed his fingers to his temples, trying to shut out the death rattle, so he could think of what he had to do next.

Lady didn't give him a moment's grace. "Give me a hand."

She shut the open eyelids, the stare already blinded. Then she let the man's head drop gently to the bruised and rust-colored grass. She settled Ronnie's curled form next to him, smoothing out her dress, unable to straighten slender limbs that death had already made rigid. He helped her, unthinking, his hands and movements patterning her own, echoing her effort. When she was done, she took off the long cotton slip from the dead woman and spread it across both their faces to keep away the flies.

"Shall we burn them?"

He straightened, putting his hands to the small of his back. He stared at the battle scene, the carnage, the carrion of what had been a sturdy community making a comeback. Crows flew overhead, skimming the roof of the manor house, headed for the slaughter in the front yard. Their harsh calls jarred his effort to think clearly.

There were too many dead. He shook his head. "No," he said. "Just Charlie and Veronica. I'll take care of them later." He walked away, taking stock of the fallen, trying now to note more than their faces, if they had any left, bloating under the sun. Lady Nolan followed after, her steps hesitant, and he knew her thoughts as well as if they were his own: someone, somewhere, might still be alive. Charles had lived this long. She did not note, as he did, that someone else had already walked through here, dispatching mercy strokes to a fallen enemy.

He found two of the Protectors, Alderman and Wyethe, huddled together. They were old men and it was an odd thing to him that, in death, they looked much younger than he could remember them in life. Lady went to one knee beside them. She gently caressed Alderman's bald pate which had sunburned before he'd died. Blade wondered if Wyethe had gone down stammering in his mildly confused way.

"Leave them," he said. "We're lucky most of the wedding guests had gone home already along with several of the Protectors, or there'd be more dead."

He walked in the back of the house. Furniture was overturned, and there were one or two bodies in here. But the house had stayed mainly intact, though it held the sticky sweet smell of blood going bad. He looked about, examining the inherited richness of a DWP's life, of the continuity of a lifestyle going all the way back to the Disasters.

Lady stayed in the doorway, beveled glass French doors framing her. Only one pane had been smashed. Its shards bediamoned her dusty boots. "It looks like they didn't even touch the house." She ran a hand up the framework.

"Nobody's touched the bodies outside, either. There's been no looting." Why, unless Denethan had been interrupted? And if he had, by whom? The approach of the two of them would scarcely frighten off an army.

"In spite of everything, I'd kill for a hot bath." Lady's face flamed a little as Thomas twisted to look at her, but he said nothing. Life went on and though she'd blurted out feelings neither had expressed aloud, the two of them still lived.

"We forgot the plant." She paused inside the house. "Maybe I won't have hot water, after all."

The refinery and pumping station. He looked to her. "Denethan couldn't kill the rest of us more completely than to shut down the stations."

"And he had little chance of getting through its defenses unless he took out Charlie first."

Stepping gingerly over the corpses and congealing pools of blood, he went to the kitchen tap. He turned it on. It howled once or twice, but water flowed smoothly—clean water. He sniffed it. Odorless. He touched the tip of his tongue to it. Dowsed water tasted better, but this was serviceable. He straightened.

Where was the conqueror? Surely he had more in mind than scattering the bodies of the defeated over the face of the earth. yet . . . He made a fist. "Where is he? And what is he doing?"

At his shoulder, Lady said softly, "Why destroy what he can occupy?"

"Out of Oz? He'd come here?" Visions of the desert nation moving in while the other counties were too confused to stop them filled his head.

"Why not? God knows the Mojave is a hellhole."

"But he was made for it."

She moved past him, took a glass from a cabinet and poured herself four fingers of water and drank it without stopping to breathe. She looked at him over the rim of the empty glass. "Any other ideas?"

"None I like. I'm searching Charlie's office. We'll move the bodies out and you can take a bath while I find out if the pigeon coop is intact. I need to get messages ready." He paused at the edge of the kitchen. "Don't move around much, just in case— just in case Denethan's booby-trapped the place or something."

Her face lightened. "Now that I can understand."

With a grim smile, Thomas left her peering carefully about the kitchen cabinetry looking for trip-wires.

Charlie's office was redolent with his presence. The great oaken desk, the leather couch, the decanter of "serious" liquor. Thomas brushed a hand over all of it, seeking trouble spots as well as memories. Nothing looked touched or bothered, yet nothing would be the same again. He saw the paneling that hid Charlie's private files ajar.

The open seam told him that here, at least, the enemy had taken spoils. He eyed the seam carefully, saw no traps, and pushed it with the toe of his boot. The wall closet creaked open.

The file drawers stood half-open, emptied. Blade flipped through the tabs. They'd taken everything—from the post-Disaster census a hundred years ago to Charlie's latest reports on the desalinization plants. Records which, from the DWP's standpoint, were irreplaceable. But nowhere in here would Charlie have committed his plans for the children to paper. Those had stayed in his mind and other intangible places.

Thomas kicked the panel open wider, looking back into the office. The bookshelves looked the same, including Charlie's collection of family bibles—his genealogy trees, hidden in plain sight. The precious and well-worn *The Way Things Work* had been left behind. He let out a grateful sigh.

Then why take everything else?

The Lizard of Oz was more incomprehensible than ever. Unless . . . he remembered Bartholomew's strident conversation. Betrayed, Charlie had said. Not attacked. Betrayed.

Thomas snapped a drawer shut and left the wall closet, closing the panel behind him out of habit. He was not worried about his own past. Charlie's list of enforcements had also been mental. His executions were a matter of public record. But whoever's job it would be to step into the shoes of the DWP would suffer. The manuals were gone, as well as the files—books almost as incomprehensible as Denethan, but the only instructions they had for maintaining the stations. Chemicals mentioned were not all available now—repairs once taken for granted were now all but monumental—but still the DWPs had kept the water moving and kept it pure.

Now the job had passed to someone else, without the information to make it possible. Thomas realized he did not even know the succession. It hadn't seemed necessary.

As Lord Protector, he had to retrieve that information. It was Charlie's legacy and he'd be damned if he was going to let Charlie die without passing on his legacy.

"Here, here." Lady stood framed in the doorway. She'd put on a robe that had belonged to Veronica. Shorter and wider than its previous owner, the blue robe pooled about her feet and its front revealed an interesting amount of skin. He took a moment to realize he'd made the last of this thoughts public. The Protector said, "That bathtub holds an obscene amount of water. I felt selfish. Come join me. Consider it an anointment for the quest."

"The bodies. . . ."

"I moved them already." She held out her hand. "Tell me how you plan to catch up with those baby killers and I'll tell you how brave I think you are." The robe parted further to reveal an even more interesting view. "And then I'll twist your arm if you don't plan to take me with you."

Life goes on. He felt himself move toward her of his own volition, even eagerly, stripping off his scarf. She tilted her head, looking at his gills.

"Tell me, Thomas. Are those the first things to go erect . . . or the second?"

Chapter 17

Thomas woke to the stare of Lady's blue eye, gone deep and dark as the Pacific, her face moon-shadowed in the waning night. She lay propped on her elbow, one bare breast cupped by the rumpled covers of the bed which nested them both. A tangle of her brown hair dipped over her brown eye, hiding its soul from his view. But he wasn't afraid to face her blue stare this early in the morning. He smiled.

Then he jerked her elbow from under her.

Lady responded by wrapping her legs about him, entwining and pinning him to the sheets. She laughed as he drew her on top of him and then rolled over, stilling her thrashing with his own leanly muscled form. She threw her head back, crying, "I give up!"

"Oh, no, you don't," he answered, tilting his chin down so he could go for her throat. "I've just begun to fight." She uttered a throaty moan and tightened her embrace about him.

Like the Pacific, the consideration of her blue eye could not be taken for granted. Later, she watched him, and through her face was dewy with contentment, he saw the questions beginning, rising like storm-stirred foam rises to the ocean surface.

"Tell me about the College Vaults Charlie mentioned. I thought they didn't exist. I thought they were legend only. Would he have sent the children there?"

He wrapped a corner of the sheet about him like a loincloth. "They exist, and possibly. It's possible they came to get the children and got out before Denethan attacked."

"Been there?"

He did not answer.

"What about Charlie? How does—did—he know they exist? Had he been there?"

"Once."

She drew back, propping the pillows behind her and sitting up, tucking her knees in under her chin, satin coverlet hiding and revealing the most disturbing patches of bare skin. "We didn't settle whether I was going with you last night."

"It's not a question to be settled. I work alone."

"You *did.* that's not a question to be settled either. You're nothing but skin and bones now, and your Talent is all but drained off. I doubt you can even Project well enough to blur your target's vision. You need me. How far are we riding this time?"

"Not far. There'll be no need for the ghost road—besides, the mounts are too worn. They can't take it, and neither can you."

Sharply, "Why not?"

"I'm going In-City. You can't come."

Lady's mouth made an involuntary *o.* Then she shut her lips. Her rose-petal, inventive tongue nervously wet her lips. Then she said, "How far In-City are we going?"

Reaching for his breeches, he stood up, the sheet falling from him.

"Nice view," she murmured.

He pulled the pants up over his muscled haunches and turned around to her as he buttoned the fly. "Stop it."

She stopped. For the barest second. Then, "I'm as capable as you are."

"I never said you weren't. It's not your capability I'm afraid of."

"Then what are you afraid of?"

He faced her, hands pausing in the midst of buttoning his shirt.

"Tell me! Don't give me this male-female bullshit."

"I'm afraid of the city." He'd heard its death cry. Ghost road or no, he was not sure he could ever go In-City without hearing it again. Then, vigorously, because he suddenly had to do *something,* he strode outside and began to drag the dead to hastily created pyres, stacking their bodies. After ten minutes or so, Lady joined him, her face pale, her lips thinned. They worked until dawn, finding it too difficult to make one bonfire, instead lighting ten, in a ragged half-circle about the manor house. He used his anger to set off the flames. Lady said nothing as she came and took his hand. The fires burned hot and the stench made tears come to his eyes, but he held his place. The woman at his side murmured a barely audible prayer. The coyotes and crows and raccoons backed off, chattering their dismay at losing the carrion. Wild dogs crouched down in the hills and watched through their marble eyes.

Lady bathed him a second time when they returned to the house, stripping off his bloodied clothes. She bathed them as well, hanging them out to dry in the rising sun. Then she joined him in bed, trembling in sudden exhaustion. He reached out and pulled the opaque window curtains together, dimming the room to a blue glow. Veronica had always loved the many hues of blue.

She spoke directly to him for the first time since he'd walked out. "It can't be that bad. You explore the ruins all the time."

"Just the suburbs, just the edges—not the inner city, and that was a hellhole *before* the Disasters hit. If Denethan is beginning an invasion, I'll be ducking down every dodge hole I find, staying out of his way." He took her by the shoulders and spoke to her firmly. "There's no clean water under that layer of concrete and debris. I'll have to pack in every drop. And bring my meter and chemical kit to check for radiation and toxins. And torches, because under the first layer it's usually dark. There's nesters and wolfrats and worse in there."

"All the more reason I can help," she pointed out. "Your Talent stretches only so far."

He shook his head. "We already know the nesters have the eleven year plague. I'll go—it's enough that I go, knowing that when I come back, I can't take the chance I might father an aberration. I can't take you in with me—I can't expose you to that."

"It's my choice."

"Then you're not thinking clearly, Lady, we're both Talents. If either one or both got the plague, think of the abomination we could have for a child."

"I can handle an extra arm or gills."

He closed his eyes and took a deep breath, then opened them and returned her gaze. "Suppose the abomination wasn't obvious. Suppose it wasn't external, *but internal*. What kind of monster might we bring into this world?"

Her breath sucked in. Then she shook her head stubbornly. "I'd know—and so would you. Besides, who says I'm going to let you father my children?"

"I say. We've been working on it."

She reached up and cupped the side of his jaw in her creased hand, and her mouth curved gently. "No, Thomas. We've been working on love."

"Don't change the subject."

"I'm not. Isn't this what all this is about—our love for our people, our hope that we can help in whatever way we can, as well as our love for one another?"

He let go of her in exasperation.

"I'll just follow you."

"I need you to carry the word about the massacre."

"We have pigeons for that."

He pointed a finger at her. "If I take you—if—you can't argue with a word I say. Our lives may depend on it."

She smiled widely. "Don't you depend on that either. At least I have enough sense to know when not to break up a winning team." She pulled him down in bed. "Now sleep at least for a few hours."

The pigeons left Charlie's house, circling once on the morning air to catch their bearings, their wings slicing through the thin, blue smoke funnels of the still burning pyres.

Lady shaded her face to watch them go. "Alderman and Wyethe each had two apprentices," she said. "I've suggested to the counties that it might not be a bad idea to have two Protectors instead of one. We've no business weeding out Talent." Sleep had smoothed out her forehead, but there was dark blue bruises under her eyes. She had washed her trail clothes and changed back into them. She held the mule's reins in her workworn hands, hands that he could vividly remember caressing him in the night with surpassing gentleness.

She turned to the mule, twisted the stirrup in her capable fingers, and put her boot toe in. With a jump, she was mounted.

Blue smoke from the fires swirled about her momentarily. She waved it off with a tired smile. "Beauty always draws smoke," she said and waited warily for his retort.

Thomas did not. He gathered up Cindy's reins, while glancing at the ten pyres. Now, tired as he was, he was glad they had done it. He grabbed the saddle horn, clucked the black mare into motion, and did a flying mount.

He looked at her. "Ready?"

For one heart-stopping moment, he saw fear in her eyes, and thought perhaps she'd come to her senses and was going to back out. Then she winked.

"After you."

Chapter 18

Charlie's gauges were barely used, well crafted, the glass covers made by an artisan glassblower whose crystals were works of art, signed indelibly by a curlique of glass sculpture where they were sealed off. Those sculptures, a dolphin here, a fox head there, made it difficult to encase the gauges and they were often framed in wood which had been hand-carved especially to fit the gauges. Barely used, but not barely loved. The wood had been rubbed and polished so often it shone. Thomas cupped the compass, thinking of the first time he and Charlie had used it. With the exception of the radiation meter, he packed away the other gauges in their case. That, he hung about his neck, entwining the thong gently about his scarf-protected gills. The compass he slipped inside his uppermost jacket pocket. The finger bones, as if precognizant, had already moved there. Angrily, he pinched them out and replaced them in a lower pocket.

He thought he heard an angry clink of ivory against glass as Cindy moved down out of the foothills.

Lady drew even. She had her hair drawn back with the two hairpins he'd given her. "Are you going to have trouble covering two trails?"

"No. No, I don't think so. We know Denethan is after the children. It's as likely he's the one who stripped Charlie's office."

"If not?"

"The children are most important. Charlie would have told them how to get there if he had to send them off, but the College Vaults are hidden damn well. I have to hope their escorts got to them first. But they can't know about the massacre or that Denethan's on their heels." He sat back in the saddle, thinking of how he and Charlie had first ferreted them out. The fables of vast, underground caches of society had always been around, and beyond the Fire Ring and In-City, little surveys were being done by some of the counties. Charles, in his role as DWP, had been the first to come up with concrete clues as to the reality of the underground. Though it was not part of his system, he'd been able to track a massive amount of water usage to otherwise barren foothills in Claremont.

The two of them had gone north and swung around east, avoiding L.A., looking along the fringe boundaries where Charlie had charted water activity. They'd found what they were looking for, narrowly avoiding a guard of soldiers that made the DWP Forces look like amateurs. Then, they'd been invited down the maw itself. The invitation had excited his old friend. He had found truth in fable—perhaps the old world wasn't completely dead yet. He responded to the invitation with enthusiasm. Charlie had had the guts to go in—he hadn't. At the time he'd told himself it was more important to guard the DWP's back, to ensure that once he got in, he would be sure of getting out because they had no idea what or who they were going after. Charlie returned from his meetings pensive and silent, never telling Thomas what had transpired except to say, "I think our genetic program is ahead of theirs," an odd thing to conclude when it had been legend that only purebloods were entombed in the College Vaults. But Thomas had not seen or talked with legend and Charlie made it clear upon their return that the matter was never to be discussed. Charlie thought he'd done a good enough job to give him the title "Sir" when they returned. Now, seven years older, Thomas knew better.

Lady read something in his face. "If necessary, we can split up."

He reined the black mare about sharply, blocking the mule's path. "Hell, no. I've got enough on my mind wondering how to take care of you with you right here."

"You may not like the idea, but it's still an option if we need one. We can't afford to leave out any possibilities."

And, damn it, he knew she was right. But he didn't tell her so. He just seesawed the bit ever so lightly in the mare's mouth and she backed up to let the mule by.

Lady looked at him. "I can see you throttling down anger as if it were some kind of beast and your will was a club. I remember you before Gillander died, a gangly boy who used to watch when he thought I wasn't looking. You weren't angry then. Where did you find all that rage? Do you cultivate it on purpose?"

"I think of it as skill."

Her shoulders swayed easily with the mule's swinging walk. "Then you acquired it. From where?"

"You mean from whom. I was furious when Gill died. I thought that if any of the Protectors had known how to fight worth a damn, it wouldn't have happened. If I could have fought well enough, it wouldn't have happened. So when I heard about this . . . man . . . who knew a hundred ways to kill, I asked Charlie for leave from my studies to go find him."

"What did Charlie say?" She brushed a stray bit of hair from her forehead.

"He told me the man was a murderer and if I wanted the bounty, to go for it. That I'd find him nesting in the ruins about twenty miles south of here."

She gave him that two color appraising look of hers. "How old were you then?"

"Fifteen. I'd just turned fifteen and I was scared shitless. I mean, it wasn't like I was going out to find a master who would teach me everything he knew, even though that's what I wanted him to do. And it didn't seem likely I could talk him into it."

They were companionably silent, as the two beasts picked their way across a four-lane-wide track, broken and incomplete, that abruptly disappeared about twenty yards from them in a yawning chasm.

Lady made a face at him. "Tell me about the murderer. Did you catch up with him?"

"Yes and no."

"Sweet heaven," she muttered fiercely. "What happened?"

"Well, I didn't exactly catch up with him."

"You must have learned something from him!"

Thomas smiled at her. "It took me a year and a half, trailing him. Every time I got close, he'd try to kill me. I'd survive it, and I did my damnedest not to forget how he'd done it. That was how I learned. My apprenticeship was one of survival. After fifty tries or so, he took me in. He was a nester. I learned everything else I could."

"Then what?" Her attention was rapt.

"Then, when I could best him, I brought him back. Charlie read him his rights and I executed him."

"Jesus! You can be a cold bastard."

He wrapped the reins tightly about his left hand and stroked the worn leather. "No," he said slowly. "An angry one. Everything that I learned on survival, I learned from that murderer. Everything good in life, I learned from a harmless old man who died because he could never be as ruthless as that murderer."

"I'm sorry."

"Don't be. You asked a question, you have an answer. And I'll give you something more—I don't want you coming with me because that murderer told me the surest way to kill a man: take him In-City." His muscles tightened and the black mare, taking it as a signal, strode out ahead of the mule, pointing her muzzle from the ruins' edges toward the area known as In-City.

Thomas knelt down and examined the tiny, rough-shod hoof-print. "Donkeys," he said. Excitement flickered through him.

"Wild?"

"This far past the fringe of the ruins? I doubt it. There's no reliable forage deep inside there, and burros know that. I think we've crossed the trail we've been looking for."

Lady's face lit up jubilantly. The expression glowed in her eyes. "We're close to finding them so soon?"

"Maybe." Thomas straightened. He pointed out the probable pathway the donkeys had taken. "The prints are deep enough that I think they're laden, but don't go congratulating ourselves yet—nesters use burros, too. There's thistle and gorse and fox-tail growing abundantly on these outer boundaries."

Lady gave him a look he could not interpret as she countered, "but if it's them, to have caught up so soon—"

He mopped his brow against the noonday sun. "It's not impossible. Charlie probably gave the escort instructions to lay low. If so, the kids wouldn't have left until late yesterday, from whatever bolt hole he told them to hide in."

"How do you know that—"

He mounted and turned Cindy's head toward the donkey track. "I don't. But I know what I would have done in Charlie's shoes."

"Well, you could have told me. I was a little worried about . . . wasting time."

He looked back over his shoulder to catch her blushing. "Wasting time? Lady, I could have come up with about five different things to call what we did most of last night, but wasting time wouldn't have been one of them."

"That wasn't what I meant."

"Forget it. I know what you meant. Believe me, as nice as it was to sleep in a real bed with you—I wouldn't have been there if I thought we were behind by several days. I can't afford to be led around by my dick."

That turned her blush to a deep rose. Her lips, slightly swollen from the night's activities, set themselves in a firm line. Thomas turned back around in the saddle to hide his smile, thinking that he had finally had the last word with her.

The scribe bowed low, as only his sinuous form could let him. The movement bothered his aging form, but he did not heed his aches. He had served long and well—and would continue to do so until it was impossible to serve at all. Denethan turned as the scribe's action drew his attention.

"What is it, Micah?"

"We have lost a second pack to the wolfrats."

Denethan frowned. "How many have we left?"

"Two trailers, sir, although one of the war packs could be used—"

"It will have to do. I presume you have better news for me than that."

Micah's inner lids closed in pleasure. "Yes. The pack was closing in on spoor—donkeys, trekking westward, just off the Fire Ring. Your packmaster feels they're not wild burros, although they could belong to squatters."

Denethan got up from his camp stool. "Any guess where they're headed?"

The elderly scribe shook his head. Years of desert weather had given his skin a fine patina like that of burled oak, and etched years both lean and plentiful into deep wrinkles. The movements of the children sent out from the DWP's home had baffled both him and his leader. They had predicted northward, along the coast, the decoys having gone that way also. "I cannot say."

Denethan sighed deeply. "Neither do I. They can continue

west or cut north . . . or even cross the Fire Ring into In-City. Send another pack of trailers out—we can't afford to lose them now."

"The nesters—"

"If we run across nesters, kill them. They're outlaws in the local society and I doubt they'd be much more useful to us."

The scribe undulated upward, placed the palms of his hands together, saying, "Yes, sir," and backed away to leave.

"Micah—"

The scribe turned at the tent doorway.

"Have the packmaster get that pack warded before he takes it out. Anything might help."

The scribe nodded understandingly and left Denethan alone in the canopied tent. The man resettled himself on his camp chair, letting the heat of the day swirl about him as he thought. He scratched his neck gently, picking at the tiny warts that made a kind of necklace, swearing gently whenever he ruptured one with his nails. There were others who would be out after the peninsula children soon—he'd no doubt of that. He couldn't afford to let anyone else find the pair first, for any reason.

His claws paused in mid-scratch. The DWP might even have been in contact with the College Vaults. No . . . surely not.

But it might be one explanation for the course across the expanse of the L.A. basin, a desperate action for two who were supposed to be, and remain, genetically pure. Denethan was a mutant. He held no good will toward the College Vaults.

He reached the tent fold and threw it open. "MICAH! Get that packmaster and sent him in, *now.*"

The patch of green in between two leaning giants had gone wild, to seed, and had wilted now in a too dry winter. The mule and the mare cropped savagely, pulling out the grass by its roots in spots, as Thomas and Lady watched them.

"I would not have believed," she said softly, "that there were no lawns, no trees or flowers then. I know you warned me, but I wouldn't have believed it." She and Thomas had scythed as much grass as they dared, two large, ballooned bags lying on the ground at their feet. The animals would eat again when they pitched camp.

"There may have been. It got crowded, as I understand it." Thomas tilted back his head, and watched a falcon span the two spires of the buildings. "This was probably quite a coveted area. This little courtyard park may have been worth as much as one of those buildings."

"How did they *breathe?*"

He only smiled indulgently. Late afternoon shadows cast a deep purple over the backs of the two mounts. "Maybe they didn't." he straightened. "We're getting close to the Fire Ring."

"Do you think they would've crossed it? What about frightening the children?"

"I don't know. Alma has been hearing stories about the burning hills all her life . . . but Stefan, well, his mother kept him fairly isolated. I know, because she worked as chief supervisor for the tanner in my county. After she died, Charlie took him in. So he might not have the superstitions—"

"It's not superstition—it's common sense."

"Most of the hill fires are out now. Oil doesn't burn forever."

Lady took her hairpins out, shook her hair free and massaged her scalp vigorously, the luxuriant mane flying. Then she combed it back with her fingers and replaced the pins. Thomas watched her, thinking that her brown hair caught the fire of the low sun. What would she look like when they crossed the Ring?

The foothills of lower L.A. held an immense underground reservoir of oil—or had before the asteroid that sheared off Nevada had also taken part of L.A. with it, and in the process had set those reserves on fire. That disaster had further damaged an already dying culture. Now the thin lines of black smoke that flumed over the lower city were nearly gone . . . and so were the reserves. None who had lived in Thomas' grandfather's era had been able to put out the fuel fires.

Thomas stirred. Already his eyes stung from the invisible fumes of the ring.

"We'd better get moving."

Lady pursed her lips. "Murphy's had enough, but your mare's still losing flesh. She needs to be grazed tonight, if we can, and save what we cut for tomorrow."

"She may have to eat a burning fire." He thinned his lips and whistled to the black horse. She tossed a dainty head, lips stained green with grass, but came to him. The hollows above her eyes had deepened, and her flank was showing more rib than he liked.

The mule threw up his head and his throat stretched in a

silent bray, body quivering as Lady reached for his headstall. She froze.

Thomas heard the howl on the wind. "Yip-yaroo."

"Shit!"

Grabbing up Lady's bag of grass, he tossed it to her. She shouldered it and mounted the mule with difficulty, though it had frozen in a stretch for her. He tossed his own harvest across the mare's flanks before taking to leather.

The mule gave him a wild look, the whites of its eyes showing. Lady curbed him into sensibility. Thomas beckoned for her to ride after him cautiously, and they exited onto the streets.

Beyond the cupped buildings, they could hear the full-throated cries of the coyote pack. They hunted as the wilderness predators they were—silently, with only an occasional yaroo to the packmaster to indicate their direction, making it more difficult to calculate their presence. Thomas's jaw tensed as he listened, then he leaned toward her. "They're not after us. They're ahead of us, outflanking us, and the sound is going away."

Lady shook her head. "How can you tell? The echoes. . . ." She paused. He could see concern for the two children they were following dawn in her eyes. "How can we get there first?"

"I don't know." Thomas cast about. Most of the buildings in this area were fairly intact structurally, though of little worth since almost everything that could be salvaged had been except for the framework itself. If they had been brick, those would have been gone, too, though few large buildings held more than a brick facade. He pointed. "Maybe we can be a close second." He put his boot heels to the mare's flank and she leaped forward.

Chapter 19

As Thomas hunched over the mare's withers, he settled her pace down. He had no desire to founder her after grazing. Cindy shook her head in disagreement, then set her ears forward alertly. He reached out and loosened his rifle in its sheath, keeping the rawhide thong loop over it lightly. Cindy jumped a broken curb and the rifle rattled but stayed in place. He did not thumb open the firing chamber, deciding the event called for darts rather than his dwindling supply of vials. He didn't want to be handling those darts with their sharp tips until he had to. Scant blocks later, the buildings disintegrated into neighborhoods that must have existed in squalor even before the Disasters. Fractured gaps opened the walkways where gas lines had exploded, gouting out foundations close to them.

The mule kept up with Blade's mare, its long ears sweeping forward, then back. Lady's hair streamed free of her hairpins.

They caught up with the echo of the coyote pack. Thomas brought his horse to a skidding halt, and stood in the stirrups. He saw their dun and dapple shapes hurtling over the asphalt and rock, dodging broken beams. At their heels rode a man-shaped figure, reining a stocky pony recklessly through the ruins.

Thomas' lips stretched into a thin line of satisfaction. He shrugged off his grass catcher and motioned for Lady to do the same. He kicked Cindy back into a run, letting his knees guide her, trusting to the mare's own fine sense of agility to protect them as he pulled the rifle loose and knuckled open the firing chamber. Deftly, he plucked darts from his inside pocket, taking care not to touch their points.

They were fletched with mockingbird feathers, stiff and insolent as the creature itself. He flipped the chamber cover back into place and wound the rifle back with his right hand as he cradled it, picking the reins back up with his left. He swept a glance over his shoulder to check on Lady. She'd pulled out some pouches and vials of her own, the bag ends sticking out through her fist, a sturdy slingshot of some size planted in the crook of her thumb.

They were not exactly armed for bear, but close.

The dark funnels of the burning hills hung over them. His eyes smarted and his nose rebelled at the stench of crude oil. Skeletons of great towers, drums, and catwalks hung canted from their foundations, rusted against the blue-black smoke. He could see low tongues of fire licking about the structures. They angled in crossways to the hunt. Now, in silhouette, he could see the shaggy forms of running donkeys, slim figures bent low over their necks. The children and their escort. The donkeys wouldn't run far, that he knew. Behind them, fleet and tireless, came the coyotes and whipping their heels, the desert mutant packmaster.

"They're running into the Ring!" Lady shouted, her breath thin and wheezy. "They'll be cut off."

The donkeys, gray coats whitened in contrast to the smoke curtain they were plunging near, ran toward a dead end.

Thomas let out a whooping yell. The coyotes swerved, and the packmaster's pony stumbled as the rider twisted to look at them. Thomas put the rifle butt into his shoulder, steadied to focus his thoughts and the chamber, and fired at the lead tracker.

The coyote went down, rolled, and got yelping to his feet. His packmates swept by him. He put his head down and caught up.

Thomas did not wait to see if the fletched dart hung from his flank. He sighted down the barrel as Cindy thundered closer to the pack, and fired his second. Then he reined back. The psychic effort of targeting the fletches left him in a cold sweat. He rubbed the back of his hand over his mouth. He breathed deeply.

The coyote went somersaulting, tail over muzzle. Again, the wave of trailers broke around him. The predator got to his feet limping and shook off the poison of the dart, as the packmaster galloped past. He lunged in his master's wake.

Perturbed, Thomas kneed Cindy into a parallel run. Awkwardly, afraid to use both hands, he reloaded the rifle.

Lady shouted, "What does it take to put them down?"

"More poison than I've got!" he answered.

"They must be warded!"

That made sense if Denethan wanted to give his trailing packs some extra protection over dangerous ground. He said to her, "Then that's your territory! I'm spent." Spent, hell, he was as weak as a babe.

She nodded curtly. Twisting in her saddle, she pulled out a bag of herbs and targeting charms to aid psychic focus. He aimed and fired again, rapidly, determined to make enough of a nuisance of himself to draw the pack away from the two flagging donkeys in front of them. His second dart clipped the desert pony. It went to its knees with a high-pitched squeal, throwing its rider to the dirt. It tried to get back up, but the right foreleg flopped about under it and it collapsed, rolling and thrashing. Thomas would have felt for its suffering, but the poison was swift and the pony died as Blade drew even with the stunned packmaster.

A shrill whistle split the air as the lizard man scrambled to his feet and charged at Thomas. The pack turned as one and came back, slanted eyes aglow with the thrill of the chase. Cindy shuddered under the weight as the packmaster jumped her, intent on grabbing Thomas out of the saddle. Blade retrieved his shuriken. He went limp and let the long, hooked fingers of Denethan's man grab him and pull him down. As they hit the ground together, he came around with a slashing backhand.

The blade touched nothing earthly.

Thomas saw crimson as the packleader put his forearm about the Protector's neck and began to strangle him. As his vision wavered he glimpsed Lady and heard her through the roaring in his ears.

With a cry of triumph, Lady pitched her bags of herbs and charms, into the midst of the coyotes. The poignant smell of garlic and pepper flumed upward. The coyotes gave startled yelps, leaping aside. As if in answer to his pack's defeat, the packmaster tightened his armhold. Thomas made a croaking sound. His vision darkened.

Lady kicked the mule into a charge, her image blurring as

Thomas felt his senses collapse. She swung her foot out of the stirrup, and slammed the packmaster in the back of his head as hard as she could. As the being went down, she broke a packet of herbs over his skull and rode past.

Thomas sneezed. He went facedown in the dirt, eyes watering. At her shout, he rolled out from under the enemy's slack form, massaging his neck. He took a deep, shuddering breath as the coyotes attacked. He projected multiple images just to slow them down a little. The vials inside his jacket clinked invitingly.

The mule let out an angry squeal. Flashing teeth and scarlet tongues filled Blade's vision as he drew his wrist knife.

The pack leader singled him out as the mule's charge daunted the others. Thomas gripped his knife tightly. With a snarl, the coyote launched itself at Thomas' throat.

Thomas slashed at the coyote's grinning jaw. His action met with thin air. He ducked, going to one knee as the coyote's rank breath grazed his face. He smelled of carrion and Lady's mixture of pepper and herbs. "Get those wards down!" he shouted at Lady.

"I'm trying," she retorted over the noise of a mulish trumpet of fierce joy. Murphy lashed and stomped every yellow hide he could reach. They circled him cautiously, waiting for an opening to pull him and his rider down.

The pack leader came after Thomas again. Thomas had no doubt that the desert wolf intended to tear him to shreds. Blade got to his feet as the coyote went for his legs. His answering knife stroke was buffeted away by an unseen force and he lost his knife in the gravel as the coyote's jaws locked about his ankle. Sharp white teeth punctured his boot leather as if it wasn't even there. He dared not throw a vial, for both he and Lady were in the midst of the enemy.

"Lady!" he shouted a last time.

"Got it!" Lady cried in triumph. A cloud of dust cascaded over them as Thomas tried to kick free of his attacker. He clubbed a fist down on the side of the coyote's head. The beast yelped and sprang away.

About then, the remaining pack members, tired of dodging the mule, came to their leader's aid.

Thomas jumped for the packmaster's whip curling out from under the mutant's body. He snapped it in their gleaming yellow eyes. The coyotes bit and yowled in frustration at the cracking whip.

Lady fought to control her furious mule. She slung another packet into the midst of the pack as the beasts threatened Thomas. The next pop of the whip brought satisfying yelps of pain. Thomas transferred the whip to his left hand and grabbed for a throwing star. He aimed it at the pack leader's bristling throat. The predator went down with a gurgling moan. The coyotes on either side of him plunged away in startlement.

He crouched down and retrieved his knife. A big yellow brute was going for Murphy's hamstrings. He threw the knife and pivoted away, hearing it thunk home. Charlie's feisty black mare decided to charge into the festivities, her reins flying. The five remaining predators ground their bellies in the dust and snapped at Cindy's hooves. Blade reached for his boot knife and carved up one more before the pack gave up and split apart, circling and yipping in fear. Then, as one, they wheeled away back in the direction they had come, nearly invisible dun shadows streaming across the hill.

Blade retrieved his wrist knife and one shuriken. Retracing the struggle, he found two of his feathered darts as well, pulling one out of the painted pony. He knelt by the packmaster, Lady riding guard over the still form.

She made a face as Thomas clucked between his teeth. He straightened. As he dusted himself off and replaced the weapons he had reclaimed, he said, "Took you long enough."

"Somebody in Denethan's camp is very good at warding. I'd keep that in mind if you ever want to try to walk in at night."

Thomas winced as he put his foot in the stirrup to mount. The coyote bite sent a thrill of pain through his ankle. He tried to ignore the pain, thinking of matters at hand. There was no sign of any other attackers—or of the children.

Lady tucked her disarrayed hair behind her ears. "Where'd they go?"

He didn't know. But he looked toward the horizon where he'd last seen them. Lady followed his gaze. She made a sound of horror.

He'd last seen them crossing the Fire Ring.

Chapter 20

"You can't be serious," Lady glared down at him as he rigged the retrieved grass catcher to hang over her saddle horn. She leaned back, hips tight against the cantle as if she did not wish his hands to mistakenly touch her.

"We're so close—"

Thomas pulled the strap tight and met her angry stare. "No one will follow them across the Fire Ring. The smell of burning pitch is so intense, they can't be trailed, and it's near dark. Denethan hasn't got time to send in replacements yet. They'll be safe enough."

"I can't just let them go. . . ."

He put his hand on her knee. "I know where they're going. I have a pretty good idea when and where they'll turn north. We'll intersect with them."

Lady looked in the direction he had indicated. "But that means we've two or three days more riding."

"The fires will slow them. Lady, inside the Fire Ring, they're as safe as they would be riding with us."

"Then where do we go?"

His neck corded up as he swallowed through a dry mouth and took his hand off her boot. "About as deep In-City as anybody would ever want to go." Maybe she heard the fear in his voice, maybe not. At least she stopped asking questions.

The torch smoldered in her hand, its light staining the dusk. "How much farther?" she said, letting the reins drop so that Murphy could pick his way carefully.

"Tonight? As soon as I find a place that's defensible. I don't want our backs to the chasm if I can help it."

"The moon's up already." She shuddered, looking at the immense crater where the asteroid had struck. Its far edge was beyond sight and its rim still showed fire-scarring even after all these years. "I thought I heard wolfrats trailing us."

"You did, but I dropped a discouragement of powdered cayenne back there." He eased his weight, leather creaking under him, and Cindy groaned softly.

The mule flicked his ears. Then Murphy snaked around so quickly Lady grabbed for the saddle horn to keep herself atop. Thomas wheeled Cindy in the same direction.

There was no mistaking the flickering of slanted red eyes as the new menace came trotting toward them, nails clicking on asphalt. Lady sucked in her breath.

Blade slipped his hand inside his jacket, reaching for a vial. Instead, he grabbed the finger bones and fisted them, and the twilight world suddenly stilled around him. His mind whirled and his bones went chill.

"Ah, m'boy," Gillander said softly behind his ear. "Sometimes you summon the ghost road—and sometimes, it summons you."

Noise. He reeled in his saddle, as the fabric of his reality stretched and curved, and vertigo snatched his vision from him. Lady Nolan gave a soft cry and he knew he'd brought her with him—that much he could be thankful for. He threw out a hand, catching the soft cloth of her sleeve. She fumbled back and their hands pressed together tightly. he uncupped the bones and wished them back, to no avail.

"I thought you said no more ghost road."

His sight sharpened and his balance returned abruptly. "I lied," he said, unwilling to let her know of his lack of control. He braced his palm on the saddle horn and let his senses trickle out, feather light, testing the area around him.

As if she knew what he was doing, Lady said, "I could hardly move that knife. It's as if Talent can't work here."

Her voice broke his concentration, and he clenched his jaw with unvoiced anger. He'd had no more success than she. But he knew why. The compass slung around his neck still worked as he drew it forth and held it. He looked to Lady Nolan as she brought the mule even with his mount. "That way," and he pointed. The corner of his mouth quirked as he added, "We're not talking ruins anymore."

They stood on a bridge of nothingness, a golden sparkle above an immense chasm. It stretched across the abyss which pulsed and writhed below, a living thing of molten lava. Thomas looked back. Tiny slits of red flashed in the darkness. He did not know how the wolfrats had followed them, or if they had ventured into a level of hell where the beasts ruled.

"We've got to keep moving. I don't know if we're on a ghost road or not—if this is the past or a resonance of it—"

"Resonance?"

He shook his head. "An echo, a ghost, something with the ability to leech away both of us. This looks like the night the world ended. But we can cross here."

"I'm with you." She bent and ripped off a length of hem, dismounted, and blindfolded her mule.

Thomas took off his jacket and used his shirt. The black mare shuddered and stepped after him reluctantly. She would not have been any happier if she'd seen the golden smoke and ash trailing from every footstep she took.

They walked into the night. The bridge muffled the hoofbeats of their mounts. Thomas stayed cold, despite the exertion it took to walk the arcway. Every step required immense concentration as though he plowed through snowdrifts chest high. Beside him, Lady's breathing was harsh but steady. Suddenly, she slipped and let out a short scream. Her torch fell away.

He dove for her, belly first, and caught her wrists. Below her, the torch seemed to drop forever before it hit. The chasm reacted with a boiling hiss and a lavalike wave spewed upward. She hung over the vast pulsating mass below, her eyes wide. "Thomas?"

"I've got you. I won't let you go." The veins and sinews stood out on the back of his arms. "Can you TK?"

"I don't know. I'll try." She closed her eyes, shutting her soul away from him. If he dropped her now, he would be unable to see the terror in her eyes.

Blade clenched his jaw and heaved upward. Her weight grew lighter as he did, and he flopped her back onto the span. She lay there a second, panting. He let go only when he knew she was secure and could not slide back over the rim.

He hadn't had the strength to help. His fingers had been almost too numb to grip her arms. Thank god her Talent, though weakened, was still there.

She got to her knees. "Let's go."

"Can you walk?"

"Do I have any choice?" She gave a bittersweet smile. "It's too far to go back."

They slogged on endlessly until it seemed they must have walked for an entire night. Dawn had to be edging over the horizon from somewhere. Lady staggered, holding onto her stirrup. Murphy came to a stubborn halt. The mule shook his head, ears flopping noisily. "He's got more sense than we do. We're going to have to rest them."

Thomas eyed the waning night. "And ourselves." As he reached up to take off the mare's blindfold, she butted him in the chest and he dropped like a stone. The torch rolled harmlessly onto the bridge and lay there, smoldering. It threw almost as much light as a lantern. Lady came to his side. "Thomas!" She put her hand to his forehead. "You're like ice."

In contrast, the warmth of her hand was a brand across his face. He waved her away.

"What's happening to you?"

"I fuel the road."

"With what?"

"Dammifiknow. My life, I think."

"Then get us off it, now."

He looked into the miasma boiling underneath the thin fabric of the golden span. He looked back into Lady's eyes. One blue, one brown. "I can't," he said. "I didn't willfully bring us this time and I don't know how to get us back."

"Shit." She sat down next to him. She pulled her denim riding skirt off her slim hips and threw it over him. It came billowing down, filled with her warmth and her woman-scented, musky perfume. His teeth began to chatter. She lay across him, hugging him.

When his shuddering stopped, she brushed his hair back from his forehead. "Tell me how it is you do it."

"Do what?"

"Open the ghost road."

He reached inside his jacket. The bones came to his fingers reluctantly and he pulled them out.

Lady looked at what he held. "Is this a focus?"

"No. Yes. I'm not sure. This isn't a paranormal Talent."

"Then what is it?"

"Witchcraft?"

Her laughter died in her throat. "I—" she stopped. "You've always been fey, Thomas, in a way none of the rest of us are. Who else could use a pebble to project a fog? Dowse for water and never have to worry about its being clean? Know unerringly the right and wrong of things? Truth-reading is one thing, but it doesn't make justice any easier to deal out. When I Read someone, I know only if they've lied, but not what the truth is. I've seen you execute a man without blinking, because you knew it was the only thing to do."

He could barely hear her now. He felt transparent, fading.

Lady could feel him slip away, as surely as if he had gone over the rim of the bridge the way she had earlier. She reached out with her mind and caught him in her thoughts, anchoring him. As she did, she could feel the terrible toll of the ghost road.

His mind was like a great, raw wound. She could feel Denethan in it, like a festering thorn. He'd never been rid of his foe—did he even know they were still linked? She shielded him as well as she was able and when she'd finished and opened her eyes to look at him, a hint of color had returned to his face.

She took a deep breath. "I can't lose you now." She grabbed for Murphy and the mare, who stood listlessly, muzzle to the strange golden fog that encircled their hooves. She threw down their grass catchers so they could eat something. She pulled her pack down and set up her tiny brazier, set a spark of fire among the coals with a snap of her mind and made herb tea, sweetening it with a last bit of honeycomb.

With an exquisitely carved teaspoon, she fed him every last drop. Then she picked up the hand still curled about the grotesque bones. He was cold as stone, as death, as . . . evil.

Hesitantly, because she was afraid, and dammit, she, Lady Nolan, had never been afraid since the day her mentor died—hesitantly, she opened his fingers and touched the bones.

The screams of a thousand thousand dead echoed in her mind, a vibration so powerful that it could be tracked through the darkest night. The voices screamed as one, and separately, in fear and hatred and confusion.

"Dear god!" Lady dropped his hand, unable to bear the vision. No heaven or hell or rest for these people, this past. Now she knew what he meant when he talked of resonances, of ghosts, of echoes. "Thomas?"

He stirred slightly. His eyes moved behind his lids and she wondered whether he only dreamed or was caught in a struggle against the ghost road's pull. Lady took a deep breath, preparing to meditate, and offer whatever aid she could give.

Murphy's snort interrupted her. She came out of trance with a jerk, already in a half-crouch and facing the part of the bridge they'd crossed. Red slits bobbed in the darkness.

The wolfrats had trailed them. She could hear the gnash of their teeth. Wind their carrion scent. But how? How did they get here? How did they transverse the fabric of this delicate universe Thomas had woven? With the Sight, she picked them up as smoke and crimson.

Thomas moaned. She looked back to him and gasped. He had tossed off her skirt and lay on the bridge, no less golden or ethereal than it. She smothered a sob, ran a hand across her face to clear her vision, and he looked his weather-beaten self again.

"I won't lose you! I won't!" She grabbed for him, for his beaten leather jacket and pulled it up. Vials sewn into slim inner pockets met her fingers. She grabbed two out. The diamond ring fell into her hand as well. She scored the glass for easier breakage, slipped the ring onto her finger. She picked up his torch where he had dropped it and held it like a weapon. She put her body between the pack and the mounts and Thomas.

"Come and get it," she said. "If you dare."

The wolfrats edged closer. She could see them now, their hides mangey and scarred, gray, mousy, piebald, and white, their nails grasping for purchase amid the strange weave of the bridge. They snarled and squeaked and huddled behind one another, watching her with eyes that glowed red.

"Don't be shy, boys." She sent a fire-spark behind them. It spouted up like a firework candle, rarest of joys, and sent the wolfrats leaping at her.

She kicked the first one in the side of the head. It fell, skittering and scrabbling, off the rim of the pathway. She tossed the vial, heard it shatter as it hit, and green-white gas boiled up. She buried her face in her sleeve and over the crook of her arm watched two of the beasts convulse and pitch off the bridge, twitching and writhing as they went.

The gas cloud dispersed as the two remaining wolfrats shrank back, noses twitching, tails whipping about them like frenzied snakes. Then they charged as one and she didn't have time to throw the second vial.

Chapter 21

As the rats rushed her, she saw a third crouching figure rise up from the shadows. He stank like the rats, but she saw the face, the beard—a wild man like none she'd ever seen before. He gave a shout and the rats swerved. She twisted to keep them in front of her, but that put her flank to the nester. Hair sizzled and flamed as she swung the torch. The piebald beast spat as it scrabbled to get away from her.

The nester edged forward. Lady swept the night between them, the torch leaving a trail of sparks to drift on the still air.

"Don't," she said. "I won't think twice about killing you."

Orange light glinted off his fists, a knife in one of them, and an unfamiliar object in the other. *Oh, Thomas,* she thought. *Where are you when I need you?* There was no one in the seven counties who was his equal with a blade.

A wolfrat darted at her, rearing up and pawing the air with sharp nails and long yellow tusks. She swung the torch at him, but kept her eyes on the nester, sensing that he was directing the beasts' movements. She backed up a step, heard Thomas moan at her heels and knew she'd retreated as far as she could. The wolfrats hunched low, their hungry eyes burning in the reflection of her light.

"Gi'e him to me." The wild man spoke, his voice scratchy, low and guttural. She barely understood him. His teeth were broken husks of yellow in his jaws.

"No."

"He don't belong to you."

Lady watched his hands. He didn't hold the knife for throwing, but for gutting and for that he'd have to move closer. Still, it would take but a flicker of movement to reposition the weapon. As for the other thing, she had no idea what it could do, but he held it as though it, too, were a weapon. It bore a slight resemblance to a zip gun.

She held up the vial. "It's a horrible way to die."

"Who says 'm alive? This is the dark road, i'n't?"

"You know about it?" She moved slightly as she spoke, forcing the rats to circle back, moving them between her and the frenzied man.

The wild man danced on one bare foot so callused its sole was like horn. Then the other foot. His odor fairly steamed from him. "He's marked," said the wild man. "The road runs where 'e does. I been told to mark him agin—so th' road's ours."

He gave a whistle and the rats charged her. With a curse, Lady moved back and tripped, her weight crashing across Thomas. He erupted upward, throwing her free. Recovering, Lady dove toward the rats as they came for Thomas, and thrust her torch into their faces.

They exploded into flame like dry straw. With mewling cries, they clawed and tumbled at one another. Regaining her feet, Lady kicked them over the edge of the bridge. Her underpants caught fire and she dusted the sparks out, unable to help Thomas who danced hand to hand with the bearded man.

They strained against one another, eyes glinting like those of wild animals with reflections of the torchlight. Thomas momentarily pushed his opponent back, his tanned face pale, his lips pulled back to bare his teeth.

"I hate to disappoint you," he said. "But I've already been marked a second time." He twisted his wrist, and the crescent scar of the dolphin's teeth, still pink in healing, came into view.

The wild man gave a cry as if he'd been struck. With a roar, he broke loose, knocking Thomas back. He raised the hand with the unfamiliar weapon. Lady cried out and threw the vial just as the weapon smoked and popped loudly. The bearded man disappeared in the white firelight of the magnesium mixture. Engulfed in its searing light, he staggered backward off the bridge and screamed his way into the abyss.

Thomas went to his knees and then fell, and ivory bones clattered out of his hand as he did so.

The golden span disintegrated below them. With screams, nickers, and brays of fear, they fell.

*   *   *

He blinked his eyes open. It was morning again, and they were sprawled in a broken concrete ring, the streets of yesterday barely spider tracks upon the face of the world he was most familiar with. Blood pooled under his arm and it hurt like hell to move it, but he did, as he sat up.

Lady got to her feet. Her jaw dropped in dismay as she knelt down and began to tug his jacket off. He fingered the hole.

"God damn it."

She slapped his hand away. "Help me get this off before you bleed to death."

"Can't bleed to death—a weapon like this doesn't even exist now. Look at this. It pierced both sides of my sleeve—"

"Meaning it went right through your arm. Help me with this thing or so help me I'll cut it off."

With a wince and a curse, he shrugged the jacket off. His upper sleeve was soaked, clinging to his bicep, and he saw a blossoming of flesh with a tiny purple center crying tears of crimson.

Lady made a sound through her teeth. She ripped the bottom half of his sleeve off even as he said, "Hey! That's my best shirt."

"Now it's your second-best shirt. Why don't you try focusing on getting that blood flow to clot up a little while I take care of the rest of this?"

He took a deep breath. The air was clean, quiet. The noise in the ruins was generated by pigeons, sparrows, and an occasional red-tailed hawk keening past. The wind whispered through conduit towers. Even the squeak of wolfrats down below sounded familiar. Home. He closed his eyes for a second.

"Hey! Don't you pass out on me."

"I'm not." He winced and hissed through his teeth as she tightened the bandage. Her efficient hands wrapped the cloth about and knotted the ends in several places. Their gazes met as he said, "I'll remember this."

"See that you do."

Suddenly, to his surprise, both her eyes brimmed with tears. She rubbed them away quickly. She got to her feet, dusting off her long traveling skirt and donning it. "It's just through the flesh. Keep it clean and you should be fine."

He moved his arm. "It hurts."

"Of course it hurts, you idiot. You were shot. That looked

like an explosive projectile to me, like one of Charlie's old guns."

"You're probably right. Want to go back and see?"

"No."

"I missed most of what he said to you. Was he a talkative fellow?"

"No." She hugged her stomach as though it hurt. Then she turned to him. She brushed her fingertips across first his brow and then his wrist. "This is supernatural, not paranormal."

"All that supernatural is, is paranormal that can't be explained or tested yet."

"He told me *you* were the road, Thomas. It goes where you take it. You . . . polarize the forces that move upon it. Primeval, good, bad . . . you glowed in the night as though you were woven of the same fabric as the span."

"Should have unraveled me and made a fortune out of gold yarn."

She spat. His face closed then. "I was dying, Lady. I didn't expect to come back, but everywhere I looked in that long dark tunnel, I saw your face. You brought me back. I felt peace, I could have had it for the wanting . . . but you anchored me. And then you fell on me and knocked the crap right out of me and I came to, choking for my life."

Her eyes had been brimming, then her mouth quirked. She threw her head back and laughed, laughed until the tears rolled down her cheeks and Murphy started braying.

His mustache twitched. "That's better," he said. "None of this mystic stuff. We're In-City and we need to get out."

The finger bones lay on the concrete between them. He scooped them up and pocketed them. "The ghost road runs on psychic emotion. Misery, mostly. Somehow I can channel it, manifest it. I can open up and give it direction, expend it. Maybe I'm releasing souls from some nether region, freeing them to go where they have to."

"Now who's getting mystical? What about the marks?"

"Current flows between poles. Maybe . . ." he shook his head. "How the hell do I know? We've got to get out of here."

Lady wiped her face again. "How do you feel?" she asked, her voice carefully neutral.

He moved a pace. His swagger had given way to a stagger and he looked as though a stiff breeze would topple him. He held his arm stiffly. The wind whistling through the eroding skyscrapers bore a trace of winter, edged with the promise of rain to come. He pulled the compass from around his neck and cupped it in his palm. Lady was looking expectantly at him when he glanced up.

"Well?"

He shrugged diffidently. "Can't tell. I suggest we just get on our horses and ride. We're still In-City, though I'd say we're several days closer to where we want to be."

She stalked off to her mule, muttering, "And what if we're several years later?"

He pulled his jacket on gingerly. The torn flesh under the knotted bandage had started to swell a bit. He ran his right hand over his inventory. He had less than a third of what he usually carried. The knobby ends of ivoried finger bones met his touch as well. "Let's get out of here." As he rode past the broken foundation where a single spire pointed upward like an index finger, he saw the painted sign of a nester border slapped upon its cornerstone. His eyes narrowed, but he said nothing to Lady. The murderer he'd brought to justice might be dead, but his clan lived on, and now he'd met them on the ghost road, too.

In the shadows as they passed, a hunched-over figure emerged, watched cannily until they'd gone, and then went to the pool of blood still liquid and warm upon the ground. It dipped a finger, then sniffed the blood. Then, with a grin, it ran back into the shadows, intent upon fulfilling a mission.

The sunlight was slanting across the cityscape when at last they halted. Lady swung down immediately, unslung her water bag and cooking pot and filled it for the mule. The mule sucked up whatever he could get, then she did the same for the black mare. Thomas brought out his case of gauges and checked the meter for toxicity and other readings. He frowned as he packed them back away.

"How bad is it?"

"Not good. But if we can avoid eating or drinking from the immediate locale and get out of here in a reasonable period of time, we should be all right."

"What's a reasonable period of time?" She slapped the mule's wet muzzle away affectionately. "Don't slobber on me!"

"Two months.

"I'd say we can make it within your time frame unless one of us gets planted here first."

He grinned at her wry tone. "In which case, it's a lost cause anyway, right?"

She gave both mounts a refill of water, then tied her bag off. "That's all, greedy guts." Her tenor changed. "We're going to have to find water soon . . . and grass."

"It's better for them to do without."

"You can't starve them!"

"They'll absorb the toxins quicker if we can even find grazing. I hadn't planned on the two of us eating much but what we're carrying, either." At the thought of eating, his stomach clenched. "Break?"

"All right." She dropped the reins, ground-tying both animals. "Tortillas and jerky sound lovely right about now."

He scrounged through the food pack. "I even have some dried apricots."

"A gourmet! What luck." She caught the package he threw to her. "Or do you say that to everybody you wine and dine?" Without waiting for an answer, she perched on a cement block and began to unwrap the packet. He watched her, trying to remember what it had been like on the trail from Orange County to the wedding, alone, without her. The memory seemed vague and unreal.

He pushed such thoughts away, knowing they were dangerous. Dangerous to become attached, to become dependent, as he'd been with Gillander, his mentor and friend. His way of life did not encourage commitment. He turned his back so that he could not see her while he opened his own packet of rations. The last of the lemon drops fell to his hand. It melted on his tongue with bittersweet poignancy. While he ate, he turned his thoughts inward to encourage the healing of his arm. In-City, the slightest disability, be it physical or emotional, could be fatal.

Chapter 22

Lady put her hand to her mouth and Murphy danced uneasily under her, shying away from the smell of blood as the desiccated animal swung in the breeze, hanging from the end of a tether. "What is that?" she asked, turning her eyes away.

"Nester totem. It's marking clan boundaries." He kneed the mare closer. Cindy chuffed at the scent of death and minced closer to the building. His sight blurred as he leaned forward to read the sign. After a day of riding his left arm pulsed with an angry throb and the blood loss kept him light-headed. He had said nothing but could feel Nolan's two-color stare on him constantly. She was a Healer and drained by the ghost road or not, she had to know what he was feeling.

The painted sign swam back into focus. Not only was this a clan boundary, but it marked feud territory. He looked down the broken city block, where the road inclined steadily, until a green and gold foothill met his eyes. He pulled a folded piece of hide from his vest.

"What is it?"

"There's water up there," he answered briefly. "We're close to the College Vaults. This clan marking tells me the reservoir is in disputed territory."

"We're sitting in the middle of a nester war zone?" Her voice gained an edge.

"Look," and she did so, despite the garish sacrificial totem behind his shoulder. "They're outlaws. If they could work together toward mutual interests, they wouldn't be outlaws."

Her mouth tightened. "I know that." Then her tone softened. "How about some tea and hardtack?"

He swung down. "More than that. I know it's still light, but we need to make camp here."

"Need? Here?"

His mouth tightened. "I need," he said.

"Ah. Wisdom comes to the boy." She dismounted easily. "I won't argue with that, but does that *thing* have to hang around?"

"Afraid so. Actually, it's the best protection we could have. This is as close to neutral territory as we're going to get until we hit the vaults."

"It'll draw wolfrats." Her voice was partially muffled as she turned her back to him and busied herself with her bedroll and saddlebags.

"Should, but I've never seen one of these do it yet. They're poisoned. Maybe the wolfrats sense it." He reached up for his pack and the answering throb in his arm shot through him. For a dizzying moment, he clung to the stirrup.

"Thomas!"

"I'm all right," he answered. His mouth felt cottony. His vision went dark, then lightened. The mare bore his weight quietly. He could smell her heated skin, see the spidery tracings of her veins through her hide. Of all the animals that had survived the disasters, horses had changed the least. He straightened up as his head cleared. Her tail came around smartly then, lashing at him as if to disprove her good humor. He smacked her fondly on her rump. "I'm all right," he repeated. He hoisted his saddlebags and pulled them off, ignoring the thrill of pain in his arm.

Lady knelt by her tiny brazier, igniting a spark among the coals that burned but were never consumed. She coaxed the rocks into a dull glow before taking out her battered teapot and filling it from her water supply. Then she sat back on her heels and mopped her brow on the sleeve of her blouse. "A good night's rest," she remarked, "will do us both a lot of good. In the morning, I'll be able to work a Healing."

"Save it."

She glanced up at him. "You've lost color as well as blood. Heroics won't do either of us any good. Can you set up wards?"

He thought about it. The effort set his mind spinning again. It was as if the ghost road was magnetic and he a lodestone, set into a whirl trying to align true and find north . . . affected long after leaving it. "Not yet," he admitted finally. "But it's getting better." He watched her sprinkle her tea leaves and herbs into water that slowly began to steam.

"We can't use the road anymore."

"I don't intend to. We should be able to meet up with Stefan and Alma tomorrow, unless I've lost all sense of time." Their gazes met briefly, then Nolan looked back to her teapot. She thumbed the lid into place.

He pulled his map out of his vest again and smoothed it over his thigh. His jeans had gone stiff with dirt.

"Tell me," Lady said, settling back as her tea brewed. "Tell me about the College Vaults."

His brows met before he could answer and she added, "You don't like them."

"I don't know them. Charlie was the only one who went in." They dealt with Intuition, it was their bread and butter, yet he felt himself flushing as he continued, "When he came out, he got his gills cut away. He never said why, but it was as if he felt alienated by them." He put his hand to his neck and seemed surprised to discover he still wore his long scarf. "Maybe I do know why."

"But the Vaults are real."

"Oh, yes."

"Then why don't they help us?"

"That's not their purpose. Their purpose is to survive, just as ours is. The Vaults were cut into this mountain to provide storage in case of earthquake or war, the labs and other equipment were haphazardly added later. They can't manufacture the past any more than we can, or so Charlie told me."

"And you believed him."

"He believed what he said. Why shouldn't I?" Blade took up the hot tin mug she handed him. The fragrance of the tea filled the late afternoon air and for a moment, the stink of the totem could be forgotten.

"It's written in your eyes." She blew steam off her mug gently.

He shifted his weight. The concrete under his lean haunches was cold and too hard. "I don't like handing the children over to them."

"He must have had his reasons. Perhaps better medical facilities. If the Vaults have always stayed this isolated, then perhaps the eleven year plague is only an ugly rumor to them."

"Maybe. I don't believe Charlie did what he did out of the goodness of his heart. The DWP was a businessman. He expected something from them."

"Any idea what it could be?"

"No, but I'm going to ask when we get there." Thomas paused to sip his tea. He bared his teeth. "Hot."

"But good." She sat back with a sigh and looked about the city block. The jagged foundations were not fire-charred as others had been, but were toppled and devastated nonetheless. "We're almost out of In-City."

"Just about."

She laughed throatily. "My Intuition's coming back. I can feel you itching, Thomas, just sitting there. You're thinking about the ruins and what they hold."

He hadn't been as far as he knew, but now that she mentioned it, yes, he had to admit it was true. He hid his smile in another sip of steaming tea.

"What do you look for?"

"Artifacts."

Nolan shook her head. "No, I mean *why*."

"Artifacts."

She shied a piece of concrete at him. He ducked, but she'd already missed on purpose. He set the mug down beside his bent knee. His throat closed for an instant, then he answered, "I look to find out why they were human and I'm not."

She looked as stunned as he felt. "We're human."

"Not. Not like they were. Even Stefan and Alma aren't. Maybe I can't explain it, but I know I'm different. You're different. Look at the photos I found in the ruins . . . the pictures in Charlie's family . . . it's more than gills or second eyelids."

Lady sat silently, both hands wrapped about her mug. She did not meet his gaze this time. "We've got the eyelids bred out. And almost the gills. If you hate them so much, why not do what Charlie did?"

"Because it's more than just your neck. It involves your bronchials and throat and lungs. And because I like swimming with dolphins. But I look at the nesters as they regress back to the first days and I wonder if we would look like that to true humans. Like animals instead of people."

A flicker of a glance. "You always stood up for the mutations."

"It's why we're alive today. But the nesters are another matter. They're asking to be hunted down and scourged out, like vermin."

She threw her empty mug down. It rattled next to the brazier, a new dent in its side. "If they're so much better, why aren't they alive today instead of us?"

"But they are. They're in the College Vaults." His voice had gone chill. "And I'm afraid to find out what I've always wanted to know." He folded the map up. "I could do with another cup of that to wash down the hardtack. Got enough water for it?"

"If you've water for the animals."

"I do. And tomorrow, we'll have fresh water, reasonably untainted."

Lady did not reply, but bent to pick up her cup and fill the traveling pot a second time. Thomas stretched his legs out carefully and got up to tend the mounts. They nosed his hands eagerly and rolled reproachful eyes at him. He stroked their necks and soothed them with promises of grass in the morning. Murphy brayed in disbelief and tried to stomp on his booted feet.

"Oh, thou of little faith," Thomas mocked him. He hobbled the beasts loosely. His wound sent a freshet of heat and pain down his arm. Tomorrow would bring Healing and answers and perhaps fresh wounds. Then, once the children were clear of Denethan's snares and he understood the deal Charlie had made with the Vaults, he would find the raiders who'd taken Charlie's papers, the lifeblood of the water system, and avenge his friend's death. The children would draw them near, he knew that, and how close he dared let them get depended on how much stronger he could be in the morning. But if Lady knew he intended to use the children as bait, she'd kill him for it.

He awoke to a sound in the night, and by the gleam of a silver bright moon through the cityscape, saw a knife being held to her throat and knew he wouldn't have to worry about it.

Chapter 23

He killed the man before Lady could waken and blink. She lay quietly, a sickly-sweet smelling rag to one side of her face. He kicked it aside, even as he looked the night over the rest of the enemy. The silver moon was at its brightest and hung over the ruins, making shadows as sharp as blades.

"Lady, breathe! Wake up!" He checked his collar for the shuriken he had left and loosened his knife in its wrist sheath. The hilt of his boot knife rested comfortingly against his ankle. He cut the hobbles away from the mounts and gave a short whistle to calm Cindy, his mustache tickling the edges of his mouth. The black mare jerked her head up and moved a bit closer. He scratched her chin with one hand as he reached for his rifle with the other, keeping his feet planted on either side of Lady like a shield.

A second later the mule lifted his head and his nostrils flared. Murphy filled his lungs for a bray, but did not wind it. A stone rolled from the broken ceiling of a building, bounced down its side, and clattered into the street. Man and mule looked up.

"Now just where did that come from?" Blade mused. The mule's long ears flipped forward and back.

Carefully, he stepped back with one foot as he cradled his rifle and dropped two darts into the firing chambers and wound it painstakingly. He left the rifle balanced across his right forearm, almost negligently. His left arm smarted as he moved about, but he never took his eyes from the shattered rims of the concrete canyons. His Intuition flooded him. The enemy stalked him out there and he could feel it almost better than he would see it when it happened.

He set his jaw. A shadow leaped form one eave to another—he caught its arc in the corner of his eye, too late to raise his rifle. Instead, he kept his rifle loose as though unaware of the movement. He watched the mule to see if anyone was approaching their rear. The animal seemed to be more concerned with the buildings across the street. Its ears pricked forward.

Blade saw it at the same time. Rags flying as if he were winged, the nester came at them with a bellowing charge. He dropped in his tracks as Blade fired, a mockingbird fletch blossoming in his throat. He drummed his heels once or twice and died, yells frothing from his mouth into silence. Ghosts shifted rapidly in the buildings behind the attacker.

How many they sent after him depended on how many males they could afford to lose from this clan.

Thomas lowered his rifle from his chin. "I wouldn't if I were you," he called out.

"Marked man," a rough shout came back. "We've feud with you."

He could not see the challenger, but the words sent a chill down his back, and the drawn scar over his brow twitched in acknowledgment.

The mule stared intently to its right. Thomas looked there as well. Half a building seemed to have an extra column. He opened the firing chamber and dropped another dart in, knowing a single fire wouldn't do him much good. Before he could thumb the cover over, the nesters hiding by the column charged.

He put the rifle up, knowing the danger if he fired without the chamber closed—his ammo could well fire into his own face—but he had no time. Blade sighted and dropped the two nesters, one halfway across the street and the other within a body length of himself. The mule put his nose down and sniffed suspiciously.

The second one took a longer time dying, his dart having been used on a coyote, the poison diluted. Blade held no sympathy for the youth. He searched his vest and pulled out a flare vial. He couldn't put up a stand here in the open. They'd undoubtedly sent for an archer and he was a tempting target.

A fourth nester saw the disadvantage and took it, charging in on his left flank with a yell. The mule never saw it coming.

Thomas threw his wrist knife and heard it thunk home. But

the nester wrenched it out of his chest and tossed it clattering to the street. With a defiant yell, he bounded at them.

Blade let him come, carrying the battle to them, and stepped out of Lady's loose embrace, garrote in hand. A foot kick to the chin, striking the nester and sending him reeling, an easy twist to the right and Blade was behind him, garrote tightening. He wasted no time, collapsing the windpipe permanently and releasing the man. The nester dropped to the broken asphalt and writhed there, unable to breathe, contorting until he died.

There was an anguished wail among the street shadows. Blade looked up. A girl. She'd not come after them, and he'd have to leave her alive to point the way, for he hadn't time to deal with her as well. He pulled Lady off the ground. He wasted a precious handful of water, dashing it in her face, bringing her eyes into focus.

She gave a violent shudder as he threw her into the saddle. "Can you ride?"

She gathered up the reins with one hand. "I—I think so. Thomas, what's happened?"

He retrieved his knife and rifle, wiping the knife edge on the closest dead body. "Never mind. We've got to get out of here." He swung up, took his bearings, and slapped the mule into motion ahead of him. "That way."

A vial broke near them. The mule swerved as flame roared up. Cindy leaped through the wall, and heat blistered Blade's face. Thomas swore between clenched teeth, wishing he'd been wrong. The nesters had held them down until the real hunters could be sent for. Now he would be facing weaponry and ammo equal to his own—superior, if their supplies were any greater than his dwindling reserves.

His left arm began to throb in time with the drumming of the mare's hooves. The coyote toothmarks in his ankle itched aggravatingly as sweat ran down into his boots. Lady's face was deathly pale. She coughed and clung to the saddle horn with both hands, letting the mule pick its way.

Thomas trusted to the clever beast's instinct as he twisted in the saddle. He could hear other horses behind him, and got a glimpse—wall-eyed, ewe-necked wild stock, small and scruffy, tough as nails to have survived on the borders of the city. Their riders hunched, riding bareback over their withers, fists knotted in tangled manes. He turned back and listened to Cindy grunt with every stride. They had only minutes left before they were going to be run down.

He jammed the rifle butt into his armpit. He checked the street to make sure the stretch was relatively flat, before turning and standing in his stirrups to fire. The flare flashed white-hot, scattering horses and riders. One went down, rolling.

Thomas had to sit back before he could see if the fallen horse tripped up others. He heard a high-pitched whinny, truncated, behind them.

Lady looked back over her shoulder in panic. She'd lost a hairpin, and her hair streamed about her face. She clawed back strands of it to see.

"Thomas!" she cried.

"Keep running!"

If caught, she'd be raped and enslaved at best. He'd be cannibalized. He didn't fancy either of their futures.

The mule hadn't been bred for fleetness. It stumbled and began to drop back until he rode even with it. Then it lagged still farther. Lady threw him a terrified look.

"We can't keep up."

They turned a corner at flagging speed.

He drew his reins between his fingers, long leathers, and snapped the ends across the mule's cream-colored butt. The beast's ears flattened and Murphy kept running doggedly, but Thomas could tell he was breaking the mount's wind. Then they'd have nothing left but dog-meat.

"Thomas . . . stop."

"No! Don't quit on me!" He whipped the mule until its cream hide was red-striped and still the beast kept slowing, and Cindy adjusted to its pace.

". . . Make a stand," Lady panted.

"Nearly out of ammo," he yelled back.

Understanding fear showed in her eyes as she looked over. Thomas risked another look behind as they rounded a corner.

He saw a lizard man riding to the fore.

Damn! He had to have known. Denethan's raiders had infiltrated the nesters.

"Keep going," he ordered Lady.

"What—"

"Don't argue! Keep going!" He pulled on the near rein, forcing Cindy into a wild circle. He might go down, but he'd take out Denethan's man and as many nesters as he could, giving Lady a clear run at safety. A vial smashed to his left. Black, choking smoke came pouring out. His eyes teared immediately. Cindy faltered. Her nostrils were flared wine red, and froth ran from between her lips, and her black hide was spattered with foam.

But the cloud worked both ways. They never saw him until he burst out of the smoke, firing his rifle as he came. The lizard man went down as his pony was hit. He rolled lithely out of its way and disappeared behind a rusting steel beam. The pack scattered, splitting up. Thomas fired a second time and a noxious cloud, a nasty yellow-looking thing, took three of them. They died with their tongues hanging swollen and black out of their mouths.

Thomas reined in Cindy and dismounted, curbing her behind him, to face a wall front made of marble, pocked by the smog and years, but still standing. Its entryway was small and intimate. He wondered briefly what sort of building it had been, knowing it did not matter. It sheltered him now, protected his rear, and gave him a chance to keep anyone from going after Lady.

The pain of his wound stabbed at him as he tore down the saddlebags and searched through them for his extra two throwing stars. The nesters and lizards were going to find this as expensive a blood feud as they'd ever begun. The mare stood where he'd put her, head down as she sucked in air and trembled.

He listened as the nesters placed themselves. They'd figured out where he was and surely knew as well that they'd have to rush him one by one. A grim smile thinned his lips. He might actually have a chance.

He laid his shuriken out on the pavement in front of him, neatly in a row, their fractured circles of death framed by his two knives. He pulled out three vials. Two were flash-bombs. The last, a vial of poison. He squatted and pulled the cork, bathing his weapons liberally. The remaining garrote he kept coiled at hand.

The first nester died laying down a line of pitch, but he fired it before he breathed his last. The night was bathed with its orange smoke. Thomas wiped tears from the corner of his eyes with a dirty hand. The pitch burned well, well enough to bring smoke into his nook, but not well enough to smoke him out. He wondered briefly whether Lady had gotten away when a second figure wavered at the corner of his vision. Thomas reached up, caught Cindy, and brought her to her knees. The mare went down with a squeal as an arrow arched overhead and shattered against the marble wall. He gingerly picked up a throwing star.

When the rippling curtain of smoke and heat stirred again, he let fly. He never saw the man fall, but he had the pleasure of listening to his gurgled screams before he died.

The third attacker cost him both his knives—a tall, raw-boned woman with her hair tied back and a ragged scar high on one cheekbone. The first knife missed her, but the second did not. Thomas wiped at an oozing graze in his hairline—her arrow had been high, but she'd come closer than anyone.

He thought he heard a massing behind the veil of smoke and threw his flash bomb. That left him very short of ammunition. One more vial and his garrote, and his rifle for clubbing if they let him get down to hand-to-hand combat.

There was a scraping along the eaves overhead. Thomas glanced up, saw nothing, but the hair on the back of his neck prickled uncomfortably. Cindy's ears flicked once or twice, but the mare was too exhausted to do more than stay where he'd snubbed her down. Blade wondered who'd gotten above him and thought of the lizard man at about the same time he jumped.

The raider let out a hissing shout of joy as they met. Thomas kicked, the raider caught him by the heel and twisted. Thomas took the energy and rolled with it, coming back up with a back-handed slash to the face. The back of his hand grazed teeth too pointed. He had a split-second to worry about venom when the raider kicked back and his left arm exploded with pain. Blade reacted, his vision red-misted, barreling headfirst into his opponent's torso.

The raider laughed, his hands closing tightly about Blade's neck. The scarf twisted and tore under callus-scaled fingers. His gills fluttered for air and found it as Thomas drove both fists into the lizard man's balls—they weren't built any different there, he thought with satisfaction—and broke the weakened hold about his neck. Each staggered back, taking the other's measure.

Then the lizard man spoke, his lips lifting to reveal his

sharpened teeth with every word. "The packmaster you killed was my brother." The dun and brown speckled face of the mutant took on a malicious delight. "It is said a man who dies In-City haunts it forever."

Thomas thought of all the thousands who'd fueled the ghost road. "You might be right," he said, and attacked.

His uppercut set the raider back on his heels, his second eyelids closing a moment in bewilderment. Before Thomas could follow up the advantage, the mutant kicked, driving Thomas' right knee out from under him. As Thomas went to the pavement, his hand swept across the coiled garrote. The raider gave him no time, a rugged one-two in the ribs sending him sprawling back, grunting with pain.

He tasted the flat sweet taste of his own blood on his lips. Everything hurt. He rolled and got up, slowly this time, and heard shouts at his back. Cindy got to her feet with a piercing whinny. Reinforcements for his opponent were deciding whether to brave a rush.

The mutant hit him in the jaw. Thomas felt the blow clear through his spine as the back of his head smashed into the marble wall. His ears roared and his eyes went dim. He put his hands up in defense and caught the lizard man around the neck with his garrote as he drove in for the kill.

He pulled tight as his sight came back, but it was no good. The raider had both hands under the loop, his tough hide defending him, and Thomas had lost strength from the beating he'd taken. His thoughts reeled and he wondered if he could hold the lizard man long enough to use as a shield for getting out of there. The black mare let out a squeal of fear and shied away.

They rushed him without hesitation.

Chapter 24

Thomas strained, the cords of his neck standing out with the effort. But it wasn't good enough. He couldn't dredge up the strength to pull the garrote tight. The trail had beaten him long before the desert mutant had gotten to him. He dragged the man back with him, putting his back to the marble wall. He could feel its coolness even through his leather jacket. He faced the nesters as they came running, triumph written across their faces. The line of pitch spread on the street flickered and burned out as they jumped it and got him in their sights.

Glass shattered at his feet. Thomas swore and ducked away as the white-hot, stinging cloud brought cries of pain and fear. The raider tore himself free and went to his knees, coughing. Blade kicked him hard in the throat, and staggered back, hiding his face. He could hear Murphy's derisive bray, chiding him for his weakness.

Through his tears, he looked up and saw the cream-colored mule being herded out of the night, riders on either side, Lady tall in the saddle with her chin high.

He reached inside his jacket for the last of his vials. There would not be many survivors once he threw it. His fingertips grazed finger bones as he did so, and he wondered what his chances would be of reaching her first if he took the ghost road.

Her voice peeled out of the smoke and fire. "No, Thomas," she called. "Enough. They only want me."

His roar of denial choked in his throat.He clawed his way near and went to his knees, cupping his hand about the bones.

"Thomas! *Enough*. They came for a Healer, and I've agreed."

*   *   *

"I won't let you do it."

Lady paused in the meadow. Grass swirled about her boots and licked up the hem of her riding skirt. She was dewed by the morning, and the sunrise lent its color to her cheeks. "It's already done and you've no choice. Besides, you'll be right in there with me." The pastoral beauty of the nester campsite framed her, and at the far side of the meadow, a hide-sewn tepee awaited her.

"We're talking plague here," he said, as he finished wiping down the black mare's nostrils. She'd bled from them, but seemed recovered now, though she might never be the same again. He'd come that close to running her to death.

"You don't know that."

"I know," and he pointed the rusty-colored rag at her, "that they were willing to kill me to take you. And while you've been meditating, I've been watching them deposit bodies inside there by the litterful."

"You laid waste to half the able-bodied men in their clan."

"And if you searched their belongings, you'd probably find goods looted from half the men missing from your country."

She came close enough to put her hand on his. "Enough, Thomas. This is not for you to judge."

"No. You're right. I'm just the executioner." He took a deep breath. "This is delaying us. We're going to lose the children. We won't be able to get to them before Denethan does. Everything we've gone through will be wasted. Every life, for nothing. Ronnie, for nothing. Charlie, for nothing."

The gentle coolness of her skin soothed him into silence as she held his hand close. "Come with me."

"No." He would not become one with the press of hair and flesh inside that tent. With the stink of their retro-manhood and the reek of their crude hide clothing. His arm flamed fiercely and he knew she wouldn't have the strength to undertake another Healing for at least two days after this, but he would not join their pack.

"You don't need to fear them. They've respect for the strength you showed in defending me. They've forgiven you their dead and crippled."

"I don't fear them!" He tore his hand away from her. "I don't fear them."

"Hate them, then."

"That." He picketed the mare. "They'll steal us blind if I go into the tent with you. I like riding with a saddle, how about you? Old Murphy's spine looks like it might be real uncomfortable bareback."

"We're guests here." She gave him a glacial look from both brown and blue eyes.

"They're not even—" He bit his words off and swallowed them.

Lady waited a breath or two, then finished, "Human?"

"Don't put words into my mouth."

Lady gave a strange, one-sided little smile. "I don't have to," she said softly. "I can hear some of the thoughts in your head, remember?"

A Talent he didn't have. He shielded himself and paid attention to Murphy. The mule was travel-worn, as were they all, but his wounds from early on had scabbed cleanly. Both mounts were contentedly cropping spring grass. From behind his shoulder, Nolan said, "Your arm needs tending," and she laid a hand on it.

Shrieking pain brought him to his knees. Sweat rolled down his brow. He doubled over, gasping for breath. Lady dropped down beside him. "Oh, love," she whispered. "I didn't know." She looked up. There were nesters appearing from nowhere. "Take him to the tent with the others."

He couldn't stand up to defend himself as they gently pushed his kneeling form onto a litter and carried him into the tent. He had a brief glimpse of blue sky with white mare's tails flicking across it, and then the stench and darkness of misery claimed him.

Someone bathed him. The water was barely warm, scented with orange and lemon peel. He winced as they touched his wound. The bather made a twitching sound, distinctly female.

"Infection cleared, but there's a lot of Healing yet to be done."

Another, huskier voice, one he knew well. His eyelids flickered as he thought of waking to glare at her. "The energy in the Healing tent was too diffuse for him. But he'll live. He's like that mule of mine, too ornery to do anything the easy way. He's awake now."

Thomas opened his eyes. There was a young girl leaning

over him. Her brow was heavily boned, and a faint brown mustache lined her upper lip. Her hair was braided back, a wild brunette mass plaited into submission. Her eyes sparkled in dark delight as his gaze met hers.

Nolan cleared her throat. "I don't think," she said, "that the clansman's daughter is a suitable conquest."

The girl looked up. She smiled widely, showing teeth a mite too sharp. "You flatter me," she said. "He'll have nothing to do with me, anyway. We know the Marked Man well. If he could, he would bring every last one of us to the counties and to a death sentence."

Mindful of the lap that pillowed his head, Thomas said nothing. The girl washed his face quickly, then moved him onto the grass. She left with a rustle of hide and fur.

Thomas tried to sit up, but Nolan held him down and slid over, her lap pillowing him instead. She picked up the washcloth and continued to bathe his torso.

"How do you feel?"

"Groggy."

"The incense and drugs in the smoke do that. It makes it easier for the patient to accept Healing. Herman is now the head clansman here. You've made him a happy man—you eliminated his rival earlier."

"Good." With a grunt, he sat up. He looked at his upper arm. Pink and purple flesh was still angry, but the heat had nearly gone. He flexed it. "Thank you," he added dryly.

"My pleasure." She dropped the cloth into the basin of scented water. "Herman says to tell you that Denethan has not crossed the In-City boundary yet and those you trail are a half-day away."

"He's not only happy, he's helpful," Thomas said and shrugged into his shirt.

"Look at me."

He refused.

Lady watched him get to his feet, waver, and stood herself. "I did what I had to do."

"For animals."

"For people. People more affected by what has happened to our world than we are. I see people here who can't cope with our Talents, who fear us as though we were the devil himself. I don't know if they were driven away from the counties or ran, but I do know they found themselves within a system they couldn't comprehend." She reached out and spun him so that he had to face her. "And even if you are right, refusing to help them doesn't make me better. It sinks me so far down on the evolutionary ladder that I'd have a hell of a time climbing back up."

He looked into her angry face. "What about the plague, Lady? Just what sort of Healing did you do inside that tent?"

"There's been no talk of plague yet in this clan. Is that what you're worried about? Your precious sperm count?"

Now it was his turn to grab her. "No, dammit—I was worried about you!"

"It's my body. I'll just have to deal with it." She shrugged out of his hold, walked a few paces away to a tree where Murphy stood in the shade. She pulled his reins off the picket line. "I thought you were in a hurry."

He found his jacket hanging over a shrub. The inside pockets were woefully empty but for his finger bones. His shuriken, however, had been cleaned and replaced. He clenched his jaw, thinking of the bodies they'd been pulled out of.

Over by the cooking fires at the meadow's end, where nesters sat and talked and worked their hides, he saw a massive man stand and begin walking across the grass toward them. He was a redhead, his uncut hair a tangled mane that caught the sun and twisted its color through every strand. His homespun shirt and hide trousers were crude in every sense, but he walked with the pride of royalty.

Thomas swung aboard the black mare. She held her head well, but she walked without any spring in her step and he knew she needed more rest. He nodded his head.

"Here comes Herman."

"We've been promised free access over the In-City border to the track that leads to the reservoir."

"Why doesn't he camp at the reservoir? We're talking a day's journey at the most," Thomas said.

She frowned at him. "I asked him the same thing. He says it's death."

Blade frowned back. It hadn't been death for him and Charles, but he did not dispute her as the massive nester walked up and grabbed a headstall in each hand. Now that he was close enough to smell the man, he was close enough to see silver threading the fiery red. Herman let out a laugh that smelled of sour beer.

"I'll walk you to the road," he said, "as promised." Cindy came as coaxed, but Murphy tossed his head stubbornly and Lady had to shake her booted foot threateningly within his eyeshot to get him to move.

Herman strode at a hunting pace. They left the nester grounds far behind them, and the sun moved to just off midday in the sky before they slowed for breath. Thomas listened to Cindy pant and to Herman standing calmly and thanked whatever gods listened that this nester had not been among the ones he'd met. The behemoth pointed along the edge of the ruins. "There."

Thomas nodded. He had his bearings and Herman had taken them where he was supposed to. He gathered up Cindy's reins. She responded to his knees and moved down the slope onto the track.

He twisted in the saddle. Herman stood, grinning hugely, his massive hand still wrapped in Murphy's headstall.

"Let her go."

"I think not," Herman's lip curled back. "We need a Healer."

Blade's hand slipped inside his jacket, found a shuriken.

Lady leaned down and put her hand on Herman's shoulder. "This is not the way," she said evenly. "I am more than a Healer, I am a Protector. My honor binds me to return to my county." She gave Herman pause, and more than that, she blocked Blade's throw.

"We have feud with the county," said Herman.

It didn't matter which county. Nesters feuded with all of them. "I know," answered Lady calmly. "But we know you need Healers. There will be some who will want to come and help, if you promise their safety."

"Water rights?"

She shook her head. Herman's brow knitted. Then, "We have water enough, right now. I will think this over. If Healers come, we would have to let them go back again."

"If they wanted to. Back and forth, as they needed to."

"No bounty hunters."

She looked at Thomas over that bountiful head of hair. "No. Right, Thomas?"

He shifted weight. "It's your treaty."

Herman looked at him, skepticism in his hazel eyes. Then he pointed a blunt finger. "You are an enemy and yet our friend has marked you, so," and he made a slash mark over his brow. "We don't understand this."

"Neither do I."

"You have the power to walk in dreams. You would be wise to know if you walk toward good or evil." Herman let go the mule's bridle. "Thank you, Lady Nolan, for the Healing." He turned his back on them to prove his bravery and stalked away.

Thomas sat in faint surprise at the nester's proposal. He had never known a nester to do anything other than take to satisfy the moment's needs. Nolan reined Murphy over to join him when Herman paused, half-blending into the scrub brush, and began to turn around as if he'd forgotten something.

A rifle whined. One, two. He heard Herman thud to the ground before he could react.

No one was visible. Then, from a jagged rooftop overlying the track, a young man dropped to his feet, white-blond hair ruffled. He carried a rifle in one hand and grinned.

"Well, Sir Thomas. How was that?"

Blade felt color return to his face. He grabbed Murphy's reins from Lady's numbed hands and snubbed the mare over. "That was some shooting, Stefan. Now let's see how good you are at burying the evidence."

Chapter 25

Stefan didn't need any help burying the body. He had his own detachment which materialized shortly after he began digging. Although Thomas appreciated the assistance, he knew instinctively he did not like the six escort guards from the College Vaults.

He could not read their body type under the uniforms, but they were taller and more muscular than he and he was no small man among the people of the counties. Neither did they have the fluid grace his double-jointedness and martial training gave him. He doubted they were pure-blooded. The gene pool would be too valuable to waste on patrolmen whose duty was to kill or be killed. He relaxed a little at that thought.

Lady traded glances with him and he thought that neither of them had to be psychic to read the body language of the captain and his five patrolmen. Thomas' stomach turned and he knew why Charlie had come home quietly and had his gills removed. From the gloves they wore to the stances they took, they acted as Thomas did himself when dealing with a contaminant. Lady frosted them in return with her one blue-eyed gaze and did not thaw even when Alma joined them.

Bruises of weariness shadowed the girl's pale face. She rode her donkey as if every movement were agony. Lady helped her down and sat quietly with her as Herman, the head clansman for one great and glorious day, was buried.

"I'm sorry," Stefan said quietly as the last shovelful was turned. "He looked as if he'd been menacing you and then when he turned to circle back—"

"A mistake," Thomas said. "Regrettable and understandable."

"I sent my men on backtrack. No one has noticed he's missing yet." Remmick's speech was as stiff as his posture. Big-voiced, like his stature.

Thomas met his glance in passing. "Too bad you weren't in charge when the boy took aim."

"I was in charge. It's my failure as well. I told him to target you . . . in case it was needed." Remmick took a deep breath. His chest swelled the khaki jacket of his uniform. The cuffs of their trousers were tucked into their boots. The holsters on their lean hips were filled with a kind of weapon Thomas had only seen—stable ammo had not been found for guns of this type and he had only briefly admired their killing beauty. "So you're the gutsy bastard who drew Denethan's packs off our heels."

Thomas did not smile at the tone of grudging respect. Nothing the captain had said had pleased or amused him yet. "We did a job, but nothing permanent. Denethan's going to cross our paths again before we reach the College Vaults." He looked at Lady and Alma. Their heads were bowed close together and from the sudden redness in the girl's face and the pinched look around her eyes, he knew what the Protector was telling her.

Thomas said to Remmick, "After you picked up the children, raiders attacked the DWP settlement. There were no survivors."

Stefan sucked in his breath, sharp and quick.

The captain's eyebrows arched. "None? That is most . . . inconvenient."

"Yes."

Stefan made a cutting motion through the air with the side of his hand. "Never mind. We'll start a new county, building on what Charlie left us." His blue eyes drilled Thomas. "You taught me to cut my losses."

"Indeed. And where will you find what Charlie left you? His office was gutted as well."

Remmick stirred. "We'd be well on our way, then . . . Protector."

"Not until I'm done with them."

Stefan looked from the captain to Thomas. His eyes narrowed. "What do you want from me?"

"You know why Jennifer and Ramos were sent out?"

"To draw attention from me and Alma leaving."

Lady spoke up, her voice commanding attention, as she

walked up, an arm about Alma's shoulders to steady her. "They gave their lives for you."

"Jennifer's dead," Alma repeated, in a stunned echo.

"It was necessary." The Russian's blue eyes stared down Blade. "You were supposed to prevent that."

"Bullshit. I was sent after to draw attention as well."

"That, too. But you were supposed to be the Protector, the one who could stand against all odds—"

"Stefan!" Alma's voice was high and pure, edged with her sorrow. "They *died* for us. There isn't a county of the seven which can manage without the information taken from the DWP."

The blond youth jutted his chin out. "And what do you want from me? Tears? They won't help now."

"I came across In-City after you, not just for the two of you. You'll draw Denethan . . . and he's the one I want, on my ground and on my terms. If you're game enough, puppy, to do for your counties what Ramos did for you," Thomas said quietly.

Stefan rose to the challenge. "My counties? My counties lie across the ocean, holding the bones of my mother's parents. I was born there. *I would have survived there,* but she was always afraid. She didn't think she was strong enough, but she was. We were the only ones who made it across. It was one of your counties that killed her. I don't think I owe you anything."

Thomas was conscious of the guardsmen gathering around them. He smiled at Stefan. "Are you telling me you're not game enough?"

"Not for suicide."

"And I agree," Lady put in. "I won't be quiet while two jerks have a piss-off to see who's bravest." Behind her, Alma gasped. Lady didn't miss a beat. "Nothing right now is more important than the life these two have the potential to conceive. Damn the water lines. Let somebody else run them. Bartholomew is probably setting up details right now. His legacy can wait until you deliver the children."

Remmick shouldered in between Thomas and Stefan. "Listen to your woman, Blade. If we have Denethan closing in, standing around is the last thing we need to do." His words put a flush on Lady's face and she closed her mouth with a nearly audible snap.

Blade leaned inward. "You, captain, have the opportunity to

ambush Denethan when he least expects it. Can you afford to lose it?"

Remmick looked coolly down at Thomas from his bulky height. His dark eyes were flat and chill. "Denethan does not worry us."

"He should. How far have we got to go—half a day's travel?"

The captain nodded.

"If he's close enough, and I think he is, he'll wonder how we disappeared. He won't leave any stone unturned to find us, and that puts him at your doorstep. Then, Captain Remmick, he becomes your problem. *That* will worry you. He's a mutant. He's got no love for the old race or anything else remotely human. So let's detour and put an end to the matter."

Remmick slapped him in the ribs, saying, "Your arsenal appears to be depleted."

"But yours isn't."

"No. And, for the moment, it isn't about to be. I have my orders from the dean to escort these two in safely. The rest will have to wait. You have my word I will bring this matter to the dean's attention." He snapped his fingers. "Mount up."

Uniforms in a blur of motion separated Thomas from the others until only he was left standing. It did not matter that Remmick rode a desert ass like the others, his boots nearly trailing the ground. With a grudging shrug, Blade swung up on the black mare. His bicep gave him a twinge of pain, a reminder, as he settled into the saddle. With a last look at the nester's grave, he reined the mare after the troop, but Denethan remained in his thoughts. Under the new clarity of Lady's Healing, he realized Denethan had not been out of his thoughts since they had fought, like an ulcer that festered until it was a great raw wound, and she'd Healed that . . . now they were knit together. If he wanted his foe at hand, all he had to do was tug.

Thomas smoothed his mustache. Considering the possibilities, he rode drag to Remmick's point.

Midday, inland, with heat beginning to shimmer off the foothills. Thomas wiped his brow with the end of his scarf and wished he had not lost his hat. He could feel the sun through his thinning hair and beads of sweat trickled down his neck and temples. Stefan pulled his donkey out of formation and dropped back. His fair skin bore the stamp of too much sun, and he frowned as he looked at Thomas.

"I'm not a coward," he said.

"Never said you were." Blade watched the guards ahead. If their ears could swivel and flick toward a conversation the way Murphy's did, he'd swear they were endeavoring to listen. He was not surprised that Stefan gravitated toward him. He had taught the boy shooting, he knew how the lad thought. Confronted directly, bull stubborn, but give him time to think about it, and he would eventually swing around.

"You thought it." Stefan sighed.

"Perhaps." Thomas stood in his stirrups, stretching his legs and back a little. He looked back at Stefan. "That was a good shot."

Stefan made a slight face. "One I never should have taken. But I never thought to see you sharing the track with a nester."

"Herman," Blade said absently. "His name was Herman." He focused. "What is Remmick like?"

"Efficient. Like you and Charlie on a bad day. We've been running the hooves off these beasties." Stefan thumped his donkey's neck. "Is everyone dead?"

"Everyone who hadn't left the party. Oletha, Alderman, Wyethe, Veronica . . . several of the mayors." Shellyann's dead face passed through is memory. They'd found her protecting her son's lifeless body. "Most of the children got away . . . at least, I don't remember seeing the bodies."

"There's that, then." Stefan busied himself plucking at the stiff, wiry mane of the donkey. "We must have gotten out just in time."

"Just," he answered. "Charlie was still alive when I found him."

"I'm sorry," Stefan looked at him quickly.

He could see the truth in the young man's face. "I know," Thomas returned. "We both are. But it's possible Remmick is right. You have another allegiance now."

"Alma is my allegiance." The young man's eyes brightened. Thomas felt something in his thoughts soften at the other's emotion.

Stefan lowered his voice a little. "Have you been to the Vaults?"

"Yes. Once."

"What are they like?"

*   *   *

Five levels, beginning a hundred feet underground. Set into a mountain so cleverly that not even nesters could tell real rock from sculptured entrance. The reservoir behind the mountain peak could not be seen from the entrance, but it had sparkled like a giant sapphire as they'd ridden past it. There were no outward sentries that Thomas could see, but Lady had leaned toward him as they approached and remarked, "Every hair on my head is standing up."

His had been, also. Technology he was unfamiliar with scanned their presence. Before he could answer, a deer bolted across their track. Her tail flagged as she bounded through the underbrush and disappeared. Remmick signaled a patrolman.

"Bring her down. Venison will taste good tonight."

The patrolman vaulted off his donkey and went on foot, his long strides quick and sure. Remmick also dismounted. He went to a place on the hill where rock had broken through the dirt, its gray stone face a map of strata and geological pressure, thrust upward by the very force of its own existence. It was then, Thomas saw in dull surprise, that the outcropping was false. Sculpted by a master, but fake nonetheless.

Remmick paused in front of it. He put a hand palm down on the rock. It split as though a messiah had parted it. Thomas watched bemused as stone slid back to reveal metal and the silvery gleam reflected the sun's rays.

It also struck him that his Intuition to Truth-read had fled at a very unfortunate time.

Chapter 26

The interior cavern was cool and hushed. Not until they entered it did Blade realize the afternoon had been filled with birdsong. Now he heard nothing but the shuffle of their own booted feet and the hoofbeats of their mounts. A sign proclaimed STAGING. Three freshly uniformed men met Remmick and saluted.

He answered them. "The password, gentlemen, is new blood."

Thomas watched as the three opened up an interior door to a narrow-necked corridor. Remmick's five patrolmen then gathered up the reins to the donkeys, Murphy, and the black mare.

"Take them to stabling," ordered Remmick. "See they're given hot mash tonight and are well-rested. Take care of the mare, she's a good specimen. Have Mendes type her in the morning." He waved to the interior corridor.

One of the three stopped him politely. "Sorry, sir. The dean knows you're here. We've been requested to do a weapons check."

"Ah." The massive man considered, then gave a nod. "Sir Thomas?"

Blade spread his hands amiably. The aide who'd spoken paused a moment as if gathering his nerve, then stepped forward and began to pat him down. Thomas stood impassively. If he had not spent most of his weaponry, this pup of a sentry might have something to worry about.

The aide patted his inside pockets down several times, then turned to Remmick. "Sir, there's something in his pockets which may or may not be a vial, but it—it keeps moving, sir. I can't seem to get my hands on it."

The artificial light had lent a pallor to Remmick's face. His cold gaze raked Thomas, then he showed his teeth in a smile. "Some of these Protectors use a bit of TK, lieutenant. He's playing with you. Sir Thomas?"

Puzzled, Blade opened his jacket. The only things remaining in his pockets were Gillander's finger bones. The ivoried knobs of their ends stuck out of a seamed niche. They seemed stationary now.

The lieutenant stared for a moment, then nodded, satisfied. He turned to Lady Nolan. "Ma'am?"

Her face pinked, but she said, "Of course, but mind where you put your hands, young man."

The lieutenant patted her down quickly, found two shuriken and a bootshank knife. He handed those solemnly to Remmick who turned them over and over in his hands as though a little unsure of what to do with them. Finally, he said, "A resourceful lady."

"Always," Nolan responded. "This is a tough country."

Without further hesitation, Stefan and Alma were both searched. Stefan had left his bolt rifle with his pack and the lieutenant found nothing more, but Blade could tell from the way Alma looked at Lady that the lieutenant had not uncovered everything.

Remmick pulled some objects off a hook inside the corridor. They were clear, clumsy lenses. "Goggles, if you please. We're going through an air lock into a decontamination chamber. It will be flooded with a strange, harsh light. Keep the goggles on to protect your eyes. This is only a preliminary cleansing procedure. You may or may not be subject to others once we reach the Vaults."

Thomas watched the captain pull his goggles on and imitated him. Alma giggled at Stefan who'd suddenly acquired the expression of a bullfrog with bulging eyes. Remmick then herded them into the corridor. Before closing the doors, he said, "Lieutenant, there's a major infestation of nesters in sector Montclair Vee Twelve. Take some defoliants and clear them out ASAP."

The door closed on the lieutenant's response. Lady reached out and took Thomas' hand. Hers was shaking though she said nothing. Thomas' ears popped faintly as the next set of doors began to blossom open. As sound and light flooded them, Remmick said, "Stefan and Alma have quarters prepared for them.

But as the dean is aware of your arrival, I'm sure he will wish to see you as much as you wish to see him."

In a small voice, muffled by the goggles hiding her shapely nose, Alma said, "Can't Lady come with me?"

"I'll be along later, dear." Lady patted her hand. "Save me some hot water. You do have hot water here, don't you?"

Remmick's neck flushed. "Yes, ma'am, we do." As soon as the light faded, he tore his goggles off and bled the doors open. "To the elevators, please."

"Elevators?"

Remmick pursed his lips. "A sort of powered stairs. We're going down into the interior of the mountain." He pointed the way. Thomas followed, but not before eying the pattern of corridors they now occupied. A sign pointed to STAIRS in a different direction. He made note of it. Elevators might be mechanical, but stairs were not.

The descent was not entirely pleasant. Alma went very pale and sagged visibly under Lady's hold. She finally closed her eyes, and a fine bead of sweat rode her slender brows. Thomas lost gravity for a moment. His senses reeled as they had not since the ghost road. Surrounded by artificial things, he seemed to have no being. His stomach turned and he knew he was going to be ill in front of Remmick, who would no doubt scorn him further.

Then the elevator thumped gently and its outer door slid open. Two sentries snapped to attention immediately.

"Take these two to their quarters. Arrange for meal credits and let the teaching staff know of the additions to their schedules." Remmick, crisply ordering the two, did not seem aware of Blade's distress.

Lady watched Stefan helping Alma down the curved corridor. His voice drifted back to them.

"I'll take care of you now. Lean on me."

With a half-smile that spoke wistfully of an emotion Thomas could not name, she looked at him. Before she could say anything, Remmick strode briskly away from them in the opposite direction.

Thomas found it hard not to stare as he followed. There were sliding gates that opened and shut automatically at their approach—grills that he knew could be shut down permanently if the operator so wished—lights that dimmed or brightened to the sound of their steps—other equipment that seemed to watch them pass by—things he had seen in the ruins, smashed, half-salvaged, uninterpretable until now. And even now, not all he saw made sense. No wonder Charlie's visit here had fired him up so.

They passed a number of closed doors and one immense hall where Thomas paused to watch more than a hundred men go through their paces. It was the largest *dojo* he had ever seen. He wondered why there were no women present. Women were generally more supple. Lady's attention flashed on it as well, but she said nothing to Thomas.

They took a second elevator marked PRIVATE. It took them seconds to reach their final destination.

The room was spacious, well-decorated, and cool, but its air held a slightly musty smell as though stale. He looked up at the large-domed room, the ceiling of which defied the feeling of oppression Thomas felt. He fought an impulse to bolt as Remmick saluted the man behind the desk and was told, "At ease."

The dean was a large, florid man, with veins that had broken into tiny crimson flowers across his aquiline nose. Two chins drooped to his stubbly neck. His eyelids hooded hazel eyes. Gray speckled his thinning brown hair which he, in his vanity, had combed from just above his left ear over his balding pate to the right ear. He wore a black overrobe, with a silken purple sash hanging about his neck. No warmth came to his expression as he eyed Thomas and Lady. Without a word to them, his attention flicked to Remmick. "Decon?"

"Done upstairs, sir. In moderation."

"Good. That's something, at least." He folded his hands over neat stacks of paperwork. "Welcome to the College Vaults. Like what you've seen?"

Actually, Thomas hadn't. "You've impressed me," he said.

"Good. That's not our purpose, but good all the same. I understand Charles Warden is dead."

Behind Remmick's khakied body was a wall lined floor to ceiling with a bookcase and books. The other two walls were backdrops to paintings, some of them priceless and thought to have perished long ago. Remmick knew what he stared at, and returned his look. Cool. Unperturbed.

As Blade's attention swept the room, he knew the only

weapon he needed to control the dean was fire. Both he and Lady could provide the spark at will, if needed. He no longer felt defenseless. "Who carried you the news?" Intuition prickled the back of his neck.

"Your own hand, I presume. Some of those pigeons Charles kept were from the Vaults. We received the news. Tragic. However, the business at hand is not. We have the two youngsters whom Warden felt represented a return to a desirable gene pool. We have medical as well as educational facilities here which will greatly benefit them." His hooded eyes closed, then opened again. The might in them was that of a hungry falcon. "Warden was a brave and literate man."

Thomas had not known that Charles had kept in regular contact with the facility, but he did not let the surprise show. "It will be difficult," Thomas said, "carrying on without him."

"But bound to happen sooner or later. You lead a precarious life. Outsiders are a bit more mortal than some." The dean chuckled deeply and tailed off. His tone became crisp again. "Where were you when the attack occurred?"

"On another mission, one which he knew might take me away at a crucial time. He took his chances." For reasons of his own, Thomas did not feel like revealing everything to the dean though he did not doubt Remmick would fill him in later.

"He lost his gamble. By treachery perhaps?"

"Not by me," Thomas answered. His chin went up slightly. "Denethan has been an enemy for some time, as was his father before him."

"Ah, yes. The miscreant from the Mojave." The dean shook his head. He turned slightly in his chair. It creaked under his bulk. "Charles warned us against him when he first visited us, some six years ago. He did well to find us. Men better than he had tried and failed. None used the method he did, though. Our water intake gave us away. We've since corrected that, following his suggestions. He was a generous . . . man."

"Perhaps too generous," Lady said. "The bargain you made with him concerning the children no longer stands. We're here to renegotiate."

The dean gave her a measuring stare. "So the lady speaks," he said at last.

"I do, indeed, and very well. Our community has suffered

grievous losses—losses which the knowledge you have hidden away can help to repair most swiftly."

The dean kneaded his heavy hands about one another. Thomas noted the thickness and twisting of the joints. The man paused and said, "You hope to draw us out against Denethan. You ask that we expose ourselves to a world gone mad and savage. I have no good reason to do this."

"Your reason is humanity."

His hooded gaze took in Lady's carefully. He said, quietly and deliberately, "Your humanity and my humanity are two different things. Honor, perhaps, might dictate our actions." He looked to Blade. "An honorable man would have come to us and solicited our aid."

Thomas grimaced. "Honorable men have more time than the rest of us."

The dean traced a burled pattern on his desk. He looked up. "It matters little now. Denethan cannot find our door unless we will it. As for the four of you, we welcome the children into our colony. There're tests to be done, naturally, blood and tissue typing, but I'm sure Stefan and Alma are everything your counties hope they are. I'll arrange quarters and reoutfitting, and you can be on your way. I don't suppose you intend to partake of our hospitality any longer than necessary."

Lady moved closer to Thomas. She slid her hand into his. "No," he said, momentarily distracted. "Give me two dozen darts and a dozen vials, and I'll be on my way."

"Still Charlie's Lord Protector?"

"I am. And I'll take his massacre out of Denethan's hide."

The dean scratched his neck, fingernails rasping across the stubble. "I don't blame you," he said, finally, "although that mentality is what drove us underground. Surely you'll stay the evening."

Lady's hand gripped Blade's more tightly. "I'd like to stay permanently, with the children."

The dean smiled hugely. "and what could you possibly teach them? My dear, I've forgotten far more than you'll ever know. The outside has lost realms of knowledge. The nesters are little more than vermin. Your instincts are good, I know, but—" he spread his hands.

"I'm a Healer. I'm a Protector."

"Parapsychology is a chancy subject at best—difficult talents to verify and none that can be passed on by mere academia. Surely your county has more need of you than we do."

Thomas could feel her humiliation burning in her. He closed his other hand about hers. "We can't afford to lose you now," he told her.

She looked at him. Her brown eye brimmed with an unshed tear. The dean interrupted, saying, "Perhaps we can answer your questions tomorrow, give you something to carry back with you?"

"You can answer one now." Blade dropped Lady's hand and swung back to face the massive desk and the man who sat behind it.

"I'll try." An expression shadowed the dean's face and Remmick responded with attention.

"Are you human?"

"I beg your pardon?"

"Human. Which ones of you come from the old lines?"

"Why, my dear executioner, we all do. Every last one of us. Does that interest you? If so, perhaps you'll volunteer for some lab work."

"What kind?" Lady murmured.

"A little blood work, a few skin scrapings. Charles did the same when he was here. He did his genetic homework the hard way, but here we have medical advantages you obviously do not. The more diverse our samples, the more accurate our conclusions can be."

"Conclusions about what?"

The dean licked his lips with the merest touch of his tongue. "We're trying to determine just how aberrant the different counties have become. The plague, other factors. The Disasters didn't create your kind, Sir Thomas, it only set your ancestors free. Labs working on genetic engineering for space exploration were destroyed, but certain . . . tissue cultures were not."

"Aberrant?" Lady repeated. "Is that what you call us?"

"Dear lady, of course not. I mean no offense." The dean stood. For a big man, he was surprisingly light on his feet.

"I've shed enough blood over the past few days," Thomas said dryly. "I might as well shed some for you." With a warning look to quell Lady's rising anger, he took her arm and guided her after the dean. Under her breath, she muttered, "Arrogant son of a bitch."

Remmick marched a pace of so behind them as the dean led them to another elevator shaft and downward again. The grills they passed through were continuously marked AUTHORIZED PERSONNEL ONLY. The halls were sterile tunnels, radiating an impersonal beige aura. Their passage through them was muffled as if it were not quite real. The dean led them through a door. Its upper portion was glass, steel meshed for strength. A white-coated man turned as they entered a large, sterile kitchenlike room.

"Dr. Mendes. This is Sir Thomas Blade of Orange County and Lady Nolan of Torrance County. They're part of the escort of our new arrivals. They're in a hurry to be on their way, but they've graciously agreed to donate to our sample pool."

"My god, Gerald. Have they even been through decon?"

The dean said smoothly, "Now, now. Of course they have."

The doctor wiped his hands on the flaps of his white coat then and smiled broadly. "Good. I won't keep you, Gerald."

With an eerie grace, the large man pivoted on his heels. "But," and Lady reached out tentatively, "what if I wished to stay? Surely there's something I could do here of value."

The falcon expression went hard and cold. "Dear lady. You've been In-City. You've lived on corrupted land. I'm prepared to extend you every hospitality, but your joining the colony is unthinkable. What if you carry the plague? Our population has none of the mutations you could carry. Our program is coming along admirably. At the very least, if we suffered you to stay, you'd have to submit to voluntary sterilization. You're still a moderately young woman. Wouldn't you find that difficult? You're better off returning to your own where you can be appreciated as the unique woman you are."

Suddenly pale, Lady shrank back. "Surely your tests would show if I carried the plague or not?"

"Within a ninety percent accuracy rate," Dr. Mendes said smoothly. He smiled reassuringly. "It's the other genetic coding we have to worry about . . ." the doctor's words trailed off.

Thomas put his arm around Lady, finding her suddenly frail within his hold. "We have work to do anyway," he told her. "I don't intend leaving without you."

She gave him a brittle smile.

The dean wrung his hands. "That's settled, then. Remmick and I will leave you in the doctor's capable care. He'll see you to your quarters and Remmick will handle your affairs in the morning." He left, the captain on his heels.

The doors closed behind them. Dr. Mendes had brown eyes as cold as the corridors of the Vaults. He let out a gust of sound. "Well. Let's get started." He began bustling through a fortune of rare equipment. Charlie would have loved it in here—probably had loved it in here. Lady plucked uncertainly at a button on her sleeve. Mendes turned around impatiently. "What are you waiting for? The sooner you strip, the sooner I can get this over with."

Mendes turned his back again, readying a set of glass tubes on a pristine plastic counter. He opened and closed cupboard doors, adding to his instruments. Thomas was as baffled by the doctor's attitude as by Lady's sudden quiet. It was as though her rejection had taken all the spirit out of her.

Thomas loosened his scarf to free his gills and began to ease out of his battered leather jacket. "The dean mentioned something about genetic engineering and space exploration. What was he talking about?"

"Well, the Mars program for one, and what we called the longship, or the generational program—"

"What?"

The doctor turned. "Just how primitive are you?" His dark skin was flushed with impatience.

Lady moved then. She reached for Thomas' arm. "I think I'd like you to kill him for me."

Thomas smiled thinly. "I think I'd like to do it." He leaned over the counter which separated them from the doctor. "I'm primitive enough to do it."

Mendes swallowed. "I apologize," he said thickly. "I don't work with people often."

Lady softened, saying, "Apology accepted."

Thomas hesitated.

Mendes put in hastily, "You do know about airplanes?"

"Of course."

"That we landed on the moon?"

Thomas shook his head.

"Mars?"

Again, negative motion.

"Ah." Mendes took a deep breath. "Well, we did both. Mars was intriguing. It was felt that genetically altered people, with environmental suits, might do quite well there. And then there were those who fancied altering for ocean exploration and cleanup. Labs were doing all sorts of work. Your . . . differences . . . are the results of those programs. Some authorized, some not. Your changes are not the most drastic by any means. Some labs augmented animal, instead of human, structure."

"Did we go to Mars?"

"Not in that state, no. And the longships went out before the Disasters . . . no way of telling what long-range effect the voyage had there until they return . . ." Mendes stalled. "How about stripping down?"

When making love, it had seemed one thing, but now, in the oppressive atmosphere of the lab, quite another. As Lady began unbuttoning once more, he asked, "Is it necessary?"

"No. But we like to make visual records." Distractedly, the doctor pointed at the equipment bolted to the corners of the lab. "We put the data on disk."

"Laser?"

"Yes! Are you familiar with them?"

"Vaguely." Thomas finished taking off his jacket. "But this is as far as I'll go."

Lady threw him a grateful look as she merely rolled up her own sleeves. Mendes frowned but said, "As you wish." He took up an instrument.

Lady remained stoic but paled as he took skin scrapings and then a blood sample. She winced at the scraping. When Mendes came to Thomas, he looked at the bloodstained clothing and the bandage.

"What happened here?"

"Wounded in a skirmish."

"I'd better take a look at that." He sliced through Lady's carefully knotted bandage and kneaded the almost healed pink flesh. "How recent was this?"

"Two, three days."

The doctor's eyebrows went up.

"I'm a Healer," Lady said in explanation.

"Oh? Turn this way. I want the camera to catch that. No, angle the arm this way—that's it." The doctor looked back at her. "You did this?"

"It's one of my Talents."

"You're an augmented paranormal? Ah." The doctor turned

away quickly, but not before Thomas saw his skin grow ashen under his naturally dark complexion. He busied himself daubing glass slides from their blood samples and running them through a large white machine. It hummed for a few minutes, then its screen filled with symbols.

"Good news," Mendes said without facing them. "No plague, as yet. Sir Thomas, you're a bit anemic. Put more iron into your diet."

Lady relaxed with an audible sigh. Happily, she linked her arm through Thomas'.

The doctor pushed a button set into his counter. "That's it, that's all I need. If you'll take a seat in the room through there, I've sent for Remmick."

Lady helped Thomas on with his jacket. "That's everything?"

"Well . . . I could do a visual check for physical aberrations, but with your eyes and his gills already recorded, it's not necessary."

She nodded. "All right." She walked with Thomas to the waiting room. They stepped inside.

The door snapped shut behind them. She gave a little shudder. "I'd never get used to all this opening and shutting without my controlling it."

"I'm not too happy about it either." He examined the entryway. There was no way of opening the door from their side. His instincts began to unsettle him. The room was as sterile and barren as an elevator. Involuntarily, he steadied his gut for another dizzying drop. Lady sat on the plastic bench against one wall. She tucked her booted feet under her.

"Disappointed?" He continued stalking about the apparently seamless walls. Sprinkler heads overhead appeared to be in good condition.

"About Alma and Stefan? Yes. I hope we get a chance to say good-bye."

"Don't count on it. Remmick could hardly wait to spirit them away." She started to say something else, but he heard a door close on the other side of the wall. He motioned her silent and strained to hear.

". . . settled in upstairs. Got what you need?"

"Yes. The girl is pre-menses, so we don't need to worry about plague contamination." Mendes' voice crisp and businesslike. "The boy, however, is from a Russian gene pool. I have my suspicions. He could be carrying a genetic Trojan horse. It's happened before."

The dean's voice rumbled in answer. "As a male, he's expendable. We can carry him for a few years before we make a decision. I won't have contamination, not now, not after all this work. We're nearly pure. What about the other two?"

"In the holding tank. One of them was spiking our ESP testing equipment like crazy. Do you suppose it's possible—"

"Bah! Would they have let you put them into the tank if they could read your mind?"

Thomas began to pry at the sealed door. A fingernail splintered down to the quick. Lady helped.

"What do you want me to do with them? That abomination with the gills is dangerous."

"Kill them," the dean intoned.

Sprinklers began to hiss, dispensing a white, misty cloud. His throat closed almost immediately. He tore his scarf off completely, freeing his gills. Lady collapsed at his feet.

"Kill them," the man repeated. "Then flush them."

Chapter 27

Below the reservoir, two still forms were tumbled into a ravine from an opening that snapped shut as quickly as it had opened. The ravine held water when it rained, runoff that eventually joined a storm drain system that could still make its broken way to the ocean. Now, wet or dry, it was a feeding ground for the wildlife in the foothills and some of the bolder predators from the ruins.

Whatever the scavenger, there would be little recognizable left of the bodies once it found them. As dusk lowered a purple curtain, a large shape loped confidently down the slopes toward the ravine and the insignificant freshet left over from heavy rains the month before. It ran mostly on two legs.

It was not human, but neither was it not not-human. It cast over the ground like a hunting beast until it stopped before the two tangled forms lying helplessly in the brush. It stooped its form over them and listened carefully. As if satisfied, it hoisted one and then the other, filling each shoulder with a burden, and loped to the concrete river that ran to the ocean.

There the beast dropped its burdens. With a black-clawed hand, it traced the chevron mark on the man's brow. It gave a grunt of satisfaction before pulling together branch and brush to form a crude raft. It rolled the bodies onto the raft which bobbed in the water. It watched the two for a long moment, and scratched at its long, russet hair. Then it pushed the raft away with a large, callused foot and watched the voyagers float downstream.

Below the city, dirty water ran like the River Styx to the ocean. Its pipes were massive, concrete and no longer whole, becoming more of a spillway than a pipeline. Animals and other things found their way through the ruins above to the depths where water—even dirty water—and life could be obtained.

A notch-eared wolfrat made his way down a warren run of trash and slime, bits of ooze clinging to his coat. The notch that took off most of his ear scarred into his eye, drew it up and puckered it half-closed. But he did not need his twilight sight to find water. He could smell it. His nails clicked on old plumbing and foundation stonework as he lumbered downhill, his tail dragging behind him like some half-forgotten reptile. The wolfrat shouldered his way through a jagged crack in the pipe. The cement edges tore out more than its share of tufted hair from his mangy hide. The wolfrat's lips twitched in a snarl of pain, unvoiced, for as pain went in the world, the discomfort was minor and unmemorable. As he hung over the lip of the crack to dip his muzzle into the murky water flowing swiftly past, he sensed a movement upstream.

The pipe was massive, and the water it carried past measured untold gallons. The wolfrat's ears flickered forward. Sometimes the water also carried gifts—gifts of garbage still fresh enough to eat. Sometimes the water carried unfortunate critters who'd also come down to drink at one of the various breaches and fallen in. That was how the wolfrat had nearly lost his eye and ear—trying to fetch out a hill cat, spitting and hissing in its fury. The wolfrat lost that dinner, and the hillcat its life, drowning in the dark spinning waters before the pipe spilled it into the ocean. Better, perhaps, that it had allowed the wolfrat to pull it out, and taken its chance fighting for survival in the dry tunnels.

The tattered ears twitched again. Unless the wolfrat missed his guess, something bigger and tastier was floating downstream, coming right at him. The beast braced himself and hunkered lower, claws flexed for grabbing. If the human scent daunted him, it was not for long.

A long shape barreled toward him. The wolfrat tensed, his tail anchoring his tenuous position, nails stretched and elongated, his toes prehensile in their flexibility.

As the smaller of the two figures borne along faced toward him, he reached and snatched. Fabric tore, and fresh cuts welled up with crimson, hot blood scent spattering the water's surface. But the raft bobbed away, bumping against the curvature of the waterway, halting only momentarily.

The rat lashed out again, fishing frantically. He nearly toppled in his enthusiasm, but his claws caught—and this time
held. He drew back slowly, lest the water-burdened flesh he de-
sired break away from him again. He bared his teeth, long fangs
beginning to slaver with anticipation. His shoulders hunched as
he drew the heavy burden closer to the jagged opening in the
pipe. If the creature should begin to fight, he would lose it, he
knew. But it stayed limp in his hold.

Hot drool ran down his lips. Then the soft, tender flesh in his
grip began to separate and he lost it as it tore loose. With an ag-
gravated squeal, the wolfrat perched a moment on the break in
the pipe, then backed out quickly. He raced through the warrens, knowing exactly where the next watering hole was. He
pushed his way through moldering earth and arrived in time to
watch the raft float away right under his nose.

The wolfrat stayed perched in disappointment for an instant,
then, with a hissing sigh, lowered his head to drink. The water,
at least, was relatively fresh as water went beneath the ruined
Earth.

The dolphin swam in crystal clear seawater, felt the thermals
and scents of an outpouring of landwater into her pathway, and
made to swerve. She disliked the sting and taste of landwater in
her eyes and airhole. But she had been summoned, and so she
stayed near the spillway that erupted from the city ruins. Then
she tasted a scent she knew, and paused.

The being who had danced with her one moonstruck time
not long ago rode that landwater. She circled and searched the
spillway, the foam in her wake bouncing upon the surface like
gems. She bit the thermal wash, tasting his essence more
clearly.

She was not an ordinary dolphin, any more than he had been
an ordinary man-thing. She rose and tail-walked a few lengths
to gauge where the wash originated from. As she spanned the
waves, she saw the two dark bundles flash out of the spillway
and rise hesitantly on the crest. Then they began to sink.

The dolphin dove and sped toward the bundles. Her intuition
had brought her fishing this coast and now she was about to
snag the unexpected.

She caught the raft up and flipped them about in the water
so that their blowholes faced upward, tending them like dolphin

pups. Her keen hearing brought her sputterings of awareness. She nosed at the two. One bled, a crimson cloud upon the water. The dolphin circled, knowing that the blood was likely to attract deadly hunters.

She nosed at the favored one's appendage, more limp than a fin, but stronger, too, though not for swimming. It flopped about with her attentions. The dolphin sounded unhappily. She searched the lower tides, tasting, smelling, listening. Teeth glistening, she snapped at a barracuda drawn by the blood scent and arrowing past her. It sped away, jaws grinning in defeat. A second tried to bolt past. She punched it and after a flailing wiggle, it, too, swam off, much more slowly, fluid leaking from its gills.

The dolphin surfaced and cleansed her air, blowhole expelling with a spray that danced about her, refracting an iridescent rainbow. She pulled alongside the dark bundles, watching as they floated limply, hanging upon the raft. She took up his wrist in her jaws, gently, as she would take a dolphin pup up to his first surfacing, aware that among her people she was huge and having learned tenderness from experience. Her bite caressed the marks of their first meeting.

She recalled with pleasure the instinct that had drawn her to the sea bowls and her delight on finding a being who shared her love of the sea and beauty and things arcane.

The dolphin goddess shook with fury. What enemy had dared to injure her favorite and his mate? Her eyes blazed, and turquoise sheened about her hide as her aura flared. She emitted a cry in her despair which only her kind and the faraway gods could hear, and shook her favorite roughly as if he had participated in his own demise, too careless to know of the gift she had bestowed upon him.

He fell from her mouth, splashing into the water, and she nosed him in the ribs as she would a reluctant pup into using his airhole. Then she picked him up again and shook him, keening silently in dolphin grief.

His gills fluttered weakly. She shook him again, then heard to her exultation the same struggling sounds a weakened pup might make. Then bad air flushed from him rapidly, expelling with an odor that made her gag in disgust. As he fell from her grip a third time, it was with a thrashing and a growing awareness.

Encouraged, she turned to the mate and shook her, too, her wounds pinking the foam with every shake until the woman made a gasping sob, and her limbs jerked in startlement. She expelled the same foul-smelling bad air, then took a choking breath as the dolphin curled about them both. The goddess opened her jaws in a wide and knowing smile as they reached for her, suddenly uncertain of their buoyancy in the ocean water, and clung to her, and gasped for air. Dolphin prayers are rarely said and even more rarely ignored.

Thomas frowned as he pulled the bandaging tight about Lady's upper arm. "I don't think she did this," he said in answer to Lady's complaint. "This doesn't look like a bite pattern. More a rip or tear."

"Then what did? Did they try to mutilate me after they gassed us?"

"Does it matter? We're here, alive, when we had no chance."

She ducked her chin down, silently. A fathomless expression passed over her face, made a little puffy and swollen from the side effects of the gas used on them. She looked tired and worn and every day of her twenty-nine years.

He reached out, cupped her chin, and gently turned her face toward him. "You're a Healer," he said. "Make sure that doesn't get infected. I don't want things falling off of you."

Her lips quirked. "Any *thing* in particular?"

"Several, as a matter of fact." He smoothed the wispy hairs off her forehead. "I suppose I'll have to find a shell comb for you."

Lady waved graciously over the expanse of beach. "Take your pick."

He settled down in the sand beside her. Their clothes were spread out, drying, and he took his nudity matter-of-factly. Lady had insisted on retaining her undergarments and sat in them now, the paler portions of her skin rapidly pinking. He'd have to get her in the shade as soon as she had warmed. The crude raft—he must have woven it together before passing out when they'd been dumped outside—had broken apart when they beached.

"Where are we?"

"Best guess or for certain?"

Lady let out a gusty laugh. "Best guess, by all means."

"Probably Catalina, though I'm not familiar with this side of it." He eyed the striated cliff wall at their backs. "In high water, I'd say this strand disappears."

Lady shuddered involuntarily. "Are we going to have to swim for it again?"

"No, no. I mean really high water, like when the Santa Anas come up. High tide is going to push us back some, but we'll be all right. It's fresh water that worries me."

"Is there any?"

"Bound to be some. I saw a wild goat or two looking down at us when we came ashore. They're tough, but they still drink. I may have to swim around until I find a cove where the cliffs can be climbed to do some dowsing, but we ought to find something."

Lady rubbed her hand over his lips. "I could go for roasted goat," she mused.

"Me, too. But not just yet. That was a rough swim, hauled by dolphins or not. We were in no shape to make it across the channel. Still cold?"

"A little, but the sun feels good." She shivered again, lightly, despite her words. They lapsed into a long silence, watching the hard brightness of the Pacific as it washed against the sands of their cove. Then, she stirred and leaned up against him, drawing strength from his presence. "I dreamed that I was dead."

He did not answer her, thinking thoughts that were the same, but not wanting to deal with them just yet.

"Are you listening to me?"

"Yes."

"Then talk to me. Am I crazy?"

"If you were sane, you'd never have insisted on coming with me."

She kicked sand over his bare feet. The warmth felt good and he kept his feet buried. But he did not feel like talking just yet. The fan of Lady's hair trailed over his shoulder.

"Did we die? Or were we just unconscious, so far under we never knew what happened to us?"

"I don't know," he said, finally, after a further silence punctuated only by their soft breathing and the breaking of waves upon the beach, and an occasional screech of a wheeling gull. "I just don't know. *Kill 'em and flush 'em*. Why?"

Lady sighed. "So we couldn't contaminate them." She tickled a fingertip over his bicep. "We have to go back. We can't leave Alma and Stef with those bastards."

"That, I know." He looked out over the ocean expanse toward where he imagined he could see the shoreline. It was a long and tiring journey already made once, waiting to be retraced, and with Cindy and Lady's mule lost to them. The waters were coming in, slowly, inexorably, high tide moving up the sands, but he did not see the dolphin arcing upon them. He wondered where she went, and if she was waiting for him to come out and dance with her again. His lungs ached, and charley horses knotted calf muscles not used to marathon swimming.

"What do you have in mind?"

Thomas put his arm about her. The sun-warmed aura of her skin brushing next to his filled his mind with a giddy thought, one that he pushed away for the time being. Getting into the College Vaults a second time would be an ordeal. "We should rest here for a week or two, provided we can find water."

"So long?"

"We've been through a lot. What happened wouldn't have happened if I had been thinking straight."

Lady sat up and looked at him, both eyes blazing indignantly. "What happened wasn't your fault! Those . . . gentlemen . . . tried to kill us!"

He tried not to smile at her. She fairly bristled. "Lady," he said softly. "We're both Talents. They shouldn't have been able to entertain those thoughts within arm's reach of us."

Her lips worked without a sound passing them. Then she let herself sag back into his embrace. "All right. We rest a week. What then?"

"I'm not sure. I have debts to pay first."

"Debts?" Her voice was muffled this time, as she moved to nestle her face against his chest, and her lips vibrated teasingly against his nipples.

She was seriously interfering with his thought processes. He reached up to her shoulders and sat her back on his knees, a hand's span between them. "You saw the dolphin who brought us here . . . you know you've never seen a creature like that."

Lady's mouth curved sulkily, but she nodded.

"Well, I have. And she marked me. It was the day of the wedding. I can't pretend I understand what she is or where she comes from, but she saved us and I owe her. I think she'll collect on that. I'd like to have it settled before we leave here."

"What if she wants your children?" Lady said softly.

"Lady!"

"All right, Thomas. I'll get serious. I understand. But she just might be a mutation or something."

"No. No." He looked out at the changing tide. "No, she's something special. Man-made or maybe nature-made, but she's something special, and I owe her our lives."

"And then we get Alma and Stefan?"

"And then."

Her face became melancholy. "I hope to god," she said to him, "that there's something left of them by then."

"Me, too."

Chapter 28

Thomas kicked his way to the surface. Lady sat placidly on the driftwood raft that had replaced the old one, her hair loose about her shoulders, looking for all the world like some mermaid out of the long ago past. He sputtered a bit and caught at a log end to steady himself.

"What is it?" she asked, leaning toward him.

"Plastic netting, heavy duty stuff, strung quite a ways along here. It's probably been in place for a hundred years or more."

Her brown eye reflected compassion, her blue eye the ocean. "Why?"

"Damned if I know. A fishery boundary maybe, maybe defense. Anyway, there's a few skeletons caught in it . . . I imagine it's been the death of a dolphin or two. Even a gray whale."

"Do you think this is what she wants, for you to cut it down?"

He ran his hands through his wet hair, slicking it back off his forehead. He'd grown very tan in his weeks on the island, but Lady had woven a grass hat and merely freckled lightly. She wore her hat now.

"I don't know what she wants." He hung in the water, floating. The sea looked calm about them and there was no sight of their benefactress.

"She towed us here. You can't believe she did it accidentally."

"I haven't the tools."

"You have the knife you found in the military cache." Lady wore it now, belted at her side. He'd used it to help rebuild the raft. "The only other alternative is for you to start swimming—and push me all the way to the peninsula." Lady leaned forward so close now she was almost lying on her stomach. "You know, Thomas," she said seductively. "I think you have remarkable stamina in many things. But I don't think you feel like towing me."

He rocked the raft. "Maybe it would do you some good to go swimming."

She let out a tiny shriek and sat bolt upright in the center of the raft. He gazed at her, and let the warm feeling he felt when he looked at her, flood him. No longer did he feel that emotion as a disability. Perhaps it had happened when he'd died . . . perhaps it had happened sooner, a little bit at a time. It was a metamorphosis he regretted no more than the butterfly regretted leaving its cocoon behind.

She said, "What are you thinking? Your mustache is twitching like an otter's whiskers."

"Flattery will get you everywhere. I'm thinking you'd better hand me the knife and I'll give it a try."

She unbelted the tool and tossed it over. He unsheathed it and let go of the raft, letting the waves take him gently.

Below, it took a moment for his eyes to get used to the sting. But he'd been bred for that tolerance, just as he'd been bred to have gills. A strand of kelp, dislodged by the tide, floated past him, trailing its own leaves like a hand across his body. Bubbles streamed out of his gills, a wake of white diamonds bumping into his sight whenever he turned his head. His skin goosefleshed. The water was cold this time of year. It sapped his strength. If the net were too tough, or he became entangled in its loose strands, he was on his own. Even the dolphin goddess feared these depths. She had towed them there and left them in a spray of turquoise water.

He readied the knife as the bright yellow netting reared in front of him. It was still taut, years of the ocean leaving little or no wear on it. Barnacle scale decorated it here and there as he tried to trace its anchorage, and seaweed grew through it as though it were a trellis, but it was deadly and remained that way. The ocean had tried to adapt it into something useful and failed.

The old-timers had tempered a good blade. Made of a metal alloy he could not identify, it was tougher than just about any knife he'd ever handled. Yet he doubted its edge would be much use against the net. He reached an end and followed it down, where concrete and a plastic pole fastened it inviolably to the ocean floor.

Thomas took a deep breath and let himself surface slowly. He looked about. Lady bobbed a little distance away. She watched the cresting waves anxiously. He did not hail her. He breathed a few times to pump up his bloodstream, then dove once more.

If he cut the net loose, or even cut it into smaller pieces, those pieces would still trap swimmers. No, the net had to come ashore where nothing could become tangled. That task was impossible for him. He could not guess the weight, but knew it must be close to several hundred pounds. His best bet was to wind it up and try to anchor it about its original mooring. Such a task seemed monumental as well.

If all he did was think about it, he would go into hypothermia before he could do anything. Thomas gripped the knife tightly and began to saw at a crucial strand. It parted easily. He moved upward, cutting as he went. The last major strand at the top strained. With a cautious move, he cut that free, knowing it would sling loose.

It did, but the ocean's grip upon it kept the reaction moderate. Thomas kicked upward, cleansed and revitalized his lungs, and dove a last time. He found the other anchorage near a kelp forest as the net began to flop about him, going to and fro in the tide. He panicked and thrashed as kelp twisted about his feet. His ears rang as he began to choke, gills unable to provide him with quite enough air. Then he looked up, seeing the sunlight streaming down into the kelp forest as the weed grew tall, seemingly before his very eyes, reaching upward.

Thomas grasped the end of the netting. The tide seemed to be with him as he dug his feet in the sandy bottom and coaxed the net into the kelp, where it could anchor and trellis something good. The tiny fish living in the forest darted about him, in and out of the netting with no trouble.

It took the better part of the afternoon, surfacing and diving, to anchor the net into the kelp bed. He kept the net low, around the base of the plants so that it would not entangle the sea otter population floating above.

Lady called encouragement to him and finally helped him aboard the raft when he quit and tried weakly to crawl out, shivering. She threw a sun-warmed grass mat over him.

"Will it work, do you think?"

He'd explained to her what it was he was trying to do. He gave a wobbly shake of his head as if to say he did not know. His teeth chattered in spite of himself.

"I tried," he finished. He lay down, his head in her sun-soaked lap, and rested, the ocean rocking him to sleep.

The dolphin came at dusk, her wake phosphorescent with the iridescent fire of her aura. She leaped and caprioled for them, nearly capsizing the raft. Lady clung to Thomas.

"Is she happy?"

"I'd say so. She's dancing for us."

Lady murmured, "I'm unused to the ways of dolphins."

Thomas laughed, as if she should not be. He watched as the mammal came alongside, grinning, her eyes shining with the last of the light off the water. He ran his hand along her flank. The beast then dipped away and came up under the tow rope. As the raft shimmied into movement, Lady clenched the bundle of their clothes. Thomas put an arm about her.

"We're going home."

Nighttime. He shrugged into his leather jacket, made incredibly stiff by its debacle in salt water, even though he'd been rubbing a crude plant oil into it the past few weeks. It would never be the same unless he could get his hands on some decent saddle soap. He mourned briefly for all of Charlie's instruments and gauges, lost to the College Vaults.

He put a hand back for Lady. She grasped it.

"How far off the peninsula are we?"

"Not far at all." His hushed tones matched hers. He brought her into a squat upon the grass, damp with winter dew. "This is what I'm going to do." And he told her the plan he'd formulated while building the raft.

She made a forbidding sound through her teeth when he'd finished. "No." Flatly. Finally.

"Listen to me. There's no other way."

"No."

"Lady—"

"You'll get yourself killed."

"We're afoot. Time is against us now. For all I know, Denethan's been laying siege to them."

"I know, I know." Silence. In the darkness he could not quite see her face, but he swore that her ice-blue eye glittered coldly at him. There was a rustle of cloth. He thought perhaps she'd turned her face away. He heard a muffled sound.

"Don't cry."

"I'm not crying, damn it," she threw at him.

A night bird rose at the sound and winged away, keening.

Then Lady said quietly, "And if you can rush the catapults and get a wind raider, what then?"

"We fly to the Vaults."

"What if there're no raiders here?"

He rocked back on his heels. "Then we'll have to walk, I guess. But there's bound to be. He'll have left sentries at the catapults. Those installations are too valuable to him to abandon just because he wiped out the peninsula."

In a very small voice, she said, "I'm afraid of heights."

"Then don't look down." He squeezed the hand she pushed into his tightly. "We've got cover. Let's go."

"All right, but don't take all night. I'm tired."

In the end, it was she who found the catapult. She pulled tightly at his wrist.

"Down!"

He let her pull him down. She crouched next to him. "There."

He saw it then, a tiny carroty flame of fire. Then, blacker than ebony against the night, the catapult tower. He crept closer.

His gamble had paid off. Two immense batwing shapes rested on the crest near the tower.

"Two of them."

"We'll have to disable one," she returned.

Thomas smiled in the night. Girl after his own heart. "I count four sentries, how many have you got?"

"Five. There's one asleep near the raiders."

"Ah." He looked over the camp. "I can take out those four, if you can handle the fifth."

Silence. Then, "All right."

He knew she could protect herself. But this seemed more like murder than self-defense. He had no immediate comfort for her. They crept down toward the camp, the sweet oil of mesquite filling the air as it bruised and broke about them.

If it had been he on duty, he would have smelled it and known that something moved in the brush. Perhaps they didn't have that much mesquite on the Mojave, or perhaps they just weren't alert enough.

It didn't matter. The outcome would have been the same. He Projected, blurring their vision and reflexes, got the four, quickly, and Lady the fifth.

After cleansing it, he handed her the knife to slash the wings of the extra wind raider. He bent to lift it up so she could reach it more easily.

Five men jumped from underneath the machine and came for him. He heard Lady's sharp cry, cut off, and began to kill anything that came near him.

Blade paused in the grass, head down, breathing heavily, thoughts swimming through his brain. She was dead, wasn't she? And he alive, out of their reach, outnumbered but not out-fought. He'd reach for her thoughts in his, but that wasn't his Talent. The only thought he could reach for was that of the enemy.

What right had he to be crouched in the darkness, alive?

"Blade! Are you listening?" The deep, masculine voice pealed out in the night.

Thomas swallowed hard. His throat hurt. His heart felt as though it could burst. The enemy shouted for him, but he had not intention of listening.

Whatever the enemy said it would be lies.

"Blade! I know you're out there."

He turned his back and began to wend his way through the undergrowth, painstakingly, having underestimated the enemy before. He was wrong about his feelings. He'd disabled him-self. He deserved defeat.

"You're getting old, Blade! You set off at least seven wards crossing the hill. How many more will you set off getting back? You're not getting out of here alive. I've got her, Blade. If you want her, come get her."

He closed his mind and continued to work his way toward freedom.

*   *   *

Lady sat, her feet bound, and a ward tied about each wrist. The fetishes rattled whenever she moved. "You won't get him," she said. "He knows better."

The tall man at the edge of the firelight stood looking out into the darkness. At her words he turned back toward her, amber eyes catching the glow of the fire. "He'll come back," Denethan said. "If I have to make you howl on the wind, he'll come back."

"Never! He's a professional."

Denethan pointed a finger at his scribe. "Micah, persuade her to do some shouting."

The wizened old man squinted at Lady. He blinked slowly. "I," he said, "would do what was asked of me."

"You," she said, "should drop dead."

The scribe curled back with a hiss. Denethan pivoted on one heel. "Micah," he ordered.

The scribe reached a leathery hand into the heart of the fire and withdrew a single, radiant ember. He held it toward her.

Lady felt her heart skip a beat. She thrust with her mind, made it spark high enough that the old being dropped it with a hiss. She looked away, but she could feel its heat draw near. "He'll come back," she said to Denethan. "But when he feels like it, and then he'll kill you. For what you did to Charlie, to me, to the county."

"Charlie?" the man said.

She felt the ember's breath upon her face. "The Director of Water and Power. The massacre on the peninsula."

Denethan laughed softly. "What a monster you must think me, but that, my pretty one, was not my handiwork."

Lady opened her mouth and screamed with all her might for Thomas. The night grew still after her outburst. No answer came. She felt the blistering warmth of the coal near her left eye, the blue one, the icy cold one that Thomas had always hated.

"Wait a moment." Denethan beckoned to the scribe. The old man knelt in front of her, glowing sparks trailing from his fingers. How could he bear the heat? He moved the ember back into the fire.

She bowed her head, knowing she was right. Thomas would not return for her, could not compromise his duty in hopes of saving her. He could not. He was what he and Charlie had molded him to be, a Lord Protector, an enforcer, all the deadlier because of his psychic abilities. She had known he could, and would, leave her behind when they'd gone after Jennifer and Ramos. When they'd gone In-City. And now.

Men like Thomas did not seek out partnership. It was a liability. He'd use the ghost road if he had to—and they both knew it would kill him this time.

"Call him again."

Her voice choked in her throat. She shook her head. "He won't come," she said, her voice barely audible. "Not tonight." She dared to look up. "But he'll come back for you some day, and when he catches you, he'll cut your heart out of your chest."

"Yes," Denethan murmured. "I think he might. But that might be too late for both of us."

A figure loomed suddenly in the firelight. "Tell me why."

Lady felt her pulse throb in her throat, and hot tears sprinkled her face as he looked down at her. It was Thomas.

Chapter 29

"Because we're alike, you and I," the desert mutant said, "and we were born out of their dreams, not their nightmares, no matter what that bastard buried in the mountain told you."

Blood-splattered and weary, Thomas swayed on his feet. Then he looked to Lady.

"Believe him, Thomas."

He closed his eyes faintly. That tiny sense of Truth-read came to him, a fragile thread of an ability the ghost road had leeched from him. It told him that his enemy was honorable. He pointed at the wards on Lady's wrists. They parted with a blue spark that snapped. "Show me your hospitality and we'll talk tomorrow."

They slept till mid-morning in a canopied tent of golden silklike fabric that billowed in the wind and captured the rays of the sun. A gold and dust dappled coyote lay in the corner, his head on his paws, eyes watching them alertly, but no one in Denethan's camp bothered them.

He slept on one cot, holding Lady in a light embrace, and the desert raider slept on the second. They had lain down warily, too tired to talk, accepting a momentary truce, after Lady had said, "Thomas—Denethan did not raid the peninsula."

But Thomas had had doubts of his own and that touched on them. So they had agreed to discuss their differences when their heads were clearer, Denethan out of courtesy, he thought, and himself out of necessity. Besides, Denethan was within arm's reach should Blade change his mind and decide to kill the mutant.

He woke, Lady's soft purr upon his chest, and lay there. He kept still, not wanting to wake her. When he finally turned his head to look at Denethan's cot, he found the man watching him, eyes like molten gold. He was not a lizard—he was like the coyote, the hillcat, and then a lizard, but all gold and dun.

"You can leave her," Denethan said quietly. "Fox here will watch her. You and I have much to talk about."

He moved carefully to disentangle himself, but woke her. She yawned and sat up, saying, "You weren't running out on me?"

"Never."

She glanced at Denethan. The man stood by his cot and bowed with liquid grace, saying nothing. They moved out into the sun where chairs and a table had been put out for them.

His men treated him like a monarch, and perhaps he was, a desert lord where no one else dared to reign. His lightly scaled skin was tanned gold, and his hair was light blond, like Thomas' but thick and curled. His eyes were bronze, catlike, and warmed when he smiled. He was tall and well-muscled, taller than Thomas and more massively built, but exceedingly graceful. He walked barefoot to the conference chairs. His toes were webbed, the skin delicate, with gold tracery upon the folds. His nails were hardened, nearly claws, but, visibly, that was all of the mutant about him. Thomas sensed there might be more. He thought to himself ironically that this was the being he'd called the Lizard of Oz, a green man from an emerald city, but this man had nothing about him that was not gold.

Thomas settled himself, keeping his legs under him and his body loosely balanced. Lady took her cue from him and did the same. She graciously accepted a cool glass of juice from Micah.

In the daylight, Thomas could see much more of the lizard about Micah than showed in Denethan. Just, he supposed, as Micah could see he had gills and Lady did not. He refused the juice when offered, saying, "Tell me why we shouldn't kill each other."

Denethan put an eyebrow up. It arced elegantly over his amused eye. "It would be a waste, I think. We are both excellent specimens of our race."

"And what race is that?"

"A race that was meant to walk the stars."

"Perhaps—except that one of us is a little cold-blooded."

"Thomas!"

The desert lord waved a hand. "Let him talk. He hasn't offended me . . . yet. We are old enemies, and that weave is a very knotted one, but I'm beginning to think we are not the only weavers."

"Why?"

"Because, as Lady Nolan expressed so elegantly late last night, my troops were not responsible for the massacre on the Palos Verdes peninsula. We interrupted the real murderers and they fled rather hastily. Not, you understand, that I had not had similar intentions."

"You did not allow looting."

"I never do. We're not barbarians. We are only desert adaptive. We are survivors."

Thomas shifted slightly. Charlie's last words had spoken of betrayal, not raiders. Had the College Vault escort brought an attack force with them? And Charles, all unaware and triumphant in his dealings, welcomed them? Those who thought of the county settlements as infestations? "Did you see what happened? Could you identify who fled?"

"No. We were on their heels, but not that close. I had my men give the mercy stroke to those who were mortally wounded . . . I could not spare the attentions of my Healer. For that, I am truly sorry."

"Then why were you here? Why did you come back out of the Mojave after, what, ten years?"

Denethan paused. He poured himself a glass of fruit juice and savored half of it, making Thomas wait. Then he set the glass down. "Have you ever been to my region?"

"No."

"But you have felt the hot winds come scorching out of the desert?"

Thomas nodded.

"It can be a cruel life. Some of us are more . . . reptile-like . . . than we deserve to be." Denethan got up. His muscular form rippled gracefully with the movement. "We were mutated genetically—engineered for survival. I'm told that originally, my breed was destined for colonization elsewhere. Mars, perhaps. Arid. Cold, though, horribly cold, and my . . . breed . . . had not been quite perfected. Whatever the reason, we were created. As you were."

Thomas put his hand up to his throat. His gaze met Denethan's.

"You understand." Denethan cleared his throat and added, "There is a virus. . . ."

"The eleven year plague," Lady said suddenly.

"Yes—you know of it?" Denethan did not wait for an answer, her interruption had been enough. "It's devastating my people. The mutations are increasing, almost geometrically. We'll not survive another thirty years and remain human."

He stopped pacing. "I knew of Charles Warden's genealogy program. I came for those children, to take them home. I wanted them to save my people! We had appealed to the College Vault decades ago. Their answer was to destroy my father and decimate our population. Our answer to that was to find an easier country to live in."

"Which we already populated."

"Yes. So and thus, by trial and error, we do eventually find wisdom. I came to the uneasy conclusion that we might learn to live together. But first, the children. Plague has already struck my camps."

"And you just intended to take them."

"Yes. The decoys we tracked up the coast . . . there was an accident. One of my men was overzealous. The craft began to burn. The children panicked when our ship circled them. They chose to crash rather than be rescued. But on examination of the bodies, my men found that we had been duped. We came back, in force, to the peninsula, to find the massacre. Your DWP, it appears, had enemies."

"No one is perfect," Thomas said.

Denethan put his head back and laughed, a booming, hearty sound. When he'd finished, he said sadly, "If we'd been perfect, we wouldn't have needed your children."

"But why," Lady said. "Why all the years of raiding and terrorizing? Why the war ten years ago?"

"Did you not do the same to me? Our hold on the desert is tenuous at best, but never a year goes by that we do not fight other men for our right to live! We have the right to defend ourselves!"

Thomas got up. He shook his head. "Not from us. Not from the counties."

Denethan grew deadly still. They stood face-to-face. Then, almost imperceptibly, the desert mutant relaxed. "We are linked, you and I," he said softly, clearly, so that he might not be misunderstood. "If you lie, I will know it."

They stood, looking into one another's eyes. Thomas felt the uncanny movement of another within his soul—and looked into the earnestness of another's. Never had it been so easy to Truthread. Or so devastating.

"No one," Thomas repeated, "to my knowledge, men of the counties or even nesters of this region, has ever gone to the Mojave to raid you."

Long moments passed. Then Denethan stepped back. "Then who?"

Together, they answered each other, "The College Vaults."

Denethan began to pace again, running his fingers through his hair. Light motes, bits of gold, spun off as he did. "It has to be. I thought they had done with me. They exist for purity. You and I are monsters in their sight, nothing of humanity remains in us."

Lady added, "They tried to kill us when we brought Alma and Stefan to them. They gassed and dumped us. We were less than animals to them."

Denethan tilted his head to listen to her. "I'm surprised they did not succeed. None of my spies has ever returned from there. No one I know has ever returned from there."

"Charlie and I did, once. And we were going back last night."

This halted Denethan. "You know the way in?"

"I know the way in, all right. I just don't know the way out."

Denethan seated himself. He snapped his fingers, and Micah reappeared. "A tray of bread and cheese, and whatever cooked meat you can find. We have a lot to talk about."

Thomas told him, "First, convince me you are not still an enemy."

From out of nowhere, Denethan drew a knife. He grasped Thomas's wrist and drew it close. Lady made a determined noise, and she frowned, then reeled back in her chair. Denethan paused long enough to glance at her saying, "You have some Talent, but don't seek to fence with me." He sliced the knife across the soft flesh inside of Thomas' wrist, then did the same with his own.

Two thin lines of crimson welled up.

"We bleed the same, you and I," the desert lord said. "I'm

not so sure about those inside the Vaults. The man called dean is the same man who ruled them when the Disasters came and the Vaults were closed. How he lives decades past his time, I don't know. But I do know this . . . we are more human who learn to make peace out of war than those who cannot."

Thomas closed his eyes in thought. *Human.* He had been engineered to be the stuff of dreams, of tomorrow, not nightmares. This he knew Denethan believed with all his heart and soul to be true. Could he do less?

With an expression of pique, Lady waved her hand over both wrists, and the cuts healed. "Keep talking," she said.

Denethan ran his hands over the webbing a last time. He pulled on the buckles to double-check the security. "Now remember, when the catapult is released, it brings a disquieting sensation. Keep your wits about you or you'll never get the glider righted."

Thomas nodded, but he could feel Lady at his back, hunched in as if she could make herself small enough to ignore the sensation of flying altogether.

The desert lord eyed them both. "I wouldn't send you out without practice flights," he said, "if I didn't have to."

Thomas smiled. "Remember, I was going to steal this. At least now I get it with a set of instructions."

Denethan laughed. "I'll be behind you at launch, but ahead of you on the thermals. Follow me. I'll signal."

"Right."

The desert lord left the fuselage. Thomas got a clear view of blue sky, all he could see from his angle on the cocked catapult. He felt Lady shivering. "Is this the woman who's cursed me from one side of hell to another?"

"Oh, shut up," came her muffled reply. "Just tell me when it's over."

He felt his smile widen. A desert man leaned over his view. "It'll be a minute, fella." The mutant showed his too sharp teeth. "It's a good thing his lordship likes you. He had a fella killed this way once. Course, we launched him without the wind raider." He laughed hugely.

Lady muttered an obscenity at his back. Before he could say anything to quiet her, he heard the command.

"Launch!"

The catapult shivered. Then it jarred beneath them. He could feel the tremendous push and the wind raider quivered as it—and they—were thrown into the sky. For a moment, the earth and sky changed places and it looked as if they were going to tumble straight down. Their webbing dug into their ribs. Thomas' head whirled. Then the ship righted as he pulled back on the rudder and the wind filled the batwings.

The solar motor at the rear took hold, humming steadily, pushing them farther ahead. A moment later, the vessel shuddered as the second plane took their draft, then came up under them and passed them.

Grudgingly, Thomas realized that the desert warrior was a master with the wind raider. He took his signals and followed after.

"God," a voice said at his shoulder. "Look down, Thomas. It's beautiful!"

In shock, he followed Lady's suggestion. The panorama below was one of green and brown, laced and quilted by the tracks of the ruins. Lady was hanging over the side in delight.

"How soon did he say we'd be there?"

"Two hours, if the thermals are right."

"Look! Look, there's the edge of the Fire Ring, to the south."

To look wherever Lady pointed, and keep an eye out for Denethan's signals, made Thomas cross-eyed and a little dizzy. The better part of valor, he decided, was to watch the other wind rider. He missed little, for Lady kept up a delighted patter cross-country. He decided that he preferred to have her cowering, but the opportunity had passed.

Denethan had troops in the field, still searching for the College Vaults and the whereabouts of the children. They were hardened, battle-worthy troops, Denethan had told Thomas and Lady, more than equal to the weeks of living In-City. He had sent word ahead where they would be landing and to meet them. As they sculled now over the foothills, he could see the open area where Denethan planned to set down. It was littered with bodies dressed in khaki, and more than a few lizard men as well. There'd been warfare already.

"Who holds the field?" he said to Lady, busy gauging the thermals as they spiraled down.

"Denethan's troops." Her joy faded. "If even one of the College guard got away. . . ."

Their whole attack was predicated on surprise. "Don't even think it," he warned her. He made a warding sign over the plane and followed Denethan's bold descent over Indian Hill, where the College Vaults were buried under several hundred feet of rock.

As they jolted to a halt, Denethan made a running leap and caught the side of the fuselage, braking it to a complete stop. "A born airman," he said, and clapped Thomas on the shoulder.

Thomas did not feel joy. "How many did you lose?"

"Barely twenty. We got thirty-four of their finest."

"Any get away?"

The desert warrior did not meet his eyes as he looked about the browned grass field littered with dead. "None," he said, "that my captain knows of."

Which meant there was room for doubt.

Thomas took a deep breath. "Hell," he said. "None of this was dead certain to begin with."

Denethan caught his expression and smiled in appreciation. He reached into the fuselage for Thomas' rifle and tossed it to him.

As he strode behind the troops, it was a comfort to have a rifle and his old jacket filled with vials again. He crested the knoll and looked down on a brilliantly blue lake. "This," he said, "is the Cobal Canyon Reservoir. Follow me and I'll show you where those bastard get their water. I still remember how impressed Charlie was with their system. He pointed things out in great detail before entering the Vaults."

Thomas knelt by the filtration pump, a vial in his hand. Denethan manned the huge valve. Amber eyes studied Thomas as he thumbed the cork out of the vial. "What is that you've mixed?"

"It's a mild hallucinogenic. We call it amberose. We use it for breakout fever . . . when our adolescent Talents reach puberty—"

"I know," Denethan said. "We suffer it, too. But the drug deals with it?"

"It calms. In some cases, it can bring it on . . . with certain

Talents, it's best if they suffer breakout when it can be dealt with more easily."

"Like Firemakers."

"Precisely."

Denethan looked across the basin and said, "There's the signal." He set his feet and began to turn the cutoff valve.

Thomas tapped the vial into the last of the water the College Vaults would be getting for a while.

Lady set her full mouth disapprovingly. "I don't think they deal with Talent. I don't think they believed we could have reliable paranormal abilities. This could waken the latents. . . ."

"The more confusion the better. We can't go down and get them, they've got to come up and get us. Or at least open up. Now all we can do is wait."

They sat as the afternoon faded to dusk, then all night and into the morning.

Lady slapped her thigh. "I swear, every kind of bug left on the face of this earth has had a bite out of me."

"Not quite." Thomas pointed at one crawling up her bare arm. "I don't think I've seen one of those before."

She grimaced and squashed it. With the slap of her hand came a sharp whistle downslope, the arrogant cry of a mockingbird. Denethan's troops flattened at the lookout's signal.

"Thank heavens," Lady muttered. Then, "Oh, god, Thomas, I'm lying on an anthill."

He pointed at a clump of bracken. "Get over there, get down and get quiet."

She went, with an angry glare of her blue eye. She got down just as six uniforms crested the knoll.

Thomas had to give Denethan credit. His troops were finely trained and well disciplined. Not a one of the six uniforms had bloodstains on them or holes in them when he and Denethan and four others dressed. Lady handed him his rifle as he finished fastening the jacket.

She eyed him critically as he said, "Is my neck covered?"

"Barely, but anybody close enough to you to tell you have gills will be dead."

"Isn't that the truth," remarked Denethan. He shrugged in his too tight jacket. "Keltz—cut that up the back. Just slit it, I can't move." The fabric gave way as the raider did as ordered. He rolled his shoulders. "That's better. Ready?"

Thomas nodded. He asked lady, "Know what you need to do?"

"Yes. I don't know whether I can do it without a token, but if Alma's had enough amberose, she might respond to a summons. But—how are you going to get in there? There's several hundred feet of rock and dirt between you and the vaults. How are you going to take them out?"

"We're using the anthill method, one you should be familiar with."

"Anthill?"

Denethan grinned as he slung his rifle over his shoulder. "Stir them up enough, and they'll come get you."

Lady stepped back as shocked as if they'd struck her. "You can't ask me to call the children up through that—call them up to wade through a war zone to get to us!"

"We haven't any choice," Thomas told her. "And it's a risk for all of us—I see no other way." He reached out and took her hands. "I promise you that I'll do everything I can to see they make it safely."

Her lips trembled, but she said nothing else. She knew he would keep his promise—even if it meant trading his life for theirs.

Denethan slapped Thomas on the back. "Let's go."

Chapter 30

"It's a massacre up there, sir," Remmick reported. "They've cracked our outer doors. They're being repaired, but we can't last out a siege if the water is shut off."

The Dean of the College Vaults paused behind his desk. He'd been shuffling through papers and now put them aside with a stack of yellowing file folders.

"Arm the expendable breeders, then. Fire them up. Tell them about the abominations that are daring to attack. Do what you have to do to get them upstairs. Then use them as a shield. Send them out in wave and come in behind them. Get the doors closed however you can—but I don't want a single attacker left alive or we'll never have peace again, doors shut or not. They're animals and they hate us."

The captain nodded briskly in understanding. "And Remmick—" The guard paused in the doorway. "Be sure to arm that Russian youngster. This is as good a time as any to get rid of him."

Another crisp nod.

The dean settled back in his chair. He looked at his gallery wall where the best of the Norton Simon museum had been scavenged. The art had been brought here where it could be used to uplift and inspire the artists of a new generation.

His fat, freckled lip curled. First, that generation had to be born. Recent births were promising. He sighed. He would hate giving up his art collection and his books, and other, more intangible things. But it would be necessary to outfit the new, fit rulers of this country.

* * *

Alma lay on her bed, staring unhappily at the bland ceiling of her room. Her stomach cramped, hesitantly, tentatively, then violently, and she dug her fists into it. The hormone shots Dr. Mendes had given her were changing her—and she lay very still, frightened, wondering if she could lie so motionless that the cramps would not know where to find her, disbelieving that her own body could attack her so. She heard Stefan in the outer room, pacing. She wanted to call out and ask for a cold wash-cloth, but couldn't. Something was wrong with the water system and they had been told to obey strict rationing for the next forty-eight hours.

Now that she knew she could not have it, her mouth dried and her lips cracked just thinking of it.

There was trouble above. Nesters making trouble, they'd heard. Stefan was dying to go see what was happening, but they'd all been confined to quarters.

Alma put the back of her hand to her clammy forehead. She hated being underground. She hated the walls and floors and ceilings. She hated the chemical smelling air that pushed out of the vents. She hated the lights that never went off in the corridors even at night and shone under the cracks of her apartment door even if she pushed towels in its way. It was never night and never day, always the same.

She felt her muscles tense. Another wave of pain rolled through her. Alma bit her lip and tried to think of anything, anyone, different from here. She closed her eyes and almost instantly, Lady Nolan's face appeared in her thoughts.

Her glistening brown hair looked windblown, and Alma could see both the sky and the earth in her warm, off-color eyes. There was love and tenderness in those eyes. Alma had always been fond of the Protector. Whenever she'd visited Alma's township, she'd always brought comfort and healing and laughter, three things the girl sorely missed now. Alma was drifting into sleep with the dream of Lady Nolan when their apartment door opened.

She heard Stefan question the intruder eagerly. She did not wish to awaken, but something was happening. She struggled out of her misery as Stefan ran into the bedroom.

He carried a rifle across his chest and thrust it toward her. "We're under attack. Denethan's lizard men have come to wipe us out like they did the peninsula."

"Stefan!"

"This is my chance! They treat me like a child here, but they need my help now—"

"Fighting?"

"Yes! Upstairs."

Alma said, in a tiny voice, "I want to go with you."

"But you're sick. It could even be breakout fever."

"Let me go."

He looked shocked. "Alma. They're killing mutants up there."

"I want to go with you." She grasped the rifle. "I was dreaming of Lady Nolan—she was standing in the open, grass about her ankles, the wind in her hair—"

He tossed his head, a shock of white-blond hair falling across his forehead as he did. "She didn't even come say goodbye to you," he said.

"That's not the point! This place . . . there's no windows, no doors. I want to breathe again!"

He looked at her, plainly not comprehending. With a twist, he freed his rifle. "I have a job to do. Stay where you're told." He "about faced" and left, his issue blues straining at the backs of his shoulders.

Alma waited two seconds, then followed him down the corridor.

Denethan braced Thomas while he loaded and wound both rifles. "It's a bottomless pit."

"No. It just seems like it. We've cracked them open like an eggshell and they know we won't go away. They've got to get rid of us."

The desert lord scanned the hillside. His men lay in heaps by the oaks and furze bushes, the choppy grass turning rust-colored with blood. "They're close."

Thomas handed both rifles to Denethan, then loaded his own. His shoulder ached where the stock kicked with every firing. "One more volley and I'll be close enough to get in. From there, we're home free."

"I still think we should just drop a couple of vials down the air shaft—"

"No." Thomas checked his ammo belt. "I'm an executioner.

I kill when I'm told to, when it's part of a judgment, *but some of those people down there haven't done anything wrong.*"

Battlefield grime dimmed Denethan's golden beauty, as he looked down at Thomas, eyes narrowed. "You heard them as they died. We're less than dirt to them. *Mutants.* The only victory we can bring out of here is to do no less to them than they would do to us."

"We have an agreement. We need Stefan and Alma, and there may be others hidden below. Denethan, I've been inside the dean's quarters. It's wall to wall with books and more. I've seen the medical labs . . . maybe we can stop the eleven year plague. The doctor talked about longships that went into space and will return. Can it be true? Think of what we can regain! We can't destroy ourselves all over again."

Denethan grew silent, his thoughts hidden by his scale-patterned face. Behind them, where Lady sat loading other rifles, her face wrinkled in sudden concentration. "Thomas—I have her. I think I have her."

"Where?"

"I—I don't know." The rifle fell from her slack fingers. "Thomas! They're massing a suicide attack!"

Denethan sprang into action before Thomas could stop him.

The Protector stumbled to her feet. Blade caught her as she swayed. Her skin went chill with the effort of her summoning. Her teeth chattered and did not stop even when he draped his battered jacket over her shoulders.

"What's going to happen?" she whispered.

He looked unhappily over the battlefield, remembering past skirmishes, as Denethan brought his men into position. "A bloodbath," he said.

All he had to do was stay in one piece long enough to bring the four of them out of it alive.

He caught the sense of it the moment he spotted the rainbow of colors among the uniforms. Dropping to his knees along the wings, hoping to outflank the attack and slip inside, Thomas paused and yelled to Denethan. "Stop! They're civilians trying to draw our fire! Look for the khakis!"

If the desert lord heard him, he gave no sign. The *shoop* of rifles firing filled the air. Bolts and darts brought down the first wave of men, their fellows behind staggering over fallen bodies, their pale faces filled with determination to get to the mutants. He heard their cries, their shouts of hatred and knew that Denethan was probably right. There would be no quarter given by those from the Vaults. They fought against abominations, not fellow men.

A hole opened in the flank nearest him. It was now or never, for he saw the khaki colors massing in behind the civilians. Thomas got to his feet and made a dash for the Vault doors.

Denethan ran with him, and Thomas saw the colored vial in his hand even as he threw it.

"God, no," he cried, as the gemlike glass hurtled through the air. It smashed as Thomas pulled his shirt up over his neck and mouth, and threw himself to one side.

The toxic cloud dispersed almost immediately in the air. Inside, in the mouth of the vaults, bodies toppled like empty shells. Denethan clawed at his arm.

"Come on!"

Thomas threw off his hand, and got up, as angry as he'd ever been, but the desert lord was moving. He set his jaw and ran after him, leaping bodies that flies were already settling on. As they moved into the Vault, a khaki-uniformed troop faced them. An iron-jawed captain led them.

Remmick stared. "You!"

Thomas put his hands to his neck. "I'm a little hard to drown." He blurred Remmick's vision, to hinder his movements. Denethan gave him no chance to say anything further, as he jumped the two closest men, blade in hand.

Remmick blinked, pivoted and fled. Thomas would have gone after him, but he found himself with an empty rifle and very, very busy.

Alma caught up with Stefan in the stairwell. Her pulse pounded and she grew sick to her stomach, but she reached for him and held on.

"Don't go out there! Not yet!"

"Alma! What are you doing here? Let go of me."

She clung determinedly. "Not yet, please. Listen to them. . . ." Hoarse cries and shouts echoed down the stairwell. "They're not fighting up there, they're *dying*."

"I'm supposed to be with them!" Anger flashed in his blue eyes and he shook her off, roughly, as bootsteps echoed on the overhead rungs. Remmick jumped in front of them. The Vault captain's eyes lit in recognition.

He grabbed for Alma and pulled her to her feet even as she let out a protesting cry.

"It's you he wants. It's you he'll get, if he pulls out." Remmick looked to Stefan. "I need your help."

The blond youth hesitated, then nodded.

"I've got the doors repaired now—we can get them closed, but I need a strong pair of arms."

Stefan stood up taller. "I'm your man."

"All right. Come on." Remmick steered Alma in front of him, taking the stair rungs one at a time with Stefan leading the way.

Lady massaged her throbbing temples. She could hear everything, piercingly, even the sound of her own breathing and the blood rushing through her veins. The screams of the dead and the dying. The epitaphs, the curses, the hatred of the fighters. A man toppled at her feet. Her vision blurred, she could not tell if he was friend or foe. She brushed her hand over him, his wound stopped pumping blood and he lay quietly. Would he live? She had no way of telling. Her Talent drew her elsewhere—drew her as inexorably to Alma as she had summoned the girl to her side. She stared at the fighting ahead and knew she'd never make it—but she had to. She drew Thomas' jacket tightly about her, pinching it shut at her neck. It smelled of leather, the sea—and him. Her fingers slipped inside, snagging on one of those countless pockets, and ivoried bones slipped into her hand. Lady closed her fingers about them. Only the ghost road could take her where she wanted to go. Not understanding why she did it, Lady shrugged out of Blade's jacket, before ducking her head and invoking her path. The cries of the dead and dying fueled her way. She shuddered, rejected it, and fought for a new road. Heedless of the battle, she made her way to the steel vault doors.

The tide of khaki-clothed men forced them back and outside once more. Rifles emptied, knives came out of sheaths and blood flowed crimson. Thomas shrugged off his newest attacker and downed him with a sharp left foot to the jaw. On the follow-through, he spotted Denethan in serious trouble. A knife in the ribs eased the situation greatly and the lizard man finished the other two guardsmen with thrusts of his own.

"Pull back," Thomas said. "They're slaughtering us." He stood in the massive steel framework of the doorway. It began to shudder and sing while they stood upon the tracks. He tried to recover his focus to use his Talent, but there was little time for it. He was nearly drained. His hands and feet were better weapons than his mind.

"Shit!" Denethan leaped aside. "Get out of here!" He yelled to his remaining troops. The ones who could fled for freedom.

The Vaults began to close. Thomas felt a whisper pass him, a chill being, a ghost brushing his side. He started. The hair prickled on the back of his neck. Denethan grabbed him and towed him out, throwing him down behind a barrier of dead men.

"Cracked open like an egg, eh?"

He had no answer. The doors ground shut, tearing heads and limbs from bodies, crushing bone within its tracks. He shuddered to hear the noise. Then, two people wide, it stopped, unable to compress its fleshy barrier anymore.

Denethan looked at him, and raised an eyebrow. Thomas shook his head.

"Sir Thomas! I have a proposition for you!"

Remmick appeared in the doorway, just enough of him to present a tempting but difficult target. The captain looked about, searching for him. "You'll never get in."

"And you'll never get out," Denethan bellowed back.

"Every den has a bolt hole," the captain returned. "Don't be too sure of that. And you'll never have what you want."

"How can you possibly know what we want?" Thomas shouted. His hand went up automatically to his shuriken, then he swore quietly, for he still wore the uniform of the maintenance squad.

Remmick jerked, and a pale form filled the void of the doorway.

"That's Alma," Thomas said quickly.

Denethan yelled. "Hold your fire!" for the girl was completely exposed by Remmick's actions. The desert lord rolled to his left and began loading his rifle. "Damn his hide."

"To hell with the girl," Thomas lied. "We want revenge!"

Remmick twitched. The girl went to her knees amid a wash

of blood and gore. She began to cry. The captain reached out and tore her tunic from neck to navel.

"Take a look, Blade! She's unblemished! We already know she hadn't been contaminated by the plague! And her DNA's as pure as it gets nowadays. You want the human race back! You'll need a good little breeder like this! Put down your arms."

Denethan mentioned a physical impossibility and muttered, "If he's human, we don't need it." He got into firing position and looked at Thomas, bronze gaze narrowed. He sighed at the expression he read. "All right. I'll cover you." To his men, he ordered, "put down your arms."

"You're killing them!"

The desert lord smiled grimly. "They swore a blood oath to me—we to each other—and they'll die for it. They begged for the right to follow me here and die for it! We're not animals. That's what makes us human, eh? The will to live and die for one another? Now get going!" And he stood, rifle hidden behind a muscular leg. "All right, captain. No weapons."

Remmick looked suspicious. "Where's Blade?"

Thomas crawled on his stomach, slowly, painstaking, getting close enough to rush the guardsman. Denethan said, "We're the only ones left."

"Lizard man. I saw the Lord Protector when you rushed the door."

"Then he's probably in that gore you're standing ankle-deep in. But we'll take the girl."

Remmick's gaze flickered nervously over the area. "I heard his voice!" He started to pull Alma back inside as he yelled, "Stefan!"

The boy answered weakly. He tried to pull himself to his knees from under a pile of death. His blue uniform was charred and streaked with blood. With a cry of defiance, Alma turned on Remmick, beating and clawing at him, the shreds of her clothing about her waist, pale skin streaked with the blood of the dead. He clubbed her, once, and she collapsed with a groan over the tracks. The whining doors convulsed and began to shut again. Thomas was close enough now to smell the machinery burning.

The Lord Protector leaped. He caught Remmick by the collar. The captain responded, and Thomas felt fingers like steel crushing about his arms. He reached out with his power, his Intuition, and did not touch a mortal being. This . . . thing . . . was artificial.

The air lock and inner doors opened, filled with the dean's bulk. The man smiled at Thomas as the captain drove him to his knees. The black-robed man leaned over and picked Alma up, slinging her easily over his shoulder.

"Take him outside to finish him, Remmick. Then download. I don't want you functional if captured."

"Yes, sir."

The being holding Thomas with inhuman strength made no response as Thomas kicked him with all his might. The dean paused in the elevator, and laughed.

"You've no idea what you're dealing with," the Dean of the College Vaults said. "He's not even close to human." He was still laughing when the air lock doors shut him and Alma away.

Remmick dragged Thomas down. In his blurring vision, he saw Denethan grabbing Stefan, dragging him away from the massive pulleys. But the door still rolled on. The two wrestled, scuffling into Remmick, breaking loose the grip of one of his hands upon Thomas. Thomas tried to brace himself on the tracks as Remmick reached for him again.

The four of them fell into the narrow opening, squeezing between the doors. Denethan, with a cough and gasp, dragged Stefan out and clubbed him into submission. The desert lord then grabbed up a rifle and swung it across the back of Remmick's shoulders. Thomas felt a bone break as the guardsman continued to squeeze, carrying him across the ground like a sack of meal. There was a pause, and Denethan swung again, harder.

The plastiflesh shell of Remmick's face fell off. Thomas found his image reflected back at him from a smooth obsidian surface. There was no loosening of the grip around his throat. But he was gilled. His lungs were meant to hold air for ten or twelve minutes at a time. What he had to worry about was crushing, permanent damage. He thought of Denethan's mindstorm, and its crackling levin-bolts. Out of his thoughts, he conjured one. Fire danced on the obsidian surface, obscuring his reflection. The being, whatever it was, began to convulse with the power overload.

Denethan said, "I've got this one." He slipped his knife blade in the base of the captain's neck and backed off.

Sparks arced. The thing threw Thomas violently across the clearing, staggered about, and then collapsed onto the bloodied grass. Thomas hit the ground hard, and stayed down, panting, momentarily unable to see. He fought for breath.

"What was that?"

"An android. I've seen a few before in the desert labs. Never one powered up. Can you get up?" Denethan towered over Stefan's quiet form.

A siren cut into the sudden silence. A single, piercing note. Denethan was reaching down to help Thomas up. He froze. Klaxons shattered the noise of the battlefield.

They heard the muffled explosion. Indian Hill danced, quivering, as a massive wave rippled through the dirt and rock. Thomas staggered to his feet in disbelief.

Then someone shouted, "Avalanche! Run for it!" as the side of the mountain began to cave in.

Denethan scooped up the unconscious boy as Thomas began to hobble for his life.

"Lady!" Nowhere did he see her. "Lady!" He stumbled across his jacket on the ground, turned inside out, the pockets empty.

Gillander's bones were missing.

He remembered, then, the feeling of gooseflesh he'd had . . . like a ghost slipping past him.

She was trapped inside the exploding mountain. They'd learned the hard way that time could not protect them . . . weapons and death were just as real on the ghost road. His agony tore out of his bruised throat. "Lady!"

Denethan reared up beside him. "Sorry," he said, and swung.

The dust and smoke hung across what had been the entrance to the College Vaults like an impenetrable curtain when the ground stopped dancing. Denethan squatted next to Thomas. "Well," he said, "That's that. They'd rather blow themselves up than be tainted."

Thomas ached all over, but nothing hurt as badly as the knowledge he'd lost Lady. He said nothing.

Denethan moved past him, knife in hand, and put it to Stefan's throat. "Judging from past experience, this little bastard's no better than the rest."

Thomas kicked out, sent the knife spinning, and lay back, groaning, as broken ribs ground, and his right arm flopped lop-sidedly. The expression in Denethan's eyes let Thomas know he was very close to being killed as well.

"Leave him be," Thomas said, suddenly very tired.

"He's been taught like the rest of them."

"He grew up in my county. The short time he spent in their hands can't poison that."

Stefan moaned and thrashed on the ground. Denethan looked down. He then looked back to Thomas. "You'd better hope not. He's not human like us." He moved away.

Thomas rolled and got to his knees. The truce with the desert lord was ended. He was only as safe as he was strong. Denethan respected strength. Strength and survival.

He limped toward the mountain base, where dust still poured from above, like blue and gold smoke in the air. He didn't want to live without Lady. He'd looked inside himself and found that which wanted a home, a base, a pairing. He'd found a solution to the bittersweet loneliness that had plagued him at a wedding party a lifetime ago.

The air shivered. He could almost hear the despair of the dead. He saw a shadow among the settling motes. It grew stronger, coalescing.

It was a woman, short but feisty, her head held high as she carried another woman, smaller, more slender, in her arms.

Lady came walking out of the side of the mountain.

Chapter 31

"This means I get the pick of the litter."

Alma blushed, wrapped in a dress made of the gold-spun silken canopy Denethan had used for his tent. The gold brought out her coloring, peach toned, her dark brown hair still curled, but not short and gamine as it had been. She'd matured over these last weeks, Thomas thought. The young lady raised her chin and said softly, "Children don't come in litters," answering the big, scaled warrior. "But we will send our second son or daughter to you for fostering. I promise."

"Done." Denethan swung on Thomas. He clasped the man's shoulder none too gently. "I still stand by my offer. A dozen of my finest to go home with you."

Blade shook his head. "No. Not yet. But an ambassador in the spring will be welcome."

"Politics is a tougher battle than war."

"I know. But I'll have some help."

Lady sat on the cart seat next to him, holding the reins as two ponies stamped their eagerness to be off and away from the stench of funeral pyres. Denethan nodded. "Take care, my friend." He straightened in his saddle, made a sign, and his legion rode after him.

Lady adjusted Thomas' sling. "That one may come as ambassador himself."

"I'm expecting it," he answered. He leaned back on the cushions. "Let's take the long way home."

Stefan snorted. "Getting soft, old man."

Thomas looked over his shoulder at the back of the cart. "At least," he said icily, "I did not take all of my lumps in the head."

The boy blushed as rosily as his new bride.

Lady clucked and the cart jolted into movement. She caught Thomas staring at the debris of the hillside which had once contained the College Vaults. Those were ruins he'd have to come back and sift through, though not for a definition of humanity. He thought of medical equipment, books, and priceless paintings. Surely some of them would have survived in the deeper tunnels.

She sensed his uneasiness. "What is it?"

He made a diffident movement, cut short by the sling on his arm and the strapping about his ribs. "He's an old fox, the dean—and I never met a fox or gopher yet who didn't have a second hole." He grasped her hand. "Why didn't the blast touch you?"

"The Ghost Road's more than paranormal, it's elemental— keyed to the person who walks it. You're an executioner. You used death to fuel it. But you were dispassionate about it at first and the road could only drain you. It couldn't touch you until you made the lives you took personal. Then you were corrupted, adding to its energies. It could draw on you and wound you with ever increasing effectiveness. I, on the other hand—"

"You are a Healer."

"Exactly. I took up the bones and couldn't use them, not as you had—I was diametrically opposed to the flow. So I reached for life." She waved a hand over the hillside which was littered with scattered ruins as far as the eye could see into the haze. "For every death, there was a life born down there once. Then the Ghost Road was mine. Oh, it drained me, too, but it had much farther to go, the entire cycle from birth to death. So the blast couldn't reach me once I'd found Alma and taken her."

"Elemental. And my totems?"

"Oh, that's a mystery you're going to have to solve. But a worthwhile one. There's magic in you, Thomas."

He shook his head, then murmured, "Thank god you were able to summon the road."

She smiled prettily. "Oh, I had help. A crusty old soul who likes to give advice from behind your left ear. You'd call him a ghost. I'd call him a psychometric resonance." Lady considered him a moment before saying, "Lord Protector, you need to find a successor to the DWP, and your county lies waiting."

"I know. And thank god for Macaulay's *The Way Things Work*. We may have lost the rest of Charlie's papers, but that still survives." He leaned against her slightly. "Dying is easy. Staying alive is the hard part."

Her lips brushed his scarred brow. "And I've never known you to do something the easy way."

He smiled. "Got any lemon drops?" he asked, as they followed the long path home.

THE
LAST RECALL

PART I

Prologue, 2277 A.D.

Commander Sun Dakin pushed away from the observation window, his Asian heritage far outweighing the mix of others in his round face and almond eyes. He frowned as he looked at Commander Willem Marshall, his second officer. "We're closer than either *Magellan* or *Mayflower*," he said. "We ought to be able to spot it if there's anything out there."

The harsh, chaotic beauty of Jupiter and its moons framed his bowed body. Yet the swirling surface of Jupiter was serene compared to the worry churning inside the man.

Marshall squinted, staring past Dakin at the panorama, his own dark eyes creased in folds of dusky skin. He shook his head. "No platforms, nothing. There ought to be something by now, even if only observation satellites. Sun, what's happened?"

"I don't know." Dakin turned around again to watch as if his shrewd eyes could see what all his sensors failed to pick up. "We're not getting any radio chatter or even television waves. It's as if nothing were being broadcast. . . ."

The Earth they knew would not have been silent. The Earth they were coming home to should be alive with joyous noise, tracking them, beaconing them back. Sun Dakin's shoulders shrugged and he sighed quietly. He pivoted.

"Get the crew together. They should know what to expect. It'll be a long ride in until we're close enough to have any real idea what's happened, but they should know."

Marshall nodded. Then, "What about Dusty?"

"It's off her cycle, but go ahead and wake her. She's our se-

nior officer and should be in on this. I'll schedule the meeting
to include her."

The second officer nodded in answer and strode from the
observation deck. Sun faced Jupiter again, worry etched deeply
in his usually impassive face. Where were they? What had happened to NASA and JPL? Why were the skies empty? *Magellan* had first alerted him, and Sun knew that *Mayflower* was
anxious as well. He would have to consult with his fellow commanders before talking to the crew. *Magellan* had been suffering with minor equipment breakdown, pesky but consistent.
Sifuentes was tense and unhappy enough as it was. Unconsciously, Dakin rubbed his duty shirt sleeve, where the embossed badge read *Challenger II*. After two hundred and fifty
years, the longships were coming home . . . to what?

"Gemma. Gemma."

She had known she was waking when she began dreaming,
but the dreams were so sweet and welcome after the bitter dark
nothingness of hibernation sleep that she was reluctant to
awaken further. She clung to her wispy fantasies long after she
should have, until the voice in her ear became harshly determined.

"Gemma, wake up."

She blinked, thinking that this was serious stuff because
everyone who knew her called her Dusty, for the auburn freckles patterning her face and arms. The thought struck her fleetingly that it might be her sister who had never had a nickname
for her unless it be *twin*, and she remembered that she hadn't
heard that inner voice of her Earthbound other self in more than
two hundred years. *Gemini experiment failed*, Dusty thought
poignantly, and yawned. Her eyelids fluttered as she struggled
to awaken.

She began to shudder and grasped blindly for the heated
blankets they were dropping over her. "It's . . . it's early," she
got out through clenched teeth and tried to look up through
gummed eyelids.

"We've got a problem, Dusty. Commander Dakin wants to
talk to everyone. We'll get you back on cycle when we put you
back down." Willem Marshall's rich, calming voice was almost
as warming as the blankets he tucked into place. There was a
stinging prick as he put the IV in place.

He looked down at the fresh face of a young lady, auburn hair a mass of curls pillowing her head. The expressive gray eyes, when open and clear, would fairly dance with both intelligence and mischief. It was hard to believe Gemma Barlowe was the only original crew member of the longships still alive. But then, her sole duty on board *Challenger* had been to sleep, waken, attempt to communicate telepathically with her twin Lisa and then return to long-term hibernation again. Dusty, of course, had done with more whenever possible. . . . Marshall could not think of a more unlikely candidate to spend decades in slothful sleep. They all took advantage of hibernation to some degree although this was a mission designed to cover several generations, but it had been Gemma's fate via genetic engineering to live and age only one month every two years. He preferred to age slowly and gracefully rather than be faced with the shock of waking to the unknown.

He really did not want to be there, leaning over the coffin-like crèche when she awoke, to see the shock in her eyes, however quickly masked, when she realized how he'd aged. She would laugh and make light of his deepening wrinkles and the sprinkling of gray hair, and then she would duck her face away. She'd seen his father age and die away and his father's father before him. To catch Dusty unaware before she could drop that careful masking expression into place was to see his death in her eyes.

Her eyelids fluttered again as her body stopped its shock-induced trembling and began to warm. She reached up. Instinctively he took her hand, pressed it close between his pink palms to warm it.

"It must be important," she finally got out, "if you're waking me up."

"It is."

"How close are we to home?"

"About eight years out. Want to see Jupiter?"

"I've seen it," she said with a low laugh. Her gray eyes fluttered open, stayed open this time, studying him. "What's wrong?"

"We don't know . . . yet."

Her eyes sparked. "You're going gray, Willem."

"Tell me about it." He chafed her hand lightly.

Dusty gave a last little shudder. Her teeth chattered as she said, "You look more like your grandfather every time I wake."

He wondered briefly if she'd ever loved his grandfather. The thought took him aback, rendering him temporarily speechless. He lost his grip on her hand.

Dusty sat up, pushing aside the heated blankets. Her crew shirt and trousers were wrinkled and she frowned, looking down at them. Someone had dressed her while she slept this last cycle. She'd have annoying bruises where the cloth had creased into her flesh. She reached up and fluffed her thick auburn hair.

Marshall got hold of himself and passed her a brush. She ran it through quickly, but the thick ringlets her hair naturally grew in did not get much tidier.

"What do I have time for?"

Willem consulted his watch. "Some dinner, a shower, that's about it."

"Okay." She stood up, swayed, caught the metal railing of the crèche foot and steadied. "I'll be there in thirty minutes, Commander," she told him as she unhooked her IV expertly.

Marshall bowed his head and left her.

Both simulcast screens were activated when Dusty entered the conference room. Already apprehensive, seeing the images of the crews filling the conference rooms of *Mayflower* and the *Maggie*, as they called her, was not reassuring. She eased herself down next to Peg Davies, the botanist, who, like Dusty, seemed compelled to sit close to the door, as if wanting to flee.

Davies had cruised into comfortable middle age since the last time Dusty had been awake. Her broad plain face had begun to show ample wrinkles and she'd let her skin get weathered looking, a tan achieved only by working long hours in the solars. She made a face as if reading Gemma's thoughts. "Don't say it, girl. I know. These crow's-feet weren't here last time we spoke." She laid a callused hand over Dusty's. "It doesn't look good. Rumor is there's no traffic."

"Traffic?" Dusty blinked. She had not come on board because of doctoral-training or any particular expertise except for the fact that she and her twin sister had proven telepathic abilities, which had led to the genetic work they'd done on her during her childhood. "You mean we're not hearing anything?"

"That's the rumor."

Dusty sat there motionless, stunned. The implication of the botanist's statement iced through her. She looked around the conference table. No one met her eyes. She recognized adults who had been teens the last time she awoke. She looked at her hands, fingers interwoven tightly. She felt alone with her fear. Even if they had been forgotten, there should have been something, some stray signal they could have picked up.

Peg patted her hands again as Commander Sun Dakin moved to the podium and, in eerie imitation, the other two commanders did the same. Commander Heredia of the *Mayflower* stood, a Hispanic beauty who looked, even to Dusty, too young for the job she held. The *Magellan* had gone democratic some hundred years ago, its chief officer elected rather than being born to the post. Commander Reichert was a plain, squat thick man with heavy eyebrows that slanted down as though he carried the weight of a world on them—and it was sliding off.

Dusty felt a moment of disorientation as Sun spoke and she listened for the others, then realized that, although they spoke, the sound was not being transmitted. It didn't matter. From the disbelieving looks on the faces of the other crew members, it was obvious Peg's rumor was being validated from ship to ship.

". . . no conclusions can be reached yet, however human it is to try to do so. We're going to boost our signal and see if the recall beacon responds, but it'll be years before we know the truth. We've an eight-year ride inward until we get close enough for our sensors to be accurate, you all know that. Until then, this is all idle speculation and not worthy of us as mission members." Sun looked relatively serene about the prospect of the end of life as they had been taught to remember it on Earth. Dusty wondered how long he had spent meditating in his cabin to achieve the calmness he exhibited now.

"Bullshit," Warwick said, as he swung his legs over the chair and leaned over the high back, his chin on his forearm. Her attention swung to him and stayed, held by the compulsion to measure the years that had gone by since she'd last seen the handsome officer. "And you know it is."

Sun looked steadily at him also, a gleam in his almond eyes. Then, "You're probably right. But what else can we do? We'll be networking with the *Maggie* and the *Mayflower* in a minute."

Warwick held his peace, hazel eyes narrowed under a brow gone salt-and-pepper. Dusty hardly recognized him. He couldn't be that old—what, thirty-nine or so?—but seemed to have hit that peak just before a quick slide into middle age. She looked away quickly before he caught her watching him.

Dakin reached out, keying the sound open on the simulcast screens. The crews of the other two ships were taking it no better than they, she thought, although everyone on the *Challenger* seemed calmer. Crews mirroring their commanders?

Maggie was not in sight although *Mayflower* could just be glimpsed on the horizon and there was a little interference in the signal. Heredia tossed her mane of thick, brown hair off her shoulders. "Well, Commander? Any suggestions?"

"Send a probe out," Warfield bellowed, overriding Dakin's answer. Sun looked dismayed, then contemplative at the interruption. He gazed at Heredia's and Reichert's images.

"That's not a bad idea," he said. "We've no capability here, our probes have all been spent. Reichert, you should have a probe or two left unless I'm mistaken."

Reichert's brows sagged even further. He shook his head. "We're in no condition to be launching."

"This is not a whimsical thing we are asking," Heredia said. Her voice retained the Hispanic accent of her parentage. "It's our best way to know what happened."

"And what would you do then? Turn around and go back? It doesn't matter what meets us at the end of this run, we've got no other destination."

There were thousands of miles between them, and yet Dusty caught the distinct interplay of emotion between these two. What had gone on while she slept? She knew the M&Ms had docked briefly while effecting repairs on the *Magellan*.

Heredia's tongue brushed her lips ever so lightly. She seemed unaware of the camera close-up. "We have options," she said. "Returning is one of them. Without a homing beacon in active recall, I think we should be reviewing our options."

Reichert's jaw tightened. He looked full face at Sun. "Commander, I don't want to be the bad guy here, but I don't have the capability of putting out a probe. We're losing water."

Peg Davies' gasp near Dusty's ear echoed those being broadcast. Sun lost his expressionless mask.

"How bad is it?"

"Not tremendously bad, but consistent. Maybe half a gallon a day. We can't find the leak."

Dusty looked at the botanist. The older woman looked grim. "What's happening?"

"It's a closed ecosystem. We can't replace that water if it's boiled out. It could be a seam or rupture losing it. Eventually it comes down to water rationing or some such . . . and if the leak continues," Peg halted. She didn't have to finish her sentence.

Dusty looked back to the screens. No one on any of the three ships remembered the fourth ship which had started the mission with them, the *Gorbachev*. The *Gorby* had not made it past sixty years before it had slowly, lumberingly, agonizingly, gone to pieces, like a staggering aged beast. She wondered if *Magellan* could make it home.

"Then," Sun said, "there is little we can do until we're within range for our normal sensors."

"Eight years," said Reichert, "to confirm what we already suspect."

Heredia said nothing, her crew silent at her back. Her eyes blazed a challenge at them.

No one answered.

It struck Dusty suddenly that perhaps the Gemini experiment hadn't been a failure. She and her sister had talked for the first few decades, each sleeping and waking on a delicately timed cycle before the silence. It had been thought that distance was what tore them apart.

Dusty stood. "Wake me," she said. "When we're ready."

She did not go back down to sleep immediately, her system was not geared for it. She helped Peg with the solars, setting out vegetable beds, splicing new varieties together and looking over seedlings generated from cuttings that had never seen Earth. She ran her fingers over the purple furred tops of a vegetable similar to what her mother had called mustard greens and she had never liked. Her waking hours were precious to her and she did not like to waste them. Even eating a purple mustard green could be an adventure.

She spent many morning hours in the ship nursery, telling the stories and songs of her youth, and playing with children who would be teens when she woke again. Dusty was afraid they would not remember her if she did not play with them now.

Warfield, whom she had wanted as a lover, had been just such a youngster not too awfully long ago.

She tried not to think that the Earth had gone peculiarly quiet, though she and Peg talked about it from time to time. Peg was for war, her faith in the ability of men to govern themselves peacefully gone skeptic. "They can't even manage a marriage," she said, hand troweling a bed of newly planted cuttings. "Although . . . it could be pollution. They could have suffocated in their own refuse."

"But we were trying. . . ." Dusty countered. She trailed off. They, to Peg, and we, to her. The Earth she knew was not so far off, in either her daily thoughts or her dreams. To the other crew members, it was a thrice-told tale, handed down through generations.

Peg looked crisply at her. "We'll know soon enough," she said and stabbed some more at the vegetable bed.

Dusty fell silent and remained that way, troweling as much through her thoughts and memories as through the garden bed.

When it came time for her to sleep again, her last conscious image was that of the *Maggie*, and the *Mayflower*, as she'd seen them from the observation deck, cruising closer on the horizon as the three ships drew together for the ride in.

Chapter 1

"The best enemy is a dead one."
—Sir Thomas Blade, 2280

September, 2285

Santa Ana winds had stripped the haze from Saddleback Mountain, leaving its hump-shouldered profile easily seen from the courtroom among the city ruins. It whistled through rusting pillars where concrete had crumbled from these metal skeletons and made dust devils in what passed for roads. Unfortunately, the same dry winds had also stripped the roof from the courthouse and while repairs were being made, the court session was being held outdoors, a makeshift resemblance to civilization.

Civilization was not what it had been in the Seven Counties, even forgetting the plague and the disasters that had torn the world apart. Those days had been survived. Those who had done the surviving were not quite the same as the humans responsible for civilization either, but they tried.

It seemed to Sir Thomas Blade as he sat among the remnants that the effort was sometimes not worth the price. But he was tired today, the justice circuit over the summer one of the longest he would ride as a Protector, and he felt that tiredness like ice settling into his bones.

A rough-hewn platform had been cobbled together for the judge's bench and the witness stand, faced immediately by the defendant and his attorney and the prosecutor, backed by rows of chairs for onlookers. The horse-line had been tethered downwind, but occasional gusts wafted its pungent aroma across the crowd. Bicycles in the racks behind the platform glinted the late afternoon sun in their eyes. The winds had died down, leaving only the dry, hot day behind them, good enough weather for mid-September. Blade shifted in his chair and eyed the sky above. Faded out blue, no clouds, no sign of the rain they needed. Orange County would be a dust bowl if the winds continued and the rains did not come. Never mind the deceptive mildness of Indian summer.

He adjusted a long, silken white scarf about his neck. The wind gave him sore throats, his gill membranes outraged by the desertlike air. As soon as the trial was over, he was heading for a tall, cold beer with the judge. Judge Henry Teal would not drink with just anyone, but Blade was the Lord Protector of Orange County, and the executioner.

Blade pulled at his scarf again as excited murmurs rose from the audience. The jury panel shuffled in from the courthouse basement where they had been sequestered and Thomas knew from the looks on their faces what the verdict was. The nester crouching defiantly in his chair knew, too. He was an unkempt mass of hair and dirt and sores and did not look up when his attorney touched his shoulder to get his attention.

Thomas sat with his boots hiked up on the rung of the chair in front of him—he was surrounded by empty chairs, people who normally would not mind rubbing shoulders with him shunned him now—because they knew why he was attending the trial and what was expected of him. The trial's verdict was a foregone conclusion. No renegade nester could poison water wells and expect to walk away.

The shirt-sleeved crowd consisted mostly of farmers and ranchers. He saw a few craftsmen among the onlookers, but not many. The spectacle of a murder trial whose outcome was certain was not enough to pull them away from their trade. The farmers were here only because the wind had kept them from their labors anyway and they wanted the satisfaction of seeing a nester pulled down.

Judge Teal listened as the jury foreman talked quietly to him, then nodded. He tapped his gavel down.

"Get the defendant up to hear the verdict."

That was not how the proceedings usually went, but the nester had been far from cooperative. His attorney now dragged him to his feet and onto the platform in front of the judge's bench.

Teal stood as well. He was an aged, once eloquent man, dressed immaculately despite the warmth of the day. White and silver strands of hair were far sparser than they had been, and his face was no softer or paler than that of any of the men in his audience who earned their living out of doors. He had an eye that wandered a bit off track, making it hard to look him in the face from time to time. He looked sternly at the nester now and Blade wondered what the judge saw in this defendant who barely resembled anything human.

He leaned forward across the chair back, not noticing his hands had gone white-knuckled as he gripped it and listened to what Judge Teal said.

"It is my duty, as judge appointed to this court of the survivors of Orange County in the year 2285, to render the verdict as given me by a jury of your peers. John Doe, you stand accused of one count of murder and three hundred and twenty-six counts of attempted murder and one count of water well poisoning. The jury has found you guilty on all counts. Accordingly, I sentence you to death and order that sentence to be speedily carried out."

The nester knocked his attorney aside and crouched in his shackles. Rifles came up all over the outdoor yard and Blade heard the click of vials being tapped into barrels.

Judge Teal pointed his gavel at the nester. "I guarantee you'll find Sir Thomas an easier way to go. By the authority vested in me, I hereby remand you to his care."

With a sigh, Blade got to his feet. A slight breeze ruffled his thinning yellow-gold hair and tugged at his scarf. His leather jacket creaked as he moved forward. Dust motes caught in the wind's stirring swirled away from his shoulders like flecks of diamonds as the sun streaked slantwise across the yard. Rifles wavered, then lowered as he approached the nester.

John Doe was not his name, of course. He'd refused to give them his name and Blade eyed his face, searching for landmarks of familiarity, cheekbones, the curve of his ears, gill-marks, anything that might tell him what family the nester had come from originally. In the deep leathery creases of his forehead, Blade saw the telltale scars of what had once been a third eye, an abomination even the nesters had obliterated. Lines tightened about the nester's mouth. He was so weather-beaten Blade could not tell if the man were older or younger than his own twenty-eight years. Bruises that had once been angry blue-black were faded to yellow and there were knobs on his arms where his bones must have healed. He'd taken quite a beating. Blade was a little surprised the man had made it to a trial.

"Just tell me," Blade said softly, his voice pitched to carry no farther than the two of them, "if you did it."

The nester's eyes shifted to him. There was a quiet dignity in them. *Still water runs deep,* Thomas thought. "I don't want to die," the nester said.

"No one does." He nodded to Judge Teal. "But that's the sentence for murder and attempted murder by water poisoning."

The nester's attention flicked off. He looked back, sullen and tired. "I ain't told them nothing and won't tell you."

Blade smiled gently. Of course, the man told him, not verbally, but he Read him and knew the truth for himself. Within the nester's tumbling thoughts was the clear image of him butchering a sheep and then throwing it down the well, with full intent to foul that water. He *had* poisoned the well. As foregone as the trial's verdict had been, it had also been correct. The knowledge steeled Blade for what he had to do.

The nester went rigid then, as if he'd felt Blade inside his thoughts. He shook. Dust flew from his ragged, ill-made clothes.

"You chose this end," Blade told him. He stretched out his hand.

Tears of fury brimmed in the man's eyes but he did not flinch away. His stare bored into Blade. "Your eyes," the nester spat. "Your truth."

Blade stunned him with a chop of his hand and as the man sagged to his knees, the Protector pulled his garrote and finished him off. The man was strong. The cords on his neck stood out as the wire cut deeply, but he did not struggle. Blade did not let up until he was certain the prisoner was dead. He let go and the nester's limp form toppled to the wooden platform. He had forgotten there was an audience and felt a faint blush of embarrassment heat his face as he looked up to see them watching. His gills stirred beneath the scarf.

Someone murmured, "Coldhearted son of a bitch." He did not see who.

With a collective sigh, the crowd began to disperse. Bailiffs unwound the garrote from the nester's throat, coiled it, and handed it back to Blade as they took the body away.

Teal dropped a callused hand to his shoulder. "Come on, Thomas. The women are waiting for us. Wouldn't want the beer to get warm. I'd like to talk to you about the election before you finish your circuit."

Blade pulled himself away from the sight of the nester's heels dragging a groove into the dirt and grass as the body was hauled away. Remorse he shouldn't have felt lanced through him. *Your eyes, your truth.* To hell with it. The truth was the truth . . . wasn't it?

Another judge took the platform and gavel as a bailiff called for Small Claims Court to convene. Their job was done here. Teal never looked back.

He matched Teal's lanky stride as they crossed the court-house lawn. Teal snapped his fingers and one of the bailiffs caught up with them.

"Get Sir Thomas' horse. He'll be staying with me and my wife this evening."

That meant at least a hot bath and decent meal. "What is this going to cost me?" he said warily.

Teal stopped in the road and gave him a look, both eyes examining him. "Now, Thomas. Don't go balky on me. Lady's waiting up at the house."

The judge's distinctive gaze was reminiscent of that of Lady Nolan, but her eyes were cast, one blue, one brown, and at the mention of her name, he keenly felt the lack of her company. They had not managed to cross paths in the past three months, but two of her letters had caught up with him.

Something in his expression must have prompted the judge because Teal said, "You know I have a reputation as a hanging judge, but I've also been vested with the power to marry."

Thomas shook his head and surged back into motion again. Traffic on the road began to catch up with them as the crowd dispersed. "There's more to it than that, Henry. We're both Protectors and can't leave our counties without an overseer."

"She's gone now. And so are you."

"That's different. We're riding circuits now and you know it."

Henry made a noncommittal noise at the back of his throat as a chrome-bumpered Chrysler carriage pulled by a high stepping mule team edged around them. He waited until the carriage drew past before saying, "Neither of you is getting any younger."

And that was the crux of it, of course, Teal cutting right to the bone. Lady did not have the time to wait for him to reconcile his jumbled feelings about their relationship. Blade creased a smile across his lean face. "I'll keep that in mind."

"Do that," Teal said crisply. He hailed the driver of a flatbed sledge. "Zaldava—give us a lift, will you?"

The judge's home was near the Santa Ana riverbed, which occasionally had water in it, and now served mainly as a reminder of the edge they all lived on. It held wild bamboo and a line of pampas grass, the stately plumes wavering in the wind. There was still water there, but it had gone underground, leaving behind these green and brown tracks. Blade's palms itched. He could find the water if he had to, but it wasn't necessary. The judge's home drew off the Glassel basin reservoir and was under the jurisdiction of the Director of Water and Power. Clean water *was* power.

The judge's house, and a cordon of others, were remnants of another age, not large but spacious and convenient, built along the corridor of Santiago Park where etched boulders lined the errant river's bed. Lawns of green ran down to the park and became part of the wilderness where dense trees held back the sun. Blade had been there before, though not often. The houses that remained standing were built of stucco and stone, their yards sprawling across the broken foundations of other homes that had not withstood the ravages of time. The monied and important lived here. If he stayed until morning, he might see deer grazing on the short stalks of green and brown grass that had survived the impossible summer. Whether he stayed until morning or not did not depend on Judge Teal, but on Lady.

The dinner party had already begun when the sledge driver dropped them off. The sounds of conversation and laughter drifted over the terraced lawns. Blade gave the judge a hand down.

"You're not an easy man to talk to," said Teal, who'd hardly spoken at all during the ride.

Blade flipped the edge of his scarf back. "That all depends on what you have to say. But if you've invited me here tonight to draft me to fill the position of DWP, our conversation is already over, Henry. Charles Warden was my patron and my best friend, but I have absolutely no desire to follow in his footsteps."

"The massacre left us little in the way of candidates."

Silence fell after the judge's remark. The massacre of the Director of Water and Power and his family and most of his friends and fellow leaders of the Seven Counties during a massive wedding celebration nearly two years ago had left a large hole in their survival plan. Blade had done what he could to avenge Charles, but he knew he could never replace him.

"There's always Art Bartholomew," Thomas answered, looking up the walkway.

"We want a Director, not a dictator." The judge dusted himself off before shanking it up the walk. "When you get a little older, my boy, you'll learn that politics is a necessary evil, a system to get things done." He pointed up to the side of the house, where paper lanterns hung glowing in the purpling shade. "You'll want a bath first, of course."

His jeans creaked with trail dirt. He gave a wry bow.

Teal said, "I'll send someone up to scrub your back," and made his way to a doorway which suddenly flooded golden-yellow light upon the dusk as his wife came out to greet him.

In the still-warm late summer day, Thomas felt a shiver down his back. He shrugged it off as he trudged down the side lane to the public bathhouse. The privileged warrens of the county seat were a far cry from the wolfrat infested ruins of In-City, but they were nonetheless dangerous, he told himself. Only here it would be your neighbor who gutted you. A man without influence, or on the wrong side of it, would be dealt with mercilessly.

Death would be as certain, if not as quick.

He checked his weaponry before peeling off his trail clothes and sliding into the four-man tub of warm water. Tapers lit the bathhouse. Nighttime had fallen deeply here while dusk still held outside. The rock decking was nearly as warm as the water, thanks to the fires banked below. He sighed and let tense muscles give way to the cleansing warmth as he stared into the shadows and tried not to think of ambushes. There was a clean caftan hanging on a brass hook by the door which he supposed would do as well as anything until he could find out where the judge had had his mount stabled. The wide sleeves gave him the advantage of hiding anything he wanted to, although he reminded himself this was a dinner party among the civilized and he should be lightly armed to be suitable.

He ducked under the water and came up in a cloud of steam, gills flared in exhilaration. Droplets ran in a stream off his forehead and though his eyes hadn't quite focused yet, he knew he was no longer alone. A slight draft touched the back of his neck and evaporated as quickly as someone entered the bathhouse. From the direction of the shadowed corner, the water level climbed.

"The judge is sending someone up," he said. "It's going to be very crowded here in a minute."

The hand slid across his thigh muscles. "No, it won't," she said softly. "Because she'll be dead."

Blade shook his head. "Temper, temper." He put his arm out and gathered Lady's curves next to his leanness. "God, I missed you."

For a long couple of minutes, she told him how she missed him as well, without words. Then he answered her, and then they told each other. Water splashed and sizzled upon the rock decking.

She was scrubbing his back before she said anything of consequence, and then it was a flat, "You're a son of a bitch, you know."

Thomas stopped relaxing under the ministrations of her hands, but she did not let him turn around. "I spent a couple of weeks healing that man."

Baffled, "What man?"

"The one you throttled today."

"The nester?" Thomas closed his eyes in quick reflex. Yes, the mottled bruises, the knots in his arms. . . .

"They beat him to a pulp before they brought him in for trial."

"Lady. What do you expect . . . he poisoned a well."

"And you believed that?"

Thomas turned about in the tub and caught her wrists. Water had darkened her ash brown hair, and pinked her fair skin, but had not thawed the icy gleam in her blue eye. "I Read him," he said. "I may be an executioner, but I have never carried out a sentence unless I have Read that the verdict is true."

She had been riding circuit, like he had, for three months,

but she would never carry his leanness. She was all curves, and she'd worn a straw hat to protect her skin, so it was only freckled from the sun, not burned and tanned like his. He would never be able to feel the ribs of her rib cage under normal circumstances nor would he want to. But he could feel the strength and determination in the muscles of her wrists. He could also feel her anger in her pulse. He wanted to say to her, *don't try to change me. I don't try to change you,* but did not. It was not exactly true, anyway.

Her brown eye, warm and deep, brimmed with unshed emotion. "I worked very hard," she said, "to save him."

"I wasn't the judge or jury," Thomas returned, letting go of her wrists.

She sank into the far end of the tub, just keeping her chin above water. "I know. I know. If only it hadn't been water."

"Or if only he hadn't stuck around to be caught. They tried him as a John Doe—he ever tell you his name?"

She shook her head. One graceful, dimpled hand swept back her hair from her temple. "Did you think he would? The first day he was fully conscious, he spat in my face. He didn't have a chance and he knew it."

"Because he did it," Thomas said flatly.

She gave him a measuring look. This was an old argument between them. He killed, she healed. He could not reconcile the differences between their chosen vocations. It was a chasm that separated them, that kept him from asking her to marry him for life—they would destroy each other, he feared, if she said yes and it would destroy him if she said no. At least now they could still talk. Like partners in an elusively patterned dance, they faced each other at times, spun away at others and occasionally embraced intimately. He had missed her terribly these last few weeks of summer. He stood in the hot tub, water cascading down his flanks and reached for a bag of scrubbing sand. "I got your letters," he told her as he sat back in the water. "What didn't you put in them?"

Worry crossed her face. "Stefan is talking about leaving Alma."

"What?"

She nodded. "He can't get her pregnant."

"Who says?"

She splashed a hand of water at him. "The fact is self-evident."

Thomas paused in washing himself. "They're both young. He's just embarrassed. Talk him out of it."

"I will, but . . . I was hoping for some help from you."

"You want me to get her pregnant? Sorry . . . the gills would show." And Thomas smiled as Lady blushed at his small joke. Russian born and bred Stefan and quiet Alma were the hope of the Seven Counties—as genetically pure as any generation had ever been since the disasters. Charles Warden, his family, and many others had died to protect and give those two a chance to bring about a new future. The wedding of his daughter Jennifer had been held as a decoy for the departure of Stefan and Alma into what should have been the hands of allies.

Although Charles was his closest friend, the DWP had not lived long enough to tell Blade the extent of the plans that had gone so terribly wrong. The elitist colony known as the College Vaults was to have taken in Stefan and Alma, to protect them against the rigors of survival aboveground, the eleven year plague, and the warring mutants. But it appeared the secretive colony had been an even more dangerous enemy than any Charles could have feared. A man known to him only as the dean looked upon all the survivors of the outside as genetic aberrations and less than human. He had ordered a massacre to cover his association with them and his taking of Stefan and Alma and to throw blame elsewhere. Blade had done what he could—his actions and those of others had cracked the College Vaults open like a rotten egg, but he would never know for sure whether he had destroyed the man who had ordered the massacre nor had he been able to find out if the dean had other allies hidden within the Seven Counties. He scrubbed his hands vigorously as if the action could cleanse his mind of the memory. His voice softened. "Is there any reason why they can't have children?"

"I could use better lab equipment to be sure, but no, I haven't found any. She's awfully young—just turned fifteen. I think all they need is time and confidence."

"Then I'll do what I can with Stefan." He extended his hand. "Let me get your back."

She neared and turned. He let out a whistle. "This back is really dirty. As a matter of fact, it's probably the dirtiest back I've ever—" Lady grabbed his ankles and pulled him under, bathwater filling his mouth and drowning out the last of his words. As Thomas came up sputtering, she shot him a look and muttered darkly, "At least you know no one else has been bathing with me."

Later, she lay in his arms and they both half-floated in the water which had begun to cool slightly. Thomas said gently, because the shell of her ear was next to his mouth, "I'll go get the fire boy."

Lady shook her head. "No. Our hosts are expecting us and we've been too long already."

"They'll understand."

She stood up, diamonds running from her skin in the candlelight. "You won't give them another choice," she said wryly. She reached for the toweling. "Art Bartholomew's here."

"I thought he might be." Thomas' lip curled a little. He disliked the warty man immensely and it wasn't because of his skin condition. The man was covetous. "He's always where he shouldn't be and not where he should."

Lady watched him closely. He could not read the expression in her shadow-darkened eyes. "I thought you gave up trying to tie him to the massacre."

Thomas paused, rinsing his hair. "Reluctantly. I can't find anyone to say anything against him. He's a hero for taking the kids out of there, coincidentally or not, and I can't prove it wasn't." Bartholomew had been at the wedding, politicking and criticizing the DWP for all he'd been worth . . . should have been there waiting for his own death, but instead had taken the orphaned wards that Charlie kept housed and schooled at the compound out for a mapping expedition. Thomas couldn't begrudge the outing. It had saved many lives which the future of the Seven Counties depended upon. But what had motivated Bartholomew to leave at such a fortuitous time? He had never shown interest in the children before, or in mapping either. He reached for a second towel. "I'll be civil."

"You'll have to be. Art is here campaigning openly for the election—"

"Already? We're talking next spring—"

"Shush," she said, brushing his lips with hers. "And listen. He's lining up as much support as he can get. Oppose him too vehemently and you'll fall right into the judge's hands. He'll draft you to run against Bartholomew."

Thomas suppressed a shudder. "I've already told him I wasn't interested."

"That doesn't matter. You'd do it if the Seven Counties told you they needed you—and Teal is counting on that."

"Then I'm just delaying the inevitable."

She smiled as she began to slip on fresh undergarments and a dress she had left hanging in the corner. "Maybe. Maybe not. You're a good man, but we both know you're not qualified to be the DWP."

"Thank you."

"You're welcome. Do this hook, will you?" She bent her head to one side and lifted her curtain of damp hair away from the nape of her neck.

Now that she was fully clothed and he half, the exposure he faced seemed suddenly erotic. He leaned forward and kissed her softly, trailing his open mouth along her fragrant skin up the curve of her neck.

"Again, Thomas?" she murmured, "I take that back. You're not a good man—you're a great one." She slipped about in his arms, pulled up the skirts of her dress and kicked aside her panties. She tugged the toweling off his hips.

"If drafted, I will not run," Thomas protested. "If elected, I will not serve."

"Oh, shut up," Lady answered. "You're not being drafted. You're being seduced."

Chapter 2

Lady had brought his saddlebags to the bathhouse, so he dressed in clean shirt and trousers, dispersing his various weaponry about his body as he was used to doing. She tactfully did not watch him, as indisposed as he was to begin their argument over again. She wore weapons as well.

The smell of the open pit barbecue drifted through the evening air as paper lanterns bobbed and swung about on bamboo poles to the side and rear of the judge's house. Thomas' stomach told him it had been a long time since early morning rations on the trail. Yet, hungry as he was, he would have preferred to be back in the open, alone with Lady beside a campfire. The sound of many voices, laughing and arguing, flowed over them.

His stride hesitated on the stone-circle pathway and Lady tugged at his elbow.

"Don't go gun-shy on me, Thomas," she said softly.

It was difficult for him to pinpoint his emotions. Reluctance filled him, that he knew. But why? He liked a celebration as well as the next man—he liked a recess from the rigors of everyday life. He could pay for it with banter and innuendo as well as the next man. But not tonight. His soul felt selfish tonight.

"On nights like this, it's hard to believe Charlie's gone," Lady said. Her hand tightened on his arm. "Or that these meetings aren't being held on the peninsula, with Veronica orchestrating them. It's like the whole center of the counties has shifted . . . is wandering, looking for a new home."

Her words tightened the ball in his chest. She felt something, too. With Lady close at his side, they stepped into the wash of light and sound and smell.

A short, stumpy man with his back to them was gesticulating to emphasize his words. Hairy warts pushed aside and interrupted the strands of his hair so he was not difficult to recognize from the back, nor was his strident voice. "Rice, I ask you," he boomed. "In waterstarved country such as ours, we're raising *rice*. Think of the water consumption—the waste!"

"Now, Art," a woman next to him said. She was dusky skinned, older, elegantly coiffed, Governor Irlene. "The basin we irrigate from is for flood control. We have no one living in that area—the water would be wasted if we didn't use it for irrigation."

"But rice," Bartholomew said testily.

"It's an important grain," the governor stood her ground. "And you're right, the water usage may be to excess and we may grow other crops there in the future. But it's worth a try."

A bent, leather lean man, added, "Better than letting the nesters bleed it off."

Thomas recognized one of the ranchers from the trial. He did not wait to hear Bartholomew's response to that but flanked the group and headed for Teal. "He owes me a beer," he told Lady.

She unwrapped her hand from his arm. "I'll catch up with you later. I see one of my patients." She drifted from his side, a graceful cloud of blue among the purples of the night. She bowed her head to pass under an arbor of wisteria and away from his immediate vision.

"Sir Thomas! There you are," Teal called. He sat in a wooden patio chair, his long thin legs crossed, a brown long-necked bottle in his left hand as he beckoned with his right. He'd not changed his suit, but his shirt was open at the neck. His wife sat next to him, a younger woman, ash-silver hair arranged in naturally curly ringlets. Her face was vibrant, blue eyes fixed on Thomas. She didn't miss much and said something briefly to Teal before she got up, vacating the chair for Thomas. She followed Lady under the arbor and out of sight before he could greet her.

Teal fished a beer out of a bucket of cold water and handed it to him. Thomas pulled the top off as he sat down. The beer went down cool, setting off taste buds as it went. "That side of beef is about ready. You've got good timing."

"And you've got excellent taste in back washers." Thomas took another long pull. There was a very slight nick in the lip of the bottle. He worried his tongue around it. The bottles were used over and over again, each one a scarred warrior of a long life. He sat back in the wooden chair. The patio and sloping backyard was thick with people. "A side of beef, eh? Boyd send it down?"

At the mention of the Santa Barbara cattleman, Teal motioned downslope. "He's here, somewhere."

Even in the summer evening, Boyd would be wearing a jacket, cut both to hide and accommodate his tail. Thomas glanced about, but the cattleman did not immediately come to view. "He's running more beef down here now than he is in Santa Barbara. Trying to talk him into relocating?"

"Could be. He's got a son left to take over the ranch."

Blade's mouth tightened. He'd executed the elder boy. Neither Boyd nor his bald wife Delia had either castigated or forgiven him for doing it. That was years ago, he barely remembered the younger boy. Santa Barbara was not officially one of the Seven Counties although they had sent a candidate in for Protector training. It struck him that he didn't want to be here, he wanted to be there, home, working with the candidates. At one time, there had been seven Protectors for the Seven Counties. Now, five struggled to fill the posts. If their old enemy Denethan had wanted to attack, there could not be a better time.

But the reptilian mutant from the Mojave was now their uneasy ally. Perhaps Protectors were an endangered species.

Thomas drained the last of the foamy beer from the bottle. Maybe that's what made him edgy. He didn't like being obsolete. He set the empty headfirst in the cooling bucket.

"Well, Thomas! You've been doin' some thirsty work!"

Blade looked up. Two-handed Delgado grinned down at him, range dust still embedded in his shirt and dusting the chaps over his jeans. He reached forward and they grappled briefly, each testing the weary strength left in his acquaintance's grip. Delgado was, of necessity, right-handed, his left wrist showing the seamy scar where a second, weaker left hand had been sheared off when he was a teen. He'd lost a hand and gained a nickname. The primary left hand would never have the strength of a normal hand, but Delgado more than made up for it. He flashed strong yellow-ivory teeth at Thomas now.

"Left your garrote in your packs, eh?"

Thomas dropped the handshake. "No, actually, I've always got one on me." They'd drawn a crowd during their boisterous welcome and now Blade heard a woman gasp. There was a rustle of skirts as she turned abruptly away.

Into the abrupt silence, Teal said, "Pull up a stump and sit down."

Two-handed never stopped smiling. "No, thanks. Got saddle sores as it is. Thought I might borrow Thomas for a minute."

"Borrow away, as long as you return him." Teal narrowed his gaze at Thomas. "We've things to discuss."

Two-handed drew him away from the bustling crowd on the patio, and into the deep purple shadows at the far side of the manor house. "Ah, Thomas. In trouble with the judge, eh?"

"Never you mind. You're the one that's going to be in front of him one of these days, for throwing too wide a loop."

The cowboy shrugged. "Those days are over, my friend. I'm running the herd for Boyd Kelley now."

"Are you?" Sheer pleasure surged through Thomas. "That's great. The judge was telling me he might move his operations down here."

"Looks good to me. We're getting spillover rights from the Prado Dam and Corona County is hotter n'hell but fair grazing, for all that." Delgado pulled a battered and tarnished flask from his shirt waist. "Want some hard stuff?"

There were men it was dangerous to refuse an invitation from. The mutant chieftain Denethan was like that. So, too, Delgado. Thomas reached for the flask. The beer was already buzzing warmly in his gut, but it wouldn't hurt to send a chaser down after it. The hooch went down hot and fiery, like swallowing an explosion. Thomas gasped for a second, his gills fluttering for breath. His eyes watered. He handed the flask back.

"Good stuff," he rasped.

"No, it ain't," Delgado said, and grinned. "But it's better than nothing." He took a long pull before capping the flask and returning it to the inside of his shirt. He looked away. "I'm not one to be tellin' you your business, Thomas, but I'm not one for forgetting either. It was you got me off that rustling charge—"

"Not me, Two-handed. You didn't do it."

"Not that time. Th' good Lord didn't mind me getting my reward, I'll tell you, but you wouldn't allow it. So I'll say this and say it quick. There's something that's rank about the nester you offed today."

Your eyes, your truth. Thomas' skin crawled as the man's epitaph echoed in his memory. "What do you know?"

"Nothing more I can say. Just a word to the wise." Delgado slapped his shoulder. He turned and disappeared toward the fringe of trees marking the riverbed.

No one had kicked when he'd executed Boyd's boy, a kid who had been essentially good until he'd gone wrong. But first Lady and now Two-handed were reprimanding him for carrying out a legal sentence on the nester. Not to mention his own nagging instincts.

But what was a Protector without Intuition?

"Dying is easy," Thomas muttered. "It's living that's hard."

He snatched at a mosquito as it hummed toward him, big as a black bumble bee, and slapped it away. Then he returned to Judge Teal's domain, where he presided over the patio as if it, too, were a courtroom.

Whoops and shouts interrupted his return. Some idiot had roped a wolfrat and those who'd already had too much to drink were making bets over who could ride it to a standstill as though it were a bucking horse. Thomas watched sourly as the rodent stood with glowering eyes and dared anyone to get close enough to try, twisted hemp harness biting into its shaggy flanks. Its scaled tail whipped about, tripping up the booted ankles of anyone edging near. It was pegged down, but circling.

Teal had been laughing. He looked at Thomas. "What do you think, m'boy?"

Wolfrats were In-City scavengers. They ruled the toxic wastelands and concrete canyons of In-City. They were shrewd, feral killers. "I think," Blade said, watching the creature, "that you'd better find out where this one was caught and wipe the whole nest out, before your pretty little park gets marked out as territory for those bastards. They'll go through your deer like a hot knife through butter."

The judge looked contemplative for a moment. "I think you're probably right." He signaled one of his staff. "Sit down and let's finish what we were discussing before Patty rings the dinner gong."

Thomas drew close to the judge, but he did not sit. His nerves were too taut for that, his insides too warm. "The ribs had better be pretty damn good if you're trying to talk me into running for DWP."

"You've never minced words, Thomas."

"No."

"Me neither." Teal looked across the brick patio. Art Bartholomew still had a crowd, though they came and went, new listeners eager to replace old ones, his strident voice barely audible across the space. "You don't have much choice. We're talking about a change of county seat as well . . . that's one of Art's main platforms. It's been proposed we shut down Charlie's house and the school."

That jolted Thomas. "Shut down—"

"Just long enough to move them into Quaker County. Art is presuming he'll win, of course."

"We have other staff there. He's talking about pulling everybody out?"

"The orphanage, the schools, the cartography section, everybody."

"Who's going to man the pumping station?"

"Whoever wants to. The water down here is more important. Art's talking about centralizing the county seat, making water operations more accessible. He says the reservoirs need closer supervision."

The heat in Thomas' stomach seemed to be nearing his throat. "He wants to close off the nesters, he means. Judge, granted the pumping station isn't crucial for agriculture, but it's our only working model to reconstruct the other systems by and the Palos Verdes community is a vital one. We've the textiles which are dependent on the wind generators, and there's the fishing community—"

Teal held up a seamed palm. "I know. I know." He leaned close. "The only way to stop Bartholomew is to oppose him."

Thomas looked away in desperation. The wolfrat gave out a shattering squeal as one of the dinner guests approached. His tusklike teeth snapped the air, just missing the man's boots. He vaulted the beast's withers and straddled him.

"Sometimes," the judge said, "you've got to do what you've got to do."

"I'm not a DWP. You need somebody with a strong mechanical background and a good analytical mind. I'm Intuitive—that's what being a Protector is all about. I'm not your man."

"Then find me one, and you'd better make it quick." Teal raised his voice. "Leo, get down from there. You look like a damn fool."

The cobbler perched on the wolfrat looked up, face pale and lips thinned, but he stayed atop the wolfrat as though his life depended on it. Thomas' gaze slid away, saw the adoring girl watching Leo, and looked back. More than Leo's life evidently rode on the wolfrat's back.

The vigorous belling of the dinner gong pealed through the air. The wolfrat bolted in response, springing airborne. The pegging rope broke with a snap. The cobbler's audience scattered with a scream as the wolfrat lunged free. Leo flew backward, head over heels, and landed with a hard bump.

Thomas jumped forward as the wolfrat's eyes blazed with the knowledge that it was now free. Its razor jaws snapped and tore sleeves and skirts, victims just escaping its mayhem as it plunged through the crowd, on a direct path toward Thomas. It gave a bull-like squeal.

Wolfrats never forgot a quarry. He'd been trailed for weeks through In-City ruins by the monsters. The corner of his mouth quirked now in wonderment. Had he eluded this killer once before?

He reached for his power. He sent a spear of fear and amazement at the creature, hoping to slow it down long enough for him to reach his weapons.

His touch did more than slow it down. The wolfrat slewed to a halt, sides heaving, glowering eyes shuttered in reaction. Before Thomas could do more, a shuriken sliced through the night and sank deeply into the wolfrat's mangy neck. Lady stood, hand still outstretched from its throwing as the poisoned edge did its work and the creature fell to its side. It kicked its way into death.

Teal stood up. "Get that pile out of here."

The quiet crowd galvanized into action. Lady retrieved her throwing star and tucked it back into the waist of her skirt. Two

or three of the judge's staff materialized and dragged the carcass off into the dark. Thomas watched them go.

At his back, Judge Teal said quietly, "Thank you, Thomas. I
have little doubt the beast was after me."

Thomas blinked. He turned on his heel. He said nothing, his
mind examining the idea that the wolfrat had single-mindedly
been bent on running him down. But the judge had been behind
Thomas. Suppose someone had scent-baited the creature and
turned him loose on the judge's property? Bad luck the creature
had been roped and hauled in for sport. Good luck the wolfrat
had gotten loose. Bad luck a pair of Protectors had been in the
way to spoil a nasty accident.

Teal clapped his hands together. "I think I heard the dinner
bell! Ladies and gentlemen, let's barbecue!"

Blade moved forward then, thoughts clicking. He paired
with Lady. "Nice work," he said.

"You, too. I didn't know you could stop a full grown wolfrat
in his tracks like that."

"Neither did I." He patted her waistband. "I hope you
washed your hands."

She gave him a smile. "I'll let you lick my fingers clean."

"I knew it," he bantered. "You're still mad at me about the
nester."

The joy left her face. "Yes," she said quietly. She did not
speak another word as they shared a warm, damp towel and
were seated together at the long dining table.

Mosquito nets had been hung, big black spidery webbed
nets to protect the diners. There were four massive tables and a
scattering of small ones on the side lawn. The smoke from the
pit barbecue hugged the ground like evening fog and even
Lady's ire could not shake. Thomas' appetite. It had been too
long since breakfast.

Thomas looked up to see Art Bartholomew's warty face
beaming across the table at him. "Sir Thomas! It's been a
while."

"Not long enough," Blade responded.

Governor Irlene had accompanied Art to the table. She
leaned forward on one elegant elbow awaiting the platter of
meats which was being passed down and now looked in astonishment at Thomas. "You can't mean that."

The expression in the man's gray eyes flickered. "No

doubt he does. We'd all like to put the massacre far behind us. I believe that unfortunate wedding is the last time Thomas and I met."

"You believe correctly."

If Art had taken offense, he did not show it. He had other interests he wished to pursue. "That trail led you to the College Vaults."

He knew well that it did. The discovery of the fabled underground society had been the talk of the Seven Counties for months. Thomas retrieved the meat platter as it was passed to him and held it for both Irlene and Lady to make their selections.

"The man who ran it, the dean, I think he called himself— do you think he was human?"

Human, Art said, but what he meant was *human,* old human, pure human. Thomas watched as Lady picked out several choice cuts for him and then passed the platter down the table. Art Bartholomew's intense gaze had never left his face.

"I think," Thomas answered slowly, "he might have been. They kept their society closed. Even the eleven year plague seemed to affect them little."

"And he took the whole community with him," Art said. "All those people, out of spite."

"Yes." Blade did not elaborate. After the explosion, there had been a few prisoners, people Denethan's troops had absorbed quickly. The Mojave mutant community needed fresh blood more than the Seven Counties. Blade had let them go. His whole definition of humanity had been redefined by example of the dean, anyway. He saw in Art's face now an echo of past feelings.

Boyd, an elbow down from Lady, busy buttering an ear from the last of the corn harvest, said, "The eleven year plague passed us by entirely. What luck did you have down here?"

"Well enough," Lady said, smoothing her napkin over her lap. "We only had one unwanted pregnancy. We're letting that one run its course. Some mutations are favorable."

Her voice and unspoken accusation fell into Art Bartholomew's silence. The genetic engineering that scarred all their bloodlines was especially prey to the wild virus that cycled through their communities approximately every eleven years. It altered their aberrant DNA even more—wildly unpredictable and unwanted. Men and women affected chose sterility rather than pass on those aberrations. Plague babies were commonly abominations and were killed rather than suffer life. Lady had always been against that. Life was life, she said. Who were they to judge its quality?

Again, Art chose to reinterpret the obvious. "Your county is indeed fortunate. We, too, got off lightly. Perhaps the virus is losing strength or perhaps we're adapting against it."

"That would be good news," Irlene said. She passed down the squat clay bowl of barbecue sauce. Its mustard and honey aroma along with other flavorings in the tomato blend perfumed the air. "Only one, Lady? Really?"

"Yes. We have hopes the plague is done this cycle."

"Can I make an announcement to that effect?"

Lady Nolan smiled brilliantly. "Ah," she said to Irlene. "Politics raises its ugly head."

The governor had the grace to blush. Lady added, "It would be premature. Perhaps when the candidates are promoted, we can make a statement."

Art cut his brisket slices neatly. He speared a chunk and looked up at Thomas. "If the plague appears to be leaving us, perhaps now is a good time to schedule a salvage run to the Vaults. Surely the explosion couldn't have destroyed everything."

Though the other diners had been engaged in lively conversations of their own, this drew their notice. Thomas felt the pressure of their attention. This is what they had come to, so hungry for any crumb left behind no matter how corrupt. And yet, he'd known that some day he'd be asked to go back to the College Vaults. He had unfinished business there. But not yet. He wasn't ready yet. He and Lady had nearly died there, not once, but twice.

"No," he said. "Not everything, but I think the timing for such an expedition should be considered. Those foothills can be treacherous in rainy season. Maybe next spring, after elections."

Art's face never changed as he swallowed the whole chunk of meat on his fork. Then he speared a second bite and that one he chewed. "But you agree an expedition is called for?"

"Yes."

A victory was a victory, no matter how small. Bartholomew relaxed. He never saw the next blow coming.

"I understand the nester I executed today came from your corner of the counties. How did the water situation get out of hand in the first place?"

"What do you mean?"

Thomas shrugged. He took a slice of freshly cooled bread and used it to butter his corn with. "I mean that nesters don't readily foul water. It sounds to me as though you have a range war threatening to blossom under your nose."

Bartholomew's position concerning nesters and water was well known. He'd threatened many times to cut them off despite the policy of the Seven Counties. "If they needed water," he bit off, "they'd scarcely be poisoning it."

The cattleman from Santa Barbara let out a laugh that was too loud. "Thomas, you've got a mind like a coyote, but the councilman has you there. If you've been hinting he's been too busy politicking to help run his county, you've got him. But damnitall, man, as you said yourself—even a nester knows better than to poison water. He deserved what he got."

"Oh, there's no doubt of that," Thomas said deliberately. "I Read the truth in him."

There was a sudden pallor to Art's warted expression. He sat back in his chair, sucking his teeth for bits of meat. He met Thomas' expression silently. Blade merely smiled and began to eat his corn. There was nothing like the implication of a Protector's powers to strike fear in an ordinary man.

Lady and Irlene took up the gap in conversation, comparing a new herbal compress for headaches. Comfrey was said to work wonders. Thomas ate in relative silence, his thoughts on Two-handed Delgado who was ramrodding Boyd's herd for him, and Boyd, and Art Bartholomew. No nester would readily poison the only water that was available to him. Unless it was already bad.

Your eyes, your truth.

"You haven't been listening to me," Lady said, placing her hand gently over his.

Thomas looked up suddenly. "No," he said. "I haven't."

"I asked if you were headed back to Char—to the school after you finish the circuit."

"They've requested my help in promoting the candidates, so I guess I'll have to."

Governor Irlene smiled. "No rest for the wicked, eh, Thomas?"

"It appears not." He stood. "I've been on the road since before dawn and I think, ladies and gentlemen, I shall call it a night. Judge and Mrs. Teal, the meal was excellent and so was the company."

Judge Teal gazed at him somberly. There was a hint of disappointment in his nod. Thomas pushed his chair out and left the diners, weaving his way through the other tables. He skirted the splash of blood which marked the wolfrat's fall.

The edginess which had driven him all night suddenly had a name to it, and that name was justice.

"Thomas!"

He stopped for Lady. She was slightly out of breath when she caught up with him on the pathway between the bathhouse and the stables.

"You'd have thought I asked you to marry me, the way you left the table."

"Did you? I wasn't listening."

"No, dammit." She brushed her ash brown hair from her temple. Both eyes, brown and blue, looked angry. "You're not going back to the school."

"No." How she knew, he wasn't sure, but he thought that even without a Protector's Intuition, she would have seen it in him.

"Where are you going and what are you going to do?"

"I'm taking the nester's body back to his clan. I think there's something going on that we don't know about, and we should."

She stood in a flicker of moonlight. She said nothing until he asked, "What do you think?"

It was then he saw the tears of regret in her eyes. "I think," she forced out, "that you're doing too little too late." With a swirl of skirt, she left him alone in the night.

Chapter 3

No one protested when he took the nester's body. The counties had mounted a guard, but people had been drifting in and out of the courtroom basement all afternoon and evening to view it and the guards seemed to think it was about time someone took the exhibit off their hands. The basement cold room had kept the corpse in fairly good condition, but Blade had no hope that it would stay that way on the journey. He swaddled it, putting fresh herbs and flowers in the wrappings to preserve it as well as he could. A travois would be the best method of transporting it, but his gelding wouldn't pull a cart and Blade thought he might object to dragging the travois. So he bought a burro, signed the credit chit in the judge's name, packed it, and left.

Nester clans stayed close to the ruins, where they scavenged a way of life, and were left alone by the survivors who'd cast them out. They camped in the foothills, above flooding, where it was easier to pool water safely during the rains. But the dry spring and summer months always drove them back to the Seven Counties for clean, reliable water. Even a nester wasn't in a hurry to die from tainted water.

As DWP, Charles Warden had made an art of water testing and purification. He could predict with uncanny accuracy which basins would be safe to reservoir in and which would not. That knowledge had died with him because most of his papers and journals had been carried off as well. Though Thomas had gone all the way to the College Vaults in search of his papers as well as for vengeance, he'd failed. But the common sense Charlie'd taught—runoffs or basins located near old garbage dumps were never to be touched—would live on after him. He'd finally managed to convince the nesters as well,

though the treaties between them were chancy at best and what
one clan held to, the next would not.

Blade knew a few of the favored runs, but not all of them,
and he'd not found a fetish or totem on the nester's body to tell
him which clan he'd come from. So all he had was his brief
conversation with Two-handed Delgado to point his way. From
Delgado's comments, this nester had probably been a scrub
rancher—he could haunt the ruins all the way from Claremont
to the fringes of Orange County, or anywhere in the foothills
and dry valleys between. A nester might herd goats or sheep or
even chickens in the foothills.

Outside the city boundaries of what had once been Santana
and Orange, he pointed his gelding's head east, toward the
Prado Dam. The canyon run into Corona County and then the
deserts beyond was a flood plain. Although it appeared the cities
had been built the length of the pass and up into the foothills,
there was little left now but broken foundations and few of
those. The seasonal torrential rains of December and January
had carried away the last traces of civilization. On the other
hand, providing you had a fair weather eye, the plain made a
good area to graze and run cattle.

Both Harley and the burro protested the lateness of the hour
and the darkness of the path Blade took. Harley, named for the
venerable motorcycle which could still be utilized if gasoline
could be found and if it was in good enough repair, was a stubborn, short in the front, wide in the rear chestnut whose intelligence could sometimes be questioned. But he was indefatigable
and even though he moved reluctantly out of the fringes of Orange County, the horse's umbrage was not based on tiredness.

Rather, it came from coyotes and wolfrats.

Blade saw the predators, too. With a rattle of tall grass and
dried eucalyptus leaves, coyotes, moonlight catching an occasional flash of their dun or green eyes, slipped past them nearly
unseen. He could hear their yips from the foothills and ledges
above him. Sand and pebbles sifted down on Blade from time
to time. Coyotes were circumspect hunters. He didn't fear them
unless he had an injured animal and the smell of easy prey became too tempting. He figured they had winded the corpse he
freighted, but the meat wasn't fresh and the human smell daunt-
ing. The burro flicked his shaggy ears back and forth, neat lit-

tle black hooves clapping obediently behind Harley's ground-eating pace.

Blade took his rifle out of its sheath under his left knee and checked the chamber. He had a general vial in place, a bullet that would explode in a fire flash when shattered. It wasn't lethal, but startling. It would scare off most predators. He resheathed the rifle but didn't snug it all the way in. Harley pulled at the bit, protesting yet again their pilgrimage into the darkness.

Thomas stroked the gelding's neck. The horse calmed under his touch. He knew what he was doing.

This time.

He'd been fourteen the first time he'd ridden out into the night. He'd left behind his fate, he'd thought, and gone in search of a killer, a nester raider, who'd broken all treaties and cared nothing for the fragile balance of the Seven Counties. It wasn't his job to go for the man's bounty, but he'd taken it upon himself anyway. He'd only been known as Thomas then, for a Protector generally took his last name from his mentor. It was an easy, convenient way of identifying the training as well as the abilities of the Protector. Lady Nolan, for example, had the healing skills a Nolan was famed for. She could also TK, Fetch, or Throw, and she could Project imagery fairly well.

When he was fourteen, Thomas had found all his abilities broken. He could never be a Protector as his mentor had been killed in an assault by the Mojave mutants. Thomas bore the blame for that death though Gillander had literally moved Time itself to save the Palos Verdes community and the offices of the DWP from Denethan's attack.

He'd driven the boy away, sent him for help, a spindly, vague, sometimes vain and silly old man who wore suspenders gleaned from In-City, their elasticity as spent as his own life. And though Thomas had gone and warned Charles and the troops of a night raid, he'd never forgiven himself for leaving Gillander to die. Neither, apparently, had the old man. He haunted Thomas from time to time.

Thomas had not been able to return to study under another tutor. The powers of ESP had forsaken him, blocked by trauma, and would not open up no matter how coaxed. All because one old man had taught him a tremendous amount about life, how fragile and precious it was, and not one whit about how to kill to protect it. Not how to protect life from raiders like Denethan and the nester he tracked. In revolt, Thomas turned in another direction. The man he rode out to find and bring back to county justice had known, it was said, a hundred ways to kill a man.

The first and quickest way, Thomas found out, was to take him In-City. The treachery of the ruins and its predators he learned to avoid the hard way. He found the Butcher a thorough teacher—every time Thomas avoided a trap, he learned a lesson. The Butcher taught him not only the many ways a man could be killed, but also about the nesters and their clans. He learned how they staked their territories and marked them with fetishes, how they hunted and thought . . . and hated.

In the end, he'd caught the nester and avoided being contaminated by In-City, and he'd learned how to protect the fragility of life Gillander had taught him to love. He returned to the Seven Counties, took his last name from his weapon of preference, a blade, and became Charles Warden's executioner. His Intuition bled back into him slowly until he also became a full-fledged Protector, no longer denied his destiny.

He was tied to the ruins now, as marked by them and Butcher as by the scar that quirked his brow. But the creature that had done that was another story altogether.

Thomas reined to a halt now. He stroked his brow in remembrance as he looked over the broken road sketchily illuminated by a three-quarter moon. Chasing after the Butcher had changed him irrevocably, more than anything he'd ever encountered in his life, even training as a Protector. He'd gone back to the ruins time and time again, gleaning them, taking instruments with him that warned of the radiation and toxicity so that he took no more chances than necessary. It was a risky harvest, but never riskier than the night a beast had risen on two legs out of the dark, claws slashing across the campfire at him.

Wards laid down by the Protector had not swayed him nor had the fire. The claws that swiped across the corner of his eyebrow could have taken his head off at the neck if the creature had been so inclined.

It had vanished even as blood had filled the sight of his left eye. Shaking, he had sat down by the fire he'd so carefully constructed, and tried to staunch the flow. He'd been marked—marked as the creature's own—without warning or omen as to its meaning. He might have been a god or he might have been signed as prey. He still didn't know, nor had he ever seen a creature like that again. It resembled nothing in the realm of his experience, as used as he was to the results of genetic engineering and mutation.

Years later he'd been marked again, in the sea, but that debt he had paid, and though the teeth marks on his right wrist worried him from time to time, the dolphin goddess who'd scarred him demanded nothing of him. Those markings and those experiences had changed him forever into something he had not foreseen. The dolphin had been a mystical experience. He swam with her now and then when he returned to the coast. Her turquoise and silver beauty paced him above wave and below, for he was one of the few survivors left unashamed of his gills or their ability to take him where man was no longer meant to go. He would never forget the day Charlie had gone under the knife to have his gills cut out.

He understood now what he had not understood then, what it meant to be human, and he wished that he could have told Charlie so that his friend might not have suffered the stigma of his heritage. Too late. Always too late.

As for what Lady wanted of him, he did not know if he could provide it. She had her methods for fighting to protect the fragility of life and he had his. He loved her the way she was. It cut deeply that she could not do the same for him.

Harley stumbled, bringing Thomas sharply into the here and now. Behind the chestnut, the little burro tugged at his lead rope as if to remind him that the animals should be sleeping now, and grazing in the early morning, or he would not reach his destination by midday.

He found hard rock to guard his back, with no overhead ledges or brush to conceal potential stalkers, pegged the burro out, and hobbled the gelding. He laid his wards out with a murmur and a click of the stones, banked a fire despite the mild Indian summer night, rolled into a groundsheet, and slept.

He was deep in dreamless sleep when Harley's sharp nicker of cold fear shattered the quiet.

Chapter 4

Somewhere it was written that cockroaches were going to inherit the Earth. Thomas knew he'd seen it and the evidence chittering in front of him would support that statement. He kicked his rifle loose from its sheath, scrambled to his feet, and grabbed it up. Harley was making admirable speed even hobbled, but the little burro was at the rope's end, braying in terror.

Cockroaches came in several sizes. In-City roaches were usually ankle- to knee-high, but this out-country dumpster size easily qualified as a "tank," big enough to make even a wolfrat reconsider. Antennae whipped at Thomas as mandibles moved. A string of slime dropped from a hairy jaw. The scent of the corpse had drawn it and it was hungry.

A fire flash wasn't going to deter it for very long. Thomas dropped the vial out of its chamber and patted down his jacket, searching for something with a little more kick to it. The inside flaps of his brown leather jacket were lined with sleevelike pockets, filled with vials of this and that, handy little concoctions. He slid his hand inside. The knobby end of a crooked finger bone slipped eagerly into his grasp. The last thing he needed now was a fight with witch power and his haunt. "Oh, no, Gillander, not now," he said and dropped the bones hastily back into a pocket. Another fumble for a vial with its embossed seal telling him what it contained and he grasped it in triumph.

The burro let out a squeal as the tank charged. Almost dwarfed by its shrouded burden, it spun at rope's end and kicked out. Thomas dropped the vial into the loading chamber and cranked the rifle. The roach sliced a second time and caught the burro along his shaggy withers. In the night, the blood looked blue-black as it welled up. The roach skittered around into position to charge again.

Thomas shot into the dirt at the creature's cable-width legs. The vial shattered on impact and exploded. In a shower of dirt and gravel, the roach flipped in midair and came down on its back with a death rattle of shell and insect anger. He helped it along with his wrist blade.

The little burro stood stubbornly at its pegging rope's full length, ears flicking forward and back in uncertainty. Thomas approached it, talking gently, and wrapped an arm about its shaggy neck. He could feel its heart thundering in its body. He pulled another vial from his jacket pocket and uncorked it between his teeth. The medicinal smell would stay on his mustache until he had a chance to wash, he thought ruefully. He poured the vial over the burro's shoulder and watched as it fizzed and a cloud of foam rose. The little beast shuddered under his ministrations, but Thomas knew the liquid didn't hurt, not really. And the carrion poison of a cockroach would be far more lethal. When the gash stopped foaming, it bled cleanly for a moment, then clotted abruptly.

Thomas slapped the creature's neck. "You'll be fine, old son. Now," he whirled, peering into the gloom. "Where the hell did Harley go?"

Harley had gotten pretty far down the canyon by the time Blade caught up with him. He'd kicked his fire site apart and moved camp with the search, knowing that neither animal would rest well with the roach carcass twitching all night. Plus, where there was one, there were bound to be more. He hiked with his saddle and tack thrown over one shoulder, rifle in the other hand, eyes squinted against the darkness until he sensed before he saw animal heat.

Harley's ears flopped forward and back in embarrassment as he walked up. Lather dried the gelding's neck and flaked off as Thomas thumped him in greeting.

"Even handicapped, you made pretty good time, old man."

The horse bumped him in the chest.

"I'm glad to see you, too. Your saddle was getting heavy." Thomas dropped it. "The bad news is, you now get pegged out like a common donkey." Harley snorted in disbelief, but Thomas was true to his word before dropping back down in a hollow of dirt and sand to sleep what he could of the remaining night away.

He could not put clarity into his dreams, but there was a sound, a hissing voice calling and it was that hiss that woke him again.

"Thomassssss."

His eyes had gone gummy. He got up on an elbow and rubbed at them, trying to see in the purple-gray night. The fire he'd banked before sleeping roared in a gout of flame—cool flame—and the illusion of a skull rippled in it. Cavernous eye sockets blazed orange. Thomas could see through the haunt to the rocks and scrub brush. He sat up with a yawn.

"Gods, Gill. It's too late for antics. What do you want?" He would not look directly at the phantasm, keeping its vision in his peripheral view. The ghost of his mentor, weighed by spectral motives rather than the goodliness of natural flesh, could not be trusted.

"Thomasssss." Like rain drops hissing on hot rocks, the specter's voice boiled up at him.

"Gillander." Thomas kept his voice flat and neutral.

With abruptness, the fire subsided to its banked embers, and the fleshed, if translucent, outline of an elderly man sitting cross-legged floated above it. The pants were dark, cuffs frayed, knees threadbare, the shirt light, with a ticked design, sleeves rolled to the elbow. The suspenders were bowed out, their stretch leeched away by the years. Thomas knew the figure well. But its face remained gaunt, as if the aspect of flesh was laid over it too lightly. He could see the skull dominating its expression. Fire danced deeply in the eyes. Gillander, irascible in life, loved scaring the hell out of people in death.

"Getting careless." The ghost grinned. The teeth bared all the way to the jawbone.

"Getting tired. What do you want from me?"

Gillander rubbed a rawboned hand through his thin thatch of hair. It had been yellow-white when the man had been alive and taught him. Now it was nearly colorless. "Maybe I'm here to avenge the dead, boy." He pointed at the shrouded burden across the burro's back.

"I have nothing to fear from you. I carried out the sentence on a guilty man."

"If you really thought so, you wouldn't be here."

"I'm satisfied he's guilty. Maybe I just want to understand why he did what he did." Thomas pulled out his canteen, took a swig of water, spat it out, then took a fresh swallow.

Gillander made a snorting noise through a nose that had been broken three times in life. Its high, knobbed bridge gave a look of arrogance to the man. "Last time we talked, you were in search of what it meant to be human. Now you're trying to define truth?"

"Maybe." Thomas shrugged into his groundsheet. The dirt had chilled down considerably during the night. "What's your excuse?"

"Maybe I like finishin' a job I started. You raised these old bones by walking across them. You're strong, Thomas. You've got talents they haven't even classified yet. You've got *magic*. Do they know that?"

Thomas had been drifting into looking the ghost flush in the face. He blinked now and angled his gaze back away. "It's possible some of them guess."

"Lady, now, she ought to." The phantasm hiked up his pants cuffs. He had never worn socks with his down-at-the-heel boots and there was a flash of cadaverous green-gray skin. "You have work to do, boy. Deliver the body and git home. There're students waiting to be taught. That's your life's work. Learn and pass it on. We've got a whole civilization's worth of know-how to catch up with and pass on. You're wasting time. Use the road, Thomas."

A cold wind touched the back of Blade's neck. "No."

"I taught you how to move Time itself. Do it. Do what you have to do and get home."

Thomas felt his skin prickle. This was precognition, even if it came out of a ghostly mouth. But even this could not drive him to use the Ghost Road. He could not control the passage if he did. The road wove its way through a time and place unknown, its beginning and end anchored God knew where, fueled by the anger of lost souls. He had used the road before only because life and death drove him to it. He would never use it again. "Never again."

"The more fool you, then. God gave you Talents. You'd not cut your gills, would you?"

Reluctantly, the answer was drawn from him. "No."

"Then use the road. It was meant for you, boy."

Thomas looked at him. The flame points in the sockets' depths flared slightly. "You walked the road and it killed you. Do you want the same for me?"

"Part of me does," the phantasm admitted. "I'm a lonely old man. But the best part of me says that what you have is a gift meant to be used. Find out how. You may need it."

The ghost's honesty fazed him. Thomas licked dry lips and said, "Rest in peace, Gill, and leave me alone. Consider me warned."

"Pshaw. I could kick you in the ass and you wouldn't know where it was." With an abrupt blink, the specter was gone.

In the cold silence, Thomas sat quietly. Then, he reached forward with a stick and stirred the fire's coals, sifting the embers about. A sharp hiss spat at him. He jumped in spite of himself. "Shit!"

There was a disembodied laugh. As it faded away, Thomas knew he was truly alone.

Get home. Why? What was going to happen? He lay back down, watching the cloudless sky overhead. The stars were brittle and brilliant. He named them to himself, saw a few he did not recognize, and drifted to sleep for a final time that night.

He knew when he was in nester territory by the red-tailed hawk that had been flayed, its skin left on a lone fence post, its natural beauty dulled both by its death and by the clay paint upon its feathers. The Prado Dam overshadowed them though it was another quarter day of leisurely riding away. He surveyed the rangeland about it. It was sere, overgrazed, the grass burned to brown husks, with mesquite woven abundantly through the range. The foothills were blackened with char marks from last year's fires. This year would be worse, until the rains came.

He reined the gelding upwind of the burro and dismounted Harley, dropped the reins into a ground tie, and squatted down. He took his battered leather hat off and wiped the sweaty band marks across his forehead. He had no need to find the nesters now. They would find him. He squinted into the late afternoon.

His muscles hadn't even tired of his hunkered down position when they appeared, loping over the flat, their faces burned dark by too much sun and wind. Grass stalks split and shattered under their pounding feet, bare soles callused hard as rock.

They circled him quietly. Unwashed and heathen, they were

no more fragrant than the corpse he brought back to them, their sweat profuse and sour. He drew his lips tight in concentration, tapping his Protector abilities, and projected trust and calm toward them.

The lead nester, his brown-streaked black hair thick and matted upon his head and face, the whites of his eyes startling against the color of his skin, jerked a thumb. "What be that?"

"It's a dead man."

"His name?"

"You tell me. He was a son of a bitchin' water poisoner, but he was one of yours." Thomas rose to his feet slowly. They'd encircled him, but he could smell them almost sharper than he could see them.

"You kill 'im, Blade?"

He was not surprised they knew his name. His light yellow-blond hair and mustache and white scarf set him off. "I executed him."

"He tell you the truth?"

Straw stalks rustled as someone moved behind him. Blade moved his wrist ever so slightly, loosening a knife in its sheath. "That he did. He poisoned the well. Now you tell me the rest of the truth."

The nester relaxed. He waved the other runners from around Blade. "He come t'listen," he said. "Bring him in." He turned and ran back the way they'd come, toward the eroded and charred hillside to the north.

Thomas caught up Harley and swung aboard. The gelding loped at an easy pace on the heels of the nester pack, snorting now and then at the dust they kicked up.

The nester encampment on the lee side of the foothills was small. The hide teepees staked out would hold no more than six families. The stench of middens in the hot afternoon sun told him this was an old camp, due to be moved shortly when even the nesters could not tolerate the smell. A dented and primered Chevy truck rested on the ground, freight packs leaning up against its wheel rims. Three slat-sided and wormy looking horses cropped the bare hills nearby. There were looms set up between the trees and women hunched over them, ignoring the dirty children rolling around at their feet. They scarcely looked up as the pack entered camp.

He smelled possum stew and though he hadn't eaten at mid-

day, he knew he wasn't hungry. From the looks of the clan,
there wasn't much to go around. He dismounted Harley and
tied him in the shade of a tree. He let a nester take the burro's
lead rope from his hand.

"The burro stays with the clan," he said. "It's for the
widow."

The man's brow raised at the gift of wealth. He nodded
briskly and towed the animal after him. One of the women
stood up suddenly and her wail broke through the camp. She
lunged into a run, made awkward by her advanced pregnancy
and the bone structure of her right leg, which seemed fused at
the knee. He could not guess if it had been a birth defect or an
old injury. Were it not for her weaving skills at the loom, even
the nesters might well have found her a liability. Thomas turned
away as she reached the burro's flank. Her grief grew louder.

The pack leader motioned him into the shade of a tree and
presented him with a dipper of water. Blade took it without hesitation, knowing that its untested condition might well cost him
a day or two of intense gastric problems, but he had vials for
that. It was these people who had to live with it.

The dark-haired nester nodded in approval as Blade drank it
down. "Clean water," he said to Thomas. Thomas did not dispute him. Water enough to wash the trail dust down his throat.

He looked into the barrel. The level was low. "Not much."

"No. The cowmen let the wells go dry. They say the herd
strays into our territory after water. We take too much meat. So
they want to leave us no water at all. The man you brought back
found our well gone alkali. He killed a sheep and threw it in."

"Deliberately?"

"Yes." The nester headman led him to a stump. They sat.
The nester tapped his chest. "I'm Clancy." He flashed a grin.
"Black Irish."

The last startled him. In a land where they struggled to survive, where the meaning of what it had meant to be an Ameri-
can, or even a Californian, had long been swept away, this man
reached for roots older than the disasters. Thomas did not
know how to take this. Finally, he nodded. "Clancy, who was
this man?"

The dark-headed nester scratched his chin reflectively. "He
didn't tell you, did he?"

"No. But I was not the judge or the jury. Nor did he tell his name to the woman who healed him, who wanted to save his life."

"We called him Kurt. He was younger than I. He wanted to force the cowmen to dig new wells, to replace the water they took from us. He never poisoned anyone. They killed one of their own."

Thomas had guessed as much. He dug his boot heels into the pebbly earth. "They took wells from you?"

"Yes." Clancy flashed him an annoyed look.

Thomas held up his hand. "I have to be sure of this, Clancy. It's against our treaties to deny you water. You have chosen to live outside our society and laws, but you're survivors, just like us. You have water rights."

"We don't need rights. We can take what is ours." Clancy straightened in stubborn pride.

"Your nester clan is known," Thomas said, by way of acknowledgment of this prowess. He couldn't afford to fight his way out of camp and neither could they. He stood. "Thank you, Clancy."

"You won't share dinner with us?"

He shook his head. "I have a long ride ahead of me." There wasn't much he could do immediately for the lot of the nesters, but he could and would bring pressure to bear against Boyd and Delgado. They had forced the nester into action that the community had found intolerable. Water poisoning was inexcusable. It was a fact of life that wells dried up or went bad. But it was a convenient fact of life for the cowmen who didn't want their herds straying into nester territory looking for water. As Thomas looked out over the camp population, he didn't see any evidence of beef-fed youngsters. These people were subsistence. How much beef could they have stolen?

Thomas had a lot of respect for Boyd, but he knew Boyd hated nesters. His own tailed ass made him more prejudiced than most. Blade would have to find a way to deal with him gracefully. A sense of failure stabbed through him. Was the man he executed innocent or guilty . . . and in this case, was there a truth to be found and Read, crystal clear, among all the events? Had he failed himself as well?

The sobbing woman reminded him that, as Lady had told him, he was found lacking and too late. Thomas took a deep breath. In the meantime. . . .

"Clancy, your middens are overflowing, your wells have gone dry. I suggest you find a new camp."

The nester nodded in agreement. "We will bury Kurt, then load the wagon. There is a well over the hill. It will last for a short while." He paused. "Pray for rain, Lord Protector."

That, and other miracles. Thomas did not respond aloud.

Clancy gave him a sharp look. "If we aren't given treaty water, there are those of us who will take it. In the north hills, there is a man . . . a counties man . . . he talks to us like you do."

Thomas' interest came back to him abruptly. He was not aware of anyone who worked with the nesters. "What can you tell me about him?"

The headman's expression became cagey. "I would not tell you, but you are Blade—and you had balls enough to bring Kurt's body back." He lowered his voice a little. "He was found near the ruins of the hidden people."

"What hidden people?" Thomas kept his voice even, but suspicion pricked at him.

"Where the big battle took place—about a year and a half ago. You and the desert chieftain fought together."

The College Vaults. Someone unaccounted for. "Tell me about this man."

Clancy shrugged. "He calls for strength out of weakness. I heard that he is a big man, massive . . . he's stolen a lot of beef." The nester grinned at that.

The Dean of the College Vaults had been a mountainous man, fat and unconditioned. "Does this county man have a name?"

"I haven't heard it. The northern clans say he does not like the Seven Counties. They are divided over him. Some say their totem, the Shastra, guided him to them. Others doubt it. He says they plan to steal all our water . . . and we should band together, under one headman. What do you think, Blade?"

Thomas wasn't familiar with any particular totem of the northern clans. But if it had been the dean they'd found, he had definite opinions on that. "I think this man sounds like trouble. I think your clan should think about it before they let another headman replace you. You've done well for them."

"That I have. You had better think on him, too. He's got a bounty on you." With that, Clancy left him and went to the sobbing woman who had unshrouded her husband.

Thomas stood, paralyzed by the implications. A nation of nesters could well bring the Seven Counties to their knees, particularly as divided as they were now in the absence of a DWP. It was not a threat any of them had thought they ever need to worry about. A nester was by nature antisocial and paranoid. It wouldn't be easy to band them together.

If he had a bounty on his life, it had to be the dean. No one else knew him as well. It appeared the dean was going to try to finish what he had started.

Perhaps it was time he did the same.

Chapter 5

Lady caught Quinones by the elbow. The administrator turned about and blinked at her with his extra set of eyelids. The effect was incredibly owllike, bolstered by the round-lensed glasses he wore. She dropped her hold on him quickly.

"I was told Sir Thomas is back," she said. "Have you seen him?"

She watched as Quinones fought to control his trembling. He had a peculiar nervous system, one that went into convulsions if shocked and he'd been known to fall over in a dead faint, harmless though spectacular, on a regular basis. "He c-came in late last night," he stuttered. "He's already been through the kitchen and bathhouse this morning."

"That's all I need to know." She spun about, her skirt hem kicking up with the movement. As she trotted briskly in the other direction, he called after her, "T-tell him that Denethan's ambassador is looking for him, t-too. It's urgent!"

Lady hurried down the pathway, wondering what could have lit a fire under Shankar, Denethan's ambassador, whose usual approach to life was as uncannily lizardlike as his appearance. Shankar's preferred activity for the day was to bask in whatever sunny spot he could find, but Lady had noticed that the ambassador had a profound ability to eavesdrop when he appeared to be comatose in the sunshine.

It was only late September and yet the early morning rays seemed to slant a little off the Palos Verdes peninsula, heralding the cant of the earth toward winter. She lifted her chin a little to catch the smell of the ocean on the breeze. A brief image drifted across her senses, a vision of herself and Thomas strolling in a pink-hued sunset along the beach, just the two of them. . . . Lady skirted a group of arguing farmers en route to the Warden manor, her daydream vanishing. She looked to the ridge above, where sentries were on duty, more as a formality now than as a necessity. Raiders from the Mojave were a thing of the past. She scanned for Thomas who, cautionary as ever, was likely to be out testing the sentry line.

She did not catch a glimpse of either Thomas or Shankar. Her next bet, then, was the school. The children loved Thomas, for reasons he could not fathom, and that amused Lady. He was always bringing back tidbits from the ruins, toys or gadgets they would pore over and guess the uses of. The entire laser disk library was due to Thomas' efforts. The children adored him for Mickey Mouse alone.

She paused on the slope. From where she stood, she could see the classrooms. Doors stood open, dark openings into what she liked to think was the soul of the Seven Counties. The classrooms were empty, quiet. The realization sent icy fingers across her Intuition. The Counties were changing, shifting. The Warden dynasty had been a glue that held them together. Now many were complaining the Warden manor and Torrance County were too far north and west of the others and that the county seat should be shifted accordingly. Few parents wanted to send their children such an inconvenient distance to be fostered. Only the orphan wards would have no choice, but Lady foresaw that changes were coming.

She stirred uncomfortably. She was a creature of habit, of nesting. She did not like the idea of change, particularly when it seemed to be a destiny she could not guide.

Where she stood now overlooked the road leading to the manor house, the lone house left standing on this block, with its massive, crescent driveway. The '98 Caddy convertible rested in the front, preparatory to being hitched up. Its metal and chrome frame, massive in its antique beauty, caught the gleam of the early morning. The car was one of several that had been restored by Charles Warden, inasmuch as he could, the last of a century of behemoths. Later decades saw cars and other vehicles made of biodegradable materials which were useless to the survivors. Her glance flicked over the car, then came back. Someone was slumped quietly in the front seat.

Lady broke into a run, propelled by the ground slope she'd been standing upon. She reached the side of the Caddy breathless, the fine strands of her hair breaking loose from its weave and drifting about her face.

Thomas looked up at her. His mouth pursed under his silky mustache, but he refrained from comment.

"The last place I'd have looked for you," she got out, and slid in as he opened the car door.

"It didn't work, then," he said mournfully. He tucked a longer strand of hair behind her ear.

"Antisocial so early in the morning?"

"Please," he said. "There're nearly three hundred people here already, with another fifty or so due in today. *All* of them politicians."

"Really, Thomas!" She laughed softly. He had the gift of making her laugh, as well as of making her cry. She grabbed his hand before he could move it out of her reach. "We've testing yet to do this morning and Quinones says Shankar is looking for you."

"Shankar has found me," the man said. His weathered blue eyes watched over the Caddy's hood, up the length of road which would take them to a point where the Pacific Ocean could be seen clearly and without break, Catalina Island on the southward horizon. Because of the moisture from the ocean breeze, grass and shrubs were abundant here, evergreen and Monterey pine, gorse and eucalyptus, citrus trees and ficus, everything imaginable. Everything but homes and the people who had once populated them. Of them no legacy remained but broken foundations. She wondered if he saw what she saw.

Curiosity prodded her. "What did Shankar want?"

"He has heard from Denethan. The old coyote has finally sent his son out to be fostered."

"That's wonderful! We need that . . . we need a visible sign of the alliance."

He scratched the corner of his mouth thoughtfully. "Yes and no. Shankar's tight-mouthed about the boy, but I gather he's a handful even among the Mojavans."

"We'll put him in school."

"I think we'll have better luck harnessing him to your mule and letting Candy break him." Thomas stood up. "Well, so much for peace and quiet. Gird yourself, milady. The fray awaits us." He handed her out of the Caddy, gathering her up in a rumple of skirt and literally tossing her over the car door. She went with a girlish squeal and considerable loss of dignity, but landed on her feet.

"Thomas!"

His eyes sparked and he gave her the briefest of grins as he landed beside her in a puff of driveway dust. He waved to the house. "The fray is that way."

"How well I know." Lady gathered herself and they walked to the doors of the flagstone manor. "I, however, can beg to be excused. Candidates are waiting for me."

"Who's up?"

"Well, Barbara's made it this far. She can Read fairly well and Project and Block. That's about it for her, but it's all we can hope for. And then there's Stanhope. He's got more to him, I think, than anybody we've seen in a long time. He straightened a broken leg for setting last week with very little pain or disruption to the patient. He Reads well, too. More importantly, he has a significant amount of Projection and Empathy, which means he'll be able to teach future candidates."

"Someone named that boy well." he held the door open for her. The smells of breakfast and the sound of voices enveloped them.

"Gillander did, actually, as I remember."

Thomas stood, stunned by the sudden lack of sunlight and by the futile expectation of waiting for Veronica Warden to glide forward to greet him. It never failed to hit him that Ronnie and Charles were gone from this place. Lady put her hand on his wrist and squeezed comfortingly as she sensed his confusion. He caught himself. "Who else?"

"Two or three others. Plus we have five more candidates to think about next spring."

"That many? After the dearth we've had? Where are the genes coming from?"

"Out of the woodwork. How should I know? Just be grateful."

There had been only seven of them, barely one for each county and none for the wide expanse of land between county centers. Now, suddenly, there would be an abundance of Protectors . . . in a time of peace when Protectors were needed least. He tasted the irony of it. "Why don't we work the room long enough to be polite? I'd like to go with you."

"All right. I want to find out what happened with the nesters."

He would not bring it up, because of their argument weeks ago when he'd left, but was relieved she had because he wanted her advice. Thomas looked down at her. "All right," he said agreeably.

The foyer opened up into a spacious living room and dining room, the far walls of tempered glass extending the horizon as far as the Pacific. The horizon was muddied now by the clusters of people standing and talking, drinks in hand despite the time of day. Thomas made Governor Valdees his target. The chunky man, his thick, brutish brown hair liberally salted with gray, stood with his back to them, his voice cutting through closer conversations. Governors were responsible for the military and revenue structure of each county while the mayors handled trade and city planning, with the DWP being the power that wove them all together.

"So, I said, what *is* the difference between horse shit and a nester? And he says to me, no one minds stepping on a nester!" As the conversation broke up in laughter, Thomas gained his objective.

Valdees turned to him. "Sir Thomas! You made it for the ceremonies, after all! Good to see you."

One of his audience, Governor Irlene, smiled coolly. She wore a dusky pink riding jacket over her trousers. Her glance slid over Lady and Thomas wondered why sudden enmity showed. He was not aware that the two had any history. She extended her hand. "Thomas, you missed one hell of a barbecue by leaving so early. That wolfrat rodeo was only the beginning."

He shook her hand, acknowledging that Judge Teal threw a good party; however, his eyes were on Valdees. The governor shifted uncomfortably. "Is there something I can do for you or is this visit merely social?"

"Actually, Governor, there is something you can do for me. When are you next exchanging duty shifts for Boyd's troops?" Military coverage for large operations was still standard though raiding had dropped down considerably.

"Near the Prado?" Valdees looked surprised. His shaggy eyebrows did a small dance. "Several days after I return home, probably. Why do you ask?"

"Send a courier with them. Suggest to Boyd that his military protection hinges on opening up his wells and keeping them open. Remind the cattleman that we have a water rights treaty with the nesters and you've got the guts to enforce it."

The room was suddenly quiet. Across the room Art Bartholomew lifted his chin as though it aided him to hear.

Lady muttered, "My god, Thomas, I thought you came in to mingle, not start a war." Valdees heard her, but few others could.

The governor's expression remained guarded. "Is there a problem I should know about?"

"I executed a man for poisoning a well. He did it. I have no guilt. But what we were not told at the trial was that the water had already been allowed to go bad and new wells hadn't been opened up. Boyd's getting water from the Prado, he doesn't care if he loses the wells—but as long as he leases his rangeland from the counties, he has to abide by our treaties the same as anyone else would. I think he needs to be reminded of it."

The amber liquid in Valdees' glass shook almost imperceptibly. He said, "I will do that, Lord Protector."

In the background, from a direction Thomas could not pinpoint, someone muttered, "Nester lover."

He looked around. No one hated nesters worse than he did—miserable curs who refused to cooperate and accept responsibility for mutual survival. But as long as they lived, there was a possibility they could change, could come back. They were not like animals who went feral and remained unreclaimable. And, there had been Clancy's warning. "I would like to remind anyone within earshot that the nester clans would be of considerable size if they decided to form a nation."

"What's the matter, Thomas—inventing new enemies now that we've got a truce with the lizards?"

Before Thomas could retort to the man who had spoken out, Art Bartholomew interrupted. "Who says we've got a truce," he yelled back. "We've been at war with Denethan since he came to power. I say we've all been duped into doing nothing while he regroups. Just because we had a common enemy does not make him our ally."

A hiss came from the shadowy corner of the room, by the kitchen doors. Thomas looked and saw Shankar, the Mojavan ambassador, draw his sinewy body to his full height.

"I take offense at your remarks, Mr. Bartholomew."

Art looked at the ambassador. His lip curled. "Take whatever you what, Mr, Ambassador. Just tell your raiders to stop stealing chickens from my farmers."

"You have no proof!" The scaled man drew close, the teeth he bared a little too sharp for comfort.

"No proof?" Bartholomew bulled his way out of his rank of listeners. "I've got shed skins—you name it, I can prove a lizard was there!"

Shankar fairly shook with rage. He turned to Thomas. "Lord Protector!"

Thomas put up one hand. "This is not a dictatorship like the Mojave, Mr. Ambassador. Mr. Bartholomew is allowed to think as he wishes. He's only in trouble if he decides to act upon it." He smiled at Bartholomew. "He has to weigh his actions against reactions to decide if it's worth it or not."

Art Bartholomew's warty face turned livid. "Don't threaten me," he said softly, "Lord Protector or not."

"It's not me you have to worry about. It's those untrustworthy Mojavans," Thomas returned. He drew Shankar aside. "As for your assumption of their guilt, I wouldn't dare suggest you look in other directions. Never mind that the nester recipe for chicken reads: first, steal a chicken." Looking beyond Bartholomew, he could see and hear the laughter, and the audience they had gathered began to turn away as the tension was defused.

He brought Shankar with him as he stepped close to Bartholomew. He pitched his voice for their ears alone. "Art, you've been breathing down Shankar's neck ever since he arrived here. This may not be an alliance you approve of, but the Board of Mayors and Governors voted for it by a majority. I know you want to be DWP, but I suggest to you strongly that you not run on a platform of action or prejudice against those we must survive alongside."

"Well spoken, Sir Thomas," Shankar began, but Thomas shook him to silence.

"As for you, you fork-tongued old rogue, you quit needling those short of temper whose support we both depend on. Bartholomew has opened wells in his southern and easternmost reaches for you, and you need them. So may I suggest, *gentlemen*, a little compromise in temperament?"

Bartholomew's mouth twitched. He leaned close as well and his brows narrowed to a vee. "No more chickens," he said.

Shankar spread webbed hands. "I am sure I know not of what you speak."

"Right. There are probably feathers all over your quarters. All right, all right." Art put his hands up. "Pax." He rocked back on his heels. "I'd like to speak with you privately, Sir Thomas, later."

Thomas felt his eyebrow go up. "All right. If not today, then tomorrow. I've told Lady Nolan I'll help with the last of the candidate testing."

The man with skin like a pebbled streambed nodded and stalked away. On Thomas' right, the Mojavan ambassador said, "With skin like that, he's probably one of my cousins and doesn't even know it!"

That possibility would explain a lot of Bartholomew's bad attitude, Thomas thought, but he said only, "Oh, I think he knows it all right. A little rape between enemies doesn't help truces."

"All the same," and Shankar put his webbed hand on Thomas' shoulder, "I cannot prove it now and all you have is my word, but the day of the massacre, I was one of my chieftain's trackers. Those who killed here and left met with a small party upon the trail leading from the peninsula. Then those trails went in far different directions. I am told that Bartholomew was conveniently not here for the massacre. Too bad, eh? And I wonder if it was he who doubled back to meet with the killers." Shankar took his hand from Blade's shoulder and moved across the room to where French doors stood open and a wet bar was doing brisk business on the patio and veranda beyond.

Thomas stood in cold silence, unaware of Lady still with him until she said, "There's no proof and I'm not at all certain I trust Shankar."

"Perhaps not," he got out, finally. "He's shrewd enough to play on my suspicions. I would trust him more if he'd been Denethan's original choice for the post—but when Micah fell ill, Shankar was sent instead. The Mojavan treaty is no more popular with some of them than it is with some of us. If I knew Shankar's game, I would know whether I could trust him."

Lady drew him away. "I'd say we've made our appearance. And while I'm talking to you about fulfilling social obligations,

I'd like to ask you if you've ever heard of 'small talk.' Or if you ever indulge in it?"

He gave a soft laugh. "Sorry."

"Sorry nothing. I thought you were going to immerse us in World War V—or however many we're up to now." She smiled at someone who waved at them. "I presume this all has to do with what you found when you took the body back."

"Not all of it," he began, but she interrupted to tell another woman, "Molly, we're late now for our candidates, but I'll see you later," as the woman accosted them. The woman gave way gracefully as Lady steered him out the French doors. He snagged up what looked to be a tumbler of lemonade as they passed the refreshment table. Shankar had found an empty patio chair in the sun and lay curled up on it despite his diplomatic suit and ruffled shirt, his eyes closed in oblivion.

"Don't you believe it," Lady muttered. She found a tumbler of iced tea before guiding Thomas to the barracks where the wards lived.

It was called a barracks, but it was actually another full-sized two-story house which had been gutted to make it all bedrooms. The number of children living there varied, as did the fortunes of all the counties. When Thomas had been young, the blistering plague had filled the house, parents dropping like flies. Today the barracks held seventeen youngsters, as he recalled, or it had before he'd embarked last spring on his judicial circuit for Orange County. Two lower bedrooms were for the fostered youths, and they would be empty now.

As they walked the well-worn pathway to the barracks, he told her about his decision to take Kurt's body back and what he'd met on the trail. She listened silently, then made him repeat what his ghostly visitor had said.

Her eyes mirrored concern as she looked up at him.

"He's right. You've got a Talent, an effect, that you can't control and yet one that can be very beneficial."

"It's deadly, Lady. It leeches on me, you, anyone who uses it."

"But to circumvent time . . . to be able to travel in two or three days what would take two or three weeks. Think of the communication possibilities. No more rumors—we'd have facts. Think of the healing possibilities, to be able to have someone right there when an outbreak of diphtheria or cholera occurs. Of all the things I've seen of the old world, that's what I miss most. The ability to take action."

"It's not teleportation."

"I know that. But it's something you can do and it's something you owe it to the rest of us to learn about."

He stopped in his tracks. "I don't know what the ghost road is, but I do know it can kill you almost as quickly as bad water. I don't owe that to you or anybody else."

"But, Thomas, it's got other possibilities, I know it—"

"Then you map out this psychic wonder."

Her eyes flashed and pink colored her rounded cheekbones. "You're the only one who can call it up."

"You did—once."

"That was different. I couldn't do it again, and it only worked because you'd already begun the process. I just . . . substituted for you."

He remembered a mountain fortress, its only entrance a stainless steel doorway into an elevator shaft, the bodies of Mojavans and humans alike beginning to bury the doorway as they fought to break the Vaults open to save their own, even as the mountain rumbled its explosive ending and smoke and dirt rose to obliterate his vision. Thomas took a deep breath.

His heart had been thumping in his chest. He projected calmness for both of them. His beat began to slow. He reached out and smoothed a stray bit of hair from her forehead. "I never want to lose you to the road again. I didn't think you were coming back, let alone with Alma."

"That's where you were wrong," Lady said. "And once the precedent has been set. . . ." her voice trailed off.

Pounding footsteps on the path interrupted what he would have said next, and it was just as well, he thought ruefully as he drew away. A slim and pretty young woman ran toward them, her brunette hair on the fly. She wore a rose and brown print dress that accented her youth and freshness. He stopped what he was saying to appreciate what he saw.

Lady put an elbow in his rib cage. "That's Alma, Thomas."

"My god," he murmured. "I've only been gone five months."

"She's at that age," the woman said, "when we all change tremendously."

"Sir Thomas! Lady!" the girl cried breathlessly. "You're late."

Lady caught Alma up as she careened heedlessly into them.
A ribbon was supposed to be holding the fall of her hair back—
it had come loose and only an accidental tangle kept her from
losing it altogether. Lady gave Thomas an amused look over
Alma's head. "How can we be late," she said, "when you can't
start without us?"

The girl gave a little giggle in response and answered by
tugging on both their hands. "You know what I mean. Come on,
come on!"

They let her pull them down the pathway.

"Greta is soooo nervous and Stanhope is very cool, just like
ice, and the others—I don't know why they don't all have
hiccups—" Halfway to the barracks, Thomas interrupted her
chatter.

"Where's Stefan?"

She came to a halt. The prettiness and color fled her face
abruptly. The gleam in her almond brown eyes went out. "He's
out somewhere." She turned then, but he'd already seen what
he'd already seen.

He traded glances with Lady. She shook her head slightly, so
he said nothing further. It was just as well, because the barracks
doors split open then and a wave of children rushed out.

The gaiety he'd come to expect did not greet him. Instead,
their voices were shrill and worried. Lady pushed forward and
grasped two boys by their shoulders. Thomas knew Stanhope,
his dusky skin and dark eyes marking him.

"What is it?" asked Lady sharply, trying to make sense out
of the chaos.

"It's Roanne," Stanhope got out. "She's started the trial
without you."

"That's impossible," the healer snapped. "Where's
Franklin?"

"Gone to the well for water. She went into a convulsion—"

Lady pushed Stanhope into Thomas' arms. "Only one Protector to watch them, and he's gone?"

Thomas caught up with her as she passed into the house.
"Lady, come on, the well's maybe fifty yards away, if that.
They're hardly abandoned—" but the woman ignored him as
she vaulted the stairway. He pressed Stanhope into a standstill
position.

"Stay here with the others. When Franklin gets back, send

him up. All right?" He sent out confidence. Stanhope would know a projection when he received it, but that would not dull its effect, not at this age.

Stanhope was sixteen, nearly a man. He nodded solemnly, "All right."

Thomas mounted the stairs at a dead run. He and Lady reached the bedroom at nearly the same time.

Lady knelt beside the twisting body on the modest navy blanketed cot. The girl was not pretty—older than Alma by a year or two, her face blotchy with acne, perspiration pouring out of her like water out of a rain cloud. Her good dress was stained and soaked already. Someone had removed her ankle boots, tucked her stockings inside of them, and left them waiting beside the cot. A washbasin sat next to them.

"Breakout fever?" The stress of crossing the thresholds of both puberty and psychic powers sometimes put a terrible strain on the body's immune system. Promising Talents had died in breakout fever.

"Hardly," Lady said, wringing out a rag and placing it on the girl's pasty forehead. She knelt beside the cot "Roanne's Talent is barely existent. We're testing her today only out of kindness and necessity." Lady took the rag off and rinsed it again. "No wonder Franklin went for water."

Alma gained the doorway behind them. "Lady?"

"Yes?"

"Is she—"

"I don't know," the healer said tersely. "Now go join the others."

"Yes, ma'am." Alma turned away.

Lady twisted on one knee. "Wait! Alma, was there any problem when you came out to get us?"

"Nothing. I didn't even know Roanne was lying down—"

Thomas looked at Lady. "Awfully quick," he said.

"Yes." Lady chewed on a lower lip. "All right, honey," she said. "Go see if you can hurry Franklin up. We're almost out of water here."

The girl's body seemed to swell up even as they watched helplessly. Lady dredged every drop of fresh water she could out of the laving basin, but there wasn't enough to wash Roanne down properly for cooling. She unbuttoned the dress front as the girl heaved for breath.

Suddenly, Roanne went stiff as a board. Her breath rattled out of her chest.

"My god, Thomas," and Lady threw him a stricken look. "I think she's dead!"

Chapter 6

The girl suddenly went limp, sinking back into the cot. Thomas searched with his Intuition but met a dark, chaotic pool of thought. Lady placed her palms on the girl's rib cage and began to pump in rhythm. "Can you breathe for me, Thomas?"

He hesitated. Who knew what disease the girl carried? He shook off his hesitation, moved to the side of the cot and leaned down, arranging her head and cupping her jaw loosely. But as he took a deep breath, Roanne fought for one of her own. Her eyes flew open.

Lady stopped pumping. The girl's eyes rolled up and then down until she stared out at them, unseeing.

"Path of the dead," she said. The tone of her voice brought up the hair at the back of Blade's neck. "Riding, riding, too close. No warning. Massacre."

"She's seeing Charlie's death," Thomas said. He felt sick to his stomach and took a step away from the cot.

Lady frowned. "Maybe. It could be Precog."

"Foresight? Thought she had little Talent," he answered.

"I could be wrong! That's why we bring in other testers for the candidates." Lady sponged up the last of the tepid water and mopped the girl's forehead. "We're listening, Roanne," she said soothingly.

With a gut-wrenching noise, the girl turned away and retched, spewing all over the flooring to the side of the cot. Thomas jumped back to avoid the spray. Lady wiped Roanne's face clean and brought Roanne's face back toward hers. The girl never blinked, her eyes wide open now as if she were dead. The healer repeated, "We're listening."

Thomas was spooked. He backed up, saying, "Not me. I'll get Franklin." He turned away.

"Blade! She's Projecting her own fear, can't you feel it?"

Sweat had beaded up on his forehead. He could feel the nerves quaking in his hands. Abruptly, he blocked himself and the near panic that had threatened to overtake him like an unstoppable tide washed away. "I didn't even feel her," he said in wonderment.

"No."

There was the sound of boots in the stairwell and a rich, young voice called up. "I'm here. How is she?" as Franklin Brown stepped into the room. He handed a pail of cold water to Lady and answered himself, "Oh, my god. What's happening?"

"We don't know."

The round-faced, rotund young man went for a mop and came back, applying himself to cleaning up as Lady wet the rag thoroughly, washing Roanne's face, neck, and wrists. Thomas washed her feet and ankles. The girl took another deep, shuddering breath.

"Warning! No warning."

Franklin turned, mop in hand, his dark hair falling into his eyes. "Is that her?" he asked.

"Yes. Spectral voice?"

The young Protector shrugged. "I don't know—I've never heard one. That's not Roanne's normal voice."

Lady bathed the girl's thick neck where her cords stood out in tense agony. Thomas stood impatiently, but he could not blame Franklin for not knowing the answers to their questions. Franklin had been an apprentice of Alderman Brown, one of the Protectors slain at the massacre, and though well-trained, he was not experienced in his position. Strain drained away his normally calm attitude. Thomas would not add to that strain.

Roanne bolted upright on the cot. She grabbed for Lady's hand. "They're coming, oh, they're coming and this time I'll die!" She blinked several times and then began to sob.

Blade looked at Lady as she took the girl in a heartfelt embrace and held her tight. The wards were raised here, schooled, and graduated, but Roanne hadn't left yet because she had shown some potential for Protector Talents—and she was one of the wards who had survived the College Vault attack.

"That's not regressive memory," he said suddenly. And he

knew what it was Roanne was seeing. Knowledge galvanized him into action. "That's Foresight—and if she's right, we're all in trouble. Franklin, take care of her, get the kids together and keep them here! Use whatever Talents you can to protect yourself."

He grabbed Lady's wrist, hauling her to her feet, dragging her out of the room and downstairs.

"That's one of the nastiest bouts of breakout fever I've ever seen," he said to her as he tugged her along.

"What's wrong?"

"We're about to be raided—and Roanne didn't see much hope for our chances this time, either." He paused at the doorway. He pointed at Stanhope. "Shutter the windows and barricade the back door."

"Yessir."

Lady balked at the doorway. "I'm staying here."

"We need a link of Protectors up at the house. Franklin's got a handful of raw Talent here. He doesn't need your help."

She looked back, torn. Her fear showed in her expression. "Roanne saw herself die."

"Lady, I need you up at the house."

She gave then, so quickly he almost went over backward. He caught himself. He could see nothing between the barracks and the house. But his senses roiled . . . a raiding party was thundering down on them. Lady sensed it, too. Her skirts boiled about her ankles as she began to run. They bolted for it.

"Shit! The one time I don't hassle the sentries."

"It's not your fault."

"And my rifle's in the stable with my packs. Shit, shit." He reached out and steadied her as she stumbled. They flew over the last ten yards of lawn. He vaulted the refreshment table, yelling, "Raiders!" Lemonade fountained across the patio as tumblers went flying. Celebrants scattered into a drill too well known.

Governor Irlene met him on the patio. Lips tight, she said, "I'll get the troops." She brushed past him en route to the stables where the peninsula troops were quartered because of the size of the gathering.

Shankar had left his sunny spot, but his nemesis loomed in the French doors. Thomas looked about. He pointed at Bartholomew. "Get everybody in that you can, and keep away from the glass."

The knobby man's warts bristled as he said, "What is it?"

"Raiders. We might have enough time to meet the attack."

He paused belligerently in the door frame. "I don't see or hear anything. There's been no alarm sounded."

There was a *shoop* and *thunk* as an arrow parted his hair and buried itself deep in the doorjamb. The shaft quivered from the impact.

Bartholomew ducked sharply indoors, commanding, "Everybody down and into the hallways—get away from the windows!"

Thomas pulled Lady into a crouch with him. The bricks were already very warm from the morning sun. He could feel the heat reach his face. He edged backward. The patio's low rock wall gave them some cover, but it was barely knee-high. Lady brushed her lips across his temple in farewell. "I'll go inside. I'll do what I can."

What Lady could do was a hell of a lot. "I'm for the stables and weapons rack."

"All right." She crawled into the house quickly, even her careful movements drawing another two quarrels, one into the wood and the second bouncing off the glass doors above her as she reached up for the latch.

He stood up and made for the stables. He could feel her cloaking, a warding against objects, not a shield he would care to stand up and dare the enemy with, but helpful now. He could smell smoke, pungent and thick, and he heard the scream of panicked horses and mules. The stable was on fire, flames licking its crest. Fire arrows had led the attack here. Their only luck lay in the fact that it was the roof which had caught first. The tremendous heat of combustion was bleeding into the sky, not building up inside the barn. It would give them some time—but only a few minutes. A barn was extremely flamable and every second counted.

There was already a bucket line forming from the horse troughs in back. Irlene led the troopers. She looked up as he ran past, aiming for the weapons rack in the tack shed. Her voice yelled after him, "Get the animals calm, and we can try to get them out!"

Thomas rounded the corner of the barn. Its side faced a wide expanse, all open, all now unguarded, and he saw the raiders.

He crouched down on one knee as they swept in over the

broken roadway and across the lawns. They weren't Mojavans, though his Intuition had told him that—when Denethan attacked, he did so with Projections of dark, abject fear so thick it could almost be sliced with a knife. Talents like Denethan's were why Protectors like him existed. He felt a kind of relief that an alliance he'd staked his integrity on was still intact. Now he had a different enemy to face.

With screams of hatred, the raiders charged at the stables, boot heels pounding the ribs of their ponies. Dirt and grass clods flew through the air. They were nesters, but they might have been comancheros from a laser disk movie. Blade hit the dirt, Projecting peace and coolness to the panicked beasts within the barn. His only hope to protect the water line would be to get them out of the line of fire—but he knew Irlene wouldn't leave until the animals were gotten out of the barn. He felt Lady's shielding leave him abruptly and knew the main house was under attack as well.

He gathered himself and stood. He built his own cloak, not of invisibility, but of inviolability and repugnance. The eye glancing at him would slide away, repulsed, unseeing. Nesters pounded past, whooping and hollering. their crossbows in hand, fetishes swinging from the chestbands and the bits of their horses. Their matted hair swung wildly. Clay streaked their faces, not in ritual painting, but just for the additional horrification of their already bestial features. He saw fresh scalps hanging from the saddlebag straps. He thought he knew why the sentries had not triggered their alarms.

A nester bore down on him. Blade saw the man's wild eyes and though he was close enough to smell him, knew the man could not see him. He pulled his shuriken out and threw it, turning away to catch it as he Fetched it back even as it completed its arc across the raider's gullet. The nester's throat blossomed crimson. With a gurgling cry, he lurched from his saddle, dead before he hit the ground.

Thomas got to his feet, running. Too-hot wood exploded, showering him with splinters that caught fire as they rained down. He cupped his arm over his face and found the swing doors.

Blade kicked the barn door open. A trooper was shoulder to shoulder with him before the door stopped bouncing. He knew the man, Kopek, a grizzled veteran. "Get them out before the lower level catches. That hay'll go up like plastique."

The trooper nodded.

Harley let out a shivery neigh. The stall holding him was half stove in as the animal had exhausted himself trying to kick free. Lather dappled the gelding's neck and flanks. He rolled a wild eye at Thomas as Thomas stepped in and grabbed his halter. He mounted bareback. His packs were slung at the stall's rear. He ground his knees into Harley's ribs and backed the horse in close enough for him to sling his packs over the gelding's withers and pull his rifle out.

His rifle had been customized to hold three smaller vials. He packed the chamber, cranked it. Harley lunged out of the stall as soon as Blade freed him. Smoke stung his eyes. He leaned over the gelding's thin neck. Mane whipped his face and eyes. The horse plunged for the open doors with a grunting neigh. Other mounts being freed by Kopek jostled them as they speared into the fresh air.

He lost the Projection for calmness then, unable to hold it indefinitely without the ability to concentrate. Behind him, he could hear Kopck's hoarse, smoke-choked voice cursing at the beasts as they raised their voices in panic.

He swung past Irlene and shouted, "Get someone in there to help Kopek!"

She nodded her heat-burned face and continued passing buckets. Harley shook his head, foam splattering her as Thomas kneed him away.

Rifle in hand, mane knotted in his left fist both to guide and steady himself, he rode out toward the broken roadway. He could see the nesters regrouping and exchanging ammo. With a whoop of his own, he drew their attention, let go of Harley's mane, and squeezed the gelding's barrel tightly with his legs.

The chestnut was running on sheer nerves. Blade aimed his rifle over Harley's bobbing head and fired, swiveled, fired, swiveled, and fired again. Without bothering to watch the results, he threw himself forward onto Harley's neck and slipped to the left wither as he turned the horse in the same direction. He was no longer a target and the swiftly dodging Harley ran as though he knew his life depended on it.

Behind him, a wall of flame roared up, eating away green lawn and weed, succulent and wild Shasta daisy, rushing toward the raiders. Charlie, he thought, would have killed him for using those defoliants if he'd been alive. The river of fire would not stop for a half mile. His only hope was that the broken road would be a firebreak between the chemical and Warden manor.

He pulled himself upward on Harley's back and grabbed to keep both himself and the saddlebags steady. He circled the gelding, popped open the chamber and dropped in two lethal vials. He did not want to be downwind when those bullets shattered and released their deadly contents. Blade looked up and slowed Harley's pace, watching as the raiders split up into groups and came round to outflank both him and the militia. He could not see who directed them, but he'd marked several different clan fetishes and that they even rode together surprised him.

He could not see the orphan barracks for smoke and dust and confusion—and did not know if a Protector gave the house an illusionary shielding, or if the nesters had broken through.

He thought of Roanne's unreal voice proclaiming her own death. He'd gotten Lady out, but the others were still in there. Perhaps trapped. Yet the vials in his rifle contained undiscriminating death—he would be no help there. Shrill screams came from both directions, and, in the end, Thomas whirled Harley uphill, to where nesters formed a line against Warden manor.

Harley gave a sudden grunt and wheeze and launched himself into the air. Thomas saw a downed nester's face flash under the horse's hooves. He dragged his boots up out of the man's grasping reach. There was a dull thunk as a rear hoof hit something solid coming down and then they were away. Blade never looked back.

The air stank with the pungency of the defoliants and smoldering death. He steered Harley clear of it, eyes watering, but slowed the gelding down to a walk. He used the cloud bank of smoke as cover, getting as close to the back of the line as possible.

An upper turret of the manor was on fire, black smoke roiling out as crawling figures on the roof dumped water on the hot spot. The nesters had trenched themselves behind the bodies of their mounts—some dead, most of them hog-tied and thrown on their sides. They were unaware of him. The chemical fire he'd started was now a blackened mass, embers and ashes and smoke drifting around.

It was mid-afternoon. The wind off the ocean should blow soon. It would change the direction of the wind blowing now. The only question was: how long would he have to wait and did he have the time?

He shrugged his white scarf about on his jacket collar, where it lay sodden with sweat and fear around his neck. Harley put his head down, blowing for air. Stick figure fire fighters became agitated on the Warden manor roof, and dark smoke began to billow up in earnest. He could hear the screams of the occupants. Breeze or not, he would not leave Lady to that death.

A cold tickle across his forehead. His scarf billowed up sluggishly, a damp sail to that omen.

Harley was spent. Blade dug his boot heels in viciously, hand fisted deep in the horse's mane. "C'mon!"

Between curls of smoke he rode. Harley was wheezing with every jump—they had to hear him, had to know he was bearing down at their backs. He did not care.

He pumped both shots as nesters yelled in fury. They scrambled to their feet to turn about, crossbows and rifles now aimed at him. He squeezed his knees and gave Harley the signal to jump as the vials shattered on impact.

The gelding refused. He ran at the line, bulling his way through as a cloud of yellow-green gave out a fatal hiss and obscured the fighters.

They broke through. Harley stumbled, going downhill toward the crescent driveway. Thomas held his breath, as weak as that first stirring of ocean breeze had been. His scarf snapped outward behind him as they staggered into the driveway, a line of death at his back.

Lady met him at the door. Her face gray with psychic fatigue. She literally fell into his arms as he dismounted and reached for her.

"They're leaving."

He nodded. "Kill enough of them and they will."

She looked over his shoulder. "You said you'd never use that stuff—that or the defoliant."

"I guess I lied." He smelled the ash and smoke in her hair, and the underlying gentle herbal smell that was always Lady. He pressed his jawline into the soft mass of her hair, and held her tighter.

From somewhere to his flank, Governor Irlene said,

"They're on the run. The troopers are after them." She sounded out of breath.

"Good. And Kopek?"

"He . . . didn't make it out. The hayloft collapsed on him."

A pang went through Blade's tiredness. That shouldn't have happened. "A damn shame," he said.

"Yes," the governor responded. She waited as Blade released Lady and stepped back. "You've got some real heroes among the new candidates."

"Where's Alma?" Lady said immediately. She gathered up Thomas' hand as if she could not bear to lose all contact with him. She turned on one heel to face the governor as she did.

Irlene had shed her new dusky rose riding jacket. Her undershirt was smudged and torn. She did not answer Lady, looking at Thomas as she said, "They broke in at the barracks—"

His thoughts raced. What he had hoped was illusionary shielding had been disaster.

"Three wards are dead, the rest are safe. With the exception of four who are missing."

"Who's dead?" he asked evenly. Lady's hand gripped his as if for life.

"Roanne, baby Tranh, and Valentin. The baby died of smoke inhalation from the fire. Roanne was guarding the door. Franklin said she put out some admirable effort before they slit her throat."

"Wh-what about the missing?" said Lady. Her throat sounded dry.

Irlene looked at her. She frowned. "Alma's one of the missing. Nesters took four of the wards with them."

Blade wheeled and grabbed for Harley's mane. "I'll be back—"

"No." Irlene's voice was sharp. "That's not necessary. Troopers rode out on their heels—they won't get far."

Blade looked at the woman. "Irlene," he explained, "they don't need to get far. Those children were bait. They won't be kept alive any longer than they need to be. They're just trying to pull enough troopers after them to pay a decent blood price."

The governor's jaw tightened. "Then," she said, "we don't need any more fools riding into a trap."

Lady had lost his hand when he'd moved so suddenly. She

reached out now and put her hand gently over his arm. "She's right," she said.

He knew they were right. He dropped his arm from Harley reluctantly. "Damn. I know it."

Irlene looked at Lady. "We're still here. We still have Protectors waiting to be passed, and sworn in."

Lady put fingers to her forehead as if stilling an inner pain. She smiled weakly. "You're right, Governor." Her lips tightened. Thomas knew she hated the implication, but the governor was right. Life goes on.

Chapter 7

"I know you're tired," Franklin said soothingly to Stanhope, "but we've got to complete your testing."

The tall boy nodded. There was an underlying pallor to his naturally dark skin, a fatigue that all of them who had used their Talents to Protect felt. Their abilities came out of a deep psychic well—difficult to dredge up and difficult to return to often. Thomas understood the effort Stanhope would be making.

The white bandage sling stood out against his blue tick shirt and dark trousers. He'd dislocated a shoulder trying to fight off the raiders who'd taken Alma and killed Roanne. He'd acquitted himself well and, as far as Thomas was concerned, he'd already passed any testing required of him.

Blade had not had his own testing from Gillander, and just a summary testing when he'd returned with the Butcher for his bounty. Ironically, if he'd undergone a ritual testing, he might never have been made a Protector, his own abilities had been so dammed up at the time, but no one alive had known that. He caught Lady looking at him and wondered if she was sharing his thoughts, however briefly. She was clever at that.

She smiled faintly and looked away, once more intent upon the young man who faced them.

The barracks had lost a bedroom wall and door to fire and axes. The windows and shutters were thrown open to air out the smoke and smell of battle. Tomorrow, carpenters would be in here measuring, cutting, and hammering new boards in place. They could not match the plastic paint that had coated the house originally and wore like iron. The repaired wall would stand out like a scar across a woman's face, a reminder of what had happened here.

Franklin looked at them. "The three of us will each devise a test of a Talent which Stanhope may or may not be known to have. His reactions and abilities will be what we judge."

In other words, they were going to judge him as much on what he couldn't do, and how he might handle that when it was asked of him, as on what he could do. Thomas nodded to show he understood.

There was a shuffle of shoe soles from the other room. No one dared stand in the doorway, but Thomas knew the rest of the children had their ears pressed to the wall in curiosity, to listen to what was happening to Stanhope. He said, a little too loudly, "There are going to be a lot of flat ears in the barracks tonight."

Franklin grinned. "No doubt. All right, I'll begin. Judges, please remember that we will all evaluate all test results, not merely those we've conducted personally."

Stanhope blurted out, "C-could we just get started?"

Lady laughed softly. She put a hand on his knee. "Franklin's just telling us the rules."

The boy looked up at her. "I'm just edgy," he said, apologetically.

Thomas answered dryly, "I wouldn't know why."

Franklin got down on one knee beside the youth in the chair. The room was bare except for a simple four-legged table with a few objects resting on top of it, nothing remarkable, and a few stools. It seemed odd to have the wind and no wall at their back, but under the circumstances, no one complained.

"Stanhope, I want you to Fetch the rice bowl from the table for me. And it must not drop or break before you release it in my hands."

There was a sharp intake of breath from the other side of the wall. The whites of the boy's eyes showed as he glanced toward the doorway. "All right," he said numbly. He closed his eyes briefly.

Franklin murmured softly, "Just build that phantom arm we talked about. Just build it . . . and reach. Nothing that you can imagine is outside your grasp."

They watched the young man who sat immobile in his chair, the starkness of his bandage setting off the richness of the face bowed over his chest. Thomas thought he would be a handsome man . . . there was character in the squared jaw and flat cheekbones. His neck was scarred where gills had been cut out—many of the survivors had that attribute. It was, after all, what had kept them alive in the beginning. They had gone back to the ocean after the disasters, most of them living on and around Catalina for the first years, filtering back to the mainland only afterward. Now, generations later, those gills were not necessary. He did not know if Stanhope had had his gills cut for cosmetic purposes or medical ones. Those not utilizing their gills, or born with immature ones, faced disease and pain through them, and surgery was an attractive alternative.

Stanhope opened his eyes and looked across the room to the table. He held out his hand. The rice bowl rose steadily and answered his movement, floating across the distance to settle in his palm. He handed it to Franklin who said nothing and let no emotion show on his Asian moon face.

Stanhope might more properly have sent the bowl to Franklin, but then he would not have been able to maintain the control the Protector said he wanted of the Fetch. Normally Thomas would wonder about the confidence, or lack of it, prompting such a control choice. Today, after all they'd been through, he knew the boy had to be tired.

Lady said, "Thomas, you're up."

She had a set to her mouth that told him she didn't wish to be argued with. Whatever she had in mind, then, would be extremely taxing. Thomas shrugged. He moved from the young man's side and hunkered down in front of him.

"I could teach you dowsing, but I won't. Why?"

Surprise blossomed in Stanhope's eyes, but no more than the startlement in both Franklin and Lady's faces. "I—I don't—"

Thomas held up a finger, silencing him. "Think it over. You'll have an answer."

The boy blinked. He sat very quietly, so quietly that Thomas knew how hard his heart pounded, for he heard it like a drum within his own senses, and he could feel the steady throb of the boy's wounded shoulder. Thomas hid his smile then, for he knew the boy was Reading him, or trying to, for an answer. He firmly shut the boy out.

Stanhope's face reflected abrupt dismay. Then he said uncertainly, "You can't teach me to dowse because it's illegal. And . . . and I've heard you say that any fool can learn to dowse, but finding *clean* water, that's the hard part, and that's the DWP's job. So, I guess, that's why."

Thomas stood up. Stanhope's flint brown gaze followed him. "Am I right?"

He smiled. "Tell you later."

Lady gave him a puzzled stare. "You, too," he said to her.

She made a face before pulling up a stool to sit opposite Stanhope. "Okay," she said. "Two down and one to go. How are you feeling?"

"I think I'd like to sleep for a week."

They all laughed. "We know the feeling." She patted his knee. "I'll make this quick." She was wearing an apron over her good blue dress now and from its pocket she withdrew a house rat. It was as big as both her fists together, a small cousin of the wolfrat. This one looked about tamely, unafraid. Its whiskers trembled as it tasted the air, and its tail lashed about.

She set the rat on Stanhope's knees. "I want you to kill it," she said. "Burn an ulcerous hole in its side, turn its flesh to decay. Or maybe you'll choose to close its throat up and choke it to death. Or still its heart. However you want to do it. But kill it."

The beige furred creature had been somebody's pet, no doubt, for it sat now on Stanhope's lap totally unafraid. It looked up with dark eyes, whiskers still atremble.

"I can't—" Stanhope seemed out of breath. "I can't do that!"

Thomas stood very still, wondering what her game was. She was a Healer and she had hoped Stanhope would follow in her tracks. Was she trying to show the boy the other side? Or was she speaking to Thomas as well, things she should not be saying to him in front of others? Anger and hurt both welled in him and he fought to keep them from showing. He must not upset or influence Stanhope in any way.

"Of course you can," she coaxed. "Remember when you set that leg. How you felt where it was wrong and you just 'nudged' it back into place. Now I'm telling you to feel where it is right . . . and 'nudge' it out of place."

Stanhope twisted his head to one side. "Nooo," he said. "I

couldn't—" His eyes got wide as his thoughts explored the possibilities.

He *could.* Thomas knew the thought as if he'd originated it himself. He could turn the heart inside out instead of calming it. He could shift bones, clench guts or lungs. He could *kill.* He watched as Stanhope lifted a hand and cupped it over the rat, torn between petting it or crushing it.

The boy looked at Lady again. "I—I—"

"You can do it," she said evenly.

She could do it. She had, in desperation once or twice, to save lives. It was not a Talent Blade had or wanted, but it was a Talent that could exist. Why would she think using a Talent to kill any cleaner than using your hands? Why would she expose him to ridicule like this, through a candidate's testing?

Stanhope sighed deeply. Then he sat up straight. "No," he said. "I won't do it."

Lady reached out crisply, scooped up the rat, and deposited it back in her apron. She stood up and walked out of the room without another word.

Stanhope looked after. Then he bowed his head again and Thomas beard the boy begin to sob.

Franklin dropped his hand to his student's shoulder. "We'll be back in a few minutes," he said gently, "to tell you if you passed." He hurried after Lady Nolan.

Thomas hung back. He put his hand on Stanhope's head, over the tightly knit hair. "It's not over until it's over," he said.

The boy looked up, wet streaks over his face. He just shook his head.

Lady stood in the kitchen, drinking a dipper of water. In the doorway, he caught up with Franklin, who seemed afraid to approach the Healer. Thomas good-naturedly jostled him aside. But the young Protector remained in shock. Lady looked over at him.

She set the dipper down on the sink. "What is it, Brown?"

"Good god, Lady. Did you have to destroy him? Wouldn't it have been enough to have just failed him?"

"Who says I failed him?"

"But—but—"

She nailed him with that blue-eyed, brown-eyed stare. "Would you rather find him capable of destroying you? A

Healer is a Healer. Not a murderer. Not a cold-blooded killer.
But the very Talent that makes one a Healer can be turned inside out, corrupted, misused . . . if the person holding it is capable of doing that."

"Shit," Franklin said and sat down weakly on a kitchen
stool. "You mean you passed him."

"Of course, I did. With flying colors. He knew exactly what
he was capable of, and repudiated it." Lady briskly took the rat
out of her pocket and put the animal in a tiny woven cage. She
looked at Thomas. "I'd say he passed the Fetch as well, but
I'm baffled as to what you were doing."

"Just checking his common sense. Sometimes a Protector
has to rely more on that than anything else."

She snorted in a most unwomanly way and added, "You
should talk."

He shrugged ruefully, moved past her to the sink, and got a
dipper of water himself. The barracks reeked of smoke and it
was drying to the throat. He would not say to her in front of
Franklin what he wanted to say. Was he such a monster to her
that she would scar Stanhope forever to keep him from turning
to Blade's path? How could she love him if she despised him
that much?

Franklin touched the back of his hand to his forehead. "I
judge him passed, as well, then. One down, three to go."

They reached their last candidate late in the afternoon.
Thomas paced unhappily by the open wall as Barbara came in
and sat demurely. She was dark-eyed and dark-haired, a
homely placid girl, her hair braided back. She was all practi-
cality, always had been. She looked up at him now and flashed
a smile that was dazzling.

He did not smile back, but nodded at her. She dimmed her
expression a bit, then settled herself in the chair. As the last,
she'd been listening at the wall while Stanhope had been raked
over and then Barnaby and then Sue and now it was her turn.
She thought she knew what to expect. Her abilities were bare
minimum, Thomas knew. She could Project, Block, and Read
the truth—the least that could be asked of a Protector. She
might open up some more Talents in her later years, women
often did.

Thomas looked out. The troopers had not come back yet

and he did not like it. The longer he waited for someone else to do his job, the less his chances of bringing Alma back alive. "Let's get this over with," Blade said.

"What's the matter?"

"I've got two hours of tracking light left. No one's come back yet. I'm going to have to go out and get them."

Lady paused, something unseen passing between them. Finally, she turned to Franklin. "I'll start."

Franklin nodded.

Thomas paid little attention as Lady had the girl Truth-read a statement she made, or as Franklin had her Project the visual hallucination that the wall had been repaired. The illusion was weak, not her best strength, but she also Projected confidence, an emotion with it, something not many could do.

Thomas had not decided yet how to test her as the hallucination faded. The girl swiveled about again to look at him and he stopped pacing as the wall resumed its wrecked appearance, his boots grinding in the debris.

As quick as the young people were, they had not yet caught on to the pattern of the three testers. There had to be at least one failed question among the three—to see how the candidates coped with failure as well as success. Stanhope's had been spectacular, the other two very quiet. Barbara had passed both Franklin's test and Lady's. It was now up to Thomas to choose something at which she'd obviously fail, to gauge how she dealt with frustration. For a relatively ungifted Talent such as Barbara, the frustrations would be far greater than her successes.

He paced over in front of her and stopped. He pulled his cuff back, exposing the scarred markings on his wrist. With his left hand he touched first his wrist and then his brow.

"Discern the meanings of my markings," he said.

Barbara looked at him. One of her braids lay over her shoulder. In concentration, she pinched the end of it between her thumb and forehead and absently began chewing on it.

Lady looked at him, her own eyebrows quirked. Franklin leaned against the far wall, boredom overlying his serene expression. He shrugged when Lady turned to look at him.

Thomas blocked himself abruptly before he could feel the first tickle or stir of any attempt to Read him, but the girl did not outwardly appear to notice. She lipped the blunt end of her braid absently as she focused on the problem.

There was a stir at the manor house. Thomas could see doors opening and the patio filling, jostling with people. He stared hard, as if he could see all the more closely what was happening. Lady noticed. She swung around and looked, too. Had someone returned?

The candidate reached out shyly and took his right wrist. "A road is anchored," she said, "by its beginning and end." Reaching up, she touched his brow. "Two more marks you must have to know the road's real destination. Earth and water you are—fire and air you must travel to."

Thomas stood in stunned silence. She could not have passed his block. How did she come up with what she'd said?

Barbara dropped her braid abruptly. "Did I pass?" she said nervously.

As his jaw dropped, Lady snapped, "Of course you have, Barbara."

Before she could say anything further, the room filled with yelling and dancing youngsters. They bore Barbara away as if she'd conquered the world, carrying her still seated in her chair, shoulder-high through the crowd. The three Protectors watched them go.

Lady called after, with little hope of being heard, "The naming ceremony is at sundown!"

Stanhope thrust his head around the doorway. "We know!" He bolted after the confusion.

Franklin said, "I'd better go make sure they live that long." He disappeared as well.

Thomas' gaze met Lady's. Her earth-brown eye glimmered with compassion, but he swore he saw amusement in the blue. "What the hell was that?" he got out.

"Her equivalent of baffling them with bullshit?"

"No." He shook his head in denial. "She was talking about the ghost road, dammit. There was no way she could have known and nothing else she could have been talking about. I kept myself totally blocked and I assume you did, too."

"So we pass her as a Protector and list Prophecy as possibly one of her latent Talents." She hooked her arm through his.

"Let's see what's going on. Maybe there's no need for you to take a tracking party out."

Her skin was cool and her manner quiet. She did not expect good from what they walked out to meet. He knew that, and he knew he should be bracing her, protecting her, but all he could think about were the words Barbara had spoken.

"Earth and water," he repeated. "The beast and the dolphin."

"Maybe. It's standard symbolism."

"But how did she *know?* How many people have we told about the road?"

"Only a ghost here and there," Lady said lightly. He looked at her face then and saw the glimmer of an unshed tear in her eyes.

"I'm sorry," Thomas said immediately. "It's not important." At least, not then it wasn't.

Art Bartholomew met them on the pathway. "Riders," he said, "Out front."

"The troops?"

"Some of them."

The man's enigmatic answer perked Thomas' attention. He drew Lady with him, weaving through the crowd that had gathered.

The manor house had lost a turret to the roof fire. As they brushed their way through, its rooms also stank of the smoke and fighting. They gained the driveway and, for a moment, the view stunned him.

The desecration of the chemical fire was vast and ugly, a gouging black stain upon the hillside and slope. The broken roadway had contained it somewhat, but the scarring ran all the way to the butte above the ocean, where a natural lookout cropped over the rock and sand. Charlie would have been appalled. Blade took a deep breath.

Lady nudged him. He looked to his left, where the riders approached. They were ragtag, bedraggled, the troopers, their ponies and mules with heads low, some limping. Bandages wrapped arms and legs, bloodstains the badges of combat. The nesters had led them over hill and dale, and it was a miracle any of them had come back at all.

"I should have gone with them," Blade said.

"You can't be everywhere," Lady admonished. Her voice lightened. "Oh, my god. He's got Alma!"

The lead rider carried the girl across his horse's withers, balanced lightly in front of him. Blade's eyes narrowed. He could not tell if the young man was nester or trooper, captive or rescuer. As they neared, he could see the three other wards had been found as well, riding double behind other troopers.

He did not know the young man in front. The rider carried a nester war lance, feathered with numerous clan fetishes and decorated with fresh scalps. Only, as the rider turned into the manor driveway, Blade identified the scalps as nester. He looked back to the rider, a man no less barbarous than the nester he'd stolen the war lance from.

He was young . . . between twenty years and Alma's age, but he rode his horse with natural grace and he was obviously the leader of this triumphant group. His shirt was of cotton, wide sleeved, open throated, his trousers of soft doeskin bleached almost white by the sun. Lady caught her breath as he kicked his heels into his mount and galloped at them, war lance flashing in the late afternoon sun.

"God, he's beautiful," she murmured, then looked guiltily up at Blade. "But arrogant," she added.

Thomas looked back to the youth as he pulled his horse to a plunging stop in front of the crowd. Dark blue eyes, their color as clear as gems under raven wing brows, swept the crowd. He handed the girl down and dismounted. He wore black leather gloves, the cuffs wide and folded back. A headdress of feathers, as thick and luxurious as a mane of hair, swept back from his brow to his broad shoulders. The feathers caught and echoed the color of his eyes, dark blue, dappled with teal and then shot with light gold and turquoise. There was amusement in his eyes as he looked about.

"We ran into a group of your troopers," he said. "They appeared to need our help." He let Alma go as if presenting a gift to the enclave.

Alma stepped into Lady's ready embrace. She let out a little sob as the woman gathered her in. "He saved me," she said. "They had us staked out . . . they're were going to do—" she shuddered. "Then they rode up."

The young man stopped behind Alma. "I'm looking for Sir

Thomas Blade," he said. He stabbed the war lance into the dirt between them.

He stepped around the women. "You've found him," Blade answered.

"Good," the rider said. The feathered headdress stirred, rising as hackles might rise, then higher, and Thomas saw that the plumage was part of him, rather than hair, as the plumes came up into an incredible crest framing his handsome face. The young man put his hand out. "I'm Drakkar," he said. "Denethan's son."

Chapter 8

Thomas stared wordlessly at the gloved hand. Drakkar kept it extended and said, a little too loudly, "Shankar! Didn't you inform our hosts I was on the way?"

The Mojavan ambassador moved out of the shadows, pushing his way through a crowd reluctant to let him pass. He bowed deeply and sinuously before the young. man. "I most certainly did, young chieftain. But you find our hosts in disarray. The raiders have done much damage. . . ."

The gaze of those deep blue eyes surveyed the manor and outbuildings. A finely chiseled nose widened at the scent of char and charnel that hung faintly on the ocean breeze. The corner of Drakkar's mouth pulled up in amusement. "Not as much," he said, "as they could have."

Indeed not. In Denethan's raiding years, communities caught as unaware as they had been would have been razed to the ground. Thomas unfroze at the ironic tone. "No," he agreed. "And partly thanks to you. Our children are more important than wood and stone." He still did not take the young man's hand.

Drakkar said, "I forget myself." He stripped off the soft gloves and hooked them in his belt. There were several gasps as his hands and inner wrists were revealed. Talonlike spurs curled at the base of his palms. Thomas had no doubt they were strong and lethal, with poisonous pouches just beneath the skin to feed venom to the spurs. They could rake a man to death or drop him with just one touch. Drakkar seemingly ignored the gasp of revelation and reached out his hand again.

There was a spark as their hands met, unseen but not unfelt. Thomas was thinking clearly, *So you're Denethan's boy,* and from the sudden amusement on the other's face, Blade thought he'd been heard as clearly as if he'd spoken aloud. *Talent, in this one.* Someone moved in the crowd. Drakkar looked away alertly, then back as they dropped hands. His feathered crest deflated slowly, dropping back down to carpet his head and shoulders once more.

Shankar jumped into place at the young man's elbow, starting a receiving line of sorts, introducing Drakkar. Thomas became aware of the low murmurs at his back and knew that the young man and his party were causing a stir. The Countians had become used to Shankar, but the lads who dismounted now were pure Mojavan, their faces and bodies lightly scaled, their skins of dun and gray and green, snakelike, their arms with more joints than any human had a right to—human, yes, but altered to be not-human. Blade remembered Denethan, the man he'd hated passionately long before they'd ever met—and Denethan, to his shock, had been handsome . . . gold and dust, more like the hill cat and the coyote than like a snake, but he'd had that faint diamond pattern to his skin as well. His eyes had been the color of bronze, his thickly curled hair as blond as Thomas', and he'd looked down on Blade's height though Thomas was a tall man among his people. As Thomas examined Drakkar, he could see Denethan's bone structure and good looks underlying—but who the hell had his mother been? Where had he gotten those unnaturally blue eyes and what had caused his avian evolution?

"I see your barn is gone." Drakkar's attention returned to him.

"But not our hospitality." Governor Irlene gave a brittle smile. "Finley, Kozinsky, take their mounts and stake them out on the horse-line." The troopers she ordered moved around the fringe of the crowd to do as bid. They halted in front of the Mojavans. There was a moment of silence, then Drakkar's men gave over the reins of their mounts. Franklin came forward and gathered in the three pale-faced children standing in Alma's and Lady's wake. He herded them back to the barracks, clucking and encouraging them like a mother goose shepherding her goslings. Alma started after them, but Lady plucked at her sleeve, drawing her back, saying, "Stefan went out, too . . . but they haven't come back yet."

Strain and exhaustion showed in her soot-stained face. She

could only nod weakly. Lady slipped an arm about her waist and kept it there.

Beyond them, Shankar brought Drakkar forward, continuing introductions and receiving only polite murmurs in exchange.

Valdees stepped forward courageously. Shankar gave a little hiss and said, "This is Armand Valdees, Governor of Orange County."

The stocky man pumped Drakkar's hand. "There is enough of a building left standing to house our ceremonies. You've caught us preparing to swear in a new generation of Protectors."

"Ah," said Drakkar. "Baptism of fire, eh?" His mouth twisted again as weak laughter followed his words. "It looks as though you could use a few more."

The sun had begun to dip low over the ocean. Its slanting rays shone across the older man's balding pate as he took Drakkar by the arm and drew him across the courtyard. Drakkar gave a signal. His men dropped into formation, flanking them. Blade watched as Shankar also fell into position as Valdees continued his animated conversation. Guests they were, but wary ones, and that was well for as Drakkar drew out of earshot, the comments Thomas heard were not all welcoming ones. Old enemies appearing on the heels of new enemies . . . even Blade felt suspicion. The appearance of Drakkar's troops across the trail of raiders seemed a trifle convenient.

Only Lady and Alma hung back, seemingly disinclined to return indoors. Thomas halted.

"Dinner?"

"We'll take it privately, I think." Lady smoothed Alma's tangled hair from her still pale face.

"I want to wait for Stefan," the girl said.

"Oh, he'll be back as soon as the nesters stop running rings around them. With you and the others returned, the clans will be heading back to their territories right about now." Thomas would have believed her more, but her dark gaze had gone after Drakkar, keeping him in sight as long as she could until he disappeared through the manor's oaken doors.

"You're sure. . . ." Thomas hesitated. "You're sure they were nesters."

She looked over at him. Lady's arm about her waist kept her

braced and on her feet. She wrinkled her nose, then nodded emphatically. "Nothing," she added, "smells like a nester."

He'd his own opinions but wanted them confirmed.

"What are you thinking, Thomas?" asked Lady sharply.

"Nothing that the majority of us aren't thinking already. Drakkar's heroism is much appreciated but a little suspect." He pulled the nester lance out of the dirt. An aura of pain and death came with it. The scalps were still fresh. Drops of gore had puddled on the ground.

"I'll take that," Lady said, reaching for it. "You'll want to look at it later."

He let her take it, though Alma shrank away from it. She gave him that two-color look as plain as any message. They had woman things to talk over and wanted their privacy. Thomas smiled ruefully and left.

The room had polarized into factions by the time he entered the manor. The festive atmosphere of the morning was gone, replaced by weary fire fighters and Countians who were hungry and tired. Drakkar appeared not to notice the division as he worked the room, shaking hands formally. He had an eye for the young ladies shuffling forward to meet him, Thomas noted. Trouble, and more trouble.

He saw Shankar and hooked the ambassador. "Why, Sir Thomas," the man said, his voice too soft and oily. "What can I do for you?"

"You can tell your young chieftain to get back on his horse and go back to the Mojave or our alliance won't be worth a damn. I'm not going to let him splinter my people."

The ambassador sighed sharply. "It wouldn't work," he said, dropping all pretense. Thomas was surprised to see overt unhappiness written all over Shankar. "Drakkar passed me this."

He handed a tidy scroll to Thomas. It was addressed to him in the finely written hand of Micah, Denethan's elderly scribe. Micah had recovered from his illness enough, apparently, to resume some of his duties for Denethan. The seal had been broken and it was obvious Shankar had read it first.

Thomas let his eyebrows go up and looked at Shankar. The ambassador merely shrugged. "Read it," he said.

My dear Thomas. Into your capable hands I send my son Drakkar as a visible token of the alliance between ourselves. I

*ask that you look as deeply for the humanity within him as you
have looked in all of us. My reign here is being challenged and
it is not safe for Drakkar to remain with me. The nesters have
acquired leadership. I have my suspicions as to who or what
provides it and will inform you as soon as I've confirmed it. In
the meantime, know that our treaty has opened a rift among my
people and that my rule is an uneasy one. I have sent Shankar
an antidote for the poison in Drakkar's spurs. He has been
named for drago or draco, in Latin, the dragon. Watch your
back. D.*

A chill went down his back. Thomas let the scroll snap shut
in his hands. "Antidote?" he said.

"The boy has been known to duel. The, ah, antidote is fairly
effective."

"Shit."

The Mojavan ambassador looked visibly startled. "Pardon?"

"You heard me. All I need is to be up to my ass in politicking and intrigue." The scars on his wrist and on his brow itched.
He looked across the vast room of the manor as the French
doors were thrown open and the scent of dinner flooded in.
Diners began drifting outside where tables had been set up on
the lawn scarred by the fighting of the afternoon. The smell of
roast pork wafted their way. It reminded him that it had been a
long day, and he was achingly hungry. "Let's eat, Shankar."

The ambassador bowed. "A worthy idea. A hot meal
changes the perspective of many problems."

Thomas had already tucked away a plateful when Lady
brought Alma and seated her at the end of his table. The girl had
bathed and changed clothes. Now she was wearing a light blue
shirt and brown and blue skirt that had undoubtedly been bor-
rowed from the Healer, for it was cinched up tightly at the waist.
The Protector also had a habit of wearing colors that echoed her
eyes.

Thomas caught her gaze and raised an inquiring eyebrow.
Lady merely returned an enigmatic look that meant nothing and
everything. She filled her plate and he noticed that she watched
Drakkar closely without seeming to.

Alma was quiet as she passed her plate for steaming chunks
of pit-roasted meat. Drakkar, seated three chairs down on

Thomas' left, did not miss the appearance of the young lady he'd rescued.

He paused, fork halfway to his mouth. "Feeling better?"

She snatched her plate back and eyed it intently. "Yes," she said quietly. "Much. And thank you."

"It was chance, but a fortunate one." Drakkar took his bite. He had good teeth.

A commotion rose on the patio, the stomping and shuffling of booted feet. Thomas turned, one hand going to his collar, fingertips brushing his throwing star. By torchlight, he could see a dusty, ragged band of troopers and riders. Sunset had just bled out of the sky, a purple haze settling over the house and lawns, but he knew Countians when he saw them. A tall man with white-blond hair led them, and his tiredness and worry was etched deeply in his face.

"It's Stefan," Alma said, pushing away from the table and getting to her feet.

Thomas dropped his hand from his weapons. He noted that two or three of the mappers had accompanied Stefan and the militia. They all looked as if they'd been beaten with a stick. The mappers, a generation of surveyors and cartographers hand-trained and inspired by Charles Warden, were all boys fast approaching adulthood. Theirs was a profession that, twenty years ago, no one could have been spared to follow.

The Russian-born Countian approached the table. "Sir Thomas," he said, and his throat sounded as if caked with dust. He cleared it and tried again. "You found them." His eyes avoided Alma, but he clearly knew she stood waiting for him.

"No," Blade answered, "but they've been brought back. Were you decoyed?"

"Yes and very successfully, too, I'm afraid. We lost three raiders to booby traps. They took us all the way down to the Fire Ring. We never saw them, but they led us by the nose . . . until we caught up with them." He left unsaid what had happened then, but Blade rejoiced at the silent implication. Stefan took off his hat and turned it in his hands, examining the brim closely. He looked up, pale blue eyes avoiding Alma. "They came to kill as many of us as they could."

"I know. You did well."

Governor Irlene spoke up. "That they did. Clean up and get some dinner before it gets cold."

Alma said, "I've saved you a plate, Stefan."

He looked at her then. "That won't be necessary," he said, turned on his heels, and followed the other boys down to the bathhouse.

Alma dropped back into her chair. She stared down at her plate.

Lady slid a hand over hers and squeezed gently.

Thomas saw that Drakkar, without staring, had missed nothing, despite the chatter of diners between them.

"Damn," he muttered to himself. He thought Shankar, next to him, made a kind of hissing noise deep in his throat.

A full moon rode the sky that night. The stars of Indian summer peppered the cloudless bowl. The only veil pulled over the silvery disk was an occasional sputter of smoke from the avenue of torches upon the lawn. The tables had been cleared and taken down. Blankets replaced chairs. Over the murmur of talking, the only loud noises were chinks of glasses or long-necked beers.

A hedge of night-blooming jasmine marked the slope of the manor house off from that of the barracks. Against its backdrop, Lady Nolan solemnly waited to swear in and name the candidates for Protector. A dusky-skinned boy stepped forward to meet her. His eyes shone in the torchlight.

"I am Stanhope Nolan," he said, declaring his training and his Talent with the choosing of his last name. Excitement greeted his opening statement. Healers were rare and needed. Counties would be vying for his permanent assignment, but Stanhope had a year on the road facing him before he would be allowed to pledge his allegiance to any one county.

Lady took his hand and they faced the Countians, but Thomas, sprawled on the grass, jaw propped on one elbow, listened without hearing. His thoughts warred with his fatigue. There was a changing of the guards of sorts, as Lady and Stanhope left the center of attention, replaced by Franklin with the next four.

She left Stanhope's side, the boy's eyes still shining, and joined him. The hand she gave him to hold was chilled. He sat up. He ground the bottle of beer into a clump of grass to steady it, so he could cover her hand with both of his.

She said nothing and although he wanted to ask her why she

had done what she had done with Stanhope during the testing, he could not. If she said that she despised him because he was the executioner, what would he do then? He would lose her for good. Better to have her now and wonder when she would leave, than to have already lost her. The breeze shifted slightly, bringing the scent of the burned out barn with it.

His thoughts chilled him then. He realized that his own musings were already leading him away from her. It was him leaving her rather than the other way around.

She half-turned to him, her lips parting gently as if to say something, when Stefan dropped down on the lawn behind them. He smelled sharply of horses, sweat, and lye soap. Lady closed her mouth firmly, no longer about to say what she had been about to.

"It's time," the young man said, without preamble. He was not good-looking in the way that Drakkar was. His features were too bony, eyes a little too small, worry lines already cutting into his lean features. He kept his light hair cut short, emphasizing the rawboned nature of his face. "I want to take a mapping expedition out, Thomas." He should be addressing a mayor or a governor, not the executioner, but Blade knew well why he came to him first.

Lady looked daggers at him, though the night shadowed her face.

Thomas let go of her hand. He sat up and crossed his legs nester-style. "You have a wife," he responded mildly.

"I also have a dream," Stefan answered. "And now's the time to follow it before I have responsibilities to keep me from it. Alma's young, we have no children—" He stopped, expressionlessly.

"There are other surveyors."

His voice took an edge. "I'm one of the oldest. I've been with you as far as the College Vaults, and we need to map beyond. There must be other enclaves, other survivors, unless we're isolated geographically. We need to know and we're ready to volunteer."

Thomas scratched at an invisible patch of dirt on the knee of his jeans. "You're talking about a lifetime vocation."

"Done a little bit at a time. A job I can pass down to my son." Stefan's voice choked up.

If the nesters united, they could effectively wall off any av-

enues to outside exploration. The mapmakers needed to go now
before those passes were closed by warfare. He could not argue
with the logic of Stefan's timing. And someone like Thomas
needed to go with the mappers, to assess what was happening
with the nester clans. He was the only authority on nesters he
knew.

He stirred.

Lady must have sensed his thoughts. "No!" she said urgently.

"He's right," Thomas told her.

"No. No, Stefan, don't do this. Don't tear yourself away
from Alma. She was terrified today."

The young man met her gaze unflinchingly. "You don't want
me to leave," he said, "because you think I'm genetically pure.
Well, I'm not. I'm probably sterile. This is the only way I can
leave my mark on the Seven Counties. At least give me this."

"It's not your failure alone," Lady argued. "It takes two.
Alma's very young. She began maturing late . . . she—"

"She's better off without me!" Stefan interrupted. He
grabbed Thomas' arm. "Let us go. Take us as far as the Vaults
and let us go. Charlie trained us for this. It was your dream
once, too."

Damn the boy. Damn the boy for remembering too well all
the years he'd worked with him. He'd taught Stefan how to
shoot, to track. How to follow the lay of the land.

Thomas stood. He had not wished to interrupt the ceremonies, but he and Stefan had a lot to talk about, and it was better done privately. "Where's the lance?" he asked of Lady.

She would not look up. "In Charlie's den."

"Come with me," he told Stefan. He wanted another look at
the war lance. If the Dean of the College Vaults was still alive,
and if the dean was behind the nester raid, it was certain he'd
sent Thomas a challenge. He wanted to be sure he read it aright
before he answered it.

Chapter 9

Return to Fall, 2283

He'd always been a big man. He remembered that, as well as seeing the fact for himself when he reviewed the records. Now he was tall, but emaciated, his fleshy bulk gone to stickpin arms and legs. Living among the nesters would not flesh him out again, but he'd begun to get his strength back in wiry muscles. He owed the clans his life, he supposed, if living among the ruins could be considered a life.

He approached his past through the broken foothills which he had known as the San Gabriel Mountains because the nester clan which had taken him in camped by the San Gabriel Reservoir. There had been clans living in the shadow of the Vaults themselves, but he had ordered them destroyed for the vermin they were. It had been weeks before this clan had found him and taken him in.

They were still vermin, but this time they were useful vermin.

He rode horseback, and the inside of his thighs chafed horribly and the bone of his butt ached with every bouncing step the horse took. The animal was ewe-necked and its spine stuck up like a range of volcanic rock even through the crude saddle, but it was better than walking. A clansman, the only one he could convince to come with him, trotted obediently behind him and on a lead behind the nester were two burros. The dean needed Ketchum far more than the nester needed him, though he would never let the beastman know that. Without him, the dean doubted he could find the encampment again or deal with the recalcitrant little Nazarene donkeys.

Every time he saw the burros, he thought of the wild ones

who'd run the China Lake military base and how much trouble there'd been every time the herds had to be thinned down. This was a memory ingrained in his first self, not an experience of this body, but accessible to him anyway. Animal rights people would protest, the military forces would embarrass themselves, the hunters would line up in their four-wheelers to go shooting along the desert flats—who would have thought, a couple of hundred years later, the burros would survive and the military would be dead.

Not him. He would not have bet on it.

He would never have bet he could have been turned out of the Vaults, either.

His horse stumbled on the jagged, brown stalks of grass that framed the dry hills. He reined it to a stop, stood in the stirrups to take his weight off his butt, and the nester rode up beside him.

The hill was still scarred with the battle fought here. The explosion had collapsed the far side of the mountain in on itself, but here was where the funeral pyres had been stacked, and great mounds of ash and bone littered the meadow. It had only been a few months and with no rain over the summer, the green was yet to come. It would be well fed when it did come.

The nester's round brown eyes were wide with awe. "Dean," he said. "The mountain is dead."

"This part of it is. We go around to the base of the hill along the creek bed."

"Ah," said Ketchum. "You have a second hole there." He spoke in the manner of a tracker used to the ways of wily animals.

"Indeed I do." He stared at the begrimed and hair-matted man until the tracker looked away, afraid to meet his eyes. The dean felt a surge of triumph at that. *I am Mowgli*, he thought, *staring down the wild animals. I am man and he is not.* He let the pleasure of the domination flood him for a moment. He had not been able to convince anyone else to accompany him—his status with the clan was uncertain, but it would not be after his return from the Vaults. Deposed from the Vaults he might have been, but in the land of the blind, the one-eyed man was king. There was science enough buried in the underground labs to keep him immortal and make him king over any subjects. And when he was done with the nester clans, the Seven Counties would pay for destroying the last stronghold of modern man.

He'd see to it personally.

He settled back in the saddle and turned his horse downslope. Ketchum made a chirping noise to his mount and dropped back into place obediently, the two fractious burros lingering behind him.

The self-destructive devices had done an excellent job, he discovered. Bellydown like a snake he crawled back into the dubious womb which had given him birth and rebirth. The escape tunnel had partially collapsed on itself after he'd gotten through. It gave the dean a certain amount of satisfaction to know that his new leaner self was gaining ground where he could not possibly have gone before. The long hot summer of lean rations had done him a favor. The light on his headgear flickered once, but he did not falter as he inched forward through the soft dirt until he found the plasticomb walls of the tunnel again.

Ketchum would not enter with him, though he held the far end of a rope that the dean untangled from his belt as he crawled forward. The man was abominably suspicious, constantly praying to the Shastra, some shaggy-haired beast he claimed watched over them. The dean had identified vague ursine and canine genes in the totems he'd been allowed to see. He'd been told it was the Shastra that had brought nester hunters across his path to save him from dying. He remembered no such creature and had been an agnostic throughout his various incarnations. But the backing of such a dubious demigod had served to give him personal magic and kept Ketchum at bay. That was just as well, for the dean wanted whatever magics he salvaged from the Vaults to be his and his alone though he doubted the stunted intelligence of the man would be able to comprehend much of what he would have seen in the ruins. Still, the dean coveted these ruins as his and his alone, the salvage as his legacy. The closed community of hundreds had died, silently, at his behest. He had intended it that way and he wanted it kept that way.

He reached an interior wall of the Vaults. Taking the rope off his waist, he anchored it on the open bulkhead. He stood, knees cracking as he did so, back still cramped because he could not stand up completely and had to walk hunched over. His light picked out the signs and international symbols, but he knew where he was. He had spent several lifetimes here. He scrounged through labs, picking through tools and utensils that were irreplaceable. He took his time, unworried whether Ketchum survived outside.

He finally found the utero chambers and dropped the makeshift packs he'd made and stuffed with salvage, uttering a cry of dismay.

This part of the Vaults had been constructed to survive even the self-destruct. It was to have been the hope against all defeat. Now it sat on its foundation, tilted, cracked like an egg. The stench from the chambers was appalling. The dean put a sleeve to his face, as if he could filter it away. The dead . . . thing . . . within had been his incarnation. Now he had but one life to live, and that was the life he possessed at this moment.

The man put his head back and let out a howl. It was muffled by the fallen concrete and plasticomb and tons of mountain. No one heard his anguish but himself. He fell to his knees, his face dampened with tears. He put a hand out to embrace himself. The plasticomb was as chill as he imagined the cadaverous flesh before him.

It was himself inside that cracked, treacherous womb, and he mourned all his possibilities with this death. He had survived it all—the meteorites, the limited nuclear exchange, the dust which had covered Earth like a shroud for decades, the famine, the plagues, the earthquakes which seemed little enough after all else—cloned and recloned, it had been planned for there to be a Dean of the College as long as the College Vaults existed.

He tried to pull himself together. A glimmer from his flashlight picked out the imprinter. It seemed intact, though its lines to the utero chamber were now useless. He crawled forward across the rubble, one arm over his face to mask the stench that grew stronger as he approached the chamber. The unit's panels flared into life as he touched them.

The dean ripped the imprinter/recorder out of its sockets. The wiring was intact as well, leads and probes falling away from the failed clone's decaying flesh. He stood up, and held the unit in his trembling hands.

He would go on. It would even be through flesh of his flesh, though his skin crawled at the concept of mating with a nester woman. No. There would be someone more suitable. When the time came, he would know it. And the machinery and the scheme would not fail him. The dean would continue to be immortal, as he had been meant to be.

He wrapped the leads around the small box and stowed it carefully in his pack. As he left the lab, the debris stirred up by his movement began a small avalanche, shelves tumbling down, and another unit bounced to the floor by his foot. It was heavy and squat.

The dean bent over to retrieve it. His fingers shook again as he brushed the dirt from its face. It was the recall beacon unit for the long-term space probes sent out at about the time the College Vaults had first been sunk into the mountain. His fingernail scraped across the plastic face. A window pulsed at him, a steady red light. He frowned, eyeing the instrument. This had been part of his life's work, to watch and monitor and hope that the longships might return as had been intended.

With the edge of his sleeve, he quickly wiped down the unit. It, too, was self-contained and self-powered. He was not lost—not himself and not his mission. Tears brimmed in his eyes. Their heat spilled over and down his face. The unit was functional. Its reading told him that a signal had been intercepted. He held it close to be sure he was reading it properly.

Something had set the unit off. Had it been blinking when he entered the lab and had he been so struck by the utero chamber that he'd failed to note it? He wiped his face. Panic swept him. Had he failed in his mission after all these years? When had he last checked the sender/receiver? He could not remember . . . years, perhaps. He had been occupied with dealing with the discovery of the Vaults by Charles Warden, a brilliant if not quite human man, and all the implications of that discovery—the dean rubbed his face harder in hopes of damming his tears.

The return of longships meant the return of humanity to the Earth. No more adapted mutants, no plague-virused-DNA freaks . . . *humans!* His chance for a genuine renewal. The Earth's second chance.

The dean flipped open a window on the unit. He paused but a second before activating the recall beacon switch. Its range was limited, not beyond the asteroid belt at best, but in order for the unit to be receiving the inquiry as it was now, the longships had to be within that range. If they had called, he had answered.

He was confirming their mission done, their need to be home. Somewhere on Mount Baldy—or perhaps it was Palomar, he could no longer remember such fine details—a silo was opening and antenna and dish should be responding, and equipment beaming that recall into the depths of space.

He snapped the window shut. Now two lights danced on the unit's face. The dean smiled grimly. If the longships were returning, he had perhaps two years, maybe a little less to prepare for them. They would be the scourge of the Earth.

And, if not, if the unit had been set off initially by accident, it was still an amusing piece of work to dazzle the nesters with.

Dusty struggled to keep her teeth from chattering as she woke. This time it was like swimming to the surface of an unforgiving, iced-over lake, wondering if she could break through.

She blinked several times, thoughts disoriented, unable to remember for a moment who it was who would greet her . . . shipmates from years past swirling through her inner vision, confusing her as she tried to focus on a face she did not recognize at first.

Then she realized it was Commander Dakin, Sun, who smiled down at her rather than Willem's dark and friendly face. She put her hand up, still inarticulate.

"It's all right, Dusty. I'll wait for you."

She managed to nod. The dialysis shunt in her ankle stung fiercely from the alcohol swab. She clung to his hand, a firm-boned hand with slender strength, his skin oddly dry. She wondered what had happened to Marshall, worried a bit, and then decided Sun would tell her when he was ready. Or, more aptly, when she was ready.

Sun reached behind him for the warmed blanket and tucked it about her. The blanket helped. Her shivers slowed to a convulsive shudder now and then. Finally, nothing.

She had been dreaming of her sister. Those dreams were always deep and underlay her waking periods as though she still hoped, in those regions of her mind and heart where she was unsure of her thoughts and motives, that Lisa was somewhere to be reached.

Sun's almond eyes came into abrupt focus. There were tiny, tiny lines at the corner as if he'd been staring into the sun. He wouldn't know about that, of course, every port on the *Chal-*

lenger was well screened for brightness and radiation. Perhaps he had been standing at the helm like a steersman of old looking across a sea of stars.

Dusty laughed softly at the idea. The noise seemed to startle the commander.

"Are you all right?"

She caught herself and sat up in the crèche, holding the warmed blanket to her chin. Her nose still felt icy. "Where's Willem?"

"At the con. He's fine, Dusty." Sun stepped back as she reached for the latch on the crèche and opened the side up. His gaze went to the timer on the dialysis unit. He said, "You're not ready yet."

"I know. I just wanted to . . . sit up." To clear the cobwebs, to touch you, to understand why you're here and Willem isn't, she wanted to say, but didn't dare.

The lines about his eyes relaxed a bit. When she saw they had, she said, "Give me the bad news, Commander."

Sun stepped back another pace and shook his head. "You've been asleep six years but you're still sharp as a tack. I look at you and think, she knew my father."

"I knew your great-grandfather," Dusty snapped. "What's that got to do with anything? What time is it—how close are we and *what's happened?*"

He put his hand out again, this time in warning and supplication. He did not want her standing and falling. "All right," he said quietly. "The good news is . . . we've got a recall beacon homing us in. It's to one of the alternate landing sites, out by Lancaster/Palmdale."

"We do?" Her heart missed a beat. It hurt. She put her hand to her chest in reflex, not noticing that Sun observed the motion and worried. She thought of herself in terms of experienced time, not the age she would be if she had lived all those years instead of hibernating. "What's the bad news?"

"It's the *Maggie*. Reichert lied to us . . . he had the capability to send out a probe and he did." Sun hesitated. "Can you watch the screen, Dusty? I want to put something up for you."

She felt cold again, achingly cold inside. She knew the Earth had to be dead, all her family and friends dead, all her memories silent. Reichert had gone and gotten confirmation for her.

She wiped her forehead, forcing her curly bangs off her brow. "How bad is it?"

"It's worse than you could possibly expect," Sun said flatly. He turned the lights down and the screen on.

"The *Maggie* launched the probe with a booster, so it made its turnaround time far faster than we could. We picked these pictures up about a year ago."

Dusty watched, but she understood nothing of what she saw. Nothing that she was seeing was a clear shot at first, so Sun interpreted the visuals for her.

"The good news is, the rain forests are back," he said almost bitterly. "And that's because, as near as we can tell, mankind has been wiped off the face of the Earth. We've picked up nuclear strike zones and also some rather odd impact zones in the western United States here and here, one in Russia and one in South America—from the craters, we want to say a meteoroid strike of significant impact, but whether those were the crowning blows or what, we can't say."

Dusty frowned at the black and white shots. "Nobody left anywhere?"

"Not that the probe picked up, which means whatever is left of civilization is either fairly small or gone underground."

"What triggered the beacon?"

"We don't know."

The shots came in tighter. She recognized the world turning slowly in its orbit as the probe swung around. "What about nuclear winter?"

"That's a good possibility. Equally good is a dust shroud, based on the Nemesis theory, from meteor impact. We don't have a Nemesis here and now, but the basic theory holds. A lot of life would have been affected by a heavy dust cover that could have lasted, oh, decades."

She looked at the screen. No sunlight, no vegetation. No food chain for existence. Mankind might outlast it a year or two on reserves, but never decades. Not *en masse*. "Mass starvation."

"Mmm," Sun said. He looked at her. "That's still not the worst."

What could be worse? She returned his look. He thumbed the screen to a pause and said, "We've lost the *Maggie*."

"What?" The words burst out of a throat gone suddenly numb.

"Shortly after the probe pictures were transmitted. Reichert said they'd been losing water. We knew they were having difficulties but—" the commander's voice came to a halt. He took the video off pause. The transmission changed abruptly from that of the probe to a view off the *Challenger*'s port side, where the *Maggie* cruised alongside, several hundred miles away.

Suddenly there was a tremendous flare-up. Explosion, implosion, she couldn't tell which—and the longship was gone. This death was silent, too. "Oh," she breathed. "My god."

"We think it was suicide. We think that Reichert filmed the transmission to be sent on to us while they reviewed the information, sat down with his command, and made the decision. They had nothing to return to. They had little likelihood of making it elsewhere. They decided to—end it. Sun turned the screen off altogether and panned the lights up. "I'd like to think it was an accident, but my heart tells me it was not."

Dusty sat, stunned.. "Then it's just us and the *Mayflower*."

He nodded.

She looked at the empty screen. She thought of all the promises, all the interviews, all the intentions. JPL, NASA, the President of the United States and the President of Russia, the long-range plans. She remembered all the meetings, all the hopes, as if it was yesterday. "It better be worth it," she said. "Someone out there owes us."

"We'll be down in about two more years. Late summer, early fall, give or take a few weeks."

Dusty disengaged the dialysis shunt and stood up. "Good. I'm staying awake for this one."

Sun smiled slightly. "I thought you might," he answered.

Chapter 10

Late September, 2285

"Remind me never to ask for your help again," Lady said bitterly. She threw him a pack as he put up an empty hand.

The noise in the newly rebuilt barn gave them privacy as nearly twenty others saddled up. Leather creaked and horses and mules gave protests over tight cinches and heavy packs.

He lashed the saddlebag into place without comment. Lady was in one of her moods and he knew better than to interrupt her before she'd run her course.

"You," she said heavily, "were supposed to talk him out of this, not organize it."

Harley stomped as if to punctuate her words. Puffs of dust rose from his hooves. Thomas pulled a last tie into place and leaned on his forearms across the saddle. "Stefan is right. This needs to be done. I told you that before. Why should I talk him out of something that needs to be done?"

"He has a wife. None of these other boys—or you—do." She met his gaze evenly, no emotion in her eyes, blue or brown.

"She's young, he's young. They'll survive. Or would you rather they stay together and beat each other into the dirt over whose fault it is they can't have children?" Thomas took a deep breath. "I can't talk him into staying, Lady. I did try. And I'm not so convinced he's wrong. Alma's hardly more than a child herself. Let her grow up a little more. Let Stefan mature a little. Then we'll see what happens to the hope of the Seven Counties."

Lady put her hand out and held onto the stirrup as if she

could stay the expedition with that one gesture. Her cheeks were flushed and her light brown hair had escaped all attempts to tame it that morning. "All right," she said. "That's his excuse. What's yours?"

Thomas had been tightening Harley's cinch as the gelding had a bad habit of blowing out. He strapped the buckle down and dropped the stirrup into place abruptly. "I don't need an excuse," he responded. "Unless you want to face a nester nation in all-out war."

"And you think you're the only one who can make a difference."

Harley caught the tenor of her voice. His ears went back and he shifted in the box stall, his hooves rustling among the straw.

Thomas caught up the reins. "If I don't go, we'll never know, will we?" The edge in his voice surprised him, he had not meant to get caught up in Lady's bitterness.

She let go of the stirrup and stepped back so he could lead Harley out of the barn and mount up. They walked through the crowd of high-spirited young men and their families, girl-friends weeping excitedly as if they played a part and were determined to play it well, fathers thumping their sons on their backs solidly, and mothers standing quietly, resignedly, in the shadows of the hayloft. The smell of new buckskins and freshly oiled rifles permeated the hay and dung atmosphere of the barn. Lady's nostrils flared slightly as if grateful for the fresh air as they stepped out into the new morning.

"Shall I send Alma to beg?" Lady squared off with him. Her blue eye had gone icy. Its glare pierced him.

He shook his head, speech momentarily surprised out of him. She looked down. She plucked at the worn seam of her riding skirt. "Don't," he said, as she inhaled slightly as if for a long speech.

Lady stopped. She looked up as if expecting something from him. He wasn't sure what it could be. She said quietly, "All right, then. Got enough vials?"

He patted down the front of his jacket. "I hope so. I don't intend for us to do any fighting. My main job is to get these boys past the basin, and then they're on their own. They're surveyors, not troopers."

"See you remember that," Lady responded softly. "Good-bye, Thomas." With no further words or gestures, she left.

He watched Lady and saw the steel determination in her spine and walk. She would not run after him. She would not offer him a second good-bye. She was done with him.

For the moment. Thomas sighed, gathered up the reins and swung aboard. Harley grunted as his rider settled into the saddle. He slid a hand down the horse's neck and wondered, just briefly, what he was doing leaving Lady behind.

The yard filled with milling horses and mules as the boys came outside, their entourage following them. Harley sidled away from the commotion and Thomas let him go. As they dipped into the shadows thrown by the corner of the building, a lithe figure darted out and caught at the horse's nosepiece.

"Sir Thomas," Shankar hissed. "A word with you, please?"

The Mojavan ambassador looked more than a little rumpled. His shirttails hung out and there were creases as if he'd slept in his clothes. That did not surprise Thomas—Shankar had been extremely busy with Drakkar the past few weeks. Denethan's son was consumed with the desire to learn all he could about the Seven Counties, firsthand if necessary, and seemed to be in motion constantly. "What is it, Shankar?"

"I beg of you—a last minute addition to your party. The experience will be good for my charge—who, may I remind you, was sent to your fostering care, and who, I may also remind you, curries as much dislike as like—"

"Shankar," the young man scolded as he rode forward out of the shadows, frowning slightly in the brightness of the daylight, "is that any way to ask for a favor? Sir Thomas, what he and I desire is that I be allowed to accompany your mapping expedition."

The surveyors had a two-year mission ahead of them. Harley snorted at the Mojavan's blue-black horse and dodged aside as Thomas answered. "I doubt your father wants you in peril and out of touch for the next two years."

Drakkar's dark brow went up. His crest rustled as if stirring. "You misunderstand me. I don't want to join the mappers. I had in mind riding with you."

"To the Vaults?"

"And to the nester boundaries."

Thomas considered. Doubtless, Denethan was as concerned

about the recent nester unrest as he was—and the boundaries of the territory. He would send spies regardless. Why not take advantage and keep Denethan's boy in sight where, hopefully, Thomas could also keep him under restraint? Nor could he afford to forget that Denethan had sent him for protection as well.

As if following Blade's train of thought, Shankar blurted, "And you will need to keep him away from his enemies as well."

"Old enemies or new ones?" Thomas asked dryly.

Drakkar's mouth quirked as well. "Either are just as deadly. And then where will your treaty be?"

"On the heads of fools," Thomas answered. He looked the young man over. Drakkar was equipped for just about anything. "I don't want to do this," he said.

"I promise you, any trouble and you can send me back."

"We'll see about that. All right, Shankar. You've got a vacation. I'll take Drakkar with me, BUT," and he pointed at the Mojavan. "Any trouble and there won't be enough left of you to send back."

Drakkar's dry little smile flashed into a sudden grin. He said to Shankar, "Like Father, is he not?" and spurred his horse forward.

"Not so fast. Dismount and let's see how you're equipped."

Gem-blue eyes blinked lazily. "Why, of course, Sir Thomas."

Blade swung back down, sure that even though he was going to be given a look through the young man's saddlebags a certain amount of sleight of hand would be hiding valuables and other important items from him.

Lady watched as the Mojavans approached Thomas and, from the gear on Drakkar's horse, guessed that the boy intended to go with the mappers. She turned from the shelter of the patio to make her way to Alma's room in the barracks. What was it about the promise of adventure that drew men, a lure even more tantalizing than sex? Her nose tickled. She rubbed it vigorously, thinking that she herself would jump at a chance to go though she knew the tedium, as well as the danger, of the long ride ahead. The difference was that she had not been invited. Thomas had never, not once, entertained the idea of her going.

Nor had she ever asked.

She wasn't sure why. She knew they had reached an impasse in their relationship. There was more than sex to be had, but neither of them were quite sure what, or what they wanted. Until they reached beyond and defined it and began to obtain that—there was nothing else. Either what they had would continue to grow, or it would die. Without being told, she sensed that Thomas hesitated to reach out, and she knew that she could not develop their relationship alone. It took two, just as fulfilling sex did. She doubted, even if she dared to ask Thomas what the problem was, that he would have an answer.

What she hadn't anticipated was that the process of breaking away at this point could be so painful. She felt as if her soul had been taken in two hands and torn asunder. Without future or commitment, hopes or promises, none of those exchanged between either of them, she had already crossed the line between lover and beloved. She loved Thomas and she could not tell him until he was ready to hear those words, until he was ready to explore all that went with it. And now she was letting him go again. He'd been gone all spring and summer riding the justice circuit and now she was letting him go again.

Franklin beamed from the kitchen as she entered the barracks. "Everyone hit the trail?"

"Not quite. I think they're waiting for a military salute."

He gave her a quizzical look as she mounted the stairs to Alma's room. She gave a perfunctory knock on the door that stood ajar.

Alma sat on the window ledge. She could see a slanted view of the stables from where she sat. Lady joined her.

The girl turned to face her. "There's no hope, is there?" she asked.

"No. They're going and that's that. And despite the dust and smog and In-City treachery and cold and rain and saddle sores, they're convinced it's going to be a glorious adventure."

Alma smiled briefly. She tucked a strand of her long, dark hair behind her ear. "And they'll be right."

"Ummm." She reached over and patted Alma's knee. "He did ask. Stefan wouldn't stay."

Alma's face paled slightly. "I didn't think he would," she said slowly. "What's wrong with me?"

"Nothing. Absolutely nothing. We need for you two to be together, to bear children—we haven't the luxury of hoping you might love one another. I hope you can forgive us."

Alma fell into Lady's arms. She sobbed two or three times, then subsided into nearly silent tears. After a long moment, she withdrew. She dried her eyes on her sleeve. "That's not good enough. I'm sorry, but it's not. And it's not your fault, it's mine."

"No."

The girl would not look back at her, just kept staring out the window as the mappers all mounted and leaned out of their saddles, saying their last good-byes. Stefan had not yet put on his hat. His height and his white-blond hair stood out like a beacon. She took a deep, steadying breath. "I'll be all right, Lady. Could you . . . leave me alone for a while?"

Lady hesitated. She wanted to tell the girl that she needed comforting as well, but she did not want to burden Alma further. "Just have Franklin give me a call. I'll be in the classrooms."

Alma nodded her understanding as the woman left, closing the door behind her.

As soon as the latch clicked into place, she reached under the fold of her skirt and brought out the fleecing shears she'd hidden there. The heavy scissors knocked aside a jar of walnut oil as well. Alma fumbled for it, praying the wooden seal would hold. Using the glass window's reflection as a mirror, she cut her hair short and then carefully applied the staining oil to her ashen face. She rubbed her hands together briskly, staining them as well.

She tore off her skirt to reveal old, worn buckskin breeches underneath, and reached under her cot for the bulging pack sacks she'd stored there earlier. Lady might take Sir Thomas' leaving in stride, but she would never be so calm, so resigned. Stefan was her husband and she was determined to follow.

Lady was going over the classroom books when she saw a movement by the pasturing yards. She paused, head up, alert, wondering if the sentries had let an intruder through again. Her senses flared. She felt someone where no one should be.

The fine hairs rose on the back of her neck. She checked her wrist sheath, twisting the knife loose in its casing. She went to the classroom door and made her way down the building's length, back to the wall, holding her breath.

A pebble clicked around the corner. She reached out and grabbed, dragging her opponent into the sunlight, bunched shirt filling her left hand and the knife in her right.

A tan slim boy writhed in her grasp, a horse shying at his back. The horse backed up a step or two as its reins dropped to the ground. In her grasp, the boy struggled. The big brown eyes, wide with fright, rolled up at her.

"What—"

"Don't stop me," the boy pleaded. "I'm going after them."

Lady's jaw dropped. She knew the voice and the eyes, even if the exterior fooled her. "Alma! My god. What are you doing?"

But the girl had already told her what she was doing. Alma stood in silence now, her lips pressed stubbornly together. Lady let go of her shirt and replaced her knife.

"That's a good way to get yourself killed," she said.

Alma picked her hat off the ground and dusted it of by whacking it across the knee of her trousers. "I figured if I could get by you, I could get by anybody."

"Well, you didn't get by me."

"You're better than I figured."

Lady took a deep breath. "And so are you." She had thought of several things Alma might do. This had not been one of them.

"Going to call Franklin?"

She looked at the girl/boy, her slim chin lifted defiantly. "No," Lady said finally, "I'm not. Go ahead. Follow him. Join them if you can—but the first time you pee, you'll be found out."

"I'll not. And I've got herbs to roughen my voice."

Lady laughed gently. "Be that as it may, you asked for it, you go get it. If I let you go today, you've a chance of catching up with them. If you run away tomorrow or the day after, then you'll be traveling alone and you'll never make it. I'll not have that on my list of sins!"

Alma's expression was one of total surprise.

Lady nudged her. "Go on—and hurry!"

The girl/boy scrambled to catch up the mule's reins. Lady stepped back as Alma left in a hail of dust and grit. She blinked, eyes tearing, from the dust she supposed.

She'd had the guts to follow Thomas once.

But not this time. What had happened to her?

Chapter 11

A bell tinkled in the mews as a pigeon made its way into the cote, the brush of its body against the chimes alerting the handler to the arrival of a message. The tired bird was caught up and relieved of its tightly wound scroll and, in due time, the missive was passed on.

The dean paused in his study of the map crudely drawn on a stretched donkey hide. A fawning nester brought a tray in and weighted on the tray was a scroll. The dean slapped away the intricately carved geode that held it down and snatched up the paper.

A wolfish smile came to his features. He looked up at the clansmen gathered around the map framework.

"The bait's been taken. A salvage team has left the center at Palos Verdes." He looked at them, his human glare beating down the animal in their eyes. "He'll come to you. Either tell him what we've discussed or say nothing at all. Anything else will be the death of you and your clan."

A chunky, pock-faced boy faced him. "If we break the pact, we'll lose our water."

"Stay with me and you'll never have to beg for water again."

The boy who was nearly a man brushed greasy braids from his forehead. *Dreadlocks*, the dean thought, a holdover from his distant past. The chieftain did not hesitate to meet his eyes. "I do not beg," he said. "But water is life."

"*Clean* water is life. Do they give it to you? Or must you give up everything else you have for it—lands, family, honor? Once we are united, the Countians will be unable to stop you from taking anything you want." The dean let his gaze sweep the room. The other nesters flinched from it.

A balding man, the side fringes of his hair grown long and brushed over the top of his head, grunted. He picked his teeth with an ivoried nail before saying, "Where are these strangers you promised us? The new weapons?"

"They're coming."

A grumble among the nesters. The dean straightened up. He lifted his chin and tilted his head to one side. He pointed at the transmitter sitting in the corner. "I called, they answered. And they will come. Soon." And even if the longships did not, the transmitter had served its purpose. It had convinced the nesters that there was a humanity even above that of the Countians, demigods, to whom all Earth would be held accountable. By the time the dean's word had been proved wrong, he would still hold the power of the united nester nation in his hands. All he had to do to keep them in his power would be to give them water.

Such an easy thing.

He waited until they filed out of the tent, still grumbling among themselves, before reading his note again. A surge of triumph went through him. Blade was in the forefront of the salvage party. He had him, he had him! The dean crumpled the note in his hands fiercely. Blade would go to the Vaults. It would be the death of him and his party. *He* would be there first. He would make sure that the twisted catacombs of the ruins would be a death trap.

The flap of the tent rustled. Ketchum stepped back in, the only nester chieftain silent among those who'd listened to him. As the dean's fortunes had risen, so had the tracker's.

"Is the man Blade among the salvagers?"

The dean weighed his options of lying and then, realizing his very hesitation in answering marked him, said, "Yes."

"He is a Protector. He has powers even you cannot explain."

"He's a freak!" The dean swung away angrily. "There's nothing he can do that will keep them alive with the traps we'll set. I want to leave in the morning. Get the animals and packs ready." He looked back, in spite of himself.

Ketchum's eyes were earth colored, with flecks of light green highlighting them. The green sparked now, weirdly, as the glow from the lanterns of the tent caught it. "What do you fear, big man?" the nester asked.

"Fear? What do you mean?" The dean responded quietly but inside, an inner voice raged, *death, you fool, dying!*

"I fear bad water. A stronger chieftain. A plague baby. More than two hands of wolfrats attacking. What do you fear?"

The dean felt like laughing bitterly but held it in. No matter how much he'd worked with Ketchum, the nester could not comprehend mathematics beyond the numbers of his fingers. He did not dare let the nester know he laughed at him. The dean swallowed tightly. "I fear a lot, Ketchum—but not him. *Not him.*"

The tracker moved to the tent flap. He stood there, blocking a cold fall wind. "Perhaps," he said, "you should."

"Blade has never been liked by you nesters."

"No. But he respects us, respects our treaty, respects our basic right to water. I don't like him, Dean, but I do fear him. The Shastra does not approve of you. I fear him also." With a whisper of wind through summer-dried evergreens, the tracker was gone.

The dean went to his writing desk and sat down. He watched the recall beacon's dual lights blinking on alternating current until they nearly hypnotized him. Then he broke away with a curse. He unrolled a hide, stretched and thinned until it approximated parchment. The message would be brief, but necessary. It was time he began to cultivate allies within the Seven Counties. There would be those eager to form new alliances once the strength of the nester nations was apparent.

He dipped his ink pen and began to write, muttering to himself. "Just think, my friend, you may be the only one left who knows how to spell." He gave a low and bitter laugh.

Chapter 12

There was someone riding drag to Thomas' point, and he didn't know who that someone was. He'd left Palos Verdes with eighteen boys and, unless he could no longer count, would pitch camp with nineteen on the second day. He didn't think the extra kid a real danger, but it made him uneasy, and so he reined about toward sundown and had the boys make camp early.

The lone rider trotted in and found everybody waiting for him. He reined back on his weary horse so hard it damn near sat down on its haunches. Without being told to, Drakkar had gotten to his feet and edged behind the boy, though the broken landscape Thomas had chosen pretty well walled off any attempt to escape unless the damn horse could sprout wings.

The rider was young and soft, a scholar probably, dark bushy hair and complexion showing his Hispanic ancestry. His mouth opened and then pinched shut. Thomas eyed the sheepskin thrown over the saddle to help prevent saddle sores. This was no nester, unless their ability to disguise themselves was far more devious than he'd ever run into before.

With Stefan and the other boys watching his back, he approached the rider and stood with one hand lightly on the horse's headstall. The horse was heavily lathered and blowing.

"Either," Thomas said lazily, "I set someone a lot farther back on drag than I remembered, or you've been trying to catch up with us."

"Yes, sir. Ah, no, sir. That is," and the boy plowed to a halt. His voice was low and hoarse, at the edge of breaking. The broad-brimmed hat he wore shadowed his young face. Hadn't even started to shave yet, by the looks of it. Not that that both-

ered Thomas. Half the mappers in the party weren't shaving
regularly. He stroked his mustache.

"Where are you from?"

"Laguna Hills, sir. My family came up with the trading caravan. I heard about the mappers. I—I wanted to go, so I took a
remount and rode hard to catch up. Don't send me back, sir."

"Most of my boys have spent a lot of years in classrooms
getting ready for this trip. What have you got to contribute?"

The boy's mouth worked soundlessly before he got out,
"I'm good with mounts, sir. And I can cook."

Bottom, the heavy cheeked, peach-jowled young man who
was their trail cook let out a snort. Thomas gave him a look
over his shoulder. The chunky red-blond boy hunkered back on
his heels as he banked the fire, but his smoky green eyes
blinked resentfully at Blade.

"Geography? Geology? Cartography? Anything else?" the
Protector said sharply when he turned back to the rider.

"I—I haven't been tested yet, but I kinda got a Talent for
Healing. Nothing much, but things knit better with me around."

The lad's voice was small. Humble, Thomas thought. He
couldn't sense anything out of the ordinary, no danger, no
threat, and he was too far out from Palos Verdes to send this
rider back alone.

As if sensing his dilemma, Drakkar spoke up. "I'll keep an
eye out for him, Sir Thomas." Denethan's heir looked at him
over the horse's rump. His feathered hair caught the lowering
sun keenly. The plumage looked almost metallic in the last
shafts of light, and his eyes burned their deepest blue.

Drakkar would keep an eye *on* the boy as well. That passed
unspoken between them. Blade thought it over another long
moment. "All right," he agreed. "What's your name?"

"Diego, sir."

"Put your horse on the line for grazing and make sure it's
tended before you settle down yourself."

"Yessir."

Thomas walked away to see if Bottom had managed to coax
up a brew of tea from his hesitant fire.

Drakkar watched the man stalk off and let out his breath
through his teeth. Shankar had gone too far by sending a spy
after him. Was he never to be out of sight of his father? He'd

come to the Seven Counties to be polished and faceted like a
fine gem. So let him be tumbled with the rocks and pebbles on
his own until that polishing was accomplished. And, if this was
one of Shankar's spies, he was not so certain Shankar was entirely on his father's side. So he would let the boy know that he
knew what the game was. He spoke, and dropped his cupped
hand across the gelding's rear.

Alma dared not let out her breath until the Protector had
walked far away from her. When she did, and Drakkar spoke,
she damn near jumped in the saddle.

The man slapped a familiar hand across the horse's rump.
As he walked past, he leaned close and said, quietly, "I know
who you are. The next time you take a remount, don't steal one
of *my* horses. And, just like I told Sir Thomas—I'll be watching you."

He brushed past, his scent one of horse and woodsmoke and
sage. Alma gulped down her fear and gathered up her horse's
reins. If he knew who she was, why didn't he tell Sir Thomas?
And what price would she have to pay to keep that silence? Unless, and her mouth tightened, the arrogant being thought she
had trailed after because of *him?* He couldn't, could he? Did he
honestly think he was such a gift to women that she'd come
cross-country to follow him, in spite of the fact that she was a
married woman? Well, if he did, she'd . . . she'd . . . just have
to take advantage of that. Thoughtfully, Alma wheeled her
horse around and headed the weary gelding to the drop line.

She wondered if Sir Thomas suspected. She knew of his reputation for Truth-reading, but he had not put her through that.
On the surface, then, she must have convinced him she was
what she said she was.

She put the reins in her teeth and swung down with a groan,
muffled by the salty leathers in her bite. Using the sheepskin
was the only smart thing she'd done so far. Without it, her legs
would have been chafed raw. As it was, she didn't think she'd
ever walk again. Clinging to the saddle with both hands was all
that kept her on her feet.

She looked up to see Stefan overshadowing her. He was
frowning, facing into the western sky.

He took the gelding's reins, tugging them gently from her
mouth. "First days are the hardest," he said. "You must have

eaten a lot of dust back there. I'll bet you came up from Laguna Hills by wagon."

Afraid to speak, even with her newly coarsened voice, Alma merely nodded.

Stefan gave a tight grin. "Thought so. You've got a soft butt, kid. Well, Sir Thomas means what he says. Rub your horse down and water him before you come over for chow." He flipped the rein ends over the rope-line and sauntered away.

Alma ducked her chin over her shoulder, trying to look at her rear. Would they all know she had a soft butt? Feeling somewhat mystified, as if she'd entered a fraternity she did not know had existed, she began to unbuckle her horse's girth. She felt vaguely disappointed that Stefan had not recognized her in spite of her chopped off hair, and hat, and oil-tanned skin. She would have known him anywhere. What was lacking in her that he couldn't look into her eyes and see her looking back?

She pulled the saddle off, grabbed a grooming cloth out of the pack and began rubbing the gelding down vigorously. He rolled an eye at her, flipped an ear which was oddly folded over, and leaned into her as she rubbed. She hardly noticed as she went over in her mind the months of marriage within which they'd shared everything a man and woman could share—how could he not know her? It was true they'd separated months ago and he'd scarcely seen her since, but she'd not forgotten him, how could he have forgotten her?

Unless he did not love her or unless she was that easily forgotten. Weariness and dust slapped up from the gelding's hide filled her eyes until she could scarcely see. One of the other boys trudged past with a water bucket for her. There was pity on his brightly sunburned face—Rubio it was, she knew him, and now the apple shine on his face matched his name. He didn't recognize her either nor would she have expected him to. The hide bucket sloshed within its collapsible frame as the gelding nosed at it eagerly.

"He'll founder if you let him drink too much," Drakkar said easily, quietly, before she'd even felt his shadow fall across her. He held a plate of something smelling remarkably good in his gloved hands. He wore the gloves most of the time. She thought of those raking, poisoned spurs and shuddered without looking up.

"I know that," she said irritably. "But there's not enough water here to founder a mouse."

"Ummm," he said. "There is that." He shoveled a forkful into his well-shaped mouth. "Looks like you've done well by him. We'll move the line later, to open up new grazing. They've got enough within reach to keep 'em quiet until we've eaten."

She finished, pulled the tack off, the bridle off his head, but leaving it buckled around his neck as the others kept theirs, and pulling the heavy saddle off to the side where the others were stacked. She was aware of Drakkar's burning gaze at her back every step of the way. She walked to her dinner, her legs bowed and gait stiffening with every step.

Thomas sat back as the last of the light faded from the canyon tongue they'd taken root in. The boys were trading ribald jokes, the younger ones laughing too loudly and too shrilly at punch lines they did not always understand, the weaker ones quiet, the road already taking its toll on them. Mentally, he was separating them out. If he was lucky, there would be twelve sturdy youths to send onward from the College Vaults. If not . . . he did not see how any survey party could survive with lesser resources. Jenkies left with his younger brother Bill to reset the horse-line.

He worried about sending boys to do a man's job, but he thought that the younger ones were tougher, unwilling to believe that anything was impossible, more resilient, quicker to mend, all factors that would make up for the lack of experience. Stefan was as close to man-grown as they had and he would have to have the experience for them all.

He picked something out of a tooth with his fingernail. "Stefan, set sentries." The young man would need to take command before he officially turned it over to him.

Drakkar looked up sharply across the campfire before Stefan even said his name.

"Drakkar, take the first watch."

"No." The young man shook his head. Feathers rattled like porcupine quills.

All joking stopped abruptly. A distant coyote's tentative yap sounded throughout the camp.

Thomas said, "I beg your pardon?"

Drakkar answered evenly, "I think not."

Stefan sat stiffly. He'd windburned in the two days, despite the hat he'd worn, and his cheeks blazed as crimson as the campfire. "You ride with us, you'll do duty with us."

Thomas thought to say something else, and changed his mind. He settled back to see how the two would work this out.

"Perhaps," Drakkar said. He stretched out on his packs and crossed his leg at the ankles. "But I won't stand first watch, tonight or any other night."

"You'll do what you're told," Stefan said. He had a slight edge to his voice, inherited from his mother's accent, and it sharpened now.

"Then you're an ass," Drakkar said, "to put being in charge over being intelligent. I probably have the best night sight of anyone in camp. You're wasting my abilities at twilight and first watch." He rolled over as he flipped a blanket over him. "Wake me for second watch."

Shocked, Stefan looked to Thomas. He seemed uncomfortably aware of the stares of every other mapper in camp.

Thomas shrugged. "He's got a point. Would you rather be right or in charge?"

The new boy, Diego, who'd not said a word since stumbling in for dinner said, "One would hope one could be both."

Stefan cleared his throat abruptly. "Right. We'll give Drakkar second watch tonight. Anybody else with good night vision or any other Talents to add?"

Thomas listened as Stefan fielded comments from the boys. Then he dealt out new assignments. With a smile, Blade leaned back on his pack. He would not sleep particularly well regardless of who Stefan put out on the rocks, but then, that was his duty. When most of the boys were asleep, he'd go set his wards and then settle to rest.

Drakkar's arrogance bothered him. And he missed Lady. No, tonight would not be a particularly restful night.

Chapter 13

"This is In-City," Thomas said, reining up. He waited as the boys grouped about him. Drakkar pulled up off to the side and slung a leg over his saddle as if bored. Stefan took his hat off and mopped his forehead with the back of his cuff. Indian summer had turned suddenly to cold fall nights, and the resulting ground fog had swaddled them all within its clammy folds. The wreckage of the inner city rose out of that fog with an eerie unreality. The smell here had changed too, tinged slightly with sulfur and mildew and decaying things, instead of sere grass and salt ocean.

He waited until all the boys had pulled close: Jenkies and his brother Bill, wiry, mousy-haired boys with violent brown freckles all over their bodies; Diego, still and secretive; the cook, Bottom, who tended to be somewhat of a bully; Montez, the cobbler's boy, who repaired their stepped-on reins and snapped girths with the same ease his father showed with a needle; Jeong, the weaver's son, intent on mapping even these known regions, his Asian yellow fingers always stained with ink; scarlet-faced Rubio whose sunburn was painful to look at; and a dozen others he was getting to know as well as the palm of his hand.

Jeong pulled out a scroll of paper and began writing and sketching feverishly even as Thomas began speaking.

"They call it In-City, but its real name is Death. Some of you have been down here before, in spite of the fact it's off-limits. Don't let that fog fool you—it doesn't take nature to hide its danger. You've been raised in the neighborhoods outside the major manufacturing centers and old In-City structures. There's a reason for that. In there, like the landfills, you've got a toxic waste situation that poisons everything about it. It's seeped into the earth itself. There's no clean water or forage. There are areas where toxic fumes can billow up, exploding out of the concrete walkways. And there's simpler deaths. There's rusting wire forms inside those chunks of concrete. Let your horse step on one, or yourself, and the chances of getting lockjaw are pretty good. The subway system tunnels under most major streets and if one should collapse under you, your mount's got another good chance of snapping a leg. And there's wolfrats, coyotes, sidewinders, black widows as big as your hat. The quickest way to kill a man is to bring him In-City unprepared."

Machander looked across at Blade. He was a good-looking young man, dark hair in a widow's peak over a wide forehead. A birthmark on his right cheek marred those good looks with its purple splotch, but he seemed unaware of his blemish. He said mildly, "But you're a ruin crawler."

"I know what I'm doing. I take my gauges with me, watch the radiation and toxicity levels—and I like killing wolfrats. But I don't recommend any of you take up the hobby. This is also nester territory and they'll kill you if In-City doesn't."

A late morning sun burned the haze away, corroding it from the ruins even as they watched it. Concrete canyons ran as far as they could, shoulder to shoulder, dispersed only by the streets and alleyways. Broken spires poked upward, yawning maws gaped downward. A loping figure crossed what had once been a street. From their distance they could see it was a wolfrat, half as big as the mounts they rode. The boys drew in their breaths almost as one, as if afraid it would scent them.

Blade pulled Harley about. "No one rides alone," he said. "Pick a trail buddy and stick with him. Know where he is at all times because he's there to protect your back and you're there to protect his." He heard the fervent murmurs at his back as eager as if the boys were choosing up sides for a stickball game. "Stefan."

"Yes, sir." The young man kicked his horse even with Harley.

"Check your gauges. Tell me what you think about the readings."

Stefan pulled at the hand-blown and sealed gauges hanging about his neck. He read his compass, then checked the other gauges. "This area appears okay, but—"

One of Thomas' brows went up. "Yes?"

"It wavers. Varies. As if we're getting bad air through here, but not on a steady basis."

"That's good. You're right. There's a natural deposit of methane gas that runs under much of the L.A. basin. It breaks through here and there. We're not as far from the Fire Ring as you think. So we're talking not a manmade problem here, but a natural one. Methane's only deadly if it's all we're breathing, but it is highly flammable. Don't strike any matches before you check your gauges." The Fire Ring burned in what had been Signal Hills, drawing ever steady fuel and life from what must have been a vast underground store of petroleum at one time. The immense towers and drums had been smoldering for as many generations as anyone could remember.

Stefan's icy blue eyes flickered. "I won't," he said. He dropped his gauges back onto his chest. "Makes you wonder how they lived."

"Actually," Thomas answered, "quite well. Until the Disasters hit." He raised his voice. "Everyone got a partner?" There should be an odd man out because of their numbers, someone forced to partner with him.

Bottom said, his chunky face mottled with anger from being spurned, "I d-don't, sir."

"You do now. Fall in behind me, the rest of you line up accordingly." The cook joined him, packs and pots and pans rattling on the two mules he led. Thomas pulled his hat down tightly. "I don't want any heroes."

Drakkar, who was holding his horse back to ride drag gave a tight smile as if receiving a private message. In his shadow was young Diego. Diego had toughened up over the past week, but Blade still felt uneasy about the youngster's presence. The boy stayed to himself, was painfully shy, and body conscious, and though Blade no longer felt him a menace personally, Diego knew that his own youth and inexperience could jeopardize the company. The fact that Drakkar looked out for him was the only saving grace of the situation. Blade felt that Drakkar could probably look out for most of them without raising a sweat. The Mojavans were tough—had to be—because of their native territory. The desert was almost as unforgiving as In-City. Drakkar met his appraisal with a faintly mocking smile.

"Stay close," Thomas finished. He put a boot heel into Harley's flank and moved him onto the path he'd chosen that would take them along the fringe of In-City. This was their initiation, the threshold they had to pass before Blade felt confident enough to let them go on alone. He'd go inward to take them to see the great crater itself, awe inspiring to see the cavernous hole responsible for the death of L.A.

Despite the hard riding and teaching, he did not sleep well at night. He set his wards much as Stefan set his sentries; Blade did not place stock in either of them. There was too much here to protect—his wards were spread far too thinly. As for the sentries—how many nesters could a fourteen- or fifteen-year-old boy kill if jumped from behind? If he had been trained by Blade, perhaps two or three. But trained to be a mapper, it was doubtful if the boy could even get a shout out in time. Why set a sentry, then? Because even some hope was better than none.

And despite those reservations, he found himself tumbling into a deep, exhausted sleep ten days into the trail. Sleep came welcome, took him soaring into the sky. He spread his wings and dreamed he was a bird coasting over the devastation, keen eyes picking out the signs of resurgent life. Even in the devastation, greenery was beginning to erupt through the asphalt and concrete cracks. The smoldering streams of ash and smoke from the Fire Ring had begun to thin. Dared he hope to dream of rejuvenation?

Then his soul winged eastward and northward until, exhausted, he sought an encampment and a cote, chimes ringing as he brushed his way inward to safe nesting. A huge, pasty, beefy hand reached for him. Thomas looked up from his bird's eyes to see the massive man he'd known as the Dean of the College Vaults reaching for him with a low, feral chuckle. He leapt, but his wings were pinioned against his side. Cruel fingers twisted about his neck. His bird heart drummed wildly inside his chest and as he struggled, the chimes rang and rang and rang. . . .

Blade bolted awake with a low cry. Sweat covered him from boot top to chin. His hands were groping at his side. Shaking, he brought them to his forehead where he rubbed away the last of the dream from his eyes. Then, like a piercing echo, someone in the camp screamed.

*   *   *

He was on his feet and halfway to the sound, knife in hand, when he heard the hissing like an overflowing tea kettle and knew what it was that attacked in the night. The boy beneath the wolfrat struggled valiantly. Fangs gnashed and the beast's beady red eyes glowed like the last of the campfire as it slithered around to face Blade, trampling its victim beneath it.

"Help!" the boy panted. "Get him off me!"

It was Watkins, a boy he'd only come to know recently, a geologist and a promising mapper. Also a lazy boy, slow moving and introspective. Even as Blade moved to protect him, he thought that Watkins had probably fallen asleep on duty. A red cloud flowed blackly in the night beneath his head, but the boy still clawed and kicked, alive enough that Thomas had hope for him.

The attacker snapped at Blade as he swung his knife through the darkness. It came forward, but not enough to free the boy. Thomas licked his dry lips. Salt from his sweat-soaked nightmare met his taste.

"Come and get me," he said. He was aware from the noise behind him that the rest of the camp were awake now and struggling to get to their feet.

"Move aside," Stefan called softly. "I've got my rifle."

"No. Watkins is still kicking. He'll block your shot." Literally, as the boy began to bicycle his legs furiously into the wolfrat's stomach.

Like a gigantic snake, the creature's tail whipped through the dust. It kicked back, claws slashing. Watkins let out a cry of hurt and rage.

"Get him off me!"

"Save your breath," Blade counseled. He attacked again, knife edge meeting yielding flesh. The rat's fetid breath hissed over the back of his wrist, yellowed tusks just missing him. He followed his cut with a vicious kick from his left boot. The wolfrat grunted as the blow caught it below the ear. It rocked back. Watkins scrambled free. He crawled out on hands and knees and then hunched over, vomiting into the brush.

Blade shouted as the rat charged him, "Get clear, Watkins, run for it!"

The wolfrat's tail snapped out. It cracked across the boy's back, knocking him to his side. Blade met the beast full face as it reared up, talons raking the air. Its red glare seemed unnatural in its snarling, lethal face.

He closed with it once. His knife moved, leapt out, and returned, a smooth motion much practiced. As he jumped back out of the wolfrat's reach, it stayed reared on its haunches. Its forepaws clawed the air. Then, as if in surprise, it clawed at its own throat as it began to gurgle and blood spurted into the night air. It toppled.

Stefan was at Thomas' side and they reached Watkins together. The boy's scalp had been raked back from his left ear. That was, apparently, what had done all the bleeding. The pain from it reached him now and he retched again in reaction to the wounding.

His shirt sleeves were in tatters. Thomas let Stefan roll him over and then pick him up, the man staggering under the weight of the boy.

"Doc!" bellowed Stefan. He half-slid, half-strode down from the rocks.

Thomas said, "Get him fixed up well enough to ride." He raised his voice. "Jenkies!"

The spotted boy appeared out of the dark. "Sir Thomas."

"Break the horse-line down. Get everybody tacked up and mounted as soon as you can."

Jenkies gulped. "But why?"

Drakkar was already in motion doing Thomas' bidding, grabbing gawkers by the elbows and steering them toward the nervous horses and mules. "Where there's one wolfrat," the Mojavan prince said to the wrangler, "there's more. That's why."

Diego joined the Healer at Stefan's elbow. Trout, a tall bony fish of a boy, was cleansing the wound before Stefan even had Watkins at the fireside. He was not a Protector, just a stitch 'em and set 'em Healer, and a hard worker. As Trout worked on stitching the scalp back in place, Diego pushed back the boy's torn sleeves and began to daub ointment on the ragged scratches. Watkins kept up a litany of yelps.

Stefan leaned over him. "Put a sock in it, Watty."

The pale boy stopped a moment. "I—I'm hurt."

"Yeah, and if it wasn't for the Lord Protector, you'd be dead. I submit to you that there are more wolfrats where that one came from. You wouldn't want to be attracting them, now, would you?"

The boy let out another "Ow!" as Trout took another stitch in open-mouthed concentration that reminded Blade of a hooked fish. Diego said, "Think of this." He put his hand on the boy's forehead and Watty gradually quieted.

Stefan watched them oddly. Then, he said abruptly, "What are you doing to him?"

"Nothing. I just . . . quieted him a little." Diego's face was shadowed under the hat he wore at all times, but Thomas thought he saw fear and resentment hidden deep in those eyes.

Trout said breathily, "Almost done."

Watty's face was moon-bled pale, his eyes large. Stefan shifted uncomfortably before telling Diego, "Thanks. Better go get saddled."

Quietly, Diego stood and found his horse at the line.

Thomas turned thoughtfully from watching them and jumped a little to find Drakkar at his elbow, also quietly observing the fireside scene.

Denethan's heir looked keenly at him. "That boy," he said softly, "isn't what he appears to be."

"No," said Thomas. "He isn't." He gathered up his reins as Jenkies brought Harley to him. "The question is: what is he?"

"He's not one of yours . . . a Protector candidate?"

"Not that I know of. Is he one of yours?"

"Not that I know of, though I thought so at first. I think he bears some very, very close watching." Drakkar spun away to find his horse and tack.

Thomas stood, disturbed, watching Trout finish with Watkins and help the boy to his feet. He could not afford enemies or sabotage among the company. He did not like his thoughts.

Chapter 14

Alma rode soundlessly behind the trail of boys. The night had paled, giving way to gray twilight before dawn. Her eyes felt gritty and gummy and she only wanted to tumble into her blanket and sleep.

She wondered how it was she had managed to soothe Watkins into relative calm, but she'd done it before with animals and had seen Lady do it many a time. Was it a Protector Talent? She prayed not. She had seen what the demands of duty had done to Lady and to Sir Thomas. They had little time for themselves and the dangers of using a power burned out . . . she shuddered in memory of the recent nester attack and the toll it had taken. She had her destiny and that was enough of a burden. All they asked of her was that she bear children, a seeming impossibility. She would not worry, but she knew that she was special, her physical form showing no signs of the adaptive aberrations that many of the survivors carried. It didn't matter that she was a little frailer, that her sight was not as keen or her stamina as great. She was purer. If only she could convince the others that it was not a gift, but a curse. Her life was not her own.

It would help if she could bring her husband back home. She couldn't do anything until they were far enough along that Sir Thomas couldn't send her back—at least, not alone. She watched Stefan's rigid back through the nighttime gloom as he rode several pairs ahead. The company was stilled, as if their very breathing could draw a pack after them. She wondered if he could feel her watching him. Even if he could, what good would it do her? He saw nothing but Diego when he looked at her.

The very hairs at the nape of her neck where the fleecing shears had cropped her hair close but unevenly seemed to prickle. She stirred in the saddle, half-turning about.

Drakkar's mocking stare met her glance. She turned back in the saddle and pulled her hat down lower. And what had that troublemaker from the desert been thinking? She swore he was telepathic. He seemed to act even before Sir Thomas ordered, finished sentences that had just been begun, and then there was that crooked smile which no amount of trail dust and discouragement could seem to wipe off his face. If Drakkar told her he was the devil himself, she wouldn't be surprised. Talk about the Warden compound and classrooms had been veiled and secretive. The dragon boy, they'd called him, with those poisonous talons, feathered crest, and burning blue eyes. He had a quick, sharp tongue and the men in his guard had been as fierce to protect his name as his body. She had grown up thinking that Denethan was the devil himself and any son of his would bear his curse.

It was said that Denethan had sent him to Sir Thomas to keep him from being murdered. She could believe that. He could provoke a stone into arguing. She set her lips. He had not given her away, but she did not doubt that he knew her secret. Was he interested in making a fool out of Stefan? She'd seen Drakkar dispute Stefan's leadership. What did the arrogant Mojavan want from them, all of them, anyway?

She put her mind to ignoring that stare that bored into her back, as uneasy as it made her. Was he thinking about unmasking her, or about payment to keep her secret? Her nerves felt tight, stretched like fine wool being spun into yarn. She unclipped a gourd that bumped her knee and took a sip, the water flavored with a bitter herb that kept her voice rough and coarse, a crucial part of her disguise. And surely, after all the riding she'd done these past few days, her butt had firmed and hardened like the rest of them.

She put her heel to her horse. Rubio and Watty were talking about the great crater in hushed, subdued tones as though they were going to view a great monument or one of the wonders of the old world.

"A man would die if he fell in't. It's city blocks long and wide, and almost as deep. And if he slept by it for more than a couple of days, he'd glow in the dark."

"Go on," Rubio countered.

"It's the truth. Radiation." Watty flipped his hair from his forehead. The bandage turbaning his head gave him a rakish look. He held his bandaged arm a little stiffly. Rubio had taken charge of their two pack mules.

"I'd like to take a chunk of it with me. D'you think it would kill me?"

Rubio said, "A man wouldn't live that long. A nester'd scalp him first."

"Probably." The two boys lapsed into silence.

Watty added, "I'll ask Sir Thomas anyway."

She'd seen the crater. It was respectable. More so, if one knew that it was responsible for the demise of the world as men then had known it. It was another obstacle for the company to traverse, besides dealing with the lack of safe water and forage. She thought she knew what Sir Thomas was doing: molding a company, seasoning them, letting them know they could depend on each other, as well as training them for In-City. The mappers didn't know what they would face beyond the College Vaults once they turned north. Vast amounts of wilderness, perhaps, forever changed by the death and rebirth of the world. There would be other In-Cities, different but just as treacherous as this one. Blade used whatever was at hand for his classroom. Survivors of the Seven Counties already knew how precarious life could be.

The only good thing about seeing the crater was that they would turn south and east and would soon pass beyond the point of no return.

Ketchum was waiting patiently, sucking on a long straw of dried grass much as if it were an unlit pipe when the dean wiggled backward out of the tunnel. He'd beefed up more than he thought, though he would never again return to his former mountainous self. He flexed his back and shoulders as he stood. This new bulk was muscle and it made him all that more intimidating. He stood head and shoulders over most of the nesters and Countians, the product of better nutrition and all around good health.

The nester gave him an unfathomable look. The man's face was dirty. He did not believe in wasting water to wash himself while on the trail. The dean pulled a handkerchief out of his trousers and mopped the sweat and dust off his own face. He was no longer a one-eyed king in the land of the blind. He had all his faculties. Now he could reach out to other lands and take them all. Then the winnowing would begin. As the chaff is separated from the wheat, so must the human be separated from the beast.

He had no doubt he was up to the task. His seed would be the foundation.

"Did you do what I told you?"

Ketchum spat out the straw. "A sharp-eyed man will spot the trail. Too plain and the Protector will suspect the traps you've laid."

The dean wiped his hands as well before folding his handkerchief neatly and putting it away. He looked back at the tunnel. "They'll never know what hit them," he said. "Most of them will die. A few may make it through. I rather hope they do." He relished the thought of a maimed Sir Thomas Blade coming after him for vengeance or lingering for days in a pool of blood and body parts, cursing his name. He smiled tightly.

The nester put his reins in his hand. The horse jerked its head up and backed away, the whites of its eyes showing in fear. The dean growled and snubbed the horse close in order to mount. As he settled in the saddle, he looked at Ketchum.

"You ride on ahead. I'm going to stay here for a day or two."

A frown creased the dirt-crusted face as the nester swung astride his own pony. "The Protector is close. They swung below the crater two days ago and headed north yesterday."

The nester network for gathering news was formidable. The dean did not doubt its accuracy. He gave a slight grunt.

"Then I won't have long to wait. I want to see them ride in."

"He will scent you."

"I doubt that." The dean pushed away the nester's superstitious fear of Blade.

"You do not know the man."

His hands balled into fists upon the reins. His horse came to a halt with a whicker of pain and fear. "You have nothing to worry about. He's a freak, Ketchum, and I have everything I need to stop him."

The tracker's eyes scanned him. The dean sat tensely until the man nodded thoughtfully.

"Perhaps," he said, "you do. I will wait for you in camp,

Chieftain." He made a sign of respect, wheeled his pony about, and put heel to it.

The dean reined back hard, until his horse foamed at the mouth pinkly, to keep it from following. Ketchum's fear would not keep him from the pleasure of watching Blade and the others fall into his ambush. Nothing would keep him from that exquisite enjoyment.

Stefan had taken his hat off. The expression in his light blue eyes was one of heated exasperation, but it was not for Alma. He never looked past Drakkar to see her. The mappers were afoot and dispersing, setting up camp rapidly. Blade was gone, putting wards on the fringe boundaries of the sleeping area and the two men were nose to nose. "You won't take first watch, you won't clean up the cook site—I'm getting a little tired of your nonparticipation, *Mojavan*. The welfare of this company depends on cooperation." Stefan's voice dripped with sarcasm. He had said Mojavan, but he might as well have said *mutant*.

Drakkar spread his gloved hands. "You have whatever you want of me."

"I want someone to start digging the latrines."

"Except that, of course." Drakkar examined a bit of lint on his folded cuff. He looked remarkably calm and unruffled, but from the rear, Alma could see a restlessness among the feathers lying flat upon his head and shoulders, as if a breeze disturbed them.

"And what's your excuse this time?"

Drakkar lifted his head. "I simply don't care to do it."

"You don't care to do it," Stefan repeated flatly. "You're too good to dig latrines. Why? You shit like the rest of us."

"Perhaps, but my Talent lies more in other areas. I had hoped you'd ask for volunteers."

Alma was too familiar with that pale anger under the tanned face, the pinched nostrils, the slash of red across high, flat cheekbones. She hoped Drakkar was as familiar with the danger signs as she. She held her tongue, afraid to interfere. The other boys about the camp were watching discreetly, pausing among their various chores.

"Volunteers? And what would you be good enough to volunteer for?"

"Let me take the horse-line out for clean water. We're low on supplies and won't be in the foothills for another day."

"This is In-City."

Drakkar made a diffident movement. She could not see the expression on his face from where she stood, behind and to the side, but she was certain the hidden anger on it matched Stefan's. "If I say I can find clean water, I can do it."

"If you can find water, don't you think you might get your hands dirty digging for it?"

"I don't see," Drakkar said mildly, "why you're so set on my performing one task over another. I have the Talent to find water and we could use it. Let someone else dig the latrines."

"Because we can't afford for anyone to be too good to do the down and dirty jobs. If you were falling off a cliff, I wouldn't want to be too good to give you a hand—or the other way around."

Drakkar tilted his head slightly. Alma could see the feathers ripple. Their panoply of blues and greens looked like a mirage in the sunlight. "You have a point," he said slowly, reluctantly. "But as neither of us is falling off a cliff and water is necessary, perhaps I could dig . . . latrines . . . tomorrow."

Stefan took a deep shuddering breath and Alma tensed, afraid of the explosion that would follow. Then Sir Thomas' level voice cut through the air, and she saw him crouched on a concrete block, just above the level of their heads.

"Commendable and right, Stefan," the man said. "But Drakkar offers us what we need most now. We've had the horses on tight water rations the last three days. I want fresh mounts when we hit the foothills—that's nester territory and we may have to outrun a raiding party."

Stefan let out his breath. He took a step back, saying, "To-morrow, then."

Drakkar nodded. His crest subsided as Stefan stalked away. His boots punctuated his frustration with puffs of dust and gravel.

Blade jumped down lightly and straightened up. "Take Diego with you," he said. "And don't take more horses at a time than you can handle."

The Mojavan nodded. Alma hesitated in his shadow, caught up for a moment in Sir Thomas' intent stare. She felt a blush heat her face and ducked her head, shying away from his observation and running a little to keep up with Drakkar's lean, long-legged movement.

He reached out and caught her by the elbow just when she thought she was in the clear.

"You were going to get in between them."

"I—I couldn't let them fight. It wouldn't be good for the rest of us."

"You thought it was coming to that."

"Yessir. Drakkar doesn't know how far he can push Stefan."

"And you do."

"Y-yessir." Hard to meet his face and yet try not to, try to keep the brim of her hat shading hers. Fear of discovery lanced through her. Her heartbeat pounded in her ears.

He let her go. "Next time, let them do what they have to do. They're both grown men. They'll learn how to pull with each other."

"Yessir." She bounded off before he could say anything else.

Thomas watched Diego take off in Drakkar's wake. He thought long and hard, and wished Lady were with him. That keen blue-and-brown gaze caught more than he did, sometimes. If he hadn't overheard the conversation, if he didn't know Diego was who he was. . . . He shook his head. His vision had gone double for a moment, a curious overlay of images, and he thought he'd seen Stefan and Drakkar squaring off over Alma, her pretty petite face obscuring Diego's. If he hadn't heard the argument over camp duties, he'd have thought they were fighting over her.

"You've been alone and in the sun too long," he muttered to himself. He trailed in the general direction of the others. Drakkar's defection to finding water meant it was his turn to dig latrines.

Alma watched Drakkar find water. He dowsed for it, something she'd seen done only once or twice in her lifetime, both times by Sir Thomas, because the Director of Water and Power had forbidden the practice. Water could be found that way, yes, but clean water . . . she watched him dig down and let it bubble up. His packs were slung over one broad shoulder and he slipped a hand into it and found a set of vials molded together like panpipes. He dipped the vials into the small puddle. He held the vials up to the sunlight and watched as the chemical changed color.

He nodded in satisfaction. "Good," he said. "Grab a shovel, Diego. We want to widen and deepen this as much as we can."

"How can you tell?"

His attention snapped to her. "Water is life in the desert. How can I not know?" He got to his feet, buckskin knees already dampened with the growing font. He began to shovel vigorously.

Alma tied her string of horses to a thick shrub. Although browned and dulled by the long summer and hot fall, its branches were still pliable. It lived. Maybe its roots fingered all the way into that underground moisture. She had her camp shovel pushed into her belt and worked it free. She stood opposite him and six paces away began to trowel up the packed dirt. Before long, the puddle had spread to her, and a pond began forming.

The horses behind her scented the water and were milling about. She felt their thirst like it was her own, as sweat poured down her brow, soaking into her hat and runneling into her eyebrows. Drakkar motioned for her to follow his lead. They moved several times, going about in a crude circle.

Drakkar threw her a grin. "Now the fun part," he said, and jumped in. He began to shovel out the muddy bottom.

Alma watched open-mouthed for a second.

"Come!" he ordered. "We've got to deepen this as much as we can. Horses can't stomach too much silt in the water."

With an awkward, sideways leap, she joined him. The shock of the jump ran clean through her boots. She grabbed her shovel tightly and began to dig. As they worked downward, the water seeped through to meet them, rising rapidly. Soon, they were knee-deep in water, and then waist-deep.

"That's it," said Drakkar. "A little muddy, but that'll settle. Out you go."

He grabbed her about the waist to hoist her from the watering hole.

She struggled to get out of his way as soon as she saw him reaching for her, but it did no good. He was behind and flanked her, and his movement brought them together abruptly. His arm crushed about her.

Her heart seemed to stop. Then she felt it beat once, ponderously. The feel of him this close took her back to the afternoon he'd rescued her, and she had ridden home in front of him, carried in his loose embrace.

Drakkar sloshed backward a step. *"Shit."* he said. "So that's who you are."

They each slogged to a bank of the pond and pulled themselves out. Drakkar watched her with accusing blue eyes, his crest half-erect.

"What the hell are you doing out here? No," and he squeezed his eyes shut. "I thought you were someone Shankar had sent after to spy on me. I should have known, should have thought. You've been watching Stefan like a hawk after a chicken. Damn it! Why didn't I know!" He watched her again.

"Don't tell. Please." Alma took her hat off wearily. "I can't let them send me back."

"We've come too far," Drakkar said. "Anyone else know?"

She'd been careful and lucky. She shook her head. "No."

"Well. That's that, then. No spies at least. You came after Stefan, didn't you?"

"We're married." She spoke defiantly.

That mocking smile half-returned. "I heard it was in name only." He put his hand up as she stammered wordlessly in anger. "Save it. If I got involved every time my father fought with one of his wives. . . ."

"Involved! Who asked you?"

"No one," he said somberly. "But I know and now I've got the burden of the secret. I'm to protect your back, remember?"

"And I yours. I'll do my job, okay?" She got to her feet. Water and mud dripped off her. The string of horses stamped and tossed their heads up and down, eager for water.

"I don't think it's wise to keep secrets from Sir Thomas." He stood as well. "Not to mention that this will probably set the whole camp on its ear."

She stripped the tie rope off its anchor. "And why would that happen?" She led the horses down to drink as the foaming water reached the brim of the pond.

"Because you're a woman, stupid." Drakkar led his string of horses and mules over. The horses plunged their muzzles into the water. The mules were a bit more circumspect, their long ears going forward and back before they dipped for a drink.

"And what is that supposed to change?"

He grinned. "How we dig the latrines, for one thing."

Heat blazed across her face. "Don't do me any favors. No one knew anything around here and wouldn't have until I told Stefan."

"And when and what are you going to tell Stefan?"

"Well, I—I wanted to wait until I knew Sir Thomas couldn't send me back. And then . . . then . . . I didn't know what to say." Her anger cooled suddenly. "I thought he would know me. I thought he would just look at me and *know.*"

"I would have," Drakkar said softly. She looked up sharply, but he had turned away by then, fussing with one of his charges.

"What would you do?"

"Truth?"

"Yes."

Those dark, impossibly blue eyes looked at her across the water. "I'd be madder than hell to have my wife trailing after me, nagging me to come home. Embarrassed, in front of the other mappers and Sir Thomas."

"But I—"

"You're doing all the wrong things for all the right reasons," he said.

"How can this be wrong?"

Drakkar made a noise in the back of his throat. Then, "He's got his pride, dammit. And so should you."

"What's pride got to do with it?"

He blinked in the late afternoon sun. "Everything. And nothing, I suppose, to you. But it would matter to Stefan."

Alma examined her hat for a moment. It did not seem possible that the Mojavan could know who she was and yet not know who she was. She said softly, "Neither of us have room for pride. We could not love or marry anyone else, even if we wanted to. I'm the girl your father started a war over."

"You're the—you're the one Charles Warden sent to the Vaults?"

"Stefan and I, yes. It's not my fault—it's nothing I asked for and I'd change it if I could."

His face had paled unnaturally. "Don't ask to change it," he said. "You've got the genetic background to bring us back. I remember when my father found out about you. He raved for days. So you and Stefan have this sacred obligation and you've come to remind him of it."

She could not tell him all of her shame, this arrogant prince who looked at her so strangely now. Her stomach felt hollow. "What else could I do?"

"Wait for him to come back. If it was me, I would. And if he doesn't . . . there's nothing you can do to make him come back." A mule lifted a sopping wet nose and pushed at him, setting him back on his heels. Drakkar rubbed its muzzle gently.

"I can't wait for him. It could be years."

A sadness drifted over Drakkar's expression and disappeared. "Then I guess you have to do what you have to do. I'll keep your secret—but if you take my advice, you'll at least let him have a taste of the adventure he came for."

She looked at him sharply. "What do you mean?"

"Don't say anything until we've had a chance to look over the College Vaults. If you're dragging him back home to be a husband, it'll be his only chance to do something extraordinary. Trust me.

"He's a fool," Drakkar added suddenly, "if he doesn't go home with you." He gathered up his lead rope. "Come on. We've got five more shifts to water before dark. I won't be treating you any differently than I would anyone else."

"I don't expect you to. But," and she paused, gathering up her own line, "what do you want out of all this?"

"Want? Why should I want anything?" He frowned deeply. "Say it's out of the goodness of my heart. I do have a heart, only my father's physicians say it's misplaced. I'm a mutant, you know." He stalked past, his boots flinging off bits of mud and sand.

"Drakkar!" Alma called, and then stopped. His back was ramrod stiff and she knew he wouldn't listen. She hadn't meant to insult him. Was every word a woman said deliberately misconstrued by a male listener? "Damn." She hurried after, certain he would give her the all mule and donkey line to water next and those donkeys could be difficult to deal with. Not much different than Stefan and Drakkar.

Chapter 15

Thomas saw Drakkar stomping out of the wash, jerking his string of horses and mules behind him. He leaned on his shovel, enjoying reading the body language of Denethan's son. While it was evident that Drakkar had Talents that no one else had and which should be used to the fullest good of the survey party, it was galling to watch him duck out on duties the other boys had no choice but to take. Drakkar had no chance in a poker game, he mused—his crest had flared up, betraying his emotions, and Thomas had only to wonder what had crossed the Mojavan. That he'd found water was evident, his riding clothes clinging damply to him.

Thomas idly saw Diego slogging after Drakkar, decided the boys had had an argument, looked him over, and returned his thoughts to Drakkar. Then, as though he'd been hit, he looked back to Diego. His Intuition hit him like a wall of bricks. A man in anger has an unmistakable walk—and so does an angry woman. Startled by revelation, he bellowed without thought.

"Alma! What the hell are you doing here?"

Illuminated by firelight and protected by night shadow, Alma looked beautiful though she'd been crying. The girl had her hat off now, her short, jagged hair fluffed about her face. Thomas couldn't tell trail dirt from nut oil staining and didn't care. Alma's large eyes dominated her face and he was glad he could once again recognize the soul behind them.

He had separated them from the rest of the camp and the startled remarks of "Holy shit, Diego's a *girl!*" had finally died out and the boys were showing a considerable amount of interest in Bottom's jackrabbit stew. The clamor had grown quieter the moment the girl had been identified as Alma. Muffled remarks drifting across the way now reached him as, "*Shit,* I knew it was Alma all the time."

Drakkar lay on the far side of the campfire, long legs stretched out in front of him indolently crossed at the ankle, his arms folded across his chest, back propped against his saddle and gear. Thomas couldn't read his eyes. All he was being given was a well-chiseled profile.

Stefan hunkered down, setting off more sparks than the old dried logs and chips the fire used for fuel. His white-blond hair had spiked up when he'd run his hand through it in exasperation and the sweat had dried it that way. Thomas stifled a sigh. What he wanted here was a happy ending and it was patently obvious he wasn't going to get it.

Alma had been talking through muffled sobs. Her voice trailed off into silence. No one said anything for a few moments. Thomas opened his mouth to speak, but Stefan cut him off.

"I don't appreciate the interference," he said, looking at Blade. "You encouraged her to come even after we talked and I made it clear what I wanted to do."

"I had nothing to do with it. She just told you that only Lady knew she was leaving the Warden compound."

"Lady, you, you're both the same."

Thomas started to argue that vehemently and stopped. Instead, he said mildly, "If I had been planning to send you home to your wife, would I have groomed you for survey leader?"

Stefan's lip curled slightly as he answered, "You don't intend to let any of us go. We should have known that. Our blood is too valuable to the counties. You were going to let us go as far as the Vaults, tease us with stories of unexplored land, then rope us together and haul us back home."

Blade figured to hell with it. "I won't deny your value to the counties. Our population has never been high enough to lose good men. But this expedition was agreed upon, and you're going as far as you have the skill to get. Of course, it's going to be a little difficult riding with your head up your ass, but you might find a way."

Drakkar snickered.

Alma said, "Stefan, *please.* Nobody sent me. Nobody knew about me. I came because I—I couldn't see any other way to get you to come home." In spite of her speaking out, she cringed when Stefan glared her way.

"Get this straight. *We* don't have a home to go back to. We're not the perfect genetic pair anymore and I don't have to return to you. I'm sterile, Alma, and that gives me back my life."

Her mouth opened in a sad *o*. Her eyes brimmed with another tear fall.

"We don't know that," Thomas said.

"*I* know it. I've been her husband for two years. Does she look pregnant to you? Look," and he surged to his feet. "Do what you want to with her. Just make sure birdman here keeps his hands off her."

Drakkar turned about slowly to face him. He smiled. "You can't have it both ways, whitey."

Stefan's fists balled and then unclenched. He strode away from the fire and disappeared in the darkness fringing the encampment.

Alma buried her face in her hands. Thomas reached over. "He's hotheaded, always has been. He'll cool down. Let him think about it."

She looked up. She might have been all right, but Drakkar said, "How could you let him walk all over you like that?"

"Keep out of this," Blade snapped.

Drakkar got to his feet. He took his gloves off and slapped them against his thigh. "You should not," he said to Alma, "let others do your fighting for you." He looked at Blade. "I've got the horses to finish watering." He sauntered off without a backward look.

Alma dabbed at her eyes with the cuff of her shirt. She met Thomas' look. "He's right," she said. "First I went to Lady, then she went to you."

"It wasn't your fault. Stefan's been treated like a bull in a breeding pen. Neither of you needs that kind of pressure." Thomas stirred up the fire. "I'd like to leave you riding with Drakkar, if that's all right. He's the best man in a fight around here, outside of myself."

A sniffle. "All right. You're not sending me back?"

"You know I can't spare the manpower. You'll go back with me from the Vaults." Thomas stood. "I've ridden with Lady, so I'm not the kind to expect you wouldn't pull your own weight.

Stay out of Stefan's way and let his temper run its course. He may change his mind after we've been through the Vaults."

Alma said nothing in reply. She sat, folded over as though she had received a mortal blow to the vitals. As Thomas strode away, he reflected that perhaps she had.

Thomas reined in. Harley came to a halt and snorted, blowing snot and foam through the air. The gelding showed his teeth at Stefan's mount as the young man answered Blade's signal to come forward and join him. The two horses leaned on one another and Stefan's mount threatened to cow-kick Harley until Stefan reined him away. It was definitely fall. The cool tinge of the late afternoon air made even these trail-weary horses dance about a bit.

Thomas looked across the Claremont-Montclair strip. They had just crossed the broad expanse of what had once been a major highway, an artery of the L.A. basin. It was more a hazard than a thoroughfare now. Huge gaps that could snap an unwary leg yawned in the road. Thomas breathed a sigh that he'd gotten the party across safely. Now he frowned at what worried him.

"What is it?" Stefan asked. His tone was strictly business.

Blade indicated the broken cityscape, foothills rising behind it. "Because of the reservoir back in the hills, this is prime nester territory. Remember? We should be running into totems soon. Fetishes, at the least."

Stefan took off his hat, mopped his forehead with the back of his hand. "I didn't recognize the lay of the land," he said shortly.

Thomas hadn't expected him to. He'd been two years younger, greener, and in the company of a guard from the Vaults. "You wouldn't. We're coming at it from a different approach. But these streets are still territory, for all that." Blade sighed. "I don't like it."

"Where could they have gone?"

"Back into the Angeles Crest, maybe. More water back in there, after a long dry summer. Or. . . ." He let his thoughts trail off. Would a nester nation still have clans marking individual territories? What was he facing in these foothills, answering the challenge the dean had sent him? "We may not see anything, but they know we're here." He eyed the sky overhead. Sparrows darted aimlessly over the cityscape. He watched a lone crow make its way north. "Stefan, I'm going to put you mostly in charge."

"Where are you going?" The towhead's attention snapped toward him.

"Right here. But I'll be using some Talent and I'll need the backup to catch details I might be a little slow on."

Stefan nodded.

Thomas continued, "Tell Bottom to take your trail buddy, you're switching with him."

"All right."

He twisted in his saddle, looking toward the rear where Drakkar and Alma rode an informal drag. "And tell those two to keep up and stay alert."

His lips tightened, but Stefan nodded again, pivoted his horse and rode back.

Blade returned to surveying the cityscape and the foothills. Unless the nesters had one hell of a shaman, he thought, they would no longer be seeing what they thought they were seeing. Painstakingly he began to gather the elements of the illusion he wanted to project. He could not keep it up for more than the length of the ride, but that was all the time he needed. By night-fall, they'd be camping at the ruins of the College Vault.

The dean cupped his field glasses to his eyes. He blinked, vision doubling, his eyes watering. He adjusted the glasses with a muffled curse, knowing the signs of age and hating them. He scanned the city lines below. He picked up Blade downslope, only Blade, in spite of nester intelligence that he'd come with a full party, and the dean didn't like that. If they'd split up, where were the rest of the riders? He had plans for all of them.

He shifted on the ground. Rocks and pebbles dug into his lean flanks. He enjoyed the sensation. It reminded him of his rejuvenation into vitality. Propped on his elbows, he eyed the sky instead, thinking of Ketchum and his tracker instinct.

Behind Blade for a block, maybe further, birds continued to be startled into the air.

With a dry laugh, the dean lowered his binoculars. How the mutant screened off his party, he couldn't begin to guess, but they were there, invisible, trailing behind him. He almost wished that, in the past when he'd had Blade in his labs, he'd done a little more thorough experimentation. He'd like to know how the trick was accomplished.

"I've got you," he said softly. He began to laugh again. He dug in for a long night.

Thomas reached out and touched the fetish hanging from a tortured branch of the live oak. Summer-dried leaves cupped and shivered in the evening breeze. The fetish was old, faded, as dried as the oak leaves beginning to drift groundward. No nester would leave a fetish as old as this hanging. A weak fetish meant a weak chieftain. Old and shriveled meant the power was gone as well.

The encampment was deserted, nothing to mark that a nester had ever claimed this reservoir basin except the bare spots where the shacks and tepees had rested. The basin had been abandoned a year, maybe two years ago. Who could be strong enough to drive or order nesters away from a water resource this constant and this pure?

Stefan shifted in his saddle. "The boys are hoping to go swimming if there's enough light and before it gets any colder," he said. "They're getting kind of rank."

Blade could use a bath as well. The reservoir was low, way down its banks and lapping onto a shore, but there was plenty of water for bathing and swimming. The mappers were tired and giddy—they'd come this far, to the first of their goals, and they could use a little celebration.

He turned on a boot heel. He felt as if he was being watched. Had been watched all day. *Are you out there?*

He got no answer. He rubbed the back of his neck. His Intuition was gone, having fled in fatigue, and there was nothing he could do but take precautions. He'd gotten them this far. He looked at the broken crown of what had once been a proud mountain. It would take the morning light to dig out an entrance. "All right," he said to Stefan. "But I want a double guard posted tonight. They're expecting us. Sooner or later, there's going to be trouble."

There was a whoop from many mouths at his reply. Thomas found himself blinking in a cloud of dust as riders thundered past him, to draw to a halt and leap headfirst from their saddles into the reservoir. Dinner would be late tonight.

*   *   *

Alma was sleeping when Thomas found her. He touched her shoulder gently. "The boys are all out. There's good light yet and the water is fairly warm. Stefan's set up a guard so you can bathe."

She set her mouth, then asked, "You put him there?"

"No, he volunteered. Come on . . . do you want a bath or not?"

She suddenly wanted a bath so badly she could taste it. She grabbed up her pack with an extra set of clothes and sprinted down the rocky pathway toward the basin where the boys had made so much noise.

She sat down on the slope, after kicking pebbles out of the way, and shed clothes and boots so quickly they went flying. There was a bag of scented soft sand and she dug it out of the bottom of her pack, hoping it would help scrub her stained skin clean. Cautiously, because the slope was very rocky, she made her way to the water's edge.

She put a toe in. It was cool and she shivered as a sudden feeling hit her, an evil oiliness washed over her. Alma stopped and looked about. There was no one to be seen. Stefan was doing his guard duty discreetly. Shaking, she pushed herself into the water and began to scrub as soon as she could crouch down and douse herself. She was afraid and could see nothing to be afraid of.

The dean lowered his glasses. Branches and grasses bent underneath him now since he had changed his vantage point. His hands trembled as he placed the binoculars on the bower in front of him.

Blade had brought a woman with him. Not just any woman, but a young woman, firm and slender, without blemish. *Without mutation,* as near as he could see. He had seen nothing like her since the demise of his people in the Vaults. Flesh of his flesh, blood of his blood—not imaginable among these freaks—he shook with emotion as his mind ran through the possibilities.

He snatched up the glasses quickly. He would have to separate the woman from the others and he knew just how he would do it. He gathered himself and leapt down from his bower. By night he moved yet again and found a new place to lie in wait.

*   *   *

Watty took the telescope Thomas had left with him and opened it up. The instrument sparkled in the morning sun and its brass casings smelled of oil. He eyed the exploring party as they picked their way around the base of the mountain and along a dry creek bed. Disappointment still ached keenly through him—he'd not made the cut to be with Blade and the others going in. He wished now he had not found the trail leading around the mountain's crumpled remains and downhill to what appeared to be an escape tunnel. But Blade had been most pleased with his discovery.

He had stood looking at it a long time. "He's been back," the Protector said, "a couple of times. Not too recently, by the looks of it."

"Who?" several boys had asked, jostling to read the mysterious signs that Sir Thomas could read and seeing nothing remarkable except perhaps a deer trail.

"Someone," the man replied enigmatically, "we're not quite ready to meet yet. But it looks like Watty here has found a way down. There'll be a tunnel mouth at the other end of this trail."

Watty remembered smiling in triumph then and when they'd clambered down and found an entrance. He did not smile when Blade had numbered them off by ones and twos and he was in the party left behind. Sir Thomas had clapped him on the shoulder.

"Someone," he'd said, "has to stay back. We'll need an anchor in case there's trouble."

But the girl had gotten to go. Watty's mouth quirked as he watched her walking to the rear of the party. He liked her, but he didn't think it was fair she could be included in the count just like anyone else.

Bottom sat down next to him on a sun-warmed boulder, just missing squashing a lizard. As the creature skittered off, the cook said, "What's happening?"

"Nothing yet. Everybody just got down to the creek bed."

The burly boy squinted a little. He grunted, "I can see that well myself."

Watty was not about to accept insult with injury. "Look, Blade's scouting the entrance out first."

Bottom smelled like bacon grease and woodsmoke. Rivulets of sweat ran off him. The climb to the butte where Sir Thomas had placed Watty as a lookout was not that bad, but the big young man had had trouble making it. Watty knew that Bottom wouldn't leave without a reward of some kind. If not interesting information about the exploration, then a mean tweak of some kind to Watty.

He put the brass telescope to his eye again. "Thomas has got the tunnel cleared. Wow. Looks like he's got to crawl in. He's putting the rope around his waist and there he goes."

"Yeah?" Bottom mopped his face. The rest of the left-behinds were policing camp. He didn't seem inclined to rejoin them.

Watty counted off the bodies crawling into the foot of the hillside. Alma was next to last. He watched as she began to bend over.

"What's that?" Bottom said.

"What's what?"

"A puff of dust from the top of the hill there," the cook began, but as he pointed, there was an ominous rumble. Suddenly, the mountaintop began to slide down, tons of dirt and gravel raining on the dry creek bed below.

"Shit!" Watty rocketed to his feet. "Bottom, run get the others. Bring the latrine shovels. There's been a slide."

As the heavy boy rolled to his feet and lumbered away, Watty collapsed the telescope and began his own frantic out of control slide down the butte toward the opposite cliff face.

Alma had jerked upright and thrown her hands over her head. She disappeared under dust and rock as he watched in horror.

Chapter 16

Thomas crawled forward in the soft, giving darkness of the tunnel, fighting his desire to stand in spite of the limited nature of the shaft. He felt as much with his Intuition as his hands as the weak beam of his light peered into the gloom. Every crawl of the way, he could feel the greasy presence of the man he'd known only as the Dean of the College Vaults. The man's aura had rubbed off onto this tunnel and its crumbling soil like slime off an eel-snake smothered anything it touched. He caught himself breathing through tightly clenched teeth. He knew the man had been here, and far more frequently than the trail outside indicated. And Blade knew that the dean had left death for him wherever he could.

He was startled but not surprised when his ears suddenly popped, and then he heard a low moan registering through the mountain.

"What is it?" Stefan yelled at his heels, his voice gone shrill with fear.

"I don't know. Explosion of some kind is my guess. Pass it down—see if we're caved in somewhere back there." He fought a momentary panic against being trapped. But he wasn't trapped, the innards of the Vaults lay before him and if the dean had survived in salvaging the installation, he would, too. He lay still in the tunnel, listening to his heart beat and feeling the sweat form on his brow.

Stefan crawled up to wrap an iron hand about his boot ankle.

"We've lost Jenkies and Alma in a slide. We think we're being dug out—we can hear the shovels and the dirt keeps shifting."

His heartbeat skipped a measure. "How bad?"

"Nobody knows. They're just—gone."

Lady had pulled Alma out of death in this mountain. It would be ironic if he'd brought her back only to lose her again. He scrabbled about on his elbows, slipping a hand inside his jacket to see if he could find a light crystal as the torch fastened to his hat grew yellower and weaker in beam. His fingers slipped about finger bones instead.

Gillander oozed out of the dirt walls. He absorbed the waning light and grew more solid.

"Thomas, my boy," the ghost said, pleased.

"Go away. I've no time for you." Thomas searched frantically for another set of rechargeable batteries before he lost all illumination. He found them and snatched his hat off, fumbling for the flashlight.

"Don't go waving your mustache about at me." His mentor sat nester-style upon the tunnel floor. His thinning hair wavered about his bony pate as if it were a halo. "I'll not take your temper, young'un."

Thomas slid the fading batteries out and quickly dropped the newer ones in place. The ghost lit up the tunnel in the absence of actual light. He screwed the flashlight back together quickly and replaced it in the loops of his hat band. The newly restored light shone out brilliantly. Gillander paled in its strength. He looked, Blade reflected, ghastly.

"Use the Ghost Road," the specter said, sympathetically. "Neither boy nor girl is dead, but they are buried. Only you can get to them in time."

"No," Thomas said shortly. The Vaults were resonant in hatred and death. The Ghost Road would be well fueled, but he knew he could not control it.

"You've got no choice," hissed Gilander.

The man took a deep breath. "I've every choice in the world," he answered. *If he was willing to lose Alma and Jenkies.*

He could hear a muffled noise behind him, then Stefan shook his leg to get his attention.

"They're being dug out," the young man called to him. His voice was stiff with emotion. "Alma's all right. Jenkies has a broken arm, probably."

"We'll back out as soon as the mouth is clear. Pass it down." Thomas swallowed a hard lump in his throat. He closed his eyes. "Get out of here, Gillander."

He could feel the ghostlight burning through his eyelids until they were as thin as paper.

"Never you mind," his old teacher said. "I'll have my time."

The tunnel went black. His flashlight sputtered as if the specter had sucked out the juice of its batteries, then the beam came on strong again. It scarcely mattered. He would crawl backward before he could crawl forward again.

Alma sat, holding onto Jenkies' arm, while Trout wrapped the splints into place. Thomas paced.

"Who set it off?" Drakkar asked. He was combing his feathered crest with a peculiar instrument, preening himself of dust and dirt.

Thomas knew only that he had not, though he had been expecting trip wires. Bottom, his face mottled with the flush of excitement and exertion, said, "I saw it—I saw a puff of smoke from the top of the cliff face."

"Where?"

The sweaty boy drew him by the elbow out into the creek bed until he could point upward. Thomas saw the fresh exposure of the cliff face. "Blasting cap," he said.

"D'you think so?" The cook took a deep breath. "Watty never saw anything."

"I can't be sure, but that's what I would have done." And, he would have done it with a remote. He looked around, scanning the creekbed and opposite butte. Brush and drought dulled evergreen met his eyes. He hoped for a flash of metal but saw nothing.

If the dean had been watching them, he was gone now.

"Jenkies, you and your brother and Alma go back to camp. The rest of you stay here and keep this tunnel mouth shored up while the rest of us go back in."

The mappers whooped. Thomas put a hand up. "That doesn't mean you'll be coming in with us. That slide was just a welcome present. He'll hit us again and hit us hard once we're inside. You can count on it."

Watty had the brass telescope slide inside his belt. "And you can c-count on us." He blushed at his stammer of excitement.

Alma said softly, "We'll be all right."

"Okay, then, let's split up. Get some deadwood to use for shoring planks, nothing fancy."

Bill helped his brother to his feet. Trout finished knotting a sling and tugged it into place. "That should do you."

Jenkies was so pale his freckles had bleached out. He nodded. Alma put a hand gently on his shoulder. The boy's color evened out.

Bill said, "Let's hike it." The three of them started up the dry creek bed as it curved toward camp.

It was so easy it was pitiful. The dean picked off the two boys with his dart gun and the girl stood alone, shockstill, as the boys dropped. They convulsed on the ground, green foam coming to their lips and then they were still, curled at her feet.

The girl let out a choked sound. She looked up in horror as the dean left the shelter of the shrubbery. He smiled as he checked the fletch of his last dart before firing again. It would be a pity to use the wrong dart on his quarry.

She turned to run. As the dart buried itself in her flank, he said, "I doubt anyone would hear you scream."

She dropped to her knees. As the mild poison invaded her bloodstream, the cords on her throat stood out. No amount of effort would bring out the scream she tried to issue.

He swept her up before she keeled over to the ground. She had large, luminous eyes, he thought, as the poison glazed them over. She fought to keep her lids open, watching him in trapped silence.

He smiled. "Don't worry, my dear. I don't intend to use you as bait to bring Thomas Blade to his knees. He won't survive what's ahead of him. You're the one I want."

She understood him, he thought in triumph. He was sure of it. He had seen the look of utter terror in her deep brown eyes just before they had rolled back in their sockets in unconsciousness. He hoisted her light weight a bit more comfortably in his arms and took care not to leave tracks leaving the camp.

He found himself humming, in a slightly off-tune voice. Every cloud had a silver lining. He had a lot of ground to put behind him before sunset.

She awoke, stiff and sore, a pain in her ribs as though she had run hard and gotten a sideache. Her mouth felt dry and gummy. Her eyelids stuck together when she first tried to open them.

Then, before she could actually see, she remembered the sight of Jenkies and Bill toppling in foaming agony, their death throes at her feet. The breath in her chest caught now as she remembered the man who'd emerged from the brush and the shadows, overlapping with that same man's image as she opened wide her eyes.

He had his head turned, unaware she'd awakened, but she knew him, though he'd lost his mountainous flesh. The hooded eyes, looking away from her, she could never forget. The years of exile from his underground retreat had sculpted a new man out of his corpulent body. He was lean and looked hard muscled under his shirt and jeans. His salt-and-pepper hair, thinning in middle age, had been pulled back and was French-braided to the nape of his neck where a nester clasp held it in place. There was an aura of power about him that she had not seen in many men besides Sir Thomas. But this power was corrupt.

He was polishing a piece of equipment balanced on one muscular thigh. She did not recognize it except that she'd seen similar equipment in the Vaults the months she'd stayed there. She knew him—would he know her? He'd taken her in reluctantly, a breeder to join the dozens of other women breeders, unskilled and useless to him in general because she did not have a College education nor did she want to obtain one. Her outside bloodlines had been suspect. She had been kept in virtual isolation and quarantine despite testing negative for the mutating eleven year plague. Stefan had been the one who'd appreciated their captivity, not she.

She glanced about the campsite quickly, trying not to betray herself. The sky was a purple-gray. They were in a thickly wooded area. Her hands were bound in front of her and she lay on a coarse blanket over boughs of some kind—pine she thought, their bruised scent was thick about her. She could smell woodsmoke and the man's scent as well, his sweat mingled with citrus.

He moved. She shut her eyes quickly and went limp despite her fear. There was a moment of quiet and then the dean said, "You're awake, my dear. I can tell the difference. While you slept, you purred like a kitten. Did you know that?"

She had no idea what he meant. She opened her eyes and saw him watching her. Dark, flat eyes, with no human expression in them that she recognized. Gooseflesh rose on her arms and crawled through her scalp.

The man smiled. It was only a drawing of the mouth and cheeks. No warmth opened the eyes. "But you wouldn't know what a cat was, would you? I believe the wolfrats killed them off some time ago. Perhaps up north, in the mountains, we might find a big cat, a cougar, or two. Perhaps not."

She would know the voice, if she had not already recognized the body or eyes. It pooled around her like toxic, stagnant water. She felt sick to her stomach. Droplets of perspiration ran down the back of her neck. The knot in her side ached fiercely.

The dean held onto his mechanical box and polishing rag. He looked about. "You could scream here," he said, "and I don't think anyone would hear you. But while you were asleep, I fed you deiffenbachia juice. It quiets the nerves and mutes one very effectively. You may feel a little nausea, but that will pass."

She was familiar with the plant. She tried to think about it, felt her thoughts swirl away in confusion and vertigo.

"The potion on your dart may also cause some numbness in the limbs. I used something quite different and more lethal on the boys."

Alma closed her eyes tightly a moment.

"Ah, no," the man said. "Do not shut your beauty away from me."

The abrupt change in his tone frightened her. As she opened her eyes, he had gone to one knee, creeping close to her. Close enough to touch. He still cradled the box in his large hands.

"This," he said lovingly, "is our future. Blade was looking for this today, to destroy me. But I already had the imprinter. If he'd known that, he would never have taken the risk to go underground. But I found it first. It's of no use now . . . but it will be. Everything I was, everything I am, is locked in here. Do you understand?"

Alma shook her head. Her body answered with a quavering, frail movement, like an aftershock ripple.

He held it up patiently. She could see its face, windowed with colors and gauges. There were fine wires wrapped tightly about its core. "This holds the memory of the first dean, and the second, and the third and the fourth. And it will hold mine, when I'm ready to pass them on. It's like a loop you see, the snake that swallows itself, perpetual, I'm always me, with all the new knowledge and experiences I've gathered."

He spoke intensely, but she still understood little of what he was telling her—and worse, what she had to do with it. He tapped it. "And when the time comes, our son will have it all. Flesh of my flesh and blood of my blood."

It was like a blow to her throat. She could not swallow or breathe. She heard her pulse drumming loudly in her ears. She felt herself cringe backward, the movement barely perceptible, but he saw it as well.

"You would do well to fear me. I'm pure. What is the best I can hope of our issue together? You're from the counties. I can thank God the plague has run its course—but you could be contaminated, still. I saw you bathing. Your perfection was apparent, but it could only be skin deep. Will you throw gills or a third eye? Not scales, I think—the desert bastards carry those genes. The Mars expedition adaptive. If I'm very lucky, perhaps the boy will simply be double-jointed." The dean laughed, a little too loudly. He put aside his imprinter box and fumbled at the laces of his jeans.

Alma got out a sound, a tiny moan. She tried to roll away, but the bower beneath her was as deep as a feather mattress and only cushioned her struggles. Pine needles worked their way through the blanket and stung her through her shirt.

The dean worked to get himself hard. He smiled down at her. "You'll be the mother of a new nation," he said. "And when we have a daughter, she will also become my wife. We'll do the best we can to bring back the pure blood. It's our duty."

He stopped stroking himself. He brought out his knife and slit her trousers away, so quickly that she could scarcely flinch. He cut her leg, a thin red line welling up. He leaned over and licked the scratch, from her calf to her thigh.

Alma tried to buck away from him. He laughed and ripped off her undershorts. She tried to club him with her bound hands. With a movement that wrenched her shoulders, he pulled her hands up over her head and hooked the thong over a pine bough end.

"I'm pure," he said. "Someday you'll thank me for this."

Her body would not answer her outrage and anger. She could not kick and though she was nearly numb from the waist down, she felt *him* as he shoved his way in. He was immense.

Her mouth opened in a dumb cry of pain. He rammed himself deep into her.

"I'm pure, *bitch*, pure, *whore*, pure, *scum*. . . ."

She tried to shut her ears to the litany of filth he poured over her as he tore into her body. The pine boughs crushed beneath their weight. He shoved his hands under her buttocks to hold her closer as he hammered her flesh. She turned her face away, panting for breath, as he began to bite at her neck. With his teeth, he tore first her shirt and then her undershirt away. Alma felt the hot wetness of tears spill over her face as he savaged her nipples. "Pure . . . pure . . . pure. . . ."

Suddenly, he was spent. He fell limp atop her. She couldn't breathe. She felt his seed brimming out and over her thighs. Her flesh felt torn and ripped everywhere he'd touched her. Feeling returned in burning agony. She could move and heaved away from under him.

Her stomach revolted and she vomited all over him, spewing bitterly. He cursed and jerked aside. The movement of his heavy form jerked her hands free from where he had hooked them.

Alma lunged for the box. He grabbed for her, but the slickness of his come covered her thighs and she slid out of his grasp. The imprinter was heavy when she picked it up. High impact plastic. It was the only thing she had. She smashed it down in the dean's face as he jumped at her.

He went down with a grunt.

The sky had gone black. Firelight illuminated his crumpled form. She looked down. Blood as well as bodily fluids stained her legs. She held her violated flesh a moment and pulled her hands away, wet with blood. Her blood, then. She did not care if she had killed the man or not. She dropped the imprinter in the dirt next to him. Its case was undented. She staggered to the tethered horse and yanked the packs stacked next to its peg. She pulled on a spare set of buckskins—immense on her and she cuffed them four times over and tied a crude knot in the waistband. Her own boots lay next to the packs.

She took the horse, the packs, the water, everything. She looked at the belt of sky she could see between the treetops. Thomas had taken great pains to point the night stars out to them. She found a direction and reined the horse back toward the ruins of the College Vaults. The beast broke into a running trot, then slowed as she could not ride upright in the saddle, but hunched over the cantle, her nose hitting the horse's neck as it bobbed up and down with its stride. The reins went slack in her hands, but the horse picked out a steadier path.

She did not know she had gotten her voice back until she heard the jagged noise of a woman in great pain crying, and realized it was herself.

Chapter 17

The dean woke in blinding pain. A kick in the shoulder, more acute than the agony of his ruined face, brought him struggling to his knees. Ketchum leaned over him and handed him a waterskin. The tracker's face was dispassionate.

The dean saw in a glance the girl and all his equipment were gone. His knee rested on the hard case of the imprinter. She'd left behind all that mattered, he thought, and took a deep swallow from the waterskin. He ripped a sleeve of his shirt off and dampened it for a compress.

One cheekbone was crushed and his nose incredibly painful to touch as he put his face to the wet cloth. Tears rushed soundlessly to his eyes.

Ketchum said, "Blade do this?"

"No," the dean answered. "One of his riders."

"I thought not. The Protector generally kills his enemies." Ketchum looked over the camp. "Do you want to go after him?"

The dean could hardly think. He wanted the girl back, but not at all costs. Not at the costs of his painstakingly built leadership. Let Ketchum think he'd been ambushed by a male rider. He'd found the girl once—he'd find her again. She was only a small portion of his ambitions. He touched his face gingerly. He looked up at the nester. "What are you doing here? I sent you back to camp."

"And so I went, Chieftain." Ketchum inclined his head respectfully, a respect which he did not otherwise radiate. "But your equipment began a new magic and so I thought to bring it to you. I consulted the Shastra and was given this vision."

"What?" The dean mopped his face carefully. The nester had not mentioned the mythic creature in months. He thought he'd beat it out of him. The fact that a nonexistent beast had probably saved him increased his melancholy. His journey was always to be one step forward and two steps backward, it seemed. He wrung the cloth out and redampened it. His nose felt the size of a melon. "What the hell are you talking about?"

The nester held out the recall beacon. It was wrapped in a reed box of the finest makings and it had rested so in the dean's tent as though at an altar. "This."

The beacon's sequencing lights had a new addition. The dean dropped his compress, forgotten, and reached for the beacon. It was tapping out a code he did not know, but the panel that now lit up sent a light through him like a searing fire.

It was an incoming code, requesting destination.

"My god," he said. His voice was low and choked in his throat. "They're coming back." His hands shook. A readout translated the code and he watched as words played across a tiny screen. They wanted verbal confirmation. He couldn't give it to them, but he could send a landing code back. They were close, only a few months, weeks away. He looked north and east. The dry lake beds at Edwards had brought in many a shuttle.

The longships were coming home.

And he would be there to meet them, with a nester nation at his back. The world would be his.

Chapter 18

Thomas emerged from the tunnel feeling as though he'd been birthed into another world. The light panels glowed an eerie red, a half-light he could see by although not well. The corridor floor was canted and halfway down to his left, he could see where the wall had collapsed upon itself completely. He moved aside so the boys could come in behind him.

He'd relented and left all but two, Ngo and a young boy they called Bugsy, to guard the shoring and the guide ropes. Those two out, plus Jenkies, Bill, and Alma left him fifteen to shepherd through the wreckage. When Drakkar emerged, it was with great caution, his crest half-aroused. He looked to Blade.

"Emergency lighting," he said.

Thomas knew only that the Mojavans had some defunct military installations in their region. He wondered what kind of salvaging Denethan had done. "What do you know about this?"

Drakkar gave him a shrewd look. "About as much as you do," he answered shortly.

Blade turned away, thinking that the only thing more devious than a Mojavan for an ally was a Mojavan for an enemy.

Stefan said, "We should split up. I know these lower levels."

Blade didn't like the idea of splitting up. It gave him too many directions to watch at one time. But he stifled his gut reaction. Stefan had obvious talents in the Vaults the rest of them did not share. "Only if you take Drakkar with you."

The Russian-born youth's face drew taut. "Don't you trust me?"

Blade pivoted slightly, his headband light coming to rest on Drakkar's face as it followed his movement. "Yes," he answered. "It's him I don't trust."

Drakkar gave a mocking half-bow.

"It's not a matter of trust," Thomas continued. "The two of you are better skilled at keeping your party alive. That slide was rigged. There'll be more traps in here. I want no more casualties. Understood?"

Stefan and Drakkar considered one another in the twilight. "Understood," Stefan said reluctantly.

Drakkar pulled his gloves on tightly. "Naturally," he answered.

Thomas took his torch out of his headband, toggled it off, and replaced it in an inner pocket. The dean's old offices would be on this level—that's why the escape tunnel led here. He cast about in the soft lighting, unable to get his bearings. Finally, to hide his momentary confusion, he counted off the boys again, taking the larger group of the mappers.

He explained to them what to look for—trip wires, snares, mines, and whatever other traps he knew the dean had the technology at hand to set for them. But the Vaults were still alive, with their remnants of a technology he could only guess at—and if they had defenses that could still be triggered, he knew the dean would use them. Jeong sketched something quickly and handed the pad to him.

Thomas frowned at it. "What's this?"

"Beam outlets. We can't see them. I saw them used on one of the CD programs you brought back. On the program, they crisscrossed like this, forming a barrier or gate. Break this barrier and alarms go off. They project from here to here—see?" And the boy showed him.

Thomas looked at the drawing. "All right. You can bet our traps won't set off alarms, though. Break a net of these and you're likely to be fried in your footsteps. Everybody take a good look at the sketch. Good going, Jeong."

Drakkar barely looked at the sketch. "I already know what I'm looking for," he said, in response to Thomas' questioning expression. "Jeong's right. Those things are invisible, quiet, and deadly."

The boys silently took a second look, their faces bled of previous doubt.

"All right. Find anything, give a whistle." Thomas let out a shrill, piercing whistle.

Drakkar answered with a similar one.

"What about if we're out of earshot?" In the half-light, Watty's birthmark looked as though a mortal wound had opened up on his face.

"We're not getting that far apart," Thomas told him. "We're working this side of the corridor and they'll work that side. Let's go. Remember, we've got crew on the outside and at camp waiting for us."

Thomas loved ruins. They were ingrained in him. He'd broken the rules and gone exploring as long as he could remember. He never quite lost the childish streak in him that hoped one day he'd cross a threshold and find out who he really was. He'd been in the Vaults long enough to meet several men in touch with the past, his past, and had known. He tucked his scarf in lightly about his gilled neck. They had looked at him, and known, and instead of telling him wondrous secrets about why he'd been remade the way he was, they'd tried to kill him.

They'd almost succeeded.

He paused in the corridor. Boys came to a stop behind him. Dirt and debris that brushed the flooring lightly seemed concentrated here. He knelt down and breathed lightly over the innocent looking litter. The dust skittered away and leaves stirred, to show a fine wire cutting across the passage. The wall light above shed little illumination on it.

"Watch it," Blade said. He pointed about the wire to them. They jostled his back, eager to look. "Don't touch."

Montez pulled a leather strap out of his daypack. He handed it to Thomas. With a nod, Thomas motioned them back. He looped the strap about so that it would trigger it and leaned as far as he could.

With a jerk, he tripped the wire. There was a blinding puff of smoke and gas from the wall light. Its plasticase shattered into shards that, face-high, would have maimed someone.

"Holy god," Montez said, and crossed himself. Blade returned the leather strap to the cobbler's son before moving up the corridor.

"Thanks."

"Don't mention it." He looked down as he carefully stepped across the debris, afraid to scuffle his feet. His companions followed suit.

Thomas found a doorway. It had been cracked out of its

track and stood half-open by the explosions which had destroyed most of the Vaults. He pointed at Bottom. "Get it open," he told the husky boy.

Bottom wedged his frame in the space and gave an immense heave. The door gave, cracking aside like an eggshell. The cook staggered forward a step.

Thomas said, "Freeze, Bottom. Not another step."

Even in the blood-colored light, he could see the older boy pale as he realized what Blade meant.

Thomas eased past him. The room had been a lab, rather like the medical lab he and Lady had briefly been examined in. It had been stripped of anything but cupboards and counters. He saw nothing of any importance and no traps. Jeong stood next to the sweating Bottom in the doorway.

"Can I come in, Sir Thomas?"

He nodded. The thin boy wedged himself through, sketching as he walked.

Thomas watched him, bemused. "What is it you see that I don't?" he asked as Jeong walked by, immersed in his drawing.

Jeong looked up. "Architecture, if nothing else," he explained.

"Ah. Maximum storage in minimum space."

"Something like that." He tapped a cupboard door. "High impact plastic," he said. "Wears like iron. We can't salvage much of that now. Most of the later plastics are degradable."

Thomas hid his amusement at being lectured by the boy. "When we open this place up, we'll get the cupboards and counters out." His voice was solemn.

Jeong nodded absently. He continued walking, his inkpen flying in his fingers. Thomas waited until he was done before escorting the boy out.

They investigated two more rooms, sterile cells without any idea of what they'd been used for or their basic function. Piles of ash littered their floors. Thomas thought privately that they might have been used for record storage, their contents triggered to self-destruct with the rest of the building. He could see no other explanation. He wondered at a code that would destroy information before sharing it with intruders. He wondered if that had been the fate of Charlie's papers, papers which held so much information about the offices of DWP. The dean's office had been a library, a museum of books and paintings and other artifacts. Had it, too, been destroyed?

Thomas threw his hand up, coming abruptly out of his thoughts. The passageway in front of them was buckled and holed from the explosion, a doorway just beyond the worst of the damaged flooring, looming blackly in the light. The air smelled dead. Acoustical tiles from the ceiling littered the floor. He felt a prickle of apprehension along his gills. He scratched his upper lip thoughtfully.

He'd made Watty gather some fist-sized rocks. "Give me one of those rocks," he said now.

Watty tumbled one into his waiting hand. He sized up the floor and pitched the rock.

He hit the mine on the first try. He wasn't sure there had even been anything there until the flare and explosion rocked the corridor. Acoustical tiles rained down on them, their white dust filling the air. Watty coughed and choked until Montez beat him between the shoulder blades.

Thomas leaned against the wall. A good-sized abyss replaced buckled flooring. The dean was no longer toying with him. And that also meant that whatever that door opened into, Thomas was determined to investigate. If the dean wanted him out, then Thomas wanted in.

But he didn't want to take the boys in with him just yet. The dean was almost certain to have left other traps in the general area.

"Listen up," Blade said, as soon as the coughing and confusion died down. "I'm going in, but I want you all to stay out here until I say to come in. Even then, don't take my word for it. Watch your step."

The boys nodded somberly. Montez's eyes were so large in his round face that Thomas thought of a barn owl. He shook the image out of his head and left them. Behind them he could hear Bottom's worried voice.

"Anybody else know how to whistle like Blade does?"

And Watty's shy voice answer, *"I do."*

Then silence.

Thomas examined the still smoking ruin of a floor. The mine had been highly concentrated. The hole was about three feet deep, and the edges of the flooring material were charred and incredibly smelly. The smoke that drifted up was damn near toxic. He untucked an end of his scarf and put it over his nose as he sidestepped the damage and surveyed the door. It was open, buckled out of its frame. Beyond, he could see a shadowy interior which, although wrecked, was intact.

This lab had been meant to withstand the self-destruct, he thought. So though its contents were damaged, they had not been removed or further salvaged. A huge chamber, like a gigantic egg, had cracked and he saw something slumped in its shadowy interior. All around the room, cabinets stood open . . . their insides still partially filled with supplies. He saw charts on the farther wall. Cables. Leads. Equipment.

A treasure.

What must it have cost the dean to leave bait like this open and waiting for him?

Blade began to move forward to lean inside the doorway to search for traps. Instead he froze, thinking rapidly. So far the dean had done nothing he could not do, although perhaps the dean's handiwork had been a little more spectacular. But explosives were something that Blade could reproduce and had, on many an occasion.

What he could not do would be to string a web of invisible rays across a doorway.

What if Jeong had been right and such technology existed? Drakkar hadn't doubted it for a moment.

Thomas ducked his chin down and examined the doorframe, such as it was. Then he spotted the small heads, studding the jam at irregular intervals. He had never seen anything like them before and, in truth, they did not resemble the outlets Jeong had drawn so quickly. But he knew that, if nothing else, technology evolved. His ancestors had had some very efficient means of killing themselves.

Taking care not to penetrate the barrier he imagined, he shifted to one side. "Watty," he called out. "Pitch a rock through here, underhanded."

The boy pulled out another fist-sized rock. He pitched it toward the door. As it sailed through, it seemed to be in slow motion. Then, caught up in midair, it pulverized to white ash. Thomas swallowed.

"Sweet Jesus," said Bottom. "Lookit that!"

"I told you," Jeong called out.

"That you did," Blade answered evenly. He paced back a

step. Could the web be deactivated? How could he fight what he couldn't see? Then he smiled to himself. Why not fight fire with fire?

He backed off, taking a jump over the mine damage in the corridor. He patted down his vest until he found the vial he wanted. He took it out, grasping the slim glass. "Get down," he told the boys.

"What?"

"I said, get down." He waited until the noise and shuffling quieted, never taking his eyes off his target. When he threw the vial, he aimed it with inner, as well as outer, vision. Then he hit the floor, arms cradling his head.

The door frame blew apart with a shattering blast. It echoed itself a second later. When the smoke cleared, there was little left of the original framing, and nothing whatsoever of the network of hardware for directional beams.

Trout had said nothing till now. The Healer in an awkward boy's body shambled to his feet. His pursed mouth worked soundlessly a moment, then he got out, *"Damn."*

"And that's an understatement," Bottom said heavily as he got to his feet.

A piercing whistle split the corridor. Thomas answered, wondering if the other party had found something—or was just worried about the explosions. He had been unaware of any detonations in Stefan's wake, but as the corridor had curved and because of the nature of the building materials, thought that lower register noises were fairly well muffled. He gave a second whistle signal, used by troopers, meaning "all clear." Stefan should catch his meaning.

He approached the room cautiously, saw nothing else immediately suspicious, and entered.

The half-light did not do the room justice. He slipped his hand inside his jacket and got his small beam. He thought of Lady and what she would have wanted him to bring from here. The supplies here had been gone through, but many vials and packets and bags remained intact. Medicines? Chemicals? He did not have the background to know, but she would have.

The thin ray of light crossed the chamber he'd seen from the doorway. It was this which projected the carrion smell, though faintly. He stepped to it, then flipped the light away from the mummified, decaying flesh within. A cage of some sort? A healing chamber, with its patient left to die instead? He had no way of knowing. He knew only that it had failed if life had been its purpose.

"Sir Thomas!"

He turned on his heel. Montez leaned inside the door.

"What is it?"

"Stefan just sent Rubio back as a runner. They've found the library. And a packet of papers he ID'd as Warden's."

"Any trouble?"

Montez grinned, large eyes crinkling at the corners. "He says Drakkar singed a few tailfeathers getting them."

"I'll bet he did. Okay, I'll make a last sweep through here and then we'll pull out." Thomas took a deep breath.

"What was this place?" Montez said.

Thomas shook his head. "I don't know." He left the chamber and made for the wall charts. What he saw there froze his breath inside him.

He reached toward the drawing and tables. LONGSHIP GENERATIONS AND ABERRATIONS it read. And he saw upon it his own evolution. How far from human he'd come— and how long the road back would be.

He'd once asked Denethan what it was to be human. The mutant from the desert whose burden it was to be reptilian as well had replied that he thought it was the intent, not the skin, that structured humanity. He hoped the Mojavan was right. If not, the journey would be impossible for him.

He put a hand out, uncertain of taking the chart down. What kind of an impact would it have on the Seven Counties? His hand hesitated. Then he snatched the object off the wall. It had a plastic skin. He rolled it up and put it inside his jacket pocket.

The boys had begun to gather cautiously outside in the hallway. He turned, ready to leave, when something caught the corner of his eyes. He turned and fixed the poster in his vision, staring.

It was a beast. Ursus and canus read below it, actually, with more diagrams of the genetic crossovers that had been done. It reared on two strong hindlegs, massive arms, shaggy and yet— shining in its bestial face was an incredible intelligence and compassion. He thought he recognized it for a fleeting second . . . *something rearing out of the night, from the ruins, swiping at him, catching his brow as he ducked away.* He touched his eyebrow, felt the tiny chevron of a scar.

It had been man-made, just as he had been. What was it—what was the purpose behind such bastardization? Blade wet suddenly dry lips. He crossed the room and tore down the poster, determined to take it with him as well. Like a hair, a thin wire drifted down from its edge as he did so.

Too late, Thomas saw it. Too slowly, he reacted. Too close, he hit the floor. The sonic blast went off. Deafened, he dropped into a black pool.

Chapter 19

He woke to being carried, slung like a sack of grain, between the boys. He could not hear and his sight was gummy, blurred, the boys' faces passing in and out of his limited vision . . . or perhaps it was he who passed in and out. They'd swaddled him in their shirts and when he came to again, they were still carrying him and he could not get a hand free to tell them he was all right. Trout's pursed mouth worked open and shut, soundlessly, like a fish on a hook.

His body ached all over and his ears rang loudly and furiously within his head, though the rest of his hearing was stone silent. He tried to speak and found his throat incredibly dry and stubborn. He choked instead, and the crowd of boys stumbled to a halt.

They looked down at him, ensnared between them. In the half-light of the tunnel, he could see their pale faces. Trout immediately went to his knees. He spoke to Thomas, but Thomas could not hear him.

Trout pointed to his ears. Thomas shook his head. The Healer's expression became even more worried, if that was possible. The healer put a hand up and mimicked something trailing from his ears and throat. Then he put a gentle finger to Thomas' neck and withdrew it, stained almost black in the rosy light.

Thomas blinked. He focused on what Trout was attempting to show him. Blood. He was bleeding from the ears and from his neck gills. What that meant, he was uncertain, except that the blast had injured him. He tried to swallow again, felt the trickle of dampness down the back of his throat. Trout dampened his mouth with a wet cloth that someone—Bottom he thought—thrust at the Healer.

He tried to say, "What happened?" He did not know if he got the words croaked out, but Trout smiled feebly and pointed to Thomas' ears and shrugged, meaning Trout could not tell him.

Blade smiled back with irony. "Find a spot to hole up. Meet up with Drakkar in a room we've already cleared." Or that's what he thought he'd said. Trout nodded emphatically and got back to his feet.

Slung between the boys—he tried to count how many bore his weight and gave up—he could at least feel no broken bones grinding against one another as they moved him. The ringing in his ears grew louder and he could feel himself drifting again. They hadn't far to go. He let himself drift.

He dreamed of swimming with the dolphin who'd marked his wrist. The ocean was gray and deep, and he was using his gills and holding onto her to keep pace with her, her wise eye large and gleaming in the dark water. A silvery gleam of bubbles trailed about them as she pulled him deeper, until he feared that gilled or not, she would drown him. She twirled to the surface, curving and looping, he within the embrace of her movement and the water, holding tight until he could see the sun shining through the water, spiking downward, searching for his face. They burst out of the water, leaping together.

"I think he's conscious again." A muffled voice, much distorted. The torchlight moved from his eye level.

He blinked. No dream, that sun. Trout had been checking his pupils. His eyes watered briefly. Trout leaned close. "Can you hear me?"

The boy sounded far away and dim, the ringing in his ears strident and almost overriding it. But he heard him.

"How long?" His own voice, a dried out croak.

Trout looked baffled.

A handsome boy squatted down beside the healer. His feathered headdress lay calm and unruffled upon his shoulders. Thomas blinking, remembering Drakkar. The young man's lips curved a little. "He means, how long has he been out? In other words, what's happening?" He looked to Thomas. "Not long, old man. Minutes, probably. We've got everyone holed up in what must have been the dean's study. I found some of the DWP's papers. We're just cooling our heels and taking a lunch break, waiting for you to come around."

"Good. Water."

Trout pressed a skin into his hand. He wedged himself upward to drink. Trout looked at Drakkar. "How'd you know what he meant?"

"My father's the same way. Got knocked ass over appetite in a raid and the first thing he'd wanted to know when he woke up was what he'd missed."

Thomas would have laughed, but he was in too much pain. Trout took the skin away. "No broken bones," he said. "But you were hit pretty hard. You were bleeding from the ears and gills. I think . . . I think if you hadn't had gills, you'd have lost your hearing for good. But they let go as well, maybe relieving some of the pressure. I think so, anyway. But you've burst both eardrums."

"You can't carry a tune now, except in a bucket," Drakkar said.

Or swim so deep. A poignant loss swept over Thomas. "Trip wire," he got out. "Never saw it. Set anything else off?"

The two boys traded looks.

Drakkar stretched his hands out. "Funny you should mention that. But I think I'll let Stefan tell you. He's out on patrol. He should be back any minute."

Trout added, "Think you could eat? Bottom's made soup."

His stomach clenched in apprehension, but Thomas forced a nod. Trout helped him sit up. He did so with a groan that made every boy in the room stop what they were doing to look at him.

And it had been quite a room to take their attention away from. The bookshelves had been toppled, but there were still books here, leaking all over the floor in a ruin of bindings and torn pages. There was still a painting or two left on the wall, though Thomas could tell quickly that most of the paintings had been removed. The immense wooden, polished desk that the dean had sat behind had been rifled, and was now perched upon by two boys playing with gadgets of some sort that had been left behind. As Blade surveyed the damaged throne room, Trout brought him a battered tin cup full of steaming liquid.

His sense of taste seemed to have been blasted along with

his sense of smell and hearing. He could tell it was hot and that was about it. There were chewy pieces floating around in it that might have been pemmican, but he could not tell. His stomach appreciated the soup far more than his mouth did.

Stefan came in with Machander. They both grabbed a cupful of soup. Machander stayed with those who gleaned pages from the spilled bookcases. Stefan came to Thomas. His white-blond hair was combed with dirt. The dust spilled down his face in lightning-like markings. He looked tired.

"There was probably more than one trigger," he said, "and one of us would have tripped it sooner or later anyway—"

"Cut the crap," Blade said. "What did I set off?"

"A truly massive interior slide. We aren't getting out the way we came in." He sat down nester-style and blew across the top of his cup to cool the soup.

Stefan's feeble attempt to make him feel better for leading them into disaster didn't work. Thomas bolted down the last of his soup. His ears fuzzed out a bit, then began ringing as strongly as ever. "Air?"

"Good, so far." Stefan gulped down his soup. He examined his battered mess cup. "Sir Thomas, I can't believe the dean would sacrifice his only entrance just to trap us."

Thomas felt himself smiling. It turned into a grimace of pain, then faded. "Nor can I, and I don't think he did. What about the shoring?"

"Probably gone."

With Ngo and Bugsy as well. Blade rubbed a hand over his face. He could not depend on outside help to dig out, unless he could reach the three he'd sent back to camp, Alma, Bill, and Jenkies. He'd not done his job. The dean had hurt him and hurt him badly.

Machander came over hesitantly. In the rose-colored half-light, the birthmark that stained his face looked as though he'd taken a mortal wound. He stood uncertainly.

"What is it?"

"I—I know we were supposed to stay together, sir, but I—I found a tunnel that doesn't make any sense."

"Doesn't make sense?" Drakkar had gotten to his feet. The Mojavan's plumage flared a little.

"No, sir. That is . . ." and Machander flushed slightly. "It's off cant to the rest of the building, sir."

Blade studied him a minute. Machander's apprenticeship had been in architecture, though the boy had made it clear he wanted a taste of adventuring before designing buildings. He might have a feel for the structure of the Vaults. "Wait a minute. He might have something."

Drakkar snorted. "Too convenient."

Stefan stood up as well. "Where did you find it?" he said to Machander.

"It's right off this room."

The buzzing in his ears grew louder as he turned rapidly to Stefan. Thomas froze in place a moment, then the ringing subsided enough so that he could hear conversation again. "This could be genuine. The dean would have an escape tunnel as close to his offices as he could manage. The old fox would be likely to have more than one bolt hole."

Machander ducked his head. "It's filled, sir," he mumbled.

"Filled?"

"Soft dirt. We could dig, but. . . ." his voice trailed off.

They only had so much time and so much manpower. Which tunnel to dig—and which would be a deathtrap? Both? Likely, if the dean could have rigged it so. Thomas strained to get up. Trout put a firm hand to his chest.

"Stay down, sir," he said quietly.

The soup was busy making a pleasant, hot, and drowsy knot in the middle of his stomach. Stefan scratched his chin where a fine beard was beginning to come in.

"I think we could all use a break. Most of the boys are tired. We should sleep if we can, then decide on which tunnel to attempt. You should be able to scope it out, then." His gaze rested on Thomas' face.

Drakkar looked as if he wished to argue, but the dark handsomeness of the young man's face closed tight instead.

Thomas could feel himself start to drift. "All right," he agreed. He lay back on the makeshift pillow they'd made for him. He closed his eyes and listened to the others shuffle away.

He contemplated the inside of his eyelids. The dean was a vengeful man. He would not leave much latitude for them to live . . . but Thomas felt that he'd seen too much of the Vaults. The salvage in them was too vast to scuttle them just for revenge. No. The dean would take them down however he could and still leave the remnants of his past life intact.

No more explosions, then, in all probability. Thomas felt his dreamself flicker at the edges of his thoughts. The dean had already shipped him out of here once, for dead. He could still hear the hissing of the gas through the pipes, flooding the chamber in which he and Lady had been trapped. . . .

Thomas jerked to awareness. Bad air. This portion of the Vaults had been all but sealed off. There were labs honeycombed all through here.

Bad air would finish what the dean had begun. All it would leave in its wake were corpses. Blade struggled to sit up again. Without help, his battered body refused to obey. He thought of calling for Stefan or Drakkar and stayed silent. He would not send either down a tunnel he had not inspected himself. He needed assistance, and from the outside. There was no way to reach Alma or the boys.

He slipped a hand inside his jacket. The finger bones came eagerly to his hand as if they'd known his conscious decision to take them up.

All right, Gill, he thought bitterly. *I've no choice but the road this time.* He could only hope it would take him where he needed to go.

Alma woke, retching down the side of the horse's neck, its dank and sour smell in her face and mingled with the animal's sweat. She gritted her teeth and stopped herself by sheer force, willing her stomach to quiet, and pulled herself upright in the saddle. She looked at the strip of starlight through the sparse evergreens. She was headed east, more than that she could not tell.

She shuddered. She would miss the reservoir and the Vaults by miles. Would they be out looking for her yet? Would Sir Thomas light bonfires? Would Stefan care at all that she'd been taken?

The gorge rose in her throat again. She swallowed heavily. The horse stumbled in the brush and came to a reluctant stop, as if responding to her own uncertainty. He stood, flanks heaving. She felt pity for him. Nester horses were not as well bred or cared for as she was used to. This one looked as if he'd never been well pastured or wormed. Lather and the wet strings of her vomit plastered his mane to his thin neck.

She rubbed a hand over his withers. "At least I'm lighter than the rider you're used to," she murmured. The horse shook his head. Foam spun out from his teeth.

She ached all over. She felt dirty and crusty and *sore*. "God," she said. "How am I going to get back?"

A branch snapped. Alma started, twisted in the saddle. Something was out there, in the shadowy night behind her, something big enough to break branches. Her heart began to pound. Had the dean followed them?

The horse threw his head up. He made a moaning sound deep in his throat, a noise of exhaustion. Then he began to stumble into motion again. Alma clung to the saddle and listened as something moved in the brush behind them, driving the horse.

Coyotes ran in packs, she told herself. And wolfrats haunted the ruins. The only predator she could think of was the one she'd just left for dead. Her breath caught in her throat, and she pounded her heels into the tired horse's flanks, pushing him into a laboring trot.

Behind her, in the night, a great beast came to a stop. It had been lumbering easily on fours and now reared upward. Its shaggy flanks heaved in what must have been a satisfied noise. Its cupped ears flicked forward and back, catching the direction of its quarry. It was not a hunter, but it drove them all the same when it dropped back to all fours. Its bulk bent saplings and crushed dry brush as it passed. A soundless calling had sent it on its task and it rushed to complete it. The foreclaws on its paws did not hamper its speed. And, if the claws had been measured, spread, the pattern of their striking would match the chevron mark on Thomas Blade's brow.

The sky had lightened to purple-gray and the birds had awakened when the tired horse went to its knees, throwing Alma over its shoulder and rolling onto the hard ground. She landed with a loud grunt, air whooshing from her. The horse got back to his hooves and stood, head down, breathing gustily. As she blinked away her momentary confusion, she listened past the bellows breath of the horse.

The forest stayed quiet. Whatever it was that had been driving them steadily all night appeared to have retreated. Alma took a deep breath and forced her stiffened body up.

The horse had stumbled at the far edge of the reservoir's lip. As the sky lightened, she could see the water's expanse before her, growing from black to purple to gray-blue. Her exhausted mount began to move to the water as if drawn. She trailed after it.

The buckskins clung to her as if pasted on. Heedless of the chill, Alma rushed past the horse and into the water. She began to scrub herself, shivering, movements frantic as if she would wash away all that had happened to her.

The horse thrust his muzzle into the water, sucking it up noisily. Alma stopped her wash. She let him swallow three, four, times convulsively, then she took him by the bridle to lead away before he could founder himself.

The beast went stiff-legged on her, the whites of his eyes rolling in stubborn disobedience.

She threw her entire weight on the reins. The horse gave way reluctantly as she kicked him in the stomach. She sloshed along the shore line until she could find a shrub strong enough to hold him and snubbed him there. The beast gave her a mournful and resentful look.

"You'll thank me someday," she told it. The horse looked doubtful.

Alma waded back into the water. She could smell herself and the smell of the dean's assault on her. Ice-cold or not, she would not leave until she'd cleansed herself. She scrubbed until the buckskins sagged about her, stretched by the weight of the water and by her vigorous attention. She fisted one small hand in the waistband to keep the trousers up and leaned over to scour her hair. The smell of bruised pine rose in it. She nearly choked on the aroma. She would never be able to breathe that fragrance again without thinking of what had happened to her.

Emotion welled in her suddenly. Overwhelmed, Alma sank to her knees in the bitter-cold water. What was she going to do? No one would ever look at her in the same way again. Why hadn't she fought? Why hadn't she done something, anything, to stop it? Her self-trust had been violated. She felt useless and helpless. She began to cry. The spilling tears felt scalding hot on her chilled face. She could never go back and face them as long as they knew.

Alma dug her hand into her eyes. She couldn't tell them. As long as they didn't know, they would treat her the same. She staggered to her feet, stripping off her sodden clothes. Her pack would be in camp. So would the dead bodies of Jenkies and his brother. She would tell Sir Thomas they'd died defending her. It was the truth.

She simply would not tell them their defense had failed.

Gasping at the cold morning breeze as it struck her, she strode down the shore of the reservoir, the nester pony draggling behind her. Her determination flagged when she reached the camp. Scavengers had been at the camp. Alma would have sicked up again, but her gut was empty. She dry heaved until she could scarcely breathe. Then she found her pack and a clean set of trail clothes. She would have to build a cairn for what the coyotes had left of the two boys. She pulled the poisonous darts from their flesh—the coyotes had worried at their extremities, staying away from the contaminated wounds— and set the weapons aside for Sir Thomas to examine.

She ducked her head and put together her latrine shovel. Between the thin scrapings of the dry, hard ground, and the rocks she could find, they would have a burial. Alma paused, thinking. Blade had always said that dying was easy. It was living that was hard.

She bit her lip and began to dig.

Alma wrestled a last rock into place. It was easily midday. Heat shimmered off the reservoir, striking her like a dagger. She wobbled back to the horse line and sat too abruptly. Her arms trembled from the effort she'd gone through. The nester pony put his head down and licked at her arms. For the salt and water, she supposed. She pushed his muzzle away.

She should eat something. Somewhere, somehow, things had to go back to normal. She put her face in her hands. She did not think that would ever be possible.

Thomas gripped the bones in his hand. Buoyed by the knowledge that Lady had once walked through this mountain, *through an explosion,* on the Ghost Road, he levered himself to his feet. The color had gone gray, lifeless, all warmth from the bodies asleep around him. He and he alone walked this road. He reached down for the strength to fuel it and found such hatred and anger that he nearly fell under its blunt force.

The dean and his people had hated long and deep. The ghost road flared under his feet with a black heat that rippled as it stretched before him. He let his senses encompass all that it had to feed him. His mind felt as though it were a black cloud stretching outward and upward. The strength of the anger made him gasp.

Rarely in his life had he underestimated an enemy. The dean had resources he could barely guess at. But whenever and wherever he touched on the ghost road, the dean was there, a filament that ran through the entire fabric of the Vaults. No man could live that long . . . could he? No one man could hate that much . . . could he? Thomas felt himself repulsed. Yet he forced himself to reach after that resonance because it was the one which would lead him free of the Vaults.

Like a snake whipping toward him, a tendril of darkness came after him. Thomas paused, steeled himself, then reached for it. A shock thrilled through him. He clenched his teeth and stood, grounding himself in his powers and himself as it threatened to burn away all that he had ever known.

A ghost was an echo of what had been. Here on the road, it was as real a presence as he was, and he'd never dared reach for such a thing before. It had always been his hope to pass by, as quickly and unseen as possible. The road was a distortion of time and distance and he'd used it only to get from one place to another far faster than mortal flesh had been meant to do.

Now he grasped that which would trap his existence for its, swallowing him down and absorbing him forever. He knew what death was and would swear that was what speared him now, icy and absolute, its touch piercing him the second he'd taken the ghost into hand. This was no Gillander, reluctant to have him, yet at the same time covetous of his life. This was an enemy bent on annihilation.

But the dean was alive, was he not? Then how could his ghost grasp Thomas now?

The snake threw a loop around him, tangling his ankles. Blade tore a morning star from under his collar and sliced it away. The metal bit cloud so quickly, he damn near sheared off his boot shank. He stomped himself free. With it came a loosening of the emotions cutting through him.

He kept hold of the filament, reeling it in, and when the apparition of the dean reared before him, he stopped. He knew the man only because of his size—taller even than Blade, but this was a dean who was literally a shade of his former self. He'd gotten lean and muscled. Thomas would not have recognized him at first. But then the man turned, looked behind him and, although he could not possibly have seen him, the hooded eyes fastened on him.

He would have recognized that calculating look anywhere.

"Show me," Blade whispered. "Show me your bolt hole."

The dean turned back and Thomas followed.

It was the tunnel Machander had sniffed out. Both the dean and Blade passed through the soft dirt as if it had not been there, although Thomas felt the weight of it, like walking through waist-high mud. The tunnel took several abrupt turns. Thomas felt his link with himself stretching thin as the overpowering hatred of the man threatened to inundate him.

At the tunnel's end, a trap. He watched as the dean dropped to one knee and prepared it. Then left through a bulkhead door which could only be opened one way—from the outside.

The filament snapped in his hand.

Thomas stood and felt the weight of the mountain bearing down on him. He could have brought the boys here all the way, only to meet defeat at the end. The tunnel's seal could only be opened from the outside. The trap would have obliterated and confused all that. They would have died here, pretty packages to be laid at the dean's feet whenever he chose to return.

Alma, he thought. If he could draw her near. If he could lead her to this point, from the other side, Alma could free them.

For the briefest stretch of time, he'd seen the other side of the door. The dean had stepped into open space. She would not have to dig to find the bulkhead.

Lady had always had a tenuous link with Alma, although the girl could not really be said to have Talent. But it was that link which had saved her life once before, if only he could draw on it now.

He was a good sender, if not a receiver. He built his image

now of Lady and Alma together, reaching for him on the pathway between the Warden manor and the barracks, in happier times, Alma rushing to meet them, reaching for Lady and then him. . . .

To draw on his Talent while on the Ghost Road leeched him. He could feel his strength draining away like muddy water down a bathtub drain. He felt himself stagger and go down. The weight of the mountain leaned on him, grew close, bled away his air. He would lose the road entirely and find himself enmeshed with the soft dirt currently blocking this passageway.

He would die here.

Alma.

She heard her name. She lifted her face from her hands, felt the air caress her tear-bloated features, and saw nothing. But she heard. She looked toward the ruined crown of the mountain which held the Vaults. A mule pawed the dirt. One of the pack donkeys let out an earshattering bray.

Through it, she heard her name again, whisper soft. *Alma.* She stood up and cast about. What could make a sound she could hear through anything?

It was not something she could put a finger on, but it sounded like Sir Thomas. It held his confidence, his determination . . . the hardness that permeated his manner. His stubbornness, Lady had called it. That man, she'd said to Alma more than once, would float upstream if he fell in a river.

A third time, she caught her name, and more. *Follow.*

She stood, hesitant. To leave the camp again, alone. The thing which had been in the brush might still be out there, although the horse-line did not look uneasy.

She took up her shovel which was big enough to dent the skull of just about anything she might connect with. She went in search of a voice that could pass through stone and time.

She followed it to the broken mountain and, there, began to search for a hidden door.

Alma stopped in frustration as the voice left her.

"Come back!" Her own echoed. "Dammit, how can I find you?"

Faintly, softer than whispers, softer than any noise except

the beat of her heart and the velvet flow of her blood in her veins. *Alma,* he answered. She followed it again.

He knew when she'd heard. He knew when she'd gotten to her feet and come in search of him. But then he lost the strength to call her further. The road sucked him dry like a spider does its prey. If he moved, he'd shatter, mummified to brittle dust. If he called her again, his soul would spool out of his mouth with his voice, to be lost forever.

The road would have him if he did not withdraw now. He'd lose his anchor and die.

He knew when she smashed her fist into rock and bramble, yelling, "Dammit! How can I find you?"

He could not leave his task unfinished. He dredged up the last of his strength and called her to him.

When he heard the shovel hit the outside of the door with a dull clang, he knew he'd done it. He let go of the road abruptly. The tunnel imploded on him, dust motes striking him with the force of hammers. He could feel himself whirl away, unraveling with the speed of light.

"Sir Thomas? Sir Thomas?" Trout, making faces at him as he tried to wake him. The boy's cold, dry hand across his forehead. Drakkar leaned from the other side.

Thomas groaned.

"He's alive," Drakkar said, and grinned.

His head pounded. His mouth felt like it was still filled with the ashes of the hatred that fueled the road. The Healer took his hand away. "We're all awake now. Bottom says it's been a night."

The cook's stomach was the best timepiece they had. Blade struggled awake and found his sides strapped firmly, so firmly he could scarcely draw breath.

"What . . . is this?"

"In case your ribs are broken. And Jeong found something else that might help. Take two of these with a little water."

He peered at the capsules. "What is it?"

"Something called aspirin." Trout looked tremendously pleased. "We can't formulate it now, but it's in a lot of our older literature. We found packets of it in the desk drawers. Should be good for the pain."

He needed to get on his feet. He took the two pills and swallowed them dry while Drakkar fetched a water skin. The aspirin was horribly bitter. He made a face. Then, "Where's Stefan?"

"Having a look at Machander's tunnel."

"Good. Tell him that's our way out. But the two of you have got to lead the dig. There's a trap, near the end. There's a door—and it should be open by the time we get there. Help me up." He put a hand out to Drakkar.

Denethan's son looked at him curiously. "What makes you think the door will be open at the other end?"

Blade grinned. "What makes you think it won't be?"

Chapter 20

"You had no business dragging Alma into it!" Stefan paced in anger, his voice loud enough to be heard throughout the camp, and he did not care who heard it.

Thomas, bolstered into a comfortable position, took a long sip from his cooling mug. He said, "We needed her on the outside. You boys found and disarmed the last trap. Nothing happened."

"She could have been killed if that bulkhead had blown."

The Protector commented mildly, "You all could have been killed."

Alma looked up as Stefan pointed. Trout had bandaged her hands where the cairn-building had left her blistered and cut. Purple shadows lay under her eyes. "I was there because I was needed."

"We couldn't have gotten out if she hadn't been," said Drakkar. He sat cross-legged atop a flat boulder, the late afternoon sun glinting off him. "That door had been rigged to open from the outside only. We're lucky we only lost the four. You knew the risk going in."

Stefan turned. He glared flatly at Drakkar. "Alma didn't know. She wasn't part of the company."

Drakkar shrugged. "You're like a coyote in the corn," he returned. "You've made it damn clear you don't want her—but you don't want anyone else to have her either."

"What's that supposed to mean?"

"It means," Alma answered, her voice taking an edge, "that you don't want me to have a life beyond you. And that most of your anger now is guilt. I don't want it!"

Stefan's voice dropped. "It's all I've got left."

"Then keep it." She levered herself to her feet. She stalked away, in the direction of the horse-line.

Thomas watched her go. "She's had a rough time of it," he said to Stefan. She'd told them all how the nester raid had killed Bill and Jenkies who'd held them just long enough to let her escape into the woods. She'd not come back unmarked, her face bruised and hands scarred, but he had confidence she'd be all right.

"And I'm responsible, right?" Stefan clenched his hands. He raised his voice to yell after her. "You've got what you want. Here, in front of these witnesses—I divorce you. I divorce you!"

Alma stumbled. She caught herself and kept walking, until she was out of their view.

Drakkar said, "I witness."

Stefan spat. Thomas put his hand up. "That's enough, you two. Let's leave her some shreds of dignity. As a Protector and executioner and officer of the courts thereby, I witness your decree, Stefan. The bond of matrimony is now broken. You're both free. I hope that's what you really wanted."

Stefan leaned over, snatching up his hat from its resting place atop his saddle and pack. Without a word, he strode off in the opposite direction. Drakkar watched him go, then opened his mouth.

Thomas pointed at him. "Not another word," he warned. "You're a diplomatic disaster, running through the Seven Counties like a rooster in heat. You quit jousting with Stefan for power. He's got nothing you want or can have."

The Mojavan snapped his mouth shut, then opened it to mumble, "Not anymore, anyway."

"Leave Alma alone. If she wants you, she'll let you know. But you're Denethan's son and if I were you, I'd consider any plans that might already be made for you."

Drakkar climbed down off his boulder. He smiled ruefully. "For an old man," he said, "you've still got your smarts." He managed to saunter off in a direction the other two had not taken.

Thomas watched him go, wondering if he had his smarts indeed. The deaths of the four young men ground at him. They should not have died. He'd taken too much on himself, spread himself too thin. He had had no right to shoulder onto the youngsters the risk he'd taken for himself, even though they'd asked for it. He was of half a mind to cancel the mapping expedition. They'd planned to split up in the morning after a short memorial service for Bill, Jenkies, Ngo, and Bugsy. Fourteen of them would go on.

If they were going to go, now was the time. The nesters had pulled out, vacated the area, leaving clear passage. As soon as Blade and the others were spotted trailing back, that advantage would be lost.

If there was a world waiting out there, it would be cut off from them the more they hesitated. He had no choice, as he saw it, but to let them go. Stefan, for all his hotheadedness, would be a good leader. They had comported themselves well. He sipped at his tea. He could ride in the morning, bruises and all. Those packets of aspirin had worked quite well. Too bad they'd been unable to find more. That was something of the old world he'd like to see restored.

Thomas stretched out his hand and set his empty tea cup aside. He looked at his flesh. The blood on it was invisible to everyone but him. He had some of Charlie's valuable papers in his pack and a chart showing the genetic outcrossing and engineering that was his legacy. And he had tried and been defeated by the ghost road for a last time. It would have killed him if he had traveled it physically instead of astrally. Despite Lady's urgings and those from Gillander, he would not be trapped again. He was not used to failure. It gave him a burning sensation in the pit of his stomach. He settled back and closed his eyes, wondering what he was going to say to Lady when he returned.

Alma brushed past Bottom at the edge of the woods. The cook seemed oblivious to her, except to say, "Bring some extra deadwood back with you. Campfire's running low."

She nodded and kept going, afraid he would notice her brimming eyes and tear-roughened face. She looked hideous when she cried. No one called anything more after her as she plunged into the brush, tree limbs snatching at her sleeves.

It was even worse to have no one notice. She stumbled to a knoll which was still covered with a slight thatch of summer grass and sat down, curling around her knees. *I divorce you.* She fisted her small hand and rubbed her forehead. What she needed was for someone to hold her tightly, someone to make her safe. She had her secret and intended to keep it, but there was no comfort to be had for her actions. Nothing. She might as well have died.

Drakkar paused in the woods, watching. The girl was not for him, and he knew it, but he watched nonetheless, sensing her pain and fragility reaching out to him. He would not go to her, not now, knowing that if he did, it would be far worse for her when the Seven Counties and the Mojave tore them apart. She was genetic promise, and he, a plague child, was genetic curse. They could have no future.

Ah, Father, he thought. *Why did you send me here?*

And even though it pained him to keep a silent watch over her, he stayed until long after she departed.

PART II

Chapter 21

"Thomas, you haven't been listening to a word I've been saying." Lady put her pen down, the ink from its carved tip squibbing a little on the table. She pushed her chair back abruptly and crossed to his side of it.

"I'm sorry," he began, but she folded her arms and perched on the table's edge.

"Don't make excuses to me." She stopped him in midsentence. "You've that look on your face. You're a million miles away chasing the dean."

He looked up at her. She wouldn't have been a Protector if she couldn't have sensed his preoccupation. That did not surprise him. What surprised him was the anger she fought to contain.

He stood up, putting their eyes more on a level. "I've got to go back. We've got nester raids on the fringe areas, and the fetishes they're leaving behind tell the story. He's done it—I don't know how, but he's done it. He's got more than half the free clans in the basin under his influence, maybe more."

"You don't know that for sure. You don't even know it's *him*."

He rubbed his rib cage. Small knots of pain soothed away. Four cracked ribs and a permanent partial hearing loss in his left ear had been his legacy from the expedition. He counted himself lucky. "I know," he said slowly, "that if I had done from the beginning what my instincts told me to do, if I had done what I've been trained to do, none of the boys would have died. None of Denethan's men would have died years ago. Only the dean would have died."

Her two-colored gaze narrowed, sharpened. "I was not

aware," Lady bit off, "that you serve as judge and jury as well as executioner."

He turned away. "There's a first time for everything. It should have been done."

"I didn't know that and I don't see how you could have! The Vaults were meant to keep safe the best our world had to offer. Even if we had suspected what we were walking into, we would have done our best to have salvaged as much as we could."

He put the length of the writing table between them. A few stray pieces of paper drifted down as he leaned his hip to the planking. "You and I are different from most people. We should have known."

"And what would you have done then? Killed everyone else you could get your hands on? No. That wasn't the solution."

He looked at her then. "We're facing an all-out war now. The nesters will outflank us once they've joined forces."

"There's always the Mojave," she pointed out.

"Chancy allies at best. Shankar hasn't said much to me since we've returned, but he gets his messages at regular intervals. I gather Denethan is neck-deep in trouble."

"What does Drakkar say?"

"The dragon boy says as little as he can." Thomas tugged at the ever-present scarf about his neck. He felt constricted, dry, and brittle. "We shouldn't argue," he finished and bent down to pick up the papers he'd displaced.

She took the papers from his hand. "No," she agreed. "I should just kick some sense into your butt."

Thomas felt himself grin wryly. "You and what army?" He grabbed her wrist and pulled her into an embrace. She did not yield to him and he let her go carefully. "What is it?"

"Thomas, you're infamous among the nesters. They know you're quick and strong and respect you. As much as you despise what they've become, you still stand up for their basic human rights. Go if you have to—but go to talk to them. You're probably the only man who can."

The warmth he'd been feeling fled abruptly. He paced a step away. He shook his head. "It's gone beyond that. I can't even talk a treaty with them the Seven Counties would agree to abide by."

"The counties," and Lady's voice was deceptively soft, "would stand behind the treaty of a DWP."

"No! We've been all through that. I'm not fit for the position."

"I wouldn't necessarily agree with that, but yes, we've been through all that." Lady reached for a packet of ribboned papers on the writing table. Her short, work-efficient nails plucked at the ribboning without opening it. "Call for a temporary DWP. You can do it. Boyd and the others will bow to you, at least until they can finish jockeying for the election. They all know it will behoove them to be appointed now . . . easier to be elected later. They'll back you for this, even if it's only long enough to entrench themselves."

Thomas felt the idea gnawing at him. Lady knew the inner workings of the counties better than he did. He spent too much time circuit riding and too much time staying neutral. He never knew who he might have to execute next. "Then it doesn't matter who gets appointed, as long as they back me."

"Well, it matters, but it's not crucial at the moment. Not as crucial as keeping a war out of the Seven Counties. Go in under truce, talk a treaty—and do whatever you have to do to obtain it, even if the dean stands between you and peace."

She met his gaze unflinchingly. "Even if I have to eliminate the dean to do it?"

"Whatever it takes. Better one man than legions."

"But you would rather I didn't kill him," he countered.

Lady tilted her head slightly, giving him the full stare of her icy blue eye, the business part of her gaze. "I'm not fool enough," she answered him, "to think the dean can be cured by a hug and a laying on of hands. But if he were whole, he'd be invaluable to this community. His education, his personal history—think of it."

Thomas already had, and had come to the conclusion that anything the dean might have to offer would be as corrupt as he was. But he did not say that to Lady. One of her eyebrows quirked, daring him to respond. He kept his tongue. There was a rap on the door and Quinones entered dartingly quick without waiting for answer.

Even a psychic mute could hear the charges, the tension, in this room. The man came to a quivering halt as his nerves got the better of him. He looked wildly at Lady.

"It's all right," she said soothingly. "What is it?"

"For Sir Thomas," he got out. "Judge Teal is here to convene with the nominating committee."

Blade felt his thoughts stagger a bit. The judge had to have been on the road a good six days. He looked at Lady, who had blushed in a becoming fashion.

"That's wonderful," the healer said, and walked Quinones to the door. "See he's made comfortable at the compound. We'll meet him before dinner."

Thomas barely waited until the door closed. "Nominating committee!"

"Yes. You suggested a week or so ago that one ought to meet when you presented your report on the Vaults. Didn't you? That's scheduled for tomorrow."

He now had an idea why she'd kept him bottled up all day with paperwork. He closed his mouth at her audacity as she returned to the writing desk. Then, grudgingly, "I've been set up."

Lady replaced her ink pen in its holder and capped the inkwell. She gave him a dazzling smile. "Don't fuss, Thomas. In the words of the immortal bard—at least, I think it was him—united we stand, divided we fall."

Alma's footsteps hesitated on the alleyway, the soles of her shoes catching on a pebble, throwing her off stride. Her shopping bags fell from her hand. She leaned against the back wall of the bakery, her senses filled with the overwhelming smell of yeast and dough as it rose for the evening's late baking. She felt a hundred years old. The building's solid warmth felt comforting as it braced her. If she hurried, she could catch the dinner hour cart up to the Warden compound, but her body betrayed her. She couldn't move another step if she had to.

A dull throbbing pain rose in her ankle. She bent over and ran her hand over the joint. Already it was swollen and the pain, though not sharp, was constant. Hot tears filled her eyes. She blinked them away. It served her right. She would be skulking down alleys when there was a perfectly good main street, with sidewalks and gutters, she could be using. But she hadn't felt up to the jostle of the foot traffic, the stares of folk as they recognized her—the pity she thought she saw in their eyes.

A divorced woman. Not proven fertile. The hope of the Seven Counties, and there she was, scarcely seventeen years, and barren. That's why he left her, you know.

Oh, god, she thought, straightening up and clinging to the corner of the building as if it could save her. What would they think if she'd told all that had happened to her? She shuddered so violently she had to catch her balance to stay on her feet.

"Alma—are you all right?"

She jumped with a half-scream. She caught herself with a hand to her mouth, stifling her startlement. Drakkar retrieved the fallen shopping bags in a fluid stoop. He handed them to her.

"I didn't mean to frighten you."

Her heart pounded in her chest. Her ears rang with her pulse. Vomit pushed up the back of her throat with the suddenness of her fear. She took a deep breath and backed away a step before he could touch her. She couldn't stand the thought of— anyone—touching her. "I'm fine. I just . . . gave my ankle a wrench."

"What are you doing back here?"

"Taking a shortcut to the cart stop." Alma gathered her nerve to brush past him. "I'm in a hurry, Drakkar."

He caught her by the elbow. His deep blue eyes reflected an unfamiliar emotion as he looked at her. He did not let her go even though she tried to free herself.

"I'll be late."

"I'll take you up later if you want. Alma, you don't belong in the shadows."

Those tears sprang up again. Damn her, what was wrong with her eyes? The DWP should declare her another water source! She blinked furiously. "I'm not in the shadows, I'm in a hurry."

He let go of her arm abruptly. "Then go. You're free. Free of Stefan and free of me. But you remind me of a hunting bird I had once. A red-tailed hawk. When I left boyhood and became a man, Micah presented me with a falcon, more befitting my status. I couldn't stand the thought of anyone else flying my little hawk, though, so I freed it. It didn't know what to do when the gear came off. It stayed to its perch. We tried to shoo it away and it came back. It didn't seem to comprehend its freedom."

Alma felt her cheeks grow warm. She looked down the tunnel of alleyway, toward the streets she'd avoided, wondering if she could bolt away from Drakkar, and knowing she couldn't. Reluctantly, she asked, "What happened?"

"It nearly starved to death. The falconer wouldn't feed it. We hoped it would leave in search of game. Finally, one day, I took it out. My beauty was so weak, I had lost all hope for its survival. Then, on a butte overlooking the dry wells, with the sun so low in the sky I couldn't see the horizon, I flew it one last time. The effort, I thought, would kill it painlessly. I had to cast it into the air with all my might to get it to leave me."

He looked at her then, keenly, and she found it hard to swallow. "And then?" she said.

"And then another red-tailed hawk flew overhead. They circled a moment, and I could tell the other hawk was a potential mate, and luring it away from me. I whistled for my bird, trying to recall it in spite of my original intentions. It never faltered. It never came back." Drakkar sighed abruptly. "Meaning, I suppose, that love and the mating instinct is even stronger than that for food, at least in red-tailed hawks. My little hawk had traded its love for me for a greater freedom and a greater love."

A dizziness swept her. She shifted weight to keep her balance. She felt Drakkar's presence suddenly overwhelm her. Alma cleared her throat. "A pretty story," she said.

"One with a moral. Take your freedom, Alma. You'll never know what is waiting for you out there if you don't."

A bell rang out, signaling the arrival of the transport cart. Biting her lip against a stab of pain from her ankle, she launched herself down the alleyway, calling back to Drakkar, "I know there won't be a cart waiting for me if I don't hurry!" She ran awkwardly, shopping bags hitting her skirts, and feeling his unrelenting stare after her.

Drakkar stared for long moments after she'd been gone from his sight. He found it difficult to believe he'd ridden nearly two weeks with her, unaware of who she really was. She radiated a sexuality now that was like a heady perfume, alerting all his senses, and it was totally unconscious on her part. Her short cropped hair had filled out, now cupping her head with its dark, curled beauty. Her eyes had looked as large as pigeon eggs, he thought, and chided himself for startling her. He moved his head, felt his feathered crest brush his shoulders. *I am a hawk, circling you. Will you have the strength to see and fly away with me?*

Drakkar took a deep breath. He had other business in town.

Shankar showed signs of being involved in some most unambassadorial activities. One of his guard had passed him the word that he'd located what he thought was a private cote, used by Shankar to house the pigeons carrying messages he did not wish Drakkar to see.

Drakkar was not a blind man. Shankar acted in his own behalf as often as he acted in that of the Mojave. His father was not pleased. Perhaps, and Drakkar stirred himself into action, he could find a way to make his father happier. It was always wisest to nip revolutions in the bud.

He kept to the alleyways, following his guard's directions.

Chapter 22

"Do you like it?" the dean said, smoothing down the front of his caftan. A violent wind shook the chieftain's quarters. It had been blowing steadily all day and might well for weeks.

Ketchum stared. The black robes had been hand painted by some of the finest nester artists. Fetishes were hand stitched to the patterns, along with beads and pyrite flakes and quartz gems. He thought privately that the fetishes would take a great deal of trouble to keep fresh and potent, and that the robe would be difficult to ride in. But he said only, "It reflects your power, Dean."

"As well it should." The man held up a shield of polished metal, scavenged off the hood of a truly old vehicle, an item of inestimable value in itself. It reflected his image adequately. The violent dip of one cheekbone, the ruined bridge of his nose, the mottled bruising now faded to a light shadow, he regarded those imperfections as he would a warp in the hood's surface rather than his true reflection. "As the clans pledge their allegiance to me, the decoration will be increased." He picked a stray bit of feather off the black cloth.

The tracker more and more did not approve of this man. He could not understand why the Shastra had brought him to them, or why it did not bring the man down when its power had been usurped. The Shastra was shy with its powers, not often seen. In Ketchum's own lifetime, the beast had only been seen twice, both times during forest fire, appearing and then leading clans to safety. The shamans claimed to speak with the beast, but Ketchum thought privately that that was more a rattle of bone and seed than speech. As for himself, he had seen the beast once, the night he had ridden to bring the dean his box of lights.

He would have followed the beast, but something had not been quite right about its appearance—it had not come to him, he'd decided, and therefore he would not follow. Finding the dean wounded had settled the matter. He would put more store in the shamans had one of them had been able to tell him he would be seeing the Shastra while doing the duty they claimed the Shastra had sent him on, but none of them had predicted that happening that night.

Privately, he wondered if perhaps the Shastra had not taken its anger out on the dean rather than one of the Protector's riders, as the dean had claimed. But signs in the camp did not uphold his theory. If anything, it indicated that the Shastra had followed the dean's attacker. Rather than dismiss the idea, Ketchum merely put it aside, waiting for the day when the Shastra would deal with the dean chieftain. It was the main reason he stayed.

The dean looked up at him suddenly. "As soon as the wind dies down," he said, "we'll have a landing time."

Ketchum could not comprehend a machine that stayed in the air, circling the earth. But he'd been told by those in a position to know that such machines had existed and might still exist. He did not allow his skepticism to surface. "Give us three travel days," he reminded.

"If I can. If not, we'll have to run the horses to death and go from there. I *will* not be late for their return. Do you understand me?"

Running a horse to death would not accomplish the dean's desires, but Ketchum only inclined his chin as if in agreement. The wind spoke to him as it snapped tent ropes, making them sing quivering notes, while branches rattled and dust peppered the hides of those unwary enough to be outside. The wind would stop blowing when it willed. It would take a prophet to know when that would be. It would take a prophet to keep the dean from being late.

But Ketchum did not believe in prophets and kept his tongue silent because the dean did.

The plot room on the *Challenger* was empty except for Sun and Dusty. Dakin rubbed his eyes. He'd gotten lined in the last eight years, she thought. She pushed away the remnants of a birthday cake—hers—she'd celebrated two actual years of wakefulness, making her all of the ancient age of twenty-seven. She slouched back in her chair and waited for him to speak.

At last he tapped a fingernail on his folder. "It's not pretty," he said.

She looked at the surveillance file. Most of the personnel aboard the ship had been banned from the surveys. After what happened to the *Maggie*, Dakin wanted no talk, or even thought, of mass suicide, no matter what they faced on the earth below. Without thinking further, she reached for the folder. Her sister had been in Pasadena, near the JPL facility. Silent, all these years, in spite of what they'd been molded for and promised.

Dakin let her slide the folder from under his slender hand. She opened it and hunched over it on the table top.

Dusty looked at it and felt as though she'd gone blind. She stared a moment, then looked up at her commander. "I don't understand."

Dakin reached out and shuffled photos. "Look at the computer enhancements and reproductions. They're better."

An auburn hair drifted down from her shoulder and lay curled across the photo, a crimson line across an aching crater. "What is it?"

"Four strikes. Meteors of incredible size. Two in North America, one in Asia, and one in Europe. We guessed as much from the probe Chandler sent out, now we know. The dust cloud raised must have shrouded the earth for nearly a century."

She stared at a landscape that reminded her of early lunar photos. "This. . . ." her throat felt dry. She tried to swallow. "This is the farmbelt. Iowa, Kansas, Nebraska, Illinois. . . ."

"A dust bowl. The Mississippi runs through mudflats. The wind has stripped away most of the topsoil. It could be reclaimed, now, if there were enough people with know-how. But the people are gone, too."

"Animal life?"

"Some. Mainly close to the riverbanks. Vegetation and trees on the fringe areas."

Her hands were shaking. "California. What about California?"

He guided her to the photo. "The strike was in Nevada, but there was a—a bounce, I think you'd call it—in the L.A. basin."

Her sister, dead. Not silent all these years, but dead. Dusty put her hand to her mouth and felt sundered. Alone for the first time since her birth. She sensed, rather than felt, Dakin's hand sheltering hers.

"You knew it. You had to have known it."

"I thought. . . ." Dusty choked. "There was a bunker. Another lab below. I hoped, maybe . . . god," and she rocked in her chair. "I don't know what I thought." She caught her breath. "All those people, dead."

"Actually, Peg was right. They might have made it, even with the dust, but there were some nuclear strikes in the third world, accidents probably, set off during famine rioting—and then there was all the pollution and no longer the technology to continue cleaning it up. We'd made a start. We just weren't around to finish it up." He moved his hand. "We've got everyone covered, all the land masses." He started shuffling out photos, but Dusty put her hand over her face.

Muffled, she asked, "Is there still an England?"

"Near as I can tell. A lot of snow cover. I'd say the Earth is pulling out of what might be termed a nuclear 'fall,' or maybe even a nuclear spring. We've seen some massive rainfall in the L.A. basin over the last two years as we've pulled closer. It's mostly lost to run off."

"Orange County is an aqueous basin," she said, dredging up long ago memories.

"What?"

"I mean . . . the water is there, if they know how to drill for it."

Sun added somberly, "And if they can keep it clean. Anyway, we've got definite signs of civilization south of the L.A. area and around the perimeter of the strike. There's some minor sign in the San Francisco Bay area and quite a bit in Vancouver-Seattle. Also, near what used to be Portugal. England, perhaps—Dusty, there're outcroppings all over the world. We're not extinct. We hung in there."

She closed the file folder. "When?"

Dakin looked up, startlement crossing his Asian features quickly, like lightning. "What?"

"When do you think it happened?"

"Well . . . that's a tough one. Judging by when you lost contact with your sister, maybe seventy-five years out. We can't really tell because your telepathy experiment was strictly experimental." He smiled thinly. "Fantastic ESP power is still part of science fiction."

She did not let his comment sting her. She'd faced that all her life. She sat back in the chair again. She looked up at him. "What are you going to tell the others?"

"Everything I've told you. We've got a fix on our recall beacon and we can put a shuttle down at Edwards, on the dry lakes airstrip, as soon as the weather dies down. There are other strips we can use and the communication from Edwards is strictly low-level. But they're the only ones to have responded at all. The feeling is a gut-level one, but we'd like to put down in the U.S.A., if we can."

America, reduced to villages and vast stretches of ruined land. All the trees they'd planted since the turn of the century . . . Dusty sat in memory.

He swept the file away from her. "We've got quite a job ahead of us."

Her gaze flickered. "What?"

He smiled. "We have the know-how. We *can* do it."

She felt a yawning emptiness inside of her. "Can we?"

"If it's hospitable at all. Just because *they* can live there doesn't mean we can. They may have mutated, adapted to a hostile environment. We won't know until we send a team down. Marshall and I will be presenting this tomorrow, so I'd appreciate it if you didn't say anything until then. It looks bleak at first."

She stood up. "I'll say. Who's on the assignment to go down?"

"We're not making assignments. This survey is strictly on a volunteer basis." Sun's almond eyes did not reflect any emotion.

Dusty suddenly sensed there was more he had to say to her. She dropped back down in the chair. "What is it?"

"We're beginning to experience some mechanical failures. And, because of the nature of the base we're landing at, anybody who goes down can't come back up. We don't think we can effect a shuttle relaunch. The survey team is on a one-way trip, Dusty. I can't order anybody to do that. It has to be volunteered," Dakin finished.

"What kind of mechanical failures?"

"The stress of maintaining an orbit, of maintaining the *Chal-*

lenger . . . we may be faced with the same kinds of problems the *Magellan* faced. We don't want that to happen. I'd like for us to have the option of leaving orbit and returning, eventually, to the habitable planets we scoped. That's virgin territory where we already know we can colonize successfully. We may want to go on, instead of trying to stay here."

"An option," Dusty repeated.

"The more we have, the better off we are."

"And whoever volunteers for the survey team loses all options."

He nodded.

Dusty shook her head. "I wouldn't want to be in your shoes, Dakin."

"Me neither." He smiled. "Heredia is laying back with the *Mayflower*. She's agreed to let us do all the initial surveying."

"Agreed? Who'd she have to kill for that privilege?"

"She beat me in chess." Dakin stood up, tucking his file under his arm.

"I'm going." The words burst from her before she'd thought about it. Dusty looked into Sun's shocked expression.

He made a negative sign.

"You said it was a volunteer survey."

"That decision is to be asked for tomorrow! And we don't need to finalize it for several days. No matter who volunteers, we'll need a balanced team."

"I can shoot. I'm one of the best drivers you've got. And I know the territory," Dusty said wryly.

He scratched an eyebrow thoughtfully. "That you do," he answered slowly. "I can't argue with that. Dusty, you're our oldest living crewmember—"

"I'm everyone's oldest living crewmember."

"I don't know if we can let you go."

Her redhead temper began to flare. She felt her skin tingle, knew her face blushed.

"On the other hand," Dakin continued coolly, "it doesn't look like it's going to be easy to make you stay. Let's see what tomorrow brings."

She would have to be content with that.

Chapter 23

"It's the wind," Blade said. "Makes everybody testy." He put a hand to his throat scarf again. His gills had warned him: dry and chafing. If he'd asked Drakkar, the boy would probably have told him as well. November, and the Santa Anas came in earnest. Mules planted their hooves firmly to the ground and refused to go out in it. The eucalyptus trees were losing branches everywhere, their brittle drought-parched limbs giving way to the onslaught. The jarcaranda trees were the same and even the vast oleander shrubs were bent near to the ground. The ocean could barely be seen from the panorama of the Warden compound. A brown haze curtained it from view. Dust, Thomas thought. Good topsoil, blown to hell. They'd have weeks of this. It would let up for a few days and start all over again. "We'll never get a DWP appointed in this."

"Thomas, don't start looking for excuses," Lady said. She took him by the elbow to draw him inside the schoolroom.

"I'll go in when I'm damn well good and ready."

Her mouth quirked. "You're the one who's testy."

"Have a right to be. Teal's been at me all night. He wants me for DWP and he's not about to take no for an answer."

"He'll just have to," Lady said firmly. "I have in mind Gray Walton or Irlene."

The tall, elegant governor came to mind. "I thought you didn't like her," he said vaguely.

"Her? Whatever gave you that idea?" Lady drew him along. "Of course, I remember telling her that if she looked at you in that suggestive way of hers one more time, I'd scratch her eyes out."

"Oh?"

"Quit grinning, Thomas. They're waiting for us."

Actually, less than a third of those concerned had seated themselves inside the main lecture hall of the school, but it was obvious Lady was using diplomatic tactics that seemed obscure to Thomas as she managed seating arrangements. He perched, rather than sat, on the edge of the lecturer's desk, and thought of Gillander and how many times he'd been called in for troublemaking or malingering in this room. Those student days were less than a dozen years ago, but he felt as if it had been a lifetime.

He did not feel comfortable making a report on the College Vaults expedition, but he hadn't much choice. He thought of the charts he'd brought back as well as Charlie's papers. He'd kept the charts from Lady for reasons he could not define except that they bore both a truth and a lie and he wanted to keep them to himself until he could discern which was which. And the beast haunted him. Was it an ancestor of the same one which had marked him instead of slaying him? And if so, why? For what purpose had it been created? What had the nesters made of it?

It was hot in the classroom. He took a slow look over his shoulder. Lady Nolan was preoccupied. He took the chance to make good his escape and stood in the windy breezeway. Drakkar bumped into him.

"Have you seen Shankar?"

"No, not today." Blade looked the Mojavan up and down. "Good god. What have you been into? You look and smell like you've been rolling in pigeon shit. You didn't make dinner muster last night."

"No," Drakkar said. "I didn't. And yes, this is pigeon shit."

"I think," Thomas added, "you'd better hit the bathhouse and then come back as soon as you can. If they ask, I'll need you to corroborate the expedition."

"Shankar—"

"Can wait."

There was a burning look in Drakkar's eyes. Abruptly, it went out. The boy's jaw squared off before he answered, "Very well." He turned abruptly and left. Thomas watched him speculatively. Where had the boy been and into what?

As he turned back to the classroom, Lady threw him a disapproving look through the open doorway. He smiled in return. The wind gusted up again, filling his teeth with grit. Lady ducked her face away in amusement as if knowing what had happened.

Drakkar had returned before the lecture hall filled. On his heels came Art Bartholomew and Boyd, with Two-handed Delgado on Boyd's heels, guarding him. They exchanged glances, the driver's one of apology. His passage by was swift, but not before Blade had counted no less than four strategically placed weapons about the man's body.

He wondered what Art Bartholomew feared in this crowd.

Drakkar smelled damp. He cleared his throat for Thomas' attention. "Where's Alma?" he asked when he saw he had it.

"Bed. She's not feeling well."

"Her ankle?"

"No, not really." Thomas gave Drakkar his full attention. "Why?"

"Just, ah, wondering. What is it?"

"I'm not sure," Blade answered. "We think it might be breakout fever. Alma's always been a touch fey, though not really powered to any extent. But we could have awakened something with what we went through. You do have breakout fever among your—ah—" He stumbled on the word 'kind' and Drakkar supplied, "sensitives."

The Mojavan continued, "Yes. It's quite common. It can be deadly."

"Stanhope's sitting with her."

Drakkar's plumage rustled. "Good," he said, and looked away as if unconcerned.

Thomas let the remark go by. He could not fault Alma for Drakkar's interest. Since coming home, the girl had been a virtual recluse. No, she had not led Denethan's boy about.

The room stilled suddenly. Thomas took the time to reenter and sit by Lady. Shankar oozed into the room, grabbed a shadowy corner and stayed there. Thomas saw Drakkar's cross look. He wondered what kind of bad blood was between the two Mojavans. What had Drakkar been up to last night?

Lady nudged him for attention as Quinones came to the podium. The man looked visibly nervous. He smoothed a wing of hair back with a palm that was undoubtedly damp. He blinked several times and looked about.

"Ladies and gentlemen. It has only been a few months since the ceremonies. Most of our repairs necessitated by the raid have been effected. We've called you because of matters that require your immediate attention. Sir Thomas Blade has asked to speak to you."

Thomas took a breath, got to his feet, and moved forward.

Alma woke with a jerk and a shudder, gasping for breath. It took a moment to recognize her own little room. It took another moment to realize her limbs were free, her voice audible, her nightmare behind her. She gave another convulsive shudder.

Stanhope's hand covered her forehead. "Fever?" the young Healer asked.

"No. Dreams. What are you doing here?"

He smiled. "Lady asked me to sit with you."

Alma felt guilt and shame that she should be diverting Stanhope from his tasks. "Go on," she said quietly. "I'm all right." She plucked at a loose thread on her quilt.

The Healer sat down on the three-legged stool pulled close to her elbow. He shook his head. She saw furrow lines across his dusky forehead. "I don't think so," he answered. "Nausea, dizziness, bad dreams. What Sir Thomas put you through could start breakout fever. Or you might just have picked up a bug. Many a trade caravan has been sidelined by outbreaks of dysentery."

Alma laughed in spite of herself. "Stanhope! I'm fine. I just . . . feel a hundred years old."

"Stress and depression. Stefan's leaving. . . ."

"Maybe." She closed her eyes, not wanting to see her reflection in the Healer's eyes.

The stool scraped the floor. "Or maybe," said Stanhope eagerly. "You could even be pregnant. That would bring Stefan back." Before she could stop him, he leaned over her, laying his palms on the coverlet over her stomach. His eyes half-closed in concentration.

"Oh, Stanhope. I haven't been with Stefan for months. He . . . he couldn't—" Her voice ground to a halt. She could feel the tension in Stanhope's hands. His warmth felt like two coals burning into her. His eyes snapped open. He looked at her.

"Then who?" he said. "Who is the father of your child?"

She did not remember screaming, but her throat ached raw and the doorway of the tiny barracks room filled with children, all curious, all looking in. Stanhope shooed them away and kicked the door shut after long moments while she practiced the basics of breathing again. In, out, in, out.

Stanhope approached her cautiously. Alma wrenched herself upward in her bed, bracing her back against the wall.

"You don't know," she said wildly. "You can't possibly tell that way."

"Some of us can. There are tests, if you're far enough along. I think you are. Seven, possibly eight weeks. *You* should be able to tell *me*."

Her flesh had been so bruised, so torn. Her system, always irregular, and the trauma. . . . She hadn't thought anything at first. She grabbed for Stanhope's hand. "You can't tell anyone. You can't."

"But, Alma—"

"Promise me."

His dark eyes mirrored his reluctance. "All right," Stanhope answered. "But this should be good news."

"I have to find a way to tell the father, first. Then, we'll let the news out." Alma's thoughts raced ahead of her words. Rape. A child of rape. Bile burned at the back of her throat. "Let me take care of this," she got out.

Stanhope's worry softened. "All right. But you go to Lady as soon as you can. You're going to need to change your eating and sleeping regimen. We want a healthy baby!" He got up and moved to the door. "I'll let you sleep."

She felt numb. Like a stone. Like someone had planted a stone inside of her. "All right," she repeated. "I'll take care of it."

He left her alone in the room.

But she wasn't alone in it. Her nightmare filled her waking mind as her rapist pounded himself into her flesh again. She shuddered again and began to cry.

Thomas left the schoolrooms, in a press of flesh congratulating him for Gray Walton's appointment and his delegacy. He fought off the momentary claustrophobia he always had in like situations—so many weapons, so many opportunities for them to strike—and smiled when Lady showed her teeth to him, prompting.

It had only taken two days to accomplish the impossible.

Gray's admitted fairness had helped immensely. He was a compromise candidate that all factions finally agreed upon. Bartholomew was not greatly pleased, but had acquiesced. And Gray, undoubtedly briefed by Lady before the proceedings had begun, had promptly tabbed Blade to go out and try diplomacy with the growing nester nation before all-out warfare became inevitable.

Judge Teal drew most of the crowd away from them by demanding the bar in the manor house be opened, and a hospitable round for all be poured. The judge gave him a last look, keen eyes measuring him as if to tell him that it wasn't over yet. Teal was not a man for compromises with justice and welfare.

Blade watched the man walk away, his older body still elegant within the lines of his suit. "He's not done with me yet," he remarked to Lady.

"Nor am I." She looked around. "Have you seen Drakkar and Shankar? I didn't like the looks of Drakkar when he caught up with his father's ambassador."

"I didn't see them."

"They were first out the door. Bolted for it, I'd say."

Lady's instincts were nearly as good as his. "Then I'd say we'd better find them."

Drakkar caught Shankar at the edge of the barn. He'd stripped off his soft-cuffed gloves and the ambassador edged away, shrinking inside his clothes, as he reached for him and caught him by the shoulder.

"Shankar," Drakkar said.

"Young chieftain," Shankar returned. He blinked at the bared wrist, so close to his neckline. "I have many duties awaiting me, Drakkar, not the least of which is notifying your father of this afternoon's events."

"My father will wait," Drakkar said. With his free hand, he patted down Shankar's body. He found a wicked-looking shiv, dropped it in the dust and kicked it aside. Inside the stable, a horse whickered shrilly. Drakkar continued his search, dipped his hand inside a pocket, and came up with tiny rolls of paper.

"Pigeon scrolls," he said.

"All blank, my lord," Shankar breathed.

"But the ones I have are not." Drakkar let the blank scrolls rain into the dirt. He pulled a missive from his front pocket. He

began to read: "Settlement satisfactory. Confirm your agreement to our terms. Instructions for your deployment to follow."
He returned the scroll to his pocket. "I went through a lot of pigeon shit to find this. Tell me, Shankar. Why would my father
send such a message? Are you or are you not already his as-
signee? Or is it possible that your allegiance has just been
sold?"

Shankar trembled wildly within his clothes. His first pair of
eyelids dropped down. "I know nothing of what you read." He
threw an arm up over his head as Drakkar shook him violently.

"No? Just as you knew nothing about Micah's sudden illness, leaving this post vacant so you could conveniently claim
it? Our Mojavan rebels have had a wealth of information from
the Seven Counties, Shankar. Who sends it to them? Who finds
it necessary to operate a pigeon cote secreted far from the Warden compound? Think before you answer, reptile. I have witnesses who have already testified as to your actions."

With a sinuous movement, Shankar slipped himself of his
jacket. Drakkar found himself holding an empty garment as the
ambassador went to all fours.

"You are a boy," the ambassador snarled. "You understand
nothing of the real world! Your father is about to be overwhelmed and he does not even see the tide that is coming." He
scrabbled about in the dust.

"Go for your knife," Drakkar spat out. "Let me see what
you're really made of." His feather crest rose in rage.

Chapter 24

"My god, Thomas," Lady breathed. "Drakkar's fighting bare-handed against Shankar!"

Blade was already slowing to a walk. He'd seen the wicked spurs free of their gloved confines. "I'd say he has the advantage," he replied, even as Shankar's shiv caught the sunlight as the ambassador lunged at his princeling.

Blade admired Drakkar's quick, space-efficient move out of the way, without a strike. The boy's mouth moved. He knew, hearing them, that the words were calculated to enflame Shankar further, so the wily ambassador would lose all rational thought and coordination. He put a hand out to catch Lady's wrist. "He's baiting him," he said. "He wants the ambassador alive."

She slowed reluctantly to his pace. "But," she answered, "does Shankar know that?"

Blade looked about. "I don't want any witnesses. We got enough shit over Drakkar while trying to get Gray nominated. If the Mojavans cause any more trouble or can't present a united front, we're going to lose all our backing for the alliance."

Lady dropped back a step. She said, "Keep them in the shadows. I'll ward the stables as best I can. Mind those spurs! Accidents happen."

He left her behind as he approached the fighters.

On dusty trails in the inner counties, he'd often seen road-runners baiting rattlesnakes. The encounter he watched now reminded him of those encounters, though this time it was the bird with the venom to be watched. But Shankar was a lizard man, with most of the dominant reptilian traits so reprehensible to the Countians. His movements were oddly jointed, incredibly fluid, and his speech had sunk into a low hissing of anger as he danced about Drakkar. The two wove a spectacle even as he felt Lady drop a cloak of seeming about it.

She joined him. "Put an arm around me," she said.

He did so, felt her body trembling from the effort of illusion. "What are they seeing?" he asked, his attention on the two fighters.

"Why us, of course. Kissing in the shadows."

He would have chuckled, but just then Shankar made a deadly strike. He caught Drakkar smiling, mocking him, even as the shiv hit home, skated off a rib, and ripped cloth.

"Damn!" Drakkar whirled away. His face went dead white, his eyes large in his face.

"Come closer," Shankar hissed. "Let me strike again."

Drakkar took his hand away from his right flank. He showed his teeth in a smile that was reminiscent of Blade just before a fight. "You'd be dead, old man, but I want you alive. Traitors are best served warm."

"Traitor? Your father doesn't know the meaning of the word. He knows nothing of friends or enemies."

Drakkar made a swift move, snagging Shankar by the collar of his shirt. "He'll know *you*."

There was a slight rip of cloth. Then Shankar twisted about, shiv stabbing upward. He impaled Drakkar's wrist on the blade.

Drakkar made no noise. It was Lady who screamed, and cut her panic short with her hands as the two men suddenly entwined about one another, tumbling down in the dust. Drakkar jerked his wrist free of the shiv. The spur stayed direct and menacing. Blood streamed down his open cuff.

Lady swayed. "Thomas," she said lowly. "Stop them. I can't . . . hide this much longer. . . ."

He took his arm from her as both men grunted, their bodies flailing, legs entangled. Drakkar had the shiv at his throat, his jaw clenched as he forced Shankar's hand away. Lady's legs folded up and she collapsed into a gentle sit-down at Blade's feet.

The wind gusted. Dust rose, obscuring faces, as bodies rolled. He hesitated, unsure of whom he reached for, his wrist knife coming smoothly into his own palm.

A boot toe kicked him sharply in the ankle as he stepped in.

The pain rocked him a second and he lost sight of whose face was on top as the fighters rolled again. Then he saw Drakkar, left wrist crimson, fighting Shankar to the ground, hand clenched about the other's forearm, the shiv paralyzed between them.

The point was at Drakkar's eye, but Shankar could not force it home. Drakkar's face showed the strain, but a savage joy lit his features. Shankar's arm shook. The ambassador kicked up, planting a knee solidly in Drakkar's solar plexus.

The tactic worked. Drakkar deflated and recoiled abruptly, but his hand remained clenched about Shankar's as the point of the shiv dropped. It stabbed brutally at his shoulder, ripping through cloth and flesh.

Drakkar had him a second time, both at counterpoint to one another, shiv frozen, its tip dripping blood between them. They held one another off, sinews tight, faces intent.

Drakkar suddenly smiled. "My tailor," he said, "is going to hate you." He struck, cracking Shankar's arm across his kneecap, and the knife went flying.

Shankar's eyes widened, then narrowed. Drakkar caught him up and drew him with him as he knelt in the dust. Shankar kicked and twisted, but could not free himself from the hold. Drakkar looked up and saw Blade for the first time.

"Politics," he said.

"At the very least. What happened?"

"Our dear Shankar has been running his own messenger system for some time, perhaps since he first arrived. He has two masters, maybe more. Father would like to know who."

Blade resheathed his knife. "I wouldn't mind knowing either," he said.

Shankar showed his too sharp teeth as he gulped for breath. "I'll tell you nothing."

"That," Blade said, approaching him, "is where you're mistaken."

Shankar reached for Drakkar's wrist. With an abrupt movement, he drew the poisonous spur across his throat.

Drakkar dropped the Mojavan as though he'd been struck. He got to his feet. "Damn."

The ambassador began to convulse in the dust. Lady struggled to her feet. "Where does he keep the antidote?"

"In his quarters." Drakkar turned after her. "Wait, Lady Nolan. There's not enough time."

Shankar began to strangle, his lips going blue, his eyes bulging. They watched as the ambassador died a horrible death. Drakkar, hands shaking, pulled his gloves from his belt and tugged them on, despite the gaping wound in his left wrist where he'd been impaled.

Lady reeled and Thomas caught her up, steadying her. "Illusion gone," she said weakly.

"Son of a bitch," Drakkar said. "I wanted that information." He looked at Thomas. "What are we going to tell the others?"

"I'd say," Blade answered, looking him up and down, "you look battered enough for me to say you defended yourself against an assassination attempt. You'd better get that rib scoring and wrist looked at. The shoulder's negligible, but you're right. Your tailor is going to hate you."

They were suddenly surrounded by a crowd, voices rising in excitement and curiosity at Shankar's twisted corpse in the dust. Thomas moved Lady back as Drakkar's guard bulled their way through. He was not too familiar with the guard as they'd kept to themselves, but now the headman went to one knee in front of Drakkar. Blade made a point of memorizing the triangular, too sharp face, the mottled tan, and sienna patterning of the skin, human and yet inhuman. *Tando*, he thought. *That's the one called Tando*.

"My lord. Are you all right?"

"I will be."

"What happened here?" Bartholomew's voice rose over the general clamor.

Drakkar turned, found the warty man's face in the crowd, and said coolly, "I was attacked. I defended myself."

Tando got to his feet and signaled the other three to pick up Shankar's body. The nails of the hands and his lips had gone blue-black. Two-handed Delgado said, "Ain't never seen a knife wound do that before."

Drakkar's crest had settled around his shoulders and the boy's face remained deathly pale, but he looked steadily at the drover. "Then I suggest," he said, "you don't pull a knife on me." He tried to push his way past, following his guard.

"Witnesses," demanded Bartholomew.

Thomas squeezed Lady's shoulders and guided her tired

steps with his. "That's a matter for the DWP," he answered, "but we saw everything." As they stepped through, the crowd began to disperse. "The boy needs a Healer. Let him go. You'll have the story tomorrow."

Lady's strength returned step by step. He said little, walking with her. He'd seen more than he wanted to, actually. Knew more than he wanted to.

Including the fact that Drakkar always kept a bottle of antidote on him, in case of accidents. Now was not the time, but there would come a reckoning when he would ask Drakkar why he'd not used it on Shankar.

Drakkar had almost made it to the barracks on his own when he went down, writhing in the dust. Tando dropped his share of the ambassador's corpse and dove to catch his prince. He looked up.

"Poison," he said. "The devil's blade was poisoned as well. His own works against it, but—"

The barracks door flew open. Alma and Stanhope stood in the dimly illuminated doorway. Lady grabbed Tando's shoulder. "Get him inside," she ordered. "As quickly as you can."

Her stomach miseries seemed insignificant in comparison to the sounds she heard emanating from the room designated for Drakkar over the next few days. And, though hers stemmed from a kind of fight for life, his were genuinely a hard fought battle. Lady and Stanhope rarely left his side and she could lie awake at night and listen to him moan between bouts of retching as they tried to purge his system.

She lay in bed one gray morning, listening to the wind die down. The sudden calm following the days of blasting punishment from the Santa Anas brought a cold clarity to her thoughts. It was strange, she thought, that Drakkar's valiant battle for life gave her no inspiration to fight for hers. She rose from her cot and went downstairs, then into the drying shed for the herbs grown in the manor gardens. No one took heed of her. She had no real occupation in the compound, but they were used to her helping out with the wards and with the Healers and not an eyebrow was raised, even when she dipped into the toxic supplies.

She drew a bucket of fresh water from the pump, went inside, and heated a teakettle on the always warm stove. As the

water heated, she prepared a teapot with the herbs she'd chosen. Chamomile, for its soothing qualities. Orange zest and
clove for their pleasing flavors. Honey, for sweetness. Oleander, just a touch, for its deadliness. She would be ill, very ill
from that. And then she added a pinch of herbs said to cause
abortions in newly conceived mothers, guaranteed to slough off
unwanted babies during plague years. When the water boiled,
she poured it over the mixture to steep and fixed a tray to carry
it upstairs.

She carried her tray upstairs to the privacy of her small room
and set it down on the writing table by the window. She shut her
door. With the wind down and Drakkar sleeping at last, it was
quiet, very quiet. The teapot steeped, steamed, and then cooled.

It was very, very cold when finally she stirred enough to
touch a fingertip into the brew to test it.

She shrank back from the tray. Alma rose and walked to the
window, where dawn was in earnest and the compound had
bustled to life. She looked across. Rape was not unknown, particularly in areas where nesters raided. It was a crime which had
never died out. She knew her disgrace would be accepted, if
painfully. If she could bear it, the shame would be bearable.

But she could not. Not Stefan's child. Not a lover's. But
seed of a being she found so vile the thought of him made her
wish she'd more than just hit him. Made her wish she'd
pounded his face into a featureless blob, skull in splinters, brain
and blood seeping out. . . .

Alma spread her hands open and looked at them, as if she
might see his blood on them.

She would have to be strong. She would have to treat this
like a plague baby, an abomination so wrong it would be cruel
to bring it to term, no matter how prized children were. She
only wished she could have asked Lady for the forbidden
recipe.

She might have used too much oleander. The flowering
shrub was incredibly lethal. If something went wrong. . . .

Alma turned from the window. She found her writing paper
and pen and ink and sat down to write. If all went well, she
would destroy the letter. If not, then Lady would read and understand.

She put away her pen and ink and poured a cup of tea. She
saluted the morning with the drink and put it to her lips.

*   *   *

Morning sun woke Drakkar. Its heat drifted across his face and he fought to get his gummy lids open. His ears popped slightly and he realized the pressure front which had been bringing in the hot, merciless winds had changed. Like a sea gone suddenly calm, it was quiet outside.

And though the back of his throat burned as if it was on fire, the convulsions and retchings had fled, leaving him feeling weak as a newborn. Drakkar turned his head on his pillow. He did not recognize the room. He must be in the orphan barracks. Lady Nolan sat in a rocker, Sir Thomas' battered leather jacket draped over her chest, her mouth slack and her breathing gone deep in a way that was almost a snore, but not quite. *Clever woman,* he thought. *You saved me.*

Thirsty as he was, he didn't feel like waking her. He stretched out a hand that wove and dove its shaky way to a goblet of water sitting on the bedstand.

A crash of china made him jerk. There was a second crash. Drakkar swung his feet out of bed. Lady Nolan heard nothing, sleeping the sleep of the innocent and the exhausted. He pulled himself to his feet and lurched to the door. He could hear a dull thud. He looked down, half-expectant that it was his own uncooperative body bitting the planking. His vision wavered.

A feather touch. A consciousness like that of perfume brushed past him. He knew it instinctively and reached out to catch Alma, but there was nothing tangible of her in the hallway.

Drakkar stumbled to the next doorway and managed to get the door open.

Her body lay slumped on the floor amidst shards of stoneware. He reached for her, his own weakness upsetting a writing table between them. A feather-light piece of paper drifted to the floor. It was that his uncoordinated hand grasped instead of Alma's limp arm. His gaze ran over it, unseeing.

Then Drakkar's attention flew back to the words. He had no time! Leaving her there, he shambled back to his room and woke up Lady Nolan by yanking her to her feet.

"My god." She dropped Thomas' jacket at Alma's feet as she knelt by her. "Let me sniff what's left of the teapot."

Drakkar handed it to her and then managed to get Alma up

in his arms and lift her formless body to the cot. Lady Nolan sniffed the small amount of tea still in the pot, a mass of leaves and herbs sodden at the bottom. Her tongue flickered out and tasted it fleetingly.

Lady Nolan dropped the pot, unheeding as it smashed at her feet. She looked at Drakkar. "She's pregnant. She tried to abort it. She's dying, Drakkar, *and I can't help her.*"

His own senses reeled. He croaked, "Something. You must be able to do something."

The Protectoress shook her head in denial. "No. If the infusion was weak enough, perhaps . . . but Alma's got to want to come back, and I don't think she does."

He looked at the still, childlike form on the bed. Not voluptuous like most of his conquests had been. Not overtly feminine or seductive. But even in deathlike coma, her eyes dominated her face, huge and beautiful, shuttered for death. He took up her cold hand in his.

"Pregnant," he said. "Whose?"

"She was raped," Lady said, her voice vague and troubled. "Raped while you were trapped in the Vaults. The dean hunted her down and trapped her as well. It can only be his, she says." The woman looked at him with her disturbing blue and brown gaze. "Is it?"

He scarcely had blood enough left to blush, but he met her look. "I have never touched her."

"Perhaps if you had, we wouldn't be in this dilemma." Lady ran a hand through disheveled hair. She took a step forward. Something tumbled out of the brown jacket at her feet and rattled across the planking. He saw what seemed to be ivoried bones as she stooped to pick the item up. She clenched her hand about it. "I'm going after her;" the woman said abruptly and swung about to Alma's form.

"What?"

Lady looked over her shoulder. She was already loosening Alma's clothes at the throat and wrists. "I'm going after her. She's got to be saved and the baby, too. It will be similar to a healer's trance—have you ever seen one?"

"Once, but—"

"I haven't any time! If I'm not awake in minutes . . . five or ten . . . go find Blade. He's at the bathhouse, sleeping, probably. The wind's been bothering his gills. Tell him I've taken the Ghost Road after Alma. Got that?"

"Yes, but—" Before his bewildered eyes, the woman pulled up a chair, grasped the bones tightly in both hands and fled her conscious form. He could have sworn he'd felt her go, striding by like righteousness itself, in pursuit of life.

Drakkar righted the small table and sat on it before he lost all balance. He'd never seen a healing trance that didn't take a great deal of meditation and preparation first. Lady was exhausted after dealing with him. She should never have worked with Alma without another Healer. He sat silently, acutely aware he could be losing both of them.

It wasn't until he'd ticked off nearly ten minutes that he noticed Lady had not been breathing.

He bolted for the door and took the staircase in leaps, scattering children by threes and fours, his body finding strength in fear. He was yelling before he reached the bathhouse.

Thomas stood over Lady. Drakkar had never seen the man afraid, even when the College Vaults had closed in lethally about them. He saw it now and wondered.

Thomas turned around. His face had gone white underneath its weathered tan. His mustache worked a moment, then he got the words out. "How long ago?"

"Fifteen minutes, at the most."

"The Ghost Road, she told you."

Drakkar nodded. He sank back onto the writing table, unable to bear his own weight any longer. He watched as Blade took up Lady's hand and wrenched the bones from her grip. The man waited a moment as if that alone might pull her from her comalike trance. Nothing happened.

Then Blade sank to his heels in front of Lady as if he might pray for her. Instead, he said, "Damn you. You know I can't do this. *I told you I couldn't do this any more.*"

"Do what?"

The man ignored Drakkar. He took the bones tightly in his hand. He said, "Believe nothing you see. Don't let them take our bodies until you know for sure our flesh is corrupting. Understand?"

"Shit, man, what are you going to do?"

"I'm going after them. And I can't tell you how I'm going to do it or where I'm going to find them. And I can't tell you if I'm going to come back or not. But, by god, I'll do the best I can." Thomas ducked his head and let out one, last hoarse word. "*Lady.*"

Oath or benediction?

Chapter 25

"What are you looking so hanged about?" Stefan bit off, as he pulled his horse about and watched the company mill into their designated rest area.

Watty twisted in his saddle. He worked his face around, but it was too late; his thoughts had already seeped into his expression and his expression had done the damage. As the others filed past them, he mumbled, "Nothing."

Stefan joined him in watching the others. The horses showed their ribs, even the mules looked scruffy and the little, tough donkeys were pulling at their leads, over-ready for a rest. The supplies pack had diminished astonishingly, supplies meant only to supplement what they could not get off the land.

Stefan took off his hat. There was a wide, white slash across his forehead where the skin hadn't tanned. Two deep creases in the folds of his eyes looked permanent. The last two months had aged him into an adult, trail-hardened and weary.

"We're not failures, Watty. Get that through your head, all right? We're not going home because we *failed*."

Watty tried to stand in the stirrups to ease his back and aching thighs, but his legs melted like butter at the attempt and he flopped back down in the saddle seat. His horse grunted in protest. He didn't say anything, afraid of Stefan's temper.

Stefan said, "Look. We've gotten farther than anyone else. We weren't prepared to cross the abyss because no one knew it was there. Even if we had gotten a rope bridge across, what would we have done with the remounts? Or Trout and the others who are sick? Now we know what we're up against, next trip out. Or we go up the coast. Boyd comes down from Santa

Barbara. We know there's no passage above him, but maybe we can angle inland from there. Right?"

Watty felt each word as it was pounded into him. He looked up then, met Stefan's intense light blue gaze. "I dunno," he said. "I'm just a kid." He reined his horse sharply away and went to join the others before he fell out of the saddle.

Stefan jammed his hat back on. He sat on the ridge a minute, watching the mappers dismount. Six weeks out, two weeks back. Going out had been at a snail's pace as they mapped and noted the terrain. Coming back, they couldn't cross the ground fast enough. He took a deep breath. Despite the skills Sir Thomas had been teaching all of them for years, they hadn't been able to live off the land. And with Trout sick and three of the others nearly as ill, they were burdened as well as short-handed. He guessed they might make the counties in another week. Home was another matter. If the nesters let them through. If Trout didn't die and the others worsen.

Jeong joined him on the ridge. The lanky boy was on foot and sketching as he came. He looked up. "I think we've gone as far as we can go today."

He was too tired to feel any more anger. "This is just supposed to be a break."

"The mounts are exhausted. There's good grazing here—they need it." Jeong looked up. Stefan was surprised to see the sketch was of him looking over the camp on the ridge. In the quick, competent lines, he thought he saw a defender, a sentry on duty.

But it was only himself.

"How's Trout?"

"A little better. He has to be, otherwise we'll have to make a travois for him. He can't ride sitting up much longer."

The trouble with Healers was that they couldn't work on themselves except for basic herbal doctoring and Trout was barely hanging on. Stefan let out his breath in a long drawn out gust. "All right. Tell the boys to pitch camp for the night."

Jeong nodded, turned heel, and sauntered down off the ridge, taking his time, drawing as he walked. Stefan stayed where he was. Watty had been right, of course, in the privacy of his thoughts. The abyss had defeated them. An immense crevice running as far as they could see across the fall-burned foothills, it had brought them to a stunning halt. They had scouted it on horseback for several days and had not found a passable point, nor any sign of the crevice's end. Too wide to jump and too long to ride around. They could have bridged it hand over hand, but there was no wood to build a real bridge to bring the animals across. That, and the barren land, and Trout's illness had brought him to the decision to take them home. Next spring, god willing, they'd start out again. In the meantime, he'd have to pound their successes into them, give them heart, not let them give up. None of them would think of themselves as failures if he had anything to do with it.

He wondered if Alma would be waiting for him. He knew he had no right any longer to wonder, but he did just the same. The trip had taught him a bitter lesson. He hoped it wasn't too late.

His horse whickered as the other mounts were hobbled and put out to pasture. He could feel its hunger and fatigue. He squeezed his knees, bringing it down off the ridge, to join the others.

The screens in the conference room were dark. Nothing they could have shown would have been much more spectacular than the water planet the *Challenger* circled, dominating the windows. Dusty had gotten there earlier, and sat, hugging herself, unable to tear her eyes away from the sight. *Home.* Not a history or a myth to make the 250-year voyage more bearable, but her home. The cloud-shrouded view drew her complete and total attention. She could see changes in the coastlines and continents facing her, though they were subtle. But how subtle to those who'd once inhabited those geographical areas, to be seen from an orbit this far out?

Commander Dakin sat in a chair, his profile enigmatic. Fewer than ten people finally took places in the room. She knew without looking about who they'd be. Marshall, of course, denying the gray in his hair. Herself. The enviros Klegg and Palchek, both middle-aged but fit. The mechanic Reynolds who, without knowing it, reminded Dusty of an Amazon. Dusty didn't think sexist mythology like Amazons had gotten into the ship's library. She'd have told Reynolds herself but wasn't sure if the bronze-skinned, dark-haired woman would have thought it was funny. There was Kerry, who split her occupations between accounting and medical. Dubois, from communications and whose hobby was cartography, sat biting a nail, his dark hair in spikes, careful to sit with his back away from everyone so that the thinning spots could not be seen. The last two volunteers were both from agra, a botanist and a zoologist. From the unhappy looks on their young faces, Dakin had twisted arms to get Colby and Goldstone here.

A balanced team. Volunteers and the volunteered. None of them had been alive to explore the Alpha Centauri regions. None of their grandparents had been alive to remember Earth. She knew they cared, everybody aboard ship cared, but these had cared enough to make a trip without options.

Colby and Goldstone were talking, low-voiced, everyone else was silent, waiting for Dakin to speak. He held his silence a long moment before finally looking to them.

"I guess that's everyone." He swiveled his chair about. "Under the circumstances, a good turnout. The pressure front kicking up some high winds in the landing area has broken up and we can expect calm weather the next two to three days. We'll be going down in two. Marshall—"

Willem's dark face looked to the commander expectantly. "You're in charge of the Away Team."

Marshall nodded, satisfaction glimmering deep in his caramel brown eyes.

Sun looked at them all. "I want reports at 2200 hours, on a daily basis. Avoid confrontations, there aren't enough of you to put up a fight. What are you expecting down there?"

Goldstone said, "Cockroaches as big as horses."

Everyone laughed. Sun smiled patiently before adding gently, "We may find subhumans as well. The Earth has gone through a lot. We don't know what to expect. I wish I could tell you to give two yanks on the rope and I'll pull you right up, but—" he spread his slender hands. "We've exhausted our capacity to relaunch on the shuttles and I don't think we're going to get any help from the locals."

The ship's cat entered with a plaintive meow and leaped onto the table. He butted an insistent yellow head on Sun's hands. The commander gathered in the striped tabby and the animal sat, gently kneading Dakin's lap. Dusty watched, distracted for a moment, thinking of how much her sister Lisa had loved cats.

"What equipment are you going to let us take down?"

"Well, there's the hover. It's pretty old, but it's reliable and there's no worry about fuel as long as the solars get enough exposure. We've two ATVs as well, for smaller forays. The shuttle itself has the portable lab setups—and I want you all to wear enviro suits. Maintain a quarantine just as if you were returning. I think that's necessary."

Marshall said quietly, "Weapons?"

"Handguns, rifles, stuns. Anything more and you'd be facing a war and I think your best bet would be to get in the shuttle, fire it up, and 'drive' as far away as you can get."

Reynolds said, "That'll be hard on the ship, sir."

"Better the ship than you." Sun put the cat down and stood up. "We all owe you a debt. You're doing what our fear won't allow us to."

Dubois spat out part of a fingernail. He added, as if the event had been punctuation to his sentence, "What about later? What if we find out there's something worth reclaiming? Are you coming down then?"

Sun did not answer immediately. Then, "If the crew votes to."

Colby's and Goldstone's faces went pale. They were young newlyweds, each a shadow of the other, white faces, dark hair, slender bodies. Colby had warm hazel eyes and Goldstone's were dark brown, otherwise Dusty had always had trouble telling them apart. They held hands tightly. Dusty looked away. She had trouble dealing with the despair on their faces, as well.

The dean looked over the dry lake beds. The low-lying hills to the east and north were in purpled shadow. The beds wavered in mirage illusion. The quonset huts and buildings across the landing strips were hunkered down, rusting and degrading dinosaurs, skeletons that might have come to drink at the mirrored pools and died of the illusion. Satisfaction and hunger rode his gut together. He swung down from his horse. "We made it, Ketchum."

The tracker said nothing. There was a dour look on his begrimed face. The dean arched an eyebrow. "Still sulking over that mare?"

They had lost one of their horses during the last day. As soon as the wind had died down, they'd set off at dawn and just as the dean had threatened, he'd spared nothing getting them here on time. Ketchum's boots were stained with the blood from the knife he'd drawn across the painted mare's throat to put her thrashing agony to a quicker end. The nester looked at the dean.

"She was the first four eyes I have had," Ketchum said, "who was not blind in one of them."

"Bah." The dean unslung his waterskin. "God never intended for a horse to have four eyes." He tilted his head back as he lifted the waterskin. Ketchum stared at his wattle of a throat and thought of putting his knife to a better use. He looked away.

"When are they coming?"

The dean replaced his waterskin and opened his pack. He took out his robes of black and garish decoration, donning them quickly. Then he took out the box of magic he had carried with him.

Ketchum knew mechanicals when he saw them. This box had never particularly fooled him, though the shamans would make a great fuss over it. But he had brought it to the dean on more than one occasion. As nearly as he could tell, it never did anything but flash lights.

The dean stroked the casing. The flashes had slowed, becoming a longer, more intense pulse. He looked skyward. The readout said 1700 hours. "At dusk, Ketchum," the man said, sinking to his haunches. "They're coming in just before sundown."

Dusty clenched her teeth. She wrapped her wrist in her shoulder strap as the shuttle swept downward and she could feel the push of real gravity, as though the world had a skin and they were a needle trying to penetrate it. She closed her eyes, her stomach churning against the feeling.

The other crew made fun of her from time to time, that she was not a military brat, born into the service and into the mission. Now none of them were although they were conscripted at sixteen and served a facsimile of military training aboard the ships. But she was just as born to it as their forefathers had been—her grandfather had been a Navy pilot during the Vietnam War, her father had been one of the last aircraft carrier captains of the twenty-first century—and she and Lisa had drawn his attention early.

Their twinship had been rare even among identical twins. They'd spoken their own language and they had always been able to live in one another's skins, so to speak. So they were barely out of toddlerhood when their father and mother had volunteered them for service.

Unlike the other crewmembers, whose genetic engineering

had been ingrained into them, spliced in unknowingly from the earlier moment of creation, she could remember the hospitals and labs. They hadn't suffered much—she knew their mother would never have allowed it—but there had been some fear and deprivation and pain.

The outgrowth was the ability of the twins to be even more telepathic with one another and to voluntarily put themselves into a sort of suspended animation. They had known from their first year of school that their destiny was paired with that of the longships. Their fate was to be separated for the duration of the trip, only their minds reaching out. Lisa would sleep when Dusty slept, family and friends living and dying and turning to ashes while they communed and rested and communed again.

Only she'd lost Lisa. Now she had nothing. Her mind stayed forever devoid of another presence except her own fleeting thoughts. She was empty.

Her stomach gave up on a corkscrew maneuver that strained her body against its straps and as she fought to contain herself, a sense of displacement swept her. A darkness more complete than the absence of light created by merely shutting her eyes welled up inside her head. She heard a man's voice, clear as a bell: *Where the hell are you?*

It was a voice she'd never heard before. Her loneliness arced through her. She wanted to answer, but her thoughts scattered like clouds in a high wind and her mind spun away as if knowing the voice was not meant for her.

Dusty opened her eyes. Sweat dripped off her forehead. Her ears popped. Dubois grinned at her. "Sick?"

"No." They'd reached the lightness of atmosphere. The sun's glare was dazzling off the form-fitting silver material of her enviro suit. She closed her eyes again. Wishful thinking. There was nothing down below with a voice for her to hear.

And she was airsick, dammit. She clenched her teeth tighter as the shuttle spun downward.

Reynolds' alto voice. "What are you doing, sir?"

"Conserving as much fuel as I can. This isn't going to be a one-way trip if I can help it." Marshall's thick, rich tones, filled with quiet determination.

Dusty smiled in spite of herself.

*　　*　　*

Thunder boomed. Ketchum moved away from the small campfire he'd been nursing. He looked up. "No clouds," he said. "No rain."

But the dean was grabbing for his binoculars. "Fool," he said, unthinkingly. "That's not thunder. That's a sonic boom. She's coming!"

Ketchum squinted. He could see nothing angling in over the hills, but the dean was striding across the parched earth, hand up, pointing, his voice rising louder.

"She's coming in! There she is! Look at her!"

A low rumbling could be heard and then even Ketchum could see the white form in the sky, like a bird on the glide. It came lower and lower and then, as the rumbling could be felt in his bones as much as in his ears, the thing touched down.

The dean let out a whoop. Streamers of dust burst from the earth like flame and the object roared down on them, bigger, ever bigger.

Ketchum got to his feet and wiped his damp palms on his trousers. The dean had finally done something that impressed him and it was roaring down on them like a vengeful god from the past.

The dean paced back. "Slow 'er down," he cried. "Slow 'er down!"

The chant seemed to help as the great winged object began to slow. Still it came head on, and Ketchum swore he could feel the sun's heat off its body, dancing in shimmering waves.

Then the object slowed rapidly, and when it came to a halt it was a good six or seven hundred yards away.

The dean dropped his binoculars to his chest. He turned slowly on one heel. He gave Ketchum a thoughtful look.

"In the next few hours," the big man said, "you will see and hear a great many things you will not understand. It's best if you simply keep your peace."

Ketchum nodded, wordlessly. He felt as if his voice had been ripped from his chest. Perhaps the Shastra had been right to bring the dean into their lives after all.

The object's flank opened up like a smaller wing rising. There was a flash of metal. People began to descend, people dressed in brilliant colors of silver and bronze and pewter. Their heads were engulfed. Ketchum felt his knees and bladder turn to water in his fear. They came out of the belly of the object and faced them.

The dean began to walk toward them. Ketchum felt another strange emotion for the dean who was not afraid. He trailed in the man's wake.

They approached until they were close enough to see faces within those helmets. Women's faces, men's, bare of beard like the Countians, young and old—they stared at the two of them. They carried mechanicals, some of them did, with hoses and flashing lights, casting them about in the air. The woman to the front—young woman—tore her helmet off, thick red hair bouncing to her shoulders.

"Welcome," the dean said. "Welcome home."

Chapter 26

"Dammit," Kerry got out in her lightly accented voice (still Southern, after all these years, passed on by her family as diligently as any ship's skill). "Git yoah helmet back *on!*"

Dusty answered, "This air's better than what I was born into! Hold your water, Kerry."

Palchek muttered, his voice thinned by the helmet comm, "Lots of molds, though. That wind packs quite a kick."

Remembering, she said, "Santa Anas used to drive everyone crazy. Anyone with bad sinuses could expect migraines."

Klegg remarked, "Let's hope that's all these molds can do," seconding Palchek's worry. He swung his computer pack about, picking up readings.

All the bickering came to a stop as the two lone figures came near and the tall one, in a black caftan wildly decorated in a style reminiscent of Africa, threw open his arms crying welcome. Dusty heard Marshall say, "Get a look at him."

"Him, hell," said Goldstone. "What's that standing next to him? Retro-human?"

And tall, muscular Reynolds took a step closer, muttering, "I wouldn't want to meet either of them in a dark corridor."

Marshall came to Dusty's elbow. He hesitated, then took off his enviro helmet, too. "Commander Willem Marshall, of the U.S.S. *Challenger*."

The berobed man bowed. "Gerald Conklin, dean emeritus, the College Vaults, Claremont, California." He looked up, intently, and Dusty was struck by the intensity of his dark eyes, despite their hooded lids. "I've waited my whole life for you to return."

* * *

The man's tent was scarcely more hospitable than the outdoors. All of them could fit if they crouched elbow to elbow, but Reynolds and Dubois elected to rest outside, an informal guard, giving up some room. They did so, keeping an eye on the dean's scruffy companion, as he did on them.

The dean passed out water as if it were fine wine. He did not seem to care that his guests were cautious about drinking it. He said, "Go ahead, test it, please. I pride myself on the quality of my water. Southern California no longer blooms like the rose in the desert as it once did, but there is water if one knows where to find it. We have much heavier rains than we used to, but the runoff is tremendous. And as for the air quality," the man gave a bleak smile. "I think we're finally getting rid of the smog."

Marshall took a stiff drink. His cocoa hands showed pink around the knuckles as he gripped the glass. "I thank you for your hospitality. This . . . isn't exactly what we were expecting."

"If you scoped out the planet coming in, I imagine you expected the worst. And it is bad, I won't spare you that. But we survive, in pockets here and there." The dean leaned forward conspiratorially. "That's why I'm here. That's why the Vaults were created, sunk in a mountain's roots. We were intended to maintain a civilization no matter what happened."

The dean had not brought an entourage of civilization with him. Dusty cradled her water uneasily. Perhaps it was his hawk's eyes, always looking through her as well as at her, as though his primary vision was some sort of . . . prey . . . miles off.

Marshall set down his goblet. "It was you who set off the recall beacon, wasn't it?"

"Oh, yes. Once your signal activated it." The dean pushed forward the compact and battered box, flashing lights gone, replaced by a steady green line. The box was silent now.

"How is it that you knew what to do?"

The dean spread his hands. "Given the vast civilization around us?" He chuckled dryly. "Please let me explain, Commander. You see, the longship mission predates me—"

Dusty shifted on her hips. The ground was hard. She looked about the tent restlessly. Goldstone caught her eyes. There was amusement in the harsh lines about his mouth, hidden amusement at what the dean was saying.

The dean swung about suddenly, his attention gone from

Marshall, nailing Goldstone with those predatory eyes. "Am I boring you, sir?"

The zoologist rocked back on his heels, embarrassment lighting up his craggy features. "Well, no, ah, not at all."

"Good. Because the technology that endowed the Vaults was about four decades more advanced than that of the longships, and we were making very rapid strides in that time period. I was barely old enough to be aware of the ships' launching—four of them, weren't there?"—he did not bother to look to Marshall for confirmation—"and I spent my life's work in education readying for the position which I held up until a few years ago when the Vaults were destroyed. You were born on ship. I was born here."

Dusty stirred. "So was I."

The dean's keen look flickered over her. "One of the first crew?"

"The only one on board this ship. My sister and I were experimenters in long-range telepathy and self-induced suspension."

"Ah." The man said nothing for a long moment. Then, "We have much in common, except perhaps that you are the original flesh, and I am flesh of flesh, so to speak."

"Come on," challenged Dubois. "You'd have to be—what, nearly three hundred years old."

"This incarnation is about fifty-three years old, but I *am* the Dean of the College Vaults. Surely cloning was not unknown when the ships launched."

Kerry and Goldstone both flushed, and the medic said, "Cloning was perfected in the early part of that century, but ethically it was shunned."

"It was deemed necessary for the continuation of our purpose. My great-grandfather was extremely fond of sourdough bread. Are you familiar with it? A dough is made. It leavens, a loaf is broken away from it to be baked, more ingredients are added to the remainder, it leavens once again—never entirely consumed, a sourdough starter can last for decades. The first dean was a "starter," if you will. I am flesh of his flesh, imprinted with all his memories as well as the complete life memories of each incarnation after that. I have forgotten nothing."

The fetishes and loose decorations on the dean's dark robes

rattled with the intensity of his speech and emotion. Dusty found she could not bear to look at him.

Marshall said softly, "What happened to the Vaults?"

"I lived underground for over two hundred years," said the dean. His intense gaze swung back to the team commander. "It was difficult, knowing the struggle those above engaged in, but we had been given our mandate and we were determined to fill it."

"There was more than one of you?"

"There was an entire city. All but myself perished when the fascist members of a survivor community cracked us open like an eggshell, determined to suck out all we had fought to preserve." The dean's voice went bitter.

"Like him?" Klegg said, jerking his head toward the tent's exterior.

"Him? Oh, Ketchum. No, Ketchum is an independent man, a member of a clan nation commonly called nesters. They've been outcast because of their refusal to kowtow to the dictatorial authority of the others. But all . . . all suffer genetic aberrations that render some scarcely more human than a brown lizard. Extensive genetic engineering had been done for the space program, in hopes of making colonization more effective on Mars and in other longship launches. Some of those aberrations made it possible for survival even after the Disasters hit. Now . . . they mutate at an incredible rate. There is a virus that attacks the transposable genes in the DNA structure. They never know what can occur. The plague surfaces about every decade or so. If humanity has survived, it's paid an incredible price to do so." The dean stirred, as if aware of the sorrow his words had laid over the group. "It's gotten quite dark. I propose that we have a hearty dinner, then retire. I'll have Ketchum strike another canopy. I'm anxious to hear your stories and to know the whereabouts of the other longships, and what your plans are. You've brought vehicles with you. I'm sure, that are far quicker than horseback. To prove my veracity, I would like to take you on a tour of what is left of my College Vaults and to look over the L.A. basin in general. There's a lot of work to be done once we clean out the scourge of the Seven Counties. I bear the blame for much of the destruction, you know. When they first came to me, it was my decision to open up the Vaults. I thought perhaps the last two hundred years had purged away

certain . . . tendencies. They had discovered our water source. I
hoped to ally with them . . . and was betrayed for my trust."
The dean looked up. "You have the weapons to prevent a similar tragedy. I have the numbers. It will be a fortuitous alliance
this time."

Dusty became aware that there was the crackle of a fire outside, and she could smell meat roasting over it. The dean's companion must have gone hunting, and quite successfully.

Marshall stood, his dark face reflecting no expression. He
had to hunch a bit in the tent's interior. "Dinner would be
most welcome, but we'll spend the night aboard the shuttle,
thank you."

"Ah. I'm most anxious to see what you have—"

Kerry put her hand up. "I'm sorry, Dean Conklin. Because
of quarantine, we can't bring you aboard just yet." Anger light-
ninged across the man's face. Just as quickly, it was erased. He
inclined his head. "I see. And please, just call me dean. It's all
I answer to."

Dusty rocked forward and got to one knee. Perhaps she was
still uneasy about the man or maybe it was just her weariness,
but she felt as though he'd just asked them all to refer to him as
a king rather than a simple college administrator. *There are layers here,* she thought, *that might well be fatal to strip away.* But
they would have to. Before bringing down the *Challenger* and
the *Mayflower,* they would have to know what kind of world it
was they were returning to.

Dusty climbed on board the shuttle, aching in every bone
from sitting on the hard, unforgiving surface of the dry lakes.
Reynolds stumbled on the ramp behind her. She reached out
and caught up the mechanic's hand. In the boarding light
spilling out into the night, she could see quite clearly the
pinched lines about Reynolds' strongly handsome face and the
beads of sweat on her forehead and upper lip.

"What is it?"

The mechanic stifled a groan and swung aboard. She shuddered and rubbed her arms gratefully. "I never thought I'd be
glad to be pent up." She looked about the shuttle's interior.

Kerry came up, her braid swinging with the motion of her
lithe body. She laughed. "Rey, honey, you've got agoraphobia."

"Ah what?"

"Fear of wide open spaces. You're ship-born. You're used to finite borders, except through windows."

Dusty looked from the petite medic to the Amazonian mechanic. She grinned. "You're afraid of wide, open spaces, Reynolds!"

The woman passed a hand over her still pale brow. "Shit," was all she answered before turning and making her way into the bowels of the shuttle.

Kerry watched her go. "You know," she said thoughtfully, "if we come down, that's a problem a lot of us are going to have to face." She disappeared after Reynolds.

Dusty stayed in the passageway as Dubois and Klegg, Polchek and Marshall did some surveying about the shuttle's immediate exterior. The medic's words troubled her, just as Dakin's had. *If.* Options.

This was her home. It was obviously not that of the others. She had to face the possibility that neither of the longships would opt to land and settle. She was a member of the *Away* Team. Not the Home Team.

Marshall spoke to them briefly before they retired. He said, in a quiet, tired voice, "Every answer brings up new questions. I've just talked with Dakin who's advised us again of the need for neutrality. The ship's library has no record of a College Vaults project, so we can only speculate on whether the man is lying or not."

Colby spoke up, the young woman usually reticent and deferring to her more outspoken partner Goldstone. "He seems well-educated. And the other man . . . Ketchum . . . would appear to be the throwback the dean indicates he is."

Before Marshall could answer, Dusty said, "I don't trust him."

The commander turned to her. One of his soft-knit, graying eyebrows went up. "Senior officer. Relying on hunches again?"

"It's my job."

"Umm. Well, I'd say the morning light is going to reveal a lot. We'll get information from the dean, offload the hover, and take a look-see ourselves. In the meantime, I suggest you all get a good night's sleep. Reynolds, get an NL-program from Kerry to help you deal with your reaction to being out in the open. We need all team members at their optimum." He clapped his hands together softly. "Good night, one and all."

*   *   *

Dusty woke early. She used the refresher sparingly and dressed quickly, anxious to get another look at the landing site. But Marshall and Dubois had beaten her to the observation deck.

Dubois had just let out a low whistle and Marshall's forehead was heavily creased.

"What is it?" she asked, drawing near.

"We're surrounded," said the communications officer. "As far as the eye can see. It's like a damn cowboy and Indians video."

She looked out the window. The vista outside was dotted with teepees and canopy tents and slow, smoking campfires everywhere she looked. "My god," she said.

"I think," Marshall commented, "the dean has decided on a show of strength."

Chapter 27

The moment he stepped onto the Ghost Road, Thomas was afraid. Reality bled away slowly, like a draining carcass, until all colors but a sepia overtone were gone. He was not in the barracks' tiny room and yet he was, poised before a vault of nothingness. He stood for a moment, clutching the finger bones in his left hand, right hand near the knife on his belt. By taking the bones from Lady and using them himself, he did not know if he'd severed her road or even put himself on the same one. Or was there always only one road? Could he go forward or she back?

He could no longer see Drakkar or the body he'd left behind. He didn't like traveling the road this way—he much preferred to go in the flesh—but he had no choice if he was to follow Lady. *The spirit is willing, but the flesh is weak.* . . .

He took another step more solidly into the road and found himself in a void, suspended over thin, black air, his sight as good as gone, his ears deafened, his voice mute—he gripped the bones tighter.

"Gillander!" He expended all his tension in a singular eruption of sound.

A cloud of sickly green and blue began to coalesce near him. Thomas backed up half a step. The cloud stopped its formation. A mocking voice said, "Back on my turf again, eh, boy? If you want to catch your lady, you'd best hurry up!"

He could see, then, a cable stretching ahead of him, like the tracings children made with sparkler fireworks in the evening air. Three cables actually, although one was so faint as to be nonexistent and the other followed it rapidly into nothingness.

But Lady's cable—he knew it had to be hers, silver-blue entwined with sable—stretched out vibrantly before him.

"Go on, Gill," he said. "I've got this one."

The emanation dissolved. Ghostly, mocking laughter followed him.

Blade swallowed tightly. He began to draw on the only energy he knew that could fuel the road. He gathered the hatred and death of the millions who had once lived in this area. The hours of their death and despair filled him, gave fuel to his effort and substance to the span which supported him. He sucked in the bitterness until he could taste its bile. He was death, oh, yes, he knew that well, Protector and executioner, yes. He was death in his own land, but the ones he held himself responsible for had been clean ones. This spew that he took in from the Ghost Road sickened him. He breathed out and in again, deeply, trying to cleanse the ache from his lungs. This was a discipline Lady had begged him to master, yet every time he used it, he left a piece of his humanity behind. She had never understood his reluctance. Now he had no choice. Thomas began to run after the cables, taking a pace he knew he could hold for hours. He did not like astral realities. Life was tough enough.

The Ghost Road could, as nearly as he could tell, telescope or fold time and distance. But to travel it leeched his own time—his life's span and energy. He didn't know how to anchor it or how to force it in any particular direction. But he did know that primal forces, very basic ones, could intersect violently with it. Wolfrats, coyotes, even sharks had run it. Traveling it in the Vaults had very nearly trapped his life force inside solid rock. And traveling it years ago had still not saved Charles and Ronnie or even their daughter Jennifer.

He *would* not be too late this time.

He ran into a void that was like running into a night sky. He felt as though he paced uphill; yet there was only above and below. The firmament ahead of him was starstruck, pinpoints of brilliant fire that shot away from him and faded even as he ran after them. The cables stretched ahead of him like a rope bridge across eternity.

He ran.

He ran until the breath sucked from his lungs couldn't be sucked back in. Until he had a stitch in his rib cage as bad as any he'd ever experienced. Until the sweat flowing off his face obscured his sight. He plowed to a halt and bowed over, his hands on his knees, gasping.

Finally, when he had breath enough, he said, "God. I must smell like a horse. I sound like one." He straightened slowly. His lungs wheezed and he coughed once or twice.

He could have been running for half a day or for two. The road was like that. He couldn't keep running forever.

He put a hand on the silver and sable strand pulling away from it. A shock ran through him. He let go of the wire with a grunt as if Lady had kicked him in the gut. He stood and rubbed the flat of his stomach.

There was a sound in the void. He turned, baffled by his bad ear, casting to see if he could tell what it was and where it had come from. It was . . . nothing and yet, he could hear it . . . a vibration, a belling beyond his sensory capacity, a somethingness beyond his perception. The darkness around him welled and buckled. His legs went out from under him as whatever it was roiled about him, under him, through him (a thousand spears of ice), left him shivering and shuddering on the pathway, on hands and knees. Gone.

What had it been?

A shadow, vast and energetic, among shadows. He grasped for Lady's cable, afraid he'd seen death. His fingers met emptiness.

The strands were gone.

Thomas roared, "Where the hell are you?"

The void swallowed up his despair as if it had never been.

Dakin said, "He wants you to do *what?*"

"Make war on the mutant society down here that he calls the Seven Counties. He's got cause. I've seen the damage they did to the installation called the College Vaults. A direct hit wouldn't have touched the facility, but they got in by subterfuge and blew it up from the inside," Marshall replied. The shuttle com room had been cleared but for the two of them. The others had tumbled exhausted into their cots and hammocks. Dusty hung onto his elbow. A day riding the hover had left her skin feeling dry and tight, grit permanently wedged between her teeth, and a keen desire to throttle Klegg and his partner.

Also with an aching hole through her heart and soul. All that could have been left of her sister was gone, blasted away in the aftermath of the Disasters. The dean had been vague about what had happened—ensconced below, he probably had not been aware of everything that had happened. A meteor hit, even a glancing blow, had left an immense crater in what had been the greater L.A. basin. Earthquakes and toxic pollution, riots and the inability to raise technology again to deal with the after-effects had destroyed the country she'd known.

The enviros had been ecstatic examining the path of destruction, mapping out pools of gas, radioactivity, toxicity, even botulism. They had hung from their straps on the hovercraft as it skimmed over the area, collecting info and readings by the seat of their pants. To their morbid fascination, the dean had replied only, "They say the quickest way to kill a man here is to take him In-City."

His flat, laconic acceptance of the hover helped to convince Marshall and Dusty that he was what he said he was—a single man of many lives. But that did not convince her he was entirely sane.

And trapped within her thoughts was that other voice. Indubitably masculine and powerful, she found it intrusive and yet . . . her own thoughts incredibly alone when she could not hear it. Was it the dean, product of a civilization forty years more advanced than the one she remembered? He watched her with a predatory keenness that disturbed her. She knew that Marshall would never have bowed to his demands alone, even under siege from the hundreds of warriors who had faced them in the morning. They could simply have shut up the shuttle and stayed aboard until the demands of water and food had driven the nation away.

But it was the witnesses they had borne with them that Marshall had listened to that day. They had lined up man by man to speak to Marshall. They had told of generations of being outcast, shunned, held to a substandard of living by water rationing. They bore on them marks of extra limbs, eyes, gills, privation, famine, and pestilence. And these were only the men. The women and children had been left in the safety of camp.

A voice droned into her musings. She looked up at the screen. Dakin's half-irritated, half-amused glance was fixed on her. "I'm sorry," she said. "I'm dead on my feet."

"And I could have sworn those were gears I saw churning."

She gave a rueful smile. "I don't necessarily agree with Marshall, sir," she returned.

"About what?"

"About anything. This . . . dean's . . . story. He crawls out of the ruins of this underground repository and the nesters take him in and heal him. Once healed, he looks around and sees the terrible conditions under which they've been forced to live and decides to liberate them? He's as old as I am, basically. Why did it take him two hundred and fifty years to decide to help his fellow man? I think he's out for somebody's ass and needs an army to help him collect it."

Marshall cleared his throat as Sun's face split into an open grin. Dusty felt her face grow warm. The *Challenger* commander answered, "Plain speaking, as always."

She shrugged. "I don't trust him."

Marshall rumbled, "I'm not sure of my stance, either, Commander, except that we can't afford to dismiss. him. He has the loyalty of a significant amount of manpower—and we need to be able to explore this area freely."

"I agree. How many is significant?"

"We scanned maybe three hundred men. Add women and children and those nesters the dean says are still outland, double it—maybe two thousand."

The commander's face went smooth. "Two thousand in an area that once supported millions prosperously."

"I understand the Seven Counties numbers closer to five thousand."

"Still a drop in the sea of humanity." Dakin appeared to sigh though she could not hear him. "Marshall, I agree with your assessment. We can't afford to antagonize this man even if we're of dubious feelings about him. We're extremely vulnerable away from the shuttle."

"I hear that one," Marshall countered. He scratched the corner of a soft brow. "I don't want to take sides in a war to wipe out whatever is left."

Dakin's image began to blue as he closed down transmission. "Unfortunately," the commander's sad voice lingered, "we may not have much choice if they're committed to warring upon us."

Chapter 28

The dean sat cross-legged upon the fragrant stuffed pillows of his tent. Ketchum hunkered down in the dirt and dried grass across from him. Dinner had been cleared. Most of the nation had been sent back to their campgrounds. The shuttle and its occupants had shut themselves up for the night. Both were intent upon the pipes in their hand. After the puffs of blue-gray smoke filtered away gently, the dean took a deep breath.

"I think I have them where I want them," he said.

Ketchum, for whom the world had changed immeasurably in the last few days, not only stopped puffing his pipe, but took the time to clean the burning weed from its clay bowl and crush the last sweet embers out upon the ground. Then he looked up. He had washed his face that day and taken care to plait his unruly hair into a sort of war-braid. It did not disguise the craggy bestiality of his face, but nothing that he did would. He put the clay pipe carefully in his shirt pocket. "Where is that, my chieftain?"

"In the palm of my hand. They doubted my story until they saw the Vaults for themselves."

Ketchum could not be convinced to travel on the hover. Instead, he had watched the machine leave and return in one long day, a distance that would have taken a week on horseback. He had a sense now of how his ancestors could have become so careless and had lost everything. Life had been too easy for them. Ease made a man careless. It had made the dean careless, and he had lost the College Vaults because of it. He made a mental note to himself not to fall in the same way. "They believed you?" He had not seen belief in all their faces. He wondered how the dean could have.

"They saw the destruction! It was graven in the earth, a testimony they could not overlook."

Ketchum felt the mellow influence of the smoke phasing through him. He relaxed from his hunkering stance to a cross-legged sit. His legs had gone pleasantly numb. "They will help you attack the Seven Counties."

"Not yet, they won't—but they will soon." The dean took a deep draw. "I've arranged a little demonstration for them. My valued ally in the counties has met with an untimely end, but another has sprung up in his place. My longship returnees have not seen how far the human race has sunk." He gave a tight smile, showing his teeth. "I've no doubt Denethan can be goaded into showing them."

Ketchum allowed himself the luxury of a returning smile. The lizard men of the Mojave would shock the new people as nothing else had. The morning would bring interesting times.

Drakkar sat uneasily, watching the still forms of three people who'd formed the core of his existence among the Seven Counties. His fight wounds still ached and he could feel the burn of a fever flickering out even as he sat vigil. None of them breathed or stirred and yet—the blood did not pool blackly in their bodies, their eyes moved under their lids as if they dreamed violently and only Alma looked pale, as if she might have gone to meet death. He did not dare sleep himself, for fear Franklin or Stanhope might enter and misunderstand the scene. An afternoon and a night and the best part of another day had gone. His stomach made a twitch of hunger.

He paced the room stiffly, beads of sweat forming upon his brow. He paused to drink from a pitcher of water on Alma's bedstand. It was tepid like the temperature of the room. He stalked about restlessly, listening to other footsteps in the hallway past the bedroom door. No one noticed that he was missing from his room. He might well have been as cold and silent as the friends he watched.

It was beyond hope that Alma would have come to him when she found herself in trouble. But if she had, none of this would have come to pass. Dishonored, the Seven Counties would never have frowned if he'd courted her. Perhaps they would even have gladly discharged her burden into his hands. Or, if she had begged him to help her keep her secret, he would have married her and taken her home to the Mojave. Fortune had not given him that opportunity. He looked beyond the window pane and saw that the day had grown long shadows, and a pale moon hung on the horizon, before its time.

He sat and tried to rest again.

A boot heel smudged the planking outside the door. Drakkar stopped his musings, his crest coming up alertly as he realized the significance of the noise. He had no knife but had pulled Sir Thomas' from the belt sheath when the door swung open cautiously.

Tando came in sideways. His face showed little emotion beyond that of its scaled patterning as he saw the still forms of Sir Thomas, Lady Nolan, and Alma. A pigeon scroll was poised between the tips of his fingers. The Mojavan wore his nails a little long and sharpened to a point like claws.

"You are well?"

"I'll live," Drakkar said and heard with surprise how weak and tired his own voice was. "More than I can say for Shankar." He did not replace Thomas' knife, but sat back with it across his thighs.

"What happened here?"

"A seeing trance." Such things were not unheard of among the sensitives under Denethan's rule. It was the best explanation he could muster. Tando seemed to accept it. He dropped the scroll in Drakkar's palm. The fine gold seal had not been removed. Drakkar opened it and read carefully. Nesters were attacking viciously upon Denethan's borders. He was having to expend time and energy to repel them. It was a necessity that might divide his power enough to leave him open to the rebels. The scroll was, in effect, a warning to Drakkar that his father's leadership had reached a crisis it might not weather. He was inquiring if the Seven Counties had yet made a decision to move against the nesters in force.

Drakkar sighed. "Send out a pigeon. Tell him 'No.' Wish him luck from me."

"That is all?"

"That," said Drakkar wearily, looking at his friends in their stillness, "is almost more than I can spare." He would not have killed Shankar and brought the rebels to their knees, but once having felt the slow acting poison on the ambassador's blade, knew he could not have left him alive to work his ill. Now wheels were in motion he could not turn or brake. He was as helpless to aid his father as he was to help Alma. He watched Tando leave as quietly as he had crept in.

Like the arc of a falling leaf, Alma's chest moved in a breath. Then she ceased movement again. It might be morning before another one of them breathed again. He closed his burning eyes.

Thomas stumbled to a halt. He went to his knees, collapsing like a paper tent in a rainstorm, folding up like a newborn colt, and lay there, fighting only to breathe. He lifted his hand and placed it on the strand carrying Lady's colors. An electricity shocked up. He felt her presence as vividly as if she stood there with him. He levered himself to his knees holding onto the cable. He had been running the road without anchor, beginning or end. Now he knew he had to find her quickly. He was spent, and if he was, they must be also.

He fixed her in his thoughts as if he were dowsing for her soul, for the clean water purity of it behind the crustiness of her exterior. He closed his eyes as if he held a dowsing rod and searched for the wellspring that was the woman.

The span trembled behind him. Thomas' eyes flew open. He lost his grip on the strand. The upheaval that had passed before was buckling the void again, a nothingness beyond the dimness, only this—this nothingness was full, filled with . . . with something he could not touch with any of his senses. It sought out his fix on Lady Nolan and took it away from him, robbing him of his anchor and hope. It left behind a shadow, a reflection so dark he could see its silhouette clearly. It was a man, a nester perhaps, walking with a feral grace, back the way he'd come.

Thomas took a gulping breath. "Shit," he said strongly and keenly. His hands felt like ice. He tried crossing his arms and warming them in the pits of his sweat-soaked shirt, but there was no warmth left in him. Something tremendous had crossed his pathway. Had it moved along another road, a road where only Lady was real?

He shook off his fear. The specter had passed on. He grabbed for the strand of sable and silver again and got to his feet. He could run no more. He stepped out on the road. He reached for the second strand, the faint tracing that was Alma, always fading and yet not diminished completely.

He found his anger and fresh energy and went after them.

Lady sat in the void, cradling Alma, the girl sprawled across her lap. Her ability to come and go had been stripped from her long before she'd felt Thomas take the bones. She could do nothing more than stay on the road she'd created, fueled from the fierce joy of birth and life with all its miseries, and hang on to Alma. She did not know if it had been hours or days.

She took her sleeve and wiped the dew from Alma's face. The girl stirred. Her eyelids fluttered.

"Let me go," she begged.

"No. Not you or the baby."

Alma opened her eyes. Huge eyes, Lady thought. Windows to her soul, if one knew to look into them. "*He raped me,*" Alma whispered hoarsely.

"I know. But the baby is innocent flesh. He may be the only good thing the dean has ever left in this world."

Alma looked away. "No good can ever come of this."

"He was never genetically altered. He was never contaminated by the eleven year plague. His sperm is the only thing about him that's not corrupt. You're no longer barren, Alma. Your promise is about to be fulfilled."

"Not with his child!"

"You have no choice now." Lady hugged her close. "If you had told me earlier . . . but now . . . Alma, I can feel his soul burning to live as fiercely as yours does. Let me bring you back. I can purge the poisons out. You'll live. He'll live."

"No." A vicious shudder wracked the slender girl. "If the baby lives, he'll come after us. He'll pound the Seven Counties until he has what he wants, and what he wants is this child!"

A low, deep voice from the shadows about them said, "I agree." Thomas stepped into their sight. Even in the dim sensory confines of the ghost road, he radiated light. His hands seemed full of it.

Lady swallowed down the sudden, hard knot in her throat. "Thank god."

He held out the finger bones. "Lose something?"

She smiled wearily. "Nearly everything but the hope you'd

come after us." She gathered up Alma, prepared to get to her feet.

But Thomas' face was not creased with welcome. His expression was drawn. He shook his head. "I won't take her back if she doesn't want to go."

"Thomas!"

He looked at Lady. "No," he said. "I won't do it. I should have killed the dean the first time we met. My mistake has cost hundreds of lives. There is nothing good that can come of him."

Alma shuddered again. Her pale fists were clenched and pushed into her stomach. "He's right."

Lady hugged her fiercely. She looked up, saw Blade's implacable face. She knew she could not move him. "Then," she said, "you'll have to return without all of us."

"You have no right to interfere with her choice!" Thomas' voice cut across the ghost road.

"I have every right! I'm older. I understand life, she doesn't! She's been beaten and broken and humiliated and terrorized. What in god's name makes you think she can make a decision like this?"

Thomas tilted his head slightly. "What makes you think she can't? It looks to me as if she already has."

"Not before I caught her on the Ghost Road. It's all of us— or none of us. Now you make the decision."

Alma grabbed her wrist. "Lady, don't. He loves you. He came for you."

"I came for both of you," Thomas said. "But not the . . . other."

Lady cried out, "You can't deny him."

"My Talent is death. Yours is life." He took a step. She saw with alarm how weak he was, that it had taken all his effort to remain standing. The road had taken nearly all he had to offer.

"I can't do it without you." Her voice caught. She turned her face away, hiding it as she bowed over Alma.

He caught her wrist and brought her to her feet. Alma tumbled out of her arms. They looked at each other searchingly. Lady knew then that it would never be the same between them. He caught Alma and hauled her to her feet as well. Lady saw then what he had woven into each hand, like a kind of rope. "We're going home." He dragged her a step in the direction he'd appeared from.

She could not fight his desperate strength. "Alma!"

The girl hung back.

"It's your choice," Thomas said, finally. "I won't kill it now. I may have to later."

The girl looked at him. "If he's . . . some kind of monster?"

Thomas nodded.

"He's . . . my son."

"I know that."

Her face crumpled and she let out a tiny wail. "What should I do?"

Lady reached out and took her hand, opening it to show the strand that Thomas had lain across her palm, her lifestrand, her colors, faint and commingled. "He's already part of you," she said softly, the tip of her finger disturbing the weave gently, separating purple from dark blue. "I'll be there with you. We'll understand, Alma. You're not alone."

The girl stood transfixed, looking at the colors interwoven with her own. She had felt the shock of her existence the moment Sir Thomas had put the cord in her hand. Now she felt the flickering tug of another presence.

Something young, and unformed, something fresh and untouched.

She looked up into Thomas' level gaze.

"I'll do what I have to," he repeated.

She looked to Lady. The Healer nodded. "As I will."

Alma took a deep, quavering breath. "That's as much assurance as any life gets, isn't it?" She took a step forward to join them.

Chapter 29

Trout died on the outskirts of Orange County. They buried him in the shade of a stand of eucalyptus, the peeled bark scenting the cairn with its pungent fragrance. Machander, his face tanned so dark his port wine birthmark barely showed now, planted geranium at the cairn's base. Winter rains were coming and the geranium would get a foothold. Once established, the flowering plant would grow and blossom through heat and drought. The boys stood around until Stefan finally mumbled a prayer of sorts and each of them said what they felt like saying.

Watty felt more like crying. He didn't, though. He watched Jeong make a sketch of the cairn and grove and the haggard boys standing around it. He saw it before the boy flipped the cover over his sketchbook quickly. The drawing shocked him.

He looked away quickly from the sight of their failure as it was etched into their faces, their posture, all of them. Their failure to map anything truly unknown, or even to have survived the trek. Their failure to have saved Trout.

Stefan broke the silence a second time. He put his hat back on. "We'll move a lot more quickly now that we don't have to use the travois. Break it down and let's get going. Two more days and we'll be having lunch in Judge Teal's backyard."

Home. Home in the Seven Counties. Soon they would be hitting the fringe of the cattle and sheep herds, and then the farms. Now they were crossing the broken terrain at the southeast lip of the foothills. They had swung east of the College Vaults, avoiding nester territory wherever they could. Stefan had been becoming increasingly tenser. The nesters appeared to be reclaiming old clan territory with a vengeance.

"Come on," Stefan urged. "Or Bottom won't have meat for tonight's dinner."

That prodded them all into motion. The burly cook shoved Watty aside and broke down Trout's conveyance single-handedly. They were not happy when they hit the trail again, but they were headed home.

Stefan took his hat off, exposing his too-white forehead, and took the telescope from Watty's hands. They lay on their stomach in a wash. A brown alligator lizard took off over Stefan's back, but the young man never felt it, his gaze too intent on the base of a foothill.

Watty squirmed in the dirt. Ants tickled his underside. He rolled onto his flank to scratch.

"Stay down! And be quiet."

The boy tried to do as ordered. He lay quiet for maybe a minute or two before asking, "What's happening?"

"I'm not sure. That's a nester gathering, but they've got a machine, a good-sized one. Bigger than a car shell. I've never seen anything like it."

Watty's curiosity peaked. "Is it working? What is it doing?"

"It isn't doing anything." Stefan froze suddenly. The lines of his body became tense.

"What is it?"

"Son of a bitch. It's *him*. He's lost a ton of flesh . . . he looks lean and mean, but I'd still know him."

"Him who?"

Stefan took the telescope from his eye and looked back at Watty. "It's the one called the dean. The one who tried to kill all of us."

Watty let out a low whistle.

Stefan put the telescope back to his eye, muttering, "I could end it all right now."

The flesh crawled on the back of Watty's neck. "What are you talking about?"

Stefan began scooting backward out of the wash. "The best way to kill a snake is to cut off its head. I think I can save all of us a lot of future grief by taking care of that bastard now. Get the guys together."

"What? Why?"

"We're attacking the camp." Stefan snapped the telescope back into its case. "Now come on, *hurry*, before they find out we're here."

"But they haven't done anything to us."

The tall man stopped. Watty looked up at his creased face. He noticed that he no longer had to look up as far as he did before. He put his shoulders back defensively.

Stefan said coldly, "That's one bastard you don't give a chance if you don't have to—and I don't have to. Stay to the rear if you want to." He pushed past Watty and began to order the boys together.

Bottom stared at Watty as though he'd known Watty had protested. The burly cook said flatly, "The son of a bitch as good as killed Trout. Jenkies and Bill. Ngo. He owes us."

Watty was afraid to say anything. He just stood by his horse as they unpacked them and loaded their rifles, checked their longknives in their sheaths, put together a rough plan for raiding the camp.

"Jeong," Watty finally said.

The artist looked over, no expression on his face or in his almond eyes. He gave a shrug.

Bottom swung up, cradling his rifle. "Hell," he said. "You're probably still a virgin."

Watty felt his blood go hot. He ducked his head down and gathered up the reins to his mount. A thick hand grabbed his shoulder. He looked up. Bottom was staring at him.

"Just stick by me," the cook said. "You'll be fine."

Watty swallowed past the hard knot in his throat and swung up.

Dusty sat in a passenger seat on the hover. It had settled down to the dry ground and brush like a massive beast lying down on its stomach. She found a packet of fruit drink in her bag, opened it and sucked it down, wondering if she'd ever get rid of her sore throat. Lack of humidity, Kerry'd said. The ships maintained as nearly perfect a climate as they could. The real thing was hot and dry and windy, though the dean swore that rainy season was within a week of reaching them.

"Rain now," he'd said, "was like the monsoons."

Monsoons in Southern California. She never thought she'd live to see it. Klegg checked his instruments. He was running numbers through his keypad. He looked up as she took a deep breath.

"Could be rain," he said. "And the barometric pressure's dropped a little. Nothing today." His skin was a bright pink, sunburned by overexposure.

"And you'd love it if it was acid rain," she said and smiled back.

The enviro wrinkled his nose. "We have been a little bloodthirsty, haven't we?"

"A little. This is our motherland here and you guys are ecstatic about the thousand deaths she died."

He ran a hand through spiky hair. "Occupational hazard. The ship maintained a norm that was almost boring. And my grandad worked on the last ground drop, so what's left for me? I forget you had a personal acquaintance with the area."

"You're forgiven." She crumpled her drink pack and restored it to her bag for recycling. Old habits were hard to break, she thought ruefully, as she remembered the recycling plant was strictly a shipboard function. She watched the dean and Ketchum and a handful of other nesters showing what they claimed was a well site to Marshall.

There was a dull booming, as of thunder. She looked up across the broken expanse of landscape, and frowned. Klegg looked up, too. "What the hell—?"

A wall of fire exploded in front of them. She rocked back, heat raking across her face. Klegg grabbed her by the elbow and threw her to the lee side of the hover. At the rear of the conveyance, she could hear Reynolds' deep voice.

"Incoming! Riders, armed, about a dozen."

The nesters scattered. Those who could get to the bony, slat-sided creatures they called horses mounted in a flying leap. Others ringed the dean, ready to defend his body with theirs.

The dean called out, "Don't touch the flames. It's akin to Greek fire. It'll spread to anything it touches."

The curtain of fire set heat waves rippling across her view as she looked across. Marshall crouched by the hover's nose. "Hold your fire," he said.

"We're outnumbered." The dean pulled on Marshall's elbow. "You have to give your men the liberty to protect themselves—and us. Those are Countians coming in. They won't leave any of us alive."

The hover swayed as Reynolds climbed it, gaining the lee-side at the fair end. Dusty looked and saw her resting her elbows on the roof, aiming at the riders coming in.

There was a melee on the field as the two forces engaged. Horses and mules squealed and circled one another. Dust rose, obscuring forces.

"Christ," Klegg said. "They're using *knives*."

Bullets, Dusty thought, must be beyond them. Then what was it that had exploded in front of them? A vial of some sort? Thrown or catapulted? She saw a man go down. The body was trampled under the wheeling hooves.

The raiders swept in. The dean bellowed, "Pull out! Take your team and pull out!"

Marshall looked over his shoulder. She could see the indecision in his face. He did not wish to abandon anyone. He turned toward them. "Fire as necessary," he said.

Watty stayed in the rear. The whoops and calls of his buddies rang as they pounded over the brush and plain. Stefan had his rifle wound and shot his glass toward the machine, whatever it was. The vial splattered on impact, sending up sheets of flame. He cradled his own rifle, afraid to fire, thinking he'd never sent a bolt into anything but coyotes and wolfrats or game. Nothing human, or remotely close to it.

They were flanked by a handful of nesters. The outcasts crashed into them, blades flashing. Watty saw Machander sit straight up in his saddle and then roll backward in a blossom of crimson. His left arm flopped disjointedly after him, nearly severed from its joint. He hit the dust with a scream drowned out by the trample of hooves.

He heard Stefan curse. Saw the rifle swing around, butt first. Saw the nester collide with it and, as his face disappeared, leave his saddle with a gurgle. And then Watty was too busy to watch out for anything but his own ass. He fought and stabbed and hit and ducked and then a handful of them burst into the clear.

His horse paced Bottom's. The cook's face was mottled purple with anger. He reined his horse onto the heels of Stefan's. "I'm going to get that son of a bitch," the big boy said.

They swept across the plain. Stefan was riding without hands, winding his rifle for a set of bolts. He was going to ride down the dean's throat. Watty swallowed and held on for dear life.

There was an explosion. He felt a cold breeze pass his ear. "What—?"

Jeong was on Watty's left. He threw up an ink-stained hand to the side of his face. Blood spurted out between his fingers. Another explosion and both mule and boy went down.

"Jeong!" cried Watty. The horses swerved. He felt a sharp sting in his shoulder as if slapped but nothing more.

And then they were within earshot of the machine, the dean, and the others. He saw strange faces and clothes, and weapons in their hands, bearing down on them. Stefan let out a yell of pain, tumbling away.

Bottom grunted. He rolled over, hitting Watty and dragging him out of the saddle, going down. Crimson splashed into the air, a wave of blood. They hit the ground with a thud, Bottom covering him.

The burly cook said, "I'm bleeding enough for both of us, kid. Stay down. They'll think you're dead, too." His chest gurgled as he fought for a breath. "When it gets dark enough, get the hell out of here."

It was all Watty could do to breathe. He didn't wait until dark, but scuttled away in the dust and the shadows, sobbing with the pain that now flared in his sodden shoulder.

He was the only one left alive.

Chapter 30

Lady Nolan came awake with a gasp and then a shuddering, deep breath. She bolted from the cot where she had been embracing Alma's still body, waking Drakkar who lunged to his feet with a startled curse.

She made it to the door and bellowed, "Franklin! Stanhope!" with a voice that would not be denied.

Alma came to, eyes rolling, the whites showing, and began to cough and choke almost immediately.

"Get a basin for her," the Healer snapped. Her burst of energy sapped, she nearly collapsed coming back to the chair where Sir Thomas' inert body sprawled.

Drakkar grabbed the basin from the nightstand and held it to Alma's mouth, not a second too late. She began to spew a black and bilious mass into the bowl. His eyes watered at the stink and his own stomach revolted at the sound of her retching. In the corner of his vision, he saw Lady Nolan sink to her knees beside Sir Thomas' body.

"Breathe, damn you," she sobbed. "Breathe!" She made a fist and slugged him in the chest.

Alma gave one last, gut-wrenching heave and sagged back into the cot. Drakkar put the basin aside and grabbed a cloth, the one he'd used to soothe her forehead while she had been . . . gone. He wiped her mouth gently after daubing her brow.

Lady Nolan continued to half shout, half cry. "What's wrong?" he said to her.

"He's not coming back," she answered bitterly. The doorway suddenly filled with Franklin and Stanhope, the man and boy splitting up. Stanhope had a kit in hand.

"What is it?" he said to Lady. He set the kit on the table, ready for work.

"She's taken an abortive, oleander, among other things. We've gotten most of it out. Give her a hot mustard purge and set her in a healing trance. She should be okay. I've lost Thomas in a healing trance."

The lie startled Drakkar, but he said nothing, stroking Alma's hair back from her face.

Lady took a deep breath, steadying. Her eyes were red and swollen as she looked up to Franklin's moon-round face. "I can't reach him!"

"Sir Thomas has always gone his own way. Maybe you're looking for him in the wrong direction. I'll anchor you," Franklin said quietly. His gentle hand entwined with hers.

Drakkar left Alma. "I've had enough of this sensitive shit." He stepped over them and kicked the chair back, sending Thomas' body lolling onto the floor. "Doesn't anybody know basic CPR?" He knelt down and placed the palms of his gloved hands on Thomas' chest. He began to pump as he'd been taught. He saw Lady's mouth open and shut in outrage, but he had no time. The first time he paused and exhaled into Thomas' airway, there was no response. Back to pumping. Exhale again. Nothing. The body resisted him. The throat seemed convulsively closed to all his efforts. Again, through the sequence. Then again. He was going light-headed taking in and expelling extra air. Again. Then he could feel it. The air going in instead of meeting an invisible resistance. He inhaled deeply a second time and breathed.

Sir Thomas came to with a gulping, grasping motion, pulling Drakkar off his chest. He struggled to the wall and sat up, bracing his back against the frame. A set of dried finger bones tumbled out of his hand and onto the floor. He took several more deep breaths before the color came back into his face.

He looked at Lady. "Never again," he said.

In the corner of the room, on the cot, Alma began to cry softly.

Dusty refastened her hair clip at the nape of her neck. Her hands felt numb, an unfeeling that went all the way through her. She sat down wearily on the bumper shield of the hover.

"He won't let us get near the bodies," she whispered to Marshall.

The Away Team commander patted her on the knee. "It's for the best."

"No." She shook her head vigorously. Her thick auburn hair threatened to come loose from its clip again. "I got a look at most of them . . . they're boys, Marshall. The oldest couldn't be more than twenty, twenty-two. What were they doing? Why did they attack?"

Kerry was lying down across two of the passenger seats. She lifted her head, the dusk obscuring the expression on her face. "Most of them were gilled."

"Gilled?"

The medic nodded shakily. She put a hand to her temple. "Immature. Another one I got a look at had had neck surgery, crude, but evident."

"Gills?" Marshall rolled the word about again. He looked at Dusty. "Gone back to the sea? Could they have survived the dust shroud by going back to the sea and farming it? We had sea lab projects."

"If the El Nino came down and kept the waters warm. . . . I don't know. The El Nino does extend into the coastline, but it's an erratic current. I can remember the weathermen complaining about it. It affected sport fishing and weather fronts . . . too much of a good thing. Wouldn't the kelp beds have died back without sunlight?"

"I don't know, Dusty." Kerry gave a bleak smile. "One thing's for sure—none of them are going to answer any questions."

Dusty looked out where the nesters were piling bodies any which way on a pyre of deadwood and mesquite. She'd never smelled burning bodies before. The thought of it made her intensely sick to her stomach. "His men came back with pack mules and donkeys. Raiders don't carry packs, do they? And those kids were really weatherbeaten. Cowboys, maybe?"

Marshall gave an impatient grunt. "It doesn't matter why they were out here, they attacked us without provocation."

Dusty hugged her knees. She said thoughtfully, "Who knows what kind of history these people have between them?" She kicked her legs free and shinnied down off the hover. Casually, hands in her enviro suit pockets, she sauntered toward the pyre. The dean was engaged in what she could only term looting, going through the saddlebags and packs brought in by Ketchum and some of the others. Ketchum stood alone in the darkness, building the pyre with bodies and more wood. The dry oily mesquite would go up like gasoline, she thought, as she came up behind him.

There were empty packs at his feet. He tossed the last body on the pyre with a grunt and reached for the torches lit and stuck in the dirt at his feet.

Dusty leaned over as something fluttered out of the boy's jacket and struck the ground near her feet. She picked it up even as the nester threw a torch into the bonfire and the brush roared into flames.

She held a book of sorts. She flipped open the cover. Primitive paper, coarse and vanilla-colored, filled with charcoal and ink sketches. She recognized faces of the dead. There was talent here. Dusty looked up, remorse swelling in her throat. Which one of the bodies had been an artist, a quick and clever drawer of line and feeling?

The hot wind of the pyre set pages to flipping in her hands. She saw maps and topographical renderings. Knowledge flooded her. These boys were explorers, pushing outward from their homes toward the unknown. The artist was committing every step of their journey to these drawings.

A last page glowed in the fire's illumination. A man, a lean man, hair below his ears and a slight mustache, a man with a scarf about his neck (hiding his own gills, she thought), with competence and danger written into the very lines of his form the boy had sketched. He was most definitely not among the dead. Who the hell was he?

"No!" Ketchum grunted and tore the book from her hands. He threw it into the heart of the blaze before Dusty could snatch it back. She watched in despair as the legacy of the unknown artist joined the fragility of his flesh. She backed up a step, the smoke and smell of the burning bodies reaching her.

Her eyes smarted. Ketchum glared at her before turning to jam his torch into another corner of the woodpile. Dusty fled back to Marshall and the others, too shaken to speak. She had found no answers and still more questions. Why would a group of scouts, of surveyors, attack without mercy?

She buried her face in her hands as she sat down next to Marshall, trying to filter out the stink as the night wind carried it to them.

Reynolds put an arm about her shoulders. "What is it, Dusty?"

Dusty only shook her head, unable to voice her feelings. The Earth and its people had become unrecognizable to her.

"What did you take from her, Ketchum?" the dean asked as the fire burned down and the forms of bodies had been reduced to sticks of char. The glow of the fire had brought out a sheen of sweat across the man's face. Ketchum saw him lick it away greedily from his upper lip, as though the smell of cooked flesh had been enticing. His flesh crawled and he looked away.

"It was nothing, Chieftain," he answered. "Papers."

"Papers? What kind of papers?"

"Papers, all stuck together. Like the shamans have—"

The dean's hooded eyes opened a bit wider. "A book?"

"Yes." Ketchum nodded. "A book."

"What did it look like?"

"Drawings and maps," the tracker said. "I cannot read."

The dean grunted. He took a stick and prodded the embers. "Drawings of what?"

"The boys. The Vaults. I saw one of the Marked Man."

"Who?"

"Protector Blade."

"Ahhh." The dean lapsed into silence. He muttered as if to himself, "I can't have that. I can't have her thinking these boys are innocents. I can't have her thinking about which side to take." He looked up abruptly. "Bide your time, Ketchum. Maybe when the rains come . . . an accident for her. She knows too much and she doesn't trust me." The dean picked up the hem of his garish robe and walked away from the pyre.

Ketchum did not watch him go, though the hairs on the back of his neck let him know when his back was safe.

Watty crawled to a halt. He rolled over with a crackle of brush. His shoulder ached like fire and ground with every movement. He forced his eyes wide and looked up at a sky of stars. For a moment, they wheeled and blurred. He scrubbed his eyes with his good hand.

The night sky came into focus. By luck or by God's will, he'd been crawling in the right direction. He thought of Stefan and Bottom and Jeong and Machander and all the others. His eyes filled with hot tears and his nose swelled. Even if he could crawl all the way to the county's edge, he couldn't bring them back.

"Idiot!" he screamed. "You jerk, Stefan! You got us all killed!" His fury and sorrow stuck in his throat. He couldn't get another word out. He fell into silence in the dirt, arm flung over, his eyes as if he could shut out his memories.

He was going to die here. Then the story of what had happened to them, of what had happened to the mapping expedition, would die as well.

His shoulder hurt like fire and he was hungry.

If his wound did bleed him to death or go septic, the coyotes would get him. Watty sniffled. He felt weak in every joint. He couldn't remember how he'd gotten out from under Bottom or how he'd run so far before he'd gone down or why the nesters hadn't seen him. All he could remember was the screaming of the horses and the harsh, trumpetlike brays of the mules and donkeys and the dust that had risen like smoke from a brushfire.

And blood.

He blew his nose on the sleeve of his shirt and rolled over, endeavoring to sit up. A wave of genuine pain hit him, so strong he went sick to his stomach and his vision went dark.

When he looked up, he saw two glowering eyes looking at him from the night, not two paces away. He could smell the animal scent then, primal and musky.

Whatever it was, it was huge.

He wasn't going to die trying to crawl home and having the buzzards and coyotes pick his bones.

He was going to be eaten alive.

Watty heard the roar of his pulse in his ears. It drowned out even the growl of the beast as it reared toward him from the night. His eyes rolled back in his head and he keeled over before it reached him.

The Shastra paused before the fallen boy. It hesitated, muzzle wrinkled. It lowered itself to all fours and hesitantly shifted its weight from side to side. Then instinctively, it reached for the boy and hoisted him in its arms. It turned southward, toward the boy's original path, and began to carry him along. It had no voice or language to express its thoughts or intentions. Watty hung from its arms as if dead.

Chapter 31

They had the private bathhouse behind the Healers' quarters all to themselves, but Thomas was distracted with every move he made, every caress he served. Lady felt the sadness ingrained in their lovemaking. It was as though he said without words, *This is the last time I shall ever kiss this breast, stroke this thigh, taste this mouth. . . .*

She held back her questions until they were finished and he lay resting in her arms.

"What is it, Thomas?"

He stirred, opening his eyes and looking up at her. He sometimes found it difficult to look her directly in the eyes. She knew full well why—her two-colored vision was disconcerting: the blue stone-cold and the brown warm and compassionate, just as disconcerting as her own nature was to her.

She said softly. "I do love you," thinking of the impasse they'd come to on the Ghost Road and wondering if it would stay unbreachable. They had not mentioned it since coming back.

"And I love wild strawberries." He sat up and slid into the bath water, this time to bathe.

"Strawberries?" She was both startled and amused. "what are you talking about?"

He paused, soap in hand. "I love them," he answered slowly, "but I can't eat them. They give me hives and welts. I've been told enough of them would even kill me."

Lady shivered and drew her towel about her. He fell silent and finished soaping. She waited until he had ducked under to rinse clean and then emerged, his hair and mustache dripping.

"Is that what I am to you, a slow poison?"

"I don't know. All I know is that you . . . cripple me."

Her throat constricted.

He did not wait for an answer. "I'm leaving tomorrow. I've sent some papers to you, some things I found in the Vaults and kept back. They're controversial. You may want to withhold them from the counties."

She interrupted him. "Thomas, I—"

He interrupted back. "And I'm taking Drakkar with me. You'll have to take care of Alma, but I can't let him court her openly, not just now. Bartholomew's crowd will string him up. When we get this nester problem settled, maybe I can get some acceptance for him. I don't dare leave him behind." He began dressing in brisk, efficient moves and she just sat on the decking and watched him, unable to stop him from doing any of the things he was doing.

Thoughts ran through her head as images, snatches of visions rather than coherent words. Thomas had had a reputation as a ladies' man before they had become involved, yet he had never been anything but faithful to her. She knew the anger that ran him, that fueled his Ghost Road, that he kept buried beneath a lonely and austere exterior. She had never turned her face from all that he'd revealed to her and she wondered if he would ever find another woman who could say as much. She loved him almost more than she loved life itself. But because she was committed to life, to the protection and healing of it, she had to let him go. She could not change any more than she already had. He either must change and accept it as growth rather than crippling, or he must leave her.

She cupped her hand over her stomach. Unlike Alma, she had known almost the moment of conception. Unlike Alma, she welcomed every difference within her body, disturbing as it might be.

If she told him now, Thomas would think it a ploy to keep him from his task. He would not take the comfort from it she wanted to give. So she kept her silence and prayed to whatever gods had not abandoned their shattered world to keep him safe and bring him back, at least long enough that she could tell him then.

He had almost finished dressing. He made a quick weapons check, looking at her. "No tears?"

"Not yet," she said. "It wouldn't help. I'm not a reed in the wind that must bend or break."

"No," he agreed. "You're one hell of a woman." He paused and then opened his mouth as if he would say one thing further.

She would never know what it was, because a sharp rap on the bathhouse door interrupted him.

Gray Walton pushed in. He looked to Thomas. "I need you, Blade. We've got news."

He slung his jacket over his shoulder and followed the DWP out of the tiny building.

Lady stayed alone for a long time, wrapped in her towel and her thoughts, her visions of the past.

Drakkar sat on the edge of Charlie Warden's antique old desk, a monstrous piece of hand-rubbed work from another era, and swung his booted heels as petulantly as any child. He had a copy of Macaulay's *The Way Things Work* in his hand, his lips moving slightly as he read as Gray and Blade entered the office.

Blade snapped, "Get off that desk!" even as Gray said, "What are you doing in here?"

Drakkar snapped the book shut and slid down. He bowed. "Yes, sir," to Thomas and to Gray, said, "you sent for me?"

"The office is private," said the new DWP.

Thomas followed with, "And the desk is sacrosanct."

"Duly noted," Drakkar answered. "But the book is wonderful. Satire and mechanics in one. Well-used, too."

"It explains much of the old world," Gray said, as he came behind the desk and pulled up the enormous canebacked chair that matched it. "Gentlemen, be seated."

Gray was a black man. Not a muted brown color like Stanhope or an even lighter shade, but a glorious brown-black like a raven's wing. His family as far back as could be remembered had never married outside their color, odd in the Seven Counties in these days, where survival was more important than color or racial background. The pink skin of his palms was just as vibrant as his darker pigment and he held his hands up now to get the attention of the two he'd brought to his office.

"Drakkar," and his dark eyes looked to the Mojavan. "I know you've gotten recent, multiple private messages. Normally I'd let them stay privy to you, but I can't allow that now."

Drakkar's crest flared immediately. "Diplomacy and the alliance—" he started, but Gray overrode him.

"Listen to what I have to say first. Then I think there will be no difficulty in revealing the information I've asked you to."

Thomas had sat quietly in one of the leather wing chairs diagonal to the desk, back to the wall, half-facing the office doors. "What is it, Gray?" he asked quietly.

"Several things. First, nester forces have taken advantage of certain rebellious elements in the Mojave and split Denethan's army in two."

"Army? When did Denethan mobilize and why?"

"Actually, that's probably the first thing." Gray shuffled some papers on the desk in front of him. "We have reports he began mobilizing about six weeks ago, in response to active raiding on his borders. But you knew things were getting tense there."

Blade nodded.

"All right. The information we have is that there is now an all-out range war proceeding on several fronts northeast and east of the Montclair-Claremont foothills where the Vaults were located."

"Right after we left the area."

"It appears so. The escalation has been gradual, though, Blade, so don't feel you missed anything."

Drakkar said nothing, but he stroked the soft leather of his cuffed gloves several times. He remained standing as if too restless to sit.

"Secondly, machinery of massive size and unknown origin has been operating in and about those areas for the last week or so."

Blade's gaze snapped back to Gray Walton. "From the Vaults? Could the dean have resurrected something?"

"That, we don't know. However, the actual escalation from raid to all out assault occurred about the same time."

"Shit." Blade shifted weight in the chair. "He thinks he can do it. What are you recommending?"

Gray pursed his lips in thought before saying, "I recommend you let me finish. Thomas . . . Judge Teal has sent me a handful of missives. Our cote is overflowing with his birds! But he had quite a story to tell." The DWP paused. "Young Watkins was found by a sheepherder at the edge of his pastures, barely alive. He'd suffered a shoulder wound from a weapon we can't identify. He was feverish, barely able to talk. But he did tell the healer and Judge Teal that the mapping party had been wiped out. He's the only survivor."

Drakkar sat down with a thud. "Wiped out?" he repeated.

"That's right. By nesters and the man known as the Dean of the College Vaults."

Blade said nothing, but his face lost color under his tan.

"Watty is pretty badly injured and they're not sure if he'll pull through or how accurate his story is. It appears that the mappers met an abyss they couldn't cross and they had decided to return home. They'd lost their Healer, as well. In the run-in with the nesters, they encountered some sort of giant machine, possibly a vehicle, and weapons of great range and destruction. Watty managed to escape in the confusion. He doesn't really know how he got as far as Orange County." Gray reshuffled his papers. "Drakkar, I believe it's your turn."

The Mojavan lifted his chin defiantly. "I see no reason—"

Gray slammed his hand down on the desk. The thunder reverberated through the room. "If you can't see the importance of cooperating during a war, you young puppy, then perhaps I'd better send for a representative of your father who does!"

Blade looked at Gray in mild surprise. He held his tongue, thinking that perhaps he and Lady had manipulated far better than they could have imagined.

Drakkar's crest stayed half-erect, like angry hackles. He said stiffly, "My father could be dead by now."

"In which case, he could care less if you kept his secrets."

The struggle in Dralckar's face was obvious. He said sulkily, "Our range covers a broad area of the desert, areas you Countians find most inhospitable. Even the floaters rarely encroach upon it. About two weeks ago, there was a vast migration. Hundreds of nester warriors entered an area once known as Edwards Air Force Base."

"To fight?" asked Thomas.

Drakkar shook his head. His plumage rattled like quills.

"Then why?"

"Have you ever heard of a longship?"

The broad face of the DWP creased in puzzlement, but Thomas got to his feet. "Only once," he answered. "When Lady and I were taken into the College Vaults. They were spaceships, sent on epic voyages. Many of our genetic adaptations were supposedly developed for those ships."

"One came back."

Drakkar's words dropped like boulders into the room. Gray Walton cleared his throat before saying, "What the hell are you two talking about?"

"Space flight, Gray. We know they went to the moon and Mars. They wanted to go further, so they developed these long-ships . . . long-term flights. Generations to be born aboard the voyage. Hundreds of years for a roundtrip. I don't know how many went out—I do know that the Dean of the College Vaults believed fervently one day they'd come back." Thomas paced a vigorous stride or two.

"They came back, didn't they?" he said to Drakkar.

"My father believes that one, at least, did. The dean went to meet it. And he believes that its technology and machinery and weaponry are now at the dean's disposal."

"Anybody who can go to space and return can't be that stupid," Gray said. "How can they take sides so easily?"

Drakkar's face whipped around toward him. "When's the last time you fought a lizard man and thought you were facing anything human?" he said bitterly. "I have half brothers and sisters who resemble an eel-snake more than they resemble me or my father."

Thomas paused, then said, "Faced with that—Stefan may well have attacked the dean and his party. He always was a hot-head. He never felt we should have let the dean go after what happened at the Vaults. If he'd run across them or surprised them. . . .

"We can't know that."

"No. Is that all, Drakkar?"

"Yes," the young man said, but his eyes flickered and Thomas knew he was lying. He also knew that the young man had no intention of saying anything further.

He looked to Gray. "What do you want me to do?"

"I don't know," answered the DWP wearily. "I was hoping you'd have an idea."

"Good, because I do. I'd intended to go out and parlay with the nesters. I still do. I may have to wade through some bodies first." Blade gave a grim smile. "Drakkar, you're coming with me."

"Me? Why?"

"Because I don't have time to go on horseback. If I know

Denethan, he's got a catapult base in operation close to here. We'll need wind raiders and we'll need them tonight while we still have a strong inshore flow. The thermals should be enough to carry us over the basin and the Angeles Crest. If the dean is getting ready to face the Mojavans, I have a pretty good idea where he's based. The only way we can get there in decent time is by flying in. Well?"

Drakkar had gone pale. He looked from face to face, then, finally shrugged. "All right," he said. "But it may be too late already. My father's last message indicated that rebel forces had broken through and attacked the longship party in force. If they're human, old-time human, it may be too late to convince them there's humanity in us."

Chapter 32

Goldstone was whistling as he worked in the lab. Dusty gagged as she entered and made an effort to breathe through her mouth so the odor of the rapidly decaying body didn't affect her.

"Incredible," he said as he opened up the chest cavity.

"You're sure it's human?"

"Fairly sure. There's a pile of them out back of the shuttle if you want to take a look for yourself." He pointed with the cutting drill, its head spinning red drops about the dissecting table. His wife looked up and her eyes met Dusty's. Colby cleared her throat. He looked up. "Sorry," he said. "I get carried away."

"From the looks of this, it's a wonder you weren't carried off." Dusty forced herself to look at the corpse. The shuttle had survived a savage attack by these lizardlike beasts while the hover was out making its recon flight.

"Easy as pie. All we had to do was shut our doors and toss some sonic bombs out the window every once in a while."

She shook her head. The scaled hands were talon-tipped and, unless she missed her guess, the pouches in the wattled throat were poison for the too sharp incisors the dead lips had curled back to expose. "Are they all like this?"

"Yes and no. It's my guess the reptilian engineering was for the Mars colonization efforts. Big lung capacity, hibernation capabilities, thicker skin—who knows." Goldstone stopped. He sighed. "I don't even know if it thought it was human," he admitted.

Dusty shuddered. It was cold in the lab. She looked about. "I'll bet you wish you were in Noah's Ark."

"Don't I though. The work I could do in there!" Goldstone put his hand drill back into place, slicing with all the delicacy of a neurosurgeon. Noah's Ark was the self-contained main lab of the *Challenger*. Not only was it completely outfitted, but all the seeds of life they could bring from the Earth were frozen and stored in it, saved for the day when it would be launched as the core of a new colony.

It had everything needed to bring a world to life. It might even have everything needed to bring this world back to life.

Dusty rubbed her forearms as a sudden chill swept her. She waved a little good-bye to Colby standing quietly by her husband and assisting with the procedures.

She was tired. Sitting in the observation lounge sounded like a good idea.

Willem Marshall was already sitting there, looking out the window. She pulled up his arm and snuggled under the crook of it, feet tucked under her. They had been lovers once. Now she sat as though a child of his. He'd left a wife and child aboard the *Challenger* to come on the Away Team.

"You're thinking," she said.

"Right about that one. I talked to Sun early tonight. He's agreed that we have little choice but to ally ourselves with the dean, for the moment. At least they were civilized enough to talk first. But I don't like it, Dusty. These . . . people . . . literally went through hell to adapt and survive. Who are we to pass judgments on the remnants of civilization?"

"Is that what we're doing?"

"I think so," said Marshall heavily. "I'm afraid so." He turned toward her suddenly. "I think we've got enough fuel to get back. It'd be a one-time shot—"

"Told anybody yet?"

"No."

She gave a tired smile. "It'll be one hell of a bounce if it doesn't work."

"Ummmm. I know that."

"Is that what you're sitting here thinking about? Getting back to the *Challenger?*"

"Umm-hmm." He snuggled her in under his arm again. "What are you thinking about?"

"I don't like to give up."

"I hear that." Marshall was staring out the observation window again. "But I don't think we're wanted here."

A dull boom sounded. "What's that?"

He waited a moment, before answering, "Thunder, I suppose. You tell me."

She realized that, ship-born, he'd never heard thunder before. She sat up. The observation window reflected a stab of lightning. "Look! And listen, it'll sound again."

Another muffled drum roll.

"Rain?" asked the commander.

"Yeah. And lots of it, according to the dean. It'll all wash away." Dusty walked to the window. Her heart ached for the sound of raindrops on the insulated pane. "God. I haven't heard rain in two hundred and fifty years. I don't think I want to try to leave."

"I don't think we have much choice."

The rain came pounding down before she could respond. She felt like a kid again as it splattered the window in front of her face. Dusty stood there and watched it for a long, long time.

The bat-winged wind raider rode the forefront of the storm as it would bodysurf a wave. It bucked and fought the rudder under him, but Drakkar threw himself on it and kept it steady.

Blade didn't like flying much. He'd only done it twice in his career as a Protector and both times in desperation. Though barely motored, once launched properly, the raider could glide over the major part of the L.A. basin.

Drakkar took to flying as though he'd been born to it, which, Blade reflected, he had. Wind raiders were part of Denethan's arsenal and threat to the safety of the Seven Counties. He yelled to Blade in the front seat, "Keep the nose up!"

Blade threw his weight on the stick, but there wasn't a lot he could do. The storm had driven him farther than he'd hoped, but it was also driving them downward. The ridge of mountains along the north side of the basin rose before them. This was where he wanted to be, the Angeles Crest forest. There was water in the ridge that ran west to east from the ocean to the Mojave. And where there was water, there would be nesters.

The bat wing veered off suddenly, left wingtip dragging in spite of Thomas' efforts to right it. Drakkar shouted in Blade's ear, "We're going down!"

Blade's reply was torn out of earshot by a wind that was suddenly across and against them instead of being behind them. He could see the darkness of evergreen blanketing brown hills below them rushing up. He threw himself on the stick full weight as the raider came crashing down.

Drakkar sat up and peered out of the wreckage. A tree limb gave under the raider as he did. He spat out a mouthful of blood from a split lip and grinned. "Any landing you can walk away from is a good one."

"I'll remember that while I'm picking pine needles out of my ass." Thomas threw his legs out of the fuselage of the raider and hoisted the rest of himself over gingerly. The stand of trees that had broken their fall, and done a fairly good job of demolishing the wind raider, shivered under his weight. He was still a good six to eight feet off the ground and reminded himself that now was no time to risk a broken ankle. He looped an arm about a tree limb and swung himself down.

Drakkar threw down the packs and rifles before joining him. He shrugged on his pack. "Any idea where we are?"

"A good idea."

"Great." Drakkar sucked at his split lip for a second. "Then things are going according to plan."

"Plan?" said Thomas as he shouldered his pack.

The Mojavan looked at him. "You do have a plan?"

"Naturally. I'm going to find a nester, kill him, take his horse and ride east. You're welcome to accompany me, but you've got to find and kill your own nester. Make sure he has a horse or mule before you do it, though. We don't have time for wasted effort."

Drakkar stared at him a minute. Then those dark jewel-blue eyes blinked. "You're kidding, right?"

"Do I look like I'm kidding? How the hell do you think we're going to get out of the woods? I have one goal and one goal only—to get to the dean as soon as possible, slit his throat, and put an end to this foolishness. I'll wade through as many nesters as I have to do it."

Drakkar absorbed the words. He shook his head. "I thought when you were appointed delegate. . . ."

"I don't have time and neither does Denethan. The nesters respect one thing and one thing only: strength. They won't cut slack for anybody who can't keep up. They have no respect for community welfare. They're outcasts who live the way they do because they chose to. They're not going to let me walk up to the dean and parlay just because I ask them to." Thomas adjusted the weight of his pack. "Coming with me? We need to get mounts as soon as we can. I figure we have a day of riding ahead of us."

"Where are we going?"

"Just beyond the Vaults, slightly north and east. There's a plains area that sort of fades into the Mojave—"

"I know it," Drakkar said.

"All right. Logically, that's where the dean will pull back to establish a front line. His back is to the Vaults if he has to retreat and I'll bet the old bastard has another tunnel entrance or two we didn't find, in case he has to hide to save his ass. The nesters will bivouac at the reservoir where we camped, sweep down off the mountain, and attack."

Drakkar fell into step with Thomas' long-striding pace. "What makes you think my father will come that far out of the desert after him?"

"A couple of things can happen. Either the nesters will fall back, feinting a retreat, pulling the Mojave troops after them— or Denethan will be chasing bait."

"Bait?"

Thomas nodded with satisfaction that the youth was panting a little to keep up with him. He repeated, "Bait. He'll have the longshippers hung out to dry." He paused, looking up. "It'll be raining tonight. It should tail off in the morning. Say your prayers, Drakkar. Your dad is probably up to his ass fighting nesters right now. They'll disengage when the rain hits. And then he'll go after the bait."

Drakkar trotted in silence for a few minutes, then he asked, "How do you plan to get to the dean in all of this?"

"One nester at a time, if necessary. But I'll get to him." Blade's voice was grim.

Drakkar stopped talking, hard put to keep up with the pace. If Blade was going to run him into the ground, he began to see the logic in obtaining a mount as soon as possible.

The dull clanging on the shuttle's hull eventually stopped. Willem Marshall left the lounge, was gone a few minutes, and then returned.

Dusty knew it had been the dean who'd come calling. She

could sense the man's presence even through the thick, space-protective skin of the vehicle.

"What did he want?"

"To remind us we're parked on a dry lake bed. He says this part of the desert is subject to flash flooding—that the rainstorms are fairly intense. He recommends we move the shuttle to higher ground and closer to the L.A. basin."

Dubois had ducked into the lounge to see what was happening. His face creased into his usual sardonic mask. "And what does he think we're going to do?" he said. "Fire her up and fly over?"

"Actually," the commander said, "we've a lot of use left in the ATVs. We could tow her."

"In the dark? In the rain?"

"We've got landing lights. The solars are strong enough to stay powered up. The possibility of flash floods does worry me." He faced Dusty. "Get your rain gear on. You're one of our best drivers."

"Will do." As she turned to sprint for the cabins, Marshall could be heard telling Dubois to batten the hatches and alert Reynolds for driving as well.

It was an all night, nine-hour drive. Klegg and Dubois spelled her twice, but she took the main brunt of the tow on the port side, Reynolds with Marshall and Palchek spelling her to the starboard. The shuttle rolled behind them, an immense white behemoth, cutting through wind and rain and mud with the difficulty of its size and weight. She had swallowed more than her share of the mire when the sun came out and the pounding rain began to let up. The horizon of the Angeles Crest Mountains was illumined in front of them, dark green from the fringe of pine and golden brown from the dried grasses and brush reaching up to its crown. In the brilliant morning light, the mountains did look as though they were gold, rising out of the desert.

She braked the ATV to a halt, coordinating with Reynolds. They had climbed a small rise, a gradual grade to a butte overlooking a plain now scoured with their wheel marks. The shuttle hatch opened and Marshall climbed down. It had taken them the better part of an hour to make the mesa.

Marshall scratched his head. "I didn't think we were going to make this last haul."

She shrugged, easing the tension from her shoulders. "We could have left her down below if we couldn't have. Nice view."

He looked about. "At least we're going to see all comers," he admitted. Dark clouds were sweeping away from the fringe and the air felt fresh and clean.

Mud caked her silver enviro suit and rain gear from head to toe. He put out a finger and wiped it across her face. "That stuff is going to dry on."

"Got enough water for a bath?"

He shook his head. She knew ship stores had been falling. Dusty pushed back her poncho hood. Her hair was sodden and limp upon her shoulders.

The dean rode up and dismounted. Pleasure split his face from ear to ear. "Excellent," he said. "You have a good eye for strategic placement." He eyed her. "Dirty work, however."

Reynolds joined them. Her muscular form conveyed an aura of sexuality, even slathered with the mud. She shivered as she looked out over the expanse, however. Dusty realized she had not yet conquered her fear of wide open spaces.

The dean said suddenly, "There is a reservoir not far from here. Ketchum could chaperone you for bathing and cleanup. You could test the water if you need to lay in supplies."

Even under the mud, Reynolds paled. She shook her head. Dusty said, "I'm in."

Palchek and Dubois nodded enthusiastically. Ketchum dismounted his horse. Dubois jumped into the driver's seat of the ATV and the rest of them climbed in. A look passed between the nester and the dean that Dusty caught as the nester occupied the rear seats with her. She wondered what could have happened to cause it.

She shrugged it off as the ATV jolted into motion. "You're going to the woods," she shouted forward into Dubois' ear.

"Good. Then we'll take the scenic route!"

Chapter 33

Marshall sat in the captain's chair, going over the computer set being read out to him. He checked and rechecked it, and then mulled it over. The numbers didn't lie. He had just enough fuel to make the thrust necessary to get the shuttle off the ground and into an orbit. From there, he would have very little maneuverability to actually dock with the *Challenger*. Sun would have to do all the fancy work to pick them. But it could be done. Maybe. If the thrusters were burning cleanly enough and if there was absolutely no waste of fuel so they could burn long enough to get the payload up.

He was running the numbers through again when Reynolds ducked her head in. She was toweling her long brunette hair off. "The ATV's back. There's been a problem."

There'd been more than a problem. The front grill was bent and one of the fender shields had been peeled back like a fruit rind. Palchek was in tears and Dubois looked uncharacteristically repentent. The nester Ketchum moved back as Marshall caught up with them.

"What the hell happened? And where's Dusty?"

Palchek blew his nose lustily as Dubois lifted a stricken face.

"We lost her, Commander," Dubois got out.

"Lost her? What the hell are you talking about? You left her in the mountains?"

Palchek dissolved into rasping sobs. Dubois gave him an annoyed look and climbed slowly out of the ATV. "Willem, she's *gone*."

Reynolds had followed Marshall out of the ATV. Goldstone

and Colby flanked her. "You mean she's dead?" the mechanic asked.

Dubois nodded. He leaned against the battered ATV as if it were his anchor.

"God." Colby's voice was barely audible.

"Where's the body?" her husband said.

"We couldn't retrieve it," Palchek finally got out. His face and nose were swollen red and contorted. Marshall finally noticed that not all of it was from crying—he'd been horribly bruised about the left side of his lanky face and Dubois was favoring his left wrist and ankle.

"What happened?" the commander repeated.

"We went to the reservoir. The water tests good, by the way. We washed off, kicked back, then Dusty wanted to go exploring. So we drove upriver, one of the tributaries to the reservoir. She said—" Dubois' voice caught. He swallowed and went on. "She said we'd love it, seeing a real river, in a real forest, after a real storm. The ATV was handling well. We cut across country once we got into some rough ground. The ATV hit a boulder and bounced to a halt in a riverbed. We all got out, got some deadwood for leverage—there wasn't any problem. The river was fairly deep and swept downstream. Dusty said it was beautiful. She could hear a waterfall below us, around the bend. Anyway, we all put our backs to getting the ATV out. That's when it happened."

Kerry had come down the shuttle ramp and approached them. She interrupted saying to Palchek, "You're hurt. Commander, let me take him in and get him quiet. He could have a concussion."

Marshall nodded. Dubois waited until Palchek had limped off with the medic's help. Then he said, "We almost had the ATV out. Then one of the tree limbs broke. The ATV reared up and rolled over, right over the top of us. Dusty went under. She was swept into the deep water immediately. The ATV came down on top of me and Palchek—he was underneath, too, pinned down in the shallows. Ketchum—" Dubois faltered.

The nester looked to the dean who had been silent during the entire exchange. The dean gave a nearly imperceptible nod. Ketchum said, "I heard her head hit rock. I could not catch her. The water carried her around the bend. I could help these two, so I did."

Dubois took a deep breath. "We couldn't find her body. We drove slowly downstream. There was a series of falls—unconscious, she must have drowned and her body swept off—god, Marshall, it happened so quickly."

Reynolds said, "I'll find it."

Willem shook his head. Heavily, he said, "These things can happen. We've other problems now. Dubois, go find Kerry and get that leg looked to. The dean tells me we've got a war on our doorsteps. More of those lizard people are massing. He's sent for his nation to protect us. By tomorrow morning, we'll be up to our chins in trouble. Dusty would understand, I think. In the meantime, we have some major decisions to make."

The dean looked curiously at the commander, but bowed graciously, saying, "We shall leave you to your grief." He took Ketchum by the elbow and steered him to their encampment.

Marshall watched them go. He put out a shoulder for Dubois to lean on. He said only, "It's no mistake that we're here when and where the dean needs us. Whatever decision we make, we're going to have to watch that man."

Air trapped between her enviro suit and skin kept her somewhat buoyed up as the water swept her along. She gritted her teeth and swam as well as she could, but it was all she could do to keep her head above the white water. She'd gone rafting down the Colorado once, she and her sister Lisa, and this was mild compared to that, but as the water dragged her down again, she knew it was just as deadly.

Her chest hurt where the nester had slammed into her with the blunt end of the log he'd been using for a lever, and her right ear felt as though it had been torn ragged by her collision with a rock. She bobbed in the water, spitting out silt and foam, her throat sore. She wasn't going to make it. Cold panic swept her. She began to thrash as the river got rougher and her head went under. Dusty came up screaming. Her voice rang off the sheered-off cliffs and trees. She caught a blurred kaleidosope of wilderness and knew there was no one to hear her.

The son of a bitch had done her in. He'd made a massive heave, overturning the ATV right on top of Dubois and Palchek, pivoted, and slammed the end of the log into her, sending her head over heels out of the shallows and into deep water. It had been no accident. As she'd struck the boulder, she'd seen an expression of sad satisfaction pass over the brutal face. Then the water'd taken her and she'd been too dazed to do anything but try to stay afloat.

Dubois and Palchek must be dead as well. What had the nester wanted? Their fantastic weapons aboard the ATV? There was nothing on the vehicle but a tool box and a flare gun. And, truthfully, the flares were probably decades old, from the last exploration and none too reliable.

No. She'd seen the look pass between the tracker and his chieftain. The dean had wanted them out of the way.

Dusty coughed, spit out water, and bobbed to the surface in an eddying pool of quiet water. The lack of current surprised her momentarily. She began to tread water and caught her breath, coughing and trying to breathe through a chest almost too sore to respire. Then she vomited, dirty water spewing from her, and coughed again.

Clawing her hair from her eyes, Dusty looked about. The back eddy of current she swam in was not still, as she'd thought, though the movement was very subtle. She looked downstream and saw the river come to an abrupt end in midair. The rush of pounding water filled her hearing. That was another waterfall, and not a minor drop like the first one or two she'd been swept down.

Her arms and legs felt like mush, each weighing hundreds of pounds. If she could sink down and touch bottom, and kick her way to shore. . . . Far from shore or rock, she was slowly being carried her way to almost certain death. If she survived the drop, she knew she would be too weak to stay afloat.

The quiet pool began to pick up speed. She whirled about lazily. She could feel the change in the water's temperature. Soon she'd be in the mainstream again—and gone.

Dusty yelled. "Help! Dear god, somebody!" Her voice echoed through the trees bent over the rain-swollen river. Then, with a tremendous push as though shoved through, she was in the white-water current again, flailing for her life. She rode the crest of foam and spray and felt a dizzying second of weightlessness before she went over.

"What's that?" Thomas pulled up his scrawny excuse for a horse and came to a stop between the trees.

Drakkar had been steadily drumming a quirt cut from a tree

branch to keep his mount going. It stopped so suddenly he fell forward on its neck. The horse blinked three of its eyes in rebuke. The fourth was white-clouded and useless. He could hear a river cutting its way through the wilderness ahead of them, perhaps even the roar of a waterfall. Water sounded good about now. He said, "I could use a drink."

Blade had not stopped listening alertly. Then Drakkar heard it, too, the high thin scream of someone in great fear. It was drowned out by the sound of the river.

Blade kicked his mount into a lunging run. With a curse, Drakkar took his switch to his mount to keep up. The two of them burst out of the woods at the edge of a massive pool below a falls whose water boiled up in a fine white spray. They reined their ponies to a plunging halt at the river bank's steep edge.

"There!" Blade pointed. Crimson floated on the pool's whirling surface, dragged down and surfaced again. Rags or perhaps hair . . . he kicked off his horse, shed his boots, scarf and jacket. "I'm going down."

"You idiot! You'll drown, too. Look at that current!"

Thomas' gills fluttered in the coolish air. "I have something of an advantage," he said, poised himself on the river bank and did a stylish, curving dive into the center of the maelstrom. He hit the water with a clean cut and disappeared.

He surfaced with his arms full of silver, like an immense trout, silver and crimson. Drakkar reacted alertly, pulling a rope off the nester saddle and going down on his stomach to pull them up. Thomas put the inert body in a sling of the rope's loop, shouting, "She's not breathing!"

Drakkar pulled the rope up until he could catch the body with his hands and hauled her up on her stomach and left her facedown in the bruised grass while he tossed the loop back down to Thomas' reach. He returned to the still form, but she had begun to move feebly and the best he could do for her was hold her head slightly as she vomited out tons of river water and silt.

Thomas squatted down next to him and gently moved her thick, curling auburn hair away from her face as if she was ill. When she stopped, she said feebly, "Don't just let me lie here."

The two men picked her up and moved her to higher ground, where the grass in the shade was still sweet and clean. Drakkar left to gather firewood and hobble the horses.

She lay on the pillow of his leather jacket, eyes open, look-ing up to the sky as if contemplating it, her chest working like a bellows. When at last her breathing calmed, she looked back to him. "Thank you," she said and coughed again, belching air fiercely. Her color began to come back, revealing a delicate complexion. She found a fastening in that marvelous silver skin of hers and peeled it away from her neck. Underneath, he saw a damp shirt clinging to shapely young breasts. Though her body was hidden from him, he saw a young woman strangely fresh and unaffected. "Thank you," she repeated.

He liked her voice. He thought guiltily of Lady and found himself flushing. "You're welcome," he said, "but it takes a lot of water to drown me."

She looked at him then, really looked at him, and the color bled from her face. "Oh, my god. You've got gills."

He had his white scarf loosely wrapped about his hand, but something in her voice brought out the defiance in him. He re-fused to wrap them from sight. "God has nothing to do with it," he said stiffly. "And we'd both be dead if I hadn't."

"No . . . you don't understand. . . ." Dusty braced her back against his jacket and a tree stump. "You're one of *them*."

"Them? I'm Sir Thomas Blade, of Orange County. That them?" He shut his mouth with a snap. He sounded like Art Bartholomew in all his pompous glory. He reached out and touched the lapel of her suit. It was like nothing he'd ever felt before. He looked up. "And you must be one of them." His gaze locked with smoky gray eyes. Intelligence fairly danced in them. She was no nester or even a Mojavan. "You're from the longship."

She sucked her breath in. "How did you—"

"If you've been with the nesters, you must think us very primitive." He moved back a step and reached for his boots. If she decided to bolt, he wasn't going to run after her barefooted. "We're survivors, not leftovers."

"I didn't mean—" the woman stopped. She took a deep breath. "Yes, I'm from the longship. I'm Gemma Barlowe, but my friends and saviors call me Dusty."

There was a crackle of dried branches behind them. Drakkar said, "And my enemies call me Drakkar."

She couldn't hide the fear that sprang into her face though

her hands went up to stifle the noise she made. Thomas turned toward Drakkar.

"Quit scaring the locals," he said.

Drakkar made his mocking half-bow. "Sorry. They call me the dragon boy at home." His crest was up, though what had alerted him, Thomas couldn't tell. The plumage caught the slanting rays of sunlight and was a dazzling display of blue and teal.

"Are those . . . is that . . . yours? Instead of hair?"

"Everybody should have feathers instead of hair. Insults, like water off a duck's back, roll off." Drakkar began to stack wood into a base for a fire. Thomas was not sure if he read arrogance or hurt in the young man's features.

The young woman brought her hands all the way down from her face. "I don't know if I'm dead or alive," she said, finally. "I can't tell."

Thomas stood up, then, and wrapped his scarf about his gills as the wind took on a chill. He carefully took his jacket from behind her, bracing her against the tree trunk instead. As he shrugged the leather coat on, her eyes brightened.

"You're the one!"

Drakkar lit the fire, keeping his silence. Thomas watched him begin to prepare a pot of tea.

"The one who saved you, yes."

"No, no." Dusty got her legs under her, shapely despite being hidden by her silver shell. "The one in the drawing. God, I'm so stupid. I saw the pictures the boy drew. . . ." She looked up at him keenly. "Was he yours? Your son, I mean?"

Thomas only knew of one artist she might have encountered. "Almond eyes, hair as dark as ink."

"Yes, that's him." She was on her feet now, though shaky. "You bastard. You sent them to attack us? You sent them to a slaughterhouse!"

"I didn't send them anywhere," Thomas said cooly. "They were mappers, Surveyors. And if they attacked you, they had a damn good reason. And no, Jeong wasn't my son." Although, and he knew it even as he said it, they'd all been his sons, in a way. "Did you . . . see them die?"

She nodded, miserably. "They were just kids . . . we burned the bodies. *They* burned the bodies. Ketchum wouldn't even let me keep the notebook."

Drakkar had put the tea pot in a frame over the fire. He faced them both. "Who's Ketchum?"

"The nester who dumped me in the river. I swear he meant to. The dean told him to. . . ." Dusty pushed her hair behind her ear and moved toward the warmth of the fire. Thomas grabbed her by the wrist and spun her on her heel.

"What do you know about the dean?"

"He met us at the landing. He showed us the wreckage of the Vaults. He's been the only one here who's asked questions first before attacking." Dusty made a quick move, releasing herself as quickly as he'd grabbed her. An expression passed over his face that she could not read . . . approval? She gathered herself, ready to sprint for one of those sorry excuses for a horse.

"The dean blew up the Vaults himself, though granted we were all involved in a bit of a fracas. I don't have time to apologize to you or tell you the history of my people, or the nesters, or the Mojavans—" again, that half-bow from Drakkar, "or convince you what a son of a bitch you're dealing with. But you will take me to him."

She lifted her chin. "Or else what?"

Drakkar laughed softly. "I wouldn't argue with him. He's the executioner for the Seven Counties."

Chapter 34

Marshall called the *Challenger* again, just before dawn. Dubois, on lookout, confirmed that there were two armies camped on the plains. Sun looked tired as he came on-screen.

"What is it, Willem?"

"I want to bring us back, Commander." He quickly outlined his idea, painstakingly checked and rechecked. Dakin waited until he was done and then pain creased the normally placid face.

"No, Marshall. I can't let you do it."

"Sun, we don't have anything to come home to. These are savages living down here—savages at each others' throats. We don't even know if the lizard men think like humans."

"Save your fuel. Make a survey flight and land elsewhere. You've got whole continents to look over. Find us a home."

Marshall felt his anxiety crowding him. He didn't like losing Dusty without cause and he hated being in the middle of a war, even though he could technically just lock his doors and wait until they destroyed each other. "I can't do that and still get back."

"You were never intended to come back," Dakin reminded him gently. "You volunteered for a one-way mission."

"I volunteered for a one-way mission because I'm one hell of a pilot and I knew I could get the shuttle down with fuel to spare."

Sun massaged the bridge of his nose. He sighed. "Willem, we've begun breaking down. Slowly, like the *Gorbachev* and the *Maggie*. You may have nothing to come back to. Heredia's brought the *Mayflower* over, but she can only take on so many passengers. We're going to have to abandon ship. You're going to have to find us a place to land before then."

His chest felt as though it were packed with ice. "How long have you got?"

Dakin smiled wearily. "We don't know."

Marshall put his hand up, to turn the screen off, saying, "I'll hurry." Dakin faded from sight. Willem muttered, "Shit!" and sat at the deadened screen for long minutes.

The dean camped by the belly of the shuttle, claiming it for protection as much as anything else. He emerged in the first gray-purple hours of dawn and took a deep breath. Ketchum had been sitting nester-style by a waning campfire and stood up to greet him.

His nation had claimed the mesa top. Below, at the foot of the gradual rise, he could see the campfires of the Mojavans. He rubbed his hands together with immense satisfaction. The longshippers would help him remove the Mojavans. Then nothing could stand between him and the counties. Nothing Blade could say or do would save or protect any of his people. Then the dean would be free to return to his people, the longshippers, true humans, and the nesters would serve as the brute strength they would need to develop the earth. Many hands and strong backs.

Ketchum had been staring into his face as though reading his thoughts. He turned his face away as the dean looked keenly at him. *Still animal,* thought the man. *Still unable to meet my stare.*

The nester said flatly, "Do we fight?"

"Undoubtedly. But we don't attack first. Let the Mojavans come to us."

An uphill offense would slaughter most of the troops early on. The dean smiled in anticipation. He laughed at Ketchum's hesitation. "Don't worry so much. I have allies in those troops. They'll carry the fight to us. I have the longshippers in the palm of my hand. They'll defend us if necessary. Today, we will carve a hole in the gut of the Mojavan nation, one that Denethan will not be able to survive. Then, the counties. Water, Ketchum. All the water and fertile land we deserve."

The shuttle began to open with a faint whine, the ramp coming down. The dean smiled broadly and went to greet them.

Marshall had worn his dress suit, beige uniform contrasting sharply with his coffee-colored skin. He was flanked by Reynolds and Dubois. He inclined his chin off the mesa, in the direction of the Mojavan army.

"What is this?"

"Strength in numbers, Commander Marshall." The dean brightened his expression. "We can always hope they came to parlay."

"And if not?"

"Then," and the dean bowed graciously, "my clans and I will defend you to our last man."

"What do you suggest we do?"

"Ah," the dean said. "I suggest we wait and let them make the first move."

A sharp whistle broke the morning air. Ketchum bounded to the edge of the mesa, looked down across the plain toward the mountains. There was sudden activity among the Mojavans.

"What is it?" the dean asked sharply. He had given no signals yet.

"I don't know. Two riders, I think. The Mojavans are giving way to them."

The dean, joined by Willem and the crew, left the shelter of the shuttle to watch. Reynolds held a pair of binoculars out to Marshall even as the dean lifted his from under cover of his robes and they scanned the plains below. The nesters moved restlessly about their campfires.

"My god!" Marshall said. "He's got Dusty with them!"

On the grass plains, the Mojavans were getting to their knees, bowing low before their prince, son of their ruler. He acknowledged their obeisance with a salute of his own. It was his shrill whistle which had pierced the stillness after dawn. Halfway through the ranks of the army, he reined to a halt.

"Shankar is dead!" Drakkar said. "His followers are known to me. Those of you within these troops have but one chance left to live. There will be great happenings this day. Follow my orders and live. Betray me and betray your very existence!"

In one throat, the Mojavans roared back. "DRAK-kar!"

Dusty stirred in Thomas' arms. "A bit feudal, isn't it?"

"Feudal?"

"Kings, peasants, that sort of thing."

"Oh," he said. His voice buzzed pleasantly in his chest. "Like Macbeth."

"*Very* like Macbeth," Dusty answered. "Now what do we do?"

"We hope that the dean makes the nesters let us get within striking distance. He should, with you as hostage, even if only to get me close enough to kill."

"He wants you that bad?" Dusty asked.

Thomas laughed mirthlessly. "Oh, yes. He wants me that bad. And I want him."

She squirmed a little, uncomfortable on the horse. They had been riding double most of the night to reach the mesa and her bumps and bruises from the river were sharp as thorns. She could not have told either man the correct direction, but they'd recognized her description of the site. There was a fatalism in Thomas Blade that she could only describe as predestiny. She thought he would have known his way here regardless.

Drakkar looked at them, his crest full and his face lit by a savage joy. "They'll let us through now."

Thomas said laconically, "All the same, watch your back, boy," as he reined past Drakkar.

The Mojavan prince took pause for just a moment, then rode after them. Thomas had been holding his longknife comfortably at her chest. Now he raised it to her throat as they paused at the mesa's base.

"Be very careful," he said. "It's got an extremely sharp edge."

Dusty could feel its prick at her skin, where the enviro suit could not protect her. "I'll remember that," she answered.

"Do that."

She felt his broad chest inhale deeply. "Commander Marshall!" he bellowed out. "I have someone of importance to you. Give me passage to come up and talk with you."

Marshall had been looking intently through the binoculars. He knew the man had Dusty. He lowered them long enough to look at the dean. "Who the hell is that?"

"That," the dean answered tensely, "is Sir Thomas Blade." He lowered his glasses as well. Ketchum inclined his head and evaporated at an invisible signal from the dean. Then he turned to Marshall as the commander spoke again.

"Will he kill her?"

"He," the dean said flatly, "is capable of slitting her throat and eviscerating her before you can draw three breaths."

Marshall took one of those breaths. He studied Dusty through the glasses. Her face had a placid, resigned expression to it.

"Let him come up," the dean urged. "I've got Ketchum placed with a rifle. Get the girl loose and we'll drop him in his tracks."

At this, Marshall dropped his glasses and turned full face to look at the dean. "Just who is this man and how badly do you want him?"

The dean hesitated, then also dropped his binoculars upon his chest, letting them dangle from their cord. "This is the man," he said, "who destroyed the College Vaults. This is the man who sent a party of children to destroy us. This is the man who, because he wears a mark upon his forehead, can frighten an entire nation of nester clans. Don't be fooled by whatever he says."

Yet Marshall hesitated. Shipborn justice was swift and sure, with the threat of being airlocked to those who trespassed the law. Quibbles were minor, though sometimes debated through generations. But the crimes of their ancestors—rape, murder, maiming—were not among their sins. He felt like Reynolds trying to deal with her fear of wide open spaces. *If this is my fellow man,* he thought, *I am frightened to death of the consequences.* He remembered the *Challenger* and shouted back, "Let her go, first."

The rider's horse took the last bucking stride and halted at the edge of the mesa. Marshall could see Dusty clearly now, with the blade of the knife to her white throat. Her hair, already the color of fresh blood, hung about her face. The man who held her had taken in the number of nesters upon the mesa and placed him and most of the Away Team as well. Marshall felt his intent gaze sweep past him a second time, linger on the dean, and return.

The commander thought he'd seen everything the shattered Earth had to offer when the lizard men had attacked, but the young man who rode to Blade's flank stopped him in surprise. He wore a feathered headdress, or perhaps it was part of him, and as his horse came to a halt beside Blade's, he stripped off his gloves, revealing spurs as large as talons on his wrist.

The dean made a noise between his teeth and turned away from Marshall.

"Who the hell is that?"

"I'm not sure," the dean said. "I think that is Denethan's son. His heir apparent. Evolution beyond the reptile, eh?"

Blade moved in his saddle. "Seen enough?" he called out. "Let us approach and you'll get the girl back. She's a little waterlogged, but I've seen worse." He smiled tightly at the dean.

Marshall cleared his throat. He said to the dean, "Let them come in."

With a glitter deep in his hooded eyes, the dean held up an arm and waved the riders closer. The nesters were already moving back, however, and Marshall could hear the whispered words, "The Marked Man. The mark of Shastra," as the nester warriors retreated to their original defensive front, protecting the mesa from the troops below.

The commander said, "Everybody get aboard the shuttle."

Reynolds began a protest.

"*Everybody*, I said. I'll bring Dusty in."

Reluctantly, they left him alone. The sun had come up enough, at the shuttle's back, to cast its shadow and he stood in the tip of it. He knew the dean would use him if he could. He had not yet figured out how.

The riders came within ten paces of Marshall. He could see the tiny line of blood welling up from Dusty's throat. He wondered if she even knew she'd been cut.

"Put the knife down," he said.

The man in the brown leather jacket with a white scarf wrapped and tucked in about his neck relaxed the knife blade a touch but shook his head with a rueful smile. "I intend to ride back out," he said. He looked Marshall up and down. "So you're human."

The commander was startled. "And you're not?"

"No. None of us are, really. You're the foundation stock. We're the selective adaptives." He reached up with a free hand and ripped away the scarf. "I'm gilled. Drakkar here displays attributes which astonish even those of us used to the aberrations of the eleven year plague—a virus which mutates us beyond imagination. I will not apologize for our lack of purity."

Marshall looked to Dusty who remained placid and quiet within the man's armhold, most unlike her. There was more here than met the eye. She did not look up at him. He heard the dean move restively at his side. The dean whispered, "Don't listen to him. The Countians have telepathic powers. He can sway a mob, he can convince you."

Marshall frowned. "Why are you here?"

"To bring you back one of your own. And to convey to you a welcome from the Seven Counties where we try very hard, with sometimes spectacular failures, to be civilized."

"A civilized man does not hold a knife to the throat of another."

"Not even in the midst of two armies?" Blade's thin smile flickered on and off. "I must remember that." He lowered his knife hand from Dusty's throat and rested it lightly on the horn of the saddle. Marshall didn't feel much better. The knife point was now just below her rib cage, where an upward thrust could send it into the heart.

Thomas now said, "You were met by a scoundrel, Commander Marshall, a man who self-destructed an invaluable repository of human knowledge because he did not wish to share it with mutants. A man whose obsessive desire to gain vengeance led him to enslave an entire people. Nesters are free people. They are outcasts who have chosen to live outside our community. Because of their choice, they are often contaminated. Mutated further than any being should have to suffer. They are often deprived of pure water and careless about the pollution of the water they do have access to. What you see around you—those you see around you—have chosen their own punishment by moving outside county boundaries. There's little I could do to them to make them more miserable."

Blade raised his voice. "But I could enslave them with promises, if I wanted to. Drive them off their campgrounds and mold them into an army. Promise them water rights and farms and herds once the Countians are driven away—those who are left alive, that is."

"You lie," the dean said impatiently. He, too, raised his voice. "He lies!"

"Do I? I was sent here by the new Director of Water and Power. He wants to remind you of your clan treaties. He wants to sit with you and forge new treaties if you're unhappy. He wants to ask why you're so eager to fight with the Mojavans and with us." Thomas' voice dropped and he looked at Marshall again. "And I was given permission to remove any obstacle in my way."

Ketchum moved out of the shadow of the shuttle, where he had been all but obscured. His rifle lay across the cradle of his arm. He said, "Is this true? New treaties?"

"Yes. We're aware that some of us have encroached your pastures, taken away your wells, raided the weaker clans. We're human, more or less. We're all on this land together. We will not deny any man or woman water."

Dusty moved slightly. She lifted her eyes to look upon Ketchum. "You tried to kill me," she said.

The nester went to one knee on the ground and bowed his head. "I was told to," he said.

With a curse, the dean kicked the tracker in the side of the head, grabbing up the rifle as it rolled free. Swinging about, he fired. It was a weapon from the shuttle and the bullet struck the nester pony in the shoulder. The horse reared up with a scream, Dusty falling free, and the horse collapsed as it returned to ground, its shattered leg failing it.

Blade was already off it and running. He threw a morning star which zithered through the air, tearing the cloth of the dean's robe through the flank as he ran. But it did not faze the man himself as he tried to gain the shuttle ramp.

Dusty cried out, "Marshall! The shuttle!"

A whistle split the air. The cries of a thousand voices rang out as the armies poised to war began their attacks. Drakkar hit the ground beside Dusty, hauling her up by the elbow and throwing her at Marshall's feet.

Dubois and Reynolds, in the shuttle, began pulling the ramp up manually. The dean caught the lip of it, firing as he went in. Reynolds went down with a crimson blossom and a shrill cry. The dean paused long enough to club Dubois with the rifle stock as he passed him.

Blade jumped and caught the ramp. He hung for a moment unnoticed and levered himself over the edge. He could hear screams and shots within the vehicle. Unfamiliar with it, he could only move in the direction of the mayhem.

But the dean was familiar with it. Familiar enough to know that the thrusters were positioned toward the main front where the Mojavans would rush the mesa. All he had to do was fire them up and his war would be done, a thousand men wiped out in the blast. The nesters and longshippers who died here also would be martyrs to his cause.

He could explain everything to the longship once this was over.

A shadowy figure blocked the corridor. The dean fired, it toppled. He stepped over the bleeding body, going aft, always seeking the main bridge. With a triumphant cry, he found it.

Drakkar put his body between the girl and the commander. He pulled a vial from his ammunition belt and reloaded his rifle. He fired once, carefully, putting a wall of flame between the nesters and himself. Ketchum had gotten to his knees, using the massive front tires of the shuttle for protection.

Dusty reached for Drakkar's arm. "Where's Thomas?"

"He's gone after the dean. They're both in the shuttle."

She felt sick to her stomach. "Marshall—"

He took her in his arms. "Are you all right?"

She could only nod. Smoke and blood filled the air as well as the cries of the victorious and the dying. And then the shuttle roared to life.

"My god," said the commander. "He knows how to fire the thrusters!"

The vehicle began to shudder as it warmed up. It trembled, straining for life, and its tires began to slowly turn. Ketchum was caught under them. His cry of pain burst into silence as he disappeared.

Blade stalked after the dean. He found one body, checked it, found a steady pulse, and stepped over it. Then as he passed an alcove, he saw a woman pressed into it, her hands covering her face in desperation. He clapped his free hand upon her wrists.

"Who are you?"

"K—kerry."

He thought over what Dusty had told him, frowning. Then, "The medic? A Healer?"

"Yes."

"Down that way, behind me, there's someone who needs you. But first . . . did you see him? Which way did he go?" The gigantic vessel trembled about him, thrumming with energy.

The woman's eyes got big. "The bridge," she said. "The controls!"

"Which way?" Blade said, not too patiently.

She pointed with a trembling hand. He went.

The dean had torn off his black robes. Beneath them he wore a simple shirt and jeans and boots—the shirt straining across his back muscles and across his flanks where handles of fat still rode. He heard Thomas' whisper-soft entry into the cabin.

"Ah," the man said. "I should have known." He reached for the rifle resting against an instrument panel.

"I should have killed you," Blade said, "the day Charles Warden came home and had his gills cut out because you made him feel ashamed of them."

The dean smiled. "And I did try to have you killed. But now I have you to thank for this. So perhaps it was meant you should die today instead of those years ago."

"I think," Blade responded, "that I can throw this knife before you can pick up that rifle."

The dean did not lose his smile. "I have no intention of picking up the rifle yet," he said. "I have an army to fry first." With a harsh laugh, he moved several levers on the board.

The shuttle roared out, erupting with power, shuddering with a thunderous noise. Thomas thought he could hear high-pitched screams under the blast. He moved, but the dean had sprung back from the instrument panel, a longknife in his hand, poised to fight.

"I am Gerald Conklin," the dean said. "And I have lived and fought in more *dojos* than you could ever imagine. I was alive when the Earth died. I let my frustrations handicap me, cloak me in fat, but adversity has taken all that away from me. If you want me, come and get me."

Chapter 35

He had good moves. Thomas had to give him that. He thought he saw his last vision of Lady pass before his eyes with the first pass of the knife blade. In the cramped quarters, the dean had the reach on him. He defended, moved, and retreated. The shuttle continued to tremble underneath their feet, its roar muted.

They both attacked at once, high, and the longknives clashed. Blade could hear the complaint of his edge nocking upon the other. They both showed their teeth and shoved each over backward.

Then the dean moved swiftly. He had a feral grace that Thomas could only admire, and fear, in the close quarters. He felt himself backing back out in the corridor where the dean might still have allies behind Thomas. The notion made him careless. The dean connected.

His jacket saved most of the flesh of his underarm. Thomas bit back his pain and said only, "Bad hit, that. Not well placed to blood me."

"That will come," the dean said. He was breathing heavily. Sweat dotted his forehead.

Thomas found something to smile about. The dean might remember his moves very well—but his body was not used to exerting them.

He tossed his knife to his other hand. "Is this a fair fight? Because if it is, then I ought to tell you I'm ambidextrous—and that I use throwing stars as well as knives." He ran his hand under his collar and filled it with the weapon.

The dean's hooded eyes narrowed. Their color stayed flat and dark. "You're a freak," he said. "Something that should never have been brought to life. I'm surprised your mother didn't strangle you the moment you passed her knees—"

Thomas threw. The dean moved incredibly quickly. The wicked device passed him and sliced deep into the cabin well where it stuck. Before Thomas could react to the miss, the dean rushed him.

The man collared him with his longer reach and Blade nearly panicked to find the knife at his throat.

"Stop," he cried, and the dean hesitated. He could feel the wild thunder of the man's beating heart against his back.

"Not in here," Thomas said. "I'm the Marked Man. The nesters will have to *see* you kill me—or they'll never follow you anywhere again. Never." The edge bit into his throat.

Then the dean stopped. "You're right." He began to shove Thomas down the corridor, back toward the ramp.

The wounded in the corridor had been removed, bright, shiny slick spots marking their presence. Thomas saw them, but the dean did not, intent upon the nearly closed ramp. He slammed his side into the controls.

The ramp began to open. As it did, the sound of warfare reached them clearly. The doorway opened onto a scene of slaughter, hand-to-hand combat, men bent at impossible angles, fighting for their lives. The dean let out a harsh, wordless cry and the fighters stopped. They turned to see what was happening.

Thomas threw his weight to the side. The dean slipped into a pool of crimson, going to his knees. Blade jumped him, going for the knife, and the two of them tumbled down the ramp to the ground. He wrestled the knife away and faced the dean barehanded.

The dean let out a bellow like a bull and charged him. Thomas met him with a fist. Conklin took it solidly on his jaw, rocking back on his heels. Then he swung himself. Thomas moved, taking the blow on his shoulder. The dean stepped back and dropped into a graceful stance. There was blood in his grin.

Thomas dodged the kick, swung around, and met the blow. Their wrists jarred as they met. He leapt back and kicked as well, low this time, going for the dean's kneecap or thigh. He connected. The older man reacted with a grunt and a half-hobble out of the way.

They mixed punches again. Thomas took one in the gut that

reminded him that breathing couldn't be taken for granted. As his stomach clenched and ears rang, he dodged out of the way of the next blow. His fist found the lower back kidney.

The dean went to one knee in pain. Thomas kicked out, lashing an uppercut. The dean fell back and lay panting. He wasn't getting up easily.

"Thomas!" It was Dusty's voice. He looked out, saw the woman kneeling in the dirt, her commander protecting her. She had a look on her face that reminded him of Lady.

He looked back to the dean. The man lay prone, heaving for breath. Thomas spat to the side of him. "I'm taking you back," he said. "To the Seven Counties. Undoubtedly it'll be my pleasure to execute you." He looked up, meeting Drakkar's eyes.

Thomas turned his back on the dean and went to retrieve his knife from the shuttle.

Dusty screamed. He turned to see Marshall, the black man who reminded him of Gray Walton, taking the knife throw meant for him. It went through his throat.

Drakkar moved. He caught the dean and brought him to his knees. He raked his spur across the man's throat in a blur. "This is for the boys and Alma," he said harshly.

The dean began to choke on the bitter poison. Drakkar dropped him into the dust.

Thomas went to Dusty and the dying commander. Dusty's hands were soaked with his blood as she tried to stop the severed arteries and windpipe.

"Help me!" she begged. "You told me you have powers. In the name of god, help me!"

Thomas looked down. Lady had those powers, not he. He was battered and nearly broken. "I can't—"

Marshall raised a hand to his wrist and squeezed it with rapidly fading strength. His attempts to breathe gurgled wetly.

"Ah, hell," Thomas said. He laid his hands over Dusty's, closed his eyes, and tried to use his Intuition. Death is the other side of life, as disappointment is the other side of hope. He carried both those sides inside of him. Gillander had always told him that. He was not a half-man, a shadow man, walking the earth.

Prove it.

Was it easier to reach for death than life? He'd always said that dying was easy. It was living that was difficult.

It was knitting torn arteries. Darning slashed windpipes. Imagining the gush of spilling blood to slow, to clot. Skin to close. Life to get busy defeating death.

"My god," Dusty said. "Look what you've done."

He opened his eyes and lifted his hands. The dark man lay alive before him, a ghastly pink scar across his throat.

"Sloppy work," Thomas said. "Lady'll be upset with me." He wiped the blood on his jeans. He looked up. Drakkar had the nesters pulled back, a contingent of his father's men at his side.

"Let them go," he said.

Drakkar cocked his head.

Wearily, Thomas got to his feet. He felt drained of power. His body ached all over and his left sleeve was sodden with blood. His, this time. "Go back to your camps," he shouted. "The Marked Man sends you home! With water rights!" He moved aside so that the longshippers could get to their commander and lift him on a stretcher.

Marshall whispered hoarsely, "Not enough fuel, Dusty."

She mopped his forehead. "Don't talk."

"I have to!" The commander pushed her hand away. "We can't go back now . . . and we can't help the *Challenger*."

Thomas sat mutely, biting his lip against the pain of having his arm bandaged by the soft-spoken woman he'd met in the corridor. She'd recovered enough of her composure to stitch him up with a needle that stung like fire and was now wrapping him tight enough to cut off circulation. He listened to the redhead talk with her commander. He still liked the sound of her voice.

"Help her? What's wrong?"

"She's breaking up. Just like the *Gorby*. And the *Maggie*."

The man called Dubois wore a rakish white turban of bandage. He looked up. "When did you find this out?"

"Early this morning. I couldn't . . . tell you. Sun said for us to find some place for the *Challenger* to put down. He said . . . they couldn't wait much longer."

Thomas spoke. "You've had a rough welcome here, but we want you."

Dusty looked at him in surprise, then smiled. "Enough to fight over us."

He shrugged. "We're only human."

She punched Dubois lightly in the shoulder. "Get Sun on-screen."

"Will do."

Thomas watched in curiosity as a panel on the cabin wall warmed to a slow and then began to reflect an image. He saw a much larger cabin, apparently empty. Then a man moved painfully into the frame. He blinked. The man was an older image of Jeong, down to his slender, quick fingers.

"Dusty. I was told you'd been lost."

"I had a long swim." There was a crackling sound. The image wavered and then strengthened. "Dakin?" she asked, clearly shaken.

"Tell Marshall, it's too late. We jettisoned Noah's Ark about ten minutes ago. It's in a disintegrating orbit. It should splash down off the Pacific Coast, just south of Point Conception. We thought that appropriate. Heredia will take on a lifeboat or two. The rest of us . . . are going down with the ship."

Marshall gasped out feebly, "I'm sorry, Commander."

Dakin's focus changed. He could apparently see the other. "And I, too. Will you be all right?"

Marshall managed a nod. "I wanted to bring the shuttle back up . . . but we've had an accident here. Most of the fuel was spent."

The onscreen image wavered again. It went dark and came back very feebly. "Too late anyway." Dakin leaned close. "It was a marvelous experiment while it lasted." The screen went dark.

Dusty made a funny noise in her throat. Then got out, "Two hundred and fifty years."

Finger bones rattled in Thomas's inner pockets. He felt them tremble against his chest. "What do you have to do?"

"Do? We have to launch this shuttle, gain an orbit equivalent to that of the *Challenger*, dock, and pull our people off. If we had enough fuel to make escape velocity, which we don't, and if we could match the *Challenger*'s orbit, which we can't, and if we could take on enough people to be worth a tinker's dam, which we can't." The sardonic man in the turban punched the dead screen in front of him.

Thomas turned to Dusty. "How many people?"

"Twelve hundred, give or take a few." Dubois tried to bring the communications panel to life again and failed.

Intuition prickled in Thomas' skin. He could feel his power rising in him, like a storm about to sweep the sky.

There was nothing he couldn't do.

He grabbed up Dusty's hand. "Can you show me the way?"

She stared at him as though he'd gone mad. "What are you talking about?"

"I've got a way to travel, but I've got to know the way." He slipped his other hand inside his jacket pocket and took out the bones. "Trust me."

The Ghost Road had always been cold, but the chill as he stepped onto it with Dusty clinging to his hand took him by surprise. She began to shake in earnest.

"Stay with me," he said. His voice sounded flat and colorless. "I can't travel this road unless I know where it's going. Talk to me. Tell me about your ship." As he moved, he could feel his power shifting. His Earth fell behind him.

Her jaw chattered. "What if . . . what if we get lost?"

"Then we'd die. Would that be so bad," he said mildly. "Scattered like stardust across the sky?"

"Not if I got warm." She started to move.

"Don't let go of me!"

She clung to him. "God. I'm not cut out for this. What are you doing?"

"I'm not sure. A very wise man once told me that I had better learn, though. I should have listened to him." Thomas picked his way across the span carefully. It looked vaguely familiar. The Ghost Road was full of resonances. He remembered going after Lady and Alma, and the specter which had passed him by. He gave a sudden laugh. That dark and feral figure had been himself . . . perhaps on this very road.

Dusty squeezed his hand. "You can laugh?"

"And so can you. But now . . ." The void beneath his feet was tenuous. "Open your mind to me, Dusty. Pretend we're lovers. Let me see all the things you want me to see, and the ones you don't. Show me the way back to your life."

She came into the grasp of his arms then. The road felt stronger. He looked into her face. She gave a quavery laugh. "I'm probably your great-great-grandmother," she said.

"No," he answered. "There're no redheads in my family."

Her lips trembled. He knew she wanted to be kissed, so he did.

Their lips met with a mild shock. He felt it more than she, but she leaned back in his arms afterward, her gray eyes wide.

Before she could say anything, he put a finger across her lips. She was fire, and he knew where to find her again.

Dusty hurried after him, her shoes making no sound on the Ghost Road.

Sun sat on the observation deck. His cat stretched across his knees, purring, unaware of the disasters tearing the *Challenger* apart. Suddenly the animal got to his paws and spit, hissing at a panel in the room which appeared to be coalescing into. . . .

He sprang to his feet. "My god. Dusty!"

She stood with a man, a man in worn and bloodied clothing, his jacket sleeve gashed open, a man with gills flaring at his neckline. The commander brushed a hand over his face. "Dusty, you're dead."

"Not yet I'm not." She looked to the man. "He knows I'm alive."

"Maybe not now he doesn't."

Dakin stood. His knees felt like water.

"Have you jettisoned Noah's Ark yet?"

"No, not yet—we're locking it down now—how did you know—"

"We're early! Sun, get everybody together. You haven't heard from me yet, but the shuttle can't help you. We had a fuel burn . . . listen to me. I know the *Challenger* is breaking up."

"How did you get in here?" Sun said shakily. He brushed his thin hair from his forehead and reached down to regather the cat in his arms.

"What the hell is that?" her companion asked.

"It's a cat."

"A what?"

Dusty slapped her hands together impatiently. "Haven't you ever seen a cat before?"

"Frankly, no. Tell him what's happening and get everybody together before I lose the road."

The commander held his cat tightly. "Dusty, what the hell is going on?"

"It's metaphysics, sir, near as I can tell. It's the only way to get you off-loaded and down to Earth."

"We're not breaking up yet."

The man swung about and looked at him. If Dakin thought he was seeing a ghost, he did not think so now. The man radiated blood, sweat, and impatience. "Commander," he said, "I'm offering you a way out. It's unorthodox, but it's all we have."

"What do you intend to do?"

The man fingered the edge of his mustache. His next words were interrupted by a mechanical voice.

Dakin answered. "What is it?"

"Noah's Ark is ready to go, sir."

"All right. Launch when ready."

The voice hesitated. "Sir. . . ."

"What is it?"

"We've discovered some severe metal fatigue. The Ark is all that's holding the mid-section together."

Dakin paused. He looked to Dusty. She shrugged. He said to the unseen voice, "What if we don't launch?"

Another pause. Then, "We're going to lose her anyway. Sir, this is what must have happened to the *Maggie*."

"I understand. Prepare evacuation first, then launch on my command." He looked to Blade. "Who the hell are you?"

"I'm from the Seven Counties. I'm a Protector. I have certain abilities that you may or may not accept . . . but I think I can get you out of here."

"How?"

"By linking hands and walking you out."

Dakin's knees gave way. The observation couch caught him at the back of them and he sat down on it. His head began to shake. After long moments, the intercom came on again. "Sir, we're standing in the corridors. But where are we going to go? The *Mayflower* can't take us on."

The commander looked up, defeated. "Where are we going to go, Dusty?"

"Home, I think. Just take my hand."

"No. I've come a long way, but I can't accept what you're talking to me about."

Dusty knelt by him. "Would I lie to you?"

He put his hand on her red hair. "You'd stand on your head if you thought you could put one over on me."

"In a few minutes, after the Ark goes, you're going to get a call from Dubois. You'll see me. You'll see Marshall, who's been injured, and you'll know that the shuttle can't help you. If all that happens, will you believe he can guide us through— forget how he does it, logic won't help you there—will you come with us?"

Dakin's tired eyes sought Blade's face. "Will it work?"

"I don't know. I've never tried this before."

The commander looked down wearily. He pressed the intercom. "Launch the Ark at will."

"Yes, sir."

The ship rocked slightly. And then came a long groan. Metal cried and whined. Dakin looked up. Moments later the communications panel lit up. Dusty moved out of sight. "It's all yours," she said.

As if in great pain, he moved to the focus of the panel.

They linked hands. Like a great chain of life snaking through the *Challenger*, they caught up backpacks and pets and loved ones and wove themselves together. Dusty and Thomas moved swiftly down the corridors. A few of them refused to go. He said nothing to convince them. There was no time. Dusty took up the last position. She held her hand out to him.

He took it and stepped onto the road.

Immediately, he knew he was in trouble. He was being unspun, torn, unraveled from a firmament too frail to take the road. The drag of a thousand lives or more clutching on to him spooled him out.

And he was lost. The pathways strung out before him, a webwork he'd never seen before. They were infinite. Earth, air, fire, and water—all the elements of the road—and he had lost his way.

He had one anchor to reach for and that was Lady.

He opened his mind and called for her.

A dolphin goddess danced sparkling waters through his memory. Her wise dark eye was Lady's. A furred beast rose from the broken ruins, slashing across his thoughts. His dark eye was Lady's.

A lover entwined her legs with his on a bed, stroking the sheets aside. Her light eye was Lady's.

A child he had never seen reached for him. Her light eye was Lady's.

He touched her then. Grounded himself in her presence. She looked up from some needlework. "Thomas?" she asked gently.

Here.

Her gaze a reflection of earth and water. An echo of himself and herself. Her mismatched eyes beacons to his lost and errant ways.

Home.

"Thomas," she said again. She sat in a rocking chair and she gently cupped her barely swollen stomach. He thought of the child reaching for him. She'd never told him. She would not hold him that way.

He'd been lost and now he was found again. Anchored by her presence, he found the Ghost Road back. As he stepped forward without hesitation, the ship about them began to crumple, dissipating like vapor, burning like a comet through the skies.

"Never let go," he said and brought his burden along the road.

A panicked cry sounded.

Dusty said, "They'll never make it." She dropped hands with him, but never let go. Instead, she climbed back along a human ladder, hand to arm to hand to arm, touching, grasping all her people. She worked her way back until she found the woman, crying in desperation, and quieted her.

The Ghost Road arced about them. They were so many, they were like a ripple in the very fabric of time.

Thomas passed himself and knew who he was. More importantly, he knew where he was going.

He never let go.

Chapter 36

"As soon as we recover Noah's Ark, we'll have our work cut out for us."

Thomas lay back on the lawn below the Warden compound. His head throbbed from a night of celebration and the sun felt a little too bright. Lady had made an honest man out of him. "Do you think," he said to the ex-commander of the *Challenger*, "you could manage aspirin?"

Dakin laughed. "I'm sure we can try." He scratched the ears of the lithe orange cat lying in the sun next to him. "Ah," he said. "Ladies approaching."

Lady looked beautiful. She wore blue and brown, as she always did, and flowers were woven into her light brown hair. With pride he noted the thickening of her waistline. She had her arm linked with Dusty's and had woven flowers into her red hair as well.

Thomas lifted his head. A prickle of Intuition went down the back of his neck. He groaned. "I would get up, wife, but the world seems kinder down here."

Lady sat down and took his head in her lap. Her fingers began rubbing his neck and temples gently. "Then I'll come to you," she said.

Dusty lay down on her stomach, chin in hand.

"Drakkar is extremely disappointed that he did not have the command of the troops he thought he did."

Thomas grunted, then added, "He needs to be taken down a notch or two. The dean inadvertently destroyed most of the Mojavan rebel faction, though. They were just as eager to get control of the shuttle as the nesters were. Denethan always could fall in horseshit and come up smelling like roses."

"Drakkar's making arrangements to go back. He wants to take Alma with him, but I convinced him to wait a few more months until Denethan solidifies his rule again."

He asked, "Will she go?"

He could feel Lady's smile through her hands. "Oh, yes. She'll go."

The gentle pressure of her fingers on his temples set him drifting in thought. He said suddenly, "Any word on Watty?"

"Yes. He's doing well. He has something he wants to discuss with you. He says some sort of great beast carried him into Orange County."

Thomas felt her fingertips detour, trace out the chevron scar on his brow. She murmured softly, "You're not done yet, you know."

He knew that all too well. He turned his head, saw the commander of the *Challenger II* watching them. He had a contented look. "When is the *Mayflower* coming down?"

The contented look faded. Dakin answered, "They're not sure. They may go back out. Heredia runs a democracy. She told me they're going to take a vote. They're a bigger craft, nearly twenty-five hundred people. They're of a mind to start a colony, as they were intended to do."

"We could use them here. Or anywhere on the planet."

"We know that." Sun noted, "Dusty has something on her mind. I know that look."

Her gray eyes flashed as she looked up at them. Then she grinned. "Well, why not. I'm not a good loser. For the first time in over two hundred years, my thoughts are not alone. The silence has been banished. I thought it might have been the dean, but now I know it was you. When you took me on the Ghost Road, I knew it. When you asked me to open up my mind as a lover opens up her body, I felt it. When you kissed me, I wanted you—all of you. Dammit, why didn't you wait for me? Sir Thomas Blade, I want to marry you."

Thomas' jaw dropped agape. His head began to throb again, but Lady laughed.

"Why, Dusty," she said. "We accept. Every good woman needs a wife."

Sun Dakin continued to stroke his cat's ears. "Blade," he said. "You live in interesting times."

CJ Cherryh

EXPLORER

0-7564-0086-4

The *Foreigner* novels introduced readers to the epic story of a lost human colony struggling to survive on the hostile world of the alien atevi. In the final installment to this sequence of this series, can diplomat Bren Cameron, trapped in a distant start system, facing a potentially bellicose alien ship, help prevent interspecies war, when the secretive Pilot's Guild won't even cooperate with their own ship?

To Order Call: 1-800-788-6262

OTHERLAND

TAD WILLIAMS

*"The Otherland books are a
major accomplishment."*
–Publishers Weekly

"It will captivate you."
–Cinescape

*In many ways it is humankind's most stunning
achievement. This most exclusive of places is also
one of the world's best-kept secrets, but somehow,
bit by bit, it is claiming Earth's most valuable
resource: its children.*

CITY OF GOLDEN SHADOW (Vol. One)
0-88677-763-1

RIVER OF BLUE FIRE (Vol. Two)
0-88677-844-1

MOUNTAIN OF BLACK GLASS (Vol. Three)
0-88677-906-5

SEA OF SILVER LIGHT (Vol. Four)
0-75640-030-9

To Order Call: 1-800-788-6262